NOONSHADE

·10/09

NOONSHADE

CHRONICLES OF THE RAVEN

JAMES BARCLAY

an imprint of **Prometheus Books**
Amherst, NY

Published 2009 by Pyr®, an imprint of Prometheus Books

Inquiries should be addressed to
Pyr
59 John Glenn Drive
Amherst, New York 14228–2119
VOICE: 716–691–0133, ext. 210
FAX: 716–691–0137
WWW.PYRSF.COM

13 12 11 10 09   5 4 3 2 1

Library of Congress Cataloging-in-Publication Data

Barclay, James, 1965–.
    Noonshade / by James Barclay.
        p. cm. — (Chronicles of the Raven ; 2)
    First published: London : Gollancz, an imprint of Orion Publishing Group, 2000.
    ISBN 978–1–59102–782–9 (pbk. : alk. paper)
    I. Title.

PR6102.A76N66 2009
823'.92—dc22
                                                                    2009022623

Printed in the United States on acid-free paper

For my parents,
Keith and Thea Barclay.
Always there, always wonderful.

The NORTHERN CONTINENT

JADEN • RACHE

BloodLake

JULATSA
DORDOVER • HAVERN • CORIN

Giverne Lake

LYSTERN

Black Wings' Castle

XETESK

Pontois Plains

UNDERSTONE
Understone Pass

PONTOIS •

DENEBRE

Septern Manse

ERSKAN • HYLD •

Grethern Forest

Taranspike Castle

KORINA

Varhawk Crags

Thornewood • GRESSE

The Bluts

GREYTHORNE

ARLEN • ORYTTE

Balan Mts.

BLACKTHORNE

Bay of Gyernath

GYERNATH

Arlen Bay

Mountains of R'th Triverne Inlet

BLACKTHORNE

Cast List

THE RAVEN

Hirad Coldheart   BARBARIAN WARRIOR
The Unknown Warrior   WARRIOR
Ilkar   JULATSAN MAGE
Denser   XETESKIAN MAGE
Erienne   DORDOVAN MAGE

THE
COLLEGES

Dystran   LORD OF THE MOUNT, XETESK
Vuldaroq   TOWERLORD, DORDOVER
Heryst   LORD ELDER MAGE, LYSTERN
Sytkan   LORD MAGE, XETESK
Ry Darrick   GENERAL, LYSTERNAN CAVALRY
Aeb   A PROTECTOR
Lyanna   ERIENNE'S DAUGHTER

THE SOLDIERS
SAILORS AND
EARLS

Ren'erei   GUILD OF DRECH
Tryuun   GUILD OF DRECH
Jasto Arlen   EARL OF ARLEN
Selik   CAPTAIN OF THE BLACK WINGS
Jevin   CAPTAIN OF THE CALAIAN SUN

THE
AL-DRECHAR

Ephemere
Cleress
Myriell
Aviana

THE KAAN

Sha-Kaan   GREAT KAAN
Hyn-Kaan
Nos-Kaan

PROLOGUE

The intensity of vibration grew in his head. Within the dark of the Choul, deep beneath the jungles of Teras, those of the Brood-at-rest shifted in sudden nervousness, most of them unaware of what they were feeling.

Like an itch he couldn't rub, the humming picked at his mind and worried him deep in the core of his being. He opened a huge blue eye, pupil widening to admit the dim light from the entrance high above, picking out the hollowed damp rock, the lianas creeping down and the lichen which covered every surface. It showed him the fluttering of a wing, the shaking of a neck and the shifting of clawed feet as the Brood moved to premature wakefulness. He felt the quickening of pulses, the rumble of lungs drawing in air and the creaking of jaws stretched wide.

A great shiver coursed his body and Sha-Kaan's heart leapt. The vibration, a siren for disaster, clamoured in his skull. He came to his feet, great wings unfurling for flight, a cry forming in his mouth. He called to the Brood and led them from the Choul, charging toward the light, drawn to the great boiling in the sky where a new battle was just beginning.

CHAPTER 1

It would be a glorious victory. Lord Senedai of the Heystron Tribes stood on a raised platform watching the smoke billowing over Julatsa as building after building was put to flame. The acrid smell of the smoke was beautiful in his nostrils and through the fog it created, he could see the white and black fire his Shamen wielded through linkage with the Wytch Lords, tearing what was left of the city's heart to shreds. And there was nothing the Julatsans could do to stop them.

Ripping from their fingers and gnawing at the stone and woodwork of the once proud College city, the white fire issued from the fingertips of a hundred Shamen, demolishing building, fence and barricade. And where men and women ran in terror, the black fire picked the flesh from their bones and gouged the eyes from their skulls while they fell screaming to die in agony.

Senedai felt no sympathy. He leapt from the platform and yelled his Lieutenants to him. All that held up his progress to the College itself were the mages who still shielded great swathes of the city borders and the enemy soldiers who protected the mages from the swords of his warriors. It was time to put a stop to this irritating resistance.

As he ran toward the battle, issuing orders and watching the standards and banners sway as tribes ran to do his bidding, a wall of flame erupted ahead, the spell detonation rippling through the ground as the targets, all Shamen, were engulfed and died without a sound of their own.

"Press! Press!" he yelled. But this close the noise, muted to a roar only a hundred yards away, was as deafening as it was distinct. He could hear individual sword clashes, the cries of panic, fear and pain. He could hear bellowed orders, desperate and confident, and he could hear the thud of metal on leather, the tumbling of stone and the cracking of timber.

Beside him, his warrior guard ran a crescent of protection while he kept himself just out of bow range as did all but his most foolhardy of Shamen. The line of Julatsans was thin to the point of collapse and Senedai knew that once pierced, there would be a route straight through to the walls of the College itself.

Horns blew and his warriors surged again. Behind the enemy lines, mages were torn to shreds by the black fire, even as they spoke their spells of protection. He could taste the anguish of his foe and his Wesmen axes rose and fell, showering blood into the smoke-muddied sky.

"I want those mages to the right destroyed!" he shouted at a lieutenant. "See it is signalled immediately." The ground heaved with Julatsan magic, cold air blasted through the warmth of the day and the sky rained drops of fire, his tribesmen paying dearly for every pace they took.

A detachment of Shamen broke and ran right, arrows peppering the ground where they moved. One fell, a shaft buried deep in his thigh. He was left to writhe. Senedai watched them go, felt a thrill when their hands and mouths moved, summoning the fire from deep within the black souls of the Wytch Lords to project its hideous power on helpless victims.

But as he watched, he felt a change. The fire pulsing from outstretched fingers guttered, strengthened briefly, flickered and died. A ripple spread across the tribes. From every part of the battle ground, shouts were raised and Shamen stared at their hands and each other, incomprehension and fear on bleak faces.

From the enemy, a cheer, gaining in intensity, swept along the defensive line. Immediately, the barrage of spells increased and the defenders pushed into the confusion that gripped his warriors. They fell back.

"My Lord?" ventured a Captain. Senedai turned to the man, whose face held anxiety not fit for a Wesmen warrior, and found a rage boiling inside him. His gaze swept back across his failing attack, taking in the magic that blasted his men and the swords of the exhausted defence that fell with renewed energy and determination. He pushed the Captain aside and ran forward, heedless of the risk.

"By all the Spirits, are we not warriors?" he bellowed into the roar of battle. "Horns, sound the attack! All fronts. Magic be damned, we fight with steel. Attack, you bastards, attack!" He crashed into the battle, his axe ploughing through the shoulder of a defending Julatsan. The man collapsed and Senedai trod on the corpse, ripping the axe clear to bat it side-on into the face of the next enemy. Around him, the tribesmen responded, picking up songs of battle as they surged again.

Horns sounded new orders, wavering standards straightened in the hands of their bearers and moved forward again. The Wesmen poured back into the battle for Julatsa, ignoring the spells that handed out death and maiming injury indiscriminately, and seeing the defenders begin to wilt at the ferocity of the onslaught.

Lord Senedai dared a look either way along the lines and smiled. Many warriors would die without the Wytch Lords' fire but the day, he determined, would still belong to the Wesmen. Noting the positions of the knots of offensive casting mages, he slapped aside a clumsy thrust and forged back into the fray.

The Raven stood in silence in Parve's central square. The battle was won. Dawnthief had been cast, the Wytch Lords destroyed and their city once more a place of the dead. Above them, the aftereffect of Dawnthief hung in the sky, brown and modulating, an alien and malevolent stain suspended like some predatory beast above the land of Balaia. It was the dimensional rip to nowhere.

Away across the square, Darrick and the remnants of the four-College cavalry had destroyed any remaining resistance and now piled bodies onto makeshift pyres; Wytch Lord acolytes, Wesmen and Guardians in one area, their own fallen in another, and the reverence with which dead cavalrymen were handled was in stark contrast to the dragging and throwing of enemy corpses. Styliann and the Protectors were in the blasted pyramid, searching the rubble for anything that might gives clues to the ancients' brief but cataclysmic return to power.

The silence in the square was palpable. None of Darrick's men spoke as they went about their sombre task; the sky under the rip was bereft of birds and the breeze that gusted across the open space seemed muted to a whisper as it coiled around Parve's buildings.

And for The Raven, victory was once again tarnished by loss.

Denser leaned heavily on Hirad, Erienne at his other side, her arm about his waist. Ilkar stood by the barbarian. Opposite them, across the grave, Will, Thraun and The Unknown Warrior. All of them gazed down at the shrouded form of Jandyr. The elf's bow lay the length of his body, his sword from chin to knees.

Sadness echoed its quiet around The Raven. At the moment of triumph, life had been taken from Jandyr. After everything he had survived, his was an unkind fate.

For Ilkar, the loss was keen. Elves were not numerous in Balaia, preferring as a rule the heat of the Southern Lands. Few now travelled to the Northern Continent excepting those called by magic and even their numbers were dwindling. They could ill afford to lose elves like Jandyr. But the grief was felt most personally by Will and Thraun. Their long-time friend had died in the service of Balaia and The Raven. What had begun as a simple rescue had finished on the steps of the Wytch Lords' tomb at the end of a desperate chase to find and cast the only spell that could save Balaia from the ancient evil. Yet Jandyr had died not knowing the outcome of the casting of Dawnthief. Life could be cruel. Mistimed death more so.

The Unknown intoned The Raven's words of parting. "By north, by east, by south, by west. Though you are gone, you will always be Raven and we shall always remember. Balaia will never forget the sacrifice you made. The Gods will smile on your soul. Farewell in whatever faces you now and ever."

Will nodded. "Thank you," he said. "Your respect and honour are truly appreciated. Now Thraun and I need time alone with him."

"Naturally," said Ilkar. He moved away.

"I'll stay a little longer," said Erienne, disentangling herself from Denser. "After all, he came to rescue my family." Will nodded and she knelt by the graveside, joining the thief and Thraun, the shapechanger, in their regrets and hopes.

The Unknown, Hirad and Denser caught up with Ilkar and the quartet sat in the lee of the pyramid tunnel, the rip above and behind them, its presence huge and menacing. Further out in the central square, Darrick's men continued piling bodies ready for the pyres. Great slicks of dried blood swathed the paving stones and here and there, pieces of torn clothing blew and ruffled in the warm breeze. Styliann and the Protectors remained inside the pyramid, no doubt dissecting every rune, painting and mosaic.

General Ry Darrick walked over and joined them as The Unknown finished passing around mugs of coffee from Will's bubbling pan. There was a brief quiet.

"I almost hate to bring this up," said Darrick. "But great as the victory is, we number perhaps three hundred and there are a good fifty thousand Wesmen between here and our homes."

"Funny isn't it?" said Ilkar. "You think about all we've achieved and the result is that we've given Balaia a chance and no more. Nothing is certain."

"So much for basking in glory," said Hirad.

"Don't understate what we've done," said Denser from his prone position, hands under his head. "We have removed the certainty of the Wytch Lords' triumph and their dominion over Balaia. And more than that, we've destroyed them and given ourselves real hope. Bask in that."

"I'll try," said Hirad, the smile returning to his face.

"Remember," said Denser. "The Wesmen have no magic."

"And we have no armies," said Ilkar.

"I wonder if there'll be anything left to return to?" mused The Unknown.

"A Communion would help to clarify a few things," agreed Denser.

"Thanks for your input, Denser," said Ilkar. "Why don't you sleep it off?"

"Just saying," said the Xeteskian Mage sharply.

"I think we're a little far from Understone, don't you?" Ilkar patted him on the shoulder.

"Selyn did it." It was Styliann. The Raven started and turned. The Lord of the Mount of Xetesk walked out of the shadow of the pyramid tunnel. The Protectors remained deep inside. He looked pale and tired, his hair lank about his shoulders, the braid holding his ponytail long since gone.

"May I?" He gestured at the pot. The Unknown shrugged and nodded. Styliann ladled out a mug of coffee and sat with The Raven.

"I've been thinking," he said.

"Is there no end to your talents?" muttered Denser.

Styliann's eyes flashed. "The Dawnthief catalysts may be destroyed, Denser, but I am still your commanding mage. You would do well to remember that." He paused. "Selyn was a Communion specialist. She reported large forces of Wesmen leaving Parve in the direction of Understone just before she entered the city. They will not have reached Understone yet so we have them to face before we reach the pass." Styliann's jaw set as if his next words were battling not to be heard. "For now, we should work together."

The atmosphere cooled. The Unknown spoke. "Your last intercession, though welcome, was hardly a determined effort to help. Before that, you tried to kill us all. Tried to turn the Protectors against me. Now you want us to work together." The Unknown looked away into the pyramid, his face troubled.

"We got here without your help. We'll get back without it," said Hirad.

Styliann regarded them calmly, the hint of a smile playing over his lips.

"You're good, I'll grant you that," he said. "But you are overlooking the severity of your situation. The Raven will never reach the East unaided. Remember, Understone Pass was opened for you but is now almost certainly closed. I have the Communion range and contacts to organise passage. You do not and Darrick ultimately reports to me and the four Colleges."

"Doesn't sound like you need us at all," said Hirad. Styliann smiled.

"One can always use The Raven."

The Unknown nodded slightly. "You have an idea, I presume?"

"A route, yes; the tactics I'll leave to the General." He looked across at Darrick who had remained silent throughout the exchange, his expression changing only by a hair at the reminder of his position in the chain of command.

"Perhaps you'd better tell us your route, my Lord," said Darrick.

Hirad's head was thumping. He needed a drink. Alcohol, preferably, to chase away the pain for a while. He lurched to his feet, making for the fire.

"You all right, Hirad?" asked Ilkar.

"Not really," he replied. "My head's killing me." A cold sensation cascaded through his back, like snow shaken from the bough of a tree, gone as soon as it had come. There was a change in the air, a movement that had nothing to do with the breeze blowing warmly about them.

Hirad stopped, looking up into the sky, clear blue but for the huge rip modulating gently. As he watched, the mottled brown surface rippled violently, bubbled, punched outward and tore for a split second. A barking roar shattered the relative peace of the afternoon. Triumphant, apocalyptic, terrible.

Hirad screamed, turned and ran away blindly in the direction of the eastern forest miles away, every fear he had harboured since his encounter with Sha-Kaan realised in an instant.

So soon after victory, they faced ultimate defeat and total destruction. There was a dragon in the skies of Balaia.

It was the way he liked it best—the way of the sword. Wesmen were warriors, not mages. And though the Wytch Lords' power had seen them to victories more quickly than he had dared hope, the Lord Tessaya was confident they would have triumphed even without the white and black fires.

Now that magic, borrowed, stolen, gifted, call it what you will, was gone. The Shamen no longer held sway and the Wesmen belonged to their tribal lords once more. It was at once terrifying and exciting. Should the unity crumble, they would be swept back across the Blackthorne Mountains by the armies of the four Colleges. If he could hold them together, Tessaya believed they could take Korina and with the capture of the capital city would come the heart, soul and wealth of Eastern Balaia.

But he had to fear the Colleges against whom they now had no defence. His dream of seeing the Towers of Xetesk burn had gone, at least for now. A wry smile touched his weather-worn, deeply tanned face. There were other ways of fighting mages.

Defeat was never an option for Tessaya. Particularly when he was drinking in the glow of recent victory. And victory against mages.

Panic had threatened to engulf the thousands pouring through Understone Pass as word had spread that the Shamen had lost their link to the Wytch Lords. But Tessaya, in unwitting mirror to Senedai far away in Julatsa, had stilled the unrest, choosing to run at the head of the Wesmen pack as it exploded into the sunlight of the East.

The College army knew they were coming but was hopelessly outnumbered. Wave after wave of Wesmen had torn into the lines, their howls drowning the screamed orders, the cries of fear and the wailing of the dying. With Tessaya leading, they were unstoppable, the blood of victory pounding in their heads, their swords and axes slicing flesh and splintering bone. The front line had been stubborn but, with their bodies littering the mud in front of the pass, and the mage support destroyed, it was little more than an organised slaughter, which left Tessaya disappointed.

Sitting in Understone's inn, now cleared of bodies, he recalled the fight, the elementary defensive mistakes and the confusion of orders that reached his ears. But most of all he remembered those who had run and those who had cast up their arms and surrendered before hope was truly lost. So different from the fight at the western end of Understone Pass. There he had seen an enemy organised and prepared to fight to the last man. An enemy that had held his armies for longer than it had any right to. An enemy he could respect.

But what disappointed him most was the failure of the General, whom Tessaya had been informed was in charge at Understone Town, to live up to his reputation. Shame. He should have been another exciting adversary. As it was, he had proved as much a coward as the rest. Darrick was a name the Wesmen would quickly forget to fear.

The door to the inn opened and his elder Shaman walked in. Without the Wytch Lords' power he was no longer a man Tessaya had to watch but the Lord of the Paleon tribes bore him no less respect.

Tessaya poured him a drink, the two men sitting across a table in the shadows at the rear of the building.

"You're looking tired, Arnoan."

"It's been a long day, my Lord."

"But over now, by the sounds of it." The noise of celebration was building.

"How are your injuries?" asked Arnoan.

"I'll live." Tessaya smiled, amused by Arnoan's fatherly concern. The burn down his right forearm was sore and blistered but treated, clean and dressed. He had been quick in the dive as the FlameOrb had splashed, so had lived.

The cuts he sported on his face, chest and legs were merely trophies of fierce fighting. Still, at his age and influence, looks weren't important and besides, he found himself tiring of the attentions of women. His line would survive the war; his sons ranged from babes in arms to muscled youths. And now their father had led the tribes to victory at Understone. Where next? It was a question clearly taxing Arnoan.

"What will the morning bring?" asked the Shaman.

"Rest and building. I will not lose Understone Pass again," said Tessaya. His expression hardened. "Lord Taomi and the southern force should be with us in a day at most. Then we can plan the conquest of Korina."

"You really believe we can achieve that?"

Tessaya nodded. "They have no armies. Only city defence and reservists. We have ten thousand here, fifteen thousand within two days of the pass, another twenty-five thousand who crossed Triverne Inlet to attack the Colleges and whatever the south brings us. Who is going to stop us?"

"My Lord, nobody disputes that the military advantage lies with us. But the mage strength of the Colleges is considerable. It would be a mistake to underestimate them." Arnoan leaned forward, his bony fingers knotted in front of him.

Tessaya hefted his burned arm. "Do you think I am in danger of doing that?" He eyes narrowed. "Arnoan, I am the oldest tribal Lord, with the largest tribal Council under me. It is so because I have made a habit of never underestimating my enemy.

"The mages are powerful and the Colleges will stand against us in strength. But a mage tires quickly and without a guard is quickly slain. Losing our magic was a blow but we were born to the sword, not the spell.

"The Wesmen will rule Balaia and I will rule the Wesmen."

No help would come to Tessaya from the south. The Wesmen were routed and running for Blackthorne Town while its namesake Baron rested high in the crags above the battlefield of his victory. With him were the concussed but otherwise happy Baron Gresse and around five hundred men and mages, all dreaming of a return to their homes.

But the euphoria of the victory at Varhawk Crags would soon wear off. Their situation remained parlous. All but a dozen or so mages had been killed by the white fire, the wounded outnumbered the able-bodied and the Wesmen's defeat had everything to do with their confusion at losing the Wytch Lords' magic. Blackthorne and Gresse had merely stoked the fires of panic. If the Wesmen chose to come back looking for them, a second victory would be hard won indeed.

Blackthorne, however, considered such a return very unlikely. In the confusion at the Crags, there was no telling what strength either side had and he knew if he were the Wesmen commander, he would retreat to Blackthorne, lick his wounds and plan his next strike while waiting for reinforcement from across the Bay of Gyernath.

The Baron came to the entrance of the overhang he'd taken as his command position. There was not much room for anything but a fire at the entrance and a few of his senior people inside. Gresse was there, propped up against a wall, his head, Blackthorne knew from experience, thudding wildly and inducing waves of nausea if he dared move.

In front of him, the crags stretched away north and south. Following the victory, he had brought his men and mages south, upwind of the stench of so much death. His fallen people had burned on pyres, the Wesmen dead were left to feed the scavengers. The overhang sat at the top of a gentle rise away from the treacherous edge and scree slopes of Varhawk. On the little plateaus and shallow slopes, his men rested under a warm but cloudy sky. Fires burned in a dozen places despite the Wesmen threat and Blackthorne's perimeter guards were under strict instructions not to turn to the light until their watches were complete. In key positions, elven eyes pierced the night to give early warning of any attack and so calmed the nerves of the sleeping.

There was little noise now. The celebrations had given way to excited chatter, then a low hum of conversation, then fatigue as night fell. Black-thorne permitted himself a smile. To his right, a man cleared his throat.

"My Lord?" Blackthorne turned to face Luke, the nervous youth he had sent to count heads.

"Speak up, lad." With an effort, the Baron softened his automatically stern demeanour and placed a fatherly hand on the youth's shoulder. "Where are you from, Luke?"

"A farm three miles north of Blackthorne, my Lord." His eyes scoured the ground at his feet. "I'll be the man of the farm now. If there's anything left of it."

Blackthorne could see Luke, no more than sixteen, biting back tears, his long dark hair covering the sides of his face. The Baron squeezed his shoulder then let his hand drop.

"We have all lost people we love, Luke," he said. "But what we can take back, we will, and those who stood with me and saved the East from the Wesmen will be known as heroes. The living and the dead." He stopped, lifted Luke's chin so that the youth's shining eyes met his.

"Was it a good life on your farm?" he asked. "Speak truthfully."

"Hard, my Lord," said Luke, the admiration burning in his face. "And not always happy, if I'm honest. The land isn't kind every year and the Gods don't always bless us with calves and lamb."

Blackthorne nodded. "Then I have failed you and everyone like you. Yet you were still prepared to lay down your life for me. When we are masters of Blackthorne once again, we will talk at greater depth. But now, you have some information for me?"

"Yes, my Lord." Luke hesitated. The Baron nodded for him to speak. "There are five hundred and thirty-two altogether, my Lord. Of these, eighteen are mages and five of them are too badly injured to cast. There are five hundred and fourteen men at arms and more than four hundred of them have some form of wound from battle. Of the worst, one hundred and five cannot fight. I have not counted those who will die by morning." Luke stopped. "My Lord," he added.

Blackthorne raised his eyebrows. "And what makes you so sure these men will die?"

"Because I have seen it often enough on the farm, my Lord," said Luke his confidence finally growing. "We aren't so different, people and animals, and I hear it in their breathing and see it in their eyes and the lie of their bodies. Inside, we know when our time is near; so do animals, and it shows."

"I'll have to take your word," said Blackthorne, fascinated by the realisation that he had probably seen less death in his long life than the youngster in front of him. Though they had surely both seen enough in the last few days to last a lifetime, he had never studied it. To Luke though, death of livestock was an economic problem and a risk of his occupation. "We must talk more another time, Luke. Now, I suggest you find a place to lay your head. We face hard days and I need men like you at your best."

"Goodnight, my Lord."

"Goodnight, Luke." Blackthorne watched the young man walk away, his head a little higher, his stride a little longer. He shook his head gently, the smile returning to his face. So were the fates at birth. Another day, Luke the farmer's son might have been born a Lord. Blackthorne was sure he would be equally at home in a Castle as a cowshed.

The Baron mulled over the numbers Luke had given him. Less than four hundred and fifty men able to fight, terribly short of mages and of those he could press into action, the overwhelming majority were hurt in some way. He guessed the Wesmen still outnumbered them two to one. And he had no idea how many were still in his Town, or at the beachhead, or on the road to Gyernath, or spread throughout the East. He bit his lip, quelling the sudden flutter in his heart. Hard days. And he had to be stronger than he had ever been.

The reality was that, unless some form of organisation grew from the chaos that ran the length of the Blackthorne Mountains, the Wesmen could still reach Korina, despite the loss of their magic. The Colleges would have to step in further. Take control. And while that was unpalatable, it was preferable to the alternative.

But the Colleges were distant and the problems of Blackthorne would hardly register. He could expect little help from the north but one thing he could do was attempt a Communion with Xetesk. Communication was an advantage the peoples of the East would have to exploit if they were to win.

Baron Blackthorne yawned. It was time to check on Gresse, and to sleep. Tomorrow, there were decisions to be made. He had to discover the wider picture. Understone, Gyernath, the scattered coastal and inland villages. He had to know where any help was coming from to drive the Wesmen back across the Bay of Gyernath. And he had to find a way to take back his town, his castle. His bed. Suppressing sudden anger, Blackthorne turned his back on the night and walked under the overhang.

The Wesmen kept on coming. Thousands of them pouring toward the borders of Julatsa, scrambling over the bodies of their fallen kinsmen and heaving themselves against the stuttering College Guard. From his Tower, Barras gazed down on the confusion, saw the spells ripping into the invading army and saw them roll relentlessly on.

It was midafternoon and the only respite in the fighting had been at the moment the Wesmen's magic deserted them. That moment, Barras' heart had surged because he knew The Raven had destroyed the Wytch Lords. He had cried in relief and joy then; and he could have cried in frustration now.

Because far from shattering the Wesmen, the setback merely seemed to inflame their anger. They had attacked again with a greater fury than before, their swords, axes and warrior passion driving them on and on.

At first it had been slaughter, the College Guard able to hold as waves of spells devastated the Wesmen lines. Thousands had died under the might of the Julatsan barrage, defenceless against the FlameOrbs, IceWind, Earth-Hammer, DeathHail, HotRain and BoneSplinter.

But the mana stamina of a mage is finite without rest and the Wesmen knew it. And the Julatsans had already spent so much on shielding men and buildings on the Shamen attack fronts. The Wesmen knew that too.

Now, with the spell barrage reduced to a tactical trickle, the Wesmen were moving with awesome confidence, crashing into the ranks of the College Guard and the reservists, unafraid now of what the next mana strike might bring.

To Barras' left, the General of the Julatsan forces bit his lip and cursed.

"How many are there?" he demanded of no one, his tone thick and exasperated. There had to be well over ten thousand.

"Too many," replied Barras.

"I am well aware of that," snapped the General. "And if that is meant to be a slur on—"

"Calm yourself, my dear Kard. It is a slur on no one, merely a statement of fact. How long can we hold them?"

"Three hours, maybe less," said Kard gruffly. "Without walls, I can't promise any more. How did the Communion go?"

"Dordover dispatched three thousand men yesterday at our request. They should be here by nightfall."

"Then you may as well tell them to turn back," said General Kard, his voice bitter, his face suddenly aged. "Julatsa will have fallen by then."

"They'll never take the College," said Barras. Kard raised his eyebrows.

"Who's going to stop them?"

Barras opened his mouth to speak but closed it again. Kard was a soldier and couldn't hope to understand.

That the College might be taken was unthinkable. More than that, it was abhorrent, an eventuality that brought bile to the Elder elven mage's throat. And there was a way of stopping the Wesmen taking their prize.

But as he turned his face back to the battle at the edge of the city and saw his people suffer under the blades of the invaders, Barras prayed it wouldn't come to that. Because what he had in his mind, he wouldn't wish on anyone. Not even Wesmen at the gates of his beloved College.

CHAPTER 2

The scene in Parve's central square was one of terrified bewilderment. At the first cry of the dragon, all noise had ceased for an instant as every head, of man and beast, turned toward the rip.

Untethered horses had turned and bolted while others threw their riders or bucked and strained at rails and posts, their throats choking out cries born of base instinct and the innate knowledge of prey under threat.

But for men and elves, blind terror gave way to a kind of fatal interest as the dragon, first a relatively indistinct shape, descended. There was a definite satisfaction in the sounds of the cries and barks with which it greeted Balaian sunshine. It twisted, rolled and wheeled, wings beating the air arrhythmically, playing in the skies of its discovery.

And as it moved closer to the ground, its form became clearer, its size dreadfully apparent. Ilkar took it all in with an analytical eye, ignoring the shaking of his body, the pounding of his heart; the urge to run, fall, fight, hide, anything.

The dragon was not as big as Sha-Kaan, the beast they had met through Taranspike Castle's dimension portal. Neither had it the same colouring or head shape, though its basic form was all but identical. The long, slender neck arched and straightened, its head searching the ground, its tail flowing behind the bulk of its body.

But where Sha-Kaan had been well in excess of one hundred and twenty feet in length, this one measured no more than seventy. And where Sha-Kaan's skin and scale had glistened gold in torchlight, this one was coloured a dark rust brown, its flat, wedge-shaped head at odds with Sha-Kaan's tall skull and muzzle.

The deep and penetrating stillness that had fallen on the central square evaporated as the slack-jawed watchers realised with an awful numbing slowness that the dragon was flying downward fast. A frenzy erupted. Darrick's normally ordered cavalry scattered into the streets, horses and riders colliding, barging and weaving as they wheeled in chaos, seeking the nearest escape from the immediate danger.

Darrick, his voice hoarse, yelled for order and calm, two things he was never going to achieve. Behind him, The Raven and Styliann scrambled to their feet, fatigue forgotten.

"Inside, inside!" shouted Ilkar, racing for the pyramid tunnel but pulling up short, The Unknown all but clattering into his back. He turned. "Where's Hirad?"

The Unknown spun and shouted after the barbarian, who had covered several hundred yards and showed no sign of slowing, but the tumult in the square stole his words.

"I'll get him," said the big man.

"No," said Ilkar, an eye on the dragon swooping toward the city. The Unknown gripped his arm.

"I'll get him," he repeated. "You understand." Ilkar nodded and The Unknown ran after Hirad who had just turned a corner and was out of sight.

From the entrance to the tunnel, Ilkar saw his friend hunch instinctively as the dragon passed by, not twenty feet above the highest flat-roofed building, its bulk that of fifty horses. He saw its head twisting, looking down on the fleeing men, elves and animals, heard its bark and felt fear deep in the pit of his stomach and a clap of pain in his receptive ears, their protective inner membranes closing instinctively.

The dragon rose, banked incredibly gracefully, and turned, diving lower, mouth agape, white fangs clearly visible against the black of its maw. Ilkar shuddered, watching it move, then paled as the sun cast a great shadow of the dragon over the running figure of The Unknown Warrior.

Everything was happening too fast. The Unknown looked up as the shadow engulfed him in an instant's dusk, turned and ran at right angles to the dragon's flight. Above and behind Ilkar, the rip shimmered and tore again, a sensation the elven mage felt through a repeat of the stillness in the air. Far from unleashing its fire, the dragon abruptly swept skyward, its bellow of disappointment echoed by another of pure rage.

Hirad, tearing through the empty streets at the edge of Parve, heard the second roar. He gasped as a weight pressed on the inside of his head, already stumbling to a halt, hands covering his ears when the voice boomed "Stop!" and sent him sprawling to the ground.

Climbing toward the boiling in the sky, Sha-Kaan felt the anger grow. It had been but a blink of an eye to him since he had warned the man, Hirad Coldheart, of the dangers posed by the knowledge he held and the amulet that had been entwined in his talons for so very long. And this was how he had been repaid.

First, the theft of the amulet, then surely the use of its text and finally, the opening of an unrestricted corridor to his melde-dimension. The melde-dimension of the entire Brood Kaan.

Behind him, the Brood flew from the Choul, unhappy at the sudden break from their sleep. Thirty Kaan, flying to join those already circling the gate in the sky.

And from all corners, drawn by the presence of the gate and the surge it sent through the nerves of every dragon within its compass, came the enemy. If they could not warn away the opposing Broods, there would be a battle as had never been seen in the skies since the appearance of the one great human, Septern. Septern who had rescued the Brood Kaan, offering them the melde they sought at a time when their numbers had dwindled close to extinction.

Sha-Kaan beat faster, a warning sounding in his head. From a bank of cloud behind the rip, a single dragon from the Brood Naik swept toward the undulating mass. His speed took him beyond the rough guard, his call of victory cut off as he plunged into the gate and was lost from sight.

Others made to follow but Sha-Kaan pulsed them to hold. "I will deal," he said. "Hold them at bay. Do not surrender the gate." He swept up and around the rip, judging its size and depth before angling his wings and plunging through.

The journey was a miasma of pressure, blindness, half-grasped messages and near knowledge of what lay outside the corridor. Sha-Kaan exploded into the skies of Balaia and immediately felt the presence of two beings known to him. The enemy Naik dragon loomed large in his consciousness and he bellowed his call to fight, knowing the Naik could not refuse. The other presence was smaller, much smaller, but no less significant. Hirad Coldheart. There would have to be words. As he dived on the Naik, Sha-Kaan pulsed the command to stop.

Ilkar's skin crawled, his fear complemented by total helplessness. At every moment, he expected more stillness, more dragons, more terror. Behind him, he knew, Styliann and the rest of The Raven were staring out into the sky. For the first time in their long and successful career, all they could do was watch.

The fight was fast and violent. The two dragons closed at a frightening speed, the smaller one from below, the larger, much larger, golden animal dived from above.

"Sha-Kaan," breathed Ilkar, recognising him by the movement of his head.

Sha-Kaan tore through Balaia's cloud-scattered sky, bellowing rage and threat. He angled a wing the instant before clashing with the rust brown enemy, the manoeuvre taking him below and, as he passed the belly, he breathed, fire coursing the length of the shorter dragon.

The scream of pain cracked the air, the wounded beast spiralling upward, neck twisting, head searching for its tormentor. But it looked in the wrong direction. Sha-Kaan, his mouth closed to extinguish his fire, turned up and back sharply to come around behind his foe. While the rust brown dragon, disorientated and in pain, searched for him, Sha-Kaan stormed across the dividing space, beat his wings to steady himself above his prey, arched his neck and struck down with terrific force on the base of his prey's skull. The rust-brown convulsed along the seventy foot length of its body, claws scrabbling briefly on thin air, wings thrashing wildly, its bark turning to a gurgle as its body, now a dead weight, fell from the sky.

Ilkar watched, his breath held, as Sha-Kaan dropped with his kill, not releasing it until they had both reached roof level. Then, with a final twist and deep growl of triumph, he swung away to hover as the dead dragon thudded into the ground in the central square, shivering the earth under Ilkar's feet. A huge cloud of dust billowed up, the waiting pyres of bodies slipping, a grotesque movement of the dead.

Unease swept across Parve. A gut-turning feeling that so much was terribly wrong. In the quiet that followed the fight, the only sound clearly heard was the beating of Sha-Kaan's wings as he circled his victim. This close, the victorious dragon was truly enormous. Almost twice the size of his foe, Sha-Kaan dominated the sky, eclipsing even the rip with his raw power. Three times around he went before, with a long, guttural roar, he swept low into the square, passed scant feet above the corpse of the dragon, turned into the air and flew off directly after Hirad.

"Oh no." Ilkar started moving into the light.

"What good can you do?" Styliann's voice, though quiet with shock, still carried power, menace and cynicism.

Ilkar turned. "You don't understand, do you? People like you never will. I've no idea what I can do but I will do something. I can't leave him to face that thing alone. He's Raven."

The elven mage ran out into the square, following in the footsteps of The Unknown. After a pause, Thraun and Will did the same. Denser slumped back to the ground, his energy spent, his eyes locked on the still mound of the dragon Sha-Kaan had killed so effortlessly. Erienne crouched beside him, cradling his head.

"Gods in the sky," he whispered. "What have I done?"

Hirad lay with his hands over his ears as the cries of battle in the sky slammed around inside his head. When it was all over, he moved groggily to his knees and dared to look back toward Parve. He vaguely noted The Unknown Warrior running toward him, shouting, but his attention was fixed on the shape of Sha-Kaan, wheeling in the sky over the dead city. The dragon's sudden dive jarred him from his almost hypnotic state and the sight of him appearing over the near buildings struck a fear in him deeper than he had ever felt before. His nightmare was about to become reality. He did his part. He picked himself up and ran.

Hirad could feel the rush of Sha-Kaan's approach in his mind long before the shadow swooped over him. Once again, he resigned himself to death. He stopped running and looked up as the huge dragon, over twenty times his length, turned in the air, neck coiling and uncoiling, head always fixed on his quarry.

He stood in the air for a moment before, with a lazy beat of his wings, landing lightly on the ground, golden body folding forward so that all four limbs supported him as he towered over Hirad. Sha-Kaan's wings tucked behind him and his head reared before shooting forward to knock Hirad from his feet. Dazed for a moment, Hirad could sense the anger and looked directly into Sha-Kaan's eyes and was surprised when he didn't see his death reflected there.

The great dragon's head was still, the mound of his body sparkling in the sunlight, obliterating any other view. Hirad didn't bother to rise but thought of speaking until Sha-Kaan's nostrils flared, sending twin lances of hot foul air into his face.

The dragon regarded him for some time, feet shifting for comfort, effortlessly clawing deep rents in the packed dry ground.

"I would say 'well met,' Hirad Coldheart but it is no such thing."

"I—" began Hirad.

"Be quiet!" Sha-Kaan's voice rolled across the Torn Wastes and clattered around the inside of Hirad's skull. "What you think is not important. What you have done is." The dragon closed his eyes and breathed in, a slow considered action. "That something so small could cause so much damage. You have put my Brood at risk."

"I don't understand."

Sha-Kaan's eyes opened to spear Hirad with his massive gaze.

"Of course you don't. But still you stole from me."

"I didn't—"

"Quiet!" thundered Sha-Kaan. "Be quiet and listen to me. Be silent until I order you to speak."

Hirad licked his lips. He could hear The Unknown slowing as he neared him, his feet cracking the dead earth and vegetation. He waved his hand behind him to keep his friend back.

Sha-Kaan spoke again, his eyes great pools of blue ire, his nostrils wide and firing repellent breath through Hirad's hair from a distance of less than three feet. The barbarian felt small, though small was hardly a strong enough word. Insignificant. And yet the imperious beast chose to speak to him rather than scorch the skin from his body and the flesh from his bones.

But there was no mistaking Sha-Kaan's mood. This was not the dragon who had seemed so amused by Hirad's presence at their first meeting beyond the dragonene dimension gate at Taranspike Castle. The meeting that had led The Raven inextricably to Parve and the deployment of Dawnthief. Now he was angry. Angry and anxious. Not for Hirad, for himself. The barbarian felt he'd hear nothing to his advantage.

He was right.

"I warned you," said Sha-Kaan. "I told you that I was keeping from you that with which you could destroy yourselves and my Brood with you. You chose not to listen. And now the results of your actions stain the sky in my dimension and in yours.

"There, Hirad Coldheart, is the problem. It is typical, I suppose, that you should contrive to save yourselves while condemning Skies know how many of my Brood to death in your defence. But your salvation can only be temporary. Because when my Brood is gone, you will be defenceless. One dragon here, bent upon your destruction, is all it will take. And there are thousands waiting to tear this place apart. Thousands." Hirad gazed into the yawning depths of Sha-Kaan's eyes, his mind a blank.

"You have no conception of what you have done, have you?" Sha-Kaan blinked very slowly, breaking Hirad's concentration. "Speak."

"No, I haven't," said Hirad. "All I do know is that we had to find and cast Dawnthief or the Wytch Lords and Wesmen would have swept us aside. You can't blame us for trying to save our own lives."

"And that is as far as you think. The ripples of your actions are no concern as you rest in the glory of your immediate triumph, are they?"

"We were bound to use all the weapons at our disposal," said Hirad a little shortly.

"This weapon was not at your disposal," said Sha-Kaan. "And it was used inaccurately. You stole it from me."

"It was there to be taken," replied Hirad. "And inaccurate or not, we used it to save Balaia."

Sha-Kaan stretched his mouth wide and laughed. The sound cracked across the Torn Wastes, setting petrified animals to flight, stopping The Unknown in his tracks and blowing Hirad onto his back. The laughter stopped abruptly, its aftershocks echoing like thunder against cliffs as they smacked against Parve's buildings.

The great dragon stretched his neck, head travelling slowly up Hirad's prone form, drool dripping from his half-open maw, until it came to rest over his face.

Hirad pushed himself up on his elbows to look into those eyes that blotted out the light. He quailed, almost able to touch the fangs that could so easily rip out his life, each easily the size of his forearm.

"Save Balaia," repeated Sha-Kaan, voice quiet and cold. "You have done nothing of the sort. Instead, you have torn a hole between our worlds and it is a hole the Kaan cannot defend for ever. And when we fail, who will defend you from your total destruction or abject slavery, do you think?" Sha-Kaan's head angled up. Hirad followed his gaze to The Unknown and Ilkar, Will and Thraun who now stood a few paces away, scared but not bowed. Hirad smiled, pride swelling his heart.

"Who are these?" demanded Sha-Kaan.

"They're The Raven, most of it."

"Friends?"

"Yes."

Sha-Kaan retracted his neck to take them all in.

"Then listen, Hirad Coldheart and The Raven. Listen closely and I shall tell you what must be done to save us all."

The Lord Tessaya walked the streets of Understone, a bottle of white grape spirit in his hand. Streets churned by fight, blood and rain, now baking hard under a hot sun which set the mud into grotesque sculptures depicting the imprint of death.

All around him, sounds of celebration echoed from the lush green slopes surrounding the town. A dozen cook fires crackled and spat, smoke spiralling into the partly cloudy sky. The shouts of sparring and the harsh laughter of storytelling rose above the general level of noise, but some sounds were missing—the screams of the tortured, the weeping of the raped and the pleas of the dying.

Tessaya was pleased. For he had not come to Understone to devastate and destroy. That endgame he reserved for the Colleges. No, he came to Understone to conquer and to rule. The first step to his domination of the whole of Balaia. A domination he could enjoy alone now that the Wytch Lords were gone.

And he would not rule by terror. In a land too large for the hand of fear, that was the way of fools. His way was simple. Control population centres through weight of numbers. Install trusted men to overlord the people and instil their own rules and discipline based on his model. Control gatherings, control talk. Be visible. The iron hand. Leave little hope and prompt no righteous anger.

Tessaya chewed his lip. It was a departure from the traditional Wesmen way but, as far as he saw it, the old way brought nothing but conflict and division. If the Wesmen were to govern Balaia, they had to adapt.

Reaching the end of the village. Tessaya paused a moment and drank from his bottle. Before him ran the trails that burrowed deep into the heart of Eastern Balaia. The arteries down which he would march to victory.

Rising on each side, gentle green slopes rolled away toward the stunning flatlands that were home to Lord Denebre, an old trading partner. There, the farmland was rich, the animals plentiful and the peace complete. For now.

There were decisions to be made but first there were questions to be asked. Tessaya headed left up a slope to where Understone's defenders had built their barracks, now their prison. Two dozen canvas and wood structures, built for two hundred men. Six of them now housed around three hundred prisoners, leaving plenty of room for his men, those few that wanted shelter. Men and women were separated and the wounded Wesmen lay side by side with Eastern Balaians. Enemies they might be but they deserved honour and the chance to live after choosing to fight over the coward's route of surrender.

Walking toward the barracks, he noted with pleasure the bearing of the guards. Ramrod straight and placed at even intervals surrounding the prison huts. He nodded at the man who opened the door for him.

"My Lord," said the man, bowing his head in deference.

Inside, the barrack hut was cramped, stuffy and hot. Men sprawled on bunk and floor, some played cards, others spoke in huddles. One thing linked them all. It was the face of defeat, the humiliation of abject surrender.

As Tessaya entered, quiet spread along the length of the hut until all those scared eyes stared at him, waiting for him to deliver their fate. The contempt with which he regarded them was palpable.

"Time to talk," he said in faultless pure-East dialect. One man moved through the throng. He was fat, greying and too short for a warrior. Perhaps in the past he had been powerful but now his mud-stained armour covered nothing more frightening than blubber.

"I am Kerus, garrison commander of Understone. You may address your questions to me."

"And I am Tessaya, Lord of the unified tribes. You will address me as 'my Lord.'" Kerus said nothing, merely inclined his head. Tessaya could see the fear in his eyes. He should have been put out to grass a long time ago. It was indicative of the East's complacency that they chose a career desk soldier to command the guard of the most important tactical landmark in the whole of Balaia.

"I am surprised that you are the spokesman," said Tessaya. "Is your commander so fearful of us that he still orders you to hide him?"

"Understone's defensive general is dead, my Lord," said Kerus, surprise edging his tone. "I am the most senior officer left alive."

Tessaya frowned. His intelligence suggested the army had surrendered long before the command post was taken. Perhaps the other rumours were true and Darrick had died leading the line but it seemed unlikely in such a critical engagement.

"Dead?"

"At the western end of the pass."

"Ah." Tessaya's frown deepened. Something wasn't right. "No matter." He would get to the bottom of it shortly. Darrick was a man whose whereabouts he needed to know. "Tell me, I'm curious. Was there an incursion into my lands before we retook Understone Pass?" He knew there had to have been but an idea of numbers would be useful.

"Why are you asking me, my Lord?" replied Kerus.

"Because you are the commanding officer. You are also my prisoner. I would advise against the futility of refusing me."

"You know as well as I do that our people penetrated your Wytch Lords' citadel. That's why you lost your magic." Kerus did his best to sneer.

"But not this battle, eh Kerus?" Tessaya's face dropped to a snarl. "That is the second time you have failed to address me correctly. Do not make me count to three." He relaxed his stance enough to drink from his bottle, taking in the angry faces in front of him.

"An impressive move. Though I must confess, I had my reservations about the strength of Parve's defence. I'm afraid too many senior Shamen felt it a waste of good warriors. How many did you send?"

"Not many. My Lord."

"How many?"

"Four hundred cavalry, a few Protectors, a handful of mages and The Raven. My Lord."

Tessaya took it all in, quietly assimilating the numbers and knowing that they should have been far short of enough to trouble Parve's defence, let alone the Wytch Lords. He made exaggerated assumptions about the power of the mage contingent and still couldn't make it add up. A nagging worry edged at his mind. He'd seen the power of the spell that had taken Understone Pass, the water magic that had obliterated so many of his kinsmen. Had they used something equally appalling or even worse to destroy the Wytch Lords?

He shuddered inside. Rumours of an attempt to recover a spell of legendary power, the spell the Shamen called "Tia-fere," Nightfall, had cast doubt over the sense of the invasion three months before. But surely if the spell had been recovered, he wouldn't be standing here.

"The Raven." Tessaya mulled the name over. Good warriors. Never to be underestimated as it seemed they had been by the Wytch Lords and their council of fawning Shamen.

"Why did The Raven travel to Parve?" he asked.

"Isn't it obvious?" Kerus wore his slightly smug expression once more.

"They carried with them the means to destroy your Masters. It is also obvious that they succeeded. My Lord."

Tessaya wasn't sure the probable destruction of the Wytch Lords bothered him. All he knew was that the Shamen, having lost their fire, were once again in their proper place, occupying the shadows behind the tribal Lords and warriors.

What did worry him was the fact that a few hundred men and mages had penetrated to the very heart of Wesmen faith. An act that had to take a good deal of tactical skill, power and bravery to succeed. A chill stole across Tessaya's back as events started to fall into place. The rumours started to make sense— the Shadow Company patrolling the highlands, the dread force marauding south of Parve and the horsemen who never ceased to ride. It all happened after the water attack in the pass. The chill deepened. Only one man would have the audacity to believe he could reach Parve with a few hundred men.

"Who was the Commander who died at the pass?" he demanded.

"Neneth. My Lord."

"And the leader of the cavalry was Darrick."

"Aye, my Lord. And he'll be back, rely on that."

Kerus' words haunted Tessaya all the way down Understone's main street.

Chapter 3

B arrass was enjoying a moment of happiness, an oasis in the desert of his hopelessness, when the Wesmen made the decisive break through Julatsa's border defences.

To his eye, there was nothing more heartwarming than to see the sun rise above the Tower of the College of Julatsa. To see the darkness flee from every corner of every building, to see light sparkling from the pinnacle of each roof and then be able to look west toward Triverne Lake and see the birthplace of Balaian magic cast its shimmering pattern on the dark backdrop of the Blackthorne Mountains.

He used to believe that nothing in the world could hurt him while he could see that sight. But then the Wesmen breach shattered the Julatsan lines and he realised that unless the ultimate action was taken, he'd never see it again.

For a short time he watched in horror as the Wesmen spilled into the streets of his city, fighting running battles with the remnants of the city Guard, the spell casting desultory and ineffective. After the first breach, fractures appeared all along the line until the Wesmen advance was a storm destined to break over the College walls. He could not allow that to happen.

Barras turned to General Kard and saw tears on the senior soldier's cheeks. He placed a hand on the man's shoulder.

"General," he said gently. "Let me at least save the College." Kard looked at him, registering his words after some delay, his lips moving and his forehead furrowing deeply.

"It can't be done."

"It can. All I need is your authority."

"It is given," said Kard immediately. Barras nodded and summoned an aide.

"Sound the emergency alarm, summon the perimeter guard inside the walls, quadruple the forces at the gates. I am going to the Heart of the Tower and will bring the Council to me. We will begin casting without pause. Don't delay your actions."

The aide looked at Barras for a moment, drinking in the words he had clearly never thought to hear.

"At once, Master Barras."

Barras stole another glance out over the Tower ramparts, the College walls and the streets of Julatsa. The wave was rising, the panic spreading; the noise was deafening.

Wesmen howled in scent of victory, defenders yelled futile rallying cries and ordinary men and women ran for their lives. As the alarms sounded, discordant bells clamouring for attention, the Julatsan population turned and ran for the College gates.

Barras mouthed a silent apology and prayer to all those who would remain outside to die. "Come on, Kard. Best you don't see this."

"See what?"

"We're deploying the DemonShroud." He strode to the door of the Tower, which was opened by an attendant, and swept through, taking the stairs down two at a time, displaying an agility that belied his advanced years.

With Kard puffing along behind him, he reached the Heart of the Tower to join the Council, taking his place in the circle barely even breathing harder. It was something else Kard wouldn't understand. A mage had to be fit, no matter the age. A strong cardiovascular system was critical for casting and for mana stamina recovery.

"Will you guard the door, General Kard?" Barras asked.

"It would be an honour," said the General, who had stopped at the door, the force of the mana inside the Heart making him uneasy though he could see nothing of it. He bowed to the Council and closed the door. His presence would ensure there were no interruptions.

The Heart of the Tower of Julatsa was a chamber set at ground level, its eight smoothed greystone segments building to a point twice a man's height above the exact centre of a helical floor pattern. A single line of stone flags spiralled inward from the door to the Heart, disappearing in its centre. And from that point burned the mana light, a candle flame-sized teardrop which never wavered and cast no glow despite its yellow colour. Because only a mage could see it. To a nonmage, there was no teardrop at all.

The other seven members of the Council nodded to Barras in turn as he took up his position among them, each one standing flush with one greystone wall segment. When Kard closed the door, the darkness was complete.

Barras could feel the nervousness of the Council, members young and old. It was hardly surprising. DemonShroud was Julatsa's most difficult, dangerous and powerful spell. Only twice had it been cast before, both times well before any of the current Council had been born, and both times at moments of extreme danger for the College of Julatsa.

All knew the import of their intended casting. All had prepared themselves for the potential eventuality of its casting when the Wesmen attack began. All were aware that only seven of them would step from the Heart when it was done. None knew who would be chosen.

"Shall we have light for our casting?" the High Mage asked of the

Council. The traditional words came from directly opposite Barras. One by one, the Council replied.

"Aye, light for us to see one another and to gain strength from the seeing."

"My mage, Barras, who called us to the Heart, bring light to us," said the High Mage.

"It will be done," replied Barras. He prepared the shape for a LightGlobe, as he knew he would have to. It was a simple shape, a static hemisphere, drawn quickly from the mana channelling into the Heart. The expenditure of effort was minimal and Barras deployed the LightGlobe just above the mana candle, its gentle light banishing shadows and illuminating the Council.

Barras took them in with a slow sweep of his head, bowing to each member, drinking in their expressions and knowing that he would never see one of them again, and that it might be him taken by the demons.

To his left, Endorr, the junior. A Council member only fully fledged seven weeks before at the High Chamber. A great talent, Endorr was short, ugly and powerful. It would be a pity to lose him.

Working around the circle, he took in Vilif, the ancient secretary to the Council, stooped, hairless and close to his time. Seldane, one of two females on the council, late middle-aged, grey-haired and sour. Kerela, the High Mage, a close personal friend and fellow elf. They could ill afford to lose her at a time like this. Tall, dark and proud, Kerela led the Council with a steel determination respected by the entire College. Deale, another elf, ageing and given to rash talk. His was a face full of fear, his long features drawn and pale. Cordolan, middle-aged, portly and jovial. His balding pate showed sweat in the light of the Globe and his jowls held a heaviness. He could do with more exercise; his stamina would otherwise suffer.

And finally, to Barras' immediate right, Torvis. Old, impetuous, energetic, wrinkled and very tall. A quite wonderful man.

"Shall we begin?" The High Mage brought them all around. "I thank you, Barras, for your gift of light." And there, the normal formalities ended.

"Members of the Julatsan Council," said Kerela. "We are gathered because a critical threat exists to our College. Unless our proposed action is taken, it is certain that the College will fall. Do any of the Council disagree with that interpretation?"

Silence.

"Knowing the risks involved in the deployment of the DemonShroud, do any of the Council wish to remain outside the Heart during the casting?"

From Barras' right, Torvis chuckled, his irreverence lifting the mana-laden tension temporarily.

"Kerela, really," he said, his voice like dried leaves underfoot. "By the time we have spoken all our words of caution, the Shamen will be in here with us to assist our casting. No one is leaving, you know it."

Kerela frowned but her eyes sparkled with passing humour. Barras nodded his agreement.

"Torvis is anxious to join a new dimension," he said. "We should begin at once."

"I had to offer the chance," said Kerela.

"I know," said Barras. "We all know." He smiled. "Lead us, Kerela."

The High Mage breathed deep, taking in the Council once more.

"To you who sacrifices their life to save this College and the magics of Julatsa, may you quickly find peace and the souls of your loved ones." She paused. "Follow my words closely. Do not deviate from my instructions. Let nothing but my voice deflect you from your concentration. Now." And her tone hardened, taking on total authority. "Place your palms on the greystone behind you and accept the mana spectrum into your eyes."

Barras pressed his hands to the cool stone segment behind him and moved his vision to focus on the mana flowing all around him. The sight was at once breathtaking and frightening.

The Heart of the Tower of Julatsa was a mana reservoir, the shape and substance of its walls drawing the fuel of magic within its boundaries and keeping it there. The strongest reflectors were the eight stone wall segments themselves and the mana rolled up their faces to the apex of the Heart. Barras traced the flow, the eight streams of mana coming together before plunging in a single column through the centre of the Heart and the flagged stone floor.

Below his feet, Barras knew, the exact mirror image of the room in which the Council stood completed the circuit of power. Placing his hands on the stone brought Barras into that circuit.

Each member of the Council started or gasped as the mana channelled through them, increasing pulses, clearing minds for intense concentration and charging every muscle to the highest state of potential for action.

"Breathe the mana." Kerela's voice, strong and clear, sounded through the Heart. "Understand its flow. Enjoy its power. Know its potential. Speak your name when you are ready to begin the summoning."

One by one, the Council members spoke their names, Barras' voice confident and loud, Torvis' with a touch of impatience, Deale's quiet and scared.

"Very well," said Kerela. "We will open the path and summon the Shroud Master. Be prepared for his appearance. Construct the circle."

Eight voices intoned quietly, speaking the words that would shape the mana and begin the summoning. Barras' heart beat faster, his hands pressed harder against the greystone, his words, ancient and powerful, rolled around his mouth like oil in a drum, spilling from his lips in a single unbroken stream.

The flow of the mana changed. At first, gentle tugging distorted the shape of its course up the wall segments. More urgent pulls followed before, with a suddenness that stole a heartbeat, the mana flow snapped away from the walls and was driven, not by nature and stone but by mages. Residual flow continued to circulate but, at eye level, a circle of mana was established, maintained by all eight senior mages, a hand's breadth wide, solid yellow and absolutely still.

"Excellent," murmured Kerela, her voice quieter now, her concentration completely on the spell in preparation. "We have totality. Now, draw the shape to a column that kisses the stone at our feet."

Julatsa's Mage Council took their hands from the wall behind them and let their fingertips enter the mana circle. To Barras, it was a feeling like touching soft cloth, delicate and beautiful. As he drew his hands down in exact synchronicity with his fellow mages, forming the flawless cylindrical shape with his mind as much as with his hands' heightened touch sense, Barras rolled one word over in his mind. "Gently. Gently."

To tear the cylinder would jeopardise not only the spell but the health of the Council. This far into the casting, headaches, bleeding from the ears and temporary blindness were real risks of any mistake or backfire.

But mages were elected to the Julatsan Council for their skill and, with all mages finishing in a crouched position, the column was complete and perfect in less than a hundred beats of Barras' heart.

"Excellent," breathed Kerela. "Is everybody secure?" No one indicated otherwise. "Endorr, Seldane, Deale, Torvis. You will anchor the column. On my signal we others will withdraw. Do not resist the extra burden, keep your minds open." She paused. "On my count. Withdrawing in three, two, one . . ." Barras, Vilif, Kerela and Cordolan withdrew their hands and stood up. Barras smiled as he saw Endorr accept the rising mana stamina drain with a puff of his cheeks and nothing more. The old elf had to resist an urge to pat the young mage on his shoulder. He really was very accomplished for his age.

The four anchoring mages steadied themselves. Until the completion of the summoning, they would focus all their energies on maintaining the mana column in its perfect state. Should it breach before the summoning was complete, the forces unleashed would rip the Heart to pieces.

Kerela gazed briefly around Julatsa's central chamber, nodding in admiration.

"We are a strong Council," she said. "Our inevitable weakening is a tragedy for Julatsa." She sighed and pressed her hands together. "Come. Stand for the summoning. Barras, you will keep the portal open." Barras nodded, disappointed but not surprised at the relief he felt. As the portal guard, the demons could not take him nor risk being trapped in the killing air of Balaia.

The four mages stepped right up to the mana column, their faces scant inches from its still surface. Each mage stared directly ahead into the eyes of the mage opposite, pairing for strength. Kerela opened her mouth to speak.

"Though I say the words, we shall all create the shape. Lend me your strength." She cleared her throat. "Heilara diun thar." The temperature in the room dipped. Kerela's next words steamed from her lips. "Heilera diun thar, mext heiron duin thar." The quartet of mages plucked more mana from the air, forming a tight disc of swirling yellow shot through with blue flecks.

The disc hovered above the cylinder, spinning fast, its edges blurred.

"Slowly," said Kerela. "Draw it gently inside the cylinder." With their noses touching the perfect yellow column, the disc-mages moved the disc inside, feeling its edge stir the calm of the anchored mana shape as it descended.

"Heilera, duin, scorthos erida," intoned Kerela. The blue in the disc gained in intensity, deep pulses flaring along the inside of the column, shuddering the anchoring mages. Their grip remained firm.

The disc descended, Barras and the three controllers struggling to keep it horizontal and maintain its crawling pace against a force that sucked from below and gained in strength: the demons knew they were coming.

"Steady," urged Kerela, her voice distant with concentration. "Steady. Cordolan, you are ragged." The disc, which had wobbled minutely, steadied immediately, the flaring inside the column violent as it dropped still further, crossing the mana candle, caressing the stone floor.

"Barras, be ready," said Kerela. "Heilera, senduin, scorthonere an estolan." A black dot appeared in the centre of the disc, widening quickly. Blue mana light flowed out, expanding as the hole grew. With a snap, the disc became a thin circle of Julatsan mana, containing a flow of ferocious blue light which hammered at the apex of the Heart and spilled down the greystone segments. Whispering filled the air, taunts, demands, gentle offers laced with evil, crowding the mages with their sound. The words picked at their courage, the susurrant tone leaching through their bodies, setting skin crawling, heads spinning and drying mouths. The door to the demon dimension was open.

"Barras, are you steady?" asked the High Mage. Barras nodded, unable to speak. Every muscle in his body was taut, his brain felt as if it heaved in his skull, yet he knew he could maintain the door indefinitely. The forces trying to smash away his control and flood the Heart were not strong enough. His confidence escalated, his muscles began to relax, the pressure in his head easing. He smiled.

"Yes, Kerela, I am steady. Call the Shroud Master."

"Aye," said Kerela. "Cordolan, Vilif, step away from the column. This is my task alone." The High Mage plunged her head into and through the column, burying her face in the blue demon light. Barras saw her features strain, leaving her face skull-like in the mage light. The old elven mage held the door still. Not for Julatsa but for his High Mage, for Kerela.

For her part, Julatsa's elder mage stared full into the face of the demon gale, and with her voice as strong as the moment she had begun the spell, she spoke.

"Heilera, duis . . . I, Kerela, High Mage of the Julatsan Council of Balaia, call you, Heila, Great One and Shroud Master. Come to me, hear our request and state your price."

For a time, there was nothing. The whispering was unchanged, ignoring the summoning High Mage.

"Hear me," said Kerela. "Heila, hear me."

Abruptly, the whispering ceased.

"I hear." The voice, warm and friendly, attacked the air of the Heart. The Council members started but the anchor held firm. So did the gateway.

And then He was there. Alone. Floating above the candle and rotating slowly, legs crossed, arms clasped and in his lap. And with his appearance, the column evaporated, the anchor mages waking from their reverie of concentration as the mana flow rebuilt along its natural lines.

Only Kerela stood firm, within touching distance of the DemonShroud Master.

"Your presence is welcome," she said.

"Hardly," replied Heila. "Hardly." And he seemed genuinely sorry to be in their company.

Barras backed away but kept his mind firmly focused on the dimension door. To let it close would be a disaster. Before Heila's inevitable death in an alien dimension, he could tear their souls to shreds. Around Barras, not a breath was drawn from the Council who, all but Kerela, had retreated to their wall segments. As if distance would make any difference.

In the centre of the Heart, floated the demon and the incomprehensible part of it was that, to Barras, the appearance and bearing had no evil about it. Heila was a little over four feet tall, his naked humanoid body coloured a gentle deep blue. His head was bald, embossed with pulsing veins and around his cheeks, upper lip, chin and neck, sprouted a carefully tended beard. His eyes, small and sunken, were black and as he turned past Barras and caught the mage's eye, the elf saw all the malice they contained.

Heila's motion stopped when he faced Kerela. He frowned, brows darting in to give his face a pinched, angry look.

"I was resting," he said. "Tell me what you require and we will discuss a price."

Barras shivered inwardly. That price would be the soul of one of the Council for as long as Heila wanted it.

Kerela met Heila's eyes without flinching.

"Our College is at risk from invasion. The enemy must not breach our walls. We require a Shroud to encircle the walls, protecting those inside and taking everyone who dares touch it. The Shroud must encompass the principal mana flow of the College which must not be lost."

"And for how long will this Shroud be needed?" asked Heila.

"Until the siege is lifted. Several weeks. We cannot be definite."

Heila raised his eyebrows. "Really? Well, well." His rotating motion began again, his bleak eyes searching deep into the faces of the Council.

"There is a price," said the demon. "You understand our energies are depleted by the maintenance of a Shroud. We must have fuel to replenish ourselves."

Barras felt a cold trickle through his body. Human life reduced to fuel for a demonic conjuration. It was barbaric, hideous. It was also Julatsa's only choice. Heila had stopped and was looking at him. He fought briefly and successfully to maintain his concentration on the portal.

"And you are the lucky one," said Heila. "I cannot touch you. Shame. Your elven soul would have been my choice."

"We are none of us lucky." Barras' calm voice was no reflection of his inner bearing. "Today, we will all lose people we know. Choose and begone."

Heila smiled, his body snapped round to face the High Mage.

"You, Kerela, are the chosen. You will fuel the Shroud your College so desperately needs." There was a hiss of indrawn breath. No demon should take the High Mage. It was like felling the tree before its fruit had grown. But Kerela just smiled.

"So be—" she began.

"No!" shouted Deale, his face pale, his body shaking. "If she goes, saving the College is worthless. Don't be bloody-minded, Heila. If you want an elf, then take me. When I entered this chamber I knew I would be chosen. And when you were summoned, you knew it too. Take your rightful victim. Take me."

Heila spun to face Deale. "Remarkable," he said. "But I fear you are in no position to bargain."

"We can always dispatch you back to where you came from, empty-handed," said Deale evenly, his face slick with sweat.

"Then you would not have your Shroud."

"And you would not have the soul of a Julatsan Council member, let alone that of the High Mage."

"Deale, I—" began Kerela.

"No, Kerela. He will not take you."

Heila regarded Deale coldly. "I am not used to being challenged." Deale shrugged. "Very well." Heila began his rotation once more. "Hear me, Council of Julatsa. This is the bargain I offer you.

"The soul of Deale the elf is not so highly prized as that of either Kerela, the High Mage, or Barras, the elder negotiator. But I will agree to take him over any of you on one condition. If, after fifty of your days, you still need the Shroud to keep your enemies at bay, either Barras or Kerela shall walk into the Shroud to provide new fuel. I leave it to you to decide who it should be. If neither of you approaches the Shroud, it will be removed and you will be left to die. Do we have a bargain?"

"The price for a DemonShroud is only ever one soul," snapped Kerela. "If mine is prized enough, then . . ."

"Kerela, the College cannot afford to lose you," said Deale. "Not at this time. We need a leader. You are it. You have to stay." Deale spun to take in his colleagues. Barras could see each of them struggling to avoid his eye. "Well, don't you agree? I should be taken and Kerela should remain? Well?"

The old mage watched as first one, then another of them nodded. All reluctant, all knowing that by their agreement they saved themselves but none wishing to condemn Deale to death.

"There," said Deale, his voice strong though his body still shook. "We have agreement." He faced Heila who was regarding him solemnly, one hand on his chin, lipless mouth partly open to reveal his tiny razor-sharp teeth. "Heila, Shroud Master and Great One, we have a bargain."

The demon nodded. "Never before have I heard man or elf argue so strongly for his own death."

"When will the Shroud be raised?" demanded Kerela, looking not at Heila but at Deale, her eyes brim with tears.

"The moment I am gone and the portal is closed. It shall stand outside your walls and encompass the core threads of your mana as you require."

Kerela nodded. "Be of your words, Heila. Our friend sacrifices himself for this. Deale, the blessing of the College shall go with you. I . . . Your sacrifice is such that . . ." She trailed off and smiled at Deale. It was the saddest smile Barras had ever seen. "Find peace quickly."

"Time is short," said Heila. "You have fifty of your days. Count them, as I will." His gaze snapped to Deale. "For you, my friend, those days and any after them that I choose shall each seem an eternity. Come with me." His hand extended, stretched beyond the confines of the portal, passing through Deale's chest and suffusing his body with blue light. At the end, Deale was calm. His face displayed no fear. He jerked once as his soul was taken, his body falling to the ground betraying no evidence of the violence of his mortal death.

Heila rotated fast and fell through the portal, Barras slamming it shut behind him. There was a momentary whispering, then all was still.

"It is done," said Kerela, and her voice cracked. Tears rolled down her cheeks and she sank to the floor. Seldane walked quickly to Deale's body and closed his eyes.

"We must—" The door to the Heart burst open and Kard staggered in, hands clutching at his ears, his face colourless, his eyes wide. He should not have been able to cross the threshold, such was the weight of mana in the Heart, but the clamour that followed him in told its own story.

The stifling pressure of the fuel of magic was as nothing compared to the screams of those, Wesmen and Julatsans, that soared over the noise of battle, silencing every blade. It was a sound quite unlike anything that could be associated with the Balaian dimension. Piercing, driven cries that emanated from the depths of human bodies as souls were torn from their living frames, echoing through the skulls of everyone who heard them, grinding teeth and freezing muscle.

Kerela raised her head and locked eyes with Barras, all the horror of their actions reflected there for the old elf to see.

The DemonShroud had risen.

CHAPTER 4

As it always does, curiosity eventually got the better of fear. The return of Sha-Kaan to his own dimension removed the immediate threat of death and, by the time The Raven walked slowly into the Central Square, a crowd was gathering around the body of the dragon.

"Back in a while," said The Unknown, trotting away toward the corpse. Ever the warrior, ever the tactician, thought Hirad, watching his friend shoulder his way through Darrick's cavalry. A knot of Protectors with their backs to him parted instinctively to let him through. He hadn't gone to stare and shake his head at the enormity of it all. He'd gone to check closely for weak points; any chinks in the dragon's hide that might help them.

Hirad wasn't convinced he'd find any and for his part had seen enough of dragons for one day. For a lifetime, come to that, but that wasn't a choice that was his to make any more. He trudged back toward Will's spluttering cook-fire and the tunnel that led into the pyramid and the former tomb of the Wytch Lords. He needed something to calm his nerves and hoped there was at least a drain of coffee left in the pot balanced precariously on the shifting embers.

Ilkar had walked back with his arm around the shoulders of the nervy barbarian, not saying a word all the way. Hirad felt him tense as they neared the tunnel. Just in the shadow stood Styliann, above the prone form of Denser and the kneeling Erienne.

"Can't that bastard go somewhere else?" muttered the Julatsan mage. "His presence offends me."

"I don't think he'll hang around long after he's heard what we have to say."

Ilkar snorted. "Well, I'd like to think he'd take the quick way back to Xetesk, too. Unfortunately, we're all going the same way."

Hirad was quiet for a time. "You know, I was looking forward to joining the war against the Wesmen," he said after a while and just as they stopped at the fire. "It seemed like a return to the simple things. But this . . ."

"I know what you mean," said Ilkar. "C'mon, sit down. I'll check the pot."

Denser had heaved himself to his feet and stood leaning against Erienne, expectancy and anxiety radiating from his pale features in equal measure.

"I think you'd better come out here and listen to this," said Hirad. "That includes you, Styliann. Things aren't so good."

"Define 'not-so-good,'" said Styliann, emerging into the sunlight and absently adjusting his shirt collar.

"Let's wait till we're all gathered, all right?" said Ilkar, handing a half mug of coffee to Hirad and sitting beside the barbarian. He nodded in the direction of the dragon's body, from which Will and Thraun were coming. The Unknown hadn't finished his examination. "I don't want to report anything inaccurately."

No one had dared even to reach out a hand to touch the dragon's cooling corpse until The Unknown crouched by its head and heaved back a heavy eyelid. From another dimension, it might have been, but The Unknown knew a dead animal when he saw its eye and this one was dead.

He let the lid snap back over the milky white eye rolled up in the skull of the beast and leaned back on his haunches, appraising the dragon, which lay on its side. Close up, he could see its rust-brown colour was due to two distinct scales, one a deep red the other, less prevalent, a dull brown. He let his eyes flicker over the head, a wedge shape about three feet long from the nostrils, which overhung the jaws, to the base of the neck. One fang was visible beneath folds of tough hide that served as lips. Another, broken, lay a few feet away. The shard was about four inches long. The Unknown picked it up, turned it over in his hands briefly and pocketed it.

The bony skull wedge swept back to protect an apparently vital area of neck beneath it. Inadequately, The Unknown decided, given the multiple-puncture wound inflicted so easily by Sha-Kaan.

He leant forward again and attempted to open the jaws, levering against the huge muscles in his arms. They parted slightly but sprang back together as he sought to look inside the mouth. He glanced up and caught the eyes of two of the thirty or so men and Protectors prodding at the carcass.

"Give me a hand here, would you?" he asked. The cavalrymen practically fell over themselves in their haste to aid not merely a member of The Raven but The Unknown Warrior to boot. Together, the three of them laid the dragon's head flat on its side and, while Darrick's men held the upper jaw, The Unknown levered down the lower and looked inside, gasping at the foul stench from within.

There was nothing too unusual about its teeth. Four large fangs, two up, two down, were the mark of a predator, as were the rows of shorter, conical incisors at the front of each jaw. Crushing molars lined up as the jaw went back but it was the gum below and inside the jaws that interested The Unknown.

He counted half a dozen angled flaps of skin, each covering a hole. Working at one of the flaps, he could feel the retractor muscle move and, as he did so, a drop of clear liquid spilled on to his palm, evaporating quickly. It was all he needed to understand about where the fire came from.

He nodded his thanks to the two cavalrymen and stood up, letting go the lower jaw which closed with a wet squelch. He looked along the dragon's length and began walking slowly down it. Slightly kinked, the neck was perhaps eight feet long, letting into the bulk of its belly. It was an altogether more slender beast than Sha-Kaan, built for speed but, thought The Unknown, given the ease with which it was killed, inexperienced. Young. Elbowed forelimbs ended in small claws, an evolutionary trait that suggested a move toward a need for relative delicacy. Each claw was hooked and sharp and forged from bone, not a hardened material like nails.

Just above the forelimbs were the roots of its wings and The Unknown didn't have to get close to see the immense muscle groups that powered the animal through the sky at such speeds. At another request, ten willing men dragged the free wing wide against the strain of its contracted muscles.

The outside arc of the wing covered a length of around thirty feet and was a flexible bone as thick as The Unknown's thigh. A further twelve bones led from a complex joint at the end of the bone and stretched between them all was a thick, oily membrane.

"Hold it taut." The Unknown drew a dagger and stabbed down at the membrane, drawing a scratch which yielded a little dark fluid. Not blood, more of the oil. He dragged a finger through it and rubbed it between thumb and forefinger, feeling its smooth texture. "Interesting," he said. But the membrane, although perhaps only a half inch thick, would not tear. "Thank you," he said. And the men let it go. It snapped back against the body, a protective mechanism that transcended death, creating a breeze that kicked up more dust, merely emphasising the incredible power of the beast.

The length of its neck was a fifth of its main body. With the dragon on its side, its bulk was taller than The Unknown and he traced his fingers along the softer, paler underbelly scales, feeling the rasping roughness of those that armoured its sides and back. Again he drew a dagger, this time squatting by the belly. But again, his stabbing made no impact.

He frowned and turned his attention to the scorch mark along the flank which ran for twenty or so feet. Here, the skin was blistered and blackened, deep wounds showed in half a dozen places and a gory black ooze filled the tears and hard burns. But even this had not been a fatal wound. Not even the full force of Sha-Kaan's breath could inflict that in one strike.

"Gods, but you're tough bastards," he murmured. The search for a weak point went on.

"What the hell is he doing?" asked Denser dully. The Unknown could be seen striding along the dragon's upper flank toward the twenty feet of thin, balancing tail, poking his sword in here and there, striking hard in other places and always shaking his head.

"Working out how to kill one, I expect," said Ilkar.

"Fat chance," said Hirad.

"So why does he bother?" asked Denser, pursing his lips and lying back, his interest gone.

"Because that's what The Unknown does," replied Hirad. "He has to know, for better or worse, the enemy he's facing. He says knowing what you can't do is more valuable than knowing what you can."

"There's sense in that," said Thraun.

"This is all very fascinating," said Styliann. "But do we really have to wait for him?"

"Yes," said Hirad simply. "He's Raven." The Unknown was walking back toward them. He rammed his sword back into its scabbard, having first unlinked the chains that held it in place, hilt over his right shoulder, point below the back of his left knee, and dropped it at his feet as he reached them. He sat, frowning.

"Well?"

"Sha-Kaan was right. Even assuming we could get near it, the only soft tissue is inside the mouth and I can't see it opening its jaws and showing off its throat to help us out. Our one chance is to dry out the wings. They secrete some form of oil and, without it, I think they might crack under heat. But again, covering the area they do, that much flame is only going to come from another dragon."

"Eyes?" Hirad shrugged.

"Small target. Not viable if the head is moving. One of those things in this dimension could kill anything and any number it wanted."

"You've forgotten the power of magic," said Styliann stiffly. The Unknown ignored him.

"The hide is incredibly tough. Even on the underside and the wings. Acid might have an effect, so will certain flame- and perhaps ice-based magics. But, as with all these things, our real problem will be getting close enough." The Unknown breathed out through his nose. "The bare fact is that if one attacks and you've nowhere to hide, you're dead."

"That's not the answer we were looking for," said Ilkar.

"So going there will be suicide," said Hirad.

"So will staying here, apparently," said Will.

Denser raised a hand. "Hold on, hold on. What are you talking about now?" The Dark Mage was staring straight at Hirad.

Ilkar nudged the barbarian. "Go on then. Sha-Kaan's your friend, after all."

"He's not my friend," said Hirad.

"Closest thing to it," returned the elf.

"Oh, right, yeah. I noticed how he went out of his way to not actually burn my skin off or bite me clean in two. If that's not friendship, I don't know what is."

Ilkar chuckled. "See," he said. "Bosom buddies."

"So just because—"

"Must you?" Denser's voice cut across Hirad's next remark. "We just want to know what's up."

"You don't," said Hirad. "But here goes anyway. The situation, I think, is this." He breathed in deeply and pointed behind him. "That rip in the sky is a direct corridor to the dragon dimension. Apparently, there's a similar mess in the sky on the other side. The trouble is, Sha-Kaan's family, he called it a Brood, the Brood Kaan, has to defend the rip to stop other Broods coming here to destroy us." Hirad nodded at the dragon's corpse. "That's because they have no way to close the rip. Sha-Kaan says we have to close it."

"Oh, no problem," said Denser. "We'll just snap our fingers and the job's done. How the hell are we supposed to achieve that?"

"That was pretty much our reaction," said Ilkar. "Sha-Kaan pointed out rather bluntly that it was our problem and we'd better not fail."

"Or else what?" asked Erienne.

"Or else, ultimately, another Brood will get in here in sufficient strength to do exactly what it wants," said Ilkar. "And those of us who travelled through Septern's rip have a good idea what that means." For the Julatsan mage, the scenes of blackened devastation, the chaotic weather and air of violent death were all too easily recalled.

Movement caught Hirad's eye. Darrick had ridden back into the square, his cavalry once more under his command. He made for the dragon but changed direction at a wave from the barbarian.

"I think he ought to be in on this," said Hirad. Once apprised, Darrick's face was as gloomy as The Raven's.

"Now," said Styliann, who had remained silent and withdrawn thus far. "I accept that this rip, as you call it, represents a significant threat. I also accept that dragons are powerful creatures and we need to develop means of disabling and destroying them from distance.

"What I don't see is why other Broods would want to come here to destroy everything and why, by all the mana in the Mount, does this Sha-Kaan care if they do?"

"Now that's a good question," said Darrick.

"Ilkar?" asked Hirad. "This was where I got a little shaky in my understanding."

"Unknown, help me out if I get too vague." Ilkar rubbed his face while he thought. "There is a link between our dimension and the Brood Kaan. The very existence of certain elements here helps the Kaan to live and breed. These elements feed their psyche and that is as important to them as feeding their bellies. Their existence depends on the base fabric of our dimension remaining intact. If we go, they go. That's why they care."

"Why don't they just station enough dragons around the rip to guard it?" Styliann said sniffily.

"Well, because, strangely, they've got better things to do with their lives than die in our defence for the rest of time," snapped Hirad. "They aren't our servants." Ilkar laid a hand on Hirad's arm.

"The point is, my Lord, that they are already forced into that action," said the Julatsan. "But Sha-Kaan was insistent that, one, they couldn't guard the rip indefinitely and, two, we caused the problem and though the Kaan would help, it was up to us to sort it out."

"How long do we have?" asked Darrick.

"We don't know," said Hirad.

"That's not helpful," said Denser.

"I think the straight answer is, Sha-Kaan himself doesn't know. He just said that when the shade covers the city, it will be too late." Hirad shrugged.

"What's that, then, some kind of dragon time-keeping code?" Erienne was nonplussed.

"We're not sure yet," said Ilkar.

"Then you should open your eyes more," said Styliann.

"What?" Hirad bristled.

"Calm down, Hirad Coldheart," replied the Lord of the Mount. "I appreciate how difficult it must have been out there. But now is the time to think. There are no shadows at noon because the sun is at its highest point in the sky. Normally. But that rip will cast a shadow. No way is it big enough to shade the whole of Parve yet, but . . ."

"Oh Gods," breathed Denser. "He's saying it's not static. It's not contained. It's going to grow." He turned from them, his face fallen.

"So we've got a time limit but we don't know what it is," said Will, glancing up at the rip.

The Unknown nodded. "Yes, but we can work it out, can't we? Measure the rate of growth of the rip's shadow. It'll be rough but it'll give us an idea."

"Indeed we can," said Denser bitterly. "But there are bigger issues to settle as well."

"Like how the hell do we close it," said Erienne.

"And what is happening east of the Blackthorne Mountains," added The Unknown.

"To name but two," said Denser.

"Not being funny, but the starting point has to be your casting of Dawnthief," said Hirad.

"Absolutely," said Denser.

"Sha-Kaan termed it 'inaccurate.'" There was a smile on the barbarian's face which grew broader as the slight sank in, turning Denser's pale face to an angry red.

"And that great fat lizard would know, of course," he stormed, shaking off Erienne's calming touch. "For his information, my casting of Dawnthief saved his precious psyche-feeding dimension from its biggest ever threat. I trained my whole life for that moment . . . inaccurate. Bastard."

"Denser, you don't have to convince us. We know what you did," said Hirad. "But Sha-Kaan doesn't see it that way. He doesn't much care who runs Balaia so long as its fabric remains intact and there are enough dragonene to serve his Brood."

"But he can't expect us not to try to save ourselves," protested Denser.

"I tried that one," said Hirad. "No dice. He just accuses us of not understanding the power of the spell."

"Well, tough."

"For the Kaan and for us, yes," said Thraun.

"Right," said Will into the pause that followed. "So what are we going to do?"

Sha-Kaan emerged from the gateway into a blizzard of wings, fire and snapping jaws, the noise of a hundred cries of exultation, pain and command mingling with the whoosh of wings and the whiplash of tails. The battle covered as far as he could see in any direction, the sky full with scale and claw and enough wing to shroud Parve from the sun. It was impossible to estimate the number of dragons in the vicinity of the rip or the number of Broods involved in the battle. All he was sure of was that, barring skeleton defence of their lands, structures and peoples, the entire Brood Kaan was fighting for its collective life. There were in excess of four hundred Kaan in the sky and they were outnumbered.

Sha-Kaan roared to rally his Brood, the answering barks and cries tearing the air from all points, a surge of strength filling his mind. Sha-Kaan arced sharply upward to gauge the situation in the skies around and below him, a phalanx of guards flew with him, defending his back.

The immediate area around the gateway was charged with battle. Better than fifty Kaan flew a defensive network across its surface, denying any attacker even the slightest chance of an entry. And for those that tried, small packs of Kaan, eight or nine strong, flew attack waves, ready to drive off portal divers.

Not for the first time in his long and fertile life, Sha-Kaan had cause to thank the intensely familial nature of dragon Broods. Together, they could overwhelm the Kaan in a matter of days, but they would never hold peace long enough to organise a concerted assault. What Sha-Kaan saw were disparate groups of attackers, none with the individual strength or guile to beat the Kaan's defence which was well drilled and properly executed. It was no secret why the Kaan were the strongest Brood. They had order.

Even so, too many beats of this battle and the Kaan would weaken. He hoped he had instilled a sense of urgency in the humans and prayed to the Skies that they had the skill to close the gateway. If not, the Kaan would inevitably perish. All of them.

But for now, more immediate concerns crowded his mind. Below and to his left, three of the Brood Naik had isolated a Kaan from his attack phalanx. As he watched, helpless, the young dragon, twisting through every evasion move he'd been taught, caught blast after blast of flame. Eventually, the heat ignited one wing, the thin membrane gushing to fire as the oils which both lubricated the wing and provided a barrier against dragonfire were driven off, scorching bone and breaking sinew and muscle.

With a cry of mixed pain, defiance and fear, the young Kaan fell from the sky, spiralling out of control, one wing trailing smoke, the other beating in a vain attempt to steady its tumbling body, the tail coiling and straightening reflexively, head twisting as it sought aid. None would come. Sha-Kaan did not look to see the end but he knew what to do.

"With me," he pulsed to his wing guards. He dived steeply, silent, wings angled back and in, bulleting through the air, reaching a velocity at which he would kill or be killed. The three Naik had no inkling of what was coming. Sha-Kaan's jaws latched on to the right wing of one, pulling it wildly off balance and dragging it groundward, his huge body barely in check as it collided with his enemy, the sound of the impact clattering dully across the sky, scales grating together. The smaller beast, flailing talons, tail and free wing, barked its fury and fear, unable to turn its head fast enough to see its assailant, flame wasted on empty sky.

Sha-Kaan's momentum took them in to, for him, a controlled tumble, dragon falling slowly over dragon until with a sharp twist of his jaws, Sha-Kaan freed his victim. But the freedom was short and agonising. The Great Kaan opened his mouth again and unleashed a torrent of fire, taking the disoriented dragon across the head, neck and along the left wing.

Half-blinded, the Naik breathed a choking gout, scorching nothing but air. Sha-Kaan's jaws snapped open again and this time the fire dragged the Naik from head to tail, critically injuring wing and tail muscle. Unable to fly, the Naik dropped to its death.

Sha-Kaan barrel rolled, bellowing triumph and vengeance. He twisted his neck to assess the progress of the battle, picked another target and flew.

"The question really is, was rip formation an unavoidable side effect of the Dawnthief casting?" Styliann's question was not criticism but observation and Denser's reactive tensing eased when he saw the Lord of the Mount's expression.

The four mages still sat around the fire. Denser's pipe smouldered in his mouth and it was an effort even to suck to keep it vaguely alight. He rested in Erienne's lap, she absently stroking his hair, and Ilkar sat with them, poking at the embers with a hardwood stick. Styliann, his dark hair brushed back into its more usual tight ponytail, sat alone on the opposite side of the fire.

Out in the square, the rest of The Raven stood with Darrick, discussing the most accurate way to measure the noon shade. They hadn't long to come up with a solution. It would soon be midday.

Those of Darrick's cavalry and Styliann's Protectors not involved in guard and sentry duties had been detailed grimmer tasks. The city had to be cleared, corpses burned and every building searched for hidden enemies. Parve had to be returned to its dead state. Not a soul could remain save the volunteers Darrick would have to find to measure the shadow day by day and commune their findings.

For the quartet of mages, their talk was the heart of the problem. How could the rip to the dragon dimension be closed before the Kaan strength collapsed and Balaia fell victim to a deluge of fire?

"To answer your question, my Lord, we'll have to pull out every text of Septern's held by the Colleges," said Erienne. "It seems obvious now that the basis for Dawnthief's power is the creation of a rip into a vortex in interdimensional space. Presumably, the complete casting opens a rip big enough to suck everything in, hence 'light-stealer.'"

"And my training focused solely on control of the casting parameters, not on withdrawal," said Denser with a shrug.

Ilkar ceased his prodding of the fire. "So what you're saying is that there could have been a way to close off the vortex as you shut down the mana shape."

"Yes, but that was not detailed in the main casting texts. It might be in the Lore somewhere. Septern's understanding of dimensional magic was very deep."

"Well, it wouldn't ever be in the casting texts," said Erienne. "If you think about it, closing the vortex at both ends, which is what you're talking about, requires a new spell."

"You're assuming that nothing in the Dawnthief text and shape formation produces the same effect," remarked Ilkar.

"Well, there isn't."

"And what makes you so sure, Dordovan?" Styliann stared at Erienne straight down his nose.

"Oh, please, Styliann, we can do without your pious condescension," snapped Ilkar, surprised at his tone with the Lord of the Mount. "This is far bigger than any one College. Just listen to her."

Styliann bridled but Denser cut across any words.

"My Lord, Ilkar is right," he said. "Erienne is an Arch Research Mage."

"You have studied Septern?" asked Styliann.

Erienne shrugged. "Of course. He was Dordovan."

"By birth alone," said Styliann.

"Dordovan," affirmed Erienne. "But you don't need research to get my point, just common sense. Listen, and don't interrupt. I'm not criticising anybody." She laid a hand on Denser's arm. "All right?" Denser nodded, frowning.

"Good," said Erienne. She breathed deep. "Sha-Kaan was right in that, technically, Denser's casting of Dawnthief was inaccurate." She squeezed Denser's arm as he tensed. "But we mustn't forget Septern's original vision for the spell, though we might question why he created it."

"He was an experimenter," said Ilkar. "He just wanted to see how far he could go."

Erienne nodded. "Probably. Dawnthief, properly cast, by which I mean at full creation, duration and power, would open a vortex capable of sucking in the whole of Balaia and that includes the Southern Continent too. Let me ask you this. Would you write into the spell a method of closing the vortex when you wouldn't be around to use it?"

"So what did you do, Denser?" asked Ilkar.

"I just dismantled the shape. Rather hurriedly, I admit, but the drain on my mana reserves was critical," said the Dark Mage. "I considered that to be safer than simply withdrawing from the spell and shutting out but there was a balance. Had I not dismantled as quickly as I did, there was a danger that the shape could have grown beyond my control and I couldn't risk a backfire. Not with Dawnthief."

"And you're sure there were no other ending options?" asked Ilkar.

"You've not studied the texts beyond the mana theory, have you?" said Denser. Ilkar shook his head. So did Styliann. "No. When you examine the casting, it's quite unlike anything else you'll see. Every spell in your teaching deals with creation, catalyst if necessary, intonation, placement, duration and deployment. And that's it. When the spell shape is released, it is stable because that is built into the lore construct.

"With Dawnthief, it was different. Because there was no proper provision written for anything other than a full strength casting, limiting the power as I trained to do makes the mana shape inherently unstable. That meant I couldn't release the shape because it would have collapsed, and that is what drained my mana stamina.

"The way I had to cast meant the spell had no end other than crude reversal through dismantling. I defy anyone to come up with a better solution."

"Academic, Denser, since Dawnthief can never be recast," said Styliann. "Besides which, we are all second to your knowledge of the spell. Unfortunately, it means we can't use it as a basis for our current predicament."

"Which takes us back to our original starting point which is pooling all College papers on Septern and dimensional magics, largely one and the same thing. We also have Septern's last diaries but I suggest a return to his workshop is a must," said Ilkar.

"So we all go back to our Colleges and pilfer from the libraries?" Erienne's tone expressed clear doubt. "I don't think I'm welcome there any more."

"That won't be necessary," said Styliann. "As we near the Blackthornes, I will commune with Xetesk and issue instructions to all the Colleges to find everything they have for us. I believe Dordover and Julatsa hold the bulk of his works. Scholars there can sift the mass and we can view anything relevant at Triverne Lake."

"I think you're forgetting something rather important, my Lord," said Ilkar. "There are fifty-odd thousand Wesmen running about over there. Triverne Lake won't be an option."

Styliann smiled. "Indeed," he said. "How easily one can forget."

"We'll have to visit the Colleges ourselves," said Ilkar.

"Assuming we can reach them." Denser adjusted his position. "There are bound to be armies marauding around the Colleges. You know the Wesmen's ultimate goal."

"Yes, but they have no magic," protested Erienne.

"That won't stop them encircling the Colleges," replied Denser tersely. "There are other methods of victory than hand-to-hand warfare." Erienne frowned at his tart reaction but said nothing.

"And you haven't heard The Unknown's assessment, have you?" Ilkar raised his eyebrows. "I'll let him fill you in if you want but in a nutshell, he doesn't see we necessarily have much of a home to go to."

Styliann snorted. "No College will fall to a non-magical army, however big."

"They don't have to batter it, they can starve it," said Ilkar. "And anyway, none of the Colleges has the strength of offensive mages to halt an advance by an army that doesn't care about the level of casualties it takes. That's what is worrying The Unknown. Nevertheless, it seems our course is clear. Dordover and Julatsa must be apprised of our needs. Following that, we, that is The Raven—" he looked pointedly at Styliann "—will revisit Septern's workshop, and perhaps the Avian dimension should that be necessary. It all depends what we find in the libraries."

"So, no real problem there then," said Denser, smiling. "I can't see why we're so worried about it. Any chance I can sleep now?"

CHAPTER 5

Funeral pyres were burning for the fallen members of Darrick's cavalry. Wytch Lord acolytes, Guardians and Wesmen burned together in one corner of the square, filling the air with an acrid taint and the ash of battle's end.

Near the pyramid, which Darrick's mages had assured him was the exact centre of Parve, the General and The Raven's warriors had waited for midday. Brisk conversation had died to the sporadic remark, then quiet.

Now, with the sharp-edged shadow of the rip cast from the cloudless sky etching the ground, the stone of Parve was stained by more than blood. The shadow covered an area of around five hundred paces on the longer side, three hundred on the shorter—as far as the irregular shape could be said to have sides. It was, at best guess, ten times the size of the rip itself. The Unknown, watched by two of Darrick's Dordovan Communion mage specialists, marked the shade at four points.

Already in agreement was a calculation of noon based on the disappearance of shadow from the east face of the pyramid.

The Unknown straightened. "There we are. Today, of course, tells us nothing. Tomorrow won't either as we will have no idea of the rip's rate of growth until we have made measurements for a week or so. Are we all agreed on the calculations?"

The mages and Darrick nodded. So, after a pause, did Will. Thraun simply shrugged.

"Hirad?" The Unknown was smiling.

"You trying to be funny?" Hirad said more irritably than he intended. The Unknown walked over to him.

"I apologise. Something's wrong, isn't it?"

"Oh, not so's you'd notice," said Hirad. "I mean, all that's happened today is we've beaten what we thought was the biggest threat to Balaia, only to find there was worse lurking around the corner. What on earth should be wrong?"

The Unknown put a hand on Hirad's shoulder and turned him away from the onlooking Will and Thraun.

"That's one thing. What else?" Hirad stared at the big warrior. "Come on, Hirad. I've known you ten years. Don't pretend that's it. Not to me."

Hirad turned his head, looking over at the three Raven mages and Styliann as they talked by the fire.

"We're going to have to go there," he said, frowning. "Sha-Kaan said the rip had to be closed back to front, or something. Erienne understood. But . . ."

"I know," said The Unknown.

"Unknown, I don't know if I can."

"I'll be standing beside you. We all will. We're The Raven."

Hirad chuckled. "At least I'll be dying in good company, then."

"No one's dying, Hirad. Least of all you. You've got more lives than a cat."

"It's my destiny." Hirad shrugged. The Unknown looked at him bleakly.

"You know nothing about destiny," he said, voice low and cool. Hirad bit his lip, cursing himself for his flapping tongue. The Unknown was a man for whom that word had a truly bitter meaning.

"How do you feel?" he asked.

"Empty and alone," said The Unknown. "Like I've lost something precious." He watched a group of Styliann's Protectors who were examining the dead dragon. "You can have no idea what it's like. I can feel them but I can't be close to them, not really. They know me as one of them but can't relate to me. I'm outside of their conception yet evidently real. It's as if I'm neither Protector nor free man." The Unknown pulled off a glove and scratched his forehead with his thumb. "You don't know what your soul really is until you lose it."

"But you wouldn't still want to be one of them, would you?" Hirad too was staring at the Protectors. Xeteskian warriors, all taken before their time to the service of the College and enthralled, their souls removed from their bodies but kept alive. And kept alive to be held together in the Soul Tank, deep in the catacombs of Xetesk where the demons could reach them and punish them should they step out of line.

The Unknown had said it was both the tragedy and the glory of existence as a Protector. Never had he felt so close to his fellow men, their souls mingling in the tank, enabling them to operate as one in the flesh—the understanding of the human at the most basic level making them the awesome power they were.

But all the time, the DemonChain linking each body to the essence of the soul could be the source of unending pain. No Protector could return to his former life though he would remember every detail. The ebony mask each wore was both reminder and warning. Protectors belonged to Xetesk. They had no identity; the Dark College's deal with the demons saw to that.

Hirad shuddered. And The Unknown had been one until Laryon, the Xeteskian Master who believed in an end to the Calling, had sacrificed his life in freeing the Raven warrior.

But the legacy remained. The Unknown's time in the Soul Tank had left him permanently bonded to the remaining Protectors, some five hundred in all. And though his soul rested in his body once more and he could live mask-less, without fear of retribution from demons, Hirad knew the big man would never really be free. He could see it in The Unknown's eyes. And though he smiled, laughed and cared as much as ever he did, something was missing. He was wounded, his brotherhood cut from him. It was a wound Hirad doubted would ever close and if it did not, The Unknown would always carry with him that sense of loss.

"Hmmm?" The Unknown hadn't heard his question.

"I said, you wouldn't still want to be a Protector, would you?" repeated the barbarian.

"I can never properly describe to you what I lost when my soul reentered my body but what I gained was my former life and it was the life I loved and had chosen to live. No, I would never want to be a Protector again but nei-ther will I demand the release of those still within the Calling either. For some of them, the shock would kill them. They've been in the tank too long and their past has become meaningless. They have to want to be free."

Hirad nodded. He thought he understood. He gazed up at the rip, boiling in the sky, its white-flecked brown surface like the eye of a malevo-lent God surveying Balaia.

"I guess that's a task for later," he said. "C'mon, let's see what the mages have dreamed up."

Tessaya slept little on a night he should have slumbered deep and untroubled, cocooned in the comfort of victory and the promise of conquest. But he was restless, the fat soldier's words eating at his dreams and breaking his rest.

Darrick. The thorn in the Wesmen's hide nine years before, when the original capture of Understone Pass was first a dream, then a desire and finally a key. And still he rode, clearly instrumental in the battle which saw the dev-astation of Wesmen in the water magic which had scoured Understone Pass only a few days before.

Darrick. Through the pass and deep into Wesmen territory. To Parve, where the Wytch Lords were strongest and were beaten. There was no doubt he was pleased that the Wytch Lord influence had been removed. Though it had galvanised and united the tribes, it was a wholly unequal partnership which demanded the subjugation of the Tribal Lords beneath the Wytch Lord standard. But with the ancients gone and the power of the Shamen—which had most certainly aided the invasion—reduced once again to that of sooth-sayers, spirit guides and medicine men, the Tribal Lords could assume their rightful positions.

Yet anyone capable of orchestrating the downfall of the Wytch Lords was a threat only a fool would ignore. Tessaya wondered whether he hadn't exchanged a tyrannical master for an even greater danger to his life and leadership.

Still, as he sat up in his bed in the early hours of the morning, with the silence of Understone ringing in his ears, a mug of water in his hand to ease his throbbing head, he couldn't help but feel respect.

Respect for Darrick, his cavalry and The Raven. The latter, men surely not a great many years younger than himself but who defied death through skill and courage. He smiled. They represented an enemy he could understand and so defeat. It was his ace but a card he would have to play just right.

He knew where they must be and Parve was more than ten days' ride from Understone. Not only that, their passage to the East would be difficult in the extreme, if not impossible. Tessaya smiled again, relaxing at last. While Darrick was a man to be watched, for now at least he could be watched from a distance.

The Lord of the Paleon Tribes fought back the urge to sleep now his mind was calm. Dawn was approaching and there was a great deal to organise. Tessaya wanted all of Balaia and for that, he needed lines of communication between his armies.

With the Wytch Lords gone, messages could no longer be sent via the Shamen. Tessaya found himself smiling once more because, again, they would have to rely on the old methods. On smoke, on flags and on birds.

Tessaya had known it was likely. Despite the best efforts of the Shamen to dissuade him, he'd brought all of his messaging birds with him and had insisted his Generals do the same. His foresight meant that communication would be swift and effective but first, men would have to take his birds to each Wesmen stronghold in Eastern Balaia. There lay the risk.

If he was right, however, and the forces of the East were shattered all along the Blackthorne Mountains, his riders would comfortably reach their targets and the links could be made. Tessaya called for a guard to summon his riders, dressed quickly in shirt and leather and met them on the baked earth outside Understone's inn.

The morning was clear and bright. A cool and gentle breeze ran off the Blackthorne Mountains, which rose stark and black in front of Tessaya, stretching away north and south, stopping only to dive into the sea. He had always hated the mountains. Without the freak feature, the Wesmen would have plundered the East generations before and magic would never have been born.

The Spirits had been unkind, leaving the mighty range as a constant challenge to the Wesmen desire for conquest. Tessaya turned his tanned and weather-worn face from the unending miles of black rock at the sound of footsteps behind him. His riders approached, accompanied by Arnoan, the Shaman. Tessaya quashed a scowl. Much as he respected Arnoan, he would have to move him firmly aside from the decision-making process. Conquest was the province of warriors, not witch doctors.

"My Lord," said Arnoan, inclining his old head. Tessaya acknowledged him vaguely, focusing on his riders. Six men, lean, fit and expert horsemen in a race for whom riding was traditionally the right of nobles only.

"Three north to meet with Lord Senedai, three south to meet with Lord Taomi," said Tessaya without preamble. "You will split the birds evenly between you. To the north, you must travel to Julatsa. To the south, toward Blackthorne. I can spare you four days only to find our armies. You must not fail. Much of the glory of battles to come rests with you."

"My Lord, we will not fail you," said one.

"Ready yourselves. I shall prepare messages for you. Be back here in half an hour."

"My Lord." The riders trotted away to the stable blocks which were housed at the east end of the town.

"Arnoan, a word if I may."

"Certainly, my Lord." Tessaya gestured for the old Shaman to precede him into the inn. The two men sat at the table they had shared the day before.

"Messages, my Lord?"

"Yes, but I feel well able to phrase them myself."

Arnoan reacted as if slapped.

"Tessaya, it is the way of the Wesmen that the Shamen advise the Warrior Lords, as befits their senior positions in the affairs of the tribes." The old Shaman frowned deeply, his wispy grey hair flying in the breeze that eddied through the open inn door.

"Absolutely," said Tessaya. "But this is not a tribal affair. This is war and the Warrior Lords shall have complete control over all command decisions, choosing who they will to advise them, and when."

"But since the new rise of the Wytch Lords, the Shamen have gained respect throughout the tribes," protested Arnoan, his hands gripping the edge of the table.

"But the Wytch Lords are gone, and the respect that you saw was sown in fear of your masters. You no longer have magic, you cannot wield a sword, you have no concept of the pressure of war from the front line or the command post." Tessaya remained impassive.

"You are dismissing me, my Lord?"

Tessaya allowed his face to soften. "No, Arnoan. You are an old and trusted friend and as such, I am giving you the opportunity to take your rightful place without the eyes of the tribesmen upon you. I will ask for your advice when I require it. Until then, please do not offer it, but take some from me. The time of Shaman domination of the tribes died with the Wytch Lords. Assumption that your hold over the Wesmen still remains could prove a costly, not to say dangerous mistake."

"You are so sure that the Wytch Lords are gone. I am not so," said Arnoan.

"The evidence was there for all to see. As was the fear in your eyes when the magic was taken from you. Do not try to convince me it is any different."

Arnoan shoved his chair back, eyes suddenly ablaze.

"We helped you. Without the Shamen, you would still be west of Understone Pass, dreaming of conquest and glory. Now you have it and you cast us aside. That too could prove a costly mistake."

"Are you threatening me, Arnoan?" asked Tessaya sharply.

"No, my Lord. But ordinary men and women respect us and believe in us. Put us aside and perhaps you will lose their support."

Tessaya chuckled. "No one is putting Shamen aside and I believe in you as much as the next man," he said. "But you have a very short memory. I do not. I thank you and your Calling for the job you have done. It is now over. You are merely returning to your rightful position as spiritual leaders of the tribes. Power is not the province of the Shamen but of the Lords born to it."

"Pray that the Spirit will still support you, Lord Tessaya."

"I need no spirits. I need skill, tactics and courage in battle. Things I already possess. Tend to those who need you now, Arnoan, I will call you when I do. You may go."

"There are times when we all need the Spirit, my Lord. Do not turn your back or risk losing favour."

"You may go," repeated Tessaya, his eyes cold. He watched Arnoan walk from the inn, stance erect and proud, his head shaking in disbelief. Regretting the harshness of his words for a brief moment, Tessaya wondered whether he had made an enemy of the old man and whether it mattered if he had. He decided that, barring assassination, it did not. A short while later, he was delivering final words to his now mounted riders.

"It is critical that I receive details of ours and enemy strengths, field positions, ability to move and supply other battles, consistency of supply lines and magical resistance. It is all in the briefing notes which I expect you all to learn in case of separation or loss. There is another thing. Make the point forcefully, with my authority, that any news of The Raven, General Darrick or this dread force must be communicated to me immediately, outside of normal messaging times.

"I expect you to travel back here separately, carrying the same messages dispatched with my first birds. You will also bring back birds from Lords Senedai and Taomi. I cannot risk a hold up at this stage. Do you understand everything I've told you?"

"Yes, my Lord."

"Excellent." Tessaya nodded at each man. It was a mark of respect for courage and these men would almost certainly need that. He had toyed with the idea of sending them back through the pass and then north and south to the water crossings at the Bay of Gyernath and Triverne Inlet. But that would increase travel time by two days at least. It was time he did not have.

"Ride with courage, ride with passion, ride for the Wesmen tribes. May the Spirit aid you." The last rang hollow in Tessaya's mouth and he could imagine Arnoan's expression had he heard those words.

"My Lord." The riders turned their mounts and spurred them to the north–south trail where they split, three heading north for the College Cities, three south toward Blackthorne.

Tessaya turned and set about organising the fortification of Understone.

"I have an idea," said Baron Blackthorne. Dawn had lit up the hillside on which his men had slept. Now its light probed the cave and overhang that had served as his command post. And with the light came a slow warming of the cold rock and a fresh, crisp scent that pervaded the old dampness of the cave. It would be a day clear of rain, something for which Blackthorne was very grateful.

Gresse turned to him. The older baron was still seated, the bruising of his concussion reaching down his forehead and temples, blackening one eye as if he wore a half mask. He looked pale beneath the discoloration, his eyes bloodshot and tired.

"Will it stop this thudding in my head?" he asked, his weakened voice, just slightly slurred, further evidence of his condition.

Blackthorne smiled. "No, I'm afraid not. But it could get us back into my town sooner."

"I could do with a proper bed," said Gresse. "I'm getting a little old for lying on rock floors."

Baron Blackthorne scratched at his thick black beard and looked down at Gresse, feeling a surge of admiration for the older Baron he had quickly come to think of as his friend. Among the members of the Korina Trade Alliance, that shambolic body that did nothing but fuel the Baronial disputes it was supposed to mediate, he had been the only man who had seen the danger posed by the Wesmen. More than that, he had been the only man with the guts to speak out and the only man to believe in himself enough to ride to Balaia's defence.

He had fought long and hard alongside his own and Blackthorne's men, knowing that his lands were being plundered by short-sighted, greedy men like Baron Pontois. He had come within an ace of death as the Shamen's black fire tore flesh from the bones of man and animal alike. His own horse had died beneath him, pitching him headlong into the rock that had been the cause of his injuries. But he was still alive and by the Gods, Blackthorne would see that he not only stayed that way but reclaimed his lands. All in the fullness of time.

"We're going to Gyernath, I take it?" said Gresse.

"Yes. The Wesmen will reach Blackthorne well ahead of us and we aren't enough to lay siege or retake the town on our own. At Gyernath, we can brief the command and sail back to the Bay with reinforcements enough to cut their supply lines. And, with further detachments coming by foot and hoof, we could be back inside the walls of Blackthorne a week after arriving in Gyernath."

"Assuming the army at Gyernath agrees," said Gresse. Blackthorne looked at him askance.

"My dear Gresse, I haven't annexed the city for nothing," he said. "That army will do anything I say."

"I wish I could say I was surprised," said Gresse. "Gyernath has always given the appearance of being a free city."

"Oh it is," assured Blackthorne. "I have no authority within its borders."

"But . . ." led Gresse, a smile creeping across his dark lips.

"But travel isn't necessarily secure . . . Gods, Gresse, don't make me state the obvious."

"So, there are deals to be done."

"Of course. Like I said, I don't run the council but I do have considerable sway in the trading community."

"I bloody knew it," said Gresse, respect overshadowing the irritation in his voice. "The KTA has consistently refused to censure your actions with Lord Arlen. It now becomes clear."

"My coffers are plentiful, if that's what you mean. Or rather, they were. It depends a little on what the Wesmen have discovered." Blackthorne squatted down next to Gresse who shook his head, a smile playing about his lips.

"I think I must be the only honest Baron left," he said.

Blackthorne chuckled and patted Gresse's thigh with his left hand.

"That class of Baron is extinct and, try as you might, you will never convince me you are actually its long-lost last member. My people have experienced your brand of honesty in Taranspike Pass on more than one occasion."

"It's a treacherous place," said Gresse, his smile broadening.

"Tell me you don't levy any charge on passage to Korina via Taranspike."

"It's not a blanket fee."

"Oh thank the Gods. Not everyone pays."

"It rather depends on allegiance and cargo." The older Baron shifted. "But don't forget I provide security along the length of the pass."

"Pontois, no doubt, feels the burden of this nonblanket levy."

"His negotiations have left him a little short of a fair deal," agreed Gresse. "But if we ever get out of this mess, he'll feel the burden of something far heavier than a few gold pennies."

A soldier appeared at the overhang.

"My Lord?"

"Yes." Blackthorne picked himself to his feet and dusted himself down.

"We are in readiness. We await your orders to march."

"Excellent," said Blackthorne. "Gresse, can you ride?"

"I sit on my arse, not my head."

The soldier stifled a laugh. Blackthorne shook his head.

"I'll take that as a yes." He turned to the soldier. "You can pass that round the fires this evening, can't you? Meanwhile, we're making for Gyernath. I need scouts ahead, tracking the Wesmen return to Blackthorne. We will take the southeast trail at Varhawk Point. We leave in an hour."

"Yes, my Lord."

Blackthorne walked to the edge of the cave. The hillside was awash with action. He saw the soldier hurry to his superiors, relaying Blackthorne's orders. Voices rolled across the open space. Men leapt to their feet, packs shouldered; horses were led to their saddling areas, the remaining mages gathered themselves. What little canvas individuals owned was struck and folded. Away to the right, a soldier struggled briefly to calm a skittish horse and, here and there, fires were stoked to make the last hour of the dying as comfortable as they could be. Those unable to make the journey wouldn't be left alive, and the pyres had been built the evening before.

The Baron smiled, satisfied. Farmers, boys and regular garrison soldiers mixed in a single purpose, moving with impressive order, readying themselves for the march. The next weeks would seal the fate of the entire Blackthorne Barony. He needed them. If they could alert Gyernath, defend the bay beaches and regain the town, the south would have a strong foothold in their own lands that could be used to strike further against the Wesmen.

The smile left Blackthorne's face. For all his talk and thought, Balaia was a mess. Understone and the pass were surely in Wesmen hands; the Colleges could fall despite the loss of Shamen magic; he, Baron Blackthorne, most powerful landowner in Eastern Balaia, was homeless, chasing the hillsides with a band of townsmen, farmers and wounded, tired soldiers.

It got worse. The Raven were trapped in the West; much of the fighting strength of the East was wrapped up in lone garrison defence or fragmented between bickering barons more concerned with maintaining obsolete land boundaries than saving their country; and to cap it all much of Korina, with its distrust of mages and their Communion, would know little or nothing about it. And although the Understone garrison would have dispatched fast messengers to the east coast, they would not arrive for seven days, if at all. The hordes of the Wesmen could sweep all the way to the eastern oceans and right now, no one was capable of stopping them.

"By the Gods, we're in trouble."

"Well spotted," said Gresse from within the cave.

"Not just us, I mean Balaia."

"Well spotted."

"What will we do?" asked Blackthorne, his confidence and belief suddenly deserting him, the enormity of the problem hitting him like an avalanche from the highest of his mountains' peaks.

"Everything we can, my friend. Everything we can," said Gresse. "Just take it one step at a time. Help me up, would you? I think we shouldn't delay our travel to Gyernath any longer than is absolutely necessary."

Chapter 6

The Raven didn't ride until well into the following afternoon. Even then, Denser wasn't truly up to it but time seemed to press. It was a warm day and the open spaces of the Torn Wastes attracted the heat. Riding would be uncomfortable without cloud to cover the sun.

The second measurement of the noon shade had been inconclusive, much as had been expected. Given allowances for inaccuracies, it wasn't clear whether the rip had grown or, in fact, shrunk. The Unknown guessed it would be at least a week before believable evidence of the rate of increase of the rip's area was available.

The four-College cavalry under General Darrick was partially split. Three mages, all Communion specialists, would remain hidden in Parve. With them would be fifteen sword cavalry, whose instructions included detailed examination and measurement of the dragon. It was this small company who would provide the information The Raven had to have: just how long it would be before the rip became too wide for the Brood Kaan to defend.

That left Darrick with around two hundred horsemen and eleven mages for attack, defence and Communion. Styliann's ninety Protectors represented a formidable force and the Lord of the Mount's magic was supremely powerful.

But, thought Hirad as he sat at the head of The Raven's four warriors and three mages, he couldn't help but feel they were just too few.

Even given that the fifty-odd thousand Wesmen would be concentrated in a few likely areas east and west of the Blackthorne Mountains, avoiding them would be difficult and they couldn't hope to outfight or outrun a Wesmen army.

And there lay their biggest and most immediate problem. Having discounted traversing the sheer and treacherous range of mountains, they were left with attempting Understone Pass, which would be a suicidal folly, or heading either north to Triverne Inlet or south to the Bay of Gyernath. At either crossing, they would be forced to steal craft to reach their own lands.

The decision of which water to attempt was to be deferred until they had ridden perhaps two days down the eastern trail which led close by the Arch-Temple of the Wrethsires and directly to Understone Pass. Hirad suppressed a shudder. The Arch-Temple of the Wrethsires, where the blood of Protector, Raven and Wrethsire had been spilt but the last catalyst of Dawnthief found, was not a place the barbarian would ever wish to lay eyes on again.

As the column rode sedately out of Parve, Darrick at its head, The Raven behind the cavalry with the Protectors surrounding Styliann at the rear, Hirad shook his head.

"We're fooling ourselves," he said.

"Pardon?" said Ilkar who, with The Unknown, flanked him.

"We need to make a quick decision of what it is we actually want. We're unclear and it'll cost us."

"I'm not with you," said the Julatsan.

"For instance, do we, I mean The Raven, have to get to the Colleges? Can't scholars there do the research for us?"

"Hirad, we none of us really know precisely what we're looking for," said Ilkar.

"Yes we do. We have to find and read everything about Septern. Or rather, you mages do, since I can't. And then, we have to link that to what Xetesk knows about dimension gates and Dragonene portals. Then we have to cast something that works."

Ilkar stared at Hirad, his mouth open, his lips tugging up at the corners as he fought to avoid a smile.

"It's not like baking a shepherd's pie, for God's sake." Hirad's expression was blank. "If we have to create a new spell to close that thing, we're finished."

"What?" Hirad turned in his saddle.

"A spell of the nature you're suggesting would take anywhere between one and five years to write, test and prove even assuming we had the raw Lore and understanding to do so.

"What we're hoping to find, and this has clearly passed you by, is some writing by Septern that will either log a spell designed to close a rip or tell us where to find one. At best, Xetesk's DimensionConnect will provide background to help us understand more quickly."

"You have completely lost me," said Hirad. "Surely a rip is a rip. If you can open one, you can close one."

"No." The voice behind belonged to Erienne. She moved in between Hirad and a relieved-looking Ilkar. "We've now got three different types of rip. Four if you count the Dragonene portals.

"We've got Septern's bordered and stable rips which some of you have travelled, Xetesk's DimensionConnect which is an unstable, embryonic portal magic, the Dragonene portals which we presume the dragons themselves control, and finally the unbounded rip created in the wake of Dawnthief.

"They are all completely different constructs. To say you can close one because you can close another is like saying you can make shoes for horses because you can make them for people. All we're sure is that, at some probably base Lore level, there is a connection between Septern's bounded rips and the one in the sky. Only his work can really help us in the time we have. We don't have time for a blacksmith's apprenticeship."

"You don't think we'll find anything to answer this problem straight, do you?" asked The Unknown.

"No," said Erienne. "Whatever, we'll be taking a big chance with what we eventually cast."

"That's not good," said Hirad. "So what do we do if we can't find anything in Septern's writings?"

"Die," said The Unknown. There was a pause.

"Cheerful, aren't you?" said Hirad.

"Right though," said The Unknown. "No use pretending."

"None of this changes the original point I was trying to make which was that three hundred of us are not going to sneak across Triverne Inlet or the Bay of Gyernath, undetected by Wesmen. We need to make a decision on whether that bothers us and if it does—and it should—what we're going to do about it," said Hirad.

The Unknown stared ahead at the backs of the cavalry in front. He then turned and gazed at the Protectors behind him.

"We need to talk more," he said. "And this isn't the place. We'll be overheard and I don't think Styliann should overhear us. Hirad's right. In the rush to leave and plan at Parve, we've forgotten ourselves. We're The Raven. We make our own decisions. Privately." He nodded at the lead Protector who inclined his head very slightly, ebony mask betraying nothing. But, Hirad thought, something passed between them. Whatever it was, The Unknown kept it to himself.

The motley column crossed the Torn Wastes under a blazing sun. The signs of former Wesmen encampments littered the packed ground and harsh scrub. Blackened earth and charred wood, torn canvas, broken posts and tent pegs, lengths of rope and discarded offcuts of metal. And, here and there, the body of a Wesman who picked a fight with the wrong kinsman.

It was seven miles to the tree line and the welcoming canopy of leaf and branch over the marked trail that led from the Torn Wastes, north of the Wesmen Heartlands, through the rugged valleys and hills of Western Balaia, past the Wrethsires' plundered temple and all the way to Understone Pass.

Behind them now, the rip hung in the sky, menacing the air and throwing its shadow over the city of the Wytch Lords. A shadow that would grow to envelop them all unless The Raven could find a way to close it.

The column rode unbroken for two hours, leaving Parve far behind. Hirad felt a growing release of tension as the buildings dwindled in the distance. And it was a release that just about made up for the discomfort of the ride. The horses sweated in the heat, attracting clouds of irritating, buzzing flies that plagued mount and rider alike. Forever waving a hand in front of his face, Hirad's body was covered in a sheen of damp, beads running down the line of his back where they collected in his seat to chafe and rub.

The late afternoon brought mercifully cooler temperatures, a cover of cloud and a change in the terrain. Passing across the northern edge of a beautiful region of river valleys, lush green vegetation, great and ancient trees and fern-covered hillsides, the Eastern Balaians moved into altogether harsher lands.

The ground rose to a series of sharp peaks, littered with cracked rocks and strewn with boulders. Darrick ordered a dismount to save the horses' legs and hooves, relieved men and mages stretching as they led their mounts over teacherous slabs of stone, half buried under tough stands of long grass. To both sides, the ground fell away down steep scree slopes into wind-blasted clefts. Nowhere in sight was there any sign of habitation. Nevertheless, The Unknown was nervous.

"We're exposed here," he said.

"But only, it seems, to the elements," replied Ilkar, drawing his cloak more firmly around his shoulders, the breeze whipping at cloth and grass, the heat changing quickly to chill.

"If we're spotted, we have no obvious cover," said The Unknown. "Thraun, what do you think?" The shapechanger had spent some time at the head of the column earlier in the afternoon, advising Darrick's scouts. He walked up to join The Unknown.

"It's not as bad as it looks although we might want to ride perhaps another quarter of a mile north if we can. The scouts have reported very little habitation up here. The land is useless for all but grazing goats. We're unlikely to meet locals; the only risk is running into Wesmen warriors.

"There are limited passable trails for horses and this is one of the better ones, believe it or not. I get no feeling that Wesmen will be a problem for a day or so. I've advised three of the scouts to travel to the fork above Terenetsa. That's still more than two days' ride from here for a fast scout. We'll have a better picture in three days. Until then, the elves and me are the best chance we have of avoiding trouble."

"And you think we will?" asked Ilkar, who had come to respect Thraun's reading of land and scent.

"Yes."

Shortly after dusk, Darrick halted the column in the lee of another steep climb. The wind had blown away the cloud and, while it had dropped to a gentle breeze, the clear skies were cooling fast.

Quickly, elves marked fire boundaries outside of which no flame could be shown. Thus marked, the perimeter of the camp was established, the first guards set and the cook fires laid.

The Raven took themselves to the opposite corner from Styliann and the Protectors. As they sat down around Will's stove, waiting for water to boil, Hirad chuckled.

"I wonder how he feels?" he said. "Styliann, I mean. I know he hasn't got too many friends but there's got to be a hundred feet between him and the nearest cavalryman, and they still look nervous."

"I shouldn't think he cares at all," said Denser. "The Lord of the Mount is used to isolation." The Dark Mage was flat on his back, head propped up on Erienne's lap, she stroking his hair in what was becoming a familiar scene as he recovered from the casting of Dawnthief. Hirad and The Unknown exchanged a glance. They were the first words Denser had spoken the entire day. And it had been a detached silence, the Xeteskian riding or walking apart from The Raven. All he had got from Erienne in response to his looks had been shrugs and shakes of the head. Now, as she cradled Denser, Erienne's concern and confusion were obvious even in the uncertain light of the flames.

The talk pattered on in a broken way until coffee was poured. To Denser and Erienne's left sat Thraun and Will while Hirad and Ilkar flanked The Unknown to their right. The Unknown called for attention.

"Ilkar, Hirad, feel uncomfortable?" he asked. The two nodded, expressions stark in the firelight, eyes hidden by shadow.

"Why just them?" asked Will.

"Because it's only the three of us who have been in potential large-scale battle situations before, and there's a lot wrong with this one."

"Not so far as I can see," said Erienne. "We just have to reach the Colleges quickly and safely and this is surely the best way."

"No," said The Unknown. "Because we don't want to invite battle and this troop is doing just that, or it will be when we reach the vicinity of the Blackthornes."

"So what do you suggest?" asked Thraun.

"We have to split from them. Our course lies in a different direction."

"How do you work that out?" Thraun frowned, his gruff low voice grumbling across the stove.

"The situation is going to be very difficult when we reach Triverne Inlet, which is, I suspect, the favoured destination. We can assume the Wesmen will be supplying their armies across the water so there'll be a relatively heavy presence.

"If we stride up with Darrick and Styliann there'll be a battle. If we go through on our own, with Thraun's eyes and ears, we can take a boat and get across unseen."

"And what happens to Darrick?"

"We have to persuade him to go south to the Bay of Gyernath, maybe creating a diversion for us along the way. Either way, we have to go alone."

"The point is," said Hirad, "that we're being run as an addition to the cavalry. That isn't how The Raven operates. Not now."

"So just how do we operate?" asked Denser.

"You should know," said Hirad, frowning at Denser's flat tone. "We go into a situation, assess, make decisions and recommendations and don't expect to be questioned."

"You don't consider that a little high-handed?" ventured Will. Hirad merely shrugged.

"Just ask yourself why we're still alive after ten years' fighting. And why, particularly, we're alive when the Wytch Lords are dead. It isn't high-any-thing, it's The Raven's way."

Ilkar smiled. "Only you could be so cocky with fifty thousand Wesmen between you and your next port of call."

"It's not that, it's—"

"We know," said Ilkar. "If we do things how we think they should be done, we'll stay alive." He mimed a yawn. Will and Thraun laughed. Hirad scowled slightly. The Unknown cleared his throat.

"I'm glad we've cleared that up," he said. "Now listen. While Darrick will almost certainly see sense, Styliann almost certainly will not."

"Why not?" asked Will.

"Because Triverne Inlet represents his quickest route to Xetesk, barring Understone Pass. If he won't see sense, we'll have to leave by the back door in a couple of nights. I just hope it doesn't come to that. Styliann could still be a pow-erful ally and his sway will definitely help us gain access to the College libraries."

"I don't trust him," said Ilkar.

"Now there's a surprise," muttered Denser.

"No, it's more than inter-College mistrust. He tried to kill us at the Wrethsires' Temple and let's not forget why. He wanted Dawnthief so he could use it to assume power over the Colleges, and as a threat to the Wytch Lords and Wesmen. He wanted to rule Balaia and I'm sure he still does. God knows what this pooling of knowledge will reveal but I don't think Styliann should have any part in it."

"What, just cut Xetesk out, is that it?" asked Denser sharply. Ilkar sighed.

"You're here, aren't you?"

"You made your choice at the Temple," added Hirad. "You're Raven."

"There's something more," said Erienne. "The dividing of Septern's works between the Colleges was no freak or accident. Septern was very careful to ensure no one College had enough knowledge to be dominant."

"Was he really that good?" asked Will.

"It was the potential of his magic that he recognised as so dangerous," said Erienne. "I suspect he could see the way his research might be taken. And he was right, as Xetesk proved with their DimensionConnect. Just think of the danger when they can stabilise the gateway."

"I'm hearing everything you're saying," said Thraun. "And there's one thing badly astray in our assumptions. We're banking on Styliann's influence opening the doors to the College libraries. I mean, let's face it, if you were a senior mage and you got a request from him to sift all of Septern's work and put it together for the Lord of the Mount to examine, would you just roll over?"

"Exactly," said Erienne.

"No," said Ilkar. "No you wouldn't. And Styliann must know that."

"If he knows that, why was he so confident back in Parve?" asked Hirad.

"Well, his network is wide, isn't it?" replied Denser with a sniff. "He'll pull strings rather than make a direct approach, certainly to Julatsa and Lystern. The Dordovans might respond well to a personal request, though."

"But if he is planning to commune directly with senior mages in other Colleges, we need to stop him taking the short cut to Xetesk *and* from calling ahead to speed up the research process," said Hirad. "Fat chance."

"So where does that leave us?" asked Will.

"Out in the cold, I expect," said The Unknown. "Look, assume for a moment that Styliann determines to cross at Triverne Inlet and that he rubs the Colleges up the wrong way with his demands. We need to know exactly what action we intend to take." He looked around the fire. The faces of The Raven were expectant. He nodded, smiling slightly.

"Right. Here's what I think we should do. First, we approach Darrick. We need him on our side. He might be able to give Styliann a tactical reason to cross south of the mountains that Styliann will swallow. If not, in two days' time, when we are close to Leionu, we do as we are doing now, camp as far from Styliann as we can. Only that night, we'll leave four hours before dawn. Darrick will help us, maybe fake an attack by a Wesmen patrol or something to cover the noise.

"Until that time, if we are speaking with Styliann, we must try to persuade him to take the right course of action but it's imperative he doesn't tumble to the fact that we have ulterior motives. If we are respectful of his authority, he won't suspect us, Denser?"

The mage sat up to drink his coffee, shrugging. "I'm not sure about the diversion thing but pandering to Styliann's ego is definitely the right idea. What worries me is the Protectors."

"Let me handle them," said The Unknown. "There are ways to obstruct without disobeying."

"How do you mean?" Hirad massaged his chin.

"You wouldn't understand," replied The Unknown, and Hirad knew enough not to question him further.

"When do we talk to Darrick?" asked Will.

"Now would be a good time," said The Unknown.

"His mages are in Communion," said Ilkar. "It may pay to wait."

The big man nodded. "How long will they be under?"

"An hour or so. It really depends on whether they can find a contact quickly or not."

"Very well," said The Unknown. "We wait."

Later, Erienne took Denser away from the fire, he going a little reluctantly.

"Are you going to tell me what's up with you?"

"Nothing's up," replied Denser. "I'm just tired and I can't believe that casting Dawnthief has left us in this state."

"But no one blames you, Denser," she said, her eyes looking deep into his and her hand caressing his hair.

"It's not a question of blame," said Denser. "It's here, inside me. I can't explain it to you. It's just . . ." He trailed away, hands waving vaguely.

"I can help you. Don't cut yourself off from me."

"I'm not," he said sharply.

"No? You're so quiet and withdrawn from me. From all of us."

"I'm not withdrawn," he snapped suddenly, his voice overloud. Erienne recoiled. Denser tried to smile. "I just don't want to talk about it."

"And that's not cutting yourself off, is it?" She felt her heart tripping in her chest and took her hand from his head. "I need you, Denser. Don't leave me alone."

"I'm here, aren't I?"

"Gods, you're like a child at the moment. That's not what I mean and you know it."

"Well, what do you mean, then?" he asked, his expression sullen and angry.

"I mean that your body's here but where's your heart?"

"Here, like always." He tapped his chest.

"Damn you, Denser, why are you being like this?"

"I'm not being like anything. Why are you being like you are?"

"Because I'm worried about you!" She stormed, feeling her cheeks redden, desperate for him to understand what he was doing to her. "About us."

"I'm fine. Just let me be."

"Fine." She got up and walked away into the camp, biting her lip before she said something she regretted. He didn't call after her.

Darrick's Dordovan mages were not alone in their Communion. Surrounded by a close cordon of Protectors, the Lord of the Mount probed across the Blackthorne Mountains, connecting with one of the few aides he felt he could still trust. The Communion was short, the message stole his breath away and when he opened his eyes, he was shaking.

Julatsa was quiet. Throughout the night and into the morning, the Wesmen camped around the College walls had tried to breach the DemonShroud. The souls of those who touched it merely went to feed the insatiable appetite of the demons controlling the awful spell.

It had been as pitiful as it had been painful. Barras had listened from his rooms as the Wesmen tried to walk across the moat, then bridge it with wood and metal and finally climb above it using grappling ropes strung from nearby buildings to the College walls.

Now, with the sun high, they were building something. Barras, unable to simply hear the terrible calls of the dying, walked out to the Tower ramparts and took in the sight of the hell that he and the Council had created just beyond the walls.

The DemonShroud surrounded the College like a thin grey cloud, rising from the unbroken ground. It was ten feet thick, rippling into the sky as high as could be seen and, Barras knew, it drove into the earth deeper than men could survive. It was an awesome, oppressive conjuration. Majestic in its way and awful testament to the power demons could wield on Balaia with the help of mages. Proximity to it set teeth on edge and fear leached from its surface, covering everything in its compass with a sheen of anxiety and requiring conscious effort not to shy away from it.

He had no doubt the Wesmen would try to tunnel in at some stage during the coming weeks. He just prayed that they would see their folly before too many souls were taken. Yet, as he gazed at the Shroud, through which blue and yellow light occasionally flared and forked like desultory lightning, he wasn't so sure. Not sure at all. The Wesmen's actions so far revealed a fundamental misunderstanding of the reality of mana and dimensional connectivity. He found himself smiling a little sadly. Of course they wouldn't understand. The Wesmen had no magic. It was both their innocence and their curse.

Barras walked around the Tower, taking in the totality of the Shroud, the shifting greyness of which lent everything beyond it a washed-out aspect, dimming colours and making movement seem indistinct. It had first been employed to make the College of Julatsa impregnable over seven hundred years previously and had served the same purpose as a moat but had been infinitely more effective.

There was no way to cross the DemonShroud until the spell was ended. Any who tried, whether friend or foe, would be taken. It couldn't be over-flown, it couldn't be dug beneath. It took souls indiscriminately from man and beast. It was evil on the face of Balaia. Yet it would save Julatsa from the Wesmen and, despite the horror of the DemonShroud, the knowledge gave Barras comfort.

Inside the College grounds the Shroud was given the utmost respect, with no one who braved the walls venturing closer to its modulating edge than half a dozen paces. Those who had made it through the gates, and who now mingled with those to whom the College was their natural home, walked, stood or sat in groups, all dazed, all saddened and all affected by the dread calm that pervaded the whole grounds. Because the single hardest aspect of the Shroud casting to take in was the quiet.

Every sound the Wesmen made was dulled and far away. They had long since stopped sending arrows over the walls; it was a waste for them and an addition to the stocks of the Julatsans. Instead, they ringed the walls just beyond the edge of the moat, clustering and staring. But their clamouring at the edges of the Shroud, the hammering at the tower Barras could see them making, their living hubbub, their walking, running, cooking, talking, laughing, all of it was muted.

Barras dug a finger into each ear, unsure for a moment of whether he wasn't losing his hearing. But then Kard's voice, loud and invasive, struck up to his left.

"Good afternoon, Barras." The old elf started and turned.

"Kard. Glad to see you are well."

"All things are relative," said the General.

"So they are. What brings you out here?"

"The same as you." Kard came to Barras' shoulder. "To see the Wesmen building their folly." He nodded toward their half-built tower outside Julatsa's south gate.

It looked a rickety structure from where Barras stood but he knew better—the Wesmen were fine woodsmen. A lattice of crossed beams was strung around four tree trunks, at the base of which carved stakes would act as axles. Inside the lattice, ladders scaled thirty feet to a platform thick with Wesmen hammering feverishly at the next level of their tower, each strike muted as if heard through thick cloth.

To the left of the main structure, another team of carpenters was carving wheels while to the right, fires belched smoke into the cloudless sky. These were not cook fires. Wesmen in thick hide aprons toiled with hammer and anvil while others made moulds.

"What are they making, more weapons?" asked Barras.

"No," said Kard. "If I'm right, it'll be cladding for the tower."

"They think we'll try and burn it, is that it?"

"That and I believe they will try to push the tower across the moat, hoping the metal will deflect its power."

"Oh dear," said Barras. He shook his head. "I think we should try to talk to them." Kard looked at him askance.

"I see no reason to persuade them to stop committing suicide."

"I understand your hatred of the invading force but they are not killing themselves in sufficient numbers to make a difference to the weight of their advantage," said Barras. "But more than that, I don't think you realise what a death in the DemonShroud means. I would wish an eternity of torment on no one. Not a Xeteskian, not a Wesman, no one."

Kard shrugged. "Talk to them if you must. I won't stand in your way but I certainly won't stand at your shoulder."

"Your heart is hard."

"They have slaughtered much of my army, untold numbers of Julatsa's people and more of your mages than you can count," said Kard, his voice cold and harsh. "For every one of them that dies in the screaming soul agony you say awaits them in the Shroud, I am a little more assuaged. Just a little."

"You are happy to greet death with more death?"

"That's unfair," said Kard sharply. "It is human to seek revenge and we did not invite this. The Wesmen have chosen their path and so far as I am concerned, if they can't learn from their mistakes, that's their problem. I will have no part in putting them straight."

Barras nodded. "Perhaps I should consult my conscience further."

"My old friend, I admire your conscience and your capacity for forgiveness but this is a war in which we have never been the aggressors," said Kard. "In fact, I still can't believe it's even happened but clearly the Wesmen felt that, with the Wytch Lords at their backs, they could destroy the Colleges just as they thought they could, three hundred years ago.

"And now they've come so far they believe they can win even without the power the Wytch Lords gave them. And they may yet be right. If you must speak to them you must, but consider this. The longer they believe they can breach the Shroud, the longer their minds are deflected from moving onward and the better our chances of effective relief from Dordover. It may also deflect their minds from what I think is a rather obvious move they have so far overlooked." Kard's face was grim.

"And that is?" But Kard's reply was left unspoken. From the North Gates, a cry went up. The two men ran around the Tower to see a dozen Wesmen walking toward the edge of the Shroud, a white and red flag of truce held in front of them. Shouts echoed up the Tower and the door opened. An aide ran out.

"Kerela requests your urgent attention, sirs." The young man wiped long red hair from his brow as it blew in the breeze.

"The North Gate?" asked Barras.

"Yes, my mage."

"Tell Kerela we will be there presently." The aide nodded and ran back the way he had come.

Barras breathed deep and faced General Kard, raising his eyebrows as he saw the other man's expression, dark and fearful.

"Kard?"

"I think the obvious move may have just occurred to them."

"What is it?"

"Hear it from them, Barras, if they care to tell you." Kard moved to the Tower's door. "I'm still praying I'm wrong."

CHAPTER 7

The camp was quietening, the cooling wind biting into clothing and conversation as the night darkened to a star-lit black, when Darrick made time to visit The Raven's fire at the behest of Hirad and, subsequently, The Unknown Warrior. In carefully plotted lines across the hillside and plateau, the cavalry tents flapped gently, lantern light from within a few casting exaggerated shadows on the inside of canvas.

The General, his curly hair pressed flat across his head and his travel-stained leather armour hidden beneath a heavy cloak, sat between Hirad and Denser, nodding at Will as the wiry man gave him a very welcome mug of coffee.

"I must apologise for the time it has taken me to respond to your invitation," said Darrick, his eyes shining from his ever-enthusiastic face. "I've been in conversation with mages and scouts and you may be very interested in what I've heard. But you had something you needed to speak to me about first."

Hirad smiled privately. Darrick's tone and bearing, now that he was leading his cavalry across enemy lands, was very much that of the man in charge despite the company in which he now sat. It was easy to see why he was held in such regard by soldier and civilian alike. He simply oozed assurance, confidence and authority.

"Indeed we do," said The Unknown Warrior. "Although we might be influenced by what your mages have discovered about conditions in the East."

Darrick scratched his nose. "Tell me your thoughts and I'll match them with what I know."

The Unknown Warrior detailed The Raven's concerns and plans while Hirad watched Darrick for reaction. He shouldn't have bothered. Throughout the big man's speech, the General betrayed no emotion whatsoever. Nodding occasionally, he took everything in with a calm detachment. When The Unknown had finished, there was a pause in which Darrick drained much of his coffee, threw the dregs aside and handed his mug to Will for a refill. The thief obliged.

"Thank you, Will," said Darrick as he accepted the mug. "The first thing to say is that much of what you have said has occurred to me already, and I thank you for confirming my thoughts. I was already planning to split us above Terenetsa, sending you north and taking my men to the Bay of Gyernath. The reports of the Communion mages this evening have convinced me that I was right." He took a sip of coffee.

"The situation around the Colleges and in Understone is grave. We could make no contact with a mage in the four-College force at Understone so have to assume the town has fallen to the Wesmen. Fifteen thousand Wesmen crossed Triverne Inlet and marched to Julatsa." Ilkar started at the mention of his College's name, Hirad seeing sweat forming on his forehead despite the cool of the night. "Notwithstanding the fact that the Wytch Lord magic was taken from them by your actions in Parve, the invasion force didn't stop its march." Another sip.

"The College," managed Ilkar, his voice little more than a whisper. "Has it fallen?"

"Ilkar, you must understand that these reports are coming via Dordover and are at best inaccurate, at worst mere rumour."

"Has the College fallen," said Ilkar deliberately and Hirad could feel the chill from his body.

"We think not," said Darrick.

"*Think?* I've got to know. Now."

"Take it easy, Ilkar," said Hirad, putting out a hand. Ilkar shook his head but it was Erienne who spoke.

"Hirad, only a mage can understand what this means to Ilkar. General, please, tell us anything you know."

Darrick raised a hand for quiet and calm.

"There are reports that the city of Julatsa has fallen but that the College itself has not, but I must stress, these are unconfirmed. There is a Dordovan force on its way to assist the Julatsans but it won't be able to report for a day at best."

Ilkar stared into the fire, eyes flat slits, cheeks sucked in, ears pricking furiously. Hirad watched as the elf composed himself, swallowed hard and turned to Darrick.

"Is there no clue as to how long they can hold out?" he asked, voice steady but the shake was there, just under the surface. "Has no one from Dordover held Communion with the mages of Julatsa?"

"There has been no direct contact since the Julatsans asked Dordover for assistance. That was two days ago," replied Darrick. "The report of the city falling was given by a mage outside of the College grounds sometime yesterday, I believe. That's why I caution you to take what I'm saying with a pinch of salt."

"Why?"

"Because the Communion was broken off before it could be finished and the Dordovan mage suffered backlash. His thoughts aren't yet clear and he doesn't remember everything that passed between them yet. When I know more, you will be the first to hear."

Ilkar nodded and rose. "Thank you, Darrick." His face was white, even in the firelight, and tears stood in his eyes. "Excuse me. I need some time alone."

"Ilkar, wait," said Hirad, half rising.

"Please, Hirad. Not right now." Ilkar walked slowly away into the rows of tents and was lost in the night. Hirad shook his head.

"But if the College hasn't fallen . . ." he began.

"But it might have done by now," said Denser, quietly, his tone rising briefly from its emotionless state. "The one report is a day old. If the Wesmen sacked the city so quickly, why would they be stopped by the College? That's what Ilkar is thinking. Believe me, besides his own death, the destruction of Ilkar's College is the worst thing that could happen to him. To any Julatsan mage. It would mean the end of Julatsan magic and it's been unthinkable for hundreds of years that such a thing might happen. Leave him be."

Hirad pursed his lips. "But he's Raven. We can help him."

"Yes, but not at this instant. Right now he's Julatsan only and he's facing the loss of everything he knows. We'll help him when he comes back," said Erienne.

"If the College falls, will he lose his abilities?" asked Will.

"No," she replied. "He will always be able to shape mana to cast spells. But what will be lost is the totality of Julatsan Lore, the teaching of ages. And with the destruction of the Tower would go the centre of Julatsan magic. You can't just build another one and be back where you were. The mana imbues the Tower with magical power over centuries and it would take that long for the Julatsans to recover themselves, if they did at all."

"And how much of Septern's work is kept in the library there?" Thraun's voice brought a shiver to the company around the fire.

"Exactly," said Darrick. "Which is why you and you alone must cross at Triverne Inlet as soon as possible. You've got to get into and out of the College before it falls, if it's going to, and travelling alone will give you the best chance. The sooner you leave the column and ride northeast, the better."

"We'll stay with you another day," said The Unknown. "Ilkar won't leave until he knows the facts and those will only come with the Dordovan relief force."

"I can hold Communion with them," said Denser.

"You can't light your own pipe yet," replied Erienne sharply. "And I'm not expert enough to commune over this distance. I agree with The Unknown."

"Very well," said Darrick. "One more day and night."

"And what about you, General?" asked Hirad.

"To the south, things are slightly more promising, but only slightly," he said. "We believe that Baron Blackthorne has had some success in holding a Wesmen force from reaching Understone. His Town has fallen and he is, as far as we can make out, riding to Gyernath to swell his numbers. It makes sense for me to attempt to join with him and try, as I assume he will, to disrupt the Wesmen's southern supply lines and take back his castle. If we can make a base, we can begin to beat them back."

"Good old Blackthorne," said The Unknown. "Give him our regards when you see him."

"Be glad to."

"And Styliann?" Denser's question had Darrick blow out his cheeks.

"He also has requested to see me and I will recommend he travels south with us. Ultimately, though, he is my commander and can do as he wishes. I believe I can persuade him that his best chance of returning in triumph to Xetesk is to attack from the south with us, avoiding Understone."

"No chance," said Denser, shaking his head a little contemptuously. "He wants in on Septern's research and coming with us is how he'll do it."

Darrick drained his coffee and stood up, brushing himself down with his free hand.

"Well, no time like the present," he said.

"Good luck," said Denser. "You'll need it."

Darrick smiled. "I never count on luck. Get some sleep. We're leaving at first light."

"If you see Ilkar . . ." said Hirad.

"I'll give him a wide berth," said Darrick. "Good night."

Ilkar strode away through the precise rows of tents. He stared straight ahead, ignoring the acknowledgements of cavalrymen, the staccato sounds of laughter and talking from within which broke the quiet.

He knew his eyes were full of tears and his teeth were clamped around the soft inner tissue below his bottom lip in a vain attempt to halt its trembling. Eventually, he slowed, reaching the edge of the tents and the open area between the cavalry and Styliann.

Sitting on a flat-faced, lichen-covered rock, he fought his mind into what passed for order and breathed in the ramifications of all he had just heard. The potential end to Julatsa's seat of magical power, the slaughter of untold numbers of his brother and sister mages, and the isolation of the survivors—still Julatsan but without a focus for their energy, power or study.

And it could all have gone already. While he thought he would feel the destruction of the Tower through the mana trails, this far from Julatsa, the deaths of so many, one by one, would barely cause a ripple. He knew of none who had a ManaPulse targeting him to warn of their death.

And if the Tower fell, what then? Who would rebuild the College? Mages like him, he supposed. But where would he and those like him find the resources and sheer strength to accomplish the mammoth task that was the construction of a new Tower? And how could they hope to attract mage students to a College that had fallen to an army without magic? Surely, to lose the College in these circumstances would mean the slow end to Julatsan magic forever as its ever dwindling number of practising mages aged and died.

He wondered if The Raven could reach Julatsa in time, or whether they would be left picking over the rubble and corpses. And getting there before the College fell would serve what purpose? What could The Raven hope to achieve as the sole fighting force of the East outside of its gates? Perhaps it would be better it they weren't around to see the end.

Ilkar bowed his head and let the tears flow, hands on his knees as the sobs wracked his body. There was no hope for Julatsa. If the Wesmen had sacked the city, the College, whose walls were not designed to repel an invading army anymore, would soon follow. Then he would be truly alone, with only The Raven to support him. He wondered whether that would be enough.

"It's not necessarily over, Ilkar." The voice came to him from out of the gloom. He wiped his eyes, feeling the chill and realising he'd lost track of how long he'd been sitting alone. His backside was numbed. He shivered, cleared his vision and strained to identify the figure that approached him, outline blurred by the half light of dying fires against the background of night.

"Get lost, Styliann," he spat. "Don't presume to carp over our demise. You know nothing of how this feels."

"On the contrary, Ilkar, and I forgive you your mood." Styliann didn't pause in his stride, the shapes of six Protectors filling the space around him.

"Thank you so much," muttered Ilkar, looking away. "What do you want?"

"I've come to offer you my sympathy, my help if I can give it, and some hope." The Lord of the Mount made no attempt to sit, seeming content to stand a few paces away, respecting Ilkar's need for space.

"Well, that's a first."

Styliann sighed. "I do understand how difficult this is for you to cope with," he said. "And I do know how it feels to face isolation, believe me. I won't ask you to respond, just listen to me for a moment." He paused. Ilkar shrugged.

"I have no desire to see the balance of magic shift. That is dangerous for us all at the best of times but right now we need every mage we can get to have a chance of seeing off the Wesmen threat. My Communion tonight was inconclusive about the situation in Julatsa and all I know is what Darrick has just told me. I will, however, seek to clarify the situation tomorrow. I understand you're staying with the column for another day and if I can provide you with more detail, I will.

"Finally, the hope." Now Styliann moved a pace closer and lowered his voice. "You and I know the capacity of the Colleges for self-preservation better than any in this camp. To me, the report of the fall of the city while the College remained intact says Julatsa has found a way of holding off the Wesmen army. It is now a question of how long that situation lasts, hence your need for haste."

Ilkar sucked his lip, nodding finally.

"Maybe. Maybe. And what are your plans?"

Styliann's eyes narrowed, his jaw set. "I will travel south, separate from the column. My immediate future lies in other directions, though I will still set in motion moves to enable the release of Septern's works to you. I fear I will no longer be able to study them with you."

That caught Ilkar off guard. His head jerked up, meeting Styliann's eyes and feeling the force of his anger.

"Why not?"

"I have a little local trouble," he said. "It seems that, temporarily at least, I am no longer the Lord of the Mount of Xetesk." He turned and strode away.

"How long before you can cast, Denser?" The Unknown's question followed directly in the wake of Darrick's departure for his meeting with Styliann. Denser, who had recovered enough to spend more time sitting than lying, shrugged his shoulders and knocked out the bowl of his pipe against a log end protruding from the fire. Dislodged embers glittered briefly in the dark.

"There's not a simple answer to that," said Denser, delving into his tobacco pouch for a refill. "Damn. This is running low."

"There never is, is there?" said Hirad.

"The situation is this," continued the Dark Mage. "I am still shattered by the Dawnthief casting in a mana stamina if not so much a physical sense and it is difficult for me to retain mana to cast. And I find myself unaccountably low in spirits though I'm sure that'll pass. Contrary to popular belief, however—" he looked half smiling at Erienne, "—I am able to light my own pipe." He clicked his right thumb against its forefinger and a deep blue flame appeared with which he set alight the weed he had tamped into the bowl of his pipe.

"Very good," said Erienne, pushing his face away. "Now bring down HellFire."

"You see? Never satisfied," said Denser, his smile broadened but it was hollow and bereft of real humour. "You offer a woman one country and she immediately demands the world."

"Hardly," said Erienne. "Merely proof of your reserves beyond the immediate."

"HellFire is a little more than proof."

"It was a metaphor, all right?" Erienne poked Denser in the chest.

"Well just give me a chance, all right?" snapped Denser, swatting her hand away. Erienne started and moved back, eyes moistening. He looked away from her into the fire.

"Take it easy, Denser," said Hirad, startled by Denser's sudden anger. "She was just fooling. How about you just answer the question. What exactly can't you do?"

"Everything else," admitted Denser. He sucked his lip and reached out a hand to Erienne who pulled further away. He sighed, raised an eyebrow and continued. "I'm empty. Given that we're riding not resting, Communion is two days away, ShadowWings the same and HellFire about four to take a sample. Sorry if that's not good enough for some of you."

Hirad regarded him evenly. "I think we might find it in our hearts to forgive you," he said.

"Most gracious," Denser mock bowed from where he sat.

"Just relax a little, eh?" Hirad indicated Erienne. Denser cut off his reply, nodding curtly instead. A short silence was broken by The Unknown.

"Thraun?" Though The Unknown had not seen Thraun change, he had seen the drain on his physical being while he had been a Protector.

"No problem, but . . ."

"I know," said The Unknown. "I'm just assessing our overall condition. We will never demand it of you. To change will always be your decision alone." Thraun nodded.

"And what about Ilkar?" asked Erienne. "What he's heard tonight could seriously damage his ability to concentrate."

"Above everything else, he's the best front-line defensive mage in Balaia," said Hirad. "His ability to concentrate in the middle of battle is one reason The Raven has survived so long. When push comes to shove, he'll be as able to cast as you."

"I hope you're right," said Erienne. "But, if you'll take my advice, you'll keep a close eye on him for a while."

"Of course." Hirad spread his hands wide. "He's Raven."

The Unknown cleared his throat for attention.

"I'm glad everyone is feeling confident because this is going to be very tough," he said. "Quite unlike anything we've ever faced. We won't be joining a line, we'll be on our own in lands swarming with Wesmen. We can't afford slip ups and we can't afford to carry anyone. If any of you have any doubts about yourself, you should stay with the cavalry."

"So, we'll be facing odds no different than those we've just faced except going in the other direction," said Hirad flatly. "And you're asking us if we're confident we can pull it off?"

A smile tugged at the corners of The Unknown's mouth. "I had to," he said.

"I think what you need is sleep," said Hirad, patting the big man's shoulder. "That sort of speech belongs ten years ago. I'll take watch and wait for Ilkar."

Barras and Kard joined Kerela at the North Gate of the College, the three elder Julatsans standing shoulder to shoulder as the gate was opened. To either side of them stood men with yellow and white flags of truce on short poles and, ringing the area by the gate, archers and defensive mages waited to respond to any projectile threat. Kard thought it very unlikely there would be an attack of any kind and had shunned the offer of a HardShield, advising the mage to conserve his mana stamina.

The gates swung back to reveal the DemonShroud, wide, grey and flaring blue-tinged yellow along its visible base. Beyond it, a trio of Wesmen. They had no archer support though the two flanking warriors were clearly a bodyguard for the man in the centre.

He was a man in his late thirties, midheight and powerfully built. Furs ran across his shoulders and down his back, fixed below his neck with a polished metal clasp. He wore cracked black leather armour padded with furs around the shoulders and leather greaves covered his thighs. His arms were exposed down to fur-edged gauntlets and heavy, strapped ankle boots covered his lower legs and feet. His hair was long, dark, shaggy and unkempt, framing a heavily tanned face boasting large eyes and a chin that had felt steel in the not too distant past.

"I am Senedai, Lord and General of the Heystron Tribes and I demand your immediate surrender." His voice, though loud and deep, echoed dully against the Shroud. Kerela turned to Barras.

"You are our Chief Negotiator, perhaps you would like to establish our position."

"I fear you are passing me a poisoned chalice," said Barras grimly.

"In all probability, my old friend. But delegation is one of the few joys I have left."

Barras composed himself and took three measured paces toward the open gate and the Shroud, its innate evil sending shivers through his body, his skin crawling. It was all he could do to stand tall and keep his voice steady.

"I am Barras, Elder Council member and Chief Negotiator of the College of Julatsa. You will appreciate that we are unwilling to surrender the homes and buildings you have not already taken by unprovoked force. What are the conditions you propose?"

"Conditions? I promise you nothing but your lives, mage. And that is generous, having seen the pyres of thousands of my kinsmen burning."

"We were bound to defend our city from your groundless attack," said Barras.

"You were bound to conduct battle like warriors, using blades, not spells."

Barras laughed; he couldn't help it.

"A preposterous suggestion from one happy to use the magic of the Wytch Lords to devastate my people."

"The Tribal Lords were against such weapons."

"And that is how history will be rewritten, is it?" Barras' voice dripped contempt. "That the Wesmen Lords called a halt to the magic of the Wytch Lords to do steel-on-steel battle with the forces of Julatsa, only to be met with a barrage of cowardly magic?"

"And yet triumph," said Senedai. "And triumph we will."

"This is a city of magic. Even in your most muddled dreams did you really believe we would not respond to your aggression with every means at our disposal? And may I remind you that we still have those means."

"Magic is an evil force and it is the sworn pledge of every Wesman to see your Colleges burn and your Towers lie in rubble." Senedai jabbed a finger at Barras.

"Lovely imagery," said Barras. "But I think you'll do well to see it."

"You think so?" Senedai smiled. "There is a pitiful number of mages within your flimsy walls, even fewer men at arms and a handful of terrified women and children. All you have is this devil's barrier and I know enough that you cannot keep it standing forever. We will not even waste our arrows on you; there is no need."

"A wise choice. Our roofs are slate, our walls are stone. We left mud and grass behind us generations ago."

"Your insults are as old as your body, mage," said Senedai. "And your posturing has got you nowhere. Now listen to me, Julatsan Council member, and listen carefully.

"I have offered you, and all those within the walls of the College, life if you surrender now. That promise dies as you all will if another drop of Wesmen blood is spilt in removing you."

"What guarantee do I have that you will keep your word?" asked Barras as haughtily as he could muster.

"I am Lord of the Heystron Tribes."

"That does not impress me. And what will become of us if we do surrender?"

"You will be held as prisoners until suitable work is found for you building the new Wesmen empire. The alternative is death."

"You are giving us nothing."

"You are in a position to demand no more." Senedai gestured around him.

"But you are forgetting that you cannot break in here. The devil's barrier, as you call it, is unbreachable."

"Indeed, although our efforts are not over," said Senedai. "But we have the option of waiting for you to die of hunger, or thirst, or for the barrier to drop as you weaken. And there is further pressure we can bring to bear but I don't wish to be forced to use it. I am not a savage but, one way or another, we will bring down your College."

"I will die before I see you set foot on this hallowed ground," said Barras coolly. Senedai threw up his arms.

"That is your choice mage, and everyone should be allowed to choose his own death. But perhaps your people are not so willing to follow you into death. It is up to you, all of you. You can either live as our prisoners and we will treat you well, or you can choose to die on our swords or from the slow death that follows an end to your food and drink. I give you until first light tomorrow to decide, when I will be forced to use other methods." He turned on his heel and walked back into the heart of the fallen city of Julatsa.

Barras waved for the gates to be closed and walked back to Kard and Kerela.

"And that's what you call negotiation, is it?" asked Kerela, putting an arm around Barras' shoulder. The three began to walk back to the Tower.

"No. That's that I call winding up a Wesman Lord who had no intention of negotiating himself."

"I take it surrender isn't an option?" said Kard.

"No," said Kerela and Barras together.

"Why did you have to ask?" asked Barras.

"And what did Senedai mean by 'further pressure'?" added Kerela.

"I know and that's why I had to ask," said Kard, his sadness so complete it brought a lump to Barras' throat.

"What is it?"

"I think we'd better go inside," said Kard. "We have a great deal of talking to do before morning."

CHAPTER 8

Sha-Kaan chose to leave the companionship and quiet of the Choul, flying instead to his own structure above the ground, the great Wingspread his Vestare had created under his guidance and direction.

Though the battle had been long and hard, the superior organisation of the Brood Kaan had limited the damage and losses and left them with enough strength to maintain sufficient guard on the gateway. But the enemy would be back. And they would keep on coming back until the Kaan were defeated or the gateway was closed. Already he could sense it widening, gnawing at the edges of the sky.

The most damaged of his Brood he had sent to the Klene, havens in interdimensional space connected to Balaia. There, the Dragonene mages would serve and heal them for the next fight.

For himself, he had no Dragonene. Since the theft of Septern's amulet and the death of his Dragonene, Seran, during his first encounter with Hirad Coldheart and The Raven, Sha-Kaan had not paused to make a selection.

The Great Kaan flew with his Brood the short distance to the Choul where all but he dived into its cool, dark depths to rest, choosing the companionship of a press of bodies over the solitude of heat as was the way after victory in battle for all but the sorely wounded. For him, though, there was still work to do and he wheeled away, taking in the state of the Kaan's territory.

From the edge of the blasted lands of Keol, past the dry wastelands and scarred mountains of Beshara and across the rolling hills and plains of Dormar and into the steam-hot forests of Teras, over which he now flew, that was the domain of the Kaan. A fitting tribute to their dominance and size, and one that would soon be lost if a way wasn't found to close the gateway to Balaia.

Much of the lands the Kaan held without contest but it hadn't always been so. For most of his young adult life, three generations and more past, he had fought the Brood Skar for control of the once-fertile lands of the Keol.

He still remembered the sheer cliffs protecting beautiful deep glades fed by spectacular waterfalls. The swaying long grass in the wetlands atop the old volcanoes and ice-cut plateaus. The burgeoning woodland where the Flamegrass grew from the rich soil beneath the canopy of leaves, harvested by the faithful to feed the Kaan's fire, its verdant blues and reds a beacon for the needy. And for those who would take it for themselves. The Skar.

The Kaan had been weakening through the long rotations of the battle, their numbers dwindling without the mind support of a parallel dimension with which to meld the Brood psyche.

The Skar and the Kaan had fought in the skies, across the ground and in the lakes and rivers, banishing life from every wad of earth and swallow of water. People were slaughtered, those who did not run for the wastelands and beyond, the courses of waterways were changed forever by barrages of dislodged rock, by slides of burned earth and by the collapse of tunnels beneath the surface as Choul after Choul was found and destroyed.

On the surface, the vegetation was scorched to its roots and beyond, the richness and fertility driven from the soil and the ground baked and blackened by endless flame from the mouths of those who relied upon it for life.

The land died and the Kaan would have followed it to oblivion but for the appearance of Septern, the one great human, on the edges of the cracked and devastated land that had once been Keol, most coveted of domains.

It was Sha-Kaan who had found him. It could just as easily have been a Skar and then history would have been so very different. He had just been there beneath Sha-Kaan's low-level sweep, walking a little aimlessly, staring up at the sky full of warring dragons, staring at Sha-Kaan as he rushed toward him.

Septern had shown no fear, just a quiet resignation, rather like Hirad Coldheart had done in Taranspike Castle. An acceptance of fate. And it was for that reason that Sha-Kaan did not kill the great human. He was curious because Septern was clearly not of the Vestare, who served the Kaan so faithfully, indeed he was also clearly not of any race that served dragons—the expression on his face told Sha-Kaan that much.

Despite the battle raging in the sky above him, Sha-Kaan had landed, his curiosity overcoming the risk. For, while dragons were masters of the skies, their movement at ground level was ungainly and slow in comparison.

His decision set in motion the events that saved the Kaan by winning them the battle against the Skar and gifting them the parallel dimension they needed to develop to the next plane of awareness.

As he'd landed close to Septern, Sha-Kaan had looked beyond him and the reason for Septern's abrupt appearance became clear. Partly hidden by the hardy brush which still survived in Keol, he saw a swirling white-flecked brown rectangle that was practically invisible against the rock on which it appeared until viewed head-on. He'd known immediately what it was and as he had shepherded Septern away, his bark to alert the Kaan had changed the course of the battle for Keol.

Immediately, a flight of Kaan dragons flew to and through the gateway, sparking a desperate reaction in the Skar. The entire Brood broke off their attack, sweeping down toward the beacon that was the active gate through which their enemy had flown.

More than a dozen had cleared the gate before the Kaan set up a defensive mesh around it that drove off the remaining Skar. It was a lesson they were never to forget. Neither was the first brief exchange between Sha-Kaan and Septern one the former would misplace in his old but razor-sharp mind.

"What's happening?" Septern had asked of no one, plainly not expecting a reply from his unexpected guardian, his bewilderment plain in his tone, on his face and in the set of his body.

"The Kaan fly to destroy the melde-dimension of the Skar. Then we will win the battle for Keol." Again, much as with Hirad Coldheart, Septern's legs had given way in his surprise at the source of the answer to his question. He, too, had recovered quickly.

"I don't understand," he had said.

"The gateway through which you travelled leads to the dimension that supports the Brood Skar; we can feel its signatures. We will destroy its critical fabrics and break that support. Then we will win the battle for Keol."

Rage had suffused Septern's face.

"But they're harmless Avians. You can't . . . murderers!" And he'd run from the startled Sha-Kaan, heading back to the gateway.

"You can't stop us. It is the way." But he had not listened. And he hadn't stopped them. And he had returned. And Sha-Kaan had been waiting.

Sha-Kaan cut short his memory, arcing high to signal to the gate guard by dive and call his intended destination. Turning a full somersault, he gave the brackish low growl that signalled Wingspread and commenced a steep dive toward a particularly dense area of rainforest canopy.

Still, all these long rotations past, almost four hundred Balaian years, he enjoyed the thrill of the dive to the Kaan Broodland. There was no need to dive so fast but then there would be no excitement.

Sha-Kaan pirouetted in the air, barrelling toward the impenetrable green. A single lazy flick of his wings set his position exactly right before he swept them right back to ease his passage and he burst through the canopy at the appointed place and the valley was open before him.

Filled with mist that gently reflected the multiple spears of green-tinged pale light penetrating thin holes in the canopy above, the Kaan Broodland stretched as far as Vestare eyes could see in either direction. The rainforest canopy provided shelter and nurtured a wonderfully soft, warm atmosphere that soothed scales and softened the sounds of the lands and weather outside, leaving the Broodland serene. Sha-Kaan called, a gentle sound of peace and the Brood-at-spawn, four, perhaps five of them, called back, hidden beneath the mists.

Peace. The sounds of falling water, gently waving branches and the echoes of Broodcall calmed his mind. He spread his wings, braking in the air; the trees which scaled the valley's sheer sides hundreds of feet and leaned to create the shield over his head were shadowy and black, the mists below pale and shifting in the spears of light.

He rolled once, letting the humid warmth caress his tired body before heading down, the steady beat of his great wings creating vortices in the mist, his head, neck outstretched, seeking home. In a dozen beats, the mists cleared and the sight below him gladdened his heart and brought tranquillity to his hard-worked mind.

Sha-Kaan's Broodland was dominated by the wide, slow-moving River Tere. The river cascaded down a mighty waterfall at the northern end of the valley, broadening to its sluggish width as it coursed the floor, fed by other falls along its length until it tumbled from the southern cleft into an underground course. The sides of the valley where the trees grew were also home to the birds which fed on and seeded the Flamegrass which grew on vast areas of the Broodland. Great stone slabs punctured the grass and, where the soil was thinnest, the Vestare of the Broodland made their homes from wood and thatch.

Sha-Kaan flew the length of the valley, his calls echoed by the Brood-at-spawn, who didn't venture from their Birthing Chouls, plain, flat, low structures designed to create the exact climate in which young Kaan could be born and nurtured until fledged. Fires burned below great steaming vats of water within each of the Birthing Chouls, keeping them hot and the condensation running freely down the walls to feed the damp of the ground, beneath which more water was channelled and in which the nests were made.

Sha-Kaan turned about, a lazy, graceful action, spread his wings, angled down to slow him for landing, and shuddered the rock under his feet as he touched ground, bringing his servants running to him.

"I am uninjured," he said. "Leave me, I would look at your labours." And he looked and he saw that everything was exactly as he wanted. He sighed his happiness. Wingspread. Home.

Wingspread was a magnificent structure, its polished white stone arc dominating the valley, pushing up more than one hundred and fifty feet toward the mists above. Its low entrance halls led to the main dome where he rested and held audience. The dome itself was a perfect hemisphere which had taken four attempts to achieve to his satisfaction. It sat atop octagonal walls, each side carved with his face such that it gazed in all directions, warding evil from the Broodland.

Either side of the dome rose towers, shining columns that finished in smoking spires with balconies at three heights. Beneath each one, fires burned hot beneath water vats. Like the spawning Kaan, he desired moist heat when away from the Choul and his kin. It eased his scales, soothed his wings and calmed his eyes.

But what gave Wingspread its name was the staggering carving that stretched behind and on either side of the dome, reaching high and touching the mists almost three hundred feet above. In every detail, every vein, bone, flaw, nick and scratch, Sha-Kaan's wings were depicted sweeping up together, their tips touching just out of sight. It was a monument appropriate to his rule of the Brood.

The Great Kaan walked slowly forward, neck held in the formal "s," wings balancing his glittering gold body in its ponderous upright movement.

"Excellent," he said. "Excellent." He closed his eyes, aligned himself carefully and shifted inside the dome. The brief dimensional movement, only possible when the body was still, was a necessity in a building whose doors were not designed to admit the bulk of a dragon, but merely his servants and aides.

Inside, the close heat worked instant relaxation. He rested his body, stretched his neck across the damp floor and chewed absently at the bales of Flamegrass stacked all around the walls before snatching a goat from its tether. He took a moment of quiet contemplation, eyes roving the inside of the dome, flickering over the murals painted there of a land long gone. A land before the dragons fought for mastery. Now there were precious few pockets of original beauty left. Keol had been one and, as he considered that more work was needed on the murals, his mind drifted back to Septern and the knowledge that their meeting that fateful day long ago was linked inexorably to the plight of Balaia today and the gateway in the sky above Teras.

"Our options are seriously limited," said Kard. "I know that's an obvious thing to say but you need to know exactly where we stand."

Kerela had summoned the entire Julatsan Council to listen to Kard. They were sat around the High Table in the Tower's Council Chambers, a series of rooms which ran around the outside of the Tower, ringing the Heart.

Kard was seated between Kerela and Barras with, running left around the polished marquetry table, Endorr, Vilif, Stefane, Cordolan and Torvis. The outer wall of the room held three open windows which admitted the afternoon light and a mild breeze. Braziers on the opposite wall balanced the illumination and a tapestry at either end, depicting Councils long dead, accorded the room the weight of ages.

"If you could first detail our strength of warrior and mage, General," invited Kerela. Kard nodded and unrolled a piece of cream parchment.

"I had a platoon conduct a census. I'm afraid to tell you that it didn't take as long as I'd hoped." Kard took a deep breath. "Inside these walls, we have one hundred and eighty-seven mages including yourselves. Yesterday we had over five hundred. Our military strength is hardly better. I now command seven hundred and seventeen able-bodied men, thirty walking, hobbling and lying wounded and a dozen I am not expecting to survive until morning. Four hundred and eight children between a few months and thirteen ran in here along with six hundred and eighty-seven women and three hundred and fourteen men of varying ages and abilities.

"That's two thousand, three hundred and fifty-five altogether and yes, that's a real crowd in here but fortunately the wells are deep and enough of you took notice of my warnings to ensure there is four weeks' food. After that, well . . ."

Barras' heart sounded loud in his ears in the shocked quiet that followed Kard's summation. Every head contemplated the three-coloured table top. No one could bear to catch another's eye. The braziers blew in the breeze, guttering for a moment.

"Gods in the ground," breathed Torvis, his old, tall and bony frame hunched, his wrinkled face showing all of its advanced years. "How big is the population of Julatsa?"

All eyes were fixed on Kard once more. He shifted in his seat, clearly uncomfortable, looking at them through hooded eyes.

"Before the Wesmen attacked, including approximations for transients and the absence of mages and the guard sent to Darrick at Understone, there were somewhere in the region of fifty thousand people in Julatsa, actually within the city," said Kard. "We have less than one in twenty of the population inside the walls of the College."

Barras put his hands behind his head and leaned back. Kerela buried her face in her hands, while her head shook slowly. Stefane put a hand to a trembling mouth and tears ran freely down Cordolan's and Torvis' cheeks. Vilif and Endorr gave no outward reaction, too stunned even to cry.

Kard raised his hands. "I understand your sorrow, your shock and your helplessness, but remember that many of our people will have escaped into the surrounding countryside and will no doubt make their way to Dordover and the other Colleges.

"But yes, we lost many good men in the defence of the city and there will be a significant number of prisoners. It is this that gives us our most immediate problem."

"So what can we actually do?" There was a half smile on Endorr's face but no mirth in his eyes. His question ignored Kard's last statement.

"Our choice is straight," said Kard. "Surrender, remove the Shroud and open the gates to the Wesmen, or wait for rescue by Dordover and other forces unknown."

"Surrender is absolutely unthinkable," said Kerela. "To open the gates would be the end of Julatsa as a centre for magic and probably of all of us too. I ask you, how many of you around this table believe the words of Lord Senedai?"

"We will be walking out to our deaths," said Seldane. "You know the Wesmen feeling for magic." There was a murmur of agreement around the table.

"And if no help arrives in four weeks?" asked Torvis, his eyes recovering a little of their twinkle.

"I will, of course, work on escape plans with my senior staff, but you should know now that any escape will be bloody and must include us all," said Kard.

"Not an escape, a break out," said Torvis.

"Yes." Kard managed a smile. "It will be a question of concentrating our efforts on the assessed line of greatest weakness. One reason why that tower they are building must be destroyed. Any moves we make have to be secret until the gates roll open. I'll leave that to you. But there is something we must face with more urgency and it may sway the mood of the people within the walls."

"Surely they are happy they are alive," said Seldane.

"Oh, I have no doubt that's true," said Kard. "But most of them have loved ones outside the walls somewhere, either dead, in the wilds or imprisoned. Earlier, Senedai spoke of employing further pressure to force our surrender and the removal of the Shroud.

"He has already lost enough men in the Shroud to understand its impenetrability and deadliness. I don't want to spell this out, so I'll ask you this. If you wanted us to remove the Shroud and surrender and you had several thousand prisoners in your hands, what would *you* do to put pressure on us?"

Septern's return through the rip had been one of unbridled rage and the incongruity of it all still made Sha-Kaan's mind fill with mirth. Septern had not been particularly tall for a human, perhaps only a little more than five and a half feet in Balaian terms. Sha-Kaan, by comparison, despite his youth, had at the time stretched more than eighty-five feet from snout to tip of tail. He had since grown to be well in excess of one hundred and twenty feet and was among the largest dragons still flying. More crucially, he was still almost as quick as he had ever been.

Septern had tumbled from the gateway, brushed himself down, seen Sha-Kaan immediately and had begun berating him and his kind. A Vestare doing the same would have been killed or at the very least expelled for insubordination. He'd pointed behind him repeatedly as he spoke.

"Why don't you go through and see what your beloved, what is it, 'Brood,' has done? You have demolished a peaceful and beautiful civilisation with your damned fire and your damned jaws. How dare you assume the right of life or death over people in another dimension? How dare you? Well, I have seen to it that you will never do the same in my world. And none of your bastard murderous Brood will ever see the Avian dimension again by my hand. I just pray enough survive to rebuild what you have taken from them.

"You are not the Lords of the world, only your own dimension, though I fail to see how destroying everything in your path makes you anything other than mindless animals. How can it possibly aid you to destroy innocent people? Well? Lost your power of speech, have you?"

By this time, Septern had been standing toe to snout with Sha-Kaan as the dragon rested on the ground, head pillowed on leaves and grass, wings furled, tail curled along the length of his body and under his long, slender neck. He had fought back the desire to punish the impudence of the human, keeping in mind how vital he might be to the Kaan's survival and development.

Behind Septern, four Kaan, all that had survived the battle with the Skar in the Avian dimension, flew from the swirling brown depths of the gateway, victory calls echoing across the devastated land of Keol.

He recalled as if it was the day before, their next exchange.

Sha-Kaan waited until they had gone, scanned the sky, sniffed the air for signs of any Skar and began to talk, having pulsed a message to his most immediate Vestare to attend him.

"I will tell you three things," he said. "My name is Sha-Kaan of the Brood Kaan, your world is not at risk from my Brood and you must curb your tongue because others of my kind are not as forgiving as I am."

"Forgiving? Don't make me laugh. You call that slaughter through there forgiving too, do you?"

"I call it survival," said Sha-Kaan, using the gentle tone he knew calmed anxious Vestare.

"How is it survival? You've torn apart their homes, burned their wings and bodies, shattered their ledges and brought darkness and lightning to the sky in daytime. I don't suppose they're impressed with your justification being a need for survival since I don't suppose they'd heard of the Brood Kaan yesterday."

"But they have heard of the Skar. And they serve the Skar. For that, they were against us, however unwittingly. This is a war and they are an ally to an enemy. They took a side that was not ours." If Sha-Kaan had been able to shrug like a human, he would have done so. Instead, he raised his bony brows. He saw Septern shift, some of the tension leaving him.

"But did they, the Avians I mean, know that?" he asked.

"The Skar should have told them everything about dragons, and the reasons they were chosen to serve. As shall you be."

"Thank you, I'm sure," said Septern. "First, tell me how the Avians could operate as allies to the dragons. It doesn't make sense."

Sha-Kaan moved his head, beginning to raise himself.

"That is not a simple request to answer," he said. "And we should move to a safer place. My attendants will give you food and provide escort. I will await your arrival at the Kaan Broodlands."

"Who says I'm going anywhere but back through that rip?" demanded Septern. At last, Sha-Kaan's eyes fired and he knocked Septern from his feet with a fuel-less breath.

"I do," he said, his voice loud. He saw Septern wince and raise hands to his ears, his face pale and scared. "You and your dimension can be of great benefit to the Kaan and, in return, we can protect you from other, less tolerant Broods. And believe me, fragile human, one day another Brood would have found you, had you not so fortuitously fallen to me.

"Now, I will await you at the Broodlands and you will attend to speak to the Ancients of the Kaan. The Vestare will help you but they will not speak your language and you may not be able to pick up their thoughts. Until we meet again, calm your mind and let it open, because this world is far bigger than you can possibly conceive."

And he had unfurled his wings and flown away, feeling Septern's eyes in his back and fighting himself not to probe the human's mind. He was a great human, of that there was no doubt. He understood the magic of dimensional travel, he could control it and that made him an incredible prize for the Kaan. He had looked back once, curling his neck under him as he flew onward. The Vestare were there. They would see him safe.

Sha-Kaan had bellowed his pleasure and flown for the Broodlands.

CHAPTER 9

Kard, Kerela and Barras stood silent in the ankle-deep mist of dawn behind the shifting evil of the DemonShroud, through which faceless pale blue phantoms shot and curled. Dormant during Balaia's hours of darkness, the shapes added a new level of deep unease to the feeling of dread the Shroud evoked. Lookouts above the North Gate had reported Senedai walking alone toward the College walls, through streets where, so recently, the peaceful business of Julatsa had been conducted. Now, those streets belonged to the Wesmen and their Lord was about to deliver judgement on the Julatsan Council's decision.

At a signal from Kerela, the gates were opened and Julatsa's military and mage elders stood across the Shroud from Senedai. This time, there were no flags, no archers and no guards. The meeting was likely to be brief.

"I see your friends keep you company this pleasant morning," said Senedai, his smile sneering from beneath his moustache, the tone of his voice falling dead against the Shroud.

"I see little pleasant in our situation," said Barras shortly. "General Kard and High Mage Kerela are with me to hear your response to our decision."

"Good. So tell me the result of your discussions."

"We will never surrender our College," said Kerela flatly.

Senedai nodded and there was a trace of regret on his face.

"I expected nothing more. I respect your decision but it leaves me no choice but to force you from behind your evil mist by means other than negotiation."

"That's what you called yesterday's ultimatum, was it?" Barras growled.

Senedai ignored him. "As you can see, I have come unarmed and unaided because I want you to believe my words. If, after I have spoken, you choose to strike me down with one of your spells, then so be it. But what I am about to tell you will merely be quickened as a result."

"Here it comes," muttered Kard.

"Tell us about the state of any prisoners you hold," demanded Barras.

"Alive," replied Senedai. "But they are prisoners. They have no standing." He paused. "There are no mages amongst them. Not now anyway. I couldn't trust them not to cast the moment my back was turned."

"That's a bluff," said Kard, speaking low, his face away from Senedai. "There's no way he could tell the difference in a crowd. He'd have to see them cast."

Senedai clapped his hands, the sound echoing dully across the small cobbled courtyard in front of the gates in the quiet of the early morning.

"No more talk. Here is what will happen until you agree to surrender. At dawn, midday and dusk each day, fifty prisoners will be brought to these walls and made to walk into this barrier you created. Any attempt to stop us will result in a further three hundred prisoners being executed and their bodies brought to you for burial. Unfortunately, since we cannot pass these bodies, or those who walk the barrier, to you, they will have to be left to fester and rot in full sight of anyone who cares to look down from your walls.

"Furthermore, as each day dawns, the number of prisoners walking into your mist each time shall rise by fifty. You can stop this repatriation—" he smiled at his choice of words "—simply by hanging your flag of truce or surrender from this gate and then removing the barrier. The first fifty prisoners will be here at dawn tomorrow. I give you one more day to make the right choice. Don't make me prove my words." He spun on his heel and strode away.

Barras and Kerela looked at Kard.

"He'll do it," said the General, nodding gravely. "Have no doubt. In fact I'm surprised he gave us another day."

"Damn the man," said Barras.

"But you can't fault his thinking, can you?" said Kerela. "This is very public. And our people will see their own killed by something we created."

"But his is the force, Kerela," protested Barras. "We're the innocents."

"Yes indeed," said Kerela quietly. "But it is within our power to halt the murder and in a very short time I can see our people turning against us. We must be prepared for that."

"You're not suggesting surrender?" said Barras.

"No. But remember, most of us within these walls are not mages. They do not have the same desire to preserve the College because they have no conception of what it would mean to lose it." Kerela chewed her lip and began walking back to the Tower. "We must work out what to say to our guests."

Sha-Kaan stretched his jaws in the quiet of Wingspread, feeling through slight vibration in the walls and floor the scurrying feet of his attendant. There was much to tell him and a journey would have to be made. So much of what was to come to Keol and then to Teras was similar to the arrival of Septern all those long rotations before. But there was a key difference.

Septern had been able to produce the help they needed through his intimate understanding of the nature of the dimensions. Sha-Kaan had no such confidence in the abilities of Hirad Coldheart and his Raven.

And yet he wondered whether it wasn't all simply a fate over which none of them had any control. Skies knew it felt that way. But who could have foreseen the other chain of events that Septern's arrival at the Broodlands had set in motion?

Sha-Kaan closed his eyes once more, breathing in the damp of the earth beneath his great body and recalled the Ancients' meeting with Septern. He had arrived irritable but well and Sha-Kaan well remembered the look of awe on his face as he took in the Broodlands. There was no Wingspread then, of course, but the structures of the Ancients sprang from the ground, testimonies to their leadership of the Kaan.

The Ancients had chosen to meet Septern on the banks of the River Tere, allowing those with the need to rest in its calming flow. In addition to Sha-Kaan, invited as the one who found Septern, three Ancients met the human. Ara-, Dun- and Los-Kaan. All had been in the last flights of their long lives, scales fading from gold to a dull brown, wings drying making flying a painful and difficult process.

Septern had walked into the middle of them, craning his neck to see their faces, his eyes trailing over their massive bodies, down to the tails which twitched impatiently. Ara-Kaan had opened his mouth to speak but Septern had spoken first, chilling the proud thought in Sha-Kaan's mind. Ara had been an ill-tempered dragon at best and the current Great Kaan felt the shudder of ages through him as he remembered what followed . . .

"—I'm not happy about this," said Septern. "I arrive in good faith, after winning the trust of the Avians to let me build a rip in their land and they are rewarded by wanton destruction by your . . . your minions or whatever you call them. It was their fatal misfortune that my incomplete knowledge of the workings of dimensional magics in their land led to it being far larger than I had intended. Then, as if that's not—"

"Silence!" thundered Ara-Kaan. "Skies fall but you humans do not know when to hold your feeble tongues." The sound of Ara's voice cracked across the valley, once again dumping Septern from his feet. He looked straight into Ara's eyes, defiant.

"I understand that I'm important or I would already be dead," he said.

"Then you understand very little." Ara's long neck snaked out, his old head, eye ridges blistered, dim blue eyes losing their lustre, coming to rest directly in front of Septern's. "We already have the means to travel to your dimension, which you presented to us. There will be other humans we can talk to."

"Then burn me and find out how wrong you are," said Septern, getting back on his feet.

Ara cocked his head.

"No!" shouted Sha-Kaan. "Great Kaan, don't." Ara-Kaan paused, one eye swivelling to fix on Sha-Kaan.

"Hear him," said the young dragon. "He has mastered controlled dimensional linking. He deserves some respect."

"He is human," said Ara dismissively.

"And here, where he shouldn't be," said Dun, speaking for the first time. "Hear him." Ara relaxed his neck.

"Speak, human," he said.

"Thank you," said Septern tersely. "Please allow me to introduce myself. I am Septern, nominally a mage of the College city of Dordover in Balaia. However, I do not feel allegiance to any one College, having been blessed with an understanding of multiple disciplines."

"Excellent," said Los-Kaan, his tail absently sweeping water over his back as he sat half in, half out of the River Tere. "And so does this mean that more than one of these multiple disciplines has an understanding of dimensional magics, as you would call them?"

Septern looked hard at Los-Kaan, presumably weighing up the meaning behind the question. He shrugged.

"Yes, in theory, all four Colleges have the knowledge to develop dimensional magics. It is a subject that crosses the ethical boundaries quite freely. However, it is the individual mage who has the responsibility to forward research and precious few work in this field. Dimensional theory is new and so is mistrusted."

"But not by you," said Ara gruffly.

"Of course not," said Septern, smiling. "I originated it."

"Really," said Ara. He stretched his huge jaws, displaying his rank of yellowed fangs. "Tell me why we are so wrong about your gateways."

"Because when I went through the rip to witness your attempted genocide, I made some adjustments to the rip magic. Now, the starting point of your travel is crucial and since the rips to the Avian dimension and Balaia are linked, you have to start in Balaia to travel back there. So the rips are useless to you, aren't they?" Septern's smile became patronising, an expression Sha-Kaan had seen among the Vestare.

"By the Skies, if I wasn't sure you were speaking the truth, I would burn the flesh from your crumbling bones," spat Ara.

"That's your answer to everything, is it? Set light to the offender and hope they learn their lesson? It's no wonder you're fighting your Skar and destroying your own lands."

"Meaning?" demanded Dun-Kaan. The Ancient's tongue flicked out of his age-paled face, moistening the lids of his eyes.

"Ever tried employing this?" Septern pointed to his mouth. "You sound bright enough; why don't you talk?"

"Ah," said Los-Kaan. "There speaks one who knows nothing of our history. The time for talking has long since passed. Conquest is the only way to secure peace now."

"Gods falling, you sound like a Wesman," said Septern.

"A who?" asked Los-Kaan.

Septern shook his head. "The race in Balaia who are threatening my lands and people. But never mind that. What is it you want?" His tone was suddenly impatient. "And why do you sound like you've met humans like me before?"

"Not quite like you," said Sha-Kaan. There was the nodding of heads and feelings of humour arose in his mind.

"Why don't you answer the human's questions, Sha?" said Dun-Kaan. "It will be a good test of your knowledge."

"Yes, Dun-Kaan, it will be my honour." Sha-Kaan swept his head low, extending his neck before snapping it back to the formal stretched "s" shape, head angled down to look directly at Septern more than a dozen feet below him.

"We flatter ourselves that we are complex beings trapped in ungainly bodies that only fulfil their potential in flight. There are many among us who crave the freedom of hands that could carve and build, and a size and flexibility that allows travel everywhere," began Sha-Kaan.

"But the trade-off with size is the loss of power," said Septern.

"And we would no longer be dragons," agreed Sha-Kaan. "So the craving is limited to those moments when we watch the Vestare at work on the structures we would love to build ourselves.

"But there is much more to us than size, strength and language. We feel the press of dimensions, we can travel them without the aid of magic such as yours and we need the energies they provide us to survive and develop."

"So you don't need me."

"Ah but we do." Sha-Kaan moved closer, relaxing his torso and leaning forward, his shadow covering Septern. "Because to leave our dimension without the knowledge of where we will finish is a risk none but the foolish and desperate would take."

"But you've seen other humans," said Septern. "So you must have been to Balaia."

"We receive visions. All dragons do. I have seen the sights of countless dimensions, including yours, when the alignment has been right and they have passed through the sphere of my psyche. But for all we see, we cannot travel to these places to establish links unless we are shown the way or manage to arrive with luck after a blind flight." Sha-Kaan settled on to his stomach, folding his front legs in front of his chest, scales glittering gold as they caught the reflection off the river. Septern moved back to accommodate him. "We want you to show us the way to your dimension."

Septern scoffed. "I'm sure you do," he said. "But if you don't mind, I think I'll pass on the sort of help you offered the Avians. I like my land and at least some of the people in it."

"Stubborn human," hissed Ara-Kaan.

"I beg your pardon?" snapped Septern. "Give me one good reason why I should invite you and your fire to my dimension."

Sha-Kaan closed his eyes and drew breath slowly, amazed that this human was being allowed to speak with such disrespect to the Ancients. Though the fact was that from his perspective, he had some valid points.

"Because another Brood will eventually find the path to your dimension, and your destruction and not protection may be their desire," he said evenly.

"Why?"

"A Brood can only melde with one dimension," said Dun-Kaan as if to a slow child. "Any Brood finding a second, unprotected dimension, and believe me we all look, will destroy its critical fabrics to stop it falling into enemy hands. If your dimension and the Brood Kaan melde, we can protect you by shielding your location from all other Broods."

"And you just expect me to believe that you don't already have a . . . um . . . melde-dimension of your own?" Septern raised his eyebrows.

"We don't quite follow."

"How do I know you aren't waiting for my help just to destroy Balaia?"

Dragons couldn't smile like humans but the space in and among the quartet filled with the feelings that would lead humans to both smile and laugh. Indeed, Septern was caught up in the emotional outflow and couldn't suppress a physical reaction.

"What? What is it?"

"Let me assure you, Septern of Balaia," said Ara-Kaan, "that had you been a representative of an enemy melde-dimension, your mind would have been closed to us, marking you as such; and your charred ashes would be blowing thinly around the dust of Keol while we plundered your dimension through the gateways you built."

"I can see why you would find that funny," said Septern, stone-faced. "All right; assume I accept what you say. How do you protect us and, more importantly, what do you expect in return?"

"An intelligent question and one that might interest you as a student of dimensional theory," said Sha-Kaan. "Every dimension, and every living thing of that dimension, has a signature that marks them. We can divine the signature by melding minds with you."

Septern nodded for Sha-Kaan to continue. "Once the signature is learned by the Brood, the psyche of the Kaan can shield the location of your dimension from enemy Broods. When we are stronger with the flow of energy from your dimension, we can stop other Broods receiving visions from Balaia."

"You tap the energy of my dimension?" Sha-Kaan could see that Septern, despite his suspicion and position, was becoming interested.

"Yes," said the young dragon. "Interdimensional space is random energy and it has no direction. We feel it, all dragons do, but the chaos can only sustain our minds. A living dimension is the coalescing of energy into coherent form. To find a melde-dimension is the dream of every Brood, because it can be used to improve the minds of the host Brood, making them stronger, better breeders, more plentiful and longer lived.

"Yours, with its magic, understanding of theory, however basic, and sheer life energy, is particularly prized."

Septern thought for a long time, his brow creased, his hands wringing together. Sha-Kaan found the sight captivating. The Vestare, though valuable, did not have the mental capacity of the human and he found this mage fascinating, touching the periphery of his active mind and finding a pulsing power there.

Septern looked up at Sha-Kaan. "This signature. Once you have that, is the melde complete?"

"It is the principal step but it does not make the melde functional," replied Sha-Kaan. "Put most simply, the signature gives us the light by which to navigate to and from this dimension, assuming the alignment remains constant. Your dimension calls you too but your mind cannot hear its song."

Septern nodded. "That makes sense," he said. "But I have other ways of divining the location of dimensions or why am I here?"

"Indeed," said Ara-Kaan, bringing his head in close once again. "We will be very interested to find out your methods."

Septern smiled. "Another time. So tell me, how do I help you form the melde?"

Sha-Kaan breathed out through his nostrils, the twin streams of air playing over Septern's face. "There is nothing simpler," he said. "Know that I am about to enter your deepest mind and don't fight me. That way leads to pain and your mind is too valuable to damage."

"I'll do my best." Septern sat on a grass-covered stone. "Wait one moment." He closed his eyes. "My mind is open. Just like before spell preparation. It's as good as you're going to get."

"Excellent," said Sha-Kaan. "I won't harm you so long as you don't resist."

"Whenever you're ready."

Mirth again. "It is done," said Sha-Kaan. "Your mind is remarkable. There is a great deal we can learn from each other."

"Now what?" asked Septern, a doubtful look on his face.

"Now we can travel to your dimension. Now we can do with you exactly as we choose." Ara-Kaan's tone was edged with cold and Sha-Kaan knew a moment of fear before realising it was the Ancient's way of playing a joke. Septern's face had gone sheet white but the Great Kaan brought his colour back. "Fortunately for you, Sha-Kaan told you the whole truth. What we need from you is more people with minds open like yours. Sha-Kaan will show you another way home and instruct you in exactly what we require."

And the meeting was over then and there. The Ancients moved away without another word and Sha-Kaan was left with Septern, the first Drag-onene of Balaia.

"Come," he said. "Let me show you how our dimensions will melde."

Sha-Kaan's attendant ran into the dome of Wingspread, disturbing his memory.

"My Great Kaan, I am ever your servant."

Sha-Kaan raised his head a little from the damp ground. The Vestare in front of him was tall for his kind, perhaps five Balaian feet and, though now in late middle age, still retained the sturdy, muscular frame that typified his race. His hair, the colour of dried Flamegrass, pale and flecked yellow, was cropped above his large and receptive ears, reaching to the nape of his neck and close to his eyebrows. His eyes, the dominant feature, large, round and deepest blue, took in the reduced light of the dome with no lessening of clarity. The braided beard, a mark of his rank as Attendant to the Great Kaan, hung down to his chest.

Connecting minds, there was no need to speak.

"Your summons had an edge of urgency, Sha-Kaan."

"Humans will be coming here, Jatha, through the Septern gateway. They must not be lost to us. Their signature is our melde; we need their aid."

Jatha swallowed hard, the sweat on his forehead not purely due to the heat in the dome.

"When will they come?"

"Soon. I cannot be more specific. Theirs is a difficult path to the far side of the gateway. But you must organise Vestare to meet them now. There can be no risk of them reaching the gate before you. Travel there yourself and take enough with you to defend yourselves on the ground. There will be no cover from the Brood. It would draw too much attention. You must leave when the orb has risen three more times."

"Your wish, Great Kaan." Jatha bowed his head. "I would ask why they are coming?"

"They are charged with repairing the damage they created in our sky and removing the risk to the Brood."

"A difficult task, Great Kaan," said Jatha.

"Yes," said Sha-Kaan slowly. "Yes."

"You're troubled. Can they succeed?"

Sha-Kaan stared at Jatha, his eyes blinking very slowly, his tongue flickering over his lids.

"I don't know," said the dragon. "They are humans. They are frail but believe themselves strong. But there is something they have. Resilience. And inventiveness. And they have a magic that can aid us." Sha-Kaan settled his head back on the ground, reaching for some Flamegrass. "I need to rest. Go now and organise yourself. I will eat as darkness falls."

Sha-Kaan let his mind drift again. Septern's reign as the first Dragonene had been short-lived. There had always been something dangerous and uncontrolled about the great human and ultimately it had meant that the Kaan never learned his dimensional location secrets.

A Vestare had taken Septern to the Melde Hall, a vast underground structure only half lodged in the Kaan's dimension. Sha-Kaan himself had shifted into the hall whose doors, like those of Wingspread, would not accept anything the size of a dragon.

"Doors big enough to admit a dragon on foot are both unmanageable and unnecessary," Sha-Kaan had said in reply to Septern's question. "I don't believe I have to describe the effort not only to make them but to operate them."

The Melde Hall had been built in hope and expectation of the discovery of a suitable melde-dimension. With the news that the event had finally occurred, celebrations had been delayed while the Hall had teemed with Vestare readying it for ceremony, their shouts echoing into its depths. Several hundred had poured in and even so they barely made an impact on the emptiness. They had polished mosaic and marble, swept dust from statues and stocked the Hall, which could comfortably accommodate two hundred dragons, with Flamegrass.

Sha-Kaan recalled that he had touched the mind of Septern then, feeling the reactions of the Balaian mage . . .

Septern remained suspicious, despite the apparent friendliness of Sha-Kaan in particular. His bravado masked a deep anxiety over what he had blundered into and the price Balaia would have to pay for his agreement with the Brood Kaan.

The hall he was standing in was the single biggest building he had ever seen, hundreds of feet long, its roof lost in the dark, the braziers lining the walls only emphasising its vastness. He could barely see the opposite arch from the one in which he stood and it was only as his eyes slowly adjusted to the gloom and distance that he realised that the series of eighteen arches, each wide enough to admit the largest dragon, led to yet more space on which he couldn't focus.

Septern took a few steps into the Melde Hall, heading right around its periphery, taking in the statues of dragons and portrayals of battles, laid out in mosaic, that punctuated the enormous stone openings.

The arches themselves were wide and tall, each better than thirty-five feet wide by twenty high. The surrounds were carved with leaf and plant motifs, great creepers denoting growth, winding their way to twine, in flower, at each apex. Septern moved to the nearest arch. Looking within, totality and oblivion clashed in his mind. He'd felt the sensation before and it set his heart racing.

"You are intrigued," said Sha-Kaan.

"What is this place?" asked Septern. "The power is almost palpable."

"It is our version of your gateway. You are looking at a melde-corridor. Choose one and enter. I will be behind you."

"If it's all the same, you can go first. Call it a fear of the unknown." Septern smiled thinly.

"Or a mistrust of the Kaan," said the dragon. "Very well." Sha-Kaan strode across the Melde Hall, his wings unfurled to balance him, his feet leaving deep imprints in the soft ground, which vibrated sharply with every fall. Septern followed but the Kaan, who showed a surprising turn of speed despite the clumsy-looking half-waddle of his walk, disappeared into a corridor just left of centre as the Balaian mage looked on, shouting: "Hurry, human, the next phase of the Kaan is upon us."

To the right of the Melde Hall, another dragon appeared, standing tall before relaxing to the ground. Vestare in attendance, the movement of displaced air blowing loose grass on the ground and the hair on Septern's head. A third dragon shifted into the space directly behind Septern, ruffling his cloak and, with sudden fear of being crushed beneath one of the massive gold creatures, the mage began to run hard.

As he neared the arch Sha-Kaan had chosen, Septern heard more dragons arrive in the Hall, their audible calls combining gently to fill the space with a soft animalian music, at once welcoming and frightening. A last look revealed a Hall that seemed full of raw power, twisting necks and expectancy. Dragon after dragon shifted into the hall, the press of reptilian majesty taking his breath. He chased Sha-Kaan into the rip.

So unlike his own magically-assisted dimensional travel with its attendant pain and uncontrollable forward motion, the short—or so it seemed—journey down the corridor was akin to walking in dense, cloying fog.

Behind him, the Hall and all its sound and light had gone. All around him was the crush of what had to be interdimensional space. He put out his hands but could feel nothing. Below his feet, the outline of a path blew in the surreal light, and enclosing his body, a gentle pressure that sucked in his lungs and constricted his chest. But there was no pain.

And before he had time to truly register his speed, he stepped out into another great domed hall, this time with tall, iron-bound wooden double doors set in the opposite wall. Sha-Kaan faced him, standing in front of one of dozens of landscape tapestries that hung on the walls. Light from torches, lanterns, ornate carved candle pillars and braziers filled the room with stark moving shadows. In a dozen places around one end of the chamber, fires burned high in grates, producing a sweltering heat. And from beyond the doors, he could hear noises of dragging and shuffling and the fall of multiple footsteps.

Feelings of calm and humour filled Septern's mind. He looked up at Sha-Kaan.

"You're going to tell me this is Balaia, right?" he asked.

"No," said Sha-Kaan. "This is a construct in interdimensional space. One day, I'll explain to you how it is done but suffice to say it is akin to a pier built into the sea, with its roots anchored firmly on land."

Septern looked behind him. There was no evidence to tell him where he had entered the hall. The wall behind him was blank.

"You cannot find your way back that way," said Sha-Kaan. "You need the Kaan signature to reach the Melde Hall."

Septern nodded. "I see. And all those arches back there, they all come to places like this?"

"Yes. Eighteen to serve the Kaan with a melde-dimension. It is the maximum number we can safely shield from our enemies when all are linked to our melde."

"All right, I'll accept that," said Septern, clutching at comprehension. "How far are we from Balaia? If distance means anything here."

"It does not and that statement tells me a great deal about your understanding. As an answer, let me say that there is no need for a corridor such as you have just travelled. To enter your domain in your dimension merely requires you to identify your preferred point of entry. Using your signature, I can ensure that happens and beyond that door, we will nominate an entry point in the construct's outer chambers."

"That's it?"

"Yes."

Septern found it all so plausible. But there had to be a catch. Something that Sha-Kaan would keep hidden. As the true cost of making a pact with the demon dimension was hidden from the mages who requested it.

"And then you have all you need?"

"By no means," said Sha-Kaan. "Protection of your dimension has a price, but it is small."

"Let's hear it."

"For you and the other mages of the Dragonene calling, all we demand is that you be available and respond whenever we call you. The weak and the damaged will use these chambers to recover their strength but the corridor must be open and that means the Dragonene must be in attendance."

"I'll be a prisoner in my own house," said Septern. "Waiting on your call. That is unacceptable. No deal."

Sha-Kaan pulled his head back sharply.

"You misunderstand," he said. "Now I have your signature, if you agree to be my Dragonene, I can touch your mind wherever you are and open the portal, if I have to, anywhere in Balaia. It is you who is the key to the link but the most effective corridor will always be at the root of your power, which I take to be your house."

Septern considered Sha-Kaan's words, realising he actually had very little choice, having already given Sha-Kaan not only the signature of the Balaian dimension, but his own personal mark too.

"Why does being here help you recover? Presumably it's better than resting in your Broodlands."

"Yes," said Sha-Kaan. "I would describe it like this. At either end of the chambers is a dimension of coalesced energy. Within each dimension, the energy is still random in its direction. But the open corridor forces a flow of energy in one direction only. It is this flow in which we bask that so speeds our healing process. We call them Klenes."

Septern caught his breath. The dragon was talking about harnessing dimensional flow. It was a technique he had only dreamed about under-standing. There was one thing, though.

"But surely these flows are visible to any dragon blind-flying in interdi-mensional space? Surely they could follow the flows to your Melde Hall or to Balaia?"

"The chances are so small, I can't calculate them," said Sha-Kaan. "Not only do we shield the corridors as we do your dimension, but flying in inter-dimensional space is like walking in impenetrable fog for you. Sanctuary could be within arms' reach and you would walk by none the wiser."

"Unless you walked right into it." Septern scratched his head. "See my point?"

"Yes. But the difference is that an effectively-shielded signature is, to all intents and purposes, not there at all. A dragon without the signature would fly through the same point in interdimensional space without touching what he was seeking." Sha-Kaan snaked his neck down, giving him eye-to-eye contact with Septern. "Now," he said. "Will you agree to be my Dragonene?"

Septern nodded. "It would be an honour. One more question, though. You talked about it being important to protect the fabric of melde-dimensions. What did you mean?"

Sha-Kaan's exhalation played over Septern's face. Feelings of warmth and joy filled his mind.

"Mage and Kaan shall grow together," he said softly. "Now to your question, using your dimension as example. Balaia, of course, is just one continent in your world but the concentration of magic has lent it great structural importance. Our melde, based upon the links with the Dragonene that you will nominate and show to us through me, will rely on many places remaining intact. Your lake, the centre of your magic, is one. The centres of the ancient towers of magic in your Cities are others. The assembly of rock and stone close to your largest city, the range you call Taranspike, is yet another. And so will your house be one. Dragons could destroy it all. We must protect it from them and from powers within yourselves that could cast down mountains." Sha-Kaan angled his head quizzically, like a dog. Septern almost laughed at the absurdity of the comparison. "You are anxious."

It must have been written all over my face, thought Septern. But the solution to his problem was sitting right in front of him. He'd like to see the man that could take the amulet from Sha-Kaan.

"It's part of the reason I was with the Avians," he explained. "I've created something I cannot destroy but that I don't wish to see fall into the wrong hands in Balaia. I wanted to hide it through a dimension gate, but I got curious and that's why I met you. The Avians have one part of the secret, maybe you should have the rest."

"What is it?" asked Sha-Kaan.

"It could remove all those fabrics you spoke of. This—" he took an engraved amulet on a chain from around his neck, "—is the first part of the puzzle to unlocking it. It's a spell. It's very powerful indeed. I call it Dawnthief."

CHAPTER 10

The next night, the Parve company split three ways. Following an evening meal and the promised Communion, Styliann and Ilkar conducted a brief conversation before the former Lord of the Mount readied his horse and Protectors. The news of his usurpation at Xetesk had struck to the core of his confidence.

Glancing back at him during the day's ride through unremitting slope and summit, valley and river, Ilkar noticed that the set had gone from his shoulders and the gleam from his eyes. They had been replaced by something altogether more sinister—a hooded, brooding fury that darkened his features, tightened his lips and corded tension through his neck.

He wouldn't say where he was going, just that he had to reach friendly contact as soon as possible. That his route took him south to the Bay of Gyernath, the same route as Darrick would pursue the following morning, was clearly of no consequence. The Protectors, he said, had little need of rest and Darrick's cavalry would only slow him down.

But as he rode off, the Protectors running in a protective diamond around him, he left unrest behind. The Raven, who were planning to leave during the early hours to put them on the trail north of Terenetsa before sunlight, reducing the chances of being sighted, sat with Darrick. The General was not enamoured at the prospect of following in the tracks of Styliann.

"If he blunders into any trouble, it'll be ten times worse for us but we won't know it until we hit it."

"Take a different route." Denser shrugged.

"Yes, because there must be hundreds to choose from." Thraun smiled.

Darrick nodded, picking up the line. "Well, yes. It was a coincidence we chose the same one out of all those many options."

A snigger went around the campfire.

"I was just making the most obvious suggestion of a solution," muttered Denser.

"You should probably just stick to magic, Denser," said Thraun, his smile cracking his heavy features.

"What the hell for? Dawnthief doesn't seem to have done us any lasting good, does it?" Denser's face was angry. Darrick chose to ignore him.

"Look, it's possible to reach the Bay of Gyernath by a number of routes but all except one involve risk to horse and rider." Darrick rubbed his hands together and warmed them over the fire though it wasn't particularly cold. "And the trouble with the best route is the half dozen villages that need avoiding. If Styliann chooses destruction not detour, I could face real difficulties reaching the Bay in his wake."

"So come with us," said Hirad.

Darrick shook his head. "No, I'll not risk your mission. Anyway, I'll make it. I always do." He chuckled.

"Gods, you sound like Hirad," said Ilkar. His mood, though still sombre, had been lightened by Styliann's confirmation that the College of Julatsa had not fallen. Why not was a matter of some conjecture, but the College, temporarily at least, still stood.

"How long to the Bay from here?" asked Hirad. Darrick shrugged.

"Well, the way gets easier south of Terenetsa, for a couple of days anyway. I should think that, barring interruptions, we'll be causing trouble to the Wesmen in about ten days' time." He smoothed his hair back from where it was blowing into his face.

"We shall be in or near Julatsa by then," said The Unknown.

"What's left of it," said Ilkar.

"Can't you commune with your people there?" asked Darrick.

"No, I'm afraid I never studied the spell. It doesn't have too many uses for a mercenary mage," replied Ilkar. "And even if I could, Styliann, who is a far better exponent, hasn't raised a contact inside the College. His information came from a mage hiding outside the city."

"So how are we so sure the College is all right?" asked Will.

"Because the Tower is still standing and there are no sounds of battle."

Darrick frowned, his brow knotting under his curly light brown hair.

"I can't believe they'd just stop at the College walls," he said.

"They're scared of magic," said Ilkar. "And they've lost the Wytch Lords' influence. Arriving at the walls of a magic College is going to be a time of real fear for them because they only have rumours of the power housed inside. Besides which, I suspect the Council has bluffed an impasse. How long it will last is open to question."

"This mage Styliann contacted. Do we have his position? He could prove invaluable," said The Unknown.

"She," corrected Ilkar. "She wouldn't give an exact geographical position but Denser knows the mana shape to contact her."

"Good, we'll need to meet people like her when we get across the Inlet."

"I can see it all now," said Ilkar. "The Raven leading a band of rebel Julatsans in an audacious attack on the Wesmen, The Unknown Warrior at their head." He reached across the patted the big warrior's arm. "I think that may be beyond even us, but thanks for the thought."

The Unknown Warrior stretched and yawned. "Don't dismiss it. If a good number have escaped and the word of Dordovan relief forces arriving turns out to be true, we could liberate your College ourselves."

"I still think you're in dreamland, Unknown."

"Well, you certainly should be," said Darrick. "Get your heads down, I'll wake you in four hours."

The rout of the Wesmen back to his town gave Baron Blackthorne and his guerrillas one major advantage. The trails to Gyernath were empty and safe. He had dispatched a dozen fast riders to the southern port to alert the Council of their arrival; the Communion mages, he kept refreshed against the possibility of Wesmen attack. His sealed note also set out basic needs and requirements of men, horses and supplies. It did not say why.

Baron Blackthorne sat with the slowly recovering Gresse in a camp six days from Gyernath. The morale of his people was rising, their action was specific and no longer mere damage limitation. Now they had a goal and it was one all could believe in. They were going to reclaim their homes.

"When we've retaken Blackthorne, Taranspike is next," said Blackthorne. Gresse smiled and looked across the fire at him.

"I think our priorities may keep us near the Bay of Gyernath," he said. "Taranspike will wait. Pontois won't destroy it, after all. Just a shame he didn't place his considerable weight behind the fight for his own country."

"Damn him," muttered Blackthorne. Baron Pontois had always been smug and arrogant. Blackthorne could just imagine him laughing with his cronies as he sat at Gresse's table, having swept into the undefended Taranspike Castle to claim it as his right.

It wouldn't last. Whether it was because of the Wesmen or a force led by Blackthorne, the Baron could at least look forward to the day when Pontois grovelled in terror. Blackthorne didn't consider himself a gratuitously violent man but, as he looked over at Gresse and saw the pain and bitterness behind the bravado, he knew he could cheerfully cut out Pontois' heart and serve it to him on a bed of his own entrails.

"We need to send messengers to all the Barons and Lords, not just those within the Korina Trade Alliance," said Gresse.

"All but Pontois," said Blackthorne. "I'd rather die than have him fight beside me."

"My sentiments exactly."

"I'll attend to it when we reach Gyernath. We'll have a better idea of the numbers we need then." Blackthorne stared away into the dark, tasting the air, his lower teeth irritating at his top lip.

"What is it?" asked Gresse.

"It'll be ten to twelve days before we reach Blackthorne," said the Baron. "In that time, they can choose to reinforce or raze my town. One thing is certain, they won't wait around doing nothing. We need to cut two days off our travel or we could be too late. I don't want to crest the Balan Mountains only to see my world burning."

The candles burned late into the night in the Tower of Julatsa. The College's Council had sat in unbroken session for three hours, debating their diminishing options in the face of Senedai's threat and the spectre of disaffection among those within the sanctuary of the DemonShroud. In a break from Council tradition, General Kard had joined the meeting, his knowledge making his exclusion unthinkable.

"It comes to a mere handful of questions," Kerela summed up after hearing much pious debate concerning the vital necessity of preserving Julatsan magic and the balance it gave Balaia; the debt of gratitude the people of Julatsa owed its mages; and the long term good of the masses— Balaians in general—coming ahead of the immediate needs of those soon to be sacrificed in the DemonShroud.

"Will the Wesmen carry out their threat? Can we stop those inside witnessing what goes on outside? If we can't, how do we justify our refusal to surrender the College to save loss of life? Should we, in fact, surrender the College to save loss of life? And would surrendering the College actually cost more lives than it saved?"

"Good summation," said Barras. "I think Kard can answer the first two. General?"

Kard nodded. "First, I'll repeat for all ears what I told you as we walked from the gates earlier. Senedai will be true to his word. I think it's a moot point, though, because, unless I'm badly mistaken, all around this table are prepared to find out the hard way, in any event. I would expect nothing less. To surrender immediately to such a threat would be a poor capitulation."

Barras, who with Kerela flanked Kard at the head of the table, tried to gauge the reaction of the Council. What he saw was a hardening of focus, a resolution of minds and a determination to proceed. He was a little surprised. Compassion was a trait in plentiful supply among the Council during normal times. But then, he reflected, these times were a very long way from being normal.

"Secondly," continued Kard. "We can stop anyone seeing the murders. We already limit access to the walls for safety reasons and there are no buildings positioned to see the base of the Shroud, not even the Tower. If we ban all access to the walls, we can practically deny anything is happening."

"Unacceptable," said Vilif shortly.

"I didn't say it was acceptable," said Kard. "I said it was possible."

"You can cut out the sight but never the sound," said Stefane. "By the time Senedai is slaughtering one hundred and fifty each third of the day, the cries will be heard throughout the College. Think of the backlash when they find out the truth."

"And there will be rumours from tomorrow morning," added Cordolan. "In fact, I'd be surprised if there weren't already. No disrespect to the professionalism of your soldiers, General, but at least a dozen of them heard Senedai's first threat. People talk."

"I assure you I have no illusions," said Kard.

"Very well," said Kerela. "I think the point is, we couldn't keep this quiet, even if we wanted to, and to try would serve only to alienate our people. So, we are left with this. How do we justify our refusal to surrender?"

There was a shifting of bodies in chairs and concerted glances at anything but another Council member. Kard spoke into the awkward silence.

"A refusal to surrender sends out a very clear signal that we believe that, ultimately, magic is more important than life. And that is hard to justify. Gods, I'm not a mage so you can imagine how I struggle with this.

"But we have not yet discussed the consequences of the alternatives on a personal basis. Surrendering the College is not only wrong on a magic-balance front but on a human and elven level too. Walking into Senedai's hands means two things. The slaughter of every Julatsan mage inside these walls and the enslavement of all surviving Julatsan people. Personally, I'd rather be dead."

It was, Barras reflected, a common sentiment but for differing reasons. Kard wanted the life he knew, the Council desired the continuation of Julatsan magic and were prepared to stake almost anything to get it.

"There is something else," said Torvis, his old face carrying none of its usual humour. "Our guests, as Kerela so appositely describes them, cannot force us to remove the Shroud. Even killing us will not alter that. Unless we agree to dismantle it, the Shroud remains active for fifty days when Heila will no doubt come to call."

Kard shook his head.

"You have something to say?" Torvis scowled. "I am just laying out the facts."

"Yes I do." Kard pushed back his chair and began to circle the table slowly, all eyes following him. "That kind of sentiment leads to conflict. Saying 'we're not changing and you can't make us even by killing us' would lead me to do just that if I was hearing my friends and family dying beyond the walls. I'd kill you just to ensure you died with those pushed into the Shroud.

"If you want these people behind you for the maximum time, you have to make them believe that, no matter the suffering outside, the consequences of surrender are worse. You have to link their minds to the lives they will live enslaved to Senedai and the Wesmen. You have to remind them the Dordovans are coming, and you have to never mention the survival of Julatsan magic as an issue. Appeal to them, don't dictate to them."

"Why don't you do it, if you know them so well?" challenged Vilif. Kard stopped his movement, finishing at the end of the table facing Barras. He nodded.

"All right. I will."

While the new stockade rose around Understone and the stone fortifications of the pass were put in place by his prisoners, Tessaya waited.

Time was precious. Darrick and The Raven were on their way and the dread force would be running again. All of them heading east, all heading for battle. He had to try to stop them linking with the remaining armies in the south, with the Colleges and, most particularly, with Korina.

He knew four days wasn't much but he had expected Taomi to be close to Understone, having encountered little resistance crossing the Bay of Gyernath and on the sparsely populated route north. Senedai, at the Colleges, would have come across considerably more trouble.

Tessaya spent hours scouring the cloudy skies from the third morning onward. He looked south, waiting for the telltale dark dots in the sky that would signify his approaching birds. And on that afternoon he was rewarded. A single bird, high in the southern sky. Tessaya tied the hair back from his face and watched its approach, his keen eyes following its course as he stood in the newly completed southern watch tower.

It was definitely one of his birds. He could tell by its flight pattern, alternating gliding rests on the wing with sharp beats, fixing its position by subtle nuances in the currents of the air and in the roll of the land.

With the bird nearing, Tessaya tied the green and red marker ribbon to his wrist and waved it slowly above his head, the striped material snapping in the stiff breeze. In a flutter of wings, the grey and white woodruff landed on the rail of the guard tower. Tessaya scooped the bird up and held it gently to his chest with one arm, bending his neck to press his lips to its head and taking the messages from its legs. Then he set it to flight again, to the roost above the inn where it could rest and eat.

"More reliable than smoke, eh?" he asked of the watchman. He unrolled the coded papers.

"Yes my Lord," replied the man, the embryonic smile dying on his lips as Tessaya, having read the import of the first message, caught his eye.

"My Lord?" ventured the watchman.

"Curse them," grated Tessaya. "Curse them." Ignoring the frightened guard, he strode to the ladder, descending more quickly than was safe. His riders had not found Lord Taomi. But they had found his men and Shamen butchered and left to rot. They had found pyres built in the eastern manner. And they had found evidence of a hasty retreat southward. They would continue but their pace would be slow. To run into the rear of the army pursuing Lord Taomi would be foolhardy.

Who could it have been? The advance was supposed to be too fast for any pursuit from Gyernath to overhaul them. That left the rich Baron Blackthorne, whose wine tasted sour in Tessaya's memory. But he found it hard to believe that Blackthorne, well-armed though he was, could muster enough of a force to seriously trouble Taomi. Not without help.

He read the notes one last time before striding away toward the barracks where his prisoners were held. The fat man, Kerus, would have to supply some answers. Either that or lose some of his men to Wesmen executioners. The time for reason was past for now. Tessaya had to have knowledge of the forces he was against and he found himself able to consider almost any method to get it.

Dawn was threatening to slit the eastern sky. Barras stood on the Tower's highest rampart, looking down into the quiet city, a cool breeze blowing fresh air across his face.

At a time like this, it was easy to imagine that all was as it had always been. That no army of Wesmen was in occupation beyond the College walls, that first light would not bring the slaughter of fifty innocents. Innocents whose souls would feed the demons' insatiable appetite and sit heavy in Barras' heart forever.

But two things gave the lie to Barras' fleeting ease of mind. The oppressive DemonShroud that surrounded them, its evil casting a pall of anxiety over him; and the Wesmen's tower, now all but complete, which overlooked them.

They had been wrong about its purpose. The Wesmen had no intention of attempting to breach the Shroud using the structure, which scaled perhaps eighty feet into the sky. Its wheels were for manoeuvring it around the College walls, its steel cladding protection against fire and spell. They wanted to see inside the College and Barras conceded the common sense in that while cursing its invention.

The old elven mage, Julatsa's Chief Negotiator, surveyed the perimeter of his city, his eyesight sharp and clear in the dark before dawn, the grey veil of the DemonShroud growing visible as light began to crack the sky, a hideous reminder of the horror that lived with them every day. The Wesmen, or rather their prisoners, had not been idle and the evidence of long-term intention to occupy was everywhere.

Other fixed watchtowers were already built in half a dozen locations and now the stockade was going up. It would be a slow job. Suitable timber was not in plentiful supply close to hand and Julatsa was a sprawling city. Even so, three weeks and the ranks of pole timber would encircle them and the Wesmen would be that much harder to shift.

Barras moved his gaze to within the College walls. The Tower and its many service and official buildings dominated the centre of the grounds. In front of him, the trio of Long Rooms, where range spells were tested, stretched away from the opposite side of the stone-flagged courtyard which encircled the Tower. Each Long Room was over two hundred feet in length, low and armoured and had seen some of Julatsa's greatest successes and most awful tragedies over the course of the centuries. Now, though, they were emergency accommodation.

The same was true of all the lecture rooms, the old Gathering Hall, the principal auditorium, and the Mana Bowl where fledgling mages hoped to discover their acceptance of mana and feared the consequences for their sanity if they did not. Only the Library and the food stores remained off limits.

Despite the hour, around a hundred people milled about in the courtyard, many, because of Kard, now aware of the fate that was about to befall the unfortunates in Wesmen hands. The General had not slept. Instead, he and a member of the Council in rotation had visited every pocket of the population within the College walls, explaining the situation as completely as he could. So far, his words had caused sadness and anxiety but no anger. Barras was due to attend the last meeting but first, he had to try and buy the College some time.

He hurried from the Tower, walking quickly across the cobbles to the North Gate where he climbed up to the gate house and came face to face with a surprised guard.

"My mage?"

"I have to talk to Senedai. Excuse me." Barras walked on to the ramparts that ran across the gate. The DemonShroud's evil was all but within reach. Well beyond it, three Wesmen guards sat around a small fire in the centre of the open area sandwiched between the College and first city buildings.

"I would speak with your Lord!" called Barras. The Wesmen looked up. Barras could see them frowning. One stood up and moved closer, cupping a hand behind his ear.

"I must speak with your Lord," said Barras. He was greeted with a stream of tribal Wes and a shrugging of the shoulders.

"Imbecile," muttered Barras. He straightened and spoke loudly. "Senedai. Get Senedai. Yes?" There was a pause that seemed to last for eternity before the guard nodded and scurried off, passing an aside to his colleagues who both laughed and looked at Barras.

"Laugh while you can," said Barras, smiling back and giving a little wave. He wasn't waiting long before Senedai strode from the shadows into the firelight, augmented now with the first murk of dawn.

"You cut it very fine, elf," said Senedai, once he had stopped a safe distance from the Shroud. "I trust there will be an orderly surrender."

"Ultimately, Lord Senedai, but not at dawn. We are not ready."

Senedai snorted. "Then fifty of your people will soon be dead." He half turned.

"No, Senedai, wait." The Wesman Lord spread his arms wide and swung back.

"I'm listening but it will make no difference."

"You don't fully understand our situation."

"Oh but I do. You are desperate. You have no way out and you are trying to buy some time. Am I right?"

"No," said Barras, knowing his attempt, a long shot at best, was now almost certainly doomed to failure. "Put yourself in our position. We have much anxiety in here. Our people are scared. We need more time to calm them, to assure them of your honourable intentions. But more than that, we have to put our affairs in order."

"Why?" demanded Senedai. "You can bring nothing with you and all that you leave will be ours. Your people are right to be scared of our strength and ferocity, but the only way to prove to them we are not wanton destroyers of those we conquer is to put them in our hands."

"I'm appealing to your humanity but I am also appealing to your good sense and your reason," said Barras. "We can calm our people and that will help both you and us, but we need more time. That's one thing. But far more important to you is that the College is safe when you finally walk through the gates in triumph. Mana is a dangerous force to those who do not understand it. If you come in now, without a mage, I could not vouch for your chances of survival."

"Are you threatening me, mage?" Senedai's voice rose in volume and hardened in tone.

"No. Merely telling you the truth," replied Barras calmly.

"And yet you wait until the new day to tell me this truth."

"I am sorry, Lord Senedai, but we have never been in this position before and had no idea of the length of time it would take to close down the source of our magic. But do it we must or not just you but this whole city could be lost."

Senedai shifted his position, made to speak and then stopped, doubt creeping across his face. Barras seized his chance.

"What I am saying is this. You can start killing innocents if you want but we will not open the gates and remove our protection. This will not be because we don't care for our people. This College must be made safe for existence without mages and in the end, our responsibility is to the whole of Julatsa, not to those of its population you choose to execute. I am imploring you, Lord Senedai, to believe my words."

Senedai stared long and hard at Barras, his face betraying his doubt and the fact that he didn't have the knowledge to test Barras' words.

"I must think," he said eventually. "How long will it take you, this closing of your mana source?"

Barras shrugged. "Six days, maybe more."

"You must think me stupid," snapped Senedai. "Six days. And I have no proof of the truth of what you say. What can you give me?"

"Nothing," said Barras evenly. "Save to say that we have nothing to gain by lying to you. There is no help coming and we have no means to arrange any. I am aware of your impatience to be on your way but surely you need to be secure here first. Until we are ready, you will not be so. What we are doing will help us all."

"If you are lying, I will have your head myself."

"I accept the bargain."

"Six days," muttered Senedai. "I might grant you two or three. I might grant you none. The screams of the dying will tell you when my patience is exhausted." He began to walk away but turned again. "You play on my ignorance of magic. Perhaps I'll question one of my captive mages. Gain myself some knowledge."

"I understood them all to be dead."

"Like me, you should not believe everything you are told." He summoned a guard to him and walked from the square.

"Now that," said Kerela, "is the negotiator's touch." She and Kard stood with Barras in the southernmost Long Room while the subdued crowd gathered to hear the General speak.

"What exactly do you have to do to dismantle Julatsan magic, then?" asked Kard, a wry smile on his lips.

"I've absolutely no idea. Nothing, so far as I am aware," replied Barras. "Though I must say I was surprised he knew so little about the random nature of mana and the harmlessness of its natural state."

"Good on you." Kard clapped Barras on the back. His expression sobered. "He won't give us six days, you know. He's not that stupid."

"Even one day saves us one hundred and fifty lives," said Kerela.

"Don't dismiss the mindset of the Wesmen. Magic terrifies them at a very fundamental level. Senedai knows he's won, or thinks he does. A few more days will make little difference," said Barras.

"Terrified he may be, but that didn't stop him sacking the city." Kard adjusted his uniform, tugging down his jacket. The crowd began to quieten. "I hear what you are saying but his impatience will soon get the better of him. His prisoners mean nothing to him, particularly those who can't perform heavy labour. Expect young girls and the old to be the first into the Shroud in no more than three days."

"I tend to agree," said Kerela. "He can't verify anything you've said, he'll assume you're lying and he'll sacrifice in the Shroud even if it's only to hurry us along."

Barras nodded. He could see he would have to talk to Senedai again. The flush of his minor victory faded. Kard began to speak to the group of about three hundred in the Long Room.

"Thank you for your attendance and your patience. By now, some of you will have heard what is happening outside the walls. But for those that haven't, here is the situation and I would ask you to keep your questions for later . . ."

Barras let his mind drift. Three days. They were outnumbered probably eight to one in absolute numbers, more than that comparing fighting strengths, but at least the mages were rested. Help was coming from Dordover but the Shroud prevented Communion as it did every spell from penetrating its borders. Meanwhile, they had to make their own plans. He wasn't going to surrender the College meekly.

Now the population within the walls was aware, the real talking could begin. If Julatsa was going to fall, it would be in a battle that would live in legend forever.

Chapter 11

The Raven, or at least Ilkar and Thraun, heard a faint sound from the Wesmen encampment long before they could hear water lapping on the western shore of Triverne Inlet.

It was night, six days after their parting from Darrick and Styliann. The Raven, under Thraun's guidance and drawing on The Unknown's experience, had travelled quickly over increasingly hostile terrain in the foothills of Sunara's Teeth, the dominant northern range. Forced to take little-used trails away from villages and Wesmen staging posts, they had picked their way over sheer cliffs, through dense forest valleys, across great shale slopes, collapsed rock formations and cold hard plateaus.

There had been six days of growing worry in Hirad as he watched Denser withdraw further and further inside himself. The initial euphoria of his success and subsequent recovery had given way quickly to a sullen self-contemplation and finally a surly unwillingness to interact. Even Erienne had suffered from his moods and her gentle touch led all too often to harsh words and an angry brush-off.

"It's like he feels he's done what he was born to do," she had said on the fourth evening after he had, as usual, taken to his bedroll early. "I'm sure, deep down, he cares for me and our child but it doesn't seem enough and he's certainly hiding it. He was chasing after Dawnthief and the perfection it represented for so long I think he's lost now it's gone."

"And imminent invasion by dragons doesn't fire him at all," Ilkar had said. "Excuse the pun."

"No," she had replied. "The urgency and energy have gone from him these last few days and that's more than a little strange, given what we learned last night." Erienne had been referring to her Communion which had revealed the first meaningful results of measurements on the noon shade. Parve would be completely covered in a little over thirty days unless The Raven could find a way to close the rip. Thirty days until dragons ruled Balaia.

But that was still in the distant future for Hirad. Right now, they had to get past the Wesmen and into Julatsa. The Raven had stopped in a hollow, sheltered from the sharp wind that blew off the Inlet. Above them, trees swayed and rustled, grass blew flat against the earth and tough shrubs grappled with neighbouring bracken. They had scrambled down a long muddy slope between sheer crags, the product of a past landslide, and the hollow was filled with lichen-covered tumbledown rock.

The opposite slope was blanketed in purple-flowered heather and strewn with loose stone, only held in place by the grasp of thin earth. Here and there, stunted trees grew in the lee of the prevailing wind. Thraun and Ilkar had scaled the bank to report on the scene at the Inlet.

Hirad rubbed his gloved hands together and accepted the warm mug of coffee, happy at the decision to keep hold of Will's stove. Earlier that day, with the horses more of a hindrance than a help, they had set them free in a wooded valley, destroying saddle, bit and stirrup and anything they couldn't easily carry. After a short debate, Thraun had shouldered Will's flat-packed stove, the weight not even hastening his breath. They were all happy for its lightless warmth now.

The little wood burner sat on a flat rock, its thin column of smoke invisible against the overcast sky, the light it cast not enough to illuminate their faces, let alone betray their position. It was five hours before dawn.

"How far away are we?" asked Hirad.

"Perhaps half an hour at a brisk trot but to enter from a sensible angle will take double that. We'll have to head a little further north or we'll be seen," said Thraun.

"What have we got?" asked The Unknown.

"You'll be able to see for yourself, the light off the water isn't too bad," said Ilkar. "But basically, we estimate an encampment of around three hundred, all billeted in tents set in classic tribal semicircles around standards and fires.

"There are three watchtowers looking landward and a group of marquees in the centre of the camp that no doubt contain stores for onward transport across the Inlet. The main route is from the south. We need to take northern entry beyond the furthest watchtower but even then, it's a little tricky."

Hirad nodded. "Boats?"

"Plenty. From small sails to midsized oceanworthy galleons, although the Gods know where they got them from. We should be able to find something we can take very easily."

"What's on the opposite bank?" asked Will.

"Something more heavily fortified, I expect," said Thraun. "But we couldn't see that far. We'll be sailing right into the mouth of the Goran Falls to avoid whatever it is, anyway."

"It'll marginally shorten our journey time, too," added The Unknown.

"What about horses, the other side?" asked Will.

"We've two options," said Ilkar. "Either steal some from the Wesmen or hope that the Triverne Lake Guard are still alive. And that's not too unlikely given that the Wesmen effort seems to have reached only Julatsa so far."

Hirad rubbed a hand over his mouth. "All right, the theory's fine. Now to the practice. How do we get a boat without waking the camp?"

"Finish your coffee and come and look," said Ilkar. "Thraun and I have got an idea."

Shortly afterward, The Raven lay in a line, looking down a long bracken-covered slope that ended in the meadows and beach at the edge of Triverne Inlet. To the south, the slope trailed away to a steep escarpment and thence to the Blackthorne Mountains themselves, while to the north, the mountains and hills flattened as they approached the northern coastline a further day's ride away.

In front of them was the Wesmen staging post. It was quiet, though a large fire burned in the centre of a hexagon of marquees and around it sat a number of Wesmen. Other fires burned along the shore, illuminating the ranks of boats drawn up on the sand, but elsewhere, the camp was in darkness but for the moon's cloud-filtered reflection off the water.

The natural light gave a muddied blue tinge to Hirad's vision but he could still make out the three watchtowers, each, he had been reliably informed, holding two guards and a bell. The southernmost commanded a view along the main trail which meandered out of sight southwest and stood in front of a corral containing horses and cattle. Coops for chickens and pens for pigs sat nearby, but the animals were quiet. A quick scan of the camp gave no indication of any Destranas, but he had no doubt the wardogs would be there somewhere, probably on guard in or near the marquees to deter any Wesmen looking to boost their rations.

The other two towers, set equidistant along the perimeter of the camp, partially obscured stands of Wes tents pitched around dead fires, the standards flapping and snapping in the wind. Thraun had been right; the only sensible way in was further north where they would be overlooked by just one tower.

"All right," said Thraun. "You can see our access point. The route we need to take will be across the top of the camp, skirting the main fire and dropping down on to the beach. We have to take out the tower guards or we'll be seen. Ilkar is suggesting two people under CloakedWalks can surprise the guards and bleed them quietly. That will be the first obstacle out of the way."

"By which he means two mages," said Denser. "Which two did he have in mind?"

"You can address me directly if you want, Denser. I can understand you."

Hirad sighed. "We have to work together or we'll all be killed," he said shortly, staring at Denser. "I know things are hard for you right now, but we still have work to do and we need you. There are three hundred Wesmen down there. How long do you think we'll last if they catch wind we're on their beach, stealing their boats?"

"I am well aware of our situation. I merely wanted to know who Ilkar had in mind for his little suicide mission."

"Me and you, that's who," said Ilkar. "It might take your mind off your inner pain or whatever it is."

"You have no idea what I am feeling." Denser was dismissive. Ilkar was earnest.

"I know. But right now, you are doing your damnedest to make sure we all suffer with you. Try participating again, you might even like it. I know I will."

"Try completing your life's work and seeing it damn you," growled Denser.

"Enough," said The Unknown. "We haven't much time." His voice stilled hasty tongues. "Thraun, you were saying."

"It all hinges on the watchtower. As you can see, we can't enter from the north because the cliff is too steep to climb down and we'll be seen. We have to edge around toward the camp, scrambling down and keeping to the shadows in the lee of the cliffs." Thraun pointed out the areas he was speaking about but Hirad couldn't make them out clearly.

"Is this watchtower thing your whole plan?" asked Will. Thraun shook his head.

"In terms of getting us into the camp safely, yes, pretty much. But our idea focused on two other things. First, a backup in case we are seen and second, we were debating a little sabotage while we were here."

"Oh God," muttered Denser.

Hirad smiled. "It would be rude not to," he said. "Let's hear it."

Styliann did not travel to the Bay of Gyernath. Nor did he have any intention of so doing from the moment he left Darrick's pitiful band of horsemen. He had been approached by the Xeteskians in the cavalry but they could not offer him anything and he was not in the frame of mind to lead any but the very best in fighting speed, skill and stamina.

So he approached the fortifications at the eastern end of Understone Pass with only ninety Protectors around him. He faced perhaps fifteen hundred Wesmen warriors but wasn't unduly worried. In a straight fight, he suspected he could force surrender or outright rout but he hadn't come to fight. He had come to organise a swift passage back to the east and to promise something he had no intention of giving. Help.

His arrival caused a great deal of consternation on the platform that ran around the inside of the partially built stockade. Shouts filled the air, bows were bent and dogs barked. He was ordered to halt and did so, the fading light of late afternoon glinting off the masks of his Protectors, their quiet stillness clearly unsettling the Wesmen.

Styliann sat on his horse in the centre of the protective echelon, his hands on the pommel of his saddle, watching the Wesmen come to some semblance of order. An initial urge to run to the attack was halted, and out of the angry and threatening gathering came one man flanked by four others. He strode purposefully across the space between them until he stood only a few yards from the front rank of Protectors. Two dozen masked heads moved fractionally to watch him and his guard, their weapons held at rest but their bodies tensed for action.

The Wesman spoke in tribal Wes dialect, his accent clipped and harsh, his speech quick but confident.

"You are trespassing on lands that belong to the unified tribes. State your reason for approaching."

"I am sorry for my sudden arrival," replied Styliann, his Wes rusty but serviceable so long as he kept to the basics. "Before I speak, I ask who I am speaking to."

The Wesman inclined his head slightly.

"Your use of my language earns you some small respect," he said. "My name is Riasu. I would have yours."

"I am Styliann, Lord of Xetesk." He saw no reason to correct the slight inaccuracy. "You are in charge here?" Riasu nodded.

"I have a force of more than two thousand tribal warriors who have closed the pass to our enemies. You have the look of one such."

Styliann was sure his use of language was far more colourful but it was the best translation he could make in the time he had.

"The skill of your warriors is known to me," said Styliann, struggling for the right words. "But you have no magic. I bring you that."

Riasu laughed. "We have no need of your magic. It is evil and must die. As must you." Styliann remained impassive despite the threat.

"I know your fear—" he began.

"I have no fear," snapped Riasu, his tone hardening. Styliann raised his hands in a gesture of calm.

"Your—ah—belief. But know the truth of it. Your arrows cannot harm me or my men. Try." Styliann's HardShield was raised in seconds but Riasu merely shook his head.

"I know your magic," he said. "What do you want that would stop me wanting your head."

"Who is the leader of your armies in the East?"

"The Lord Tessaya."

"I will speak to him," said Styliann.

"If I allow your travel," said Riasu. "Something I have no wish to do. What do you want?"

Styliann nodded, unwilling to make a show of force. The very fact that Riasu had not ordered an attack on him demonstrated the Wesman's caution and fear of the force of magic, not to mention the obvious power of the Protectors. But he was concerned that this lesser Lord would misunderstand him and he could not afford to lose any Protectors this side of the pass.

"Let us sit, talk and eat by a fire," said the former Lord of the Mount. "Out here on neutral ground."

"Very well." Riasu shouted orders back to his men at the gate of the stockade. A flurry of activity resulted in firewood, a cooking pot, food and an increased guard arriving in the space between Styliann and the tribal Lord. Soon, the fire was blazing and water heating up over the flames. Declining any pleasantries, Riasu and Styliann took up positions on opposite sides of the fire, a dozen guards behind each of them. The remainder of Styliann's Protectors were ordered back as far from their master as the Wesmen were from theirs.

Styliann smiled inwardly at the arrangement set out by Riasu. He had no conception of the communication the Protectors enjoyed. If the meeting broke down, Riasu would be dead, his guard overrun and Styliann reinforced long before any help could arrive from the stockade. Still, it made him happy and that was all Styliann really wanted.

With wine and meat in hand, Riasu began.

"I will not say this is a pleasure. But I will not toss my warriors' lives away in needless fight. This is one thing Tessaya has taught us."

"But it has not halted large loss of life in Julatsa," said Styliann, preferring to keep his mind clear with a hot rough leaf tea that a quick divining spell had revealed as harmless, if a little bitter.

"I know nothing of that."

"I do." Styliann looked at the reaction of Riasu, his augmented eyesight piercing both fire glare and gathering gloom to see a flicker of doubt in the Wesman's face. "Your feelings about magic do you no help," he continued. "You hate magic because you do not understand it. If you did, you would see that it could help you."

Riasu snorted. "I think not. We are a warrior race. Your tricks may kill and maim and see things far away but we will triumph over you one day."

Styliann sighed. He could see this discussion going round in circles.

"Yet you said you would not toss away the lives of your men. If you do not listen to me, you will be doing that." Styliann cursed his lack of vocabulary in tribal Wes. It was difficult to make any emphasis and Riasu needed his eyes opened very crudely if he was to see sense and give Styliann access to the pass.

"Tell me of your bargain." Riasu moved subject without any evidence he had heard, let alone comprehended, anything Styliann had said so far.

"It is simple," said Styliann. "I would regain access to my College quickly. You wish to destroy magic. You can help me do the one and I will help you do the other if you let my magic live."

"We are sworn to end all magic." Riasu shrugged. "Why should we bargain with you?"

"You will never end all magic," said Styliann shortly. "If one mage lives, there is magic. If there is magic, it can be learned by others. And you will never take Xetesk."

"You are so sure. But if you were to die here, what then?"

Styliann kneaded his temples with the thumb and middle finger of his right hand. He should have expected this rather blinkered and aggressive pigheadedness but that knowledge didn't help his frustration.

"You won't kill me here. You haven't the strength," he said, looking Riasu directly in the eye. The Wesman stiffened.

"You dare to threaten me in my own lands?"

"No." Styliann permitted himself to relax and chuckle. "I just speak the truth."

"Two thousand men," said Riasu, jerking a thumb in the direction of the stockade.

"I know. But your beliefs—" (oh, to know the word for ignorance) "—about magic stop your eyes from seeing the truth. My men here are nearly one hundred in number and if I thought I had to fight you, I would not fear the outcome. They are magical. If you saw them fight, you would see."

"We would cut you down."

"You are skilled but you are not strong with magic. I do not wish to fight. Let me talk with Tessaya."

Riasu raised a forefinger. "Very well. A test. One of your masked men against two of my warriors."

"It will be an uneven fight," said Styliann. "I have no wish to spill the blood of your men."

"State the odds, then," said Riasu.

"One of my men will take four of yours, armed or unarmed. But this is not what I want to see."

Riasu raised his eyebrows. "Four? This I must see. And armed, I think. Let us see a real fight." He leaned to his left and spoke to one of his guard. The man nodded and ran back toward the stockade. "Choose who you will."

"Do you want this? It is wasted death." Styliann pursed his lips.

"For you, maybe."

"As you wish." Styliann rose from the fire, his food forgotten. Perhaps this was inevitable. It really depended whether Riasu took it as insult or with respect. He summoned the nearest Protector with a crook of his right index finger.

"Choose one who is willing to fight. It isn't to protect me but to prove a point so I want it to be quick and bloody, do you understand?" he asked of the masked warrior.

"I understand."

"Excellent. Who shall it be?" The Protector was silent for a moment, communing with his brothers.

"Cil."

"Give him your strength and your sight. Let him fight fast and true. There must be no error," said Styliann.

"It shall be done." The Protector turned. Cil came from the group gathered away from the fire. He walked into the light, polished ebony mask reflecting the yellow flame. Behind the mask, the eyes were impassive, fixed on the four Wesmen who gathered to the left, leaning on their weapons.

Styliann returned to the fire and stood across from Riasu. The tribal Lord was nervous and uncertain, feelings clearly not shared by those he had chosen to fight. Four large men, decked in furs and metal helmets, two carrying longswords, two carrying double-bladed axes. They came to the ready in a loose semicircle as Cil approached, axe in his right hand, longsword in the left.

The Protector, in heavy leather and chain, stood well over six feet tall, towering over his thickset, powerful opponents. He stood in an open stance, weapons down and to either side, waiting.

"You can save your men," said Styliann. Riasu half smiled and shook his head.

"They will save themselves," he said. "Fight!"

The Wesmen moved to encircle Cil, who stood motionless, not even acknowledging the two who flanked him. His head was straight, taking in the axemen who came at him from the front, weapons in two hands, wary, slightly crouched. At a signal from an axeman, one of those behind sprang forward, aiming a blow at Cil's broad back. The Protector lashed out with his axe, blocking the sweep, blade ending close to the ground. He hadn't turned or moved his feet. The man fell back and the circling began.

Styliann folded his arms across his chest. It was a matter of waiting for them to run to their own deaths and suddenly he forgot his desire to see no blood spilt. Perhaps this display was what the Wesmen needed. A little reminder that taking Understone and its Pass meant little to the mages of Xetesk.

Cil had returned to his open stance, body absolutely still. He was,

Styliann knew, listening to his brothers, feeling the ground beneath his feet and tasting the air around him.

Deciding numbers would win the day, the Wesmen attacked together, angling in from all four corners. Like two men, Cil blocked the first axe with his longsword while sweeping out and behind with his axe, catching one swordsman high in the head. The Wesman's intended blow never came and he clattered to the earth, blood and brain oozing from his skull.

Bringing his axe back sharply, he caught his next enemy's overhead on his blade and, while twisting to disarm him, placed his longsword parallel to his back to block the fourth man. Cil pulled on his axe shaft, dragging the helpless Wesman off balance. Now he moved his feet for the first time, quarter-turning left, throwing the caught axeman hard into his companion. Both men fell to the ground.

He turned again, this time to fend a stab to his side and bring his axe through, waist high, chopping through the Wesman's stomach and angling out and up through his rib cage, carrying gore in a wide arc as he rounded on the remaining two. They scrabbled to their feet but he was on them so fast, batting right with the flat of his axe into one's face while piercing the other's heart. Before Styliann could order him to stop, he had beheaded the last man.

Finished, he returned to his open stance, blood streaming from his weapons into the dust, carnage surrounding him and a shocked silence falling on the arena of sudden slaughter.

Styliann turned to Riasu who stared openmouthed at the corpses of his men.

"Now, think if all of my men were fighting and I backed it with my magic," he said. "It was you who wanted this, not me."

Riasu faced him, fear in his eyes, fury in his body and humiliation burning from every pore.

"You will die for this." Riasu chopped his hand down and arrows flew from the top of the stockade, arcing over the fire to where the Protectors stood in tight formation, their eyes on Cil. The shafts flashed in the late afternoon light, every one bouncing harmlessly from Styliann's ready deployed HardShield.

"You are testing me," said Styliann. "And that is good. But now, I will talk with Lord Tessaya."

"Do not think to give me orders," said Riasu, his face an angry snarl.

"Pick your next words with care," warned Styliann. "You are far from your two thousand men."

Riasu's eyes betrayed his anxiety, flicking over the situation in which he found himself, too close to a dozen Protectors for comfort and knowing his like number of guards would be no match whatever. "I will send word to Tessaya that you wish to talk."

"Good. I have no wish to see more blood spilled."

Riasu nodded curtly and turned to go. Styliann's next words froze him in his tracks.

"I will give you until this time tomorrow to bring me an answer," he said. "Or I will have to walk the pass anyway, whether you are with me or against me."

"I will not forget what you have done, Styliann, Lord of Xetesk. And there will come a time when you are alone. Fear that time," said Riasu. He stalked across the dirt back toward the stockade, his guards lingering to look at their fallen tribesmen.

"Take their bodies," said Styliann. "He will not harm you." Cil cleaned and sheathed his weapons and returned to the mass of the Protectors. Styliann looked after the retreating form of Riasu and sat back down by the fire. Poor fool. He would find out, probably to his cost, that no Xetesk mage, particularly not one so senior, was ever alone.

CHAPTER 12

The Raven trotted north along the gully in which they had made their temporary camp. Will's stove, cooled sufficiently by earth and boot, was packed in its leather coverings and was once more on Thraun's back. The shapechanger led the group, The Unknown at his shoulder. Hirad brought up the rear, sandwiching Denser, Ilkar, Erienne and Will between the warriors.

They had discussed a variety of options to liberate a boat but the simplest, to send in the mages under a CloakedWalk to steal a boat and bring it upstream was dismissed for the simplest of reasons; neither knew one end of a boat from the other. Further, it was the cause of passing mirth when Ilkar admitted that not only had he never learned to swim but that he was actively scared of water. Besides, The Raven wanted to cause some damage.

Ultimately, Denser had reluctantly agreed to Ilkar's original plan but Hirad harboured worries. Denser was not thinking straight and that could mean great danger for Ilkar as the two mages scaled the watchtower.

Any sabotage would follow the commandeering of a suitable boat. The fireworks Ilkar had in mind would blow their cover and require a quick getaway but the vote had carried. All were aware of the urgency of their mission but Ilkar in particular was keen to disrupt supply to the attack on the Colleges.

From the top of the gully's northern end, the way down was rocky but firm and led toward the edge of the sheer cliff, at the base of which tumbles of stone jutted from the water. They kept to the base of the cliff, hugging its shadow as it curved toward the camp until Thraun called a halt beyond the periphery of likely Wesmen vision. The night was dark this low on the ground and it was little more than a hundred yards to the first tent of the encampment. For now, they were out of sight of the tower and secure. A few yards further on, the ground fell away and would leave them exposed.

"We will follow on in three hundred counts unless we hear sounds of trouble," said Thraun. "You know the meeting point. Are you ready?" Ilkar nodded. Denser shrugged.

"Let's get it over with," he said. Hirad stared at him bleakly.

"Concentrate on your position, Denser," he said. "Any lapse could kill you both and that would be unforgivable."

"I haven't lost my eyesight or sense," said Denser.

"Just your sense of purpose," said Ilkar.

"Nor my respect for my friends," continued Denser, staring hard at Ilkar.

"I'm glad to hear it. Right. Let's get going."

Ilkar and Denser intoned quietly, moving their hands up and down their bodies. With a curt nod, Denser walked forward a pace and disappeared. Ilkar followed him and Hirad could hear them talking low as they moved off.

"Gods, he'd better not let me down," said Hirad.

"He won't," said Erienne. "If nothing else he isn't stupid."

"Just stubborn, difficult and bloody miserable," said Hirad.

"Nobody's perfect." Erienne smiled but it was forced and unhappy.

"No." Hirad looked toward the Wesmen encampment.

As agreed, Ilkar took the lead with Denser right behind him, one finger hooked in his belt. The CloakedWalks wreathed their bodies in invisibility but did not muffle their sound and Ilkar kept to bare earth, being careful to skirt the waist-high plains grass that edged the cliffs and grew in patches across the ground and away up the slope where they had first taken in the camp.

"Don't stop when we hit the ladder," said Denser.

"I won't," said Ilkar a little sharply. "I am aware of the limitations of the spell. And keep your voice down."

"My pleasure," hissed Denser.

"What the hell has happened to you, Denser?" whispered Ilkar, all his ire gone.

"You wouldn't understand," replied the Dark Mage, his voice quiet and vulnerable.

"Try me."

"Later. Are you going left or right in the tower?"

"Left, as agreed."

"Just checking," said Denser.

The camp was quiet as they approached, passing the peripheral tents pitched around their standards. The two mages slowed. From the nearest tent, the sounds of snoring filtered through the canvas. Across the camp, a horse whinnied and the unmistakable odour of pig filth drifted on the wind which gusted and swirled through the camp, rattling tentage, tightening rope on peg and blowing the odd snatch of conversation from tower or central fire.

Ilkar appraised their task. From the safety of the gully it had seemed simple enough but, closer to, the watchtower seemed tall and crowded with powerful Wesmen. Ilkar looked the tower up and down as they neared it, silent now but for their footfalls.

The tower stood about twenty feet high and was constructed from four stout central trunks sunk into the ground and packed at their base with rock for extra stability. A lattice of strengthening timbers crisscrossed their way to the roofed platform on which stood the pair of Wesmen guards. In the left-hand corner of the platform, a bell was fixed to one of the roof supports, its clapper tied off against wind and careless elbow.

"Remember, the throat or through the eye to the brain. We can't afford for them to cry out," whispered Denser.

"I know," said Ilkar, but inside the knot of nerves tightened. This was not the sort of action he was used to. He'd killed a number of times before but with the sword or with an offensive spell. This, he wasn't used to at all. "I'm going straight up."

The ladder ran up between the two poles facing into the camp and finished at a gap in the waist-high balustrade that ran around the platform. The two bored guards were leaning on its outward edge, sometimes exchanging low words but mostly quiet.

Ilkar grasped the sides of the ladder, being careful not to lose momentum. The wood creaked alarmingly, his heart missed a beat and his eyes scanned the platform for signs of agitation but the Wesmen seemed not to have heard. For now, at least, the wind was in their favour.

Ilkar's nerves became a fear which gripped him for a moment. This was a job for a warrior but none of them could hold the spell in place. Even The Unknown, who had operated ShadowWings shortly after his release from the thrall of the Protector calling, could not hope to maintain a CloakedWalk. There was a subtlety to the spell that had to be learned and enjoyed. The ability to hold the mana shape when stationary and visible, and to perform simple tasks while on the move without losing spell concentration, were nuances not quickly mastered. Simple tasks like murder, thought Ilkar grimly.

Five rungs from the top, everything started to go astray. With each step, the new wood protested, not yet bedded to its fastening. Ilkar slowed but there was an inevitability about the head of a curious guard that appeared at the top of the ladder, frowning down into the gloom beneath him, seeing nothing.

Ilkar felt Denser's hand on the rung his trailing foot was just vacating. They weren't supposed to get that close—Denser hadn't slowed, and couldn't have seen the danger.

"Move back," Ilkar urged the guard under his breath as he climbed inexorably upward, slowing still further. To slow any more would be to become visible and to become visible would be to die. "Move back." He made another step, keeping his feet to the ends of the rungs, but another creak cracked the night, deafening to Ilkar's ears. The Wesman leaned further out, peering down with intense concentration, knowing what he was hearing but confused by what he wasn't seeing.

Ilkar thought briefly about heading down but the change in direction would give him away, not to mention catching Denser completely unawares. The stupidity of the situation fell about his head.

The guard straightened but did not move from the edge of the platform. Keeping his gaze firmly set on the ladder below him, Ilkar placed his hand on the rung directly beneath the Wesman's feet and drew his dagger with the other. He really had no other choice.

"Oh Gods," he muttered, and surged upward, blade before him, taking the guard in the crotch, where it lodged. The man grunted in shock and pain, staggered back a pace and fell to the ground, dragging the dagger from Ilkar's grasp, clutching between his legs as blood blossomed to stain his leggings.

Ilkar kept moving left, knowing Denser would take the right. As the guard hit the platform with a dull thud, his companion turned, his mouth dropping open at the sight that greeted him. He started to speak but Denser's thrown dagger caught him clear in the throat, his shout turning to gargles as the blood poured from the wound.

Ilkar looked down at his victim who opened his mouth, a low agonised keening escaping his lips. He crouched, snatched his second dagger and jammed it through the man's open eye into his brain. He died instantly. The surviving Wesman clutched at the dagger in his throat as he staggered backward, his jaws moving soundlessly, his eyes wide as Ilkar switched into view.

Too late, the elf saw the danger and even as Denser grabbed at the man, the Wesman's furs dragging outward in the Dark Mage's invisible grip, he tumbled off balance, his arm swinging back where it caught the bell full on, knocking it from its mounting. The guard fell dead, Denser on top of him, but the bell, sounding dully, teetered and plunged over the side of the tower.

"If we're lucky . . ." said Ilkar.

"No chance," returned Denser. The bell struck the rocks at the base of the tower with a loud clang, the clapper breaking free to swipe at its dented surface on its single bounce. The strangled ring sounded right across the camp.

"At least the others know we made it," said Denser.

"We're in trouble," said Ilkar. "Know any Wes?" Denser shook his head. "Big trouble."

Harsh voices came from the next tower and the beginnings of spreading alarm below them were plain to the ear.

"Stay down," said Denser.

"Thanks for the tip," snapped Ilkar. "Any bright ideas?"

"Yeah, let's steal a boat, learn to sail and leave the towers alone." Denser crawled toward the gap in the balustrade. The shouts from the tower were louder, more urgent. There was a moment's silence before the bell sounded, calling the camp to wakefulness.

"Gods falling, what a cock-up," said Ilkar, raising his head to look out at the camp. Denser dragged him back down, the light of energy suddenly bright in his eyes.

"You want sabotage?" he said. "I'll give you sabotage." He closed his eyes and prepared to cast. Ilkar's face cracked into a smile.

Thraun had unshouldered his pack and was stripping off his leather before the sound of the fallen bell registered as trouble in Hirad's mind.

"You don't have to do this, Thraun," said Will, his stance edgy, worry lining his face.

"We must have a diversion or Ilkar and Denser will be killed."

"I doubt that," said Hirad.

"There are seven of us against three hundred. We have to give ourselves a fighting chance," Thraun said.

"But that's not the real reason, is it?" Will was staring up into Thraun's yellow-tinged eyes. Anger flickered across them before he shook his head sharply.

"There's no time to talk about this now." He turned to face Hirad. "Don't wait for me at the shore. I can swim. I'll find you." The shapechanger, naked now, lay down. The Unknown hefted Will's stove and Thraun's sword on his back. Will bagged the clothes and armour and slung them over his. "Best you get on," said Thraun. "I'll catch you up."

The night was filling with the sounds of anger and confusion. Hirad led The Raven quietly along the edges of the cliff. Soon, the watchtower was in sight and the shore angled sharply away to their left where the camp was built. Nothing moved on the platform.

"Where are they?" In answer, a figure rose in the tower. Denser. His arms moved outward, then clutched into his chest. Six columns of fire screamed down from the sky, scoring sudden blinding light across the camp. Each one smashed into a store marquee, unleashing frightening devastation.

HellFire. The columns sought souls. Denser had guessed rightly that men or dogs slept inside the marquees, and each column plunged through canvas to gorge itself. Tearing through timber boxes, stacks of cured meats, vegetables, grains, rope and weapons, detonating flour which flashed fire bright within three of the store tents. Their canvas exploded outward on a wave of air, sending planks, splinters, shards of wood and debris high into the night. Flame burst sideways, sheets of yellow-flecked orange snapping out, catching men and surrounding tents alike. The guards around the campfire wouldn't have stood a chance.

"Raven, let's go!" called Hirad as the camp dissolved into chaos. From somewhere on the wind he thought he heard laughter. He broke into a run, heading for the base of the tower in which Ilkar and Denser both now stood. FlameOrbs sailed out, diving into the tents at the northern end of the camp and splashing fire across tribal standards, scorching Wesman and canvas alike. New screams joined those already mingling with barked orders, shouts of alarm and the roar of two dozen blazes. Wesmen ran in all directions, carrying buckets, salvaged stores, and burned and dying comrades.

A handful of Wesmen warriors ran to intercept The Raven and gain the tower.

"Forget a shield, Erienne," said Hirad as they took up position, the mage behind the trio of swordsmen. "We need offence. And quickly."

"Right."

Hirad roared and closed with the first Wesman. The Unknown, three paces right, waited for the flanking attack.

The barbarian sliced left to right, his enemy blocking and leaping backward. Hirad followed up with a cut to the neck which the Wesman turned away but he was in no shape for the third as Hirad switched grip and opened a huge gash across his chest. Blood welled through his heavy furs and he stumbled. The Raven warrior stepped up and pierced his heart.

Turning, Hirad saw The Unknown taking on two, sweeping his blade into one's side and kicking out straight into the other's stomach. More Wesmen were gathering and Hirad weighed up their options.

"Ilkar, we need you two down here," he called.

"We've got a better idea," Ilkar shouted back. "Head for the shore, we'll see you there."

Hirad refocused on the battle. Fire raged on in the centre of the camp. Fanned by the wind, more and more tents fell victim and the anguished cries of terrified animals rose above the noise of blaze and clamour of voices. Directly in front of The Raven, twenty Wesmen broke and ran at them. The Unknown tapped his blade on the ground, waiting.

"I'll take left," he said, sensing Hirad's eyes on him.

"Will to my right," said Hirad. The wiry man trotted into position. The Wesmen ran on, their momentum the greatest immediate threat they posed, their weight of numbers enough to overpower the thin Raven line if they so chose. Hirad tensed for the fight but at twenty yards the charge was shattered.

Erienne stepped forward between Hirad and The Unknown. She crouched and spread her arms wide.

"IceWind." The temperature fell sharply as the cone of dread cold air streamed from Erienne's palms, whistling as it went and taking the centre of the Wesmen advance. Its broad front caught six men full on and they fell, clutching their faces, lips seared together, eyes frozen and cracked, their cries of agony little more than desperate hums inside useless mouths.

At the periphery of the spell, blood chilled in exposed flesh, blades fell from numb fingers and heads turned away, the whole line stumbling to a stop in the face of the sudden blast of glacial air.

As quickly as it had come, the IceWind had gone but there was no respite for the stricken Wesmen. Trying to bring some order out of the mayhem caused by the spell, they were taken completely unawares by Thraun. The wolf's approach had been silent but now he howled and crashed neck-high into the enemy, ripping the throat from one, his huge flailing paws knocking another from his feet to lie stunned on the ground.

Hirad made to wade in but The Unknown's voice stopped him.

"No, Hirad. Leave him to it. They can't hurt him. Let's get to the shore." The barbarian nodded.

"Just as we planned," he said, and headed north to skirt the first group of burned out tents. A dark shape flew over his head and ducked low toward him. He flinched and brought up his sword. Denser hovered in front of him, ShadowWings deployed, Ilkar in his arms and caught around his neck.

"We've got more damage to cause. Get the boat and get out in the Inlet. I'll fly in," said Denser. Ilkar said nothing, his eyes closed as he prepared a spell.

"You be careful, Denser," warned Erienne.

"The thought is lodged in my mind." He shot up and back, heading for the southern end of the camp. Hirad followed the flight; the black shaft of an arrow silhouetted against the light swept past them. Immediately afterward, the gates of the cow and horse pens shattered and the animals stampeded.

"Let's go, Raven." Hirad ran for the shore, leaving Thraun to his slaughter and the mages to their destruction.

Thraun could smell the fires, the fear and the blood mixed with the scent of prey animal and dog. He picked his way quickly through the grass, pale brown body blending with the colours of night, paws silent. He stopped at the perimeter of the human occupation, myriad scents vying for dominance. He ignored them. In front of man-packbrother, enemies gathered. They threatened, their sharp weapons raised. With the sound of the pack echoing in his mind and the smell of the forest forward in his memory, he charged.

The first enemy hadn't even faced him. He leapt, jaws closing on unprotected throat, left paw connecting with his chest, right beating another to the ground. Blood filled his mouth and coated his nose, his growl of pleasure the last sound his victim heard.

Panic gripped the enemy. They broke and ran. Thraun turned his head. Man-packbrother and the others were moving swiftly away. Water. His brain fought to remember. He would meet them on the water. He looked down, lashing a paw into the man he'd knocked down. He stopped moving, blood covering the wreckage of his face. Thraun howled again and set off, tracking man-packbrother, fighting the urge to chase down the prey animals that bolted here and there, their terror a tempting taste in his mouth.

Man-packbrother moved along the edge of the occupation. Thraun was inside the first line of dwellings, most of which burned, their occupants either dead or running blindly. There was no order. From his right, he heard sounds of alarm. Three enemy moved toward man-packbrother. Thraun hit them at a dead run, catching the first on his chest and sending him sprawling into the others. Consumed with the blood, he ripped and tore, his fangs chopping into flesh as he worked his head left and right, his paws beating, claws dragging.

From above, an enemy hit him with his sharp weapon. It stung his hide and he yelped, rounding on his tormentor, whose eyes widened. It had been a hard blow but Thraun's side had not split. He bared his fangs and advanced.

Denser flew back toward the blazing marquees, rising high to assess the mayhem he had so spectacularly initiated. Panicked Wesmen beat at the edges of the fires, their bucket chain scarcely making a dent in the heat and destruction. Ilkar's ForceCone had knocked the animal picketing flat on a twenty-foot stretch and in the confusion of fear and fire, horses and cattle stampeded away from the bright yellow blazes licking the air, trampling man and tent indiscriminately.

To his left, Thraun clamped his jaws on the sword arm of a hapless Wesman warrior and further on in the shadows cast by the fire, he caught the odd glimpse of The Raven, tracking toward the shore, unmolested for the moment.

Ilkar, cradled in his arms, was getting heavy. Denser was a strong man and the ShadowWings he had cast were trimmed for weight but there was a limit and the growing ache in his limbs was beginning to threaten his concentration.

"What have you got left?" asked Denser.

"FlameOrbs or another ForceCone. I want to keep enough to shield the boat," replied Ilkar. "More to the point, what have you got left?"

"I'll let you know," said Denser.

"How?"

"You'll start falling."

"Funny."

"Just get concentrating on those Orbs. If we can disrupt the bucket chain, we might get clean away." Ilkar nodded and closed his eyes, his mouth moving slightly, fingers describing intricate circles in the air. Denser leaned back to counter the shift in balance.

Denser watched the expert movements of the efficient mage, arms almost still, hands creating the shape with the words his mouth framed. Nothing was wasted, no mana stamina escaped. He was a consummate mage, his magic learned through long years and honed through sometimes agonising practice. Denser knew this because it had been the same for him.

Yet, despite Ilkar's clever use of his stamina, he was beginning to tire while Denser felt as fresh as he had before he had cast his CloakedWalk. Something had happened to him during his casting of Dawnthief. A new linking with the mana, a coupling forged deep in the core of his being. And it had given him new ways to construct his shapes. Much as Styliann harnessed mana in a way so thrifty and quick it took away the breath, so Denser had that understanding. But it was more than mere understanding. It was fundamental coexistence with the fuel of magic.

Ilkar nodded, Denser's signal that he was ready to cast. His eyes were now open, focused on the target ahead. Denser flew above the bucket chain, out over Triverne Inlet and round again, coming up the line giving Ilkar the widest target area he could.

"FlameOrbs." Ilkar clapped his hands and opened his palms. A trio of orange globes rested there, growing to the size of apples before he jerked his hands down and apart, the FlameOrbs flashing away. They grew as they fell, to the size of skulls when they collided with the unprotected Wesmen, splashing fire that consumed fur and flesh, the screams of the burning rising over the crackle of the fires that engulfed the camp.

Denser, his arms pained from shoulder to wrist, headed down to the beach.

Hirad broke into a sprint as Ilkar's FlameOrbs destroyed the bucket chain, fracturing the Wesmen's fragile organisation. He raced around the final tents before the shore, leading The Raven across the sand, the Wesmen forgetting all thoughts of saving their tents, turning instead to help kinsmen whose agonised cries split the night.

Ahead of him, Thraun paused, looked to see that Will was safe, and streaked across the sand toward Denser and Ilkar who had landed near the boats. Hirad pushed on, crunching sand underfoot, the rhythmic fall of small waves on the shore contrasting with the clamour of noise from the ruined camp. Ahead of him, Thraun brought down a Wesman warrior from behind, the man's bucket flying from his grasp, the warning sounds of his kinsmen too late to save him.

There was a dip in the level of the bedlam. The fires raged on but the Wesmen paused, making a concerted move for their weaponry as it dawned on them exactly what was happening.

"We've got to move fast," said The Unknown by Hirad's shoulder.

"Raven!" shouted Hirad. "Raven with me." He charged toward a knot of

Wesmen who had gathered near Thraun. The wolf snarled, darting in, jaws snapping, claws whistling through the air. Wary, the Wesmen kept their distance. But they couldn't avoid The Raven.

"Erienne, find a boat. We need a fast sail. Will, defend the mages. Unknown, with me." He tore into the Wesmen, sword chopping through fur and flesh. Beside him, The Unknown's blade caught the glare of the fires as it plunged into his victims. Thraun, sensing he was helped, howled and leapt, jaws burying into a shoulder.

Hirad parried an axe sweep to his head, his sword sliding down the shaft, shaving wood and chopping the gripping fingers from his assailant's hands. The man shuddered, mouth open in shock, axe falling. Hirad's next blow took out his throat. More Wesmen saw them. Thraun ran over his latest kill to attack the oncoming pack. Swords rose and fell but Hirad could see as he smashed a fist into an enemy nose and brought his blade through his stomach, that Thraun sustained no wounds.

From behind them, blue lightning arced across the sky, piercing the eyes of three Wesmen who fell clutching at their smoking faces. The attack faltered. Hirad batted aside a clumsy thrust, stepped inside, head-butted his opponent back and followed up with a stab clear through the heart. Beside him, The Unknown raked his blade across two chests, blood fountaining from a sliced artery and smashed lung while Thraun's snarls and growls accompanied Wesmen cries of desperation.

Hirad glanced over his shoulder. Ilkar and Erienne had pushed a boat out on to the water. At twenty feet long, it would easily take them all. Will was tugging at the sail stays, slightly unsteady as he stood on the rocking vessel. It was time to fall back.

The Wesmen had lost their appetite for the fight. Thraun ran at small groups who scattered, keeping them away from the beach. Hirad and The Unknown moved backward across the sand. More lightning from the fingers of Denser, more Wesmen fell, faces blackened, eyes gone.

"Get in and we'll push out," ordered Hirad. Arrows flew the gap across the beach, clattering off Ilkar's HardShield. Hirad grinned. The Raven slick as ever, an unshakeable unit.

When he hit the water, he turned as did The Unknown, running and jumping through the shallows to push the stern of the boat on which the three mages and Will sat, the cold water shocking his muscles to new life.

"Tell me if they start following us," said Hirad. More arrows bounced from the shield. The boat moved through the gentle tide and waves, the wind bringing nothing more than choppiness to the Inlet this near the shore. Behind him, he heard splashing and in the boat Will straightened. Hirad turned. Three Wesmen ran at them, circling axes above their heads and roaring battle cries.

To his left, The Unknown tapped his blade into the water, the normal ring of steel on stone reduced to a splash and muffled grate on the shingle below. They waited but the Wesmen didn't make it. From their right, the water exploded upward and Thraun surged from the surf he'd created to bear one down into the water, fangs deep in his thigh. A shout rang out from the shore and the others turned and ran, their kinsman left to float in as the tide dictated, his blood slicking the moonlit water.

Hirad yelled in triumph, exulting at the fires that scored the dark above the burning camp. The Unknown clapped him on the shoulder.

"Come on, let's get this boat moving." The old friends scrambled the few yards to the small craft and climbed aboard, Thraun paddling strongly beside them. In moments, the sail was unfurled, the wind snapped the dark canvas taut and The Raven headed back to the east. Home.

Chapter 13

Sha-Kaan and a dozen of his lieutenants flew from the Broodlands, already aware that they were almost certainly too late to save Jatha and the party of Vestare who were supposed to meet The Raven.

In the skies above Teras, the gateway hung in the sky, myopic gaze expanding inexorably. Around its surface, the guard flew their defensive holding pattern, at ease in the clear sky that day and comfortable that their vision would give ample warning time to assemble a defence to quell any attack.

But how long would the cloud stay away? How long before Sha-Kaan was forced to deploy more and more of his tiring Brood to fly patrol in the banks of thick, rain-bearing cloud that periodically swept down from the mountains of Beshara, drawing moisture to deposit on his lands? The rain fed the Flamegrass but the cloud obscured their enemies. Right now, clear skies were preferable. The River Tere, running through the heart of the Broodlands, was full and powerful and the Vestare could channel it to the beds of cultivated Flamegrass. It was in the open plains that their harvest would suffer, for the Flamegrass was greedy for moisture and wilted quickly without it.

But away toward the devastated lands of Keol, where Septern's gateway lay hidden by Vestare cunning and design, new columns of smoke smudged the sky, new fires coloured the earth. Sha-Kaan took his dragons high into the bright sky, calling barks of welcome and warning to the guard as they passed. As they flew hard over the hills of Dormar and the wastes at the borders of Beshara, the dark shapes in the sky revealed themselves to be of the Brood Veret.

The Great Kaan was surprised and pulsed a query to his cohorts. Slender and quick, the dragons of the Veret were semiaquatic, normally inhabiting the caves and seas to the north of Teras, never straying far from their Broodlands deep in the Shedara Ocean. They were characterised by blue and green colouring, thin muzzles which jetted slim concentrations of fire, short necks, four even, webbed feet and long, slightly flattened tails that powered them through the water.

They possessed poisonous spikes of bone that ran along skull and neck but their wings, small and swept back for speed through air and water, were their weakness. Gone was the reservoir of secreted oil that lubricated land-borne dragons and resisted fire, replaced instead by a veined water lubrication lattice. The lightweight system gave their wings greater manoeuvrability but, with armour nonexistent, it was vulnerable to being burned off by the scorching temperatures of dragon fire. But they had to be caught first.

The Kaan closed. Sha-Kaan could feel Jatha's fear, sensing his pounding heart and his laboured breath as he and the Vestare ran to escape the Veret. There were eight of the enemy Brood, all intent on their quarry. What taxed Sha-Kaan as he commenced his first attack dive was why the Veret had strayed so far inland and whether their interception of his Vestare was by coincidence or design.

The Veret didn't sense the threat of the Kaan at first, had no idea that above them, Sha-Kaan's fire was ready, his jaws open and dripping fuel. He glided hard down, slipstreaming a young marine blue Veret only half his own length who was chasing down a lone Vestare.

The man was neither quick nor agile enough, his dodging among stunted, blackened trees not adept enough to confuse the Veret's approach. Sha-Kaan could see him, darting left and right, back and forth, stopping and rolling, sprinting and standing, just as he had been taught. The theory was there—the momentum of dragons in the sky robbed them of the manoeuvrability to accommodate sudden changes in pace and direction but the practice against the more agile Veret was lacking.

And so it was that as Sha-Kaan lined himself up behind the young male Veret, the enemy dragon, having tracked his quarry with deft wing alignments and slight movements of head and neck, opened his mouth and exhaled two tight jets of fire that tore through the Vestare's body. The victim was hurled from his feet into the bole of a tree, his flaming corpse flopping to the ground, chest holed massively, head aflame. Around him, wood blazed in the sudden inferno and the wave of flame rolled away into the forest, igniting branch and leaf and scattering birds.

Sha-Kaan rolled slightly right and unleashed the power of his fire, ripping into the Veret's fully deployed wing as he braked to bank away from his dive. The young dragon's head jerked around in shock to snap a glance at Sha-Kaan before the fires destroyed his wing membrane and he barrel rolled into the blackened forest, dying body bouncing from the ground before driving uncontrolled into a stand of shattered trunks to lie still, a cloud of earth and dead leaves erupting into the air.

Sha-Kaan pulled up sharply, searching the ground for Jatha whose presence he could still feel, and the sky for a view on the battle. Kaan chased down three Veret, the agile blue-green animals spinning and turning as they sought to flee their larger, more powerful assailants. Below and to his left, a Veret was locked in the air with a Kaan. Spikes had punctured the softer underscales of the Kaan's neck but she held on, jaws clamped behind the Veret's head. Blood was pouring from the wound and Sha-Kaan pulsed the order to release. The returning pulse saddened him. The poison was overwhelming the dragon's system. She would die but she wouldn't release the

Veret to live. He watched as the two spiralled to their deaths before homing in on Jatha.

The frightened Vestare was still running but Sha-Kaan brought him to a grateful halt and landed just in front of him. Jatha and his remaining party were still a full day's journey from Septern's gateway. They should already have arrived and be safe, awaiting their Balaian visitors.

"Thank the Skies you have come, Great Kaan," gasped Jatha. "We—"

"Calm yourself," pulsed Sha-Kaan, allowing his mind to cool the heat in the Vestare mind. "Sit down and slow your heart; its beating is hurting my ears." Jatha slumped to the ground, heaving great lungfuls of air, the beginnings of a smile playing over his lips. In the sky above, the remaining Kaan chased the Veret away and patrolled in a holding pattern that gave Sha complete confidence.

"Now," said the Great Kaan. "Tell me why you are so far from the gateway."

Jatha nodded, Sha-Kaan feeling his pulse cease its dangerous racing.

"There is great activity in Keol," said Jatha. "My party have been slowed by the need to conceal ourselves from bands of Naik and Veret warriors. They seem to be linked in some way; it is the only reason I can think of for the appearance of Veret in the sky.

"We first saw them yesterday, flying to the south, and we thought we could evade them. But we were ambushed by Veret warriors. They are dead but our position was opened. Thus, we could be attacked as you saw."

Sha-Kaan let his head drop. Naik and Veret in alliance. The Kaan could be in more trouble than he thought. A concerted attack by three or more Broods might prove too much for them.

"How sure are you that there is an alliance?" he asked.

"They were not fighting when they met," said Jatha. "We watched them for a full day. Great Kaan, these are our lands, though we do not defend them. We cannot allow enemy occupation. It would bring them too close to Teras."

"There are greater threats than that posed by other Broods taking dead lands like Keol from us. It is critical that the humans from Balaia reach the Broodlands when they arrive here. I cannot release dragons to shadow you. If what you say proves true, I cannot afford to draw attention to you by flying in your defence, do you understand?"

Jatha inclined his head. "There is one other way." Sha-Kaan retracted his head sharply, his neck describing an "s." He hissed.

"No human shall ever ride the Kaan. We are the masters here." Sha-Kaan breathed out long. "It is your task to see them safe to Teras. Have you thought of the battle there would be if we were seen with humans on our necks? No carrying Kaan would stand a chance of survival; our place would be gone." He moved his head groundward once more. "Banish that thought, Jatha. Though I understand the desperation in which it was formed, it must never be uttered again. The Kaan shall never bow their necks to humans. We would die first."

"I am sorry, Great Kaan. And I thank you for your understanding."

"Consider that were you not so important to me, my reaction might have been different." Sha-Kaan's admonishment was tinted with humour. "You are a faithful attendant and companion, Jatha. Now, we will sweep the way ahead of you and seek out your enemies on the ground and in the sky. Do not move until night falls and we have gone. I expect your signal when you reach the gateway."

Jatha stood and spread his arms wide in deference, dropping back to one knee before he spoke again.

"It shall be done, Great Kaan."

"Skies keep you." Sha-Kaan extended his wings and rose lazily into the sky, calling to his Brood to do his bidding.

Senedai's patience broke on the fourth day. There was no warning, no new ultimatum. With the coming of a blustery dawn, heavy with cloud and the cloying damp that signalled the approach of rain, Barras was awakened by a general alarm that ran through the Council Rooms.

Instantly alert, he belted on his yellow robe of the day before, slid on boots without socks and rushed to the courtyard, dimly aware that his grey hair was wild in the wind, blowing into his eyes. He smoothed it back as Kard joined him.

"Senedai?" asked Barras. The old General nodded.

"And he's brought prisoners."

"Damn it." Barras increased his pace. "I thought we could bluff him longer."

"You've already saved fifteen hundred innocent lives. He was bound to lose patience eventually."

Behind them, the sound of running feet grew in volume. Soldiers clattered by, heading for their guard posts on the North Gate and walls. Kerela and Seldane joined Barras.

"So now it starts." Kerela was grim. Barras nodded.

"If only I could have bought more time."

Kerela squeezed Barras' shoulder.

"You bought us more time than we could possibly have dreamed of. Senedai's fear of magic is more deeply ingrained than all but you imagined. You saw that and you made it pay. Be satisfied."

"More likely he was just in no hurry then, but now he is. It worries me that something has happened elsewhere that demands his taking of the College urgently. Perhaps one of the others has already fallen." They began ascending the stairs to the gate house and ramparts.

"He is under pressure, certainly," said Kard. "But don't assume it's because of further victory. Lack of success by other armies has probably forced him to act."

The desire for conversation and the search for reason ceased as they looked down on the cobbled square before the gates. There stood Senedai, arms crossed over his chest, feet placed deliberately apart, dark cloak billowing in the breeze that accompanied the early morning chill. His hair, heavy with braids, barely stirred.

Behind him, better than one hundred Wesmen circled a group of fifty Julatsan children and older folk. All looked confused, all fearful, knowing only that they were a bargaining counter of some sort. None could know the fate that awaited them, their faces holding no panic or terror.

"I said it would take six days," said Barras. Senedai shrugged.

"And in four, you have done nothing but drilled your soldiers in full view of my observers. I will not debate this further." He raised an arm.

"Wait!" said Barras. "You can't expect to see the results of our efforts. There is no physical dismantling of magic. We will be ready soon."

"You have lied to me, mage," said Senedai. "Such is the thinking among my captains. And for that, I will have your head as our bargain allows."

"It took him long enough to work it out," muttered Kard.

"Now, how long you stay is up to you. But as the mound of corpses rises and its stench drifts across your faces, so will the hatred among those of your people left alive rise against you."

A murmur and movement stirred among the prisoners and Barras could all but feel their hearts beginning to race as the awful realisation of possible death brought sweat to bead on the back of necks, cold as the grip of night. Barked shouts from the Wesmen guards restored order, but the fear etched deeper into faces and the blank incomprehension of children tore at Barras.

"I had thought you to be a man of honour," said the elder elven mage. "Not a murderer of the weak and helpless. You are a soldier, by the Gods. Act like one."

Senedai wiped a hand across his mouth, apparently attempting to conceal a smile.

"You are a skilled speaker, mage, but your words no longer move me. It is not I who shall murder them. None of my prisoners will die under a Wesman hand or blade. I am merely releasing them into your hands. If you drop your devil's curtain, they will live." He pointed at the group on the ramparts. "You

are the murderers. Watch fifty lives be lost, their deaths on your conscience."
He raised his hand again, this time sweeping it down before Barras opened his
mouth to speak. The guards pushed through the crowd, one pair to each prisoner. They were marched struggling in a four-deep line toward the Demon-
Shroud directly under the North Gate, stopping less than three feet from the
modulating grey spell. That close, its aura must have been terrible.

Senedai walked behind the first row of prisoners almost as if he was
inspecting soldiers under his command. He stopped at the midpoint.

"Senedai, no," urged Barras.

"Take down your defence." He paused, looked up into Barras' eyes. "Take
down your defence." Barras said nothing.

"Don't give in." The voice came from Barras' left. There stood an old
mage in the front row, tall and proud, a balding pate atop fierce eyes and a
sharp nose. Senedai walked quickly behind him, grabbing his neck in one
gloved hand.

"You seem anxious to die, old man," he rasped. "Perhaps you would like
to be the first."

"I am proud to die protecting the integrity of my College," spat the
mage, meeting Senedai eyeball to eyeball. "And most of those here will
follow me gladly." He shook his arms. "Let go of me, dammit. I can stand
unaided." At a signal from Senedai, the guards released him.

"I'm waiting," said the Wesman Lord. The old mage turned and
addressed the Julatsans.

"This day, I ask you to join me in giving your lives to save the College
of Julatsa and all who stand safe behind her walls. Many of you, I know, have
no affinity with magic but, as native Julatsans, you are blessed by it and its
force for good every day. We cannot let that force die. For hundreds of years,
Julatsan mages have given of themselves for their people. Witness how many
were killed trying to defend the city. Now, in our time of direst need, it is
time to give something back. All that would walk willingly with me into the
Shroud, say aye."

A ragged response gained in volume, ending with the shrill "Aye" of a
child. The mage looked again at Senedai.

"Your words writhe like maggots in a rotting corpse. You have ordered
our deaths, you are killing prisoners. Julatsa has the right to protect herself
and your blackmail will return to visit death upon you and your kinsmen.
But we will not give you the satisfaction of seeing us beg for your mercy."

"It will not always be so." Barras could see the hatred in Senedai's face
and knew that the old mage, whose name he could not recall, had scored a
victory, however small.

"Release my people," said the mage. Senedai had no choice. He shook his head, waved his arm wearily and the guards released the arms of the prisoners they held. None moved to run and the perplexed expressions on the faces of the guards told everything. Precious few had understood Senedai's exchange with the old mage and even fewer could see why their prisoners made no attempt to save themselves.

"We will line up, each person holding the hand of those either side." The prisoners moved silently forward, the men and women upright and proud through their fear, the children uncomprehending, their voices stilled in the enormity of the atmosphere.

Barras could hardly bear to watch but knew that to flinch was to betray the act of extraordinary courage being played out in front of him. He wanted to shout for them to run, to fight, to struggle against their deaths. A part of him, though, saw that this solidarity would unsettle Senedai more than any futile fight. Now, at least, he knew the strength of will of the Julatsan people. Or thought he did.

The movement below Barras ceased. Fifty Julatsans stood a single pace from the DemonShroud, faces alive with terror at their imminent deaths and the evil pulsing from the Shroud's borders. The wind whistled around the walls of the College. Behind the line, Senedai and his guards stood uncertain, their objective about to be fulfilled but the initiative gone.

The old mage stood in the centre of the line, hands clasped with a child on his right and an elderly man to his left. He stared up at the ramparts.

"My mages Kerela and Barras, General Kard, it is with honour that we make this sacrifice. Do not let it be in vain."

"It will not be," said Barras, his voice shaking.

"What is your name?" asked Kerela from beside the stunned negotiator.

"Theopa, my Lord."

"Theopa, your name will live forever in the minds of generations of Julatsan mages that follow you," said Kerela. "I am shamed and lessened not to have known you better."

"It is enough that you know me now. And know all of us now." He raised his voice. "Come, let us walk to glory. The Gods will smile upon us, and the demons below will have mercy on our souls." Theopa's expression betrayed the lie.

Beside him, the child started to weep. Theopa bent and whispered words that would remain between them. The child nodded, her face cracking into a smile.

"Close your eyes and walk with me," said the mage, his voice loud and strong. He paced forward, the line with him. The fifty Julatsans dropped, their mouths open, screams of agony cut short as their souls were torn from their bodies.

Barras could feel the tears on his cheeks. A soldier walked by him, muttered something under his breath. Kard heard him.

"Consider yourself confined to your quarters," he grated. "Speak to no one on your way. I will deal with you myself." The soldier paled and moved on.

"Don't be harsh on him," said Barras.

"He accused you of murder."

"He was right."

Kard stepped in front of Barras, shielding him from the Wesmen below. "Never, ever believe that. The murderer stands outside these walls. And he will be brought to justice." Barras gestured Kard aside.

"Lord Senedai," he called. The Wesman turned and looked up. "May your dreams be plagued by the shades of hell every day of your short life."

Senedai bowed. "I will return at midday. More will die."

Barras began preparing. From here, he could take Senedai, burn the flesh from his bones. Kerela stopped him, breaking his concentration.

"I understand your hate," she said. "But you'll be wasting your mana on the inside of the Shroud. Better we channel our energies to finding a way to free ourselves and our prisoners. Come, Barras. Rest and think."

The High Mage led the weeping Barras from the ramparts.

CHAPTER 14

Tessaya had to know he was coming but it was both the price he was willing to pay and the risk he had to take. In truth, Styliann hadn't expected to talk his way past Riasu but the nervous tribal Lord had been so taken aback by the display of Protector power that he had sent horsemen through the pass to seek Tessaya's approval before the blood of his warriors had run cold.

To Styliann it had all served as a fascinating demonstration of the fear in which all things magical were held. Individually, Wesmen, even their Lords, were weak. Most of them. But, he considered, there were notable exceptions. For one, the man commanding the tribes laying siege to Julatsa. Undoubtedly a strong man but even he was apparently unwilling to press on into the heart of their magic, stayed by a trepidation of the unknown that no proof of might could shift. Generations of conditioning stood between the man and his conquest of a College city. Something that had never been achieved before.

And then, Tessaya, an altogether different animal. His reputation went before him and Styliann was certain that he would not so much as entertain the thought of talking to the Lord of the Mount. Death or hostage. Styliann favoured the latter.

There lay the gamble. He had his route across the mountains. He had avoided further travel with both The Raven, whom he distrusted and admired in equal measure, and with the bright General, Darrick—a man in the hero mould if ever there was one; the former because he had no wish to join the attempted liberation of Julatsa and the latter because Gyernath was simply too far. To lose the stewardship of the Mount even temporarily, was a humiliation that took precedence over every consideration.

For a while, in the aftermath of the Dawnthief casting and the realisation of his usurpation, he had suffered a crisis of confidence as his influence over Balaian affairs waned. But it had all become clear to him soon enough. Much of the modern expertise in dimensional magics lay within the walls of Xetesk, and there was a text recently released from the locked vaults beneath his Tower which he was certain had direct bearing on the problem facing The Raven. His influence over Balaia would remain crucial but only if he could regain the Mount quickly.

Thus, his chosen route. It was the most direct to Xetesk by several days but contained the largest obstacle. Tessaya. But even the fact that Tessaya expected him was not necessarily a fatal disadvantage. After all, Styliann was under guard and coming to talk. The Wesmen would hardly be massing their armies. Indeed, quite the reverse if he knew anything about Tessaya's mind. And Styliann had the advantage of knowing precisely when he would arrive, a luxury not afforded the Lord of the Wesmen.

As the sun reached the heights of the midday sky, Styliann, his Protectors and a guard of forty Wesmen moved into Understone Pass, the former Lord of the Mount the only one on horseback. The Wesmen were guides, monitors and a guard of honour, Riasu had said and at the time Styliann had found it hard not to laugh.

Did the Wesman Lord really believe Styliann could get lost in a Pass with only one bore? And what good did he think forty would be against ninety of the most complete fighting machines in Balaia? The answer to the latter was, as it turned out, none at all.

Styliann yawned and looked behind him. As at the head of the column, twenty Wesmen were marching along the pass, the light from their lanterns decorating the dark slate walls with elaborate dancing shadows as they moved. Above him, a natural fissure ran up into the heart of the Blackthorne Mountains. Up ahead, however, the ceiling shelved down sharply to a height of less than fifteen feet and on one side the path fell away into a chasm that struck into the depths of hell.

The air was damp and cool and, here and there, water dripped, the escape of some long forgotten rainfall or buried tributary. The sounds of foot and hoof combined with the slap of scabbard on thigh to echo ever louder from the walls as they closed in. Hardly a word had been exchanged, none between Styliann and the Wesmen, and the warriors' bravado had fast given way to uneasy whispers and ultimately an anxious silence. Understone Pass did that to people. The power overhead and the press to left and right stole confidence, hunched shoulders and hurried footsteps.

The column made good time and, an hour into the march, had a little more than three still to go. The barracks built into the western end of the pass were far behind and no one, east or west, could hear them.

Styliann smiled. It was time. He had no need of guides or lanterns or monitors. It would have been better for the guard had they stayed west. At least there they would have lived a little longer.

Considering his options, Styliann decided against depleting his mana stamina reserves however slightly. It was a pointless exercise. None of the Wesmen had bows—an omission none of them would live to regret. He leaned forward in his saddle, mouth close to the ear of Cil, now a favoured Protector, who marched in the centre of the defensive cordon that comprehensively shielded Styliann.

"Destroy them," he whispered. Cil's head moved fractionally in acknowledgement. Without breaking stride, he relayed the order to his brothers. Styliann smiled again as an instant's tension crackled the air before the Wesmen were engulfed in a battle they didn't realise had started until it was effectively over.

Eight wide, the front rank of Protectors swept axes from waist hitches and plunged them into the backs and necks of the oblivious Wesmen a few paces ahead. Behind, the thirty Protectors swivelled, axes to the ready and slammed into the wide-eyed rear guard.

The cacophony of shouts and cries that filled the air were calls to death, not to arms. In the front the Protectors surged on into the Wesmen guard, axes rising, falling and sweeping, blood smearing the pass, the sick thud of metal striking flesh loud in Styliann's ears.

Struggling to turn and draw weapons, the Wesmen lost all shape, the shock of the assault defeating clear thought. Even as a few faced their attackers, they were cut down by the relentless accuracy and power of the Protectors whose every pace was for gain, whose every blow struck home and who never uttered a sound from behind their masks.

To the rear, at least there was resistance, however brief. Howling a rallying cry, one Wesman stood firm, others around him taking his lead. For a few moments, sparks lit the passage adding a flickering aspect to the lantern-lit nightmare and the clash of steel on steel rang out in the enclosed space. But the Protectors simply increased the pace and ferocity of their attack, moving to strike again almost before the last blow was complete and forcing the Wesmen back in a desperate and futile defence.

With blood slicking the floor and the dismembered and hideously scarred bodies of their kinsmen littering the ground, with the impassive masks of the dread force facing them down, the remaining Wesmen, perhaps ten altogether, turned and fled, screaming warnings that no one would hear as they went.

"Catch them and kill them," said Styliann.

Half a dozen Protectors from each end picked their way deliberately over the carnage and ran east or west, their footfalls sounding impending death as they chased down their hapless quarry.

With the lanterns gone in the hands of fleeing Wesmen, or crushed underfoot, Styliann cast a LightGlobe and raised his eyebrows at the destruction he had ordered.

"Excellent," he said. "Any injuries?"

"Minor cuts to two, my Lord," replied Cil. "Nothing more."

"Excellent," he repeated, nodding. "Now. Clear the bodies over the side. I will ride forward and you will stand by me."

Again the almost imperceptible nod of the head. Immediately, Protectors stooped to drag the bodies from the passage to dump them in the chasm. Styliann urged on his nervous horse, Cil and five others flanking him, three either side. A few yards further on, he stopped and dismounted, dusted himself down and sat with his back to the north wall of the pass, the LightGlobe illuminating the rough-hewn rock.

Little impressed Styliann but Understone Pass certainly did. It represented a combination of extraordinary human and natural engineering. Built for profit and conquest, it had proved to be a millstone. He scratched his cheek below his left eye and shrugged. It was the way of so much meant for good to become evil.

"And now we wait," he said to Cil. "Or rather, you do. I have work to do." He closed his eyes. "I have need of your soul companions."

In the fading gentle light of late afternoon, Lord Tessaya took a walk around the boundaries of Understone, a worry beginning to nag at the back of his mind. It had been a day of extreme contrasts.

The message brought back by his bird had spoiled his mood but not his plans. The fast riders from Riasu at the eastern end of the pass had brought remarkable and unexpected news that could prove pivotal. Control of the Xeteskian Lord Mage was a prize worthy of the effort of containing his power. Never mind the dread force surrounding him. If he could be isolated, they could be nullified and eventually destroyed. There was no greater bargaining counter than Styliann. And he had volunteered to lend assistance in return for his speedy repatriation to his College. Fine. Tessaya was entirely happy to promise everything and give nothing. Particularly to a mage.

But something wasn't right. His initial euphoria at Styliann's *naïveté*, and the apparent overconfidence in his worth, had led to him dispatching the riders back immediately, bearing his written invitation. He had toyed with the idea of meeting Styliann with overwhelming force but had no desire to waste the lives of his men when, given a little patience, he could reach his goal without spilling a drop of Wesmen blood.

But now, with the day fast waning, Tessaya, whose tour of the reinforced stockade Darrick had built had been completed some time ago, was worried. And another circuit of the garrison town had done nothing to alleviate that worry.

By his calculations, Styliann should have been with him by now. Indeed, should have been so an hour before. And the men he had sent in to meet and replace Riasu's guard had not returned as they had been instructed to if the meet was missed.

Admittedly, there were a number of good reasons for any delay. A horse throwing a shoe, lack of organisation at the western end, a longer than expected rest break, his guards deciding to press on through the pass rather than report, Styliann causing difficulties with regard to march conditions, Styliann ensuring the deal he thought he had with Tessaya was watertight, Styliann making extra demands late in the day. Styliann.

Tessaya stopped walking and sat on a flat rock looking south over Understone. The setting sun washed a beautiful pale red light over the town, firing the light cloud cover with anger and shooting its beams to the earth. From his right, the softened sound of hammer and saw drifted on the light breeze. Below and to his left, the door to one of the prison barracks opened and a line of bowed and defeated easterners trudged away for evening exercise, flanked by axe-carrying guards.

Listening to the breeze, he could pick out the sound of voices from all corners of the town, talking, ordering, arguing. In three days the stockade, which already controlled the main east–west trail, would encircle Understone. Then he could begin work on the pass defences, so far neglected.

The small town had sprawled like oil over water in the wake of the Wesmen's occupation. Gazing across the shallow dip in which Understone's original buildings lay, Tessaya was greeted by the grey canvas that covered every inch of the gentle southward slope and the plateau to which it led. Standards from a dozen tribes and a hundred minor noble families stood proud above the massed semicircles of tents, each standing around a firepit.

For himself, he had chosen lodging in the inn with his advisors, including Arnoan whom he wished to keep a close eye on. Few of his family were in Understone. His sons fought with Senedai in the north. His brothers were long since dead at the hands of Xetesk's mages.

He scowled and stood up, straightening his jacket. Styliann. He strode briskly to the western end of the town.

"I need a scout," he demanded of the duty watch Captain.

"My Lord." The brown-bearded Captain hollered a name, the sound booming from the nearby buildings. A man came running from a working party digging a channel for a set of stakes outside the stockade. "Kessarin, my Lord."

Tessaya nodded and turned to the athletically built Wesman who wore pale brown leggings, a shirt and lightweight boots and carried a small single-bladed axe in his belt. He was young and clean-cut, a product of a lesser noble village, no doubt.

"Can you run?" asked Tessaya.

"Yes, my Lord." Kessarin nodded vigorously, fear of Tessaya overcome by his eagerness to please.

"Then go into the pass. Take a hooded lantern but use it sparingly. I need you to find the fools I sent in this afternoon. Do not make contact with anyone. Report directly back to me on your return."

"Yes, my Lord."

"Go now." Tessaya looked toward the black maw of the pass blending into the deepening shadows. He was loath to stand against Styliann and his dread force but dawn's first light would force his hand. Kessarin needed to return quickly and the thought that he might not scared Tessaya more than it should.

Styliann, with his close guard around him, relaxed and formed the mana shape for a Communion he would either enjoy immensely or curse forever. The shape, narrow and twisted like a plaited deep blue rope, spiralled away through the rock of the Blackthorne Mountains, seeking one particular mind in Xetesk, a mind which, while suddenly powerful, would be unable to resist Styliann's casting pressure.

The Communion bridged the divide to Xetesk in an instant, a little smile playing around Styliann's lips as the spell drifted over the resting minds of hundreds of mages inside the College. They appeared like small ripples in an otherwise still pond, a map of minds that, with care, the skilled and knowledgeable could read.

Styliann searched the random thoughts of sleep for one who would be active, spiking the ripples like splashes from falling rain. He was not hard to find. A man whose rise to power had been respectably swift, his opportunity grasped with both hands on the back of a spectacular spell success and, critically, the absence of the incumbent Lord of the Mount.

Styliann admired the courage of the man but he hated the humiliation and was enraged by the weakness of his own circle. When his rightful position was regained, he would need answers to a great many questions.

The Communion arrowed in, jerking the slumbering mage to a sudden and intensely uncomfortable wakefulness. A token resistance was broken almost immediately.

"My apologies for the lateness of the hour. My Lord." Styliann's mind-voice was laden with bile.

"St-Styliann?" gasped the befuddled mage.

"Yes, Dystran, Styliann. And close enough to sweep away your poorly formed shield. You should train harder in self-preservation. It might come in useful." Styliann had never been forced to take a Communion against his will.

"Where are you?" Dystran was fully awake now.

Styliann could feel the anxiety and imagined him fighting to sit upright to look about him, though the Communion held him prone.

"No need to WardLock your doors," said Styliann, voice mocking. "Not yet."

"What do you want?" asked the new Lord of the Mount.

"Apart from the obvious? A little assistance to ensure our inevitable meeting is more amicable than it is likely to be at present."

"You're coming back?"

"Xetesk is my home," Styliann said sharply, comforted by the knowledge that Dystran and his team had given little thought to the possible consequences of their usurpation.

There was a pause. Styliann could feel Dystran's thoughts roiling in his uneasy mind. How he must wish his advisers could help him now.

"What is it you want?" he asked again.

"Muscle," said Styliann. "A lot of muscle. To leave Xetesk immediately and head south toward Understone. I will meet them *en route.*"

"You're talking about Protectors?" Dystran's thought was disbelieving.

"Naturally," replied Styliann. "Calling the Protector army is a right of the Lord of the Mount."

"But you are not the Lord of the Mount," Dystran's mind-voice sneered. "I am."

Styliann chuckled. At least the man had some backbone if no conception of what he had done. Following his success with the DimensionConnect, he had been correctly made a Master. But his ill-advised leap to ultimate power would suit no one but his advisers who were no doubt using him as a stalking horse to gauge College mood and opinion. It was a shame that he couldn't see it but then they never did. Styliann's stalking horse hadn't.

"But you will grant me the Protector army nonetheless," said Styliann, his tone full of certainty. "Perhaps then we can sort out the Mount sensibly when I return."

"And if I don't grant them, perhaps you will not return. Then the situation will have sorted itself out."

"Fool." Styliann spiked the thought, feeling Dystran's mind recoil. "Do you really think that I have remained Lord for so long just to let an upstart mage like you take my Tower?" He breathed deep to calm himself. There was something he needed to know. "You have been studying the texts of the Stewardship, no doubt?"

"When there has been time," said Dystran.

"Yes. The pressures are great, are they not?"

Dystran relaxed, Styliann could feel it. "Yes. I hope we can discuss them in a civilised manner."

"Hmm." Styliann paused. "You have rescinded the Act of Giving and appropriated it yourself, I trust?" he asked.

"The Act of . . . ? No, that text is not known to me."

"Ah." Styliann felt a surge of pleasure and triumph. "And nor, apparently, to your ill-chosen advisers. But let me assure you that you will all feel its effects." Styliann terminated the Communion abruptly, shaking off the momentary disorientation.

Not rescinding the Act of Giving was an unsurprising error. Normally, there was no living former Lord from whom to remove the Act and the discovery of its power could be discovered at leisure. Normally.

Styliann smiled and tuned his mind to summon the entire Protector army as was, unfortunately for Dystran, still his right.

Kessarin was a proud man. Selected by his Captain and trusted by his Lord with a task of importance and secrecy. One that would end with a report direct to Tessaya himself.

He ran into the pass with enough oil in the small lantern for a good four hours. The wick was trimmed low and the shutter was clipped across to hide all but the merest chink of light and allow sufficient ventilation. Using the failing light of the sun which shone directly along his path, he moved quickly into the first section of the pass which angled very slightly downward.

His padded leather shoes made little sound, his small axe was strapped hard to his back and his hands were free to trace the outline of the pass, areas of which he could navigate by touch alone—as any good Paleon scout could. Silence was paramount. Lord Tessaya wanted the guard found without their knowing it, and that was exactly what he would do.

Kessarin smirked as he imagined the march, if it could be termed such, of the guard dispatched into the pass five hours previously. Obviously, there had been some delay in the Xeteskian reaching them but they should have been closing in on the western end of the pass by now, if not actually sitting with Riasu.

Kessarin somehow doubted they had travelled that far. Under the leadership of the disagreeable Pelassar, he expected to find them no further than half an hour in, at their stated meeting point. This was despite very specific instructions to move into the centre of the pass if it proved necessary. In choosing Pelassar to lead the relief guard, Tessaya had made, in Kessarin's estimation, his only mistake so far. Hardly a grave error and Kessarin would be only too pleased to report back on Pelassar's slovenly conduct and see him whipped or strung. Either would do fine.

Pelassar was nowhere in evidence at the point where Kessarin had expected him and his thirty men to be. The scout had anticipated hearing the sounds of bone dice clacking off the stone floor, of rough laughter echoing down the pass, and the glow of lanterns and torches illuminating the way unnecessarily for a hundred yards or more.

But there had been no need to slow his pace or cloak his lantern. Surprisingly, Pelassar had moved on. The scout raised his eyebrows and did the same.

Kessarin was a fit man and his pace ate up the pass. At a roughly estimated hour in, his caution slowed him to a fast walk. His lantern, hooded all the way, was pared to a thin strip of light which he shone either at the ground directly in front of him or the wall either side, never directly ahead.

His breathing was controlled and his ears tuned to hear the merest sound but all he picked up was the dripping of water somewhere far away. On it went for perhaps another half an hour, the silence supreme, the light nowhere and no sign at all of Pelassar and his men. It was then that he smelt the blood. Not a strong scent but there all the same, drifting on the breath of a breeze that meandered along the pass.

Kessarin stopped immediately, lantern slide pushed all the way across, darkness complete. He pressed himself against the left-hand wall, thinking. This was an area he knew little of, particularly with no light. He had a vague memory of an opening out to both sides and above but, in truth, couldn't be sure. He was skilled in the feel of the rock at either end but, in the middle, his knowledge was slight. There hadn't been time.

He listened closely. Still no sound of Pelassar and his men. No echo of footsteps along the rock walls, no change in the air told of imminent meeting and, straining his eyes along with his ears, no light pushed at the blackness. Just that faint taste of blood. There one breath, gone the next.

Kessarin was, by nature, a calm individual but the silence and the dark were moving in on him. Sounds he knew could not be there whispered in his ear. The cry of a child, the lowing of cattle. All distant, the tricks the mountains above played. He shook his head and forced himself to focus. He had two choices.

He could either report back the silence and the hint of blood in the air or he could move on, knowing Tessaya would be growing impatient, and find out whether his fears were justified.

Actually, it was quite simple. To find favour, he had to go on and hope that Tessaya's anger would subside as he heard Kessarin's report. He looked again into the darkness. Here, deep in the pass, no natural light would ever penetrate. He couldn't even see the wall with his nose touching it. Here, even the slightest chink of light would push back the blackness like a beacon fire. Up ahead then, he could be sure, there was no one.

He moved back the slot of the hooded lantern, aware that the limited air within the glass would soon be gone if he didn't expose an airhole. The sound was loud in the silence, like pushing open a rusted iron door. Kessarin allowed himself a smile.

With his left hand brushing the wall, he moved forward again, carefully, the light down and to his right, illuminating a slight incline in the passageway. A couple of paces further on, he stepped in a patch of stickiness that slicked across the floor.

He stopped to look, knowing it was blood, and then they simply melted out of the darkness ahead, a pale light gently illuminating their nightmare masks. One grabbed his neck with astonishing swiftness. He dropped the lantern, which shattered on the hard stone floor. He tried to speak but no sound came, his arms thrashing uselessly, his eyes staring wildly, taking in the sea of blank faces which parted to let through a tall man with black hair. Behind him floated a glowing sphere. The face came close.

"Very good," he said. "You almost had us believing you weren't there. Almost. Now, you are alone, I take it?"

Kessarin, terrified, managed to nod his head, jaw against the gauntlet of the silent masked man.

"As I thought." His head turned away. "Is it full dark outside?"

Another nod.

"Good. Cil, we have work."

The hand around Kessarin's throat tightened and all his dreams of glory fled into the darkness from which he would never return.

The only question that remained was the reception at Understone but the captured scout removed some of the uncertainty. Styliann considered that Tessaya would want to wait for the scout's report before deciding how heavily to arm his defence. At this stage, Tessaya still had no genuine cause to believe that the Lord of the Mount's nonappearance was anything other than irritating delay.

Styliann and his Protectors moved quickly, the LightGlobe faint but significant, providing light enough to see a few paces all round. That, combined with the innate sense of the enthralled warriors, was quite enough. In less than two hours, they were approaching the eastern end of the pass. Stopping perhaps four hundred yards from the entrance and hidden by a series of outcrops and shallow bends, Styliann assigned his LightGlobe to Cil, dismounted and cast a CloakedWalk on himself. He could have selected a Protector as the spell's target but the nuances of the Cloak made its retention far more difficult than a LightGlobe or ShadowWings.

"Stay here," he ordered. "They will not see me." Styliann disappeared from their view, his hand trailing the left-hand wall, a dull luminescence taking the totality from the darkness. He walked briskly, his eyes adjusting to the increasing light that filtered along the passage. It was, he guessed, around four hours from dawn. Night was full outside but, in comparison to the black of the pass, the sky was bright. Inside it was chill and damp and Styliann was glad of his cloak.

There were no obvious signs of buildup at the entrance to the pass but a guard of eight or so sat around a fire just outside. Styliann pitied them. The Xeteskian storm would see them to their graves before they knew it had broken.

He continued walking slowly forward, coming to within a dozen paces of the guards where he crouched behind a slide of rock caused by the spell his own mages, organised by Dystran, had cast to massacre so many Wesmen. The scent of death would remain in the pass forever.

None of the guard was facing into the pass, which Styliann found a little strange. Overconfidence caused carelessness. He looked beyond them to what he could see of Understone itself. Darrick's defences had been considerably strengthened and watchtowers sprang from eight places that Styliann could count. His view was partially obscured by the slope down to the base of the gates Tessaya had constructed but the glow of further fires told of more guards outside the town.

Understone was quiet. The Wesmen slept while above the sky was clear and the air was still and cool. He wouldn't get a better opportunity. Styliann, again cloaked by magic, slipped back to join the Protectors.

Understone's night was uneasy. Tessaya stalked the quiet streets, for once unsure of himself. Kessarin was among the best, the duty Captain had assured him of this. He would find the guard and report back but, if he had to travel the entire pass, he would not return until early morning, shortly before dawn.

But the situation was patently wrong. How could the delay be so great that Styliann still had not appeared? And if this was so, why had no word been sent? Never indecisive, Tessaya found himself torn. His senses screamed at him to wake every man and destroy the cursed mage the moment he appeared in the east. But his tactical brain begged him to play it softly and patiently. To wait for Styliann's arrival and greet him with open arms. Let him place himself exactly where Tessaya wanted him.

The Lord of the Paleon Tribes looked to the sky for inspiration but found none. The air was still, silent and cool. He had come to a standstill close to the inn but resisted the urge to seek Arnoan's advice. Besides, he knew what the old Shaman would say. "Bring the mage to me. Let me work my magic on him." But of course he had no magic. Only chants and potions, bones and books. Styliann could destroy him with a wave of the hand.

What should he do? He walked back up the main street to the gates of the town, climbing up the watchtower that controlled them. The two guards bowed their heads at his appearance.

"Keep watching," he said. They turned again to look at the empty black that was the entrance to the pass, illuminated to the right by the fire of the pass watch. "Has there been no sign?"

"No, my Lord," replied one, unsure whether to turn or not and ending up awkwardly half faced toward Tessaya. "They have seen nothing down there and the paths to the north and south are both empty."

"What in all the hells has happened to them?" demanded Tessaya.

Still unsure, the guard ventured a reply. "He is a mage, my Lord. Not to be trusted."

Tessaya opened his mouth to slap down the guard, whose response was not required, but found himself in total agreement. Instead of barking, he nodded and relaxed just a little.

"Yes. Why should I be surprised, eh? I'm glad to see you understand who we are expecting." He turned to go. "Be very vigilant. I cannot have this man loose."

And then the entrance to the pass was engulfed in sudden violence.

Masked warriors surged into the night, scattering the watch fire and slaughtering the guards, who plainly hadn't seen them coming. The shouts of alarm were cut off so quickly. Without a pause, the warriors continued at a dead run and in their midst, a lone man on horseback, riding at a canter. The dread force surrounded him completely, the warriors moving easily at speed. There was no fuss, no struggle and no doubt. Only a frightening efficiency of pace and stride and a total focus. Not one glanced toward Understone as the whole turned north and ran up the trail, the bemused stares of the watchtower guards following them as they ran quickly away.

Tessaya swore to break the hypnotism of the moment, slamming his fists down so hard on the tower rail that it shuddered beneath him, one timber cracking under the strain.

"Wake the tribes!" he yelled. "I want every man from his bed. I want this town empty and I want it now. Every warrior. I want those bastards caught and slaughtered. Move!"

Alarm bells rang out all round Understone. Tessaya stared after Styliann. It had to be him on that horse. Loose in the east with his damned masked warriors and heading straight for Xetesk. And even as he watched, a new chill stole over him. There went Styliann, but where was Darrick? And where were The Raven? He dismissed the new worry from his mind, knowing it would return once his fury had subsided. For now, he had but one target in his sights.

"By the spirits of the Paleon dead, I will drink your blood, Styliann of Xetesk," he growled.

But as the clamour of the waking army engulfed his ears, he thought he heard laughter echoing from the mountains in the still night air.

And so it was for the next three days. The Council of Julatsa made the awful pilgrimage to the North Gate to see Senedai and the Wesmen murdering innocents. Sacrificing them on the altar of the DemonShroud. On the first day, a further hundred died, fifty at noon, fifty at dusk. On the second, three hundred met their deaths, many with the same proud face as the old mage, but more and more with reluctance, defiance and angry words shouted at the Council who watched them all and, in their eyes, lifted not a finger in their defence.

On the third day, that unrest had shifted within the walls of the College and with the sacrifice of one hundred and fifty older women at noon, the Council turned from the gate ramparts to find themselves facing an angry mob held at bay by Kard and a line of College Guards. Behind the steel defence, mages stood ready to cast ForceCones to fragment the crowd if necessary.

At the front of the crowd of perhaps two hundred were their appointed spokesmen and the soldier whom Kard had reprimanded at the first sacrifice. The General had succeeded in quieting them but the silence had a menacing quality, every eye on the Council. Kerela nodded.

"Well, I suppose we had to expect this."

"This is hardly the time to talk to them," said Seldane.

"There will be no right time," said Kerela. "Though I had hoped Kard's talks would have a longer lasting effect."

"I suspect those that listened to them are praying rather than demonstrating," said Barras. "We were never going to convince everyone."

"What do they hope to achieve?" asked Endorr. The junior Council member scanned the crowd nervously.

"Well, let's go and ask them, shall we?" Kerela led the way down the stairs inside the gatehouse. As they emerged into the courtyard, a whisper went around the crowd. Kerela strode across the space and waved Kard and his soldiers aside. She stood, Barras at her left shoulder and the remainder of the Council grouped behind them, and looked solemnly into the faces of the frightened angry city folk whose friends were dying in increasing numbers outside the relative sanctuary of the walls.

Barras decided to let her have the first words though many naturally looked to the Chief Negotiator for comfort, or a solution, anything.

"This is the hardest time of our lives," said Kerela, and the whisper of voices stilled instantly. "Our people . . . your people are dying in their hundreds, forced into the DemonShroud by a mob of murderers who seek the destruction of this College. But to remove the Shroud now would put the life of every Julatsan at risk."

"But if the Shroud goes, the killing will stop," said a voice from the crowd. Others joined in support.

"Will it?" asked Kerela. "Why do you think the Wesmen are killing the very young, the very old and women they deem beyond child-bearing age? They are a conquering army. Those of no immediate use are merely extra mouths to feed and extra enemies to watch over. Maybe they could sell the children as slaves across the Southern Oceans but the rest? Just an expense. And right now, they cannot afford any extra expense. I'm looking around you now and one in three of you will die if the Shroud is removed before we are ready to act. Anyone who doesn't believe how selective the killings are, is welcome to view from the North Gate at dusk."

"We can't just sit here and watch the bodies pile up," said the spokesman, a youngish brown-haired man named Lorron. "You understand that."

"I do. And I am mystified that you know nothing of our plans in development. Here you stand with a member of the city Guard, to whom General Kard will be giving further instruction later, and yet he has clearly told you very little or nothing." Kerela stared at the soldier whose defiant expression began to wilt under the pressure of the old elf's gaze. "I do hope you haven't just been stirring up trouble," she said gently.

"I'll tell you our problem," said the soldier. Barras could feel Kard tense and could only imagine the look on his face. "It looks like you'll do anything to keep your College secure. Even if that means every prisoner out there dies."

"Yes, but I see you managed to find sanctuary in here. Is our accommodation no longer to your satisfaction?" The tips of Kerela's ears were reddening. Barras knew there was an explosion to come. It was just a matter of when. "Tell me," said the High Mage, her voice awfully calm. "What would you have us do?"

"Fight!" said the soldier, and a brief murmur rose around him. "Gods in the ground, what else?"

Kerela nodded. "I see. And presumably, you think we'll triumph despite the odds stacked against us, do you?"

"We can try. We have magic," said Lorron.

"And it will be used when the time is right!" thundered Kerela, the sudden power and volume of her voice jolting the entire crowd. Barras fought back an unwanted smile. Kerela continued.

"Do you think I want to stand and watch while innocent Julatsans die?

Do you really? But I'm afraid I have to. Because more than half of my mages are unable to cast through injury or mental damage caused ensuring that *you* stand here alive and well today. And General Kard has drawn up plans for an attack but the beds are still full of wounded men. Would you have me leave them to die? Are they somehow less important than those outside?

"Dordover has sent soldiers, and probably mages, to our defence. Shall we not bother to wait for them? And shall we rehearse our plans in the courtyard here under the eyes of that damned tower, giving away our intentions as we do so?" She pointed to the Wesmen's tower which, manned day and night, was even now being pushed to a new position, presumably to observe better the current dispute.

"The slaughter outside the North Gate sickens my very soul but worse is the thought that any of you believe I am complacent in my duties." Her voice lowered again. "We are few against many and our attack has to be on our terms and its timing exactly right or we will be slaughtered. I understand your impatience but, my way, we will save more lives overall. Should that not be our aim?"

"And what about the College?" asked the soldier.

"It is the hand that feeds us and the power that drives us. We will defend its integrity with everything we have. I will not lie to you. Any attack we mount in an attempt to break the siege must not leave the College at the mercy of the Wesmen." Kerela stopped, awaiting a response. "No Julatsan will die in vain. No life will be wasted while I am High Mage. Does anyone wish to say anything else at this stage?" People in the crowd looked at each other. Heads dropped.

"Good," said the High Mage. "Just one more thing before you go. I am High Mage and this College is under my direct control, along with the Council and, because we are in a siege situation, General Kard. Anyone who thinks that this is not an acceptable situation can try walking the Shroud with my blessing. Do I make myself clear?" Some nodded, some didn't. Most found their shoes very suddenly the most interesting part of the College. Kerela nodded, gathered the Council and walked away toward the Tower.

Behind them, Kard's voice rang clear. "Break it up. Get about your duties. Not you. Come here, soldier. Come here!"

Thraun stood at the stern of the single-masted sailboat, growling at the Wesmen grouped on the shore. He was in the way of the tiller and Denser, under the watchful eye of The Unknown, had to reach around his rear to control their direction. There was no pursuit. The flames of the devastated camp lit up the sky, casting dancing shadows on the water that played in the ripples caused by the wind. Cloud had rolled up to all but extinguish the moon's watery luminescence.

Hirad sat back and pulled off his boots, emptying water over the side. He was tired. Six days of hard riding and walking followed by a fight they hadn't planned. He sat the other side of Thraun and looked along the boat. The sail was full but not tight, driving them across the inlet. The Unknown Warrior was sitting opposite the boom wringing out his socks. On the covered prow in front of the mast sat Erienne and Will, out of the way of the tackle, while Ilkar, his hands gripping the gunwale, was right next to Hirad, his gaze fiercely inboard.

They had escaped but it hadn't been comfortable. Fortunately the back-up plan had worked well. Even so, Hirad wasn't satisfied.

"What happened, Ilkar?"

"Clumsy Wesman," said Ilkar, raising a smile. "I think he was trying to wrestle Denser's dagger from his throat but he knocked their alarm bell off instead."

"We had to attack before we reached the platform," said Denser, supplying the answer Hirad wanted. "Ilkar couldn't come back because he'd have lost his Cloak for a beat and stepped on me, so, with the guard blocking the entrance, we had no other choice."

"But the kills weren't clean," said Hirad.

"We're mages, not knifemen," said Ilkar a little sharply. "I have never done anything like that before and I doubt you have."

"I guess not," said Hirad. "But I still need to show you the best killing thrusts. It would have helped."

"When we're on dry land, I'll be glad to undergo training," said Ilkar. "But right now, I'm trying not to be violently sick."

Hirad laughed. The boat was barely pitching, its passage very smooth, yet there was an uncharacteristic paleness about the elf's face.

"You'll be all right," said the barbarian.

"Look at the horizon," said The Unknown. "It moves less than the inside of the boat. It'll give you some sense of stability." Ilkar nodded and dragged his gaze out over the water toward the eastern shoreline where the sea met the sky.

Apparently satisfied with what he saw on land, Thraun turned, knocking the tiller briefly from Denser's hand. He ambled up the boat, pausing to stare at each member of The Raven as he passed. Hirad met his gaze, seeing the yellow flecks in Thraun's eyes but none of the repressed humanity that Will assured him was there. Yet there was an intelligence in that stare that had nothing to do with anything animal and, curiously, Hirad felt no threat despite being one lunge from death.

He watched as the wolf leaped lightly on to the decking of the prow, moving in between Erienne and Will. Will's hand reached out and stroked the length of his back. Thraun's head turned and his tongue licked out, plastering the little man's face.

"Affectionate, isn't he?" said Hirad.

"I wonder if he'll be embarrassed to hear about that when he changes back," mused Denser, his mood at odds with his behaviour of the last few days.

"How long will we be sailing?" asked Ilkar.

"Half the night, maybe a little more," replied The Unknown.

"Oh, Gods," muttered Ilkar, tightening his grip still further. Hirad put a hand on his shoulder, patting him gently.

In the prow, Will wiped his face, anxious to keep the wolf saliva from his lips. He didn't quite succeed. He scowled and grabbed Thraun's muzzle with a hand, giving it a shake.

"Do you have to?" The wolf licked his lips and gazed mournfully back, eyes sad and far away. Will's scowl turned to a frown. "What is it, Thraun? What's wrong?" Thraun dropped his eyes to the decking. "You could change here. You don't have to wait until we land. *Remember*." It was the word that triggered the human deep within the body of the wolf. Or should have. But Thraun merely hunkered down, resting his head on his forelegs, head pointing out to the Inlet.

Will glanced across at Erienne. Worry lined her face as it lined his.

"It'll be all right," she said unconvincingly. "He'll change when we land."

"You saw him the last time," said Will. "He changed the moment we were clear of Dordover. Couldn't wait. The longer he goes, the harder it gets to remember he can." He stroked Thraun again, pushing his hand in hard against his spine. Thraun's tail flipped languidly, for all the world like a dog relaxing by his master's feet.

Will shook his head. Thraun always changed back so quickly. He hated the form of the animal, he was frightened by it. Or so he said. But this time . . . Maybe the motion of the boat unsettled him. Maybe. But he looked comfortable. *Comfortable*. That was a state he had never seen in the wolf and he'd witnessed Thraun change at least a dozen times over the years he'd known him.

"Thraun, come on, look at me." The wolf obliged, blinking. That was something at least. "*Remember*. Please." Thraun raised his head slightly, sniffing the air. He growled deep in his throat and returned to his scan of the water in front of him. Will turned to The Raven; all eyes were on him.

"Can't this boat go any faster? I think we've got a problem."

Chapter 15

It had been a sunny enough morning. The light cloud that had covered the sky at dawn had been blown away by a fresh breeze from the northwest, leaving clear blue skies, a gently warming sun and the ever-roiling and growing shadow.

The fifteen soldiers and three mages of the monitoring party in Parve had chosen for themselves one of the grand houses that lay just off the central square. It was a large, two-storey building with rooms enough for each to be shared by just two men. A well-stocked pantry and cellars, partly harvested from other nearby dwellings, made living comfortable. But not too comfortable.

Each of the men who had volunteered for the duty was aware that they were unlikely to see the Colleges again. Between them and home lay the entire Wesmen invading armies and the Blackthorne Mountains. Above them, the rip to the dragon Dimension posed unguessable threat, and in the dead city they knew that not everyone was dead.

Outside of the billet, the platoon officer, Jayash, forbade them to walk in groups of less than three. Mages had to have two guards each. Patrols leaving the relative sanctuary of the square were always six strong with a mage in support. The streets weren't safe.

Not that they had actually seen anyone. But the sounds were there. The echo of a footstep, the slap of a door on a windless day, the hurried scrabbling of hand in dirt, the ghost of a voice carried on the breeze. Some, probably acolytes, had escaped Darrick's net. Parve was an eerie place.

It was approaching noon on the eleventh day of measurement. Having long since calculated the rate of increase of the noon shade and the dimensions of Parve, it was now a question of monitoring, of completing the chart each day, of checking for errors and watching the sky.

No one had actually said it but they were the early warning system of another dragon attack. An attack they would not be expected to survive.

Jayash and three soldiers watched while the duty mages prepared the ground for the day's measurement. Inside an area covering almost a thousand paces on its long side, and seven hundred on its shorter, the paving of the central square had eight lines of metal spikes driven in to its surface. Each line represented a compass point and the distance between each spike and their progression toward the edges of the square marked the expansion of the shadow.

Jayash strolled around the perimeter of the marked area as the shadow moved across the ground, a monstrous blot on the earth that sent shivers through his body and cooled the fledgling warmth of the day.

Turning in the area, he walked along one line and back down another, noting the distance between each peg. It was not an exact science, of course. If the cloud was heavy, the shadow's edge was more indistinct and inevitably there was error.

He paused at the end of the second line he'd tracked, the one representing southeast, frowning. The final two spikes seemed a little further from their adjacent cousins than the rest, like the line was becoming stretched. He glanced left and right. If his eyes didn't deceive him, the pattern was repeated in the south and east lines.

"Delyr?" he called. The Xeteskian looked up from his conversation with Sapon, a Dordovan colleague.

"Jayash."

"Have we had a problem the last couple of days?"

Delyr shrugged. "Not really. We've seen what is a significant but probably small acceleration of the rate of shadow increase but some of it has to be to do with cloud effect blurring the edge of the shade." He glanced up into the sky, blue but for the rip overhead. "Today we'll know."

Jayash nodded. "But you've known of this possible problem for a couple of days."

"Five actually. Look, I appreciate your desire to be told every minute detail, but in scientific terms, it was not worth mentioning, so I didn't."

"But today."

Delyr smiled thinly. "You will receive instant assessment followed by a full report. Now, if you wouldn't mind, time is short." He gestured at the rip and the shadow at the base of the pyramid that was all but gone.

Jayash waved a hand vaguely and stepped back to watch. Delyr and Sapon trotted around the edge of the spike field, leaving a peg lying at the end of each line. Both mages then walked briskly to the base of the pyramid and knelt close to the sun shade marker, a long piece of polished wood fixed to the ground where the pyramid's east wall met the earth. When the last vestiges of natural shadow had left it, the measurements were made.

It was a good enough system but, Jayash considered, it had a flaw. At present, the shade was relatively small and the pyramid close. The movement of the sun between the moment the mages agreed it was noon and the measurement of the shade was negligible.

But soon, the pyramid would be covered by the rip's shadow and the agreement of noon would have to be made more distantly. What was more, the area of the shade, growing larger, would mean more time to make the measurements.

He could foresee, firstly, all his men being co-opted into taking readings rather than securing lives and later, a hopelessly inaccurate measurement, leaving The Raven with a margin of error that ran into days. Delyr seemed oblivious. He alone still thought he was going home once the rate of increase of the shade had been clearly established.

He didn't realise he'd been marked as a martyr, not a hero.

It was noon. Delyr and Sapon straightened and walked quickly back toward the spikes. The rip hung in the air, waiting, its shadow wide and clear, uncluttered by the fog of cloud, its edges hard and distinct.

Swiftly and without conversation, the two mages took up opposite positions, north and south, and began their task, leaning close to the ground to gauge the exact end of the shade and the beginning of light. Once satisfied, they placed spikes in their marks and, with small iron mallets, drove them into the earth beneath the paving of the square. Moving around the compass points counterclockwise, they repeated the operation in less than five minutes.

Jayash could see the mages' consternation immediately, saw the anxious glance they exchanged and began walking toward them. Delyr and Sapon met by the south line and measured the distance the new spike sat from yesterday's using both a length of carefully marked rope and a carved length of rod-straight wood in which they made two marks. In this way they took readings from three points before Delyr consulted a parchment he fetched from a leather bag lying on the ground.

"What is it?" asked Jayash but he knew the answer already.

"Just a moment," said Delyr. He and Sapon scribbled on the parchment, retook their measurements and entered the figures in the log. Delyr looked up.

"Instant assessment?" suggested Jayash.

"We're in deep trouble."

"Justification?"

"We'll check again tomorrow but the rate at which the shade is growing is increasing. It's not stable, or doesn't appear to be."

"Meaning?"

"Meaning the bigger it gets, the faster it grows."

Jayash pushed his tongue into the inside of a cheek. "So, time is shorter than you originally calculated."

"Yes, much," said Delyr. "And we have no way of knowing whether the rate of increase will continue to rise. I suspect that it will."

"So what's the new estimate?"

"Yes, hold on . . ." Delyr looked at Sapon who had been writing furiously. He underlined a figure on the parchment and handed it to Delyr, whose eyes widened.

"Are you sure?" he asked.

"Yes." Sapon nodded. "I'll refine it later but it's not far away from accurate."

"Well, before, we had thirty days before the rip covered Parve. We now have eight."

Jayash said nothing, just stood at the rip above, shuddered and imagined the dragons pouring through.

It was the longest night of Ilkar's life. Between them, The Unknown and Denser set a direct course across Triverne Inlet, using the stiffening breeze to drive them on a single tack toward the meeting of water and the Blackthorne Mountains on the eastern side of the Inlet. At least the Xeteskian was making good on his desire to learn to sail. Further out into the expanse of tidal sea, the swell deepened, making the quiet choppiness near the shore a distant memory. The small boat, never in danger under the stewardship of its dual skippers, pitched and yawed through the swell but made good headway, sail taut and full.

But something was wrong. Ilkar had always thought himself naturally empathic but even he was taken aback that Hirad in particular seemed to have no inkling that it was much more than the fact that Thraun had not returned to human form.

For Ilkar though, it was as obvious as the sun in a cloudless sky. He had taken The Unknown's advice and kept his eye on the horizon, feeling an initial wash of sickness slowly subside as his brain registered normality forever just out of reach. But increasingly, he found his attention straying to the boat's other occupants. It was the quiet. At first, Hirad had quipped away, talking the irrelevancies that were his trademark in relaxed situations, but received at best low chuckles and short answers in response. Ultimately, there was no reaction and he had shrugged and joined the silence. But quiet was so unlike The Raven. There had been little discussion of their direction on reaching the eastern shore save to try and find horses quickly for the ride to Julatsa. Beyond that, there seemed no plan and, without The Unknown to drive the discussion, the energy to talk was lacking.

Ignoring his protesting gut and swimming head, Ilkar turned to look at the Big Man and felt a chill in his body. Never given to joviality, The Unknown typically had his eyes everywhere in every situation, playing the role of the guardian angel with consummate skill, snuffing out threat to his friends before it became deadly. But now he was inside himself. Ilkar saw him glance occasionally in their direction, or up at the sail and even more rarely murmur to Denser to trim the tiller position or release a handful of mainsheet.

Aside from that, his head was angled forward, his eyes closed or fixed firmly on the timbers between his feet and the set of his body slightly slumped. Ilkar knew what had to be troubling him and there was nothing any of them could do about it. He had changed during his brief time as a Protector. Not because of the harsh regime under which the demons held them in thrall but because of the closeness of souls in Xetesk's Soul Tank.

He had hinted as much in the days after his release and had appeared to shake off the memories of the bonding he had undergone but now, as they returned to the East, the memories resurfaced. Because every passing moment brought them closer to the Colleges, closer to Xetesk and closer to the Soul Tank from which his soul was wrenched. Ilkar wondered if he could still hear them calling him.

"Unknown?" said Ilkar. The Big Man looked up, his eyes heavy and full of pain. "Can you feel them?"

The Unknown shook his head. "No. But they are there and I am not. Their voices still sound in my memory and tear at the strings of my heart. The emptiness has not filled inside my soul. I think it never will."

"But . . ."

"Please, Ilkar. I know you want to help but you can't. No one can." The Unknown returned to his examination of the bottom of the boat, his last words directed at none who could hear them. "To reach the dragons I will have to walk by my grave."

Ilkar felt a pang in his chest and drew in his breath sharply. He caught Denser's eye. The Dark Mage looked no better than The Unknown and Ilkar felt despair. He had hoped the manner of their escape from the camp would have rekindled his enthusiasm. But it was clear now that it was a spark derived from the innate desire for self-preservation.

Denser believed he had already served his life's purpose: Dawnthief was cast and the Wytch Lords were gone. But they had to close the rip in the sky or there would be no hiding place from the hordes of dragons that would eventually fly through it. Not for Denser, not for The Raven and not for Erienne and their child.

Why then, would he not take his place in the heart of The Raven and drive like he had done all the way to Parve? Ilkar understood very well that he must be fatigued but his mana stamina had returned and any bone-weariness was surely shared by them all.

"Thanks for not dropping me back there," said Ilkar.

"No problem. I'd rather have you alive than dead at the hands of the Wesmen."

Ilkar took that as a compliment but it saddened him at the same time. The old Denser, that which had surfaced to such spectacular effect in the

Wesmen camp, had quickly disappeared beneath the waves of his own self pity once again. It took all the elf's control not to tell him so.

"You must be tired."

Denser shrugged. "I've been worse. When you've cast Dawnthief, any other exhaustion rather pales."

"Good effort though, Denser," said Hirad. Ilkar glanced down at the barbarian, half sprawled and half asleep on his bench, a cloak under his head, his eyes closed. Thank the Gods for Hirad. At least, in his ignorance of the mood suffocating The Raven, he was not affected by it. They would need his strength and aggression in the time ahead, that was clear.

Ilkar opened his mouth to speak but found he couldn't be bothered to try and engage Denser in any further conversation. Nothing was coming back but the lethargic utterings of a man searching for a reason to keep on fighting. The elven mage shook his head. Surely Erienne and their unborn child were enough. But even she had found his mood impenetrable and their physical distance on this small boat was stark indication of the difficulties they faced.

At the bow lay the most immediate problem. Will had not taken his hand from Thraun's back nor his eyes from the wolf's head for hours. A deep anxiety crowded his face and his whisperings in the ears of his friend did nothing more than bring twitches and low growls. Thraun didn't want to listen.

What would they do if he never changed back? Ilkar almost laughed at his own question but feared the noise of his fleeting good humour. It was, of course, not their decision to make. They could not order the wolf to leave them or to stay with them. They couldn't tell him what to do. They couldn't control him. The longer he stayed a wolf, the more wild he would become. Eventually, Ilkar presumed, he would cease to recognise them. At that point, they would become as much prey as the next man and they would have to try to kill him.

Ilkar knew that was the fear that drove Will's anxiety. It was one that should drive them all.

And for his part, Ilkar himself was scared of what they would find in Julatsa. He would know if the College fell and the Heart was destroyed as would every Julatsan mage—those that lived through the experience. He was aware his city might well be in ruins. He knew the Wesmen were an occupying force. He knew the Council would not give up the College until every last one of them had perished in its defence.

But if The Raven couldn't get into the Library, if they couldn't find what they had to find, then the Wesmen, in the moment of their triumph, would have condemned most Balaians to death at the hands of dragons. Ilkar would derive no pleasure from telling them so.

He sighed deep in his chest and watched the shore unfold its detail before him, praying dry land would kindle some hope in his heart but knowing it probably would not. The destiny of Balaia was not in good hands.

Keeping far upstream from the Wesmen staging post, The Raven landed in a small cove bounded on both sides by crags and steep slopes. Above them towered the dark mass of the Blackthorne Mountains, cascading precipitously toward the Inlet, while immediately in front of them, the land angled sharply away from the rocky cove toward Triverne Lake, whose waters flowed into the sea not far from them as the mouth of the River Tri.

Splashing through the shallows, The Raven set foot back on dry land to an audible sigh of pleasure from Ilkar. He looked up at the climb into the lightening sky with what Hirad took to be pleasure.

While The Unknown made fast the boat and Denser furled the sail under his instruction, Will and Thraun scrambled away up the slope of grass-covered thinly soiled rock and crumbling clay. Will, clutching Thraun's clothes in his bag more in hope than expectation, hung on to a fistful of fur and thick hide low on the wolf's back, to help him on up.

"Why are you bothering to learn all that?" asked Ilkar, the words tumbling from his mouth before he could stop them.

Denser stopped and straightened. "What?"

"If you care so little for the future, why bother to learn to sail?" Ilkar had no option but to carry on. Denser's eyes narrowed.

"Well maybe I'm trying to establish some normality. Maybe I'm making a bloody effort. Is there something wrong with that?"

Ilkar smiled, trying to defuse the situation he'd created, aware that the eyes of The Raven were on him.

"It just struck me as a little incongruous, that's all. Don't worry about it."

Denser strode toward him. "Yes I will worry about it. Your ignorance of how I feel doesn't give you the right to make sneering little comments like that. What are you trying to say?"

"I'm trying to say that you are totally unpredictable and it's causing us all a problem. Furling that sail you are totally normal, just like the Denser we know so well. But in the next heartbeat you could close up and disappear inside yourself. We don't know where we stand."

"Is that right?" Denser's face was reddening. "And you think I know, do you? My head's a complete bloody mess and I'm trying hard to make sense of what I have left. What I want is a little patience, not clever comment, from people like you!" He stabbed a finger into Ilkar's chest. The Julatsan pushed it away and pointed at Erienne.

"And she's not enough, is that what you're saying?"

"Ilkar, that's enough. Just leave it," said Erienne.

But Denser moved in until their noses all but touched. "Don't you dare to question the way I feel about Erienne. You don't understand." He pushed Ilkar firmly backward along the shingle. "Keep away from me, Julatsan, until you have something good to say." He stalked over to the rise and began a solitary, angry climb, Erienne behind him.

"Good work, Ilkar," said Hirad, shaking his head. He climbed up slowly behind the mages, noting the clear sky and the light forging toward them from the east. They would need to find cover soon. Fortunately, the River Tri's course was lush and wooded and far enough from likely Wesmen occupation to make quick travel possible. They would still have to be careful, though, aliens in their own land.

What taxed Hirad's mind, apart from Ilkar's surprising outburst and Denser's altogether predictable one, was where they would find horses. Without rides, journey time to Julatsa would be trebled or worse and give them no fast escape option. He dug in his heels and climbed faster.

The scent of home was everywhere, bleeding from the very ground on which Thraun trod. The colours of the forest and of his packbrothers filled his head as he bounded away from the water's edge, taking care that man-packbrother should not slip from him by moving too fast.

Cresting the rise, he put his snout high into the air and sniffed. Untainted by the saltwater smells from below, the scents of the land and its inhabitants unfolded like a map before him. He turned to man-packbrother, aware he was making sounds. Man-packbrother knelt in front of him and held his face in his two hands. He growled, amusement and mild irritation mixing in his mind.

Man-packbrother spoke a word to him. He was aware it was a word without comprehension of language. It tolled in his head but the doors didn't open. Instead, a confusion of thought plundered his consciousness.

He was standing on his hind legs and there was no hair covering his face. His howl had gone and he could run upright without falling. But there was no joy in his senses, no feeling of the pack around him. He felt clumsy if strong, awkward in his understanding of the land and prey and threat around him. The memories were dim but he knew they were memories. They hurt him inside, dragged at his body and punished his being. He knew there was a way to make the hurt stop but he fought that way.

The hurt scared him, he reacted.

Thraun barked once and recoiled from Will's grasp, crouching low, yellow eyes fixed on him, fangs bared. He growled, deep, low and menacing. Will stood up in shock and backed away a pace, hands outstretched.

"Thraun, it's all right. Calm. Calm." He backed away further.

Hirad had reached the top of the slope in time to see the end of the exchange and Thraun's sudden move backward, taking him perilously close to tumbling over the edge back to the cove. Hirad held his breath. The wolf was tensed to spring, its eyes on Will's face. But to his eternal credit, Will remained what he urged Thraun to be. Calm. And Thraun eventually relaxed his crouch, shook his head, stood up and trotted away toward a stand of trees.

"What happened?" asked Hirad. Will's face was sheet white in the pre-dawn light. He shrugged. "I mean, what did you do?"

"N-nothing," said Will, with a hint of the stammer that had plagued him for days following his terrifying encounter with Denser's familiar in Dordover. "Just tried to bring him back to himself with the word."

"What word?"

"*Remember*," said Will, massaging his temples with thumb and index finger and looking after the retreating form of the wolf. "It's the word he tells himself before he changes. It's supposed to trigger his memories. It's not working." Will sounded desperate. Hirad placed a hand on his shoulder.

"He'll be all right," he said. "He's probably gone to change now, hasn't he?"

Will turned his face to Hirad, a rueful half smile on his lips and tears in his eyes. "I don't think so," he said.

"So what's different this time?" asked Hirad. "He's never reacted like this before, has he?"

"No. He hates the wolf's form. His worst nightmare is being stuck inside it forever and losing his ability to change back. But in the years I've known him, he's never tasted the blood of so many victims either. I just wonder whether he's in some kind of frenzy that won't go away and it's blocking his human side from reasserting itself."

"What can we do?"

Will sighed. "I don't know. There's no spell that can bring him back. His condition isn't magical. We'll have to wait and I'll have to keep on trying to get through to him."

"A risky path."

"The only path." Will looked at Hirad. "I can't lose him, Hirad. It would be like being dead anyway so I may as well die trying as sit and wait to die alone."

Hirad nodded. "I understand."

"I know."

CHAPTER 16

With Ilkar, Denser, Erienne and The Unknown reaching the flatter land above the cove, The Raven made headway to the Tri River valley, Thraun shadowing their progress. The landscape in front of them was beautiful, even in the half-light of early dawn, with much still wreathed in heavy shadow.

North and east, the land swept away in gentle rises, its bracken swaying and rustling, isolated groups of trees and low bush surrounding rocky pools, crags mottling the greens and browns with their stark slate grey.

South and east, in the direction of their immediate travel, the scene was altogether different. At the top of a shallow rise, the land fell away sharply into the valley of the River Tri where it flattened briefly to form great green meadows of thick grass. The river's banks gave root to thick-trunked oaks and willows, and wild hawthorn tangled the river's edge while, here and there, pebbled shallows rising to flat rock, covered in times of flood, gave sight of the quarter-mile width of the gentle flow.

To the west and south of The Raven, the black enormity of Balaia's dominant mountain range scaled to the heavens, mesa, peak and slide punctuating its descent into rambling foothills and finally the fertile lowlands of the East. Close to, its power was staggering and Hirad wondered whether Baron Blackthorne, whose family took their name from the range, ever felt as he did now. Small in the presence of extraordinary might. While the mountains stood, Balaia lived. But if dragons flew through the rip in numbers large enough to overwhelm the Brood Kaan, the Blackthornes would be laid waste, shattered. He couldn't let that happen.

Close to, it was clear that the vegetation either side of the Tri, while excellent cover, was poor walking country. With Thraun on not necessarily unwitting point duty, The Raven drove as far inland as they dared, with the light of day flying across the sky to meet them. Eventually, tired and in the open, they worked toward the water's edge, finding enough of a clearing to set up Will's stove, which The Unknown still carried, yet remaining hidden from both the south bank and their immediate north. Thraun had disappeared but none doubted he knew exactly where they were.

"It's good to be back this side of the Blackthornes," said Hirad, relaxing against a tree, rubbing his back on it and feeling the bark dig into the stiff muscles of his back through his leather armour. He loosened the jerkin straps and breathed deeply. The Unknown said nothing, merely stared into the woods surrounding them. Denser shook his head and Will said:

"It isn't worth the price we seem to have paid."

It wasn't exactly the reaction Hirad had envisaged. He sniffed and looked across at Ilkar whose glum face carried no surprise at the muted, if not depressed, expressions surrounding the stove.

"Perhaps we should sleep on it a while," ventured Hirad.

"We need Thraun," said The Unknown. "We need his tracking and his sense. If this area is patrolled, and I expect it us, we could hit big trouble without warning."

"Can't you track?" asked Erienne.

"Not really," said The Unknown. "And certainly not as unerringly as Thraun."

"What did you do before we joined you?" asked Will, his eyes never still, scouring the undergrowth for his friend.

"Nothing quite like this," said Hirad. "Generally, we rode into castles or on to battlefields in broad daylight, fought all day, collected our money and that was that. Avoiding being seen wasn't an advantage."

"Well, we'll just have to be careful, won't we?" said Denser, his voice flat.

"We don't have time to be careful," said Ilkar sharply. "If the Library in Julatsa is destroyed before we get there—"

"I know, I know," said Denser. "You don't have to keep lecturing about it."

"Why not? You don't seem to have any sense of urgency."

"I'm just saying there's no point in getting ourselves killed because we're in too much of a hurry. That would be just as bad."

"Voices down," snapped The Unknown, his voice quiet and powerful. Their progress had been slower than he'd hoped, Denser's attitude affecting them all. That had to change before they fought again. Focus was everything and, right now, The Raven lacked it. "If you've all finished stating the bloody obvious, we've got to find the best solution." He turned his head to Will. "Will, how well does Thraun understand you?"

The wiry man shrugged. "It's hard to say. He recognises my voice, that's certain, but how much he actually understands is anybody's guess. Words like 'no' and 'stop' and 'run,' I think he does but I couldn't hope to persuade him to track for us, for instance. Particularly now. This is the wildest he's ever been and he's not even been changed that long."

"Well, we have to get him to change back," said Ilkar.

"You can't. I'm not even sure that I can now. He's not listening." Will bit his lip.

"In that case, we have to assume he's gone. Sorry Will, but you know what I mean." The Unknown unbuckled his chest plate. "Is there going to be a time when he'll attack us?"

"I don't know," said Will. "I want to believe that he'll recognise me however long he's changed for. But he said himself that, ultimately, he'll just become a wild animal."

"Except much harder to kill," said Denser.

"Much," agreed Will. "But it won't come to that. Wolves aren't killers. They hunt for food and we aren't first choice."

As if he'd known they were talking about him, Thraun padded into the camp, his sudden appearance at Will's shoulder causing Erienne to start. Will himself turned and draped an arm across the huge wolf's neck and pulled his head close.

"Glad you could be here," he said. Thraun nuzzled his cheek then lay down facing the stove, snout twitching at the smells of wood, coffee and hot metal.

"Like I say," said Will. "Ultimately, he'll do what he wants and if any of you think you can stop him, well . . ." There was a dry chuckle around the stove.

"All right," said The Unknown, his face blank. He hadn't joined the brief mirth. "At walking pace, we are six days from Julatsa. We need to liberate horses quickly but we can't risk running into a large Wesmen force. Are there any local farms or villages the Wesmen may not have found?"

"No," said Ilkar. "The nearest settlements that might just have escaped are Lord Jaden's to the north but that's two days extra over hostile country in the wrong direction. Our only chance without fighting or stealing is Triverne Lake, as Styliann said."

"Surely the Lake will be taken," said Hirad.

"I wouldn't be quite so sure," said Ilkar. "It's the seat of ancient magic and a place of the most base evil if you're a Wesman. There's a standing guard of two hundred protecting the Shard at all times. They might still be there. And don't forget, Triverne isn't the most direct route to Julatsa from where the Wesmen landed a little north of here."

"Communion?" suggested Erienne. Denser shrugged.

"If I must. I need to rest first, though."

"I'll do it," said Erienne. "I am capable."

"Whatever," said the Xeteskian.

"Fine." The Unknown stretched his legs out in front of him, trying to push his own problems from his mind while clutching at the threads that held them all together. "I'm sceptical, I must say, but if we can find out through Communion, that's fine. Otherwise, I'm not sure the detour is worth the risk. We also need to contact the mage outside of Julatsa, assuming she's still there—get ourselves the latest position. But first, Denser's right, we should rest. I'll watch and so, no doubt, will Thraun. We'll push on after midday."

Dawn in Julatsa on the eleventh day of the siege of the College brought the first open conflict within its walls. Two hundred and fifty innocent Julatsans had just perished. Those first to die were rotting in the Shroud. Barras could feel the tension. It had been in the air since the first confrontation but now it had real menace to it as the Council stepped away from the gatehouse, saddened, disgusted and scared. This time there had been no show of strength or solidarity, no songs and no bravado. Just weeping, screaming and angry accusation before the agony.

The city's people issued from the buildings all around the courtyard as the Council walked slowly to the Tower, heads bowed, each lost in their own thoughts. Kard had been alert, as always, and his shouted commands to his men ensured a significant protective guard for the Council by the time the mob had surrounded them.

"Oh dear," muttered Kerela in Barras' ear. The old elf Negotiator looked quickly about him. The clamour hurt his ears, the fury of the Julatsans edging toward the precipice of violence. Weapons were brandished, fists shaken and everywhere red faces spat anger and belligerence.

Kard's shout for calm went unheard by all but those immediately around him and ignored by even them. With the mob beginning to press, despite a fragmentation of its edges caused by more soldiers pulling people away, the greying General turned a worried face to Barras.

"Your turn, I think," he mouthed.

Barras nodded and leaned into Kerela. "Time for VoiceHail," he said.

"Just a single word," she advised. "I'll pass on your intention."

"Thank you." Barras drew in a deep breath and closed his eyes, bringing the geography of the College to his mind. The mana shape was little more than a line, tracing and connecting every building. The Tower, the Long Rooms, the walls, Mana Bowl, lecture theatres, classrooms and billets. All were linked by the shape, all became receptors, conduits and amplifiers of Barras' voice. He opened his eyes and nodded.

Kerela placed a hand on Kard's shoulder and every soldier and Council member immediately placed hands over his or her ears. Before any in the whistling crowd had time to react, Barras, his voice deep on the frequency of the mana stream, spoke.

"Silence."

The word clattered over the open space, crashing into unprotected ears to rattle skulls and stun voices to quiet. It rolled off the College buildings, a word from the Gods, deafening and irresistible. Metal resonated, glass rattled in frames and a sound like thunder, like stone shaking in its foundations, rolled around the square. Silence reigned.

"We will talk or disperse, we will not shout or fight," said Kerela. Her voice, like Barras', was augmented by the mana shape still being held firm by the elf, though much lessened in power. Still, it boomed out over the mob, now motionless but for hands rubbing heads and ears. The anger inside, though, still remained. "Do you not realise that this is precisely what Senedai and his band of murderers beyond our walls want? Gods in the ground, if we kill ourselves or divide ourselves so finely we cannot fight, we will have done his job far more completely than he could do it himself." Kerela shook her head. "We must remain one or we will be unable to function."

"But soon there will be no one left to fight for out there!" shouted one. More joined the chorus and through it Barras plainly heard the word, "murderers." The crowd closed again.

"Please," said Kerela. "I beg your patience and your understanding a little longer."

"But how long. How long, eh?" A face at the front of the crowd growled the words. He was a big man, muscles bunched beneath his shirt. He carried a mace. "My mother lies out there, the stench of her rotting body in my nose every time I draw breath. My heart is in tatters and yet I have to stand here and listen to you beg more time to save your own filthy skins."

"I understand your pain . . ." began Kerela.

"You understand nothing!" spat the man. "How many of your family have died so far to protect mages who have grown fat off Julatsa for far too long?"

"And who was it that saved you from death at the hands of the Wesmen?" asked Kerela, and Barras could see her trying to keep herself in check. "The same mages who have already perished in the Shroud, waiting outside to give you the time to run in. Please do not judge us uncaring of our people."

"We are not your people," said the man, his voice carrying clear over the crowd that had paused to listen to the exchange. "And we demand you remove the Shroud and let us fight."

"When the Dordovans arrive, then we will fight. And where Kard's soldiers lead, you may follow," said Kerela, heedless of the message that might be heard beyond the walls.

"They should have been here days ago," said the man, his face reddening. "How long did you think we would swallow this lie? Drop the Shroud now."

"And if I refuse?" asked Kerela.

"We may be forced to make sacrifices of our own."

Barras' heart missed a beat and the sickness already in his stomach at the hideous sight beyond the North Gate intensified. Kerela, he could see, was unprepared for the response. He decided to talk himself, turning up the VoiceHail.

"You would kill Julatsans to force us to action? Murder more innocents?" he demanded.

"Not innocents. Mages." A ripple ran around the crowd. Clearly, not all were privy to the plan being hatched before them. "Not all mages enjoy your security."

"And what difference do you think you can make outside if we do drop the Shroud? We are already too few. Fragmenting us more would harm us still further."

"You don't care about Julatsa," said the man, and his voice rose in volume. "All you care about is the preservation of that!" He pointed his mace at the Tower and the clamour grew again. "How many more must die in the thing you created before even your stuffed heads realise what is going on. We have to stop the killing." He took a pace forward and was pushed back by a soldier. Hate in his eyes, he brandished his mace and brought it crashing down on the guard's helmeted head, the man collapsing, blood running from the helm line.

Immediately, another soldier lashed out with a sword, taking the man in the midriff. He screamed and fell and the crowd erupted in fury. They surged forward against the desperate defence of Kard's well-marshalled troops. Barras yelled for calm but even his augmented voice had no effect. Around the edges of the mob, he could see scuffles breaking out among city folk and College guard and part of the crowd broke away to run toward the Mana Bowl where many mages were billeted.

A more pressing problem, quite literally, was the surrounding throng that moved in from all sides. Temporarily, there was a yard space between them and Kard's men, whose swords glinted in the dawn light, keeping back the front rank who had no desire to die. Behind them, though, there was no such risk.

"Quick," ordered Kerela. "All of you. SunBurst. Cover the compass then be ready to run for the Tower. Kard, on the command word, shield your eyes. Pass word around the ring."

"Aye, my Lady." Kard circled quickly behind his men and the message was passed.

Dropping the VoiceHail, Barras concentrated on the new spell. Its shape was flat and, as he dropped his vision into the mana spectrum, he could see the yellow disc growing in intensity as more and more of the Council lent it their strength of mind and channelled ever-increasing mana into its expanding diameter. In a matter of moments, it covered the College and beyond, a slowly revolving disc of mana, swirling with many hues of yellow and shot through with black. One by one, the Council announced their readiness to each other by flagging the disc with their signature in its centre. When all were done, Kerela spoke.

"Now Kard. Right now. Vilif, the command is yours."

"SunBurst," intoned the ageing mage. "Flash deployment." In an instant, the mana shape was gone. Barras closed his eyes and covered them with his hands. White light deluged the courtyard, bringing a temporary blindness to everyone not shielded. Even Barras could feel its force, knowing that, though temporary, the effect was both painful and frightening. They had taken a big chance.

Screams of shock and sudden pain echoed about the courtyard and a hundred weapons clattered to the stone. Barras opened his eyes to see people collapsed on the ground or running away to nowhere, sight gone for a few moments, anger supplanted by the urge to escape.

"Let's go," ordered Kard, and he led the Council across the short distance to the Tower, seeing them safely inside before turning to bark more orders that saw his men disperse in disciplined teams to defend the College's crucial buildings. Barras closed the Tower doors and followed the Council up the long outside stair to the first rampart. There they gathered to witness the effects of their action.

Instantly, it had proved a success. The crowd's collective spirit had broken for now and, as sight came back to them, people fled the courtyard. But some remained, and anger filled the air.

"Just where are the Dordovans?" asked Endorr, his face pale. He was gazing north from where the Dordovans would most likely approach, the swirling grey of the DemonShroud filling the air beyond the College walls.

"I have no idea," said Kerela. "But that poor man was right. They should have been here by now. If they have turned back or been killed, I don't think anything can save us. We are in the endgame for this College now, my friends. We have made enemies within as well as without and the time to act is soon. When calm is restored, we must meet with Kard and name the day we try to break the siege."

"But they will kill us and take the College," protested Seldane. "Nothing has changed but that more of our people are dead and the Wesmen better fortified."

Kerela said nothing for a moment and Barras followed her gaze to the courtyard where the two fallen men were picked lifeless from the cobbles, blood slicks marking where they had rested.

"We have waited as long as we can," she said eventually. "I do not believe that Dordover will help us now." She turned back to them and the tears were beginning to run down her face. "We are going to lose our College."

Sha-Kaan felt an emotion he'd thought was forever alien to him. Returning from the Keol, his Kaan in victory formation behind him—a single, curving line in the sky forming a quarter circle—he had considered the implications of the apparent union between the Naik and the Veret and didn't like the conclusions he drew. His heart sounded heavily in his great chest. He was anxious.

First and foremost, the union meant that at least two Broods were actively talking to each other. Presumably, their initial goal, the destruction of the Kaan, was the same. Beyond that, though, he could see no future in any allegiance. For the waterborne Veret particularly, the extinguishing of Kaan life from Beshara would have little significant effect.

The Kaan and the Veret had historically tolerated one another's presence simply because their Broodland desires were so different. Why then, should they ally with the Naik to destroy the Kaan? Perhaps they felt able to live in and around the River Tere. Sha-Kaan knew this would never happen. His Broodlands were as coveted by the Naik as they were secret and secure. The Naik would not slipstream aside to let the Veret into occupation.

So, the following conclusion was that the Veret were under threat and had allied to stave off that threat. Why then, had they not come to the Kaan? And who posed a threat of substance to them? No Brood wanted the Veret's vast expanse of Shedara Ocean. They had eliminated all other marine-based Broods many cycles before.

Finally, it dawned. The Naik were capable of destroying the Veret, should they so desire. It would be an act of pure vindictiveness but it could be done. Knowing a little of the psyche of the Naik, Sha-Kaan thought it not beyond them to promise extinction if they weren't aided. And if they could promise it to one Brood, they could promise it to others.

An alliance of fear it might be but an alliance of any sort would quickly prove fatal for the Kaan. Indeed, Sha-Kaan had been relying on inter-Brood hatred and mistrust to gain The Raven as much time as possible—even up to the moment the critical size of the gateway was reached, when he knew they would be overwhelmed. An alliance, though, would bring that day of defeat much closer.

As he approached the entrance to the Broodlands, Sha-Kaan dismissed the thoughts from his mind, revelling in his moment of pleasure as he and the victory curve swept along the mist-filled valley.

Later, in the quiet of Wingspread, he mulled over the growing spectre of

Brood alliance, cursed its vengeful nature but understood its necessity if the Kaan were to be defeated quickly. Unlike his forebears, Sha-Kaan would not debate openly, choosing to announce decisions and invite criticism and further options. He found it hastened the process.

There were two actions he felt he had to take. First, talk to the Veret and find out the manner of their alliance. Subsequent to that, he had to break it, forge his own perhaps, or seek out weaker allied Broods and destroy them if he could. The latter was not a palatable prospect given the stretching of the Kaan forces.

The second action was far more personal and one which he should not have neglected so long. He was out of touch with Balaia. He had no inkling of the way its struggles leant and, more crucially, was without the healing stream that inter-dimensional space could provide him. He had to select another Dragonene.

But this was not a simple operation. With the battles raging near and in Balaia's College Cities, the chances for his Brood's existing Dragonene to recruit a mage capable of dealing with the demands of Sha-Kaan had been few. No suitable candidates had been seriously discussed.

And in itself, this presented a critical problem. The bonds he had enjoyed with Septern so long ago and the subsequent mages that had served him up to the death of Seran were all known quantities, selected with both their blessing and in the knowledge that their minds possessed the necessary strength. To force his mind into that of an untried mage, however highly recommended, risked confusion in his mind and the death of the subject.

That left one possibility. One man who he knew could withstand the power of his mind and whose colleagues could provide the necessary magic. It was a break with over four hundred Balaian years of tradition but the time to be more selective was gone—if he was to fly to speak to the Veret, he had to have the means to heal and, without a Dragonene signature in Balaian space, he had none.

He reached forward with his neck and grabbed a bale of Flamegrass, tossing it around in his great jaws as he chewed and swallowed.

"So be it," he said. "So be it." He stretched full length across the warm wet floor of Wingspread and opened his mind to search for his new Dragonene.

It was an hour after noon on a day that had chilled as the sun fled west over the Blackthorne Mountains and cloud bubbled up on the prevailing southeasterly wind. In their sheltered space, The Raven had slept, enjoying the gentle warmth of the stove. The Unknown had watched without break while even Thraun slept, his flank a pillow for the anxious Will's head.

Shortly after midday, Erienne had conducted a Communion, making contact with the refugee mage in the hills to the north of Julatsa. The spell had been relatively short and, as Erienne opened her eyes, Ilkar could see that she didn't know whether to smile or frown. It was a while before she could meet Ilkar's eye.

"Are you stable?" asked Ilkar. Communion, or rather the breaking of it, left channelled mana suddenly without focus but lying still in the mind. Its return to a more normal randomised state sometimes disoriented both caster and contact.

Erienne nodded and gave Denser a little smile. He smoothed some hair that had fallen over her face back behind her ear. Her smile broadened at the small show of affection.

"The College is still standing. The Heart is still intact," she said and paused. "I'm not sure which order to say this in."

"Does the mage know how many Wesmen are in and around Julatsa?" asked The Unknown.

"Yes," said Erienne, glad for direction. "She, that is Pheone, says that somewhere around ten thousand Wesmen are occupying Julatsa and erecting a stockade to defend it. They have reinforced since the initial victory and further tented areas to the west hold about five thousand. They haven't yet moved southeast toward Dordover."

"And what about those who escaped into the hills?" The Unknown ladled himself a mug of coffee.

"They've been ignored so far, Pheone thinks, because the College is still resisting."

Ilkar felt at once proud and devastated. His city, occupied by invaders; his people, those who escaped, forced to scavenge in the hills. But his College somehow stood against the tide.

"There's more," said Erienne. "There are knots of Julatsans all around the city, hiding in the hills and woodlands. She doesn't know how many though a group to the southeast intercepted the Dordovan force that Darrick mentioned, over three thousand foot and cavalry, and stopped their scouts running into the Wesmen lines."

"So, there is a military leader out there," said The Unknown. "Did Pheone say anything about an organised attack being planned?"

"I'm surprised there hasn't already been an assault," said Hirad. "Surely they can talk to the mages left inside the College and set up something."

"No, because no one can talk to the College," replied Erienne. "Besides, it's tough to coordinate disparate groups all around the city. Communion isn't that easy."

"Well, why can't anyone Commune with Julatsa?" Ilkar's heart raced. "Is she sure the Wesmen haven't taken it."

"Yes, she's certain, because they have magical protection which blocks Communion." She drew in breath deeply. "Ilkar, they've erected a DemonShroud."

"A what?" asked Hirad.

"Gods in the sky, have they really?" said Ilkar, eyes widening in surprise. And now he'd been told, the solution was obvious as the only one that could keep at bay an army of fifteen thousand, no matter how great their fear of magic. But with the knowledge that the Wesmen could not hope to enter the College while the Shroud remained, came the connected problem. Ilkar quickly outlined the workings of the Shroud before giving voice to the issue of which both Erienne and Denser were already aware.

"So how in all the hells do we get in?" demanded Hirad.

"We don't, not until the Shroud is dropped," replied Ilkar.

"I'd worked that bit out," said Hirad, tapping his head. "It isn't hot like yours but it does go round. I mean, when and if the Shroud is dropped, how do we beat ten thousand Wesmen into the Library?"

"We don't," said The Unknown. "We have to get them away from the College before that happens. I know that sounds ridiculous but we've got ourselves, God knows how many Julatsans aching for revenge and three thousand professional soldiers, and the Wesmen don't even seem to realise it. There's time enough because the Shade isn't growing that fast and I think we could make something work for us."

"Really? What exactly?" Denser wasn't alone in his scepticism. But The Unknown didn't have time to explain. The Dark Mage grunted and shook his head. "Communion," he said, frowning. "It's Delyr, I think." He lay down and closed his eyes to accept the contact from Parve.

It was a contact that would change everything.

CHAPTER 17

The Council Chamber was bleak and cold. Outside the College, an eerie silence had fallen. Two men lay dead, dozens would have wounds and Kard had placed instant curfew on the courtyard and grounds. Every non-essential person, was confined inside and the guard on certain doors—two of the Long Rooms in particular—was heavy.

A cordon, eighty strong, secured the base of the Tower and for the first time the remaining guard on the walls looked inward, not out.

Barras, his heart heavy, anticipated, as they all did, the battle that would ensue inside the walls if they kept up the Shroud. He didn't like it and, despite the knowledge of the College's demise, could see the fight couldn't be allowed to happen.

"Why won't they understand?" Endorr was frustrated.

"Where's your family, Endorr?" countered Cordolan, his usual jovial face a distant memory.

"You know I have no family."

"Then you can never understand why they don't understand." Cordolan steepled his hands.

"Why?"

"Because your family are not dying while you live unmarked inside these walls. The people you love the best are not in the game of chance for sacrifice. Your greatest terrors for your brothers, sisters and parents are not unfolding before your eyes."

"The point, Endorr, is this," said Barras. "We can no longer presume to uphold the College in the face of so much slaughter. I believed, as no doubt did you, that the College and Julatsan magic were more important than life. They are not. I also didn't believe Senedai would carry out his threat or would stop after one show of bravado. I was wrong.

"I saw the faces of those who died today and the anger of those who confronted us. Unless you are blind, you must see we cannot let this slaughter continue."

"That is a considerable change of opinion," said Seldane. "Not that long ago, we sat here with General Kard and agreed that nothing, not even life, was as important as maintaining the College."

"Yes, and pious, grossly insensitive and morally indefensible it was too," said Barras.

"We cannot suffer the College to fall," said Torvis. "We cannot see Julatsan magic die. The imbalance in power will destabilise the whole of Balaia."

"We can bury the Heart," said Kerela. "Our life will always beat."

"Why bother? If we lose the Mana Bowl, The Tower and the Library, we are so much lessened. What does the Heart do but give us a spiritual centre for our magic? It is our books, our architecture and our places of deepest solemnity that make us Julatsan mages. Vital though it is, the Heart is just one of them." Seldane shook her head.

"If we do nothing, there will be battle inside these walls and I will not have Julatsans spill one another's blood in my College." Kerela's eyes held an uncompromising power, just as her tears had told of the depth of her pain.

"If we step outside these walls, we will be killed and any nonmage enslaved. I fail to see the purpose of walking into their hands and leaving the College to their mercy," said Vilif.

"One thing we will not be doing is rolling over, let me assure you of that," said Kerela.

"If we fight them, we will lose," said Seldane. "We can exist here until help arrives."

"It's not going to!" snapped Kerela, thumping her hand on the table. "Do you still not see what should have been obvious right from the start? While the Shroud remains, no one will come to our aid. We have erected an impenetrable barrier. We are safe. No one knows what is happening in here and I tell you something, if I was a Dordovan, I wouldn't be rushing on to Wesmen swords with no guarantee of help from those I was supposed to be rescuing. Would you?"

There was a knock on the door and Kard entered. He looked harassed, sweat beading his face which was red and vein-shot.

"Your arrival is most opportune," said Kerela. "Please, take a drink, sit yourself down and tell us what is happening out there."

Kard nodded, grateful for a moment's respite. He unhooked his cloak and draped it over the back of his chair, filled a crystal glass with water and sat down, exhaling loudly. He drained his glass and set it down gently, a more natural colour already returning to his face.

"I'm too old for this," he said. An embryonic chuckle ran around the table.

"That applies to most of us here," said Vilif. The General smiled briefly.

"All right, we've put back the cork for now but I can't keep it there indefinitely. These people are not our prisoners, they are not disarmed and they outnumber my soldiers two to one, though that is small concern because we will not fight them hand to hand. Not if a decision, the right decision, comes from this room before noon. We have to stop Senedai's killing."

"What would you have us do, General?" asked Seldane, her tone terse.

"Remove the Shroud—"

"And leave us open for slaughter just like that?" Endorr was incensed.

"No, young idiot," snarled Kard, his demeanour changed suddenly, his voice hard, military. "The College Guard of Julatsa will never leave us open for slaughter or these buildings at their mercy. Save your sharp tongue for your spells."

"Kard, be calm," said Barras, reaching out a hand toward the General. "We are all under great pressure."

Kard nodded and straightened his uniform tunic.

"A number of events must happen in quick succession if we are to buy the time we need. And much of it falls on the mages in the first instance. If I might make my recommendations without interruption?"

Kerela smiled. "I think we can agree to that."

"Good, good." Kard shot a sharp glance in the direction of Endorr. "It is my belief that the Dordovans are hidden, probably half a day's ride or more from the city, and also probably in contact with escaped Julatsans. If they aren't, we'll fail.

"After the Shroud is dropped, mages need to complete two tasks the moment the Wesmen raise the alarm as they undoubtedly will. First, Communion to establish contact with anyone who will hear but particularly the Dordovans. We will need them and anyone else who is out there and armed to hit the rear of the Wesmen lines. We may be able to hold them alone for a couple of days, but we may not.

"Second, I need that bastard moving tower destroyed. I don't care how it's done but it'll provide access as well as vision once the Shroud goes." He paused, refilled his glass and drank.

"My soldiers are ready drilled for their positions and I need your permission to set mage defence around the walls. Lastly, Barras, I need you to speak to Senedai. Tell him we're going to come out in three days. See if you can delay any more of this senseless death. That's all."

"You want to break out in three days?" asked Torvis.

"No, two. But I don't want the Wesmen ready to receive us. Every moment we buy is precious."

"We should drop the Shroud at night, then, when there are fewer of them to see it go," said Endorr.

"Absolutely," agreed Kard. "I was thinking of the dark before the dawn. Remember, we don't want to spark trouble in the middle of the night because the Dordovans will be sleeping too. We shouldn't bring down the tower until the Wesmen realise the Shroud is gone. Again, should that buy us an hour in which to mobilise the Dordovans, it could be critical."

"But this doesn't change the fact that we are surrendering the College," said Seldane. Kard turned his head and looked long at her.

"My Lady, I have no intention of surrendering this College."

"So why are we dropping the Shroud for which, I remind you, Deale gave his life?" demanded Endorr.

"Because the time has come again to fight for our freedom. And to gamble that help will arrive. And if the times become desperate again, we can bury the Heart. Julatsa will beat life until we can reclaim it," said Kard.

"But surely you don't believe we can win?" Endorr's scepticism was written in a sneer all over his face.

"Young man, I never start a battle I believe I can't win. You've seen the energy out there. If we channel it right, and if the help outside the city hits the rear of the Wesmen lines, we can win."

"Thank you, Kard," said Kerela. "I suggest that you and Barras speak to Senedai. We will stay here and discuss the division of mages for your tasks."

As he and Kard walked, under guard, to the North Gate, Barras could feel the tension in the silent College. In the wood and steel tower, which currently stood overlooking the Long Rooms, half a dozen Wesmen leaned on the parapet, monitoring their movement with only passing interest.

"You should have been a Negotiator, General," said Barras, a wry smile on his face. "You're almost as good a liar as I am."

"I'm sure I don't know what you mean." Kard fixed his gaze straight ahead but Barras saw the twitching of his lip.

"Outside these walls, there must be ten thousand heavily armed and focused Wesmen. Inside, we have seven hundred soldiers, a few hundred angry men and fewer than two hundred mages. What do you think I mean?"

"Actually, with our estimates of their ability to reinforce, there could be as many as twenty thousand Wesmen out there."

"And do you really believe the Dordovans are waiting for a sign? Surely they'll have been recalled once Julatsa fell."

"No, I'd say they were still there somewhere. There just aren't enough of them."

"So how long can we hold them off?" asked Barras.

Kard shrugged. "Hard to say. Realistically, perhaps three days but it could be over in one if our spirit crumbles."

"But you don't think we can win?"

Kard laughed, clapped Barras on the back with one hand and pulled open the door to the North Gate tower with the other.

"I may be old, but I am not senile. I strongly suggest you place your most valuable texts in the Heart prior to burial," he said and gestured at the stairs. "After you."

Lords Blackthorne and Gresse arrived at the southern port of Gyernath too late to lend their ramshackle forces of soldiers and farmers to the battle but not to the cleanup. And as Blackthorne directed his men to their tasks, he felt a sense of relief despite the destruction and death all around them.

They had seen the fires while they were still over a day's march away, an orange glow blooming over the mountains which marked the northern reaches of Gyernath's boundaries. He and Gresse had feared the worst then, could see the sacking of the port and the routing of her army in their minds' eyes and with it, the extinguishing of their still embryonic hopes for victory.

But Gyernath had survived, the remnants of the Wesmen force scattering back toward Blackthorne. The attack had been expected, some of Blackthorne's people had brought warning, and the days of preparation they had been granted had proved the difference.

For eight days, Gyernath had repulsed the waves of Wesmen from both land and sea, eventually breaking the Wesmen spirit as parts of the old port burned and their mage strength dwindled. They had not had to suffer the Shamen's white or black fires like Julatsa but their toll had been heavy nonetheless.

Gyernath's army had lost half of its military and reservist strength to death or injury. Barely a man walked without bearing some sort of wound. And the mages, ruthlessly targeted wherever the Wesmen pierced the line, now numbered less than one hundred.

For Blackthorne, though the salvation of the port was magnificent, it meant he could not hope to take the strength he wanted to attempt the reclamation of his town.

"On the other hand, Blackthorne will be emptier of Wesmen than we expected," said Gresse, standing at the Baron's shoulder, a dull ache and occasional fuzzy vision all that remained of his heavy concussion.

"That rather depends on how many of this Wesmen force came from Blackthorne and how many directly across the Bay," said Blackthorne.

"Always the pessimist," said Gresse.

"It's easy to be pessimistic," replied Blackthorne. "Just look at the mess they've made of this beautiful port."

The two men straightened and looked down the hill toward the Southern Ocean. The whole port was laid out before them in the midafternoon light. Smoke from a dozen extinguished fires spiralled slowly into the sky. The main street, at the top of which they stood, now led through a scene of devastation. Much of the fighting had been concentrated on its sloped cobbles and all the buildings: inns, houses, bakers', armourers', shipwright offices and the premises of a dozen other trades lay in ruins.

To the left and right, the path of the street-to-street, house-to-house fighting was drawn in blood and ash. Funeral pyres were alight everywhere they looked and it was not until the eye travelled down toward the dockside piles, cranes, jetties and warehouses, that the port regained some semblance of its recognised shape. Out in the harbour, the masts of three or four tall ships jutted from the low tide water but the Gyernath blockade had frustrated every attempt of the Wesmen, not natural sailors, to break through.

But the eight days of fighting had left thousands homeless and as many orphaned or widowed. The army and city guard, those who could still walk, threw the remainder of their energies into salvaging what they could from the wreckage of the port and making as much of it as habitable as possible. All too often since Blackthorne and Gresse had arrived though, it was the sound of the unsafe timbers being dragged to the ground that drowned out the sound of new timbers being nailed over cracks in roofs and walls. Gyernath's glory was gone.

A man was striding up the slope of Drovers' Way, the main street, toward them. He was tall, middle-aged and dressed in robes of state. The mayor's emblem hung around his neck and he was clutching a roll of parchment.

"I'd say welcome, Blackthorne, but there's precious little of my town left for that," he said. Blackthorne shook the man's hand.

"But more than I can currently offer you at my own," replied the Baron. "Mayor Scalier, may I introduce my friend, Baron Gresse." The two men shook.

"I have heard of your efforts," said Scalier. "It is rare to find a man of your honour wearing Baronial colours these days. Present company excepted, naturally."

"Rarer still to find a victorious Eastern Balaian. I congratulate you on your triumph."

Scalier's smile faded a little and his long lined face took on a sadder aspect below the wisps of grey hair that blew about his head.

"If it can be described as such. We cannot sustain another such attack; we will be driven into the sea. And as I look down on the ruins, I wonder whether that might not be a blessing."

"I understand your feelings, Scalier, as perhaps no one else can. But you know that my request for soldiers and mages is aimed at finishing the threat of such an attack." Blackthorne rubbed at his beard. "I presume that parchment is your decision."

"Yes. I am sorry it has taken this long to deliver our answer; your messenger was most insistent about its urgency, but you can see we have had one or two other matters to attend to." He handed over the parchment which Blackthorne unrolled quickly, his heart beating proud in his chest as he scanned the numbers it contained. His face cracked into a huge but short-lived smile.

"You cannot afford this many men and mages. You have to maintain some defence." He passed the parchment to Gresse whose breath hissed in through his teeth. Scalier clapped his hands together.

"What for? Just look around you. The Wesmen must be stopped and you can stop them if you take the rest of Gyernath's army and its mages with you. We will position scouts and beacon fires on every route from the port. Should the Wesmen attack us again, we will have advance warning and evacuate to sea. You will command the forces of Gyernath and may the Gods bless you in your fight."

Blackthorne grabbed Scalier and hugged him, slapping his back until the older man coughed.

"What you have done gives Balaia a chance," he said. "Once Blackthorne is retaken and the camps either side of the Bay of Gyernath are destroyed, we will march back north and fight at Understone. And this time, we will have victory as a true goal. Then," he turned to Gresse. "Then will come the reckoning."

"How soon can these men be ready?" asked Gresse.

"It will take a while to provision the ships and I should think the same time for you to formulate your plans with my Captains, not to mention allowing time for rest. There is a tide that will stream out in the early hours in two days' time. You should be on it." Blackthorne nodded.

"Come, let us find an inn that is standing and drink to Gyernath and the whole of Balaia." He led the way down Drovers' Way, his head high, his mood ecstatic. There would be a victory at Blackthorne. His men, together with eight thousand from Gyernath, would sweep the Wesmen back across the Bay and into their homelands to lick their wounds. He hoped enough lived to curse their folly and to resolve never to challenge Baron Blackthorne again.

CHAPTER 18

Thraun felt it first, though Hirad didn't know it until later. Denser was still in Communion, face drawn into a deep frown, lips moving soundlessly, Erienne stroking his hair.

To the rest of The Raven, nothing was out of the ordinary, but the wolf picked up his head and made a soft noise in his throat which became a whine. He shook his powerful muzzle and stood up, sniffing the air, hackles rising, a slight quiver apparent in his forelegs.

He backed away from the stove, ignoring Will's calming hand and voice, looking left across the river and right into the brush that secluded them from unwelcome eyes. The whine continued from deep in the centre of his forehead then shut off abruptly. He locked eyes with Hirad and the barbarian would have laughed, swearing the wolf was actually frowning in worry, had not the pain seared into his skull.

He cried out, clutching his head in both hands, making to rise but falling back, first to his haunches, then flat prone his legs thrashing, facial muscles horribly twisting his expression. Dimly, he heard Ilkar's voice and felt other hands grabbing at him, trying to still his body as it heaved and tremored.

It was like nothing he had ever experienced. As if his brain was being squashed against the inside of his head by spiked mallets while, at the same time, squeezed to the size of an apple by a monstrous hand. He saw flashes of red and gold light before his eyes though the rest of the world was dark, and in his ears the sound of a thousand pairs of wings beat on his eardrums. His nose, he thought in a queer moment of total clarity, was bleeding.

The agony had a voice. Hirad heard it echo at first, unsure whether it was another trick of the pain. It came to him on a hurricane of whispers just out of reach, sliding past his numbed mind then grabbing a hold. He wanted to open his eyes but could not. His limbs too, were leaden and immobile.

This is death, he thought.

"No, Hirad Coldheart, not death." It was a voice he knew well and though it came to him from out of his nightmares, it brought strange comfort. "I am sorry for the inevitable unpleasantness. First contact over such a distance is difficult but it will ease. I will teach you."

"Sha-Kaan?" Hirad was aware his mouth was moving but his confusion of thoughts found a focal point in his bruised brain, allowing him to communicate.

"Excellent. There is no damage."

"It doesn't feel that way and unpleasantness is hardly the word I would choose to describe what you have just caused."

Sha-Kaan chuckled, a gentle feeling which stroked Hirad's aching mind.

"You have the same fearlessness I found in Septern," he said. "It is a shame you are not a mage."

"Why?"

"Because it would make our binding all the more powerful and complete."

"What binding?" Hirad felt a flicker of worry. It hadn't occurred why Sha-Kaan had chosen to contact him. He hadn't even conceived the possibility unless the dragon was in Balaia. The fact that he was apparently speaking from great distance was a cause for concern.

"There is something I must ask you to do that will help my Brood to survive. I am old, even by the standards of the Kaan, yet I have had no Dragonene since the death of Seran at Taranspike Castle. You are the only human with the strength of mind to answer my calls. I may have need of you in the time before you travel to my domain."

Hirad was stunned. He also felt a sense of overwhelming honour but curiously didn't know why he should. He had precious little knowledge of the Dragonene save that all were mages.

"But what can I do? I cannot cast a spell. Why me?"

"There are others of The Raven to channel the energies of interdimensional space and to provide for my wounds and damages. But yours is a mind that burns bright for me as those of your friends do not. Even were I sorely wounded, I could find you and reach sanctuary. I ask that you agree. I will teach you what you need to know."

"And can I call on you?"

"Should you need to, but I could not swear to answer you immediately, nor to be able to give you the help you desire, though I would expect nothing less from you."

"But what if I'm in the middle of battle?" Hirad could imagine the pain felling him as surely as an enemy axe in the midst of mêlée. He could not allow that. The Raven were too important.

"If your mind is open as it should be, I could detect whether you were at rest before contacting you."

"Then I accept," said Hirad before he knew quite what he was saying.

"Excellent. Now tell me, how goes your search for a means to close the gateway?"

Hirad quickly outlined his understanding of the DemonShroud, which was limited, and the distance they had to travel to Julatsa, which was far more complete.

"I must know more about this Shroud. Is it pandimensional?"

"I have absolutely no idea what you are talking about," said Hirad. "All I know is that nothing living can pass through it, that it stretches as high as heaven and as low as hell and all who attempt to cross it lose their souls to the demons."

Sha-Kaan was quiet for a moment but Hirad felt his presence, and his worry, no less keenly. He had a moment to reflect on the enormity of what he had done and found himself unperturbed by it. There was one thing, though.

"Why did you choose me now?" he asked.

"Because I must attempt tasks that will provoke attack and damage. I must have a Dragonene. Now to this Shroud. Let me investigate. Your mages have dabbled again in something they do not fully understand or can control. I will contact the Brood and probe the space around the city you head for. There may be a way to get through. Be ready for my contact tomorrow as your sun passes its highest."

"I will."

"Thank you, Hirad Coldheart. You have taken a solemn oath but you are not alone. There are Dragonene everywhere there are mages. Until tomorrow."

And then he was gone and Hirad realised he had no idea how to contact the Great Kaan himself. He opened his eyes.

"Gods in the ground, Hirad, what the hell happened to you?" Ilkar's face loomed over his, colour returning to his cheeks, frown relaxing.

Hirad smiled, his head encased in sponge, his eyesight not quite sharp and the ache of Sha-Kaan's presence a reminder it had not all been a dream. He was lying flat on his back, a cloak pillowing his head. A female hand reached across with a rag and wiped what had to be blood from his nose.

"How long have I been out?"

"A couple of minutes," said The Unknown.

"Maybe less," added Ilkar. There was a low growl. Thraun's muzzle appeared suddenly in his vision, the wolf's yellow eyes searching his, heavy furred brows forced together, an almost comical frown rippling the skin above them. Apparently satisfied, his tongue whipped out to lick Hirad's cheek then he moved away.

"He's happy anyway," said Hirad.

"Yes, but he wasn't. Not happy at all," said The Unknown.

"Do you mind if I sit up?" asked Hirad. They helped him to a sitting position. Denser sat cross-legged away from the group, his pipe newly lit, smoking into the afternoon sky. He wore a deeply troubled expression. Will stood nearby, stroking Thraun's flank. Ilkar, The Unknown and Erienne crowded him, Ilkar handing him a mug of coffee.

"You dropped your last one," he said.

"I don't remember." He was feeling more human now, the pulp encasing his brain fading, his thoughts sharper, as was his sight.

"So what happened?" asked Ilkar again.

"It was Sha-Kaan; he spoke to me, from his own lands. From Wingspread."

"From where?" The Unknown leaned back on his haunches. Hirad shrugged. He had no idea where the word came from. Sha-Kaan had not used it.

"Wingspread. Sha-Kaan's place, I suppose." Hirad scanned the faces of Ilkar and The Unknown. The former was thoughtful, the latter worried.

"I presume it wasn't good news," said Ilkar. "I mean, why is he contacting you?"

"How, is more pertinent," added The Unknown. "Look at you. You're paler than a two-day corpse."

"Thanks," said Hirad. "Look. I'm not sure what the news was but he's worried about getting hurt and needs a new Dragonene. Me, to be exact."

"What?" chorused the trio of mages.

"Yeah, that's what *I* said. But apparently I can be the contact and you three can do whatever he needs you to do. He picked me because he's familiar with my mind. It's very strong, he said." Hirad sat up a little straighter.

Ilkar chuckled. "Well, your head's thick enough anyway."

"You didn't agree, did you?" asked Denser. It was more of a statement than a question.

Hirad raised an eyebrow. "Well, yes, of course. I had to."

"Thanks very much," snapped the Xeteskian.

"What's your problem?" Hirad felt the pricklings of anger. "Did I really have a choice?"

"Yes, you did. You could have said no. Suppose I don't want to be a Dragonene?"

"You aren't, Xetesk man, I am. You're a . . . I don't know, you're a consort or something." It was the wrong word and Hirad knew it. He only half-regretted saying it. Denser rose.

"You have got to be bloody joking, Hirad. If you think I'm going to agree to be a 'consort'"—he ejected the word like a mouthful of rotten fruit—"you can stick it straight up your arse."

"Denser, sit down now and lower your voice," ordered The Unknown, making the ghost of a move when the mage threatened to speak again. "Your noise will bring the entire Wesmen nation down on our necks. All our noise for that matter. We are The Raven. Let's try and remember that once in a while."

"You weren't there," said Hirad.

"Hirad," warned The Unknown.

"No, hear me out." He lowered his voice. "I could feel the waves of need in Sha-Kaan. He needs me, us, as much as we'll need him. And in case you'd forgotten, Denser, if he and the Kaan die, so do we all. It is our duty to help protect him. And for that, I need your help. There was no time to consult you. I did what I had to do. What was right in here." He tapped his chest.

Denser took his place by the fire, exchanging sharp glances with Erienne.

"Well, you're right about the time thing anyway."

The Raven looked at him with virgin interest. His Communion had been forgotten.

Ilkar cleared his throat. "I ask this with all due dread, but why?"

"Because we've only got eight days to close the rip."

Darrick's heart was soaring. Eight days of exhilarating riding had brought the cavalry to within striking distance of the Bay of Gyernath staging post. His scouts reported a small force of Wesmen warriors and workers, perhaps as few as one hundred and fifty, and an intermittent stream of traffic moving in from the Heartlands trail which ran away to the west and the Southern Force, the river which ran from the Garan Mountains to the sea and guarded the eastern edge of the Wesmen's ancestral home.

It had been a ride of power and discipline, hard paced by day, resting by night. He knew the horses hadn't much left but journey's end was in sight and the destruction of the staging post would herald a short sea journey and perhaps a day's rest.

The four-College cavalry, one hundred and ninety swordsmen and archers and eighteen mages, was gathered an hour's ride from the bayside encampment. The plans were laid. The most potent risk was from three watchtowers manned by three warriors each and to these Darrick detailed his full contingent of fourteen archers and enough mage support to provide HardShields. He would have preferred to launch a magical attack but the spells he needed were very hard to prepare and cast at a gallop. The main body of the camp, large store tents surrounded in a loose circle by billet canvas, was ripe for a cavalry charge with mage-fired torches as the first attack volley.

Darrick, at the head of the cavalry astride his mount, gave his final address as the late afternoon sun began to wane.

"These people have invaded our lands and killed our people. You all know some of those who have already died. All those lost in the defence of Understone Pass, all those lost so far in the siege of Julatsa. The Gods only can know the state of Blackthorne, Gyernath and Arlen. Erskan, Denebre and Eimot.

"They have shown us no mercy. You must do the same. Kill them or they will kill you. I want this encampment burned to the ground and the charred earth left as memorial and warning. The East shall not bend the knee to the West. The Colleges shall thrive. The Wesmen shall be driven from our lands, our homes and yes, our beds.

"Are you with me?"

The chorus sent birds into the sky. Darrick nodded.

"Then let's ride." The cavalry galloped for the Bay.

The camp had quietened, The Raven sitting around Will's stove, each drawing on their own thoughts, dwelling on Denser's words. Will himself had stretched out next to Thraun, an arm carelessly thrown over the wolf's prone form. Thraun remained alert, head up, ears pricked, tongue licking his lips as he scanned his new territory.

Erienne watched them both for a moment, seeing in them a closeness she no longer seemed to share with Denser. The Dark Mage was absently flicking at dried leaves on the ground while his pipe sat between his teeth, long since dead and ignored. She frowned and sent out a gentle probing in the mana but, as with so many times before, found only a blanket covering his mind. She wasn't even sure if he was aware of his shield against her but then she wasn't sure he was aware of much but his own memories of Dawnthief and what it had done to him.

She rose and went to sit by him; he acknowledging her with the slightest of smiles. It set her body tingling.

"Do you want to walk a little way?" she asked. "Down to the water's edge? It's dark."

He looked her full in the face, forehead wrinkling, pupils dilated in the dim light. How she wished they were wide in longing for her.

"What for?" he asked.

"I would have thought that was obvious," muttered Ilkar from nearby.

"Keep out of this, Ilkar," said Erienne shortly. "Denser, please?" Denser shrugged and dragged himself to his feet, a sigh escaping his lips.

"Lead on," he said, his half gesture mirroring the lack of enthusiasm so plainly displayed on his face. She narrowed her eyes but said nothing, choosing instead to do as he asked.

"Don't stray too far," warned Hirad. "This area isn't safe."

Erienne handed aside a low branch, ducked right and moved off toward the River Tri. Despite the night, the moon gave enough light to see by and she walked briskly between tree and bush down a shallow slope that led to the water's edge.

At the shore, a mixture of fine shingle, mud and overhanging plants, she turned left and, stepping over puddles and marshy ground, found her way to a flat patch of grass a couple of paces back from the river and covered by trees. She sat down on the slightly damp ground, looking out at the wide, sluggish course of the Tri as it drove inexorably to Triverne Inlet and then out to sea. In the dimness, it looked dark grey, like a slow-moving sludge, and did nothing to lighten her mood.

After a few moments, Denser appeared, striking light to his pipe. He seemed unsure what to do.

"Sit down," she said, patting the grass next to him. Another shrug and he complied, leaving a small distance between them and only half looking at her.

"Why won't you talk to me?" she asked, not sure how to begin the conversation but knowing she had to get through to him for the sake not just of herself, but of The Raven too.

"I do," he responded.

"Oh yes, and I really enjoy our 'how are you, fine' conversations. Very meaningful. Very fulfilling." A light breeze rustled the leaves at her back and blew hair across her face.

"So, what do you want me to talk about?"

"You! God's sake, Denser, haven't you seen what's happened to you since you cast Dawnthief?" She felt anger welling up at his surly, deliberate obstruction.

"Nothing's happened," he said defensively. "I've just gained a clear knowledge of the true working of magic."

"Yes, and look what it's done to you. Taken you away from us, from me, and given you this damned superior air. Like we are beneath your level all of a sudden."

"That's not what I think."

"Well, that's how it appears. You snap at Ilkar, you wind up Hirad and you just ignore me most of the time." Her eyes were filling with tears. Only a few short days ago, she'd sat with him lying in her lap, so proud of him, so happy he was alive and simply staggered by his achievement. But her surge of feelings had struck a hard wall of hidden emotion and now she felt helpless. "What is going on in that head of yours?"

"Nothing," he said quietly.

"Exactly," she snapped. "Ever since you regained your mana stamina it's like you don't care. Not for me, not for The Raven and not for our child."

"That's not true." Denser still wouldn't look at her. She wanted to reach out to touch him but her heart lurched as, in her mind's eye, she saw him pulling away.

"So talk to me," she urged. "Please."

He sighed and she almost slapped him. But then their eyes met and she saw him fighting for the words.

"It's difficult," he said, a slight shrug following.

"We have all night."

"Hardly," he said, a smile touching his lips for the briefest of moments. "You understand magic. You understand the energy it takes to control mana and the depletion of your stamina whenever you cast. And you know that every mage searches for new ways to minimise that depletion. But I've just been given most of it on a plate. And that's just the half of it."

Erienne was desperate to interrupt but even more so not to disrupt his train of thought, such as it was. She wasn't sure anything he was saying was relevant; she was just glad to hear him talk.

"The thing is, we all have our life's work and our life's dream. I've discovered that the trick is never to achieve that dream." He looked away over the water.

"You have lost me there," said Erienne. "Why would you chase after things you didn't actually want to achieve?"

"What do you do when you've achieved your life's ultimate challenge?" countered Denser.

For a moment, Erienne had no response. "There must always be something," she said.

"That's what I thought. But what when there isn't anything as big as what you've just done?"

"I—" she began, thinking she understood. For a heartbeat, the pieces began to fall into place. But she found they didn't fit. "How can you have nothing?" she asked. "We're here because we have to close that rip, because no one else can. How can that not be important enough to you?"

"I don't know."

"If we fail, you'll die. We all will."

"But death no longer holds any fear for me. I have cast Dawnthief, I have achieved something I thought unattainable. The one thing I could go on dreaming about because I knew I would never succeed. But I have succeeded and now I am empty. If I died now, I would die complete."

Now she slapped him. Hard across the cheek, the sound ringing out on the still night air. The Raven would be on them shortly but she didn't care. Every frustration, every cold look he'd given her and every little slight in his manner boiled out of her. It made her feel no better.

"Then do it for someone else. What about me? What about your *child?*" Her tears began to flow. "Selfish bastard."

He caught her arm. "I cast Dawnthief to save everyone."

"You did it for yourself," she snarled, sudden contempt flowing through her veins. "You have just made that very clear." She jerked her arm free. "I'm just surprised you didn't go full force. I mean, why not perform the ultimate act of selfishness and take us all with you? At least that way you wouldn't have to be so damned self-pitying now." She made to go but his words stopped her dead.

"I nearly did. But I couldn't because I love you."

She turned, knowing she should slap him again for daring to toy with her emotions that way. But something in his tone stayed her hand.

"That is an extraordinary statement," she said coldly.

"But true."

"Well, you've had a strange way of showing it since."

Denser looked up at her, his eyes glinting in the dim light. "I can't be all that you need right now. If I'm honest, I do feel that I've made a huge sacrifice. Not just for you but for The Raven. But when it came to it, I couldn't betray the faith you had shown in me. All of you. And much as Dawnthief tried to beguile me into taking the world with me, I couldn't do it." He let his gaze drop back to the grass. "It's funny. I never thought I'd live to see the spell cast but, when casting, my desperation that you should live overcame the terrible desire to see my life's work completed."

Erienne sat next to him and placed an arm around his neck, stroking his face where she had slapped it.

"And now you have the chance to carry on a new life's work, my love," she whispered. "You've spent all your life learning to destroy but, you and me, we've created something. You can make sure it isn't allowed to die." She realised he was shaking. Whether it was chill or emotion she didn't know for a while but when he turned to her he took her hands in his, and his face was wet with tears.

"It's what I want more than anything but inside I feel cheated. Don't you see? Everything in my life has been peripheral to that damned spell ever since I can remember. It was drummed into me so hard there was no room for anything else. But now it's gone and I have no centre, no core to keep me wanting to live through trouble and come out the other side." He brushed a hand across her cheek. "I know how hard that must sound for you and I know it's wrong to feel that way but I do. What if I can never feel the way I did before? What if I can't want something else as much as I wanted Dawnthief?"

"You will, love. Trust me. All you have to do is try." She kissed his mouth gently, letting her tongue caress his lips. He forced her mouth open, his kiss becoming urgent, his hands suddenly at her back, pressing her to him. She warmed to his touch, wanting him but instead she pushed him away.

"It's not quite that easy," she said, feeling the heat in her face and the flutter of her heart. Their faces were close and he was smiling that genuine smile she had loved the first time she saw it but feared she'd seen for the last time.

"But all this was put here for us. A soft patch of grass, the sound of the river and a hint of moonlight. It would be rude to pass it by."

"You ignore me for days and now this?"

"Got to start somewhere." He moved a hand to caress her breast. She wanted to pull away but couldn't find the will. And as she let herself be lain on her back, his kisses smothering her in repeated sensual blooms, she thought she heard footsteps creeping back toward the camp.

Sha-Kaan rested a while. Tiring of Flamegrass, he devoured the carcass of a freshly slaughtered goat. It took the edge off his hunger.

He contemplated his conversation with Hirad Coldheart, impressed at the human's strength but unsure of the wisdom of his decision nonetheless. If it didn't work, he knew he could move on but the thought of Hirad Coldheart's inevitable death in that circumstance gave him no comfort. He had gambled and that was not something he did lightly.

And now he had to act. He crushed and swallowed the last of the bones, followed them with a bale of Flamegrass and shifted out of Wingspread, a command to attend flashing from his mind to a Kaan of whom he had need.

Sha-Kaan materialised in the river and drank long from its cool flow. Above him, the mist parted and a large young Kaan dropped into the Broodland, wings braking his descent, feet seeking purchase a little clumsily on an area of flat, pitted rock, his talons goring it deeply.

The Great Kaan picked his head from the river and rose up, his neck forming the formal "s," his torso upright, the duller yellow scales of his belly exposed, front legs flat, his wings twitching for balance. He gazed at the young Kaan who mirrored his bearing but whose head was bowed in respect.

Elu-Kaan reminded him of himself at the same age—strong, large, confident in his abilities, yet nervous in the presence of his elders.

"Skies greet you, Elu-Kaan," he said.

"I am honoured by your call, Great Kaan," Elu responded.

"I have work for you. Your Dragonene is, I understand, a mage residing in the Balaian city of Julatsa?"

"Yes, Great Kaan, though I have not taken contact for several cycles. I have been fortunate in battle." His head bowed further, though his mind was as proud as it should be.

"Fortune, it was not. Skill is your saviour." Sha felt a surge of pride from the youngster at his compliment. "But now I need you to travel interdimensional space to speak with your Dragonene, if you are able. The mages have protected their College with an energy derived from the dimension of the Arakhe. I fear that the gateway will be feeding power to the Arakhe and I cannot allow them ungoverned access to Balaia. Find out whether your portal can penetrate it but do not risk your life. There is risk in what I ask. Withdraw the moment you feel them press; they are a difficult enemy."

"I will begin at once." The young Kaan raised his head to assure Sha-Kaan of his intent.

"Elu," said Sha-Kaan. "I must have an answer when the orb darkens the Skies."

"Yes, Great Kaan."

"I will be gone from the Broodlands for a short time. I must speak with the Veret. If I do not return, you must pick up the signature of Hirad Coldheart of The Raven. It will reside in the Mind of Wingspread and you alone have my permission to enter if I should die."

"I am honoured, Great Kaan."

"You are still young, Elu, but the greatness is in your heart, mind and wings. Learn from me and become Great Kaan yourself in time." Sha-Kaan stretched his wings. "May the Skies be clear for you."

"And you, Great Kaan. Be careful. The Brood needs you."

Sha made no response. Calling his farewells to the Brood, he flew from the valley, heading north for the Shedara Ocean.

The skies were calm, the cloud high and the winds in the upper strata aided his flight. After exchanging greetings and instructions with the gateway defence, he climbed high above the cloud layer and drank in the radiance of the orb and the beauty of his world.

From the heights, the tranquillity lifted his heart and, for a beat, he could believe the world was at peace. Warm yellow-orange light flooded the sky, reflecting from the clouds and sparkling in his vision. He closed his inner lids and focused his mind below.

Nothing impinged on his consciousness. No flights of dragons moved the air contours, no clash of minds filled the void with noise, no barks told of battles to come, no cries of pain told of battles lost. Satisfied, he increased his wing beats and tore across the sky.

The Shedara Ocean filled the northern hemisphere. Where the vast lands of Dormar and Keol ended, so it began, its vastness punctuated only by islands, reefs and drifts of sand, immense on the tide, nothing in the flood. But it was a short-sighted dragon that ignored the land masses, however temporary their hold on dry air. The Veret, though marine in all their biology, chose to nest and breed in caves and hides where the sea was not forever above their heads.

Sha-Kaan knew where the Veret chose to Brood and he flew deliberately through the centre of their mind net before banking steeply up to await the inevitable response. It was not long in coming.

A flight of Veret, six strong, ploughed through the moist air to meet him, their aggression plain. Sha-Kaan defused their ire before they had a chance to close for the fight.

"I would speak with Tanis-Veret, my *altemelde*," he said, knowing the name of their Elder Veret and the link to a long-standing kinship would stay their fire. "I am Sha-Kaan."

Spiralling up through the heights, the Veret called challenges and warnings, daring him to descend toward their Broodlands beneath the waves. Their aquamarine blue scales flashed wet in the sunlight, their wings drove them up at speed, their streamlined bodies causing precious little resistance. He watched them turn, assessed the confidence of their movement and concluded he would likely be killed if they attacked him. He remained on station, circling slowly, the Veret forming a holding group around him, left, right, in front, behind, above and below. Sha-Kaan could feel their awe of him but also anger and, in one to his right, hate.

"You will not break from us as we descend. You will not call, you will not pulse," said the Veret with hate on his mind.

"I understand," said Sha-Kaan. "You realise I am no threat to you. I have come alone to talk."

"It is our way," said another, more reverence in his tone. "All visitors must be escorted to the Broodlanding."

"Care cannot be overestimated."

The flight dived steeply, reining in their natural speed to account for Sha-Kaan's less aerodynamic frame. They were heading for a small rock island at the edge of which great towers of rock jutted up in five places.

"Land centrally." Sha-Kaan was ordered. The flight pulled away. Sha-Kaan feathered his huge wings, braking quickly to drop vertically between the rock spires on to the sea-drenched main outcrop. Almost immediately, the water ahead of him rippled, boiled and exploded outward. Tanis-Veret broke surface, dragging a mass of ocean with him that tumbled back into the frothing turbulence he left behind and soared into the sky, an arrow punching through the air, a call of greeting bouncing from the crannied stone. Tanis-Veret turned full somersault and landed at the very edge of the island, tail drawing moisture from the ocean, the ripples of his exit from the water expanding still as he settled.

"There is nothing like the wind on wet scales," said Tanis. "You are far from home, Sha-Kaan."

"This is far from an ordinary situation," replied the Great Kaan. "I greet you, Tanis-Veret." He lifted his neck to the formal "s," meeting the gaze of his equal.

"And I you." Tanis' short neck couldn't form as Sha-Kaan's but he picked up his torso to sit upright, exposing as Sha did, his belly scales.

Above them, the Veret flight broke and dived into the sea, their perfect entries minimising splash and ripple as they disappeared beneath the swell.

"I do not feel we need them, do you?"

Sha-Kaan inclined his head.

"Your trust is welcome and is reciprocated."

"Speak, Sha-Kaan, though I think I know your subject."

"I will speak plainly. It is my belief that you have allied with the Naik in a battle that is not your concern nor which could possibly benefit your Brood."

Tanis looked away, a cough rippling his chest, the dulling scales a sign of his great age. He was far older than Sha-Kaan but in the tight Brood structure that was the Veret way, his authority and ability to lead would never be questioned. Only in death would a successor be appointed. For the Kaan, mind strength was critical and Sha knew that one day Elu-Kaan would beat him and he would take his place among the Elder-Kaan, revered but peripheral.

"Sha-Kaan, this is a time of great peril for the Veret. Our birthings have slumped, protection for our carrying females has to be our primary concern and this leaves too few to defend our borders against attack."

"So I was right." Sha-Kaan's anger flared. He felt some small pity for Tanis but it was overwhelmed by contempt. "Why didn't you come to me?"

"The Naik were already here. They had the strength to finish us there and then. We had no choice."

"Naik!" spat Sha-Kaan, a gout of smoke firing from his mouth. "But after. Why not send a flight to me after?"

"They would know. They knew of our trouble. They knew we would have to furl wing to them."

Sha-Kaan stared hard at Tanis-Veret, disappointment now burying his contempt. The Veret Elder was broken and bowed. He had not even the strength to try and free his Brood. Surely the Naik would finish them anyway. He said so.

"Perhaps," said Tanis. "I have to trust they will not."

"You are letting your Brood die," said Sha-Kaan angrily. "I came to offer help. Maybe I should just leave you to fade away."

"How can you help? Your Brood is stretched, a gateway to your melde-dimension hangs in the sky for all to see. You fight for your own survival."

"And you add to the struggle by aiding the Naik. Do you not see?"

"I must protect my Brood above all others, please respect that." Tanis looked skyward, his eyes nervous.

"No one is near."

"They are always near."

"Last light was the most painful I have suffered for many cycles," said Sha-Kaan. "I killed one of your Brood who chased down and fired my Vestare. Another of my Brood died in a diving embrace, punctured by a Veret. Others of my Brood either chased off or killed more Veret. We are not at war with you, Tanis; why must you fight us?"

"Because if we do not, we will be extinguished." Tanis would not look at Sha-Kaan.

"I understand your problem and the confusion it must cause you. But I am here now and my Brood will protect you if you break your alliance of fear with the Naik." Sha-Kaan moved for the first time since he landed, extending his wings and rising up on his hind legs in a gesture of intent. His massive bulk dwarfing the smaller Veret, his wings casting a broad shadow over the island and his claws dragging scars in the rock beneath him.

Tanis stretched his jaws, his brows furrowing, the spikes across his skull ridge catching a reflection off the water.

"You do not have the Brood strength to protect us from the Naik."

"But it's like this, you see," said Sha-Kaan very calmly. "We are at war with the Naik, as we are with a number of minor Broods, because they determine to fly through our gateway. They have allied with you and, we expect, other Broods they can threaten successfully. We have no choice but to be at war with these Broods too. Break your alliance. Trust me. Trust the Kaan."

"Sha-Kaan, I cannot."

"Then we will continue to destroy your Brood wherever it is a threat. And if that threat grows, then the next time you see me here, it will be at the head of an echelon. Try to avoid us where you can. I will not see the Kaan fail."

"I am sorry it is this way."

"It is in your power to change it, Tanis-Veret. Should you do so, you know I will hear you."

Tanis met Sha-Kaan's eyes again at last. "You should leave. I will not relay your message until you have cleared my skies."

"Fair winds, fair tides be with you," said Sha-Kaan.

"Beat the Naik."

"I will," said Sha-Kaan. "The tragedy is that you do not believe I will." He took to the air, calling his farewell and rose back to the relative safety of the upper layer where the winds blew the anger from his mind.

CHAPTER 19

Trees jutted into the path three hundred yards from the camp, the elbow they created obscuring the onrushing cavalry. Aware that the sound of their hoofbeats must be clearly audible, Darrick roared the order to split and charge.

In front of him, the horse archers increased their pace, a dozen swordsmen flanked them and five mages trailed them, each invoking a HardShield. They kept to the outside of the path, aiming to attack the watchtowers as Darrick brought the rest of the cavalry into the main body of the camp.

The General dug his heels in and his horse responded. He tore around the elbow at the head of his cavalry just as the first volleys of arrows were exchanged, those of the Wesmen bouncing, while those of his men hit home. He never ceased to wonder at the skill of horseborne archers. Gripping only with their thighs they compensated for the movement of a galloping horse and still managed to shoot accurately. He saw four Wesmen fall in the first volley.

The encampment was in no way prepared for an organised cavalry charge. Not for any attack, come to that. There were no close furrows of tentage, no narrowing path down which an enemy might be driven and no killing ground. Though the camp was roughly organised, it was with one goal only—to facilitate the storage and onward movement of supplies across the Bay of Gyernath. It was paradise for the tactically aware General and, in Ry Darrick, the Wesmen were facing the best.

Darrick ordered the split, holding up a gloved hand and pointing first left, then right and backing it up with a yelled command. He galloped down one side of the stores, a mirror force taking the other. Swords flashing in the afternoon sun, they rode through the camp, hacking aside the ineffective defence, slashing at rope, canvas and beam, collapsing tents on to helpless Wesmen and simply riding down any who got in their way. Clear through to the beach rode Darrick and his cavalry, wheeling in the shallow surf and pausing then to assess the damage they'd caused.

The watchtowers were home to corpses now, his archers waiting for their next orders. In the main body of the camp, cries for aid mixed with those of anger as Wesmen struggled to come to terms with the whirlwind that had engulfed them, those trampled by hooves picking themselves up if they could, the defence beginning to gain shape. But they were too few and too late.

"Mages, fire please." Sounding like an invitation, the order was met by two dozen FlameOrbs arcing across the sky to fall among the defenders, igniting their camp and stirring the chaos. Barely had the screams of the burning reached his ears than Darrick called the second charge and mêlée.

Almost two hundred cavalry rode into the middle of the Wesmen, trampling scorched canvas under hoof, bloodied swords rising and falling on the confused workers and warriors whose easy peace had been so effectively shattered. From the path, archers picked off any threat and mages using Mind-Melt, ForceCone and concentrations of DeathHail smashed fence, flesh, brain and stone. It was all over in no time.

Darrick sat at the head of his whooping, cheering cavalry, surveying the damage he had wrought. Just like old times, he thought.

He hadn't lost a man.

They waited for him, three of them, downwind but not closed of mind. They had thought to surprise him but their thoughts were crystal to the Great Kaan.

He had been flying steadily in the upper strata, the winds against him as he returned to Teras. The Naik had apparently been advised of his journey and from the right and below, he felt them coming before their challenges to battle rang out in the cold sky.

Sha-Kaan turned quickly and dived on the trio, using his altitude advantage to give him speed and angle. The Naik saw him coming and split left, right and down in an attempt to confuse but he had seen too many battles and his eyes were already fixed on his target. The Naik was small, perhaps little more than fifty feet in length, less than half Sha-Kaan's size, but used his body badly.

As Sha-Kaan closed, he saw the attitude of the enemy's wings was all wrong, body shape at odds with the direction of his travel and legs splayed. The Naik was either a clumsy flier or . . . Sha-Kaan curved away from his dive and angled back up, a breath of flame scorched the air just under his belly, a second missed by a wingspan. Roaring their disappointment, the Naik who had sprung the trap passed each other beneath him and he flipped on his back into a steep dive after the decoy who had not yet regained his shape.

Plunging through the line of the two attacking Naik, Sha-Kaan opened his mouth and poured flame down and to his left, searing the flank and wing of the struggling Naik. The beast shivered away, howling pain, a tear evident in its right wing, wind whistling through the rent in the membrane and damaged flank scales bubbling.

Not waiting for the response, Sha-Kaan furled his wings briefly, barrel-rolled away, then arced steeply right and up, head looking behind him. He could only see two of the Naik.

He rolled in the air again but a fraction too late. His snapshot all round vision picked out the third attacker bearing down from above, aiming for his exposed underbelly as he rolled. Knowing he couldn't hope to avoid the flame, he spun half circle, collected his wings and waited for the pain, his momentum carrying him on up. The gout caught him high on his shoulder and seared low across his neck. He felt scales tear and skin contract, knew he had lost some movement but refused to yield his position, knowing where the Naik would complete his move.

With the breeze of the enemy's passing very near him, he opened his armoured outer eyelids, deployed his wings and snaked his neck down his body, ignoring the yank of pain to clamp his jaws on the Naik wing. The younger dragon had great strength and threatened to break away but Sha-Kaan's balance was born of long years of fighting and his opposite pull tore muscle and membrane. He breathed fire over the ruined wing and let the crippled dragon take the long spiralling drop to its death.

Roaring in pain and triumph, Sha-Kaan beat his wings wide. In front of him, the undamaged Naik hovered, looking for a point of attack. At right angles the injured but very mobile second enemy circled tightly.

For a time, they stood off but Sha-Kaan knew what was coming. At a signal, the dragons flew, one up, one down, before angling in to the attack. It was a well-worn manoeuvre and exposed their lack of real fight experience.

Armour was for a purpose, and in a pincer attack, more dragons died for-getting this simple fact that anything else. Sha-Kaan had no intention of trying to dodge both dragons. Accepting the fact of new pain but able to minimise its damage, he reverse-beat his wings to slow his forward move-ment, furled them, lay his neck along his belly and dropped straight down.

Above him, the Naik adjusted quickly, steepening the angle of his dive and sending flame rushing over Sha-Kaan's back. Below him, though, the injured dragon failed to react and Sha-Kaan, lucky for the first time in the battle, struck the enemy's body, his tail a whip for the unwary, lashing around the Naik's neck where it established a choking grip.

A strangled gasp of flame coughed from the enemy's mouth as he fought for breath but Sha-Kaan was in total control. Continuing his plummet, he dragged the young Naik off balance, stretched his neck and beat fire into its face from close range. He dropped the corpse and dived away, wings spread, neck and back stiffening as the damaged muscle below the scales protested. He roared again but this time the enemy didn't respond.

Seeing the battle lost, the one remaining Naik turned and fled, Sha-Kaan watching him dwindle in the lower cloud, a dark shape against the pale back-ground. He didn't follow, choosing instead to drive back into the heights where he flew, more slowly now, back to Teras, his Broodlands and, most importantly, the welcome dimensional streams of the Melde Hall.

The Raven didn't move on until midafternoon. Hirad's contact with Sha-Kaan had left him temporarily fatigued but extremely hungry. Thraun and Will had disappeared into the brush, returning impossibly quickly with a quartet of rabbits and a brace of wood pigeon. These, Will prepared and cooked on the stove's hot plate, bulking the small animals with grain from The Unknown's pack, root vegetables from the river's edge and a fresh herb preparation.

It all made a decent stew but Hirad found himself missing the hunk of bread he'd normally enjoy it with. He also missed the ale and wine.

"It's a depressingly long time since I've had a drink," he said.

"Yes, my profits are surely in tatters because of your absence from my inn," said The Unknown. Hirad looked at him, hoping this was an attempt at humour but seeing it was not. They all missed Korina and The Unknown certainly missed *The Rookery*, the bar he part owned with Tomas, the resident innkeeper. And at this precise moment, Hirad would have given anything at all to have his feet up in front of the fire in the back room, a goblet of wine at his hand, a plate of meat and cheese in his lap.

But memories of *The Rookery* were tinged with sadness. The last time The Raven had been there, Hirad's oldest friend, Sirendor Larn, had been murdered. The fact that he had given his life to save Denser was scant comfort despite the Dark Mage's importance to the future of Balaia.

As he chewed a slightly gristly piece of rabbit, Hirad thought back to their fateful meeting with Denser in the grounds of Taranspike Castle and all to which it had led. So many had died, so much had been achieved and yet, as he sat hidden by the banks of the River Tri, Hirad felt their insignificance. The Raven were just seven people, and himself, The Unknown and Ilkar apart, not even particularly experienced people. But to them lay the task of closing the rip before the Balaian sky was flooded by dragons.

In normal days, it would have been difficult to persuade the doubters of the necessity of their task and their demands for open house in at least two College libraries. Now, with the invading armies of the Wesmen swarming all over the mage lands, it was a task rendered practically impossible. The Wesmen certainly wouldn't believe them and that was no surprise. Despite the fact that they were as much at risk as any Balaian, why should they believe the stories of a band of mercenaries, albeit famous ones? No one could see the rip yet. When they could, it would probably be too late. The tale was just too far-fetched and even Darrick and Styliann's words wouldn't add the necessary weight.

So The Raven were left having to hide the reasons for their actions from all they encountered simply because they hadn't the time or the patience to make people believe them. In fact, as far as Hirad could make out, the only people who would take their story seriously, besides those Styliann could convert should he choose to do so, were the Dragonene mages. But that sect was so secretive that their ear, sympathetic or otherwise, was of limited use. Not one among them would reveal themselves as Dragonene to the wider mage population, let alone to nonmages.

Hirad spat out the gristle. There was no doubting the injustice of their position but mulling on it solved nothing. The stew pot was empty and The Raven had all but finished the meal.

"It's time we were moving," said Hirad. "Will, cool the stove please. Unknown? A route if you would be so kind. Anybody needing to relieve themselves, now is the time. We aren't stopping till nightfall."

Denser grumbled, hauled himself to his feet and crackled away toward the water's edge.

"Cheerful soul, isn't he?" said Ilkar.

"Hmm. Just like his old self, unfortunately," replied Hirad. "Erienne, are you sure you want to hang around with him when you're old and grey?"

Erienne smiled. "Who says I'll go grey? At this moment, he's a little hard to love but, well, you know . . ." Hirad nodded. "But I'll tell you something," she continued. "You could help by being a little more tactful. His fuse is short."

"You're telling me," said Hirad.

"Him, tactful?" Ilkar jerked a thumb in Hirad's direction. "You might just as well ask Thraun to have slightly shorter fangs. It's not going to happen."

"Thanks for your support, Ilkar," said Hirad. He turned his back on the mage and grinned over at The Unknown who didn't respond in kind. "Which way, Big Man?"

The Unknown Warrior moved fluidly to his feet and helped Will kick dirt over the stove.

"I could be flippant and say 'east' but no one would laugh," he said. "If we've decided Triverne Lake isn't an option, that leaves us with few alternatives. My view is that we should drive straight for Julatsa. Given Denser's announcement of our dwindling time, we have to chance running into some Wesmen. Now the only reason I think that's a risk worth taking is that Thraun will almost certainly give us ample warning. We should strike away from the river now and head for the city. The ground is flattish and the cover most of the time is adequate."

"Whatever you say," said Hirad. Denser came back into the small clearing. "Bowels empty?"

"Yes, thank you, Hirad," he replied somewhat testily.

"Let's go." The barbarian gestured for The Unknown to show them the way. Thraun loped off on his own toward the river. Will, the stove tied into its leather, shouldered the burden for the time being and brought up the rear behind the trio of mages.

It was, Hirad thought, a long way to Julatsa on foot and he found himself hoping for an encounter with some unwary Wesmen.

Thraun lapped at the cool water of the slow-flowing river, feeling the liquid chill his throat as it rushed to his belly. His mind was confused but he didn't remember a time when it wasn't.

Earlier he had felt fear and he hadn't enjoyed it. He could find nothing to strike out at so he had crouched, defeated, while the huge animal power caused such pain to the man who led. The man had cried out, the power in his head and filling the space around him, flowing over the ground and covering the leaves of trees and the flowers of the bush.

Thraun had felt it before any of the men had done. They knew too little even to show fear of the power but they should have done. Because it came from nowhere. It had no face, no shape and did not breathe. Yet it was still animal. Thraun knew that and knew also that because it had no form, it was to be feared.

Only the one man had felt it and though he had spoken pain, he had not been harmed. There were no marks on his body and his mind kept its sharpness—Thraun had established that himself.

But he wasn't sure the man who led was safe. The power could return at any time. And Thraun had to watch over man-packbrother. He would suffer no threat to him. He was the man, the only man, whom Thraun truly recognised though the others around him were lodged in his memory. And man-packbrother was calm in their company, which was good. While he protected man-packbrother he knew he would protect the others. The woman who had life within her, the two men with mists around their souls and the one man whose soul was uneasy, yearning for another time though his heart resisted it.

Thraun would watch and Thraun would protect. Thraun would hunt and Thraun would kill.

He lifted his muzzle from the water and sniffed the air. The scent of the pack was strong in his head and the call of the forest lured him, its ties around him hardening, pulling him back to its heart where he would be free of man.

Julatsa's Council room was a cold place. Around the oval table, Kerela, Barras, Seldane, Torvis, Endorr, Cordolan and Vilif listened to General Kard outline the battle to come.

At least he and Barras had been successful in persuading Senedai to hold from his killing of innocents. The Wesmen commander had, though, promised to sacrifice every one of those he still held if he was double-crossed. It was a gamble worth taking—when the fighting started, a full day before the Wesmen believed the Shroud would fall, the odds were stacked very heavily in favour of Senedai concentrating all his effort on the College walls. If that was so, the prisoners had a chance.

The brazier behind Kard's chair guttered suddenly, throwing his face into shadow. The breeze, no more than a whisper of night air, spent itself and the flame brightened.

"It is critical that we cause as much damage as possible to those immediately outside the walls before Senedai's army can be mustered. The sequence will be as follows. An hour before dawn, the DemonShroud will be dispersed. Assuming the guards in the tower don't sound the alarm immediately, eight mages will attempt Communion with our forces outside the city. We have no idea how successful this will be but we can cover all points of the compass with eight. There are also some more obvious places to hide a camp and we'll target those specifically at the outset.

"To a certain extent, we will be driven by the tower guards. Should they see us quickly, the whole process will happen that much faster. If not, we will hold our attack until the alarm is raised. At this time, a dozen mages will FlameOrb the tower and both North and South Gates will be opened. Archers and the balance of mages will be sent to the ramparts while my entire College and city Guard force will get outside.

"Their job is to cause as much damage as possible to Senedai's defences and guard posts before the balance of his army arrives. At this time, they will fall back, the gates will close and be strengthened by craftsmen and Ward-Lock and the siege can begin again.

"Finally, I've hand picked a dozen men to attempt to find and free the prisoners. It's all in the cause of creating confusion. Any questions?" Kard leaned back in his chair and folded his arms. Around the table, nods greeted his summary.

"We can augment the Communion by having the casting take place in the Heart," said Vilif.

"Noncouncil and senior circle members are expressly forbidden to enter the Heart," remarked Endorr. Kerela chuckled.

"And you so young," she said. "I might have expected such an utterance from Torvis, but not you. I am pleased you seek so fervently to uphold our traditions and laws."

"Though this is not the time to do so," added Torvis.

"My feelings exactly. Unless there is further dissent, I approve the use of the Heart for this emergency," said Kerela.

Barras nodded his support and looked over at Endorr. The young mage scowled but said nothing. Barras had certain sympathy with him. His work, diligence and genius had brought him to the Council and its privileges. It must be hard to see them so easily eroded, whatever the situation.

"How will your men know when to fall back?" asked Seldane.

"Once the tower is empty of Wesmen, I will post ShadowWinged mages, three should be sufficient, above the city to gauge the buildup. I'm really only looking to bite at the guard force of Wesmen, not the army. I will not burn Julatsa to free us; there is no time and I don't believe it will be an effective tactic. If we do fall to fighting in the streets, it will benefit us as the smaller force, to fight them in smaller, tighter spaces.

"Once the flying mages see forces strong enough to potentially overwhelm us outside of the gates, we will fall back. They know what to look for and the signals have been learned."

"Why risk your men in such an action at all?" asked Vilif. "Better surely to keep them fresh and on the walls."

Kard shook his head. "I disagree. I don't expect us to be outside for long and the action will have two effects. Most importantly, if we strike first blood, it gives us confidence. I can assure you that standing on the ramparts watching an army advance is, pardon the expression, soul-destroying. Second, if we can wreak small havoc it might knock their confidence just that little bit. That, plus our opening spell barrage, could just serve to weaken their resolve."

"Hardly," said Vilif. "They outnumber us almost ten to one."

"But theirs is a fragile morale. And when the rear of their line is also struck, well, we can only guess at their reaction."

Barras raised his eyebrows. Yes, he could guess at the reaction of the Wesmen. Slaughter. But there was no way out. Even if they hid behind the Shroud for a hundred days it would still end in failure. Ultimately, their food would dwindle, more souls would be taken to fuel the Shroud and open revolt would ensue inside the grounds.

"What in hell's name did we think we were doing raising the Shroud in the first place?" he said, a feeling of desperation sweeping suddenly across his body like dead leaves over stone. There was a moment's quiet in the chamber. Kerela placed a hand on his arm as it rested on the table. It was Kard who spoke.

"Buying ourselves time," he said gently. "We all knew that from the start, our brave friend Deale included. And stopping the Wesmen from simply overwhelming us in the rout. For all our brave words and assertions, we have all been hoping for the same thing, to see an army breasting the hills to save us, our city and our College. But now, twelve days later, we have to accept that's not going to happen, at least while the Shroud remains, and it's no longer acceptable to watch the murder of our people. In a way, it would be easier to see them put to the sword, disembowelled even. At least then they would retain their souls. But in the Shroud . . . Gods in the sky, we can only imagine their torment."

"So, should we sully their sacrifice by surrendering meekly now?" asked Endorr.

Kard's eyes flashed but Barras stared him out of his anger. The General's voice remained calm.

"It is too late to do anything for those lost in the DemonShroud. But it isn't too late to save those still alive out there. Endorr, my naïve young mage, there is to be no meek surrender. Indeed, I expect you to play your full part in ensuring the Wesmen forever fear Julatsa. And if, in our battle, we all die but just one child from within these walls escapes the clutches of the Wesmen, I will deem it a victory worth the fight.

"Do I have your permission to begin?" Kard asked of the entire Council. One by one, its members nodded and said "aye."

"Then it is done," said Kard. "An hour before first light tomorrow, I will visit you here to request you disperse the DemonShroud. From that moment, I will command all forces of the Julatsan city and College, mage and soldier, man and woman. Do I have this authority?"

"Yes, General Kard, you do," said Kerela. "And you have the backing, the blessing and the prayers of all of us. Save our College. Stop our people dying."

Kard smiled. "I'll see what I can do."

Sha-Kaan's entry into the Broodlands had none of the triumph of his previous return. He slipped through the mists all but unnoticed, announcing his arrival to a ministering Vestare only as he landed. Dispensing with the usual formalities of welcome, he enquired about the use of the Melde Hall, stilled his body and switched straight inside.

There, lying flat on his flank, neck and tail both stretched out, was Elu-Kaan, all manner of cuts and scores evident on his head and neck. One wing was unfurled, its membrane marked and dry but mercifully unbroken. But it was his breathing which worried Sha-Kaan. Rapid and ragged as if his lungs had lost capacity and his every inhalation dragged their surface over teeth of stone.

Though tired, stiff and in considerable pain after his battle and bone-wearying flight to Teras, he immediately ordered his ministering Vestare to tend to Elu-Kaan. He moved his great bulk out of their way, sat down and snaked his head to the ground by Elu-Kaan's.

He hardly had to ask the question. The reason Elu was damaged had to be an encounter with the Arakhe and the reason he was not in the flow of interdimensional space was because he had clearly not found a way through to his Dragonene inside Julatsa.

Close to, Elu-Kaan's muzzle was covered in myriad scratches from the claws and teeth of the Arakhe. All but impervious to Dragonfire, they were a dangerous foe but seldom ventured from their dimension to trouble the huge animals whose souls they dare not take. But this DemonShroud penetrated the sanctity of interdimensional space and Elu-Kaan had stumbled into their innate fury and had almost paid the ultimate price.

There was no formal contact between the two races. For all that dragons were hard to negotiate with, Arakhe would not talk at all. Theirs was a simple doctrine that assumed all other races in all other dimensions were inferior to them, to be used and destroyed as necessary. Sha-Kaan, who had only one encounter with them in his long history, would concede that in most cases, they had reason to believe so. But dragons and now humans and elves had learned to either use them or deal with them effectively and this made them more unpredictable still.

Elu-Kaan's eyes flickered open as he felt Sha-Kaan's breath on his face. A dark discharge ran from his nose but this was so far ignored by the Vestare who concentrated on his wing and the scales and skin that covered his chest cavity.

"I am sorry, Sha-Kaan, I have failed you," he said, voice rasping and wheezing.

"Speak with your mind, Elu, I am open to you. Rest your throat and your lungs."

"Thank you," said Elu-Kaan, a pulse of gratitude for the honour of mind speaking with the Great Kaan accompanying his words.

"Soon you will be able to do so as of right," said Sha-Kaan. "Now, tell me of your journey and your encounter with the Arakhe. And I will hear no talk of failure. Yours was a mission of risk and that you survived at all is testament to your ability and strength. If you should tire, tell me and we will talk at a later time."

"You are hurt, Sha-Kaan."

"Look to your own injuries, Elu. I need to take your information to my Dragonene. Speak while you are able."

Elu-Kaan took as deep a breath as was possible for him. His body shuddered with the effort and the pain. Sha-Kaan again wondered what the damage could be but thought to ask a Vestare later.

"It is hard to follow the corridor without a Dragonene as beacon but I could follow the streams and markers I knew, and the signature of Balaia is strong." Elu-Kaan's eyes were closed once more and Sha could allow the frown of worry to spread across his features. Another breath, shorter this time, heaved across Elu's body. His voice faded for a moment and then recovered. "I could feel the presence you call the Shroud as I approached Julatsa and the location of my Dragonene but behind it was silence like the void we felt when the Balaians cast their spell that tore our gateway."

"Calm yourself, Elu," said Sha-Kaan as he felt the increase in the younger dragon's heart rate. He glanced across at the Vestare who worked feverishly on his chest with heated mud balms and scented steams. They would take some time to filter through the skin. One of the Vestare moved between the two dragon's heads and rested a steaming pot beneath Elu-Kaan's mouth and nostrils. His surprise at the new scent was followed swiftly by a relaxation of the muscles in his neck as the gentle fragrance of mist and leaf carried its healing properties to his lungs.

"The Vestares' skill is a blessing," said Sha-Kaan, nodding to the servants of the Kaan, who bowed in response to his notice though they could not hear the exchange between him and Elu. "Now, how did the Arakhe get close to you?"

"I felt I could move through the Shroud but as I touched its presence, I could feel the magic was strong and a link between the Balaian and the Arakhe dimension, not of the Arakhe alone.

"And it was full of Arakhe and they flooded my corridor, repulsing my fire and attacking me with their feet, their hands and their teeth. Those that bit inside my mouth hurt me. It was like ice and it quelled my fire and now it burns in my neck and deep within me . . ." He trailed off again as a cough racked his body, causing his tail to reflex and slap the ground behind him and the Vestare near him to jump away sharply. New discharge shot from his nostrils and bowled over the pot whose contents drained into the hot moist earth of the Melde Hall. It was immediately replaced by another.

"Enough, Elu-Kaan, you must rest."

"No, Great Kaan, there is one more thing," Elu's mind voice was fading and Sha-Kaan guessed the balms and scents were designed to force sleep upon the wounded dragon. "The Shroud is full of Arakhe and they are baying for the souls of the Balaians. They think they have been given a way to breach the Balaian dimension that the Balaians cannot close. We must pray to the Skies that they are wrong because there is no way we can help them, the power is too great and we are too stretched."

"But what might it mean?" asked Sha-Kaan, trying to close on the ramifications of the new threat. Elu-Kaan had the answer.

"If they can beat the mages with whom they made the Shroud, they can
expand its compass at will. It is another gateway, Great Kaan, and without
Balaians to control it, could swallow our melde-dimension as easily as the
gateway over Teras." Elu-Kaan's mind contact slipped away and, for a
moment, Sha-Kaan thought he had died. But a glance at the Vestare and
their calm ministrations told him that Elu-Kaan was merely at healing rest.

He pulled his neck away from the ground and stood. There was no time
to be lost and there was no time to rest and heal his own wounds. He had
been right. Again, Balaians, trying to protect themselves, had set in train an
event over which they no longer had any proper control. This time he could
not talk just to Hirad Coldheart. This time, the entirety of The Raven had to
hear him. Without another backward glance, he walked to his corridor and
sought to travel interdimensional space, Hirad Coldheart's signature as his
guiding beacon.

Chapter 20

B arras knocked quietly, hoping to find the General asleep but the order to come in was rasped out immediately. The old elf negotiator entered Kard's rooms in the base of the Tower, to find the General sitting by a small fire, his chair pulled over to an open window. A steaming mug rested on the sill and Julatsa's senior soldier was gazing out at the star-lit sky. Night was a release, if only because the Shroud was all but invisible in the dark and somehow less menacing, though its aura sent shudders down the spines of any within its influence. By the master sand-timers, it was about two hours before dawn.

There was nothing more any of them could do but wait until the first order came through and then the day would bring what it would bring. Throughout the College, an uneasy quiet held sway. There was not a man, woman or child that did not know their role. In dozens of meetings, all of which took place beyond the gaze of the guards in the Wesmen's tower, Kard and his lieutenants had outlined their plans in great detail.

In addition to the fighting groups and mage defence and offence, Kard had organised every member of the civilian population into a group to tackle a specific task. From provisioning soldiers on the walls with everything from arrows to bread, through carpentry and stonemasonry teams to plug and strengthen defences, to medical, stretcher, and fire teams, everyone was assigned the task most suited to their abilities.

In separate meetings, Kerela had briefed all her mages to obey Kard until the battle was either won or lost. In that latter event, all knew what would happen and those who could not directly help in burying the Heart were expected to die defending those who could. And finally, with the College sleeping its last before battle was joined, Endorr and Seldane had, at Barras' behest, moved hundreds of the College's most critical texts into or just out-side of the Heart. Now, when the Shroud was dispersed, the Heart would look more akin to a storeroom than the very centre of Julatsan magic.

Barras glanced around Kard's sparse accommodation. A single bunk lay unused against the right-hand wall. Charts, parchments and quills littered a desk beneath the other, still closed, window and the desk chair was heaped with books and diaries. These, Kard moved when he saw it was his old friend that had entered.

"Sit down, Barras, you need your rest," he said, a half smile playing over his cracked lips; his chin, newly shaved, glistening with the sweat of the fire in the warmth of the room. He removed a pot from a hook just inside the grate and filled a mug for Barras, which the elf took in both hands, nodding his thanks.

"Are you sure this is right?" asked Kard, pointing his chin in the direction of the Shroud. "Going back to battle, I mean."

"What other way is there?"

"Well, we could restrain the people and exist within these walls for . . ." He paused and dragged a sheet of paper from the desk, shaking off those that sat atop it. A couple fluttered to the floor where he left them. ". . . one hundred and seventeen days. If we ration hard and deal with our cess sensibly."

"And at the end of that time?"

Kard smiled again and shrugged his shoulders. "Well, the world will have done a lot of turning. Perhaps we could be liberated."

"And Senedai will have run out of prisoners to slaughter and the mounds of disease-ridden corpses will be higher than the walls. What's all this about?" Barras frowned and sipped at his drink. It was a herbal leaf tea with a hint of peppermint and was most agreeable.

Kard's smile faded and he shook his head, a finger on his lips.

"Oh, nothing. I was just hoping you were coming here with another solution, I suppose, one that wouldn't lead to so many of those people out there getting killed tomorrow and the next day and the next day after that."

"I didn't think doubt ever entered your head, Kard."

"It doesn't, as you well know, but, well I don't know, I hoped for so much when the Shroud went up."

"Do you wish we'd never raised it?" asked Barras.

"No, no. Actually, last night, or was it the night before?" Kard looked out over the courtyard. "Anyway, the other night, I lay there and wondered about the outcome had you not raised the Shroud."

"And?" Barras raised his eyebrows.

"You know as well as I do. The Wesmen would have been over these walls in no time. We had no mage strength, our army was routed and everyone was terrified. This way, we are rested, our morale is higher but we are still as scared, I think. At least we'll give them a bloody nose."

Barras said nothing, drinking his tea and watching the thoughts play over Kard's face, seeing the ghosts of smiles, frowns and tears. He was sorry to have interrupted the General's reverie. The old soldier was replaying his life, knowing he had little of it left. The doubts he expressed were just those of any hard-thinking man who had the sense to search for a better way out until time was up and he had to concede there wasn't one. He decided to take his leave quickly but he had come here for a reason.

"What are you doing here, anyway?" said Kard realising the same thing.

"We've been talking in the Council Room. We're going to start the Summoning now. It could be sometime before Heila reveals himself and then we have to negotiate the removal of the Shroud. It'll be difficult to guarantee it will be gone exactly an hour before dawn but it shouldn't be any later. You need to have at least the tower attack mages ready fairly soon."

"And I'll wake my soldiers too. Couldn't you have mentioned this earlier?"

"We needed to study some texts to be sure. We'll be starting presently." Barras got up to leave, placing his empty mug on the desk where it left a ring on an organisation chart. "Sorry."

Kard shrugged very slightly. "No matter. I think they've outlived their usefulness now." He shook hands with Barras, his grip strong and confident. "Good luck."

Barras nodded. "I'll see you upstairs later this morning. May the Gods be with you."

"If they aren't, we'll be with them soon enough."

"That's a grim thought." Barras smiled.

"But a realistic one."

Barras walked away to the Heart of the Tower of Julatsa.

The Raven had stopped to rest in the lee of a small incline, sheltered from the prevailing wind. Above them, bracken and bush rustled further up the slope while, to either side, the land stretched away, full of stream, bog, marsh and scrub.

They had walked well into the evening, stopping only when Denser indicated that Erienne needed the rest. The Dordovan mage herself had said nothing but the lines on her face had deepened with the late afternoon gloom and, though outwardly irritated by the attention, was soon asleep, a reassured smile on her face.

Will and Thraun had left the camp once the stove was lit and returned a long while later, Will tight-lipped, Thraun padding to a quiet spot away from his companions before lying down, a brooding look across his lupine features.

First Denser and then The Unknown had taken watches and now, with the stars straining to touch the land with their radiance, Hirad sat awake, his back against the rise, gazing across his sleeping friends and back along their path of the previous day.

While the pace had been quick, it was still just a walk and Hirad fretted on the lack of any chance to secure even a pair of horses to carry baggage and give them a break in turn from the long foot slog. But far more pressing on Hirad, despite the time constraints he knew they faced, was how they might penetrate first the Wesmen army, whose number was not known but certainly high, and following that, the DemonShroud.

He had little understanding of what Ilkar talked about but it seemed to him that they could not break the thing, whatever it was. He found himself looking forward to Sha-Kaan's next contact, hoping the mighty dragon had found a way for them to get through.

Hirad yawned, letting his jaws stretch. He shook his head and glanced around the sky. It was a couple of hours until dawn, maybe a little more. The night was mild without the breeze to chill the skin and the gentle warmth of the stove blanketed the camp.

He levered himself to his feet and refilled his mug from the pot on the stove, adding more water and grounds from the skin and sack nearby. The supply of coffee was dwindling quickly and Hirad wrinkled his nose in distaste as he imagined a return to the leaf teas he knew Ilkar would make when the coffee sack was empty.

He made to sit back down but a growl had him spin on his heel. Coffee splashed over his gloved hand. Thraun was crouched, staring at him, his yellow eyes cold and malign. Hirad met the stare, forcing a smile on to his face.

"Hey, Thraun, it's me, remember?"

Thraun growled on, hackles rising. He shifted back, resting on the raw power of his hind quarters. Nearest to him, Will stirred and woke.

"What's up?" he asked blearily.

"I don't know," said Hirad. "He—"

With a half bark, the wolf sprang away into the darkness. And then the pain gripped Hirad. Brief and intense, it swamped his senses and brought him to his knees, contents of his mug draining into the dirt in front of him.

"Hirad Coldheart, hear me." Hirad didn't know why but the voice of Sha-Kaan was close this time. And it had a different quality. Not as strong and commanding. Pained.

"I hear you, Sha-Kaan."

"I must open the portal. The Raven must hear me. Are you in a place of safety? Your rhythms and signature tell me you are at rest."

"Yes, Great Kaan."

"Excellent. It will be done." And the pain was gone.

A few paces directly in front of Hirad as he remained on his knees, and a short way down the shallow incline, a line of flickering light traced a rectangle from the ground up to a height of ten feet, across seven and back down. Inside the rectangle, all was black but to either side and above, the landscape stayed in view.

Hirad climbed to his feet, glancing around. Will was staring wide-eyed at the light, with the remainder of The Raven all stirring, sleep interrupted by an unknown quantity that bled unease over their resting minds.

"Don't be scared, Will, it's Sha-Kaan."

"It's all right. I'm all right." Will's voice had a quaver. "How is it Sha-Kaan?"

"Hard to explain right now but he's travelled from his dimension to ours to talk. Wake the others." Hirad's eyes returned to the light. Inside its frame, the dark sparkled gold like a sudden snowstorm, and then slid left, revealing a brazier-lit passageway that led to a small bare chamber Hirad had seen before.

"What is that?" asked Will. Hirad turned to him, smiling.

"The path to the Great Kaan," he said.

Sha-Kaan's voice whispered across his mind.

"Well done, Hirad Coldheart, your signature is strong. Come, bring your companions."

Hirad wasn't quite sure what he was experiencing but it was something akin to euphoria. His head felt light, his limbs empowered, his heart thumping its joy. He quashed the worry that immediately surfaced. Sha-Kaan was here.

"Here again, are we?" said Ilkar's voice at his shoulder. It held no surprise but more than a little weariness.

"But this time the meeting will be easier and happier," said Hirad.

"Well, nothing will be stolen, I'm sure," said Ilkar. The Raven were not long in waking. The Unknown came to Hirad's other shoulder, silent, face drawn, eyes flat.

"Just like old times, eh Unknown?" Hirad smiled.

"No, Hirad, not really." He led the way inside. Hirad paused, watching Denser and Erienne walk around the back of the portal.

"Fascinating," said the Dark Mage. "I can see you from the other side but I can't put my hand through to wave at you. It's as if it only really exists as you see it." He rejoined Hirad. "Will you try something?"

Hirad shrugged and nodded. "If I must."

"Walk around like I've just done. I'll stand here."

Hirad raised his eyebrows and began walking, stopping after only a couple of paces.

"Hold on," he said. "That's not right." The opening had followed him, he was still in front of it.

"Yes it is," said Ilkar. "We're behind it again, if behind is the right word."

"You're Dragonene now," said Erienne. "That portal only exists because of you and your link to Sha-Kaan."

"Oh, I see," said Hirad. He hadn't a clue what Erienne was talking about.

"Any chance of the rest of you coming in?" The Unknown's face appeared at the portal. "Come on." He turned back inside.

"Will, what about Thraun. Will he come?" asked Hirad.

"I'm only just convinced of going in myself," said the wiry little man, black hair shot through with grey, the legacy of a terror that still plagued his nightmares. "But I guess he'll follow if he's still keen to protect me. I think your dragon's presence scares him."

"He's not alone," said Erienne.

"Come on, Raven, let's meet the Great Kaan," said Hirad, adding, "Swords sheathed."

It was like walking back inside a memory. Hirad could recall with complete clarity his blind pursuit of Denser the first time they had been inside Sha-Kaan's melde-corridor. That time, he hadn't stopped to look around him. Now he did, albeit briefly.

The passageway was short and The Unknown waited at its far end, inside the small bare chamber. He hadn't opened the door. The Chamber itself had benches down either wall, a stone-flagged floor and dark green painted murals depicting fire and jungle.

Through the door was the first hall, the only part of which Hirad remembered was the fire that Sha-Kaan had blasted through the twin doors to the right. These had been replaced, any scorch marks removed and a log fire burned beneath the Dragonene crest that hung on the wall above the grate opposite him.

Hirad walked toward the crest, drawn by its symbolism, two claws beneath the open maw of a dragon breathing flame. A ghosting within the crest toyed with his eyes. He moved closer and what he saw swelled his heart. It was the crest of The Raven, blood-red background behind a silhouette of a raven's head and wing. It sat within the Dragonene symbol, proud yet subordinate. Hirad had no quarrel with the chain of command it implied.

"Well, well, well," said Ilkar, whose eyes had picked out the credit to The Raven very early. Hirad smiled.

"One in, all in," he said.

"Which way to Sha-Kaan?" asked Erienne. Hirad pointed right and led The Raven onward.

Through one of the twin doors which flanked a second fireplace they faced the crest-emblazoned, rune-carved doors that Hirad had seen destroyed what felt like a lifetime ago. But they were whole, the gold of the crest glinting in the light of the hall fire and the braziers hung around the small antechamber.

"Push it open," said Hirad and The Unknown did so, revealing the Dragon Hall, its tapestries, fires, heat and Sha-Kaan, lying flat at rest, neck stretched out toward them, tail coiled behind the vast bulk of his body. He spoke for them all to hear.

"Welcome, Hirad Coldheart, Dragonene. Welcome The Raven."

Sha-Kaan was immense. It was a fact Hirad had never truly allowed his conscious mind to accept, not since their first meeting, and it was clear to him why. His size alone was terrifying but to accept that something getting on for one hundred and twenty feet long also had mental powers and knowledge far ahead of his own was a step closer to madness. And that in addition to the physical power and strength that oozed from every pore.

But looking at Sha-Kaan for the first time as a Dragonene, the mists were parted for him. Now he could see past the bulk into the mind within. He could feel the thoughts and fears. And he knew the Great Kaan was hurt.

Hirad led The Raven forward across the tiled floor toward the damp mud and earth on which Sha-Kaan rested. Ten fires burned in grates on three sides of the dragon and the hall was full of heat and condensation. They fanned out in a natural defensive formation, The Unknown at Hirad's right shoulder, Will at his left, the mages in a line behind, Denser, Ilkar and Erienne left to right. Of Thraun, there was no sign. As they closed, Hirad could see the fire damage marks on the dragon's neck.

"Tell me what to do, Sha-Kaan," he said.

"There will be time for that later, or no time for any of us at all," said the dragon. "There is great trouble in Julatsa. Your mages there have unleashed a power they are unable to contain, though I fear they do not know it."

"May I speak?" asked Ilkar. Sha-Kaan raised his head a few feet from the ground. His old eyes blinked slowly.

"An elf of Julatsa," he said. "I would be most interested in what you have to say but be brief. Time is short."

"Thank you," said Ilkar. He stepped forward to stand by Hirad, Will giving way with some relief.

"The powers you are talking about relate to an old and established spell called the DemonShroud. The Council of Julatsa are all expert in its casting and in its dispersal. I can assure you that they have the wit to shackle the powers of the demons. The Shroud by its very nature is a closed conjuration. The demons cannot step outside its bounds. It is impossible."

Sha-Kaan was silent for a moment, his heavy bone brows arrowing between his eyes. He breathed out, a hot, sour exhalation that caught in the throat and stung the eyes.

"And is this what your Council believe?"

"It is written in our Lore and the mana structure is sound, tested and completely reliable," replied Ilkar.

"But," said Sha-Kaan, and his voice tolled like a knell of death, "the fabric of your dimension is *not* sound. The forces of interdimensional space are at work in your skies and the Arakhe, demons, are a dimensional power. They have a hold, currently contained, which the Shroud gives them. And in the moment of dispersal, as you call it, there is the potential to make that hold permanent. If that should happen, the demons could threaten your survival and our melde."

"No," said Ilkar, frowning and shaking his head. "The mana construct is wholly controlled by Julatsa. The demons name the catalyst but beyond that are forced to operate the Shroud as an extension of their dimension within Balaia constrained by our magic."

Sha-Kaan's eyes flashed and Hirad felt the brief surge of anger.

"Ilkar, I don't think—" he began.

"I'm just explaining what I know," said Ilkar.

"Then you know very little!" Sha-Kaan's voice whistled around the hall, booming from the tapestry-clad walls. "The DemonShroud gives the Arakhe access through your dimension and so the column projects from their dimension on a course through interdimensional space until it strikes another it cannot yet pierce—Skies know where that is. It is not contained within Balaia and the weakening of your fabric is feeding them more power than you can imagine because the essence of your dimension is flowing into interdimensional space where they can drink their fill. They have the strength to overpower your Council."

"Trust him, on this," said Hirad, feeling Sha-Kaan's short patience wearing thin. "I've no idea what he's talking about but I'm sure he's right." Ilkar nodded but Denser spoke up.

"One question, Sha-Kaan, if I may?"

Sha-Kaan's head moved smartly to spear Denser with his cold blue eyes.

"Ah," he said, and Hirad could taste his disdain. "The one who stole from me. You should feel fortunate that I have not chosen to take your life in return. But as we say, when the Skies blacken with the wings of your enemies, you will chew even the rotten stalks to fuel your fire. Remember that and ask, thief."

Hirad glanced behind him at Denser who had gone quite pale. His eyes, though, didn't waver or flick downward.

"Dawnthief was our only hope of survival—"

"Do not test my temper, thief, your reasons are not important. That you stole was. Speak."

Hirad sighed. Denser took a deep breath.

"I would ask how you know so much, how—"

"How can I be so sure? Because one of my strongest young Kaan lies on the edge of death after encountering the Arakhe in a place where they should not have been. They overwhelmed him in his own melde-corridor. And before you ask, yes that should be impossible."

"What can be done, Great Kaan?" asked Hirad, fearing the answer.

"We have one chance and for that, I need your human strength and magic. And your souls."

"We're bait," muttered The Unknown.

Sha-Kaan favoured the Big Man's response with a chuckle, a dry rattling sound deep in his throat.

"Yes," he said. "But bait laced with poison."

The Raven looked at each other, a general shifting unease broke their stillness.

"I will explain what you must do." Hirad looked into the Great Kaan's eyes. He saw and felt no intent to harm, only a desire to survive and to win. He nodded his head and listened.

Thraun moved warily to the opening from which the scent of the animal flowed. He knew what he saw was wrong and the thought worried at his mind as he approached. He could see into the opening, saw the lights flickering there, but looking past it, could see nothing but the land. He growled but the growl became a whine of deep-seated fear. The opening led to man-packbrother; it also led to the animal whose power so scared the wolf. But it led to nowhere—it was not the forest, it was not the open space, it was not the water or the sky.

Thraun sniffed at the base of the opening, seeing the grass become stone and tasting the odours that came from within. There was wood and oil, there was man and elf, all of which comforted him. But lying deep over the scents he knew, were alien taints he could link to nothing. He picked up his head and looked inside, seeing the lights and the stone. The trail of man-packbrother, a trail tinged by fear but not terror, was clear as were those of the other men and the elf.

He glanced behind him, heart hammering in his chest, saw the places where they had rested, all empty, took one last fill of the lights in the sky and padded carefully into the opening.

Chapter 21

Hirad regarded the face of each of The Raven with great solemnity. Sha-Kaan's words still rolled around his head, the dual dangers of which they spoke difficult to comprehend. As usual, the Great Kaan had given them a choice while giving them no option whatsoever.

They could trust that the Julatsan Council had the power to snuff out the demon threat but if they hadn't, Balaia would be deluged by demons flooding every corner on a wave of pure mana. It was the air they breathed but would kill every man, woman and child it touched; its concentration would drive the air from lungs and, worse, leave souls at the mercy of the demons, the Arakhe as Sha-Kaan called them. Balaia would become an extension of their dimension and the Kaan would lose their melde and ultimately their lives.

Or, there was a way that might threaten the Arakhe enough to deflect them from their apparent goal. But the description of the task and the risks it posed to them all, dragon and Raven, simply took the breath away. The rewards, however, were great indeed. An end to the current demon threat and a way past the Wesmen army into the College of Julatsa.

And so, Hirad studied them all. For some, the answer was easy. Ilkar just nodded and The Unknown Warrior held Hirad's gaze as if to challenge the fact that he had to be asked at all. For himself, Hirad would do the Great Kaan's bidding so long as The Raven agreed. All of them.

Will was scared. Gods in the sky, they all were. But he had suffered already from the sight of a demon and the thought of facing an untold number took the colour from his face and brought a quiver to his limbs.

"We may not have to fight them," said Hirad.

"But we will have to see them," said Will.

"We'll protect you."

"Only Thraun can do that."

Hirad had forgotten about the wolf. Still presumably outside, he knew that the shapechanger had to be with them, or Will would not be. And The Raven never fought apart. Never.

"And if Thraun is here?"

"Then I will stand by you," said Will. Hirad nodded and turned to Erienne and Denser, standing close together.

"We can't do it without you," said Hirad. "Mainly because you're Raven but we need you to help Ilkar with the mana shield or whatever it is." He was addressing himself principally to Denser but it was Erienne who spoke.

"This is a tall order but we can do it. I don't think we really have a choice," she said. She placed a hand on her belly and anxiety clouded her face for a second.

"There is always a choice," muttered Denser.

"What, similar to the one you offered us with Dawnthief?" Hirad growled. "Your turn now."

"I didn't say I wouldn't go."

"But if you do, you have to *be* there," said Hirad. "All there, all the time."

Sha-Kaan, who had remained quiet throughout the exchange, brought his huge head forward on his long neck and spoke over Hirad's shoulder.

"He speaks correctly, thief. Your skill is undoubted but if you are anything less than attuned, you will be a hindrance and a risk to us all. What do you say?"

Denser bridled at Sha-Kaan's choice of words but Hirad's frown stayed him. Instead, he managed what passed for the briefest of smiles.

"I have nothing more pressing," he said.

Sha-Kaan looked at Hirad, neck in a "u" to face him, head and muzzle alone almost as tall as the barbarian.

"Well?" he asked.

Hirad grinned. "Take it as a yes, Great Kaan."

"Excellent." The head withdrew. "Strike your camp. We will not return here."

"What about Thraun?" asked Will.

"Thraun?" Sha-Kaan looked for clarification.

"The shapechanger," said Hirad. "The wolf."

"Ah." A pulse of forest images and blood filled Hirad's mind. "I have touched consciousness with him. He is here in the corridor somewhere. He will come. His bond with you, little human Will, is very strong. Like a dragon with his Dragonene."

The tension on Will's face broke and he nodded and looked round.

"Go and find him, Will," said Hirad. "The rest of us will clear the camp."

"Hurry," said Sha-Kaan. "The Council will act soon."

Hirad led The Raven from the chamber and back, briefly, into Balaia.

With General Kard again outside the Heart, and with Endorr's LightGlobe illuminating them, the Julatsan Council minus the sacrificed Deale stood in the Heart and prepared to talk again to Heila, the Shroud Master.

The small chamber, centre of Julatsan magic, was cluttered with Barras' selection of the College's most critical texts. They were stacked high in the spaces between the eight smoothed greystone segments and covered swathes of the stone flags that spiralled inward from the door to the Heart, hiding each councillor from those adjacent as they stood flush with the wall.

Kerela frowned at the obstacles spread all over this most hallowed of rooms, and Barras couldn't help but smile.

"We always said we should expand the Library," said the old elf negotiator.

"I'll have the plans drawn up as soon as we've seen off the Wesmen," said Torvis. A chuckle ran around the Heart, easing the tension.

Kerela held up her hands to restore quiet.

"Please, my friends," she said. "We are here to disperse the Demon-Shroud protecting us from the armies of the Wesmen. Its raising took Deale from us and his soul is still under thrall to Heila and will remain so for we know not how long after the Shroud is gone. He may never be released. For the soul of Deale, I beg of you a moment's contemplation."

Barras dropped his head forward on to his chest as did they all. Deale's had been the supreme sacrifice, his soul now at the mercy, though that was a complete misnomer, of the demons. It was a sacrifice Barras and Kerela felt keenly. Heila's preferred choice would have been either of them.

"Thank you," said Kerela. "And now we will summon Heila, Shroud Master."

With eight reduced to seven, the Council's task was that much more difficult. Kerela could spare only three to anchor the column and the sweat quickly covered the brows of Endorr, Torvis and Seldane as they struggled to maintain its integrity. Despite a single dangerous flare as the disc descended, they held firm, eventually settling to allow Barras to open the gateway.

As he edged it open, a surge of ice-blue mana light powered along the cylinder, all but dragging the lid from his mind's grasp.

"Something is wrong," he said, his voice straining as he concentrated on control.

"Are you stable?" asked Kerela.

"Barely," replied Barras.

"Can I continue the summoning?" Kerela's voice was urgent.

"You have no choice." Barras could dimly feel perspiration running down his back. The mana still surged up the cylinder to dissipate against the walls or feed into the Heart construct where it added to the power the Council could draw on.

To Barras, Kerela's words of summoning were a faraway murmur as he bent all of his age, experience and sheer bloody-mindedness to the task of maintaining the gateway. Somewhere, the demons were drawing on a power that fuelled huge pressure in the mana they were projecting through the small portal and into which, Kerela placed her head to conduct the Summoning.

He couldn't understand the behaviour. Disappointment that the Council were about to force the dispersal of the Shroud, perhaps. Just being difficult, certainly. But in the deep of his mind, Barras felt something more sinister. Its root hung just beyond his reach, just beyond his comprehension. It was there though, like a marker for a thought he couldn't quite grasp. They would have to be careful.

Abruptly, the battering at the portal ceased, the column disappeared and Heila was among them once more. He was larger this time, both in height and girth, his azure blue colouring so bright it partially obscured his features. He rotated slowly for a while, arms and legs crossed and back ramrod straight, taking in the scene inside the Heart.

"I had not thought to be here so soon," he said, his voice betraying his irritation.

"We were always honour-bound to limit our need for the Shroud as far as possible," replied Kerela calmly.

"Ah, we are here to discuss dispersal, not extension."

"You are surprised?" asked Kerela.

"At the discussion, no. At the timing, yes."

"It is not in your gift to choose the time of dispersal." Kerela's tone was tense.

"But circumstances change, do they not, High Mage?" Anxiety crackled in the air. Barras frowned. Nothing had actually changed, had it?

"Meaning?" Thank the Gods for the steadying influence of Kerela. If she felt nervous, she didn't show it.

"The dispersal of the DemonShroud is not currently in our best interests. To do so now would inconvenience us." Heila's expression never changed. His every utterance carried no emotion, no betrayal of his desire. Yet every word carried with it the power of his position. Few stood taller in the hierarchy understood to control the demon dimension—a dimension in no way as chaotic as popular myth depicted.

"Inconvenient?" Kerela laced the word with total contempt. "Might I remind you, Heila, that the dispersal of the Shroud is not contingent on the convenience or otherwise to you. It is conferred following a decision by the Julatsan Council. Your agreement is sought to ensure that none of your people are caught as the Shroud is capped. It is not something we have to do. It is a courtesy we observe in the hope that you will look mercifully on the souls of those caught in its embrace. The spell of dispersal is not something you can resist."

Heila smiled, revealing close ranks of needle-sharp teeth. "I am aware of the limitations placed upon us by the construct of your mana shape and it is most cunningly crafted. All I ask is for two more days for us to reap full benefit of the power it has temporarily given us. We too have enemies to fight. If you grant me these days, all the souls of those taken will go free." There was a sparkle in Heila's eyes above the brightness of his skin, or rather the chosen colour of the mana encasing him.

Barras heard Seldane gasp and there was hesitation in Kerela's voice as she spoke.

"Heila, your offer is both generous and tempting. Very tempting," she said. "And in any other circumstance, I would gratefully accept it. However, the lives of countless thousands of Julatsans hinge on the Shroud's immediate dispersal. With due sorrow and regret for the plight of Deale and all those taken, I cannot agree to this."

Heila's brows arrowed in and his face contorted in a rage that suffused his feelings in blue swirls of writhing mana. His breath clouded in a sudden cold that swept the Heart and his fists unclenched to reveal wisps of pure white essence that voiced human screams as they were snatched back through the portal.

"We will fight you, High Mage, and souls like these will, I promise you, suffer an eternity of torment far from the heavens in which they belong. They are lost as you will be. I name you, Kerela of Julatsa. You are mine."

"You cannot touch me, Heila," said Kerela, though the demon's words had clearly shaken her. "Prepare your underlings for the dispersal of the Shroud. Goodbye." Kerela terminated the link and Heila vanished without another word. Mana howled again along the column but Barras was both ready for it and equal to it. With a solid grunt, he sealed the portal.

There was quiet in the Heart for a moment. Barras wiped wispy grey strands of hair from his face and puffed out his cheeks. Torvis and Vilif exchanged frowns. Endorr spoke.

"What did he mean, 'we will fight you'?" asked the young mage.

"Presumably, they will resist our capping and dispersal," said Cordolan.

"No," said Kerela. "It will be worse than that. The demons seek souls and something is giving them the strength to challenge us now they have a foothold in Balaia. I think they may try and break the containment."

"What?" Seldane gaped, then her brow creased. "Can they do that?"

"Ordinarily, no," said Kerela. "But ordinarily, they wouldn't feel they had the power to threaten us in our own dimension. Now, they obviously think they can."

"So shouldn't we wait these two days? Let Heila complete whatever it is needs doing?" asked Endorr. There was a murmur of disagreement from Torvis, put into words by Vilif.

"No, young Master, I think you misunderstand who are the enemies to which Heila referred. In two days, I suspect the demons would be strong enough to sweep the containment aside. Heila was presumably upset because he can no longer be certain."

"Yes," agreed Barras. "And in two days, so many more will die in the Shroud. We cannot wait."

"But his offer—" said Endorr.

"A lie," said Kerela, her expression set and determined. "Come, my friends, the longer we delay, the greater our chances of failure. Join with me around the candle and remain strong. We cannot afford to weaken or the demons and not the Wesmen will take Julatsa. And then they will take Balaia."

The Raven gathered close to Sha-Kaan, the wood and oil odours of his hide mixing uncomfortably with the sourness of his breath and the heat from the fires. They were in a defensive formation, the dragon and the humans back to back, he taking three quadrants, they the fourth. Hirad stood flanked by The Unknown and Will, Thraun beside the little man. Behind them, Ilkar, Erienne and Denser, ready to prepare on Sha-Kaan's word.

They couldn't feel the movement of the corridor, though Sha-Kaan assured them they were approaching Julatsa and he was merely waiting for the right time to breach the Shroud. Indeed, the calm was unnerving and Hirad found it hard to credit that they had moved anywhere. It was his trust in Sha-Kaan that made him believe.

"You will know when we touch the DemonShroud," said Sha-Kaan. "The walls of this hall will shake and you will stumble. I will try and steer a steady path but I must strike at the heart of their power if we are to stop them and allow your mages to close the Shroud."

"How soon?" asked Hirad.

"Very. They have begun their preparation. Your casting should commence shortly."

"Before we start, remember what this spell actually is," said Ilkar. "We're constructing a Cold Room by creating a shell inside of which mana cannot flow. We will maintain it using thread streams of mana stamina from within us. The process will be very draining. The Cold Room will not stop the demons but it will hurt them to enter it and weaken them extremely quickly. The absence of mana flow around your weapons will allow you to damage them but kills won't be quick and you should be striking to keep them back.

"We'll colour the shield pale green. You'll be able to see through it but don't step outside of its bounds or your weapons will be useless and your soul will be lost."

Hirad and The Unknown nodded. Will turned to Thraun whose wolfen eyes bored into his face.

"Stay beside me always," he said. "Don't leave my side for a moment." He drew his dual short swords, unable to keep the quiver from his arms. Thraun looked up at him, a growl rumbling in his throat.

"Are you sure they'll attack us?" asked Will.

"There can be no doubt," said Sha-Kaan, his voice tone altered as he steered the corridor toward Julatsa, along the trails and markers given to him by the stricken Elu-Kaan. "Our presence will disrupt their energies, acting like a stopper in a bottle. Your souls will attract them like dragons to prey, deflecting their attention. Soul-taking Arakhe have little discipline when temptation is put in their way." He swung his long neck around and over their heads to face them. "One more thing. Expect the Arakhe from any-where. They are not bound by our laws. They could come from above you or from beneath your feet as well as straight at you. Their touch is like fire, their bite like ice and their eyes will try to prise the souls from you. Strike hard and strike often. Show them no fear."

He locked eyes with Hirad for a moment and the barbarian felt a flow of thanks tinged with anger. Sha-Kaan blamed their casting of Dawnthief for all that had come since and he wouldn't forgive quickly.

Hirad turned to the mages. "You ready?"

Ilkar nodded. "Just keep your sword sharp."

"I wonder what colour demon blood is."

"Well, now's a good time to find out," said Denser. "Find out a lot, will you?"

Hirad smiled. "As much as I can. Let's go Raven. Great Kaan, the casting will start on your word."

"Excellent. Begin at once." Sha-Kaan returned his head forward. A ripple ran through the corridor. Hirad adjusted, knees unlocked. He drew his sword. Behind him, the mages sat back to back. They couldn't afford a fall to break their concentration.

Ilkar found he wasn't scared of the union of the three magics. Indeed, since his first enforced link with Denser, to save Hirad back in Septern's long barn, the idea had fascinated him as he knew it did the Xeteskian.

With all three minds attuned to the mana spectrum, Ilkar watched as the streams of orange-, deep blue- and yellow-hued mana indicating Dordover, Xetesk and Julatsa respectively ran together over their heads. Each mage was encased in a sheath of colour while above them their magics mixed like the plaits of a rope, each strengthening the other two.

Then, with the stream coiling and thrusting, seeking outlet, the trio tipped their heads back so that their skulls touched and clasped hands left and right to complete the circle. Erienne, who had most knowledge of mana exclusion constructs, led the casting.

"One magic, one mage," she said.

"One magic, one mage," repeated Denser.

"Just get on with it," said Ilkar, feeling the warmth between Denser and Erienne through the mana flow which now encased them all in a single tri-coloured tulip.

"I'll speak the words but we must all reinforce the shape. Keep your colours for now and push out to form one side of an equilateral triangle. Bring the sides in and rotate." Erienne's voice was barely above a murmur.

Ilkar felt a tremor through the corridor but ignored it, concentrating on the slowly moving four-sided pyramid shape above their heads. Erienne let it settle before moving on.

"Divide and angle out your sides. Allow the apex to break." A six-sided shape formed from the pyramid. "Mirror and double, base to base."

It was a fairly simple construct and now, almost formed, the two pyramids flush and rotating in opposite directions, Ilkar could see where the shape was going and where the difficulty lay. Erienne confirmed his view.

"All right; we need a spike at either end, each one rotating opposite to the pyramid beneath, each six-sided with consecutive panels of each College mana to bind it securely and to produce the shape to force mana around the outside of the whole. The pyramids must continue rotating during spike construct." She fell silent and the air around Ilkar hummed with effort.

It was a trick of the mind, the ability to maintain and construct simultaneously. Partitioning was a skill taught early but learned long. Ilkar had no doubt they'd all mastered it but this was different. If the pyramids stopped rotating, the spell would backfire with consequences Ilkar guessed would be severe. Perhaps memory loss, perhaps blindness. Maybe death.

Denser's panels appeared almost immediately, rotating opposite each other, apexes touching.

"I am secure," he said and Ilkar wondered briefly what Dawnthief had actually done to him. It should have been impossible to produce the panels that fast. But it had its benefits and gave Ilkar a target for his own panels.

Imagining a gentle breeze, he set the thought aside, knowing it would sustain the pyramids' rotation for a short while.

Despite the two-way pull on his mana flow, Ilkar, using subtle movement of his still-clasped hands, dragged mana with mind and intonation, matching Denser's triangular panel sizes. He forged them deep yellow and robust, snapping them into place instants after Erienne's. Now the pyramids held counter-rotating spikes at either end and the spell could be completed.

"Outstanding," said Erienne, though there was little surprise in her voice. She knew the extent of their abilities. "The two halves must mirror exactly in shape and rotation speed. Flatten and spread the pyramids . . . yes. Widen the bases of the spikes. Hold it. We're ready to deploy."

"I'm stable," said Denser.

"Me also," said Ilkar. Above them, the mana shape hung and spun like two large, spiked, domed helmets.

"Dor anwar enuith," said Erienne, the words of Dordovan lore sparking through the shape, mixing threads of pale orange through the yellow and blue. "Eart jen hoth." She unclasped her hands from Ilkar and Denser and held them, arms stretched, above her head. "Deploy." She brought them down, her palms slapping on the stone floor. The mana shape expanded as if a burst of air had been fired into it at enormous pressure. One half covered The Raven and Sha-Kaan, the other was beneath them, intended to slow the advance of any demons who attacked from below.

"Lys falette," said Ilkar quietly and a green washed through the shape, pale and translucent. The trio of mages allowed their heads to drop. The casting was complete. Raven and dragon breathed air untainted by mana. It tasted and felt no different but to the mages, the Cold Room was an instant drain. They could not hold it for long.

Hirad didn't have to open his mouth to advise Sha-Kaan the spell was done. A savage jolt shook the corridor, ruffling the tapestries which hung from the walls and sending sparks from the fires as log and coal shifted. Hirad wobbled and Will sprawled, tripping against Thraun's broad flank. The wolf howled in fear, unable to see the threat but knowing it was there.

"Steady, Raven," said The Unknown who had not even had to adjust his footing. He tapped his sword's point on the stone, its gentle clashing bringing clarity to mind and banishing uncertainty.

A second jolt, followed by a long rumbling through the stone of the corridor, shook dust into the air.

"Prepare yourselves," said Sha-Kaan.

Hirad and The Unknown exchanged glances. Inside the Big Man's eyes was an unease Hirad had never seen before, but with it a determination strong enough to wipe away doubt, and Hirad knew exactly why. The Unknown was a man who already knew what it was to lose his soul to the demons. That time, he had been given it back and he had no desire to lose it again.

With their souls a clarion call for any demon, The Raven plunged into the DemonShroud.

CHAPTER 22

The Julatsan Council ringed the mana candle in the centre of the Heart, arms in crucifix form, as the roar of demon mana tore around them, whipping away the holding patterns they struggled to make and forcing them to expend energy merely keeping the door to the demon dimension closed.

The casting to cap and disperse the DemonShroud had begun calmly enough and the shape that would close the Shroud and dissipate its energy back into the demon dimension, which could be likened to a crown, had been quickly made and deployed. But exactly at the moment when that shape had connected with the Shroud, the demons had attacked, sending blasts of pure mana energy through the Shroud's periphery.

As he clung desperately to his concentration and the tatters of the crown, Barras thanked the Gods that the Council mages were so exceptional in their mastery of magic. A lesser set would have lost hold completely and been blown away, their minds wrecked by the power the demons threw at them. As it was, both Endorr and Cordolan had momentarily slipped, relying on the remainder of the Council to cling on with their minds to the crown until they could refocus.

And with his thanks went a fear that, no matter how powerful they were, the Council would not be able to keep their hold for long and it was already too late to go back. The mana construct bordering the Shroud was maintained throughout its life by the demons and it was for this service that they demanded a critical soul. On dispersal, that control was taken from the demons and brought once again into the domain of Julatsa.

It was an enormous drain on mana stamina but, crucially, also meant a change to the nature of the construct. It was at this point that, theoretically at least, demons could force their way through the protection afforded by the construct and flood Balaia with mana enough to choke the life from every living thing. Mages had always known of the possibility but never had the demons had an independent source of power large enough to make that potential a reality. Until now.

But what really worried Barras was that the demons knew exactly when to strike and that meant they had an understanding of Julatsan lore and mana construction far in excess of anything he had dreamed of. It potentially also meant that they could read the trails and, if that was the case, they could counteract anything the Council wanted to do almost before it was tried.

And that left them hanging on to the crown, alternately attempting to close it onto the Shroud or clawing its shape back to prevent the demons tearing it to shreds as they clearly intended to do. Barras shuddered. The crown was the weak point of the construct but its destruction would leave the Shroud construct both changed and vulnerable. To lose the crown was unthinkable. The demons would be free.

"Kerela, we must reform the shape. The crown is losing outline. We can't close it down like this." Barras knew his voice was low but that every member of the Council could hear it through the screams of mana battering at their inner minds.

"We must regain cohesion first. The link to the Shroud is not fast," said Kerela, her voice calm and authoritative. "Endorr, we need a shield against the demon mana."

"Yes, High Mage." The strain in the young mage's tone mirrored that on his consciousness.

"Leave the crown to the rest of us. We can hold it while you cast," said Kerela.

"Withdrawing," said Endorr. Even as his mind cut away from the crown, those of Vilif and Seldane closed to take up the slack in the shape, keeping it together. Barras closed his eyes and let his mind drift carefully toward Endorr, feeling his pull on the mana as he created the shield, modifying its normal shape, used to repel offensive spells, to one that would act as a buffer to a stream of pure mana. He smiled. Endorr was quite brilliant, melding the spell shield with a ManaMask designed to block attacks on the mind.

As quickly as it had come, Barras' smile disappeared. Endorr's mana shape was ragged, the two spells linking imprecisely allowing one to flow indiscriminately into the other causing instability. Yet Endorr seemed not to have sensed it as he poured more and more force into it, its boundaries beginning to pulse as he drove toward deployment. But there, right in the midst of the rough-cut dodecahedron, a miasma of colours. Yellow conflicting with a vivid purple and a dark swirling grey that told of a potentially catastrophic weakness.

"Endorr, you aren't stable. Check your lore. Don't cast. You have time." Barras' urgent words affected concentration all around the candle. Wisps of the crown tore away as the Council were deflected by the sight of Endorr's flawed mana shape. But the young mage didn't hear him. Outside the circle of the crown's casting, he was lost in his own concentration, his lips moving soundlessly and his hands flickering as they sought to hold the shape together. Only he couldn't see the trauma at its centre. Why, Barras didn't know, but the darkness consumed the core of the twin spell linkage and casting could result in only one thing.

"Endorr!" shouted Kerela, her grip on the crown not slipping even as her conscious mind dominated in the attempt to disturb the youngster. Endorr continued to intone quietly and a ripple of anxiety ran through the remainder of the Council, reflected in the crown. Kerela called for concentration and the vital shape steadied though all eyes stayed on Endorr.

None of them could move. To do so would render the crown unsustainable—five could not hope to maintain it against the storm from the demon dimension. Endorr built toward casting, the dodecahedron pulsating bright yellow, shot through with bronze and white, but at its centre, the grey. Barras could feel the tension carving through the circle.

"Brace yourselves. If he backfires, we'll need to be strong," warned Kerela.

Why could Endorr not see his error? Barras fought to find a way through, something that he could communicate but he knew there was nothing. And he knew that to let go his mind any longer would leave the crown at even greater risk.

Endorr opened his eyes, spoke the command word and only then saw the cancer in his construct that his mind should have picked up. His face filled red as the shape blossomed outward then collapsed back on itself, simultaneously consumed by the ravaging grey within.

A shrill squeal escaped his tight-closed mouth, blood ran from his nose and ears and his whole body shook, hands scrabbling at the air, furious in their attempts to control the contracting spell.

With a flash in the mana spectrum that blanked thought for an instant, the construct imploded. Endorr's head snapped back savagely, his limbs tensed then he crumpled, unmoving to the floor of the Heart.

The glare cleared as soon as it had come and the crown was rocking. A renewed blast of mana howled through the edges of the Shroud, ripping away the linkage in a dozen places.

"Lock it down," said Kerela. "Lock it down." The remaining six of the Council fought for purchase, grappling the failing cap into some semblance of order.

"What now?" asked Seldane, her voice full of fear.

"We wait and we think. We concentrate and we become strong," said Kerela.

"Wait for what?"

"I don't know, Seldane," she said and for the first time, Barras saw the possibility of defeat in her eyes. "I don't know."

The corridor rattled as it cut across the outer border of the DemonShroud. Instantly, the green outline of the Cold Room was covered with the writing blue shapes of demons. Without the spell, the Raven's souls would already be gone but the howls of frustration and pain from a hundred sharp-toothed mouths told their own story. And for a moment, none ventured further.

"Don't wait for them. Strike at their bodies as they press against your spell. Make them fear you. Make them slow," said Sha-Kaan and as if to demonstrate, his jaws, leaking fire, snapped forward, joined by his front limbs and a thrash of his tail before the latter coiled again protectively around the mages.

The Unknown's sword point ceased its tapping.

"Raven," he growled. "Raven with me!" He swept up his blade and crashed it in an upward arc into the armourless bodies of the demons in its path. Screeches of anger were followed by the snaking out of arms and legs, claws flashing, skittering across the metal as it flashed past them. Hirad looked briefly to the right, seeing Will launch a ferocious attack, his twin short swords weaving a complex lattice in front of him. Thraun howled and joined the onslaught.

Hirad's attention switched to his own situation. The Raven's blades had maddened the demons and he could see them swarming over the surface of the Cold Room, looking for the place of easy strike. Again and again, a demon would press through into the mana-less space, only to recoil, blue colour dulled, pain evident in the cry of anguish and the contortion of the face.

But more were joining them and the desire to be the first to taste the flesh and the souls would overcome the damage caused by a flight in mana-free air. Hirad looked up. More were crowding over their heads, clamouring for blood, clamouring for life essence.

"There are so many of them. Can we beat them?" asked Hirad.

"Our role is not to beat them," said Sha-Kaan, a trimmed gout of fire withering the arm of a demon who pushed in too far. The creature disappeared. "The more we can attract, the less pressure on the Julatsan Council. We must keep them occupied. It might give the mages the opportunity to close the Shroud."

"And if not?"

"Then we were all dead anyway." Sha-Kaan turned his head and stared briefly at his Dragonene. Hirad felt the confidence flow through his body. "Fight, Hirad Coldheart. Fight Raven. Like you have never fought before."

The first of the demons braved the torture of the Cold Room and the battle for survival began.

The battering at their minds grew more persistent, like a gale turning to a hurricane, tearing at the strands that held the crown together, ripping mana stamina from their bodies and striking at their concentration. But with it came the voices and the laughter. As the demons gained strength and confidence, as the mana they hurled in great waves at the Julatsan Council sapped the will of their enemies, so they moved closer, all but daring to breach the Balaian dimension.

It was a whispering at first from which Barras could glean nothing coherent. Then slowly the volume increased and coalesced into a single voice supported by many others and carrying with it the scorn of millions. And it promised misery. An eternity of suffering for him and all he held dear to his heart. It assured him of pain, of agony and of unending sorrow. It promised him hell.

Though only if he clung on to his futile spell.

If he were to let it go, if he would allow the demons to finish their work, he would be spared. They would all be spared. Yes, a few might die out in the streets but was that such a large price to pay for the saving of the Council who were the very core of Julatsan magic? Was it so unthinkable that, after a life's selfless sacrifice he should consider himself for once? And in this case, the price in human lives now would be far outweighed by the benefit to future generations. Let it go. All he had to do was let it go.

Barras opened his eyes with a start, his heart hammering. All around the circle, the Council's eyes were closed. Cordolan even had a smile on his face. And above them, the shape of the crown slowly unwound itself. From its head, the deftly spinning diamonds flattened, dropped and disappeared. From its hub, the solidity of the lattice framework snapped and in its rim, the linkage to the Shroud frayed and was chopped away on the blizzard of demon mana.

"No!" shouted the elf negotiator and the crown teetered, its hold against the demons now held only through the mages' innate sense and subconscious minds. But that too was fading, his word serving only to damage what little concentration was left inside the minds of his friends.

"Kerela, awake," he said sharply, knowing the use of the High Mage's name would stir her but might also pull her from the circle. It was a risk he had to take and he grasped at the section of the crown Kerela controlled as the elder returned to her senses, mouthing words of agreement and acceptance that changed to curses and threats. The sweat poured from Barras as his mind clung to a larger section of the construct than he could properly control.

And then Kerela was with him, pushing him gently aside as she reasserted herself. Not even pausing to reflect, she said:

"Now the others. Occupy their hold before you speak to them. And be gentle."

Like drawing children from a deep, dream-filled slumber, Barras and Kerela caressed the minds of the hypnotised Council to a bemused, then desperate wakefulness. They could hear the demons, their voices inviting denial of reality and of a surrender to hell, first persuasive and then with agitation and finally in fury as the Council was, temporarily at least, lost to them.

Vilif was the last to return the full force of his mind to the struggle to maintain the crown. He looked terribly tired and every one of his seventy-plus years weighed on him. The upright stoop was gone, replaced by a hunched, hooded-eyed dejection. His bald head was a sickly white and his limbs were shaking. He was close to the edge.

"Vilif, we will prevail," said Barras. "Trust in the strength of us all. Keep the Heart beating."

Vilif nodded and a little light returned to his eyes. But all around the circle, the attitude of the Council members spoke more eloquently than any words. They had been mere moments from disaster before Barras awoke and they all knew it. Without help from the outside, without something to halt the demons' unbridled power, they would be lost. It was only a matter of time.

Shrieks filled the air and demons came from all sides. The attack gained and gained in intensity. Hirad had no time to see how his friends fared. He had trouble enough of his own.

From above, left and straight on they came at him, needle teeth bared behind lipless mouths, claws flashing bright in the green-hued firelight. Every face was racked with pain, every body dulled as it approached, like the burnish taken from a polished blade. Yet still they came and still they were strong.

He hefted his longsword in his right and a dagger in his left. They came at him in waves, chittering and laughing, shrieking and shouting, promising him death in eternity.

He laughed back and carved a staggered zigzag in the space in front of him while weaving the dagger above his head and the back of his neck. He felt the heavy blade slash home, heard the cry of torment and looked right to see a demon clutching at the stump of a leg. It bored its hideous eyes into him and flitted from existence.

Above him, the noise increased and he switched blades, carving out a circle above his head that drove the demons back. Behind him, five headed down for the mages. He made to lunge but The Unknown was there first, his two-handed blade scoring deep into blue hide, his movement too quick for their damaged bodies.

More poured through into the Cold Room, gasping at the lack of mana, moving to attack The Unknown's unprotected back and flank.

"Back up Raven!" roared Hirad. "Will, my left, Unknown's right, circle clockwise if at all and protect the mages."

Will broke off a stinging attack on a pair of demons that flitted about his head, backing up to stand half a pace from Hirad, the barbarian chasing off the demons who threatened The Unknown. The Big Man threw down his blade, which clashed on the stone floor at his feet, drawing a pair of long-bladed daggers from sheaths in either calf. He made up the third part of the Raven defensive triangle, hefting the daggers easily in his hands.

"Will, if it gets too heavy for you, we can turn you away. Just keep talking."

"Don't worry, I will."

Towering above them all, Sha-Kaan went about his destruction of demons with no sound but the fire snapping in short gouts from his mouth. Hirad could feel him in his mind, calm and controlled.

Above the humans, the demons attacked again.

Thraun buried his confusion in supporting man-packbrother as he struck again and again at the floating, hissing blue creatures who came from the green sky. His jaws snapped out, biting into tasteless bloodless flesh that oozed from between his jaws. He knew he caused them pain and he knew his claws damaged them but they didn't bleed and the fang punctures closed as soon as he withdrew to bite again.

He felt a fear greater than that caused by the great beast who, it seemed, was not against them, but whose power could destroy them so easily. The blue creatures were not birds yet they flew and were not men though they walked upright if they chose to. Their scent scared him. It was not of his earth. It was alien and it was bad, like death undying. The thought furrowed his wolven brow and he lashed a claw into the face of one who yelped and disappeared too quickly for his eye to follow though he tried, leaving himself open to the bite of another. It clamped its jaws onto his ear, a feeling like fire spreading through his head. He howled and shook his head, sending the creature flying to slap into a wall.

Terror threatened to swamp him and he backed up, tongue lolling, eyes seeing face after face coming for him. He whined, looked to man-packbrother who stood with the other men now.

And then the air went blue.

"They are come," intoned Sha-Kaan, confusing Hirad for just a moment. He looked at the walls of the Cold Room. The writhing bodies of the child-sized demons were gone, replaced by thousands of unblinking eyes, staring from faces the size of a child's doll. Dark brows speared in above those eyes and their deep blue features were cut harsh, skin stretched tight over square cheeks and jaws, eyes sunk into heavy sockets and mouths small and fangs set in stark black gums.

"Oh dear Gods," breathed Hirad.

"Don't let them face you down. Keep your souls safe," said Sha-Kaan.

"How in the hells do we do that?" snapped Will, his eyes flickering everywhere.

"Keep them from eye contact. When they have your mind, they can take your soul," said Sha-Kaan.

The demons attacked.

At once, the sky was full of squealing blue-winged and wingless doll-sized demons, crying their delight at the assault on new souls and their pain at the poisonous atmosphere. They filled the Cold Room in their hundreds and, for every ten who dropped to the floor spent, bodies unable to function, double that number came on. But they were weakened.

Following his friends, Hirad dropped his longsword in favour of a second dagger.

"Keep the strike rate up, Raven. Watch the mages."

His daggers fizzed through the air in a pattern designed for defence of upper body and head. The demons cluttered the air like birds and covered the floor in a mass of pumping limbs. One or two appeared through the stone but were too far gone to cause any real damage, serving only to disrupt the march of their brethren.

Hirad's blades cut and slashed through body after body, catapulting the light creatures through the air on the arc of every blow. His forearms blocked and smashed noses, claws and ribs, sending shrieking demons back to where they came from. And his feet stamped and kicked, crushing, dashing and shattering the enfeebled bodies which didn't die but which disappeared.

But on they forged, to scrabble at his leather, catch on to his flailing arms, nip at the top of his skull and tug at the soles of his boots. And where they touched his flesh, fire and ice struck pain throughout his body. He roared his anger and upped the pace of his movement.

Beside him, Will's breathing was too fast and the frightened grunts that accompanied every strike he made sent shivers up Hirad's spine. The barbarian spoke while jabbing and weaving with his daggers at the onrushing demons.

"Will, breathe deep. Focus on your targets, ignore the pain. They can't kill you if they can't reach your eyes."

"There's so many of them," gasped the little man.

"And every one you force away is one less." Hirad thrashed his left hand dagger through a line of four chittering demons, their yelps following them back to their own dimension.

Behind him, Sha-Kaan breathed tight fire through either nostril or from between his teeth, each jet searing a demon while his claws flashed in the fire-light and his tail kept up a whip defence above the unmoving mages, battering wave after wave of demons aside. His every movement was measured and every breath targeted to cause maximum damage with maximum efficiency.

Not so, Thraun. The wolf, plainly in distress at the alien bombardment, whimpered low in his throat, chasing his tail, his head flashing left and right, dragging his body round and round. His jaws clashed at air, his paws lashed out in any direction and all the time he kept an eye on Will, a frown deep in his furred brow.

The attack increased in intensity. More and more of the demons crowded into the space.

"Hold them off; we are winning the battle," said Sha-Kaan.

"Winning?" Hirad gasped as he struck out with feet and blades again. The demons were everywhere. They crawled on his legs, bit at his leather, swarmed near his head, clawing at his scalp. The Unknown, never given to exclamation, gasped as his bare arms suffered bite and scratch, Hirad imagining the fire and ice shooting through his limbs and seeing the blood that ran freely from them. And Will had all but stopped fighting. He was covered in pale blue, his arms over his head and, near him, Thraun howled and batted at the attackers of his friend while his hide was pierced again and again and his rear legs quivered under the weight of his foe.

Sha-Kaan lashed a broad swathe of fire to his right and away from The Raven, while his tail jabbed and swatted. But his great gold hide was covered with blue and his shaking body failed to dislodge the tenacious hellspawn.

"Keep going Raven, keep going!" yelled Hirad, his arms whistling around his head, the pain in his legs ignored, his daggers cutting and chopping the enemy from the air.

But now the press was from below too and demons placed hands on the defenceless mages. The Unknown shouted a warning and dived under the whipping tail of the dragon, pulling the squealing, chattering, laughing creatures from the trio whose chanting kept them still one pace from death. While the Cold Room still maintained its integrity, The Raven had a chance. But even with it, the fight was nearly over.

Will screamed. The demons were at his face.

"No!" shouted Hirad. "Get away from him you bastards!" He threw himself at the little man, bearing him to the ground, his daggers forgotten as he, like The Unknown, dragged demons from the body of a Raven man. Taking his lead, Thraun's jaws snapped in and out, crushing the small bodies in his powerful jaws.

"Sha-Kaan!" shouted Hirad over the tumult in the Cold Room. "We have to get out. Now!"

"A little longer," said the dragon, his voice choked and distant somehow. "We can win this. We have to."

But Hirad felt them at his neck and tearing at his clothes to reach the skin they could hurt and knew he was wrong. The Raven would soon be gone.

Endorr's body lay still on the floor of the Heart, crumpled into an untidy fetal position, hands clamped to his head, one knee up, the other leg splayed. A line of drool ran from his mouth and blood dripped occasionally from his nose. At least he was alive.

All this, Barras saw from a detachment of his conscious mind while the main thrust of his thought held sway in the increasingly futile fight to keep the crown from disintegrating.

The demons sensed victory and their taunts ripped at the armour of his willpower. The mana howled around him, flooding his mind with its stream, loosening his hold on the construct the Council had to maintain, and roaring in his ears behind the chiding laughter.

All around the circle, the strain was evident. Sweat, tears, frowns, grimaces and tense, over-tense, bodies created a living model of despair and imminent defeat. And on the ground, Endorr needed urgent help and there was nothing at all they could do for him. Gods, there was nothing they could do for themselves.

"How long?" gasped Seldane.

"As long as it takes," said Kerela but they all knew that was not the question she had asked.

Barras felt a tear of frustration squeeze from his eye. They were trapped. Endorr's shield had failed and they could not let go of the crown to cast a holding spell because the demons would not give them the time. Yet their hold could not last forever and, with the last of their mana stamina spent, the result would be the same as if they stopped right now.

And yet they couldn't surrender to the demons. Not while there was the remotest chance that something from somewhere would serve to aid them.

Barras bit back further tears, this time of regret. For so long, he had looked forward to a gentle old age, cosseted in the loving embrace of the College he had served all his life. Then the Wesmen had attacked and he had managed to come to terms with his death as an heroic event in the defence of that self same College.

But this? This ignominious, futile and pointless end in a closed room far from fresh air and sunshine—an end that gave hope to no one and torment to all—this end was not fitting for an elf of his bearing, nor indeed for any of the Council. What they were on the verge of accepting as inevitable was not acceptable in any way, shape or form.

He raised his head from his chest, his vision still tuned to the mana spectrum, and began to knit threads back into the crown.

"Barras?" Strain took the power from Torvis' voice.

"I will be *damned* if I let those unholy ingrates walk my College and my dimension and I will not amble meekly to my own demise." He punctuated every word with a stab from his mind that knitted more of the frail structure together, feeling the strength of desperation flooding his body.

"Great Gods in the ground, we aren't helpless," grated Kerela. "Any of you who feel you can, let's show these bastards who owns Balaia. If you can't, hang on and don't weaken." And she joined Barras, somehow reinforcing the structure and more, making it grow.

It was then that they noticed the change. So slight at first that it was all but imperceptible. But it grew by degrees; a drop in the intensity of the mana gale and a distraction in the voices of those who taunted and goaded. It would have been easy to claim the credit but Barras knew their renewed effort had nothing to do with it. Incredibly, the miracle was happening. Something, or someone, had diverted the demons.

"This is the only chance we'll get!" Kerela's voice, stoked with all its old authority, called the Council to action. "We've wasted enough of Kard's valuable time, now let's rid our city of this damned Shroud."

The crown, once so dim, blazed again.

Will's screams threatened the concentration of the Raven mages more than the flooding, swarming demons that ran over their bodies. Ignoring their own pain, Hirad and The Unknown snatched and crushed, kicked and stamped at the hideous dolls that crawled and flew to their most defenceless prey.

With one hand, The Unknown plucked at the demons who sought his eyes while the other swept away the mages' attackers, all the while crouched to avoid Sha-Kaan's blue-covered, flailing tail.

For Hirad, the task was harder. Will, his short swords long forgotten, rolled on the floor, hands scrabbling uselessly, keening wails flung out hoarsely with each breath. His body heaved and flowed with the weight of demons attacking him and Hirad felt a rising nausea as he watched their claws and feet striking home.

"Will, keep still!" he shouted, shaking his own head vigorously to dislodge a beast he felt on top of his skull. "Shit," he gasped, feeling the cold creep across his scalp and a trail of blood run down his forehead and between his eyes. The little man writhed on oblivious, the demons covering his face.

Hirad clamped a hand on one of Will's shoulders and pulled his face up, tearing the creatures off his friend, ignoring the marks they left and keeping Will's eyes from their dread stares. And all the while Thraun, bemused and terrified, looked on, occasionally reaching around with his mouth to pluck a demon from his hide, though they largely ignored him. His animal soul was buried deep.

Everywhere, spent creatures fell to vanish back whence they came only to be replaced by more, their laughter a sound of awful glee as they peeled and gashed and tore.

A claw gripped Hirad's cheek and hooked back, tearing the skin. He swore and snatched the demon from his face, crushing it in one hand. Will escaped his grasp and rolled away, rubbing hard at his sides and face.

"Steady Will." But the little man wasn't listening.

"Got to get out," he wailed. "Out . . ." He stood up and ran toward the edge of the Cold Room.

"No. Will, no!" Hirad launched himself at Will, striking his ankle as he ran. Will sprawled but rose again and Hirad could hear the demons goading him, telling him it was all right.

Belatedly spurred into action, Thraun barked and leapt after his companion, missing him by inches. Will reached the borders of the Cold Room and pushed a hand through. In that same moment, the demons and all their evil and malevolence disappeared. Ilkar, Erienne and Denser dropped their spell and the corridor was still once more.

In the quiet that followed, Hirad took in The Raven and Sha-Kaan. The Unknown Warrior sat with the relatively unscathed mages, his head a mass of oozing cuts, his arms swathed in a slick of blood. The Great Kaan rested on his belly, his scales outwardly sound but Hirad could feel his hurt and knew the demons had made him suffer for each one he had killed.

A piercing howl split the air. The Raven turned to see Thraun sitting by the prone form of Will, one paw resting on his chest, deep sorrow and blind fury clashing in his feral yellow eyes.

"Oh no," breathed Erienne.

Will was not moving.

CHAPTER 23

B arras imagined rather than heard the clang as the crown closed the DemonShroud but the wails of frustration and fury that diminished to nothing in a few heartbeats were real enough.

The Council had deployed the spell and with their release from its construction, came an intense relief and the briefest moment of euphoria. Vilif swayed and would have fallen but for the strong arms of Cordolan who was none too steady himself. Torvis, Seldane and Kerela all rushed to the crumpled but breathing form of Endorr while Barras kept the presence of mind to stumble across a line of books to the door to the Heart, pulling it open on to the pale, anxious face of Kard. A face that broke into a relieved smile on seeing him.

"Gods Barras . . . the sounds I was hearing."

"We're all right. Endorr's hurt. Bring the Communion mages, the Shroud is down."

Kard hesitated. "Endorr?"

"There's nothing you can do. See to the defence. Go. Go." Barras watched Kard go, then turned back into the Heart.

Kerela stood up and passed a hand over her forehead, her face grim. She caught Barras' eye.

"It isn't good. He's comatose." She patted Cordolan on the shoulder. "Take him to the healers, all of you. I'll wait for the Communion mages. Hurry." Cordolan, Torvis and Seldane picked up Endorr's limp body between them and carried him out of the door. Vilif, still unsteady, walked behind them. Outside, Barras heard Cordolan order assistance.

"Thank you, Barras," said Kerela.

"For what?"

"For showing us the way. All of us."

Barras shrugged. "It would have made no difference. If it hadn't—"

A square outline of light appeared near the door to the Heart. Kerela opened her mouth but Barras raised a hand to stop her speaking.

"It's all right, Kerela. I think you're going to learn something about me you never suspected." With a whisper, the outline became solid and a figure stood silhouetted against the torchlight behind. He walked quickly forward, followed by others, one, a huge man, carrying a body in his arms and trailed very closely by a large dog or . . .

"Great Gods—" began Barras.

"Barras, don't worry," said Ilkar. "The wolf is a shapechanger. He's with us."

He hadn't seen The Raven since their meeting at Triverne Lake before the casting of Dawnthief and assumed them trapped to the west of Understone Pass. But their bloodied appearance from what was, without a shadow of a doubt, a Dragonene portal threw him completely. None of them was Dragonene, he had known that when he met them, yet only a Dragonene could facilitate the opening of a portal and it was not Elu-Kaan who awaited him inside.

"How did you get here?"

"It's a long story," said Ilkar, ushering The Raven straight out of the Heart, the nonmages struggling with the weight of mana and the Xeteskian and Dordovan unwelcome inside of it. "But it'll have to wait. Two things first. We need immediate access to the Library and some urgent healing help for Will."

Light dawned for Barras. "You came through the Shroud?"

"Yes, but please, there isn't much time."

"Indeed not," said Kerela. "But there is always a moment to welcome back a favourite son." She kissed Ilkar on either cheek and squeezed his hands. "As you can see, some of the Library is here because the Wesmen are at our gates. We're soon to engage in a battle we can't hope to win but The Raven always help the odds. We have to clear the Heart now to start our Communion preparations. Come, we'll get your sick man to the infirmary and take a few minutes to talk in the Council chambers." She gestured for Ilkar to precede her, turning to look at Barras, her face not unkindly. "You could have trusted me."

"We can tell no one. It's not a question of trust."

"Later," said Kerela. Hirad Coldheart passed her, coming back into the Heart despite the discomfort caused by the mana.

"Sha-Kaan needs to speak to you," he said, addressing himself to Barras.

"*You?* Dragonene?" Barras frowned.

Hirad nodded. "Come on. Elu-Kaan is badly hurt. He needs your help." He led the way back into the melde-corridor.

General Kard walked quickly to the kitchens at the base of the Tower and ordered the Communion mages to stand by outside the Heart. Immediately afterward, he walked out a few steps into the silent courtyard, nodding his approval at the discipline of the Julatsans who had heeded the order to remain quiet after the Shroud was dispersed. He glanced up at the Wesmen's mobile watchtower, which was lit by torches all night long. He couldn't believe that the guards inside had not noticed the disappearance of the Shroud but, by their silence, he assumed they had not. On the other hand he had noted before that, in the dark, it was very hard to see the swirling grey of the Shroud and there was no doubting that people saw what they expected to see. But the feel of evil was gone and the Wesmen had so far missed that too. He only hoped that it stayed that way for another hour. By then, not only would the tower attack mages be fully prepared, their preparation for casting had already begun, but the rest of his preemptive strike force would be completely ready to enter the streets of Julatsa.

He stood for a moment, knowing that all around the walls his men were primed and ready, having seen and, more than that, felt the Shroud disperse. Behind closed doors, his army, such as it was, waited for the order to attack and were receiving their final briefings. Elsewhere, the mages who would fly point and those who would cover the run back inside the walls from the ramparts were resting and practising the shapes that would release death over the Wesmen.

A commotion behind him in the Tower had him turn, then take two paces backward in complete surprise. A huge warrior came striding toward him, bearing the body of another, much smaller, man in his arms. He was trailed very closely by what had to be a large wolf and, behind them, two of the Council hurried alongside soldiers carrying the limp body of Endorr. His jaw dropped and his hand strayed reflexively to the hilt of his sword.

"We're friends," said the warrior brusquely. "Now, which way to the infirmary? Quickly man, Will doesn't have much time." Kard found himself pointing vaguely across the courtyard to the left. The warrior nodded and ran in the indicated direction, the wolf at his heels. Just behind them, the soldiers carried Endorr. Cordolan stopped briefly.

"The Raven are here, Barras is a Dragonene, or so it seems and . . . well, go to the chambers, Kerela is talking to them, I think." He hurried after Endorr. Kard cast his gaze heavenward and ran back inside, pausing only to speak to a Lieutenant.

"You know the drill," he said. "The orders haven't changed, just that things have moved very slightly in our favour. If the alarm sounds before I get back outside, take the tower and start the attack. Do you understand?"

"Yes sir."

Kard made for the chambers.

Hirad joined the impromptu meeting between Kerela and The Raven's mages after acquainting Barras with Sha-Kaan. The Great Kaan was to return immediately to Wingspread, leaving the corridor open for Elu-Kaan to receive the aid he needed in the interdimensional streams under the watchful eye of Barras. He was introduced quickly to Kerela, Julatsa's senior mage, and

General Kard, the middle-aged soldier in charge of the College's military defence. The Unknown would stay with Will and Thraun.

"The Communion is even now under way inside the Heart." Kerela continued where she had paused as Hirad entered the room. "We have no idea who will hear us and how soon they can reach us. What we do know is, as the sky lightens, the likelihood increases that the Wesmen will see the Demon-Shroud is gone. Once the attack starts, we think we can hold out for two, maybe three days, but beyond that, the College will be lost."

"All right," said Ilkar, plainly finding the situation difficult to take on board despite the information he'd been receiving. "What odds do we have exactly?"

"I don't know exactly," said Kerela. "But a fighting level of between ten and fifteen to one is a good guess. Of course, we do have the walls and all the mages."

"It's bad," said Erienne gently. "But it's not our primary concern, is it, Ilkar?" After what seemed an eternity, Ilkar shook his head.

"Kerela, we have not come here to help in the salvation of Julatsa." He licked his upper lip before continuing. "There is a threat to Balaia far greater than the Wesmen and The Raven are charged with halting it before it consumes us all, the Wesmen included."

Kerela was quiet for a while. Denser maintained a considered silence, choosing to light his pipe and confine his reactions to noddings or shakings of his head. For once, Hirad was glad of his reticence.

"But Dawnthief. Didn't that guarantee us victory?" she asked, confusion dancing across her expression.

"Over the Wytch Lords, yes," said Erienne. "However, the casting has led to a tearing of the fabric of our dimension and it's a tear that is growing with every breath we draw. It links us to the dragons and eventually it will be too big for the Kaan to defend in their own space. Then we will have invasion by dragons."

Kerela's silence was longer this time. There was a curious symmetry with the dimensional damage they described and the sudden extraordinary strength of the demons' fight to stop them dispersing the Shroud. She examined the faces of The Raven, searching for the lies and treachery that she already knew she would not find, and for the truth she knew she would find but did not want to believe.

"What is it you're looking for?" she asked.

"Septern's texts," said Erienne almost before Kerela's words were out. "Anything that will help us close a dimensional portal. A big one."

Kerela nodded but spread her hands. "Of course, access is yours. I'm sure

Barras will confirm your words when he has finished with whatever he has to do. I suggest you begin in the Heart once our Communion is complete. Barras moved a number of key texts there and many of Septern's will be among them. But the Library contains better than a hundred of his works and associated researches. The duty mage will help you but it could be a long search."

"We have two days at most," said Ilkar, rising.

"Meantime," said Hirad. "If you'll allow, General Kard, you might benefit from talking to The Unknown Warrior and myself. If we're to fight for you, we need a say in how the defence is conducted."

Kard bridled. "I am well aware how to conduct a siege defence," he said.

"But we are The Raven," said Hirad. "And we've been in more sieges than you could ever dream of. From both sides. Please, I insist."

Kerela laid a hand on Kard's arm and nodded. "Anything that might help us, we should use."

Kard nodded. "Very well, though I doubt you'll change the structure I have made."

"So do I. But if we can improve upon one segment, it will be worth our while. The Unknown is in the infirmary."

Kard gestured at the door. "Come on. The Wesmen won't wait long."

The Unknown Warrior had lain Will on a bed in the mercifully empty infirmary, knowing that neither poultices nor any manner of compresses or infusions would help. The little man was far beyond conventional intervention.

Thraun sat up at the bedside, occasionally licking Will's face reflexively but mostly just staring, his yellow eyes moist and large, his expression plainly desperate. The Unknown stroked him absently while Will was examined, following a précis of what had caused his condition.

The infirmary was a low stone and slate-roofed structure, the walls decked in bright tapestries and punctuated by windows. It held twenty well-spaced beds in two rows of ten, though The Unknown knew it would soon hold three or four times that many wounded and be wholly inadequate. At the far end of the single ward, with piles of spare bedding stacked to warm, a fire burned in a large grate, providing the calming sight of gentle flame, and heat for both patients and healing balms.

The Unknown truly felt for Will. He knew only too well the terror of the soul being snagged by the claws of demons. Dead or alive, it made no difference. The soul belonged in the body until it chose to travel beyond mortal confines.

Will's soul was not gone but the demons had most certainly touched it. And the ice chill of a demon's claw on the core of his being was the reason

Will lay so deep in shock. It was a miracle his brain could tell his lungs to breathe. The Unknown was fairly sure the little man would die and, as the healer mage finished her attempted contact with Will's buried consciousness, the blank look on her face told its own story.

"Well?" asked The Unknown. The mage turned to him, moving aside to let two of the town's women assigned to the infirmary make Will comfortable. She was a tall woman, graceful, with long fingers and bobbed grey hair, her face wrinkled by age.

"I have never experienced someone so far down. Even though he is breathing, I find it hard to believe his soul still resides in his body. I cannot even hear his mind, let alone contact it. His brain is keeping him alive but how long that continues is anybody's guess though it will not be long." She glanced at Thraun as she had done many times already.

"Don't worry about him. I think he understands you're trying to help and he is certainly aware that Will is gravely ill. So how long?" The Unknown saw Hirad and the Julatsan General enter the infirmary, making a bee-line for him.

"Before he wakes or before he dies?"

"I think we both know it's unlikely to be the former," said The Unknown. The mage smiled sadly and nodded.

"Well, put it this way, if he doesn't begin to recover in a day, I'll be moving him to the rest house to die—we'll need the bed here and, after that time, I don't think he'll know how to come back."

The Unknown crouched by the wolf, who stared mournfully at him. "I don't know if you understand me, Thraun, but there's going to be a battle. To help Will, fight with us. We need you and Will needs time."

Thraun didn't blink but met The Unknown's eyes squarely for a time before moving past him. He licked Will's face, then lay on the ground at the head of his bed. The Unknown pushed himself to his feet, noting the cuts in his arms steadily fading under the continued influence of Erienne and Ilkar's CareHeal.

"Well, it was worth a try," he said, approaching Hirad, whose wounds had received the same treatment, and General Kard. "About this siege then, gentlemen?" he ventured. They nodded. "Over a mug of coffee, I think." He indicated the rest area at the western end of the infirmary. The fire burned brightly and several small pots hung over its flames. Once ensconced, The Unknown offered a hand to Kard, who shook it.

"I'm sorry I didn't introduce myself earlier. I'm The Unknown Warrior."

Kard smiled. "I know. I'm Kard, General of the Julatsan forces."

"This had better be brief," said The Unknown.

"Very well," said Kard. "Communion is underway to alert anyone up to a day away that we need assistance; one of your mages, Ilkar, gave me the name of one mage we know we can contact."

"Pheone," said The Unknown.

"Yes. Following that, we await the inevitable alarm from the watch-tower before mounting our attack."

"Why would you wait?" asked Hirad.

"Because every moment we can buy brings help that much closer. And without help we will surely lose this fight."

"But it's still an error to wait for them," said The Unknown. "It leaves your people on edge and removes the total surprise that is so vital to you. Attack when you are ready. Obliterate the tower before they have a chance to sound their alarms and get your men out into the streets right behind the first spell assault, assuming that's what you were intending to do."

"But—" began Kard.

"Your ideas are sound, General, and the Dordovans do need to be given the maximum time to arrive, but think of the effect on the Wesmen. Before they even know the Shroud is gone, they are being killed where they sleep and around their camp fires. And before they can mount a meaningful resist-ance, we are back inside the walls waiting for them. And then what?" The Unknown invited Kard to speak.

The General nodded. "I can see the sense in it. Then we keep them back as long as possible with spells, stop them mounting a serious assault."

"Exactly, but make sure you hit them hard to begin with. Make them scared to approach," said The Unknown. "Keep your mages moving after first strike. Don't let the Wesmen know where the magic is coming from next."

"All right," said Kard, looking a little hurt. "But we'll have to clear the wall run."

"That's fine because you can have warriors standing down all around the walls until they're called. Though you might want to keep archers behind the battlements," said Hirad. "Remember, if the flash attack into the streets is a success, the Wesmen will already be disorganised and demoralised. It'll take them several hours to organise for siege and attack. If you can damage them as they approach the walls, you can delay them still further. But you have to use the mages right."

The Unknown smiled and reached out a hand to grip Kard's upper arm briefly. "General, we're not questioning your skill or authority, just adding our experience. How many sieges have you been involved in?"

"This is my first," admitted Kard, his face cracking and his eyes lighting up. He chuckled.

"Then you have done a phenomenal job so far," said The Unknown. "We've spent a good part of our ten years fighting within or without castle walls."

"In that case, I am glad of your advice," said Kard.

"It will help us all to live longer," said Hirad.

"There's one more thing." Kard drained his coffee. "Senedai, the Wesmen Lord, has Julatsan prisoners, probably thousands of them. He promised to kill them should we double-cross him, which is exactly what we are planning to do."

"You don't think he'll be too busy with the trouble you cause to worry about them?" asked Hirad.

"That's what I told the Council but frankly I doubt it," replied Kard. "He's got at least fifteen thousand warriors out there. I feel sure he can spare some to slaughter a potential problem."

"Any mages among the prisoners?" The Unknown was frowning.

"I'm sure there are but they'll be keeping very quiet," said Kard. "Senedai would have killed them otherwise. He's ruthless as he's proved by all the sacrifices in the Shroud."

"Is any Communion directed at them? Where will they be being held?" The Unknown asked, seeing Hirad framing the same questions and coming to the same conclusion.

"In the south of the city, probably at the grain store. It's the only building big enough for the number of people I think Senedai's probably captured; and it's a secure structure, for obvious reasons. As for Communion, we can't risk it. Not just because we don't know if any mages are alive there but because we don't want the prisoners or the Wesmen getting a sniff of our plans before we attack."

The Unknown exchanged a brief glance with Hirad, who raised his eyebrows and nodded.

"We'll free them," said the big man. "But it'll require a slight change to your plans."

"How?" asked Kard.

"Just leave it to The Raven," said Hirad. "We know what we're doing."

Kard nodded. "It's your party if you want it."

The Communion had proved promising. Pheone, the mage already contacted by The Raven, was with a group of two hundred Julatsans including eleven other mages. They were picking their way toward where they suspected the Dordovans were camped and could strike at the Wesmen encircling the city in a day.

The Dordovans too had been found. Two and a half thousand foot, five hundred cavalry and fifty mages, who had been on the point of returning to Dordover because of the strength of the Wesmen massing at Understone, had been given the order to march instead to Julatsa.

Three other disparate groups of soldiers, city folk and a handful of mages, perhaps one hundred and fifty in all, had been found and advised of the siege plans. Whether they joined the effort or not depended largely on their intercepting the Dordovan force.

That left the Julatsans plus The Raven with at least one day to hold off the might of the Wesmen, who outnumbered them so comprehensively. Kard believed they could do it. It was down to troop morale, effective use of mages and, critically for the survival of the spirit within the College, The Raven liberating the prisoners assumed to be in the grain store.

The College had enjoyed its first run of good fortune since the fall of Julatsa. The news of the mysterious but very welcome arrival of The Raven had spread like bushfire through the College, bringing smiles to faces and the quoting of good omens. The Raven were also credited with the blindness that appeared to have afflicted the Wesmen in the watchtower who, an hour after the Shroud's dispersal, had still not realised the vulnerability of those they watched. For them, it would soon be too late.

A group of six mages walked from the base of the Tower. Dawn was coming though it was still full dark. The courtyard was quiet but for the cloth-muffled sounds of pans clashing in the kitchens, of cook fires being gently stoked, and of the muted protestations of the freshly greased well-chain as water was hauled from the underground course. In so many ways it was, as Kard demanded, an entirely ordinary yet artificially governed preamble to dawn.

But from behind every door, a Captain or Lieutenant watched, their men primed and ready to race for their designated gate. The spotter mages prepared ShadowWings and The Raven, already hidden in shadow by the South Gate, waited. Hirad and The Unknown Warrior hefted weapons, Ilkar and Erienne prepared HardShield and HotRain respectively and Denser, ShadowWings of his own. He would navigate. It was the best way to avoid unwanted confrontation.

The six mages walked casually across the courtyard, their bodies relaxed but their minds taut with spell preparation. For all the steel cladding on the lower levels of the Wesmen's tower, the watchplatform was still open, though netted against arrows. There was no warning. One moment they were walking, the next they stopped and a dozen FlameOrbs were flashing across the sky, the extra preparation time adding speed and accuracy to the casting.

The sudden light flared harshly across the courtyard as it moved swiftly toward the helpless Wesmen guards. Shadow followed orange light in hypnotic sequence and the briefest of hushes fell on the College before the Orbs struck home.

The Julatsan night lit up as orange fire deluged the platform, igniting wood and flesh and consuming both with equal voracity. Flames leapt upward, boiling off the roof of the tower, while on the platform itself the burning Wesmen shrieked and thrashed in their agony, one plunging through the torn netting to fall, trailing smoke and flame as he went. And as the single desperate toll of an alarm bell rang mournfully out into the night, joined by the screams of the dying, the College courtyard sprang to life.

Kard and his Captains yelled orders, soldiers and men raced to the gates which were hauled open and, first into the streets of Julatsa, The Raven, with Denser, eyes magically augmented, flying above and ahead of the runners. Behind them came a force of six hundred soldiers and city men at arms plus thirty defensive mages. North would go around four hundred swordsmen plus twenty mages, leaving the College temporarily undefended by steel but not by magic.

During the days of the DemonShroud, Senedai had stood down the force that had originally completely encircled the College walls, presumably dispersing them through the far more luxurious surroundings of his captured buildings. However, a circle of guardpoints still closed all routes from the cobbled ring that ran around the outside of the College walls where they intersected the first city buildings and it was here that the first strike would be made.

Hirad led The Raven across the cobbled ring, toward the main street that led to the industrial quarter. Wesmen guards in front of them yelled warnings and drew weapons, cries were taken up in a dozen places but the tide of Julatsans was about to sweep away the first flimsy line of defence.

"Raven!" roared Hirad. "Raven with me!" He sprinted forward, The Unknown just to his left, Ilkar immediately behind them.

"Shield up," said the elf. "Hold your casting, Erienne."

"Holding."

Four Wesmen stood in their way, their expressions ranging from uncertainty to incomprehension at the force coming at them. Hirad ran in, sweeping his sword through, chest high. His target leapt backward, hanging out his axe in a feeble attempt at a block that The Raven man knocked aside, butting the man in the face and smashing his nose. The Unknown went one better, his sword breaking the weapon of his victim on its way to lodge deep in the Wesman's shoulder. Hirad could hear the bones splintering.

With one man clutching at his face, Hirad sliced his sword up and right, taking the next man across the stomach as he raised his axe to strike, and finishing him with a stab to the heart. He reversed his blade and chopped it across the neck of the man he'd head-butted while The Unknown lashed a haymaking punch into the midriff of the fourth before stabbing him in the throat.

Denser landed behind them. "Your first left is an alleyway. Take it and then the first right. It's quiet there for now but the Wesmen are waking. We need to hurry. Erienne are you all right?" She nodded and pointed to her head where she held the mana shape for HotRain. Denser took off again and The Raven ran on, leaving the Julatsans to clear their path back.

Hirad grabbed a branch from a fire and took off down the narrow alleyway, the flickering cast by the makeshift torch just enough to ward off the worst of the shadows. Behind them he could hear the shouts of waking Wesmen, the sounding of alarms and the clashing of steel as Julatsan warriors joined battle with those who had taken their city. Detonations sounded, muffled by the blank walls of the alleyway that led them away from the main street, the light of FlameOrbs and the muted glitter of HotRain casting brief luminescence in the sky.

Turning down the next alley, a slightly wider paved street, Hirad could see Denser flitting ahead. He banked sharply right and dived low, storming back toward the rest of The Raven, landing in front of Hirad, who pulled up sharply.

"This is easier than I thought. The grain store is just to the end of this alley and across a wide square. It's guarded and there's light in every window of every building now the alarm has spread but any Wesman running is running for the College. If we're quick, we can—"

Above the ascending din of battle and the crump of spells hitting buildings and men, a howl pierced the night. It was long and full of anger and sorrow, tailing off into a keening wail and a bark that echoed out. For a split second, Julatsa was silent then battle was joined again.

"Shield down," said Ilkar. "What in all the hells was that?"

"Dear Gods," said Erienne who had clearly lost her mana shape. "It was Thraun."

"Will," said The Unknown. "Poor Will."

Another howl split the air.

"What will he do? Thraun, I mean?" asked Ilkar.

"I don't know," said Erienne. "But I think we'd better get back as quickly as we can. If he'll listen to anyone, he'll listen to us."

"But we have to get these prisoners out first. Right," said Hirad, looking to where Denser stood, his wings proud at his back. "Erienne, go with Denser if he'll hold you. Your spells are probably best directed from above us. Ilkar, FlameOrb then sword please; we can't waste another shield. We'll deal with Thraun and see to Will's Vigil later." His mind, clouded briefly by the loss of another Raven warrior, cleared to deal with their immediate situation. "Raven with me."

A third howl echoed from the walls of the alleyway. Closer this time. The wolf was loose in the streets of Julatsa.

CHAPTER 24

Dystran cursed and threw the book down at his feet. He leant on the balustrade of the Tower balcony he had assumed from Styliann and prayed hell would visit swift retribution on the former Lord of the Mount.

Knowing Styliann was probably still alive following his usurpation of power in the College, Dystran and his cohorts had known only too well the importance of the Protectors in maintaining that power. And yet, immediately below him, the entire Protector army stood silent, awesome and terrifying, on the carefully tended lawn. Waiting.

At first, Dystran hadn't believed Styliann and had fallen back into an uneasy sleep. But a frantic knocking at his bedchamber door soon afterward had led to him scurrying to the study and out on to the balcony where he saw the Protectors issuing from their barracks into the cool breezy night. With unhurried purpose, they had marched into the torchlit night, flickering orange glinting off their masks, their polished leather and the buckles of their boots and clothing.

They had assembled over the course of an hour but Dystran hadn't watched. Tearing back into the study, he had grabbed the Articles of Stewardship from its place on the shelves by the desk and flicked feverishly through its pages. The Act of Giving was there, plain for him to read. But in his pride and overwhelming sense of achievement and importance at attaining his new position, he just hadn't bothered to look.

The Lore script concerning the Act was the most modern in the College, written by Styliann and designed to make renunciation a long and complex process. By the time he had studied the text in enough detail, had gathered the Circle Seven and fulfilled the meditation process, eight days would have passed. And so the Articles lay at his feet, an open page fluttering in the gentle night air.

"We've got to stop them," he muttered.

"What do you intend doing?" asked his senior confidante, an ageing, grey-haired mage named Ranyl.

"We can WardLock the gates for a start." Dystran waved a hand in their direction.

"And they will merely batter the timbers to splinters," said Ranyl. "No holding spell is strong enough to keep them all quiet and they will respond to aggression by attacking the source of the order to strike or cast. And that's you." The old mage's voice was quiet but sure. "There are four hundred and seventeen Protectors down there, all with innate magical shielding. I know who I'd back in the fight."

"So what can we do?" Dystran's voice held a note of desperation.

"Let them go and rescind the Act of Giving. Or send an assassin to kill Styliann. Those are the only two ways to bring the Protectors into your control."

Dystran snorted. "An assassin? Styliann's soon going to have five hundred-odd Protectors around him. The whole Wesmen nation would have trouble getting to him."

Ranyl stooped and picked up the Articles of Stewardship and slapped them into Dystran's chest.

"In that case, my Lord, might I humbly suggest that you get reading?"

Below them, the Protector army moved on an unspoken command, coming to readiness absolutely as one. Dystran started, his heart thudding in his chest. Exuding power with every stride and swing of the arm, they trotted to the south gate, now under the gaze of the rudely awakened College. Dystran shook his head, his face taut with anxiety, seeing more than one questioning face turned up toward him and Ranyl.

At the gate, the lead Protector pushed the gateman firmly aside, wound the bar away and pulled open the heavy iron-clad wooden gates with assistance from three others. Without further pause, the Protectors trotted away into the dark streets of Xetesk, and Dystran could very easily imagine Styliann's laughter.

Lord Tessaya watched tight-lipped as Styliann and the dread force ran to the north while his warriors struggled to form under the harsh shouts of his Captains. He summoned his highest ranking General, a man named Adesellere.

"I want four thousand men after them before dawn cracks the sky. Do not let them escape. I want word sent through to Riasu for five thousand of the reserve to be here in one day. He should also be advised to attend me immediately. Lastly, I want you to personally organise forward defence of Understone, the pass and the surrounds. Be mindful of the south.

"I will be pushing on to Korina in two days' time. See every commander has carrier birds. Do you understand all that?"

"Yes, my Lord," said Adesellere, an old and trusted aide, battle-scarred, bald and fierce. "Do you want me to remain with the defence?"

Tessaya nodded and put a hand on his shoulder. "You are one of the very few I can trust. Send Bedelao after the mage. I will get word to my scouts north and south. I get the uneasy feeling we'll have to revise our plans. Not all of my brother Lords have acquitted themselves as they might."

"I won't fail you, Tessaya."

"You never have before." Tessaya dismissed Adesellere. He looked out over the muster area into which the General now ran, barking out orders to his Lieutenants who drove the warriors into some semblance of order. This was not as he had planned and he cursed under his breath, bringing to his mind where it had begun to go wrong.

With the destruction of the Wytch Lords certainly but there was more. The attack on Julatsa had not been swift enough and to the south, disaster had apparently overtaken Taomi. The Eastern Balaians should have had no hope but the fact was that the Wesmen had failed to capture or kill a single targeted figure.

Unless his reading of the situation was completely cock-eyed, General Darrick, Baron Blackthorne and The Raven were all still alive and fighting. And now, unless they could catch him, Styliann would return to Xetesk as a standard for the mages. Tessaya's hand was being forced and he didn't like it.

What he needed was for Senedai to occupy the College Cities, for Adesellere to halt any advance from the south and for his march to Korina at the head of ten thousand Wesmen to be swift and without error. He could still take Korina. The bloated capital city wallowed in its sense of achievement and wealth and had little time for organised defence. Yes, there would be resistance but, with the Colleges and southern armies busy, he was certain he could prevail.

But it wouldn't be the glorious march he had anticipated and dreamed, with the smoking ruins of the bastard Colleges behind him. And for that, he wanted someone to pay, and pay heavily.

Darrick's flotilla of small and medium-sized craft had crossed over three quarters of the Bay of Gyernath when a shouted alarm reached him from the southern edge of the squadron. He quickly scanned the beach they were approaching but it was deserted, yet consternation fed through the boats to his right and he could see men, or more probably elves, pointing southward.

He looked and could see nothing initially but then, as a nearby twin-masted craft cleared his line of sight, he saw them. Sails. Cruising around the Gyernath headland. First two, then four. All noise in his boat ceased as more and more eyes turned to stare at the fleet moving up the Bay toward them. As Darrick watched, he saw more sails rounding the headland, appearing like ghosts on the breeze. Silent predators, swift and deadly.

"Gods under water," he muttered. He turned to his second-in-command. "I need the elves and mages to tell me who they are and I need to know fast. Go to it." The man strode away, shouting a name Darrick couldn't catch. The General summoned his signalmen.

"Flags for course change. North-northeast immediate. If those are Wesmen, we'll need all the distance we can get."

Messages were relayed as the flotilla changed course, heading for a more difficult shore. Almost immediately, the larger fleet of predominantly three-masted vessels altered its direction in response. They were gaining and fast. Pennants flew from the tops of masts and from each stern. He could see tiny figures in the rigging and, he thought, faces lining the decks. Thousands of faces.

They would barely make land before they were caught and still more ships came into sight. There had to be two dozen and more now. If they were Wesmen, the four-College cavalry was finished.

To Darrick's left, a mage shot into the sky, ShadowWings shaped for height and glide. The General tracked her as she flew away south toward the approaching fleet, waiting to see the arrows fly high, trying to bring her down. Silence reigned. All that could be heard was the creaking of timbers, the ruffle of canvas, the push of bows through the water and the splash of oars. The mage continued on. Darrick realised he was holding his breath.

Three shapes rose on an intercept course from the lead ship; and they weren't arrows, they were mages. A cheer went up all around the squadron and Darrick's face cracked into a smile. The Wesmen had no mages. Whoever they were, they were friends.

All eyes were on the quartet of mages circling at close quarters in the sky above. Whatever they were discussing seemed to take forever and Darrick found himself grinding his teeth, impatient for knowledge. Presently, though, the mage was back on deck, excitement firing her eyes and bringing a flush to her pretty but dirt-streaked face.

She began breathlessly, her words tumbling from her mouth in a stream of delighted incomprehensibility. Darrick laughed and placed a hand on either shoulder.

"Slow down," he said. She nodded and breathed deeply, flashing a smile of her own.

"I'm sorry, sir, but the relief I feel . . ."

"We all feel it," said Darrick. "Now tell us who our new friends are."

"It is the army of Gyernath. And at their head are Barons Blackthorne and Gresse."

This time, Darrick's laughter echoed through the fleet and across the calm waters of the Bay of Gyernath. He slapped the mast against which he stood.

"I don't believe it!" he said. "This meeting will be a real pleasure." He ordered the flagmen signal a return to their original course and turned, the smile wide on his lips, and anticipated his meeting with the two magnificent Barons.

Just before midday, with the two fleets moored as near shore as their draughts would allow and with the multiple dinghies and shallow transport barges of the Gyernath force ferrying men and horses to shore under the watchful eyes of ShadowWinged mages flitting in the sky, Darrick crunched across the sand toward Blackthorne and Gresse.

The two Barons were standing side by side, watching the beaches fill with troops, determination in every move they made and in the set of their faces. As Darrick approached, they ceased their discussion and moved toward him, both with hands outstretched. Darrick shook them in turn.

"This is happy coincidence," said the Lysternan General. "I had thought to travel to Gyernath to stir the army before marching to Understone. Now I find that two of our supposedly uncaring Barons have saved me seven days and that the army stands on this very beach."

"Uncaring, eh, Blackthorne? What do you make of that?" Gresse rubbed at the stubble on his chin.

"Upstart young Generals with air for brains are commonplace. Fortunately, we are not standing before one of them," said Blackthorne.

"And nor are the pair of you uncaring, though the same cannot be said for certain of your brotherhood," replied Darrick, bowing slightly at the compliment paid him.

A look passed between the two Barons and Gresse's eyes narrowed. "There will be actions taken when this is all over. But that is for another day. Now, General, let us tell you what we have been doing and we can plan the liberation of Blackthorne."

"Liberation?" Darrick's heart skipped a beat and he looked at Blackthorne, who raised his eyebrows. "Did they not drive straight for Gyernath and Korina?"

"No," said Blackthorne. "They clearly wanted my town as a southern staging post rather than Gyernath which, for you, is lucky since you hoped to raise an army from there. Much of their force headed north to Understone but it didn't get there."

"No more summaries," said Gresse. "We should sit and analyse this properly. We want to be at the gates of Blackthorne before nightfall."

Darrick felt energised, his whole body powered and healthy. This unexpected turn of fortune changed a great deal. Not only had Gyernath been able to repulse the Wesmen attack but it seemed that the north–south supply line was not in place and now would never be. For the first time since he rode through Understone Pass to help The Raven, Darrick firmly believed Balaia could be freed from the clutches of the Wesmen.

But his belief was tempered by a growing concern. Though they had, by his latest reckoning, around twenty days, time was nonetheless short and, as the brown stain ate the sky over Parve, the noon shade grew, marking the progress toward Balaia's doom at the hands of an army of dragons. Again, The Raven had the task of saving the continent in their hands and again, Darrick had to try to support them, keeping Wesmen from their path. Now he had made landfall in the East, he had to contact them. Because, if anything befell them, only he and Styliann could pass on the knowledge of the threat to the Colleges. And he didn't trust Styliann as far as he could throw him.

Sha-Kaan sat heavily in the Melde Hall feeling every one of his four hundred and more cycles. Elu-Kaan, the Great Kaan's hope for a successor, lay on the verge of death in a melde-corridor, tended at last by his Dragonene, the old elven mage, Barras. He was doubtful whether the expert ministrations of the Julatsan or the healing flow of channelled interdimensional space would be enough but they had to try, despite Barras' personally desperate siege situation.

At least Sha-Kaan was able to advise Barras from his own painful experience concerning the nature of Elu's multiple wounds. The Great Kaan's scales were covered in tiny scratches, his eyes smarted from the touch of claws and inside his mouth the ice of their bite dulled his fires. He chewed on bales of Flamegrass, reflecting that he had escaped lightly, the human's spells critically weakening the sea of Arakhe who had attacked them. Elu-Kaan hadn't been so fortunate, stumbling across the full fury of the Arakhe and suffering horrible wounds deep into his throat. It was these that Sha-Kaan feared and that he had exhorted Barras to heal if he could.

For himself, he needed rest. Ideally, that rest would have been in his own melde-corridor under the ministrations of Hirad Coldheart and The Raven but, much though it rankled, he accepted that was not possible. So he had to content himself with first the energy of the Melde Hall and then, when he tired of its noise, the calm and quiet of Wingspread.

He ached from constant toil. The wounds from his battle with the Naik above the southern plains were not healed and the muscles at the roots of his wings protested though the wide spans themselves were furled and stowed. He looked along the length of his body, noting with displeasure the fading hue of his golden scales. Once so bright they dazzled in the orb light, they were now a dim indicator of his age and health. They hadn't begun to lift just yet and his wings maintained their full lubrication but it wouldn't be long. And part of him even looked forward to the day when he no longer had the weight of the Kaan on his broad back. But there was so much that still had to be done and the fate of them all blew with the vagaries of the wind.

Sha-Kaan swallowed the last of his bale of Flamegrass, the alarm sounding in his mind before he had resettled on the warm quiet mud. He breathed out long and deep, smoke drifting from the corners of his mouth as his irritation fed through to the glands inside his gums. He had known deep inside of him that there would be no real rest but he could have expected at least a few beats. Snatching another bale of Flamegrass, he switched out of Wingspread, the call to the Brood forming on his lips.

The sight at the gateway shook Sha-Kaan to the core. Though the guard around the roiling brown mass was doubled, they seemed pitifully few against that which they had been detailed to oppose. And the Naik were coming in strength, and with allies. Out-fliers had pulsed warnings back through the net of Kaan minds, forcing the Brood-at-rest and the Brood-awake into concerted action, implementing the defensive plan drilled into them by Sha-Kaan.

But Sha-Kaan himself had to force away doubts that it would work. The gateway had grown far more quickly than he had feared in his worst moments and now was linked fast to the sky above Beshara, grabbing at its edges as it fed its voracious appetite. A thin line of cloud now bordered the gateway and Sha-Kaan knew that would develop, bringing obscured vision as yet another problem to the defenders.

In time, the gateway would collapse, its structural instability forcing it in on itself. But that would not happen until long after the Kaan and Balaia were destroyed; and the shockwaves it would send through the whole of interdimensional space would ripple tremors through every dimension, though none worse than through the ruins of Balaia itself.

Sha put the thoughts from his mind. For now, the Kaan simply had to survive the coming battle. From every point of the sky, his Brood came to the defence of their melde-dimension and themselves while from the north, a dark blotch signified the mass of the Naik and their enslaved allies.

As he reached the vicinity of the rip and felt its pull on his mind, strong like a wind sucking him toward it, the Great Kaan knew that what was to come had to be the last. If The Raven had not reached Beshara before the Naik attacked again, all would be lost.

He pulsed greetings and orders and the first Kaan flights set out to attack.

Julatsa's stone-clad grain store sat in the middle of a cobbled square providing a natural fire break from the predominantly wooden buildings which surrounded it. History had demanded it be strong. Times of shortage in ages gone by had forced the peaceful folk of Julatsa into desperate measures and the blood of many a starving man with a dying family back home had soaked through the stones into the earth below. And though those times were long gone, the grain store stood as testament and reminder, as well as being a fully functional city building.

The Raven, with Denser overhead, Erienne now in his arms much as Ilkar had been over the Wesmen camp at Triverne Inlet, stood in the shadows of an alley that opened directly onto the square. They were parallel to the main street which led from the store, through the southern market and up to the College. Thraun had gone quiet but the hand-to-hand fighting was getting nearer and the level of noise from every quarter of Julatsa was rising. Hirad shifted grip on his sword. They were going to have to move fast and the Julatsans from the College would just have to be ready for them.

The grain store measured better than ninety feet on its short side, which faced them, and perhaps double that on its longer. The Wesmen had stationed half a dozen guards outside the main doors, which faced the alley, and watchfires ringed the square in front of the four main access streets.

When the hoped-for opportunity presented itself, Hirad seized it eagerly. A spell landed close by, sending flames lashing up into the heavens. Wesmen from two of the watchfires ran away to join the fighting that bordered the square to The Raven's left and the guards at the door were nervous and distracted, clearly unsure what they should do.

"Now Raven!" shouted Hirad and he charged out of the alley, The Unknown right next to him and Ilkar, sword drawn, a pace behind. Above them, Denser flew low across the face of the store. From out of the sky above the guards, drops of flame, just a few, lashed down, setting fur and clothing alight. Panicked, the guards ran blindly away, not realising that The Raven were also attacking on foot.

Beating at the flames that threatened to engulf him, the fastest Wesman ran headlong toward the waiting Unknown. The Big Man sidestepped smartly, left in a foot which the Wesman obligingly tumbled over and finally drove his blade straight through the prone man's throat. Beside him, Hirad ran forward to take on two more. One's gaze was locked anxiously on the sky until his companion tugged at his smouldering sleeve and both squared up to the barbarian.

"Who's first?" rasped Hirad, springing forward and opening a cut in the face of the left-hand man. "You'll do." He ducked under a wild axe swing and buried his sword in the Wesman's gut. He dragged his blade clear and rolled away from the attack of the other, who followed his movement and turned his back on The Unknown. It was the last mistake he ever made. Before his body had dropped to the floor, The Unknown Warrior had turned to face the three remaining Wesmen and Ilkar was sprinting for the grain store doors.

Hirad ran in to support his old friend, though The Unknown scarcely needed it. Angling his sword hilt in front of his face and blade down left, he caught the first axe blow and thrust upward, tearing the weapon from the guard's grasp to go spinning away into the night. He lashed the double-handed blade back down across his enemy's chest and Hirad could hear the ribs shear. The man fell backward, clutching at his ruined body with the blood pouring through his hands.

Hirad closed down the penultimate threat, clashing blades with the Wesman and kicking out straight to connect with his stomach. The man grunted but still thrust Hirad back and, though winded, held his blade steady in front of him. The barbarian smiled. Moving a pace forward, he feinted to strike right, switched grip and chopped in left. Hopelessly slow, the Wesman had barely moved his sword in the right direction before Hirad's entered his neck, cleaving all the way to the spine. He turned to see The Unknown wipe his blade on the body of the last man. He spread his arms wide.

"Good, aren't we?" he said, smiling.

"You know it," said The Unknown, the corners of his mouth turning up. They ran on to join Ilkar, who was preparing to cast. Denser and Erienne circled above them.

"Clear at the moment," said the Xeteskian. "The Julatsans have run into a little trouble just south of the market but the Wesmen aren't organised yet. Be quick because I can see a large force, probably two or three thousand, running in from the west. You don't have too long before they get here."

Hirad nodded and hammered on the padlocked, barred doors with his sword. The sound of voices, lots of them, could be plainly heard but he had to try anyway or someone would get hurt.

"Get away from the doors!" he bellowed. "No time to explain, just get away."

Ilkar stood and backed away a pace, giving the slightest of nods to Hirad who could see his face wracked with concentration, his arms tight in front of him and cupped as if to catch a ball. Hirad moved aside.

"Deploying," said Ilkar quietly. He jabbed his arms forward quickly and the tightly formed ForceCone shot from the centre of his cupped hands and thundered into the heavy wooden doors. Built to withstand weapons they may have been, but not the ForceCone of a master. As the mana shape ploughed in, they first buckled at the lock then shot inward, the padlock and chain snapping and whipping away to clatter into the wall near Hirad's head.

"Steady, Ilkar," said Hirad.

Ilkar shrugged. "I had to be sure," he said. The three Raven men ran inside to confront a sea of faces and a thousand frightened voices.

"Your job, I think." Hirad patted Ilkar on the back. "You are a native, after all." Ilkar gave him a sideways look and opened his mouth to call for quiet.

CHAPTER 25

For an instant, Thraun's eyes misted over as the life slipped away from man-packbrother. He felt it in the core of his being and the passing to the grey dust left a pit of loneliness inside his wolven heart. An agonised whine escaped his throat as he watched man-packbrother's head slip slightly to the side and his chest fall but not rise again. He looked up into the face of the human who tended him. She laid an implement aside, one which had been used to wipe man-packbrother's face, then moved a white covering to hide his still form.

Thraun could see the sorrow in her and felt the helplessness which tinged that sorrow with anger. The instant passed and Thraun's mind was deluged with animal fury. He opened his mouth and howled at the sky blocked from him by the human structure as the blood-lust soaked into him and cast about for prey.

The body of the tending woman now cascaded fear, it showed in her face and gushed from every pore. She backed away. He could smell it like he could smell the forest. It was fear of him and fear was good. It told him when a prey was beaten. But she had tried to save man-packbrother and he found himself unable to bring her down. A vestige of thought swam through his crazed mind and he bolted into the open, another howl blasting from his mouth, his body racked, muscles glowing with rage, the blood on his mind and the forest in his nose.

But outside he scrabbled to a halt on the cruel stone. Outside was fire and shouting in the dark. Outside was chaos and confusion. Humans ran everywhere and the overpowering scent of the hated ones whose flesh he remembered assailed him, mixed with the rotting stench of death. A mass of the humans, those untainted with the scent of the hated, ran toward an opening in the walls. Beyond it, the prey he desired.

Thraun ran hard toward the opening, his savage barks scattering the humans whose inbred terror of the wolf had them leap from his path. He could feel their alternate fear and relief as he ran past them, intent on the one prey, the strong-scented ones whose blood he had tasted and desired to taste again. He cleared the opening and, sniffing the air as his legs blurred beneath him, drove straight to where he knew his prey waited, a third and final howl marking his grief at the loss of man-packbrother.

Thraun ran toward the flickering light of a fire. Around it, the hated men were standing and he could feel their anxiety and incomprehension of the noise and flame the pack-humans had caused. His blond-flecked brown body slipped through the dark unnoticed, the noises covering his footfalls and the growls quiet in his throat.

Prey.

There was no desire to stalk. The pack were far away, the forest colours dim in his memory and his animal brain ablaze with the anger of something taken that could never be returned.

At a dead run from the shadows he pounced, leaping high, taking his first prey in the throat, his jaws ripping for blood, his paws braced on the shoulders. The man fell under the force of the leap but had no fight in him, his life already flowing from the tear under his chin. Thraun lapped hungrily at the blood, careless of its spurting and flashing over his muzzle and coat. Lost in desire, he didn't hear the other men surround him but he felt the sharp slap as one of their metal sticks bounced from his impervious hide.

He turned and the four of them stumbled backward, scared words tumbling from their mouths combined with frantic pointing with their arms at where one had struck him. Thraun crouched, yellow eyes smouldering contempt for their helplessness, jaws dripping the blood of their companion, his body tensed.

The men backed away further but they could not escape, not all of them. Thraun sprang again, paws thumping into the chest of his prey, snout firing hot breath over his face. His jaws snapped together, ripping the flesh off one cheek. The man screamed. His companions struck and pulled at Thraun who stepped back, lashed a claw into the prey to silence him then begin to circle, tongue lolling.

One of the prey turned and ran, shouting as he went. Thraun watched him briefly but let him go. The other two stood knowing they could neither fight to win nor both outrun the wolf. At a word, they split and ran in opposite directions but Thraun had already chosen his victim. He loped after him, through a narrow way with sheer stone walls rising either side, and ended his whimpering life far from the light of the fire.

And later, sated in mind and body, the passing of man-packbrother avenged, he cleaned his paws, muzzle and chest and trotted back to where Will lay, the lust clearing from his mind where one word pulsed at him.

Remember.

Ilkar feared for a time that the tumult wouldn't subside. The grain store was packed with men, women and children of all ages and their automatic move away from the sundered doors was reversed immediately they saw it was not Wesmen framed in the opening.

It sounded as if all of them were talking, crying or shouting at once and he worried briefly that they would be crushed in a stampede for the open air. He shouted for calm, his voice joined by Hirad's and The Unknown's, all three Raven men now with swords sheathed, aware that Denser would alert them to any approaching danger.

Inside, the grain store was gloomy but not dark. Half a dozen low-wicked lanterns lit its cavernous stone-arched space and, to his left and right, Ilkar could see areas set aside for food and washing. And though the smell of sweat and stale air within was strong and pervasive, the lack of raw stench told him that at least they were not forced to urinate or defecate where they stood and slept.

At the front of the crowd, younger men stared back at him, their faces tired and angry, their voices lost in the morass of sound. In the centre, Ilkar recognised the unmistakable aura of a mage and strode forward to speak with him. His movement caused a ripple through the crowd which swayed back instinctively and Ilkar could only guess at the treatment they had sometimes received at the hands of the Wesmen. And their fears were based in ignorance. Every day, some of their number were taken from the store and never returned. Ilkar knew where they lay and the realisation that these people, his people, did not, twisted his stomach and reignited his anger at the plight of Julatsa.

But the bodies lying outside the College were something he couldn't ignore and they represented a real risk to the rescue if the subject wasn't handled correctly.

The mage, late middle-aged and puny, tufted red hair sprouting from a narrow head, bore an expression of enormous relief but Ilkar didn't let him speak, beckoning him forward. They met and shook hands a pace in front of the crowd.

"Your name?" asked Ilkar.

"Dewer," replied the mage.

"Good. Dewer, I am Ilkar and this is The Raven. We're here to get you out of this. All of you. But we don't have much time."

Dewer gaped. "The Raven?" There were tears in his eyes.

"Yes. Look, I must have quiet. The Wesmen are close and we have to leave now. Who's in charge?"

"I'll pass the word for quiet," said Dewer. "Speak to Lallan while I hush everyone." He pointed at a tall slim man in his late fifties. He wore fine deep green clothing and a burgundy shirt, dirty and torn now but the quality still shone through. His face was drawn and tired yet proud and he stood tall, refusing to be bowed by the abrupt change in his circumstances. Ilkar walked quickly over to him where he stood a little further along the line, beckoning The Unknown and Hirad to join him.

"Lallan," said Ilkar. The two shook hands briefly. "I'm Ilkar, and these are Hirad and The Unknown Warrior."

Lallan nodded. "I recognised you as you came in."

"It is very important that your people listen to us and follow our instructions. If not, there could be a slaughter," said Ilkar.

"How many of you are there here?" asked Hirad.

"Three thousand four hundred and seventy-eight," said Lallan without pause. "We started with more but the Wesmen have been taking away the very old, very young and some women."

"I know, and that is something we have to deal with now." Around Ilkar, a ripple of excited conversation was followed by a wave of hushing sounds and then almost complete silence.

"Impressive," said The Unknown.

"We decided early that discipline was important," said Lallan. "I'll speak first, then I'll introduce you, Ilkar. They'll listen if I ask it."

The four men stepped away from the crowd and toward the door. Denser chose the same moment to sweep down to the doorway, release Erienne from his arms, kiss her and step back into the sky. Erienne ran in, breaking the silence of the crowd, their murmur a vocalisation of their anxiety.

"Erienne?" asked Hirad.

"We're in trouble," she said. "The main force of Wesmen from the west of the city has changed direction and are heading this way. Denser thinks they are under the control of the commander and he's guessed what's going on. They'll be here very soon. We've established the corridor back to the College but it's under attack in a dozen places, street to street. This isn't what Kard needs. His men are dying out here and he needs them on the walls."

"Right," said The Unknown. "Lallan, get talking. Now."

Lallan nodded and faced the crowd who quietened on his first word.

"My friends," he said, his arms aloft, palms outward. "The Raven are here to organise rescue. It is hazardous and I beseech you, listen to what Ilkar has to say and let no doubt cloud your mind. Wesmen warriors are coming this way and we have to act decisively. This is our only chance. Ilkar."

The Raven mage stepped forward. "Outside it is dark, with only wood and spell fires lighting the sky. The Wesmen are running Julatsa but we have this one opportunity to get you out of their immediate clutches. What we want you to do is this. On Lallan's word, leave here and run as hard as you can through the southern market and, by the main streets, to the College. Don't stop until you are well inside the walls. Anyone who can fight and finds a weapon on a dead Wesmen, take it; you might need it. The streets are, for now, secured by soldiers and men from Julatsa but they are under attack. Anyone who delays in the run is risking their lives.

"There are two things I must tell you. First, you will be running into a College that will be under siege. It isn't freedom, not yet, but if you are there, you can do your part to help us regain our city. Any who feel their chances are better elsewhere, are very welcome to choose another direction in which to run. But I should mention that The Raven will be standing on the College walls where the best chance lies.

"Second, as you approach the College, you will see a terrible sight. The bodies of all of those taken from this grain store ring the walls, murdered by the Wesmen in an attempt to force surrender. They gave their lives to give you a chance. Don't pause to mourn until you are inside or their deaths might end up being in vain. Lallan."

Lallan addressed the crowd again, their silence broken by the odd shouted question and the murmur of shocked sob and sorrow. He raised his voice to quell the spread of the noise.

"My friends, we don't have time for questions. We have to run, as fast as we can, and pray the Gods and our soldiers will protect us. The strong must help the weak and carry the very young. We will run in our rotas, 'A' through to 'L,' and I hardly need to say that any mages should shield their comrades. Divide and organise now, I want 'A' through to 'E' in front of these doors immediately. Go."

He clapped his hands and the hall dissolved into the noise of action. The drum of thousands of feet on the stone-flagged floor, the shouts and calls to organise and the clatter of timber as tables were shoved aside to create space by the main doors. Ilkar couldn't keep a smile from his face and he turned to Hirad and The Unknown, both of whom were nodding their appreciation. The discipline of the Julatsans gave them a chance.

Denser landed again at the doors, his voice urgent. "Come on. They're almost on the store, they'll enter through the western entrance. We have to move now or they'll overwhelm us." He held out his arms for Erienne and she ran into them. "HotRain, I think." She nodded and they took off.

The first of the rota letters were ready. Lallan, under the shadow of The Unknown Warrior, did not hesitate.

"Go, go, go! Through the southern market, follow the corridor of soldiers. Take weapons where you find them. Run!" His last was lost in the thunder of feet and the calls of encouragement that rang out and echoed in the grain store. The Wesmen's Julatsan prisoners ran free, ran hard and ran straight.

Ilkar was joined to the left of the doors by The Unknown and Hirad, and the three Raven watched the Julatsans as they made their bid for brief freedom. Above them, and moving in a lazy arc while they watched the advancing Wesmen, were Denser and Erienne. Julatsa was alive with fighting, the clash of swords, the detonation of spells and the shouts and calls to action coming at them from all directions.

"We had no right to expect this to go so well," said Ilkar.

"I'm not so sure that it is," said The Unknown. "They're moving too slowly. And look at Denser now."

Ilkar could see what he meant. Despite the selective murder of the young and very old by the Wesmen, there were still a sizeable number still alive and the pace of the column of city people was slow, scared and stumbling, the elderly supported by and slowing the younger and quicker. Behind them, in the store, Lallan's voice could be heard above the general hubbub, urging them on, exhorting them to greater effort and greater speed.

And now, moving determinedly west, Denser was tracking the Wesmen force as it neared the square.

Above the rooftops, Denser, his sight augmented, surveyed Julatsa and, more particularly, the immediate threat to The Raven. Along the secure corridor, the Julatsans were coming under increasing pressure from the waking, angry Wesmen. Pockets of fighting were continuing along its whole length as the occupying warriors directed themselves against the College defenders. Nowhere yet was the situation critical but east and west Denser could see Wesmen streaming in from their billets and camps, emerging from houses, offices and inns, belting on their weapons and hurrying to the fight, alarm bells sounding out across the city.

The weak points of the corridor were at either end and in the southern market where buildings gave way to cobbles and access to the defensive line was broader. Fortunately, the Wesmen hadn't reached those points yet, halted by fierce flank defence in critical streets and the judicious use of fire as a barricade. The Julatsans were making their knowledge of the city streets work hard for them and, so far, neither grain store nor College was assailed.

But to the south and west of the grain store, the clearly organised fast march of well over three thousand Wesmen was nearing the square and would soon engulf The Raven and their charges. Too soon.

Below Denser, the freed Julatsans continued to stream out of the doors to the grain store, urged on by the gesturing arms of Hirad, The Unknown and Ilkar, the sound of their voices rising clear into the slowly lightening sky. Denser swooped down again, hovering over the moving line, apologising as some of those below him flinched or stumbled.

"Hirad, any time now this square will be crawling with Wesmen bent on unpicking your entrails. They are barely a street away from the south and west entrances and we aren't enough to stop them on open ground."

Hirad shrugged and pointed at Erienne who rested in his arms, eyes closed, deep in concentration.

"Delay them for us, then," he said. "We aren't leaving until this hall is empty." He glanced back inside. "There are only a few hundred to go."

"Gods, you're pushing it close," said Denser.

"Too close if you don't start laying down some fire," said Hirad. "So go and make yourself useful."

Denser glowered and swept back into the sky, heading southwest.

"Come on, hurry!" Ilkar shouted, frustration edging his tone. There were only a couple of hundred left in the store and Hirad had to smile though he could hear the barking shouts of the approaching enemy.

"Calm down, Ilks. We'll be fine."

"*Calm down?* A Wesmen army is about to slaughter us as we stand at the back of a slow-moving line of infants and ancients and all you can do is stick the only man who can slow them up with little barbs from that great barbarian mouth of yours. Don't tell me to calm down."

"Ilkar." The Unknown's tone was admonishing. "Your talk will incite panic. More haste is good, blind flight is bad." The Unknown helped a frail-looking man on his way with a friendly pat. "That's it, keep up the pace. Time is running out. That's it." He leant into Ilkar again. "Don't forget, we're The Raven. While we remain calm, so will they."

"I just think we're cutting this very fine, just like Denser says," said Ilkar.

"And you are both right," said The Unknown quietly. "But like Hirad says, we aren't leaving anyone behind."

The store was all but empty. A man jogged past with a child on his shoulders and a babe in his arms, followed by two young women arm-chairing a tiny old lady who appeared in a dead faint.

"How are we doing, Lallan?" called Ilkar.

"Fine. Almost there."

Sudden illumination from behind them threw stark shards of shadow flashing across the stone-flagged square. Hirad swung round. Drops of fire fell like heavy rain from the sky, concentrating in a tight area to the south. Above the spell, the dark shape of Denser carrying Erienne flitted upward, pursued by the black shafts of arrows. None hit, so far as Hirad could see, but the clatter of wood on stone as the arrows dropped to the earth, was lost in the tumult of noise as Erienne's HotRain struck home.

Horns sounded behind the buildings, men shouted, some crying out in shock, pain or surprise. The rumbling of running feet could be clearly heard and, where the HotRain took a hold, flames licked at wood and caressed the night from the sky, augmenting the dawn.

As Hirad watched, Denser and Erienne wheeled and dived in again, fast. A long, narrow line of HotRain flared beneath them, dropping quickly. More wasted arrows flicked into the sky, tracking far too slowly to catch the speeding mage pair, who swung back toward the grain store.

Landing in a flurry of dust as the last of the Julatsans ran from the doors with Lallan's urging voice behind them, Denser set Erienne down and shook some life back into his arms.

"We're slowing them but we aren't stopping them, I—"

With a howl, the first of the Wesmen entered the square. Like a flash flood bursting into a valley they came, filling the space with the weight of their numbers and the very air with the deafening sound of their voices as they saw their quarry at last.

The released Julatsan prisoners panicked and ran, their screams tearing at the ear, any semblance of order in those at the rear of the line dissolving into terrified chaos, stumbling, tripping, pushing and forcing their way toward the northern exit of the square.

"Move quickly but *calmly*. Help your friends, don't shove them aside!" Lallan's voice rose above the barrage of noise but was completely ignored. The Unknown turned to him.

"Get yourself out of here," he said. "Don't look back. Hirad, time to act."

Hirad gauged the pace of the Wesmen approach, guessing they might just reach the street before the enemy.

"All right you three, we need some rubble to slow them down. Sorry Ilkar but some of your buildings will have to come down." He pointed at the city administration offices and barracks that ran around the northern edge of the square around the grain store.

"No problem," said Ilkar. "C'mon you two." The Julatsan ran around the thinning crowd, Erienne and Denser, wings now dispersed, hard on his heels.

"All right Big Man, that leaves you and me for the rear guard."

The Unknown nodded. "I gathered. Let's go." The two men turned and hurried after the fleeing Julatsans, shepherding them toward the exit from the square which was under heavy guard.

"Keep it going. No need for panic, we're at your backs." Hirad's voice urged and cajoled frightened men, women and children. To his left, The Unknown scooped a fallen child under one arm and sprinted forward, planting the crying girl on the shoulders of a young woman. He turned back to the onrushing Wesmen, caught Hirad's eye and yelled.

"Duck!"

Arrows coursed over Hirad's head, plunging into the defenceless civilians. A dozen fell and the line disintegrated, people running in all directions to avoid the killing shafts.

"No!" shouted Hirad. "Forward. Keep going forward." But his voice was lost. Behind him, the Wesmen roar increased, and the pounding of their feet could be felt through the cobbles of the square. "Ilkar!" His voice now a bellow, Hirad saw Ilkar turn his way. "HardShield! HardShield! Protect the exit."

An arrow whistled past Hirad's right ear, burying itself in the shoulder of an old man. He fell and others paused to help. Hirad made a hurrying motion with his arms as he hurdled the body. "Don't stop. You can't help him, he's gone already. Run on."

With The Unknown again at his shoulder, Hirad urged and pushed the Julatsans out of the square, at every step expecting an arrow to thud into one or both of their bodies. The shafts still fell but they were arced to fall into the main body of the crowd in an attempt to incite more panic. But those who hadn't broken away as the first arrows fell had clearly decided to run head-long and trust to luck, for which Hirad was eternally grateful.

Ahead, Hirad could see Ilkar had cast and that Erienne and Denser were deep in concentration, at work on the spell that would bring down the build-ings in the faces of the Wesmen. In front of them, Julatsan soldiers beckoned the crowd on, helping them to relative safety up the secured path that Hirad knew must be under increasing pressure all along its length.

"Almost there," he shouted. "Keep pushing on."

The arrows no longer fell in the crowd, bouncing instead from Ilkar's shield. Hirad and The Unknown reached the line of soldiers, stopped and spun round. The Wesmen were less than a hundred yards behind them.

"Now Denser," said Hirad. "Now Erienne." He and The Unknown spread their arms and moved backward, ushering the soldiers back with them. The Wesmen roared on, sensing blood.

"Hammer," said Denser and Erienne together.

Beneath their feet, the earth rumbled and shifted. Hirad felt a ripple travel through his body as it moved in the direction of the square, gathering in intensity.

As he continued to move back, he saw the Wesmen line falter in its charge, still forty yards distant, as it neared the buildings. Under the enemy, cracks opened as the ground moved violently, pitching Wesmen from their feet, forcing most to stop and scramble for balance. Behind them, their com-rades ploughed on, trampling the fallen underfoot until horns and shouts slowed them to a stop.

To Hirad's left and right, the buildings shuddered, loose chips of stonework and dust clouded the outlines and roof slates shifted and fell. A pause followed in which Denser and Erienne both jerked their arms skyward before flattening them in an arc to the cruciform shape. Then they turned and ran.

Without bothering to wait, Hirad did the same, closing to Ilkar's ear as he did so. "Time to go, Ilkar. Keep that shield up if you can."

The Julatsan nodded. Hirad grabbed one of his arms and led him away, all the time with one eye on the scene behind.

Slabs of stone twice a man's height burst from the ground, spearing the street in two dozen places and showering cobbles and mud in all directions.

They rose under the buildings and the feet of the Wesmen causing chaos and destruction while all the time the tremors and ripples gained strength as they focused under their targets.

With a flat crack that echoed into the lightening sky, the city administration offices slid left into the street. Thousands of stones burst from their bindings to cascade, bounce and crash down to cover the escape of the Julatsans, the clatter of pebbles complementing the rumble of the main parts of the building and the fragmenting of tiles. Moments later, barracks to the right began to rock as slab after slab rose inside, sending slate and timber into the square, scattering the Wesmen line. Across the street a fissure opened in the ground, the fault running left and right gouting dust into the air and yawning three feet wide in places.

"Let's take this chance!" roared Hirad. "Push it on, straight to the College. Come on!"

Falling back in preordered form, the Julatsan city guard closed ranks as the whole force began slowly to relinquish the corridor while maintaining the integrity of its shortening length. They had been trained for just such action. Drilled for years in fighting street to street, falling back in safety to the next bottleneck when required and striking out in guerrilla action to weaken and demoralise attacking forces, the guard moved efficiently to the College.

Inside the cordon, The Raven ran the line of city folk, cajoling, urging and encouraging while Ilkar's moving HardShield, joined shortly after by those of Denser and Erienne, provided significant protection from the arrows that fell sporadically into the running crowd.

Hirad knew the building collapses wouldn't hold the Wesmen for long and already, as the desultory arrow drop indicated, they were finding their way along parallel alleys, though not in sufficient numbers to overwhelm the well-drilled Julatsan city guard who had beaten off all attempts thus far. But there was one point where weakness in their line was inevitable and, glancing back to see the retreat under control, he made his decision.

"Unknown!" he called above the cries and screams of the crowd and the barked orders of the guard Captains. "The southern market."

The Unknown nodded. "Raven! Raven with me!" Dropping their shields, the trio of mages formed up behind the warrior pair and ran for the open space of Julatsa's southern market place where, in peaceful times, grain and fresh produce were traded.

It was asway with people, the yelling of soldiers, the running of the old and the young and the clash of weapons as the Wesmen battered at the slim line of defence, heedless of the spells that dropped death on their defenceless bodies.

Hirad headed left across the market where the Julatsan line was being pushed back, not needing to check if The Raven were with him. In front of him, he could see hundreds of Wesmen spilling into a wide access street and running to the attack. Facing them, two dozen Julatsan guard and a pair of mages, one of whom was maintaining a HardShield as occasional bouncing arrows indicated.

"Denser, we need FlameOrbs. Ilkar, relieve the shield mage. Erienne, whatever you've got to keep them back. Unknown, with me." Hirad ran into the centre of the line, pulled an injured man away with his left arm and swung his blade right-handed and overhead, feeling the metal crash through the shoulder of his target. Behind him as he squared up, he heard The Unknown issuing instructions to the Julatsan squad leader.

"Take half your men and shore up the rolling retreat to the south. Leave the mages with us. Keep the people moving. We're doing well but we're not home yet."

"Yes sir," said the squad leader. Moments later, The Unknown was beside him, his blade making the space he needed, cleaving the air in a tight upward arc, punching a Wesman from his feet as he tried desperately to block. The enemy warrior crashed into those behind him, his axe shaft splintered, his hands bloodied. Hirad smashed a fist into his next victim's face and drove his blade straight into the Wesman's stomach.

"*Sir?*" Hirad shook his head. "Are you sure he knew who you were?" He drove his sword at the face of an enemy who blocked it with his own, jumping back as he did so.

The Unknown risked a glance across at the barbarian, his double-handed blade sweeping through in a defensive arc, connecting with nothing but keeping back everything. Hirad saw the big man's mouth turn half up as he shrugged.

"He just recognised authority when he spoke to it," he said.

"Arrogant bastard." Hirad smiled.

"Big sword." The Unknown winked and hefted his blade. "It usually does the trick."

The press on the Julatsan line had eased just a little. The arrival of The Raven had energised the flagging Julatsan guard and given their adversaries pause for thought. There was not quite so much determination to breach into the square. An air of anxiety flickered across the faces of the Wesmen facing them and still any arrows bounced from the HardShield, now almost certainly held by Ilkar.

Denser's FlameOrbs exploded into the partial standoff, flitting over the heads of the first Wesmen and landing in the thick of their number, inflicting maximum damage, panic and chaos.

Though it was a sight he'd seen many times before, Hirad still had to steel himself against the horror of the magical flame that ate through armour and flesh like acid, burned with the intensity of a blacksmith's forge and was as hard to douse. Those Wesmen who could, scattered from the effect of the flames, leaving their comrades to tear at clothes, beat at flames that consumed skin and hair and die in screaming agony.

Hirad and The Unknown were ready for the fallout as the instinctive move from the centre of the spell pushed unprepared Wesmen toward them. They led the Julatsans, striking hard and fast, cutting the enemy down as they all but stumbled on to the Julatsan defenders' blades.

And before Denser's magical fires guttered, HotRain was falling among the confused ranks of Wesmen who broke and scattered backward, their wounded comrades and dead forgotten in the rush to dodge the tears of flame.

Hirad laughed. "On your way, Wesmen!" he called after them. "You'll never take the East."

He and The Unknown stooped among the fallen, their daggers finishing those who still lived before they cleaned their blades on charred furs and scorched cloth and swept up discarded axes, knives and swords, prising or chopping away locked fingers.

"We've bought a little time here," said The Unknown, glancing behind him as he reformed the line with Hirad, passing his haul of weapons to soldiers standing ready. "But just a little. Look at that movement." He indicated with a lazy sweep of his sword, flicking the heavy blade as nonchalantly as he might a stick. Hirad followed his gaze.

The Wesmen had reformed some thirty yards distant, a massive gap in the context of this conflict, at a crossroad where a narrow alley crossed the main street. Behind their somewhat bemused defensive line, Wesmen poured across the street, heading north toward the College. The numbers weren't great but it could be assumed that the movement was being mirrored on the opposite side of the southern market.

"The last thing we need is to come under sustained attack before we're into the defence from the College walls," said The Unknown. "We need more weight further up the chain."

Hirad glanced over his shoulder. The square was emptying rapidly, now populated principally by city guardsmen and soldiers.

"I think we just need to leave," said Hirad. "If we don't, we'll soon be overwhelmed anyway, defence from the College walls or not."

The Unknown nodded. "Agreed." He raised his voice just a little. "All right. On my mark, we move backward. Denser, Erienne, look after Ilkar."

The Julatsans, under The Raven's calming voices, began to back away into the square, triggering an instant reaction among the Wesmen who advanced, crowding into the street, still cautious and thirty yards distant.

"Shield down," said Ilkar almost immediately. "Wait. This is no good; they'll overwhelm us if they charge, we need to keep them further back. We need static ForceCones covering every exit to the square. Any mage that can cast, do it. Hirad, trust me."

"Always," said Hirad. Ilkar began casting. "I'll stay with him. The rest of you find those mages."

Erienne hesitated, made a half move but Denser stayed her. The Unknown turned to the Julatsan squad leader, talking over the shouts he could hear across the square as the retreat continued.

"You heard him. We've got to buy more time. Run." He moved to stand by Ilkar's free shoulder, Denser and Erienne forming a mage line behind the trio. "Now is not the time to split us," said The Unknown. "We are The Raven." He held his sword in front of him, point tapping rhythmically on the stone at his feet.

A calm came over Hirad. He smiled and faced the enemy. Beside him, Ilkar's low intonation stopped and he spoke the command word. The Force-Cone, invisible and impenetrable, hurtled toward the advancing Wesmen.

"HardShield up," said Erienne.

"Ilkar is secure," added Denser.

Numerical superiority belatedly overcame fear of magic and the Wesmen charged, angry yells spilling from their lips, axes and swords catching the first rays of morning light. But a mere handful of paces in, the charge was abruptly blunted as the leading warriors smashed into Ilkar's ForceCone which barricaded the street so effectively.

Wesmen bounced from its invisible surface, stumbling back and sprawling, those behind them, not willing to believe what their eyes showed them, hurdling their prone comrades only to discover the truth as noses were bloodied and axes sprung from hands.

Bewilderment replaced anger for a while as confused men picked themselves from the ground, gathered up weapons and moved cautiously forward again, hands outstretched, until they encountered Ilkar's barrier.

Hirad watched them with a kind of detached amusement, confident in both the Raven mages' spells. The Unknown, he could sense, was monitoring the square behind them, his eyes no doubt assessing defence of other entrances and his mind calculating when the time would be right to run.

In front of Hirad, the Wesmen quickly appraised their problem. A few ineffectual strikes against the Cone did nothing but risk sprained wrists and the arrows loosed bounced or snapped on impact, springing back toward the rapidly growing force behind.

The archers switched their attention to the boundaries of the Cone, testing its height by sending arrows up at ever steepening angles until they cleared its upper edge, plunging down merely to bounce from Erienne's HardShield, choking off the fledgling cheers of the Wesmen. They fell silent and dropped away a couple of paces. They knew they were up against magic they couldn't penetrate but knew also that they had one last weapon. Time. No spell lasts forever.

Hirad checked The Raven. Ilkar and Erienne were deep in the maintenance of their spells. Denser stood with a hand on Erienne's shoulder, his eyes open but unfocused, monitoring the castings. The Unknown had backed up a few paces to get a clearer view of the square in its entirety. He was frowning but not scowling. Things weren't critical.

So Hirad turned back to the enemy, watching their growing frustration. He caught the gaze of a Wesman warrior. He grinned broadly. The man had a smear of blood on his face and the skin of his knuckles was broken though he gripped the shaft of his axe hard. His eyes, dark and brooding under heavy brows, stared from a square face pocked by weather and skirmish. Thin lips, large ears and a mass of unruly hair framed his scornful facial cast. Hirad cocked his head, let his expression harden, then straightened his posture.

"Think you can take me?" he asked. The Wesman, apparently with a rudimentary grasp of eastern dialect, nodded. "Know who I am? Know who we are?" No response. "We are The Raven. We are your nightmare. We are your death." Borrowed words but the Wesman wouldn't know it. Hirad saw him shift his stance and retake the grip on his axe.

"Must you?" asked The Unknown, at his shoulder once again. "They'll only run faster."

"Not fast enough. What's up?" Hirad saw The Unknown chewing his lip.

"There aren't enough mages in the square. The Wesmen are peppering arrows where they know we have no shields. It's only a matter of time before one of the Cones goes down."

"And the prisoners?"

"They've cleared the square but it's slow going. And there's fighting further up the secure corridor."

"How long do you think we've got?" asked Hirad.

"How good are the Wesmen archers?" replied The Unknown.

Good enough.

A roar echoed through the square. Moments later, the first of the Julatsan guardsmen sprinted past The Raven's position, heading north.

"If we stay, we'll die," said Hirad. In front of him, the Wesmen tensed, ready. The Unknown nodded and leaned into Ilkar.

"Ilkar, we have to leave. When I squeeze your shoulder, drop the Cone and run. Don't look back." Ilkar's reply was a slight nod of the head. Denser relayed the same message to Erienne.

"Ready, Hirad? Denser?" The Unknown took in their curt acknowledgements, placed a hand on Ilkar's shoulder and squeezed. The Raven's Julatsan punched his hands outward and the Cone shot into the unsuspecting Wesmen before dissipating, knocking a dozen from their feet and causing momentary disarray. It was all the gap the Raven needed.

"Run!" yelled Hirad. And The Raven ran, Denser snatching the slower Erienne into his arms and springing into the air on load-bearing ShadowWings. Tearing left into the square, Hirad looked right to see a wave of Wesmen forging into the open space and, in front of them, a handful of Julatsan warriors and mages desperate to escape the deluge.

Ahead, the column of ex-prisoners, all pretence at order gone, stampeded toward the College while at either side of them city and College guardsmen fought grim battles with Wesmen determined to close the pincer.

The Raven trio, under Ilkar's running HardShield, took up rear station on the chase. Above them, Denser swooped in again and again, Erienne scattering HotRain to disrupt the Wesmen charge and buy precious time. And as they approached pockets of defence at entry points to the corridor, The Unknown or Hirad barked the order to disengage to the Julatsan guard.

They gained on the prisoner column quickly, the walls of the College looming large. Great sheets of magical fire sealed the path to the south gates across the cobbled space in front of the ancient school and, mercifully, hid the mounds of bodies that rotted and stank where they lay.

They were close to sanctuary, so very close, when the last alley defenders buckled under the weight of Wesmen numbers and the enemy spilled into the street, their weapons flailing around the terrified city folk.

"Denser, block that entrance!" roared The Unknown as he upped his pace toward the break that threatened to trap them. Hirad swore and plunged into the crowd, his sword slashing the spine of a Wesman whose axe had bitten into the skull of an old man, killing him within sight of safety.

The Dark Mage and Erienne flew over his head. HotRain fell, this time a downpour, a curtain of flame drops, orange, red and white splashing over stone, brick and body.

To Hirad's left, The Unknown, his momentum giving him great strength, picked up a Wesman with one hand around his neck and hurled him from the scattering crowd.

"Run. Get to the doors. Now!" he yelled. Behind them, the Wesmen army poured up the street, showers of arrows clattering off walls and pouring down into the fleeing Julatsans. Hirad chopped the thighs of another Wesman, stooped and picked up the child who had stumbled at his feet and ran, the shouts of the enemy firing into his ears.

"Go! Go!" he shouted and Ilkar dropped the HardShield and chased ahead, The Unknown just in advance of him. Over their heads, spells from the ranks of Julatsan mages arced out, fire, ice and hail tearing into the storming Wesmen army, whose charge slowed and stopped where their men were cut down by the magic against which they were helpless.

"Close the gates," called Hirad as they neared and the gatemen obliged, The Raven squeezing through the gap they left. The great iron-bound wooden gates clanged shut, WardLock fizzed across the wood and the last arrows thudded in harmlessly, their impact muted by the thick timbers.

Hirad set down the child who clung to his leg bawling, his mouth wide, terrified, eyes streaming tears. The Raven warrior wiped and sheathed his sword, feeling the gazes of his friends on him, their mouths turning up, smiling through their gasps for breath. He shrugged and patted the boy ineffectually on the head. The volume of his cries increased.

"You're safe now," Hirad said. "Quiet down."

Denser landed close by, Erienne tumbling from his grasp to snatch the toddler from Hirad's leg, holding him to her chest and patting his back, his arms thrown around her neck.

"Do you know nothing?" she asked him, but there was admiration in her voice, not anger.

Hirad smiled. "Not a great deal," he said. "Thanks." He looked about the College courtyard. It was teeming with bewildered but relieved city folk, some of whom had the presence of mind to thank their rescuers before being ushered away by College guards anxious to clear open spaces at risk from projectile attack.

Above The Raven, who leaned against the walls, the spell barrage had ceased and outside the Wesmen clamoured, kept back for now at a safe distance, wary of magic. But soon, the false calm would be shattered and already men had fought and mages had spent themselves and it was not yet full dawn.

And before they could join the battle, The Raven had texts to find but, more importantly, a duty to perform. One that wouldn't wait.

Hirad indicated the infirmary.

"Come on, Raven, we have a Vigil to observe." The mercenaries walked solemnly across the College courtyard. Of Thraun, there was no sign.

Chapter 26

Styliann felt a tiny pang of sorrow for what he had led the Wesmen into.

The Protectors had run on, indefatigable, resting only when the Wesmen behind them had to pause, and pushing on before their pursuers began again. Throughout the chase, the Wesmen never fell back by more than a few hours and Styliann was impressed by their sheer stamina and determination.

But, with the sun at its zenith on the third day of the chase, he had met the Protector army he had summoned from Xetesk and now he waited. The scouts he had posted estimated the Wesmen force to be in the region of four to five thousand but, even though he had perhaps a tenth that number of Protectors at his disposal, he knew he would win, probably losing no more than forty of his charges in the process.

Styliann surveyed the land on which he had chosen to fight. He sat on his horse on a small rise to the right of his main force of Protectors. In front of him, the ground rose gently to a small plateau, on the other side of which lay a steeper slope up which the Wesmen would soon be marching.

To the left and right, tracking through areas of low crag and woodland, a dozen Protectors swept for forward enemy scouts while two groups of forty lay ready for the flanking order when battle was joined.

That left almost four hundred to take the core of the Wesmen battle front. They stood absolutely silent below the lip of the rise, waiting for the pulsed command from Cil to surge over the top. Should everything go as planned, mêlée would be joined before the Wesmen archers could string their bows.

Styliann had chosen a reasonably narrow focus for the attack. His front line would be no more than eighty warriors wide. Narrow enough to ensure he couldn't be overwhelmed, wide enough to unleash the full force of the Protectors on an enemy who would be totally unprepared for what they faced.

He heard the Wesmen long before a silent order brought his Protectors to the ready, each with sword and axe in either hand. The tribal songs echoed from the slopes, filtered through the trees and rang into the clear blue sky on the gusting breeze. Ten tribesmen, making up a Wesmen advance guard, ran up the rise and over it, meeting swift, silent death on the blades of the waiting Xeteskian warriors before they had a chance to change their songs to warnings. The rest of the army were jogging, the pace and rhythm of the words told him that, driving hard toward their doom with victory on their lips.

Styliann smiled at the irony.

It would soon be time, and the former Lord of the Mount found himself irritated at the necessity of the fight to come. But he couldn't have the Wesmen chase him to the gates of Xetesk, as they would undoubtedly do if not stopped before. He had no guarantee that he would gain access to the city immediately and any delay could quite literally be fatal. The ground around Xetesk was too open and even the Protectors would struggle against four thousand on the fields before the walled city. No, it had to be here and it had to be now.

Styliann turned to Cil. "Engage at will." Cil nodded and faced the ranks of his brethren, still with a secure hand on the reins of his Given's horse. Styliann felt a stab of nerves through his confidence but he quashed it merely by looking again at his Protectors.

Not a word was shouted, no signals fanned through their ranks, no heads turned to await command. The thunder of footsteps grew, vibrating through the ground as the enemy closed. Individual voices could be heard through the mass of the song, whose intensity never let up as they ran. Four thousand Wesmen calling death to their enemies, beating axes against thighs, the dull thumping adding a grim beat to the song. On they came, a surge racing forward, ready to crash on their foe. They had no fear. It could be heard from every throat. They were the Tribes; the land would be theirs.

And hidden before them, the Protectors. One moment, they were standing stock still while the songs of the Wesmen and the sound of their feet rolled over them. The next, battle was joined in a ring of steel and a storm up the rise.

Wide spaced, to allow the free wielding of both weapons, the Protectors ran mute into the unsuspecting ranks of the Wesmen, whose songs died in their throats, turning to warning and battle order as the first of their number dropped lifeless to the ground. The Xeteskian thralled force plunged in with extraordinary brutality, stopping the Wesmen in their tracks with a blistering barrage of axe and longsword. Screams filled the air.

Styliann watched dispassionately as his Protectors destroyed the vanguard of the Wesmen before they had a chance to break from their ten-abreast column, the mana shape for HotRain playing in his mind.

He rode further up the rise on which he was positioned, moving nearer the battle, and was greeted with the sight of his flanking forces wading in from the left and right. They scythed through the column, cutting off a section of perhaps three hundred Wesmen.

Completely surrounded by Protectors, they were simply massacred while the Dark College force simultaneously formed a new advanced front line, again precisely spaced but with a concavity to draw the Wesmen in.

The enemy leader finally managed to force order on his men. Commands ran throughout the panicked column, which broke and moved to attack on a broader front, meeting the Protectors head on. Behind the lines, archers peeled away and Styliann quickly adjusted his mana shape, moving from the lattice that was HotRain, to the tight spheroid that produced FlameOrbs.

Before the first volley of arrows was nocked, the ex-Lord of the Mount's quartet of white-striated orange Orbs, each the size of a human skull, sailed over the closing battle lines to splash fire on the defenceless archers. Those not deluged, scattered, a pall of thick smoke rising from burning victims, cries of pain louder than the urgent orders to reform.

Battle proper was joined with the Wesmen in turmoil and fighting as much for shape as for their lives. They were scared. Styliann could see it in the set of their bodies and knew what they faced. Masks and polished steel. Death whose countenance they would never see, death that was silent and unstoppable.

The Protectors made no sound. No grunts of exertion as they struck, no battle cries, no screams from the injured and the few who died. Nothing. Just a wall of blades; flat, featureless masks and dark-stained leather, chain and plate. To Styliann's ears, the sound of their weapons was almost musical, and he watched their inexorable advance, likening it in his mind to a macabre dance.

Blades flashed in the sunlight, crashing into the Wesmen's stout defence. Axe and sword fell remorselessly as the Protectors forced the pace, their onslaught withering and awesome. The clatter of weapon on shield, the dull thud of blade on body, the sparking clash as metal found metal; all drifted over Styliann on a cloud of Wesmen blood. Three more times, at Cil's request, he launched devastating FlameOrbs into groups of archers or individual bowmen. Three times, fire washed the sky. Three times, the acrid smoke rose to mingle with the dust and the blood.

The Wesmen were brave and resolute and Styliann admired their spirit while pitying the futility of their action. And they didn't simply queue up to die. From the rear of their lines, more than five hundred broke ranks to skirt the battlefield, aiming to flank the Protectors. Watched all the way by the scouts concealed left and right, they were met by a force of the Xeteskian warriors who peeled from the line to confront them before they could pose any threat to Styliann.

Even that didn't deter them. Ultimately, it was the Protectors' defence that broke their morale.

The battle had raged for well over an hour and the Protectors had maintained their steady, silent advance, walking through the bodies of the Wesmen, never looking down to find their feet, each pace sure and certain. Those behind the fighting line directed movement, leaving them free to focus on attack, while others stooped to pull fallen brethren from the carnage.

It was a hopeless task for the Wesmen. Even when a Protector fell, their line was never in danger of being breached. Almost before the warrior had hit the ground, another was in his place, completing the defensive net.

Each Protector attacked without a flicker of a glance to his flanks. And while his sword or axe drove at his latest opponent, his chosen second weapon blocked and parried both strikes to his own body and those of the brother next to him; all directed by the soul mind whose conscious strength lay in Xetesk and whose eyes looked from five hundred faces. They missed almost nothing, gave the Wesmen no consistent target, and any hope that flickered was snuffed out by the turn of a blade at the critical moment.

Styliann saw the end. To the right of the battle line, the Wesmen mounted a desperate push. Spearmen jabbed between the sword and axemen, adding a new dimension to the fight. They roared their battle cries, summoned every ounce of spirit and hurled themselves forward.

Instantly, and almost imperceptibly, the Protectors responded. The slightest closing of their ranks, the merest quickening of their strike rate, the smallest increase of the defensive response. Wesmen axe and sword found nothing but steel; spear thrusts were caught in the gauntleted hands of the second-line Protectors, their wielders dragged to their deaths. Bodies dropped, the wounded screamed, and blood ran over the feet of those still standing. In a matter of moments, the Wesmen effort to break the Protector line was reversed, the Xeteskians punched a hole in the enemy defence and their order broke and scattered.

Across the battle front, they turned and ran, the orders of their captains ignored, the belief gone and their spirit broken. The Protectors made no move to give chase, merely standing and watching them go.

Styliann laid a hand on Cil's shoulder. The Protector turned smartly to him.

"You may take the masks from the dead. But be quick with your rituals. We must be back in Xetesk before nightfall tomorrow. There is much to be done."

They'd found Thraun curled by the foot of Will's bed. The infirmary staff hadn't dared to move the big blond warrior, instead throwing a blanket over his nakedness to give him some warmth and dignity.

And that was all they could do for him because flooding through the doors had been Julatsa's wounded and dying. Every bed was occupied; dark red had joined the light colours of the infirmary, and the wails of pain and fear mixed with the clatter of buckets, the whispering of mages, the urgent shouts of the tenders and the running of feet in every direction.

Will had lain in the bed, his face covered by a sheet, waiting for The Raven to take him and honour him, the area around him and Thraun a pool of sad quiet in the hubbub of the infirmary. There had been a Vigil but no burial. Victims of the siege were to be stored in the cellars beneath the Mana Bowl, where it was cool and dry and the air heavy with incense.

Now, with Thraun lifted on to the empty bed and left to sleep, his eyes dark hollows, his mouth moving soundlessly, framing words of grief and anguish, tears squeezing from his eyelids, The Raven took time to sit and talk in a quiet chamber in the Tower. Outside, the Wesmen gathered their forces, brought up their towers and catapults and prepared to attack, while in the skies above the sun shone down, an inappropriate warmth and freshness drifting over Julatsa.

Hirad took them all in, knowing their first action should be to sleep all day. They had had no rest since Sha-Kaan's arrival, had fought almost constantly and Ilkar and Erienne, he was sure, were both spent as far as casting was concerned. Of Denser, he wasn't so sure. The Xeteskian appeared relatively fresh and alert, his pipe, as ever, clamped between his teeth. But his eyes had that distant look that Hirad didn't much care for. Like he was thinking greater thoughts than those in his company should be allowed to share. Still, it was an improvement on the sullen disinterest he'd shown since leaving Parve.

"Will's death triggered his change back, I presume," said Ilkar. Erienne nodded.

"Had to be," said The Unknown. "But I think such speculation is not the best use of our very limited time."

"We need to try and understand or we won't be able to help him," said Erienne.

"Yes, but we've got significant problems, other than Thraun, that I am afraid some of us seem to have overlooked in the recent excitement," said The Unknown, his tone forbidding any interruption. Hirad almost smiled but quashed it. Denser and Erienne wouldn't have seen him like this, not really. This was The Unknown he needed. The calm assessor and practical planner as well as the colossal warrior.

"We came here to find Septern's texts; let's not forget that. But we don't know how long the College can hold out against the Wesmen. The task is further complicated by the fact that part of the Library is now in the Heart below us. We have no idea how long the search will take and Barras cannot spare us many, if any, mages from the College defence.

"We will have to play our part in securing the College from the Wesmen, not least to give ourselves time enough to search the Heart and Library.

"We also have to tend to Thraun until he is fit enough to travel and, when we have what we came for, we have to get out of Julatsa whether the siege is over or not. The rip widens daily. It will not wait for us and we've already been delayed too long. If the measurements are correct, we have only seven days to close the rip and the only gateway we know of is three days' ride away at least." He leaned back in his chair and sipped his drink.

"But look at us, Unknown," said Hirad. "We can't fight or cast effectively right now. We're all shattered. The first thing we need is rest."

"We've made something of a rod for our own backs, haven't we?" said Denser, applying flame to his pipe. "It was a heroic rescue but they'll merely expect more of the same."

"Well, thanks for that incisive contribution," said Ilkar. "Any other words of wisdom you'd care to share with us?"

"I just felt it needed saying," said Denser with a shrug.

"It makes no difference what people expect," said Hirad. "The Raven do what The Raven have to do. And what we have to do now is rest. I don't want to see any of us on the ramparts today unless there's a breach, which is something I doubt."

"You don't think they'll expect us to advise, or just be there to raise morale?" said Denser.

"We've told Kard all he needs to know," said The Unknown. "We have to look after ourselves for now. Ilkar, what's your condition?"

"Not too bad," said the Julatsan. "I can replenish quickly here in the College. We all can, though Denser and Erienne have to modulate the flow they accept. It's you, Hirad and Thraun who need the rest. I'm going to the Heart to start the search and I'll sleep at night, Wesmen willing. If Erienne and Denser want to help, the Library will be open to them." Both mages nodded. "Good."

"Another thing before we break," said Hirad. "The Raven do not fight apart. I don't want to see any of us fighting or casting alone. I for one, will not stand on the ramparts without the rest of you. We are The Raven. Remember that."

"You'll never let us forget it," muttered Denser.

"Still alive, aren't you, Denser?" snapped Hirad. "Think on why that is."

Styliann had lost only twenty-three Protectors, an astonishing testament to the power and skill of the soul-linked army. He estimated that almost half of the Wesmen lay staring sightless at the sky and, before he left the battlefield, birds were circling over and walking among the dead, a fresh feast theirs for the taking. The rest of the routed army would report back to Tessaya and their terror would do more long-term damage than any blade.

The gates of Xetesk were closed to the former Lord of the Mount when he arrived, not that he was surprised. Dystran had few defences left and, he suspected, even fewer friends. As he rode toward the gates, the blustery, cloudy day drawing quickly toward dusk, Styliann reinforced the natural shield around his mind. He smiled as he felt the tendrils of a spell push at his barrier. They, whoever they were, had no hope of sundering the shield but he would have been disappointed had they not tried. To remain Lord of the Mount required consummate skill at protecting the mind.

Styliann dismounted and seated himself on a convenient grass-covered rise, around fifty yards from the gates and a stone's throw from the main trail. There was a quickening of the pulse as he took in the dark-walled power of his beloved city.

To either side of the grand East Gate tower, with its ornate arched windows, multiple oil runs and three levels of reinforced ramparts, the dun-coloured walls ran away for over a mile, lost to sight as the dark closed in. Studded along their length with functional mage and archer turrets built in dark grey stone, the walls turned west for around a mile and a half before meeting the great west wall which faced the Blackthorne Mountains.

With deep foundations and internal buttressing, the walls, never less than fifty feet in height, sloped very slightly outward as they rose, over-looking an area of gently undulating grass and shrubland, cleared for over a hundred yards in every direction to provide defending mages with a clear field of vision.

And inside, Styliann could see the lights beginning to shine in the Towers of Xetesk. The sight saddened him more than he cared to admit to himself, his unwanted exile pulling at his heart.

With a hundred eyes staring at him from the walls and gate towers, Styliann considered the problems he faced in gaining entry to Xetesk. Guessing the next likely action depended very much on your point of view. The average Xeteskian guardsman looking out at their Lord of the Mount and the Protector army would be confused. The more enlightened would surmise political unrest on the Mount but none would know yet that there had been an attempted usurpation. Even Dystran was not fool enough to claim stewardship until he could parade Styliann's corpse.

Inside the Mount, those few remaining loyal to Styliann would be working on a way to see him safely into the College, knowing that he couldn't fly in without weakening his mind shield—an almost certainly fatal act. Presumably, they would be negotiating with Dystran and his aides, demanding audience for Styliann in controlled conditions, probably a Cold Room.

For his part, Dystran, because he was a dithering imbecile without the wit to govern, would be hoping in vain for some preemptive action from

Styliann and his Protectors. Anything that would allow him to unleash magical offence with the blessing of the Xeteskian public. But even then he would have to exercise caution. Any aggression aimed at Styliann would trigger the Protectors and they could do significant damage to Xetesk and the College before they were stopped. All Styliann could do was wait. He wasn't kept long.

Perhaps an hour after his arrival, and with a cool moonlit night giving Styliann's quiet camp an eerie hue, the gate tower filled with archers and mages and the gate itself edged slightly ajar. One man stepped out. The gate closed. The archers and mages remained on station. Styliann rose to his feet and walked away from the warmth of his fire to approach the lone man, Cil at his shoulder, the rest of the Protectors bearing mute witness from a short distance.

"Well, well. Dystran. I am honoured." Neither man offered a hand though Styliann had to admit some small respect that the new Lord of the Mount had chosen to meet him personally.

"What is it that you want, Styliann?" demanded Dystran, attempting to appear disinterested though the flicker of his eyes betrayed his nervousness.

"Oh, just a bed for the night. I am but a weary traveller," said Styliann, his tone caustic. "What in all the hells do you think I want?"

Dystran flinched at Styliann's sudden ire. "I cannot let you back in. The decision has been made. I am Lord of the Mount."

Styliann's lips thinned. "But I came back, didn't I? You knew that I would."

"Once I knew you were still alive and in the East, yes," admitted Dystran.

"Yes," said Styliann. "Unfortunate for you, wasn't it?"

Dystran's mouth tugged up at the corners. "A little."

Styliann studied his face carefully, letting the silence grow.

"At the present time you preside over very little," said the former Lord of the Mount. "An unrestrained rip eats at the sky threatening cataclysmic invasion from another dimension and only I and The Raven have the wit to try and search for an answer. The Wesmen are battering at the gates of Julatsa. They hold Understone and the pass and tens of thousands are poised to sweep toward Korina at will. And what have you and your supporters done in my absence?

"Rather than conduct research to my instruction or organise serious defence and send soldiers to the battle for Julatsa, you have chosen to further your own personal ends. And how sorry they will look when the dragons are taking the Towers apart, brick by brick.

"If you were half a man you would see that our dispute has to be set aside until the threats to us all are gone. Right now, I need access to the Library. The destination of the Stewardship is currently unimportant."

"The Library? Then you wish to do in Xetesk what we have so far failed to do and what The Raven are trying to do in Julatsa?"

Styliann tensed, his expression hardening. His eyes bored remorselessly into Dystran's. "The Raven have reached Julatsa?"

Dystran nodded. "Contrary to your low opinion of our efforts, we are back in contact with Julatsa following the dispersal of their DemonShroud. It coincided with the rather extraordinary arrival of The Raven who apparently then released several thousand prisoners from a city swarming with Wesmen before setting to work on searching the Julatsan Library."

Styliann laughed aloud, a reaction Dystran clearly wasn't expecting.

"Gods falling but they're good," he said. "You have to hand it to them." The humour dropped from his eyes and face. "Tell me, how long have they been in Julatsa?"

"Since before dawn this morning," replied Dystran.

Styliann bit his lip. He would have to hurry or they'd pass through into the dragon dimension without him, something he could not allow. And then the mists cleared in his mind and the answer to his problems was there before him.

"Let me make you a proposition," he said, seeing Dystran frown and make a reflexive move backward. "I think it will be to your advantage."

"I'm listening."

"Naturally."

CHAPTER 27

On the walls of Julatsa, the battle raged. Spells swept across the cobbled apron around the College, detonations shook foundations. The ring of metal, the shouts of men and women, the dull thud of catapult, the wash of mana flow as spell barrages ebbed and flowed; all of it filtered down into the Heart where Ilkar sat.

With one ear constantly tuned to the fight outside, and ever ready to react should the quality and atmosphere of the sound change, he flicked through text after text, searching for note, reference and passage discussing Septern's work.

Nearby, in the Library, Denser and Erienne taxed the librarians and archivists Barras had spared them, hoping for a breakthrough that looked increasingly unlikely as the day progressed to a blustery late afternoon.

And in a chamber as far from the sounds of death and momentary glory as the College confines would allow, Hirad and The Unknown slept. Not that they needed the quiet. Part of the career warrior's art was the ability to sleep practically behind the front line. Hirad was particularly adept at snatching rest as the blood spattered his face, his innate sense of danger always waking him before his life was threatened. No, they didn't need the quiet but Ilkar was anxious to see they rested deeply. There were hard times to come.

Ilkar rubbed his eyes and stared gloomily at the mass of books, scrolls and bundled papers he had still to sift through, next to the relatively small pile he had completed. He had known it would be difficult. Complete texts by Septern were rare and that pile of five bound volumes already sat at his right elbow, having been among the first brought to the Heart by Barras when the Wesmen threat grew. But all three Raven mages knew that much of Septern's wisdom, scribbled down on scraps of parchment, annotated on other texts or sketched on the backs of scrolls, was either lost, hidden or transcribed. All they had was reference, cross-reference and the incomplete knowledge of the archivists. Following another vague lead offered by the preceding parchment, he frowned, sighed and read on.

In Julatsa's Library, the hours crawled, though the work had a deadline neither could forget. Erienne and Denser's arrival had, despite Barras' assurances of good faith and assistance, been greeted with total suspicion by the archivists; three old men and a young student, who stared down their identically long noses and sniffed at every request.

"It takes a certain sort to organise a library, don't you find?" Denser had said soon after they arrived.

"They could be brothers of those in Dordover," Erienne had agreed.

"One magic, one mage," Denser had said, covering her hand with his. Erienne had smiled and placed a hand low down on her stomach, imagining her child moving within her though in truth she could feel nothing.

"I hope so," she had said.

The archivists' frosty attitude had warmed over the following hours as it became obvious that The Raven's mages had no intention of pillaging Julatsan secrets. Curt responses, thumped-down books and half-thrown scrolls had given way to slight smiles, words of help and encouragement and, eventually, to direct research assistance.

The archive student sat at the desk with them, poring over a referential text of Julatsan lore, every now and then lifting a nervous head as the sounds of fighting reached his young ears.

"We're in no immediate danger," said Denser.

"How do you know?" asked the student, Therus, his freckled face displaying his awe of the Dawnthief mage next to him.

"Because Hirad Coldheart hasn't appeared to order us up to the walls," replied Denser. "Keep calm. Your soldiers have great hearts. They won't crumble."

Mollified, Therus went back to his reading. Erienne smiled and Denser leaned back and stretched his aching neck, taking in the vast shelves of magical text, theoretical research, casting analysis and lore—the latter incomprehensible to him and passed to Ilkar if any potential use was indicated.

They were seated at a desk near the door to the Library, facing an aisle flanked by five-tiered shelves that, studded by more desks, ran away fully two hundred feet. Five more such aisles made up the lower level and further shelves ranged around the walls, their highest texts accessible only by ladder. Two galleries held yet more of the accumulated wisdom of Julatsa and her allies, their ornate polished balustrades reflecting the gentle illumination cast by static LightGlobes. Below he knew, but hadn't seen, older and more delicate texts were stored in carefully controlled atmospheres where the light seldom shone.

Julatsa's Library, like that of Xetesk, was heavy with age and history, its dry paper-dust mustiness a delight to the bookworm's nose. But, curiously for a building containing so much latent knowledge and power, the Library bore no mana weight. No yoke-like mass hung on the neck and, as Denser kneaded the taut back of his own with one hand and Erienne's with the other, he was very glad of the fact.

"Where are we at?" he asked of anyone who cared to answer.

"Nowhere particularly useful," replied Erienne, nodding her thanks as further ribboned parchments were edged onto the desk at her right hand.

"We have established a possible link between Septern's contained rip-building and the DimensionConnect used at Understone but nothing so far on the lore to combine the two into a closing pattern.

"Therus vaguely remembers a note in the margin of a Julatsan text pertaining to mana flow and dimensional disruption caused by rip construction but can't find it and you have discovered a way to maintain your pipe bowl at a temperature that burns the weed more effectively."

"And very important it is too," said Denser, a glint in his eye. Erienne thinned her lips.

"It's a disgusting habit."

"It's my only vice."

"Hardly."

Therus cleared his throat. "Sorry to interrupt but I've found something."

"Good?" asked Denser.

"Not entirely."

"Well, let's hear it."

The dreams chased themselves across Thraun's mind with a clarity he would be unable to forget on waking. All the thoughts, feelings, scents and urges of his lupine half played out in his human mind and, for the first time, he would remember everything.

His consciousness fought to surface through the morass of his exhaustion and grief. A pit was open in his heart, and the protestations of his strained muscles, and bruised and stretched sinews and tendons merely added symphony to his sorrow.

He lifted his lids on a reality he had previously seen only through other eyes. The white, he remembered. It was the colour of the walls, the sheets and the bandages. The people too, some lying still, others moving amongst them. Here there was comfort but it was mixed with death.

Thraun mumbled the first of a thousand apologies to the friend he had failed and whose eyes, closed forever, no longer saw the world. The sound he made moved from whisper to growl and almost immediately he felt a hand on his brow, then the cool touch of a damp cloth. He focused, looking up to the face of an elderly woman whose lined skin surrounded eyes of stunning clear blue. She smiled down at him.

"You do not have to fear retribution for what you are here," she said, her voice quiet. "Here you can rest secure."

That they should be aware of his other form had not impinged on Thraun but he was calmed by the reassurance nonetheless. He didn't have the energy to frame the words of thanks but the woman seemed to understand.

"Do not hide your grief," she said. "It is human to cry. Your friends paid him great respect and he is at peace. Rest now. There is water by your bed. I am Salthea. Call me when you need me. Rest now."

Thraun nodded and turned his face away, unwilling to let her see the first of his tears.

While waiting for Ilkar to arrive, Denser read and reread the entry Therus had found, Erienne doing the same. Its meaning was clear enough. There were other writings; important ones, detailing the living construct of inter-dimensional rips, how they sustained themselves against the buffeting of the void they travelled, how they affected the space around them, the implications of linking two dimensions and the implications of dissolving that link. To devise some kind of answer quickly enough to the problem staining the sky over Parve, they were writings The Raven needed.

Septern, said the entry in a report made to the Julatsan Council over three hundred and fifty years before, had delivered a series of lectures to a high-level symposium at Triverne Lake covering a good deal of his theoretical understanding of dimensional magic. His lecture papers he had bequeathed to the sponsoring college. It was a typically Septern-like act—he had never felt allegiance to any college despite his Dordovan birth.

It was just a pity the sponsoring college on that occasion had been Xetesk.

"Would you believe it?" said Erienne.

"Given Styliann's desire to get to Xetesk alone and unaided, yes I'm afraid I would," said Denser.

"You think he knows about these texts?"

"Without a shadow of a doubt. He and Dystran both."

The door to the Library opened and Ilkar strode in, hands massaging his neck to relieve tension. Denser briefed him.

"Next move?" asked the Julatsan, shaking his head. "What's your reading of Styliann on this one?"

"He knows what we have to do and he'll be aware of the importance of these writings. The fact that he didn't tell us about them back in Parve tells me one thing. He wants to come to the dragon dimension with us."

"What for?" asked Ilkar.

"Well, it's possible that he doesn't trust us to find the solution alone but, given our respective talents, I rather doubt that. No, I think he's curious, which doesn't worry me, and I think he wants to eye up potential gain for himself and Xetesk, which does."

"*Gain?*" Erienne was dismissive.

"All I'm saying is, if he can do a deal with the dragons, or get some guarantees that aid Xetesk, whatever, he will."

"But he can't get there without us, can he?" said Ilkar.

"Why not?" asked Erienne.

"Because we hold both the keys to Septern's workshop," said Ilkar. "So he still needs us to help him get to the dragon dimension. And frankly, I'm confident the Kaan won't just roll over to his demands. I'm not sure he quite understands how powerful they are."

"Such is the arrogance of the Lord of the Mount," said Erienne. Denser shot her a sharp glance but said nothing.

"So we'll take him with us?" he said.

Ilkar shrugged. "To be honest, I don't see we have much choice. And I'm sure Hirad and The Unknown will see it that way. We have to close the rip first and worry about Styliann's motives later."

Denser nodded. "In that case, and returning to your original question, our next move, or rather my next move, is to commune with Styliann. Since we appear to need each other, we'd better at least know each other's position."

"All right," said Ilkar. "And then we'd better wake the others and put our heads together and think of a way to get out of here."

"How's the battle going?" asked Erienne. All three of them became aware again of the noises outside.

"Exactly as you might expect. The Wesmen are making thrusts toward the walls but are being knocked back by arrows and spells. Their catapult rounds are being held off the walls by our shields and they aren't really trying to get them over and into the College proper. They know what they're doing and so do we but there's nothing we can do about it. They'll wear the mages down and they know it. And then they'll mount a serious offensive and eventually take us." Ilkar's face was impassive but Denser knew the turmoil he'd be feeling inside. Not only was he witnessing the probable sacking of his College, he also knew he'd be forced to leave before it fell.

"And the Dordovans?" asked Denser.

"Well, clearly they represent our only real chance. Estimates are they'll reach us sometime tomorrow morning but it's critical they attack in the right place. That may also present us with our best opportunity of getting away from here unscathed." Ilkar paused and scratched his head. "Anyway, I'm going back to the Heart. Erienne, any news on Thraun?"

"He's woken once but is sleeping again. Physically, he's just tired. Emotionally, who knows?"

"Keep me posted, will you?" He turned to go. "See you a little later."

Denser watched the door close behind him. "I'm going to rest, love. I'll commune after dark." He leaned forward and kissed her. "Don't forget to replenish yourself. We need you."

Erienne reached up and ruffled his hair. "Don't worry about me, I'll be fine on a night's sleep. But you be careful. Communion with Styliann is dangerous."

Barras stood with the Council on the north walls of the College as he had done for much of the day, safe under a static HardShield and on ramparts secured by binding spells against the threat of catapult and battering ram. Even though the Wesmen hadn't laid one hand on the walls, he watched the progress of the battle with an increasing sense of hopelessness.

The day had started with an outrage, the Wesmen dousing the Julatsan dead with oil flung from heavy crossbow and light catapult and setting the corpses on fire with flaming arrows.

With pallid skin and clothing tinder dry, the bodies caught and burned quickly, removing from their loved ones the chance to honour and dignify them in death. And even as the choking, vile grey-black smoke boiled up the walls, sending ash and soot to cloud the early morning sky all around the College, the Wesmen had mounted their first attack under cover of the dreadful fog they'd created.

Though a predictable move, it was nonetheless the most difficult of the day to repel. From a breathable distance away from the choking, blinding smoke, mages blanketed the area outside the walls with FlameOrb, HotRain, and DeathHail. Forced to SpellShield the walls themselves against the inevitable inaccuracy and flashback, it was an expensive and wasteful barrage, called to a halt only when cloth-masked soldiers signalled Wesmen retreat.

And thus, as the smoke cleared, was the tone set for the day. Sporadic but sustained attack on any of two dozen points around the walls. Never enough to mount a serious threat to the integrity of the walls but enough to force continued spell deployment. Senedai knew what he was doing and he kept his own casualties at a minimum while he did it.

Had Barras heard Ilkar's swift assessment of the siege, he would have agreed with every succinct point. The Wesmen had time, or thought they did, and the Julatsans would tire eventually just like they had on the city borders. And one break was all the Wesmen really needed.

Barras rubbed at his eyes. Unusually for Wesmen, he was certain they would attack all night, probably with greater ferocity, forcing more mages and soldiers to remain on the walls while keeping those stood down from true rest. And all who stood guard faced the morale-sapping enormity of it all.

In the relative calm of the courtyard's edges and even ascending the steps to the ramparts, it was possible to detach oneself from the reality of the siege. But first view changed all that. Because, standing out of spell range in the rubble of the buildings they had demolished to make their muster areas, stood the Wesmen. Thousands upon thousands of them. Waiting. Sometimes quiet, sometimes roaring their songs of victory and hate or just chanting and taunting, voices echoing harshly off the college walls.

They were a rippling sea, waiting for the storm to whip them into a tidal wave. They were locusts, poised to strip the ripe fields.

And yet they still feared the magic. It made them cautious, just as before. It was Barras' only solace. Had they not been so, surely the first attack would have proved enough. But Senedai had not committed enough of his armies.

As a result, the Julatsans, though temporarily relieved, had to beat off jab after jab, forever weakening ever so slightly while they were forced to watch the rape and destruction of their city. Fires burned in dozens of places. The sound of falling rubble and collapsing timbers filled the air when the Wesmen's voices did not, adding to the dead weight on the shoulders of every man, woman and child who heard or saw.

There was no way out but still Barras kindled the faintest hope. The Raven were inside the College, however temporarily, while outside—

"When will the Dordovans arrive?" he asked of Seldane who had recently returned from Communion.

"Their progress is slow," she said. "There are Wesmen scouting and raiding parties all over the place, now they think the fight is nearly done. They've been forced into the woods three hours away. If they can make up the ground overnight, they'll attack just after dawn. If not, well your guess is as good as mine."

"I must remember to wake early," said Kerela.

"What's your latest assessment of our magical strength?" asked General Kard. He had stood with the Council between tours of the walls with one or other of them throughout the day. Kerela nodded for Vilif to speak.

The ancient, stooped and hairless secretary to the Council raised his eyebrows. "Not good," he said. "Not good at all. HotRain and FlameOrb, while effective, are draining over these distances and repetitions. Assuming a similar intensity of attack throughout the night, I should think we'd be largely exhausted by midafternoon tomorrow. And then, my dear friend, we will all be in your very capable hands."

Night had fallen on Julatsa but, as expected, many of the Wesmen had not stood down. Still, the catapult rounds thudded against shielded walls or dropped sporadically beyond, causing occasional damage to buildings and those foolish enough to loiter in the open.

Denser, tired and yawning, sat by Erienne in the bare Tower chamber. Erienne had just completed Communion with Pheone who had joined the Dordovan force. Conversely, feeling fresh and eager, Hirad and The Unknown demolished plates of meat and vegetables and were planning to spar for an hour or two before resting with The Raven until near dawn. Thraun still slept.

"We could go on searching for days," said Ilkar. "But I don't think we'd turn up much more here. We've found some vital detail but the prize is in Xetesk and there's no point pretending otherwise." He felt angry that Styliann had stolen a march on them but somehow was not surprised.

"To be honest, it may be a blessing," said The Unknown. He took a long swallow of ale and wiped his hand across his mouth. "We've all identified that the diversion the Dordovans will cause is our best chance of getting out. Not only that, if they don't manage to break the siege, this College will eventually fall and, sorry Ilkar, but what we're doing can't be interrupted to help save it."

"I know," said Ilkar. "We all know. We are prepared." There was a brief silence.

"We have to brief Kard and the Council," said The Unknown. "We need horses, supplies, someone to open the North Gate at the right moment and, if we can get it, back up to punch through the line."

"We'll get it," said Ilkar. "Kerela is no fool. She can see the bigger picture. I'll talk to her."

"Denser. Styliann?" invited The Unknown. Denser dragged himself from his slouch and rested his arms on the table.

"It was not an easy Communion," he said. A chuckle ran around the table despite the mood. "Styliann is clearly determined to come with us though he hasn't said as much. He knows we have to have the texts he's found and says he'll meet us at Septern Manse to discuss them. We all know what that means."

"When is he travelling?" asked Hirad, only vaguely annoyed at Styliann's apparent plan. He'd gone way past being surprised at anything he saw or heard. Dawnthief and dragons did that to a man.

"Tomorrow, same as us. He may even beat us there."

"Protectors?"

"What do you think?"

"How many?" Hirad scowled.

"He wouldn't say."

"I'll let you know," said The Unknown, finality in his tone. "Erienne, tell us about the Dordovan situation."

"There's not much that's new to tell you," she said. "The Dordovans are marching slowly toward the North Gate and have been joined by a few of the disparate groups of Julatsans hiding out in the wilds. I took the liberty of telling Pheone of our need to break out and she will pass that information on to the Dordovan commander. However, their first duty is the liberation of Julatsa. That's it, really."

"Did she give you any indication of Dordovan attacking intent?" asked Hirad.

Erienne frowned. "I don't get you."

"Are they planning a broad attack front or a spear formation to drive a breakthrough?"

"She didn't say," said Erienne. "I seriously doubt she knows."

"It's of no real matter," said The Unknown. "We know our task in either instance. Right. Rest. Hirad, come on, let's loosen up and look in on Thraun. He needs to be ready at first light."

Styliann sat with Dystran in the Tower of the Lord of the Mount, dismayed at the clutter the young mage had accumulated in just a few days. Order was everything. One day, Dystran might learn that. On the other hand, the time for his education may already have passed.

Styliann sipped from his Blackthorne red, not a classic vintage but sound enough, and took in the study. Dystran sat opposite him across the fire which burned low, its warmth already in the stone. Behind the new lord, two warriors and two mages sized Styliann up with open distrust while he had but Cil for a guard. Even so, he considered he held a considerable advantage.

"So, what is your answer?" asked Styliann, placing his empty glass in the hearth and feeling the fire warm his arm.

"Your proposal is, frankly, unbelievable," said Dystran. "And since you refuse to submit to a TruthTell, I am sceptical of its veracity."

"Come, Dystran, my refusal to take TruthTell has its reasons entirely elsewhere as you well know. I am offering you everything you desire for a single sheaf of papers we both know must reach The Raven for any of us to survive."

"But you also demand the Protector army," said Dystran.

"And for that one reason alone. Protection. In case it had escaped your attention, the Wesmen have invaded in large numbers and I must reach the Manse safely. You will be free to perform the Act of Renunciation within seven days and then they will be yours once more. Mine is a simple request and remember, when I leave the College, it is in your power to prevent me from ever returning."

"And you are promising no challenge to my Stewardship?" Dystran shook his head in disbelief.

"Correct. I will sign the deeds confirming your ascension immediately after you have them prepared." Styliann poured himself another glass of wine. "I cannot see a single reason why you should refuse."

"And that is exactly why I am so concerned."

Styliann chuckled. "I am glad to see your mind still turns. Nonetheless, my offer is everything that you want and nothing you don't."

"Why?" Dystran leaned forward. "I cannot fathom why you would give up so tamely all for which you have lived."

"No, I don't suppose you can," said Styliann. He pitied Dystran's lack of true vision. Pitied it but welcomed it. "But there are some paths opened to us from which we dare not turn."

"And the noon shade is one of those things?"

Styliann inclined his head. "In a sense, yes."

Dystran looked away into the fire but Styliann could see his eyes flicking as the thoughts tumbled through his head. Indeed, he was probably in a close Communion with his aides, who had wisely elected to remain anonymous to Styliann. Dystran's silence was brief.

"The papers will be drawn up. You will sign them and leave the city immediately, returning only with my permission and carrying Septern's pages which are loaned to you for the purpose of saving Balaia. Is that acceptable?"

"Yes, my Lord," said Styliann, rising. "And now I will leave you to your work. The Lord of the Mount enjoys little respite. I shall await the papers in the Grand Dining Room."

"Food will be brought."

"Thank you." Styliann proffered a hand which Dystran took a little reluctantly. "Until we meet again." Clutching Septern's writings, Styliann left the Tower.

Later, walking back toward the waiting Protectors, Cil trailing him leading a line of six laden pack horses, Styliann gazed down at the papers and parchments in his hands and wondered at the stupidity of the new Lord of the Mount. He hadn't questioned any of the papers Styliann had selected, indeed hadn't even glanced over them. Yet they were the keys to power and influence that made Dystran an insignificant pawn.

One day, he would realise that. It was a day Styliann relished.

It was hardly night at all, not in the way Hirad understood it. He stood in the lee of the north wall, a line of six saddled, bagged and magically-calmed horses tethered nearby while the latest assault on the College raged outside. The afterglow of spells flared visibly in the predawn dark, flooding the sky where the fires from a hundred burning buildings in Julatsa already carved their signatures.

Flames and hail lashed the approaching Wesmen whose screams mixed with the orders of the lead mages who directed the fire and ice. The thrum of bowstrings punctuated the voices but the rasp of swords was missing. No Wesmen had yet scaled the walls but they were getting closer and closer.

Hirad was content to stand in the shadows and listen. There was nothing he could do and he had to prepare himself, as did all The Raven. The morning and the Dordovan attack, when it came in, would be difficult. Risky. And The Raven weren't given to taking chances.

As he leant against the wall, hand absently rubbing his horse's shoulder, the door to the Tower opened and a huge figure stooped through it followed by one much slighter. The Unknown and Ilkar. He smiled as they ambled toward him, for all the world two friends merely out for a stroll, chatting as they walked. But Hirad could guess their words, and remarks about the warmth of the morning would not be among them.

Shortly afterward, lamp light spilled into the courtyard from the infirmary and three silhouettes emerged. In the centre the tall man walked hunched and bowed, his companions always half a step ahead. Theirs was a silent march.

"Been here long?" asked Ilkar as he approached.

"Long enough to hear the strains in the defence," replied Hirad. "Feeling good?"

"As you ever can at this ungodly hour."

"Any word from the Dordovans?" asked Hirad.

"'Be ready,'" replied Ilkar.

"That it?"

"Well they didn't give a tactical battle plan involving points of insertion, pressure magic and flank defence, if that's what you're asking." Ilkar's ears pricked. "This was a brief Communion, not a roundtable discussion."

"Call yourselves mages, I don't know . . ." Hirad's humour at Ilkar's irritation faded as Thraun loomed into view.

Someone else had brushed his hair into a ponytail; its untidiness told Hirad that. It was swept back from red-rimmed eyes which gazed blankly from a drawn and terribly tired face that betrayed every tear he had shed and all that were still to come. Hirad's heart lurched as he remembered all too clearly the aftermath of Sirendor's murder. There was nothing to be said but silence was not an option.

"The pain will ease," he said. Thraun looked at him squarely before shaking his head and dropping his gaze to the ground once more.

"No," he said. "I let him die."

"You know that's not true," said The Unknown.

"As a man, I could have stopped them but as a wolf I could only really understand my own fear. I let him die."

Hirad opened and closed his mouth, discarding his reply for something more practical. "Can you ride?"

Thraun nodded, very briefly.

"Good. We need you, Thraun. We need your strength. You are Raven and we will always stand by you."

Another nod but his shoulders had begun to shake. "Like I stood beside Will and let him die?" he managed though his throat was clogged.

"Sometimes even our best is not enough," said Hirad.

"But I didn't give him that. I was lost and because of that Will is dead."

"You don't know that," said Erienne.

Thraun favoured her with a bleak stare. "Yes I do," he said, repeating in a whisper, "Yes I do."

Throughout a tense morning, the Wesmen mounted surge after surge as if sensing a change in the atmosphere in the College. They flung themselves at the walls with increasing fury and ferocity,.

Thousands were committed, their ladders and towers bumping against Julatsan stone to be destroyed by fire, their men by wind and hail. But still they came and, as the mages tired, the threat of hand-to-hand fighting on the ramparts came ever closer.

During a temporary lull with the Wesmen regrouping out of spell range once more, The Raven moved up to the North Gate battlements to assess the state of the day. Julatsa was being systematically destroyed, her useful materials pressed into new service, and anything else broken or burned. Fires flickered everywhere and the flattened killing zone was widening by the hour.

Hirad turned to The Unknown as catapult rounds whistled overhead to smash into buildings and the deserted courtyard, warranting hardly a backward glance. The big warrior was staring impassively out over the sea of Wesmen, calculating their likely chances of escape while assessing the hit-and-run tactics that so drained the Julatsan mage defence.

"Thoughts, Unknown?"

"We're relying too heavily on the Dordovans causing a wide disruption," he said. "If we don't strike from this side too, we won't break the line."

"Positive, aren't you?"

The Unknown looked at him. "Realistic."

"So what do you suggest?"

"Well, let's assume the Dordovans strike on a front from that red bear standard across to the bull head one there." He indicated two of the flapping Wesmen muster flags set about seventy yards apart. "We can reckon on there being an instant disruption of the line to either side of up to about twenty or thirty feet as men leave the front to fight behind them. If we can reinforce that break with an attack from here, even just a quick hit, we'll much improve our chances. Simple, really."

Hirad chuckled. "We've done this before," he said, his smile broadening at The Unknown's quizzical frown. "Although you weren't with us at the time. Trust me."

The Unknown nodded and turned back to the Wesmen.

The attack came without warning, just as the sun passed its zenith. The Julatsan mages were bracing for another Wesmen surge when, on the northern periphery of the city, fire bloomed and the sound of falling masonry rumbled across the sky. Flash after flash threw shadow and blinding light across Julatsa, filling the day with vivid reds, oranges and blues.

Cheers went up around the northern ramparts, mages lost their concentration and all around the College faces turned and arms pointed. The Dordovans had arrived.

For a few timeless moments, there was no reaction from the Wesmen. Then, the sound of staccato orders rattled across the northern forces facing the College. Whole sections of the line detached, the Wesmen ordering defence by tribe and standard, their places taken by their fellows, the entire muster thinning. Those dispatched to the rear headed away along the streets and an atmosphere of relief washed over the College just as one of consternation appeared to grip the Wesmen.

The Julatsans' grim expressions were replaced by smiles and hope grew from the ashes of despondency. The College defenders roared on their saviours and, with the sounds of hand-to-hand fighting filtering across the city on the back of more and more arcing spells, Hirad had seen enough.

"It's got to be now," he said. He, The Unknown and Ilkar ran down the steps to the waiting party beneath the gatehouse. The Raven would ride behind a quintet of shielded mages and in front of two hundred foot soldiers. Swinging into his saddle, Hirad took in the others.

"Ready?" Nods asserted that they were. At a signal from The Unknown, the North Gate swung open.

"Make it quick!" he urged, "The Wesmen won't stand around waiting for us."

The small force rode out at a gallop toward the Wesmen who, clearly distracted by the attack to their rear, made no immediate move.

The two central mages loosed ForceCones that had been long in preparation. The twin spells battered through the Wesmen lines, hurling warriors to either side and driving the luckless to their deaths against buildings and piles of rubble where their bodies were flattened and torn to pieces. A heartbeat later, FlameOrbs arced away from the palms of the outrider mages to spread panic and scatter the sides of the cone-formed passage. The mages wheeled away, tracked by the fifth whose shield was not needed.

"Raven!" roared Hirad. "Raven with me!"

Keeping close form, The Raven sped into the gap, swords flailing to right and left, Ilkar's HardShield over their heads and Denser and Erienne's FlameOrbs splashing killing fire further to the sides. Only Thraun took no part. Hunched in his saddle, head down, he let his horse follow, its fear keeping it from straying.

Hirad, chopping the axe arm from an enemy, bellowed his delight at the rush. Flames rose to either side, Wesmen careered in every direction, his horse threatened to bolt at each stride, yet through the line they went. Hurled stone, axe and timber bounced from Ilkar's shield, The Unknown's sword flashed light and blood as it hacked a passage and The Raven tore through the chaos, breaking through the line to a cheer from the walls of the College, audible even with the shouts of the Wesmen ringing in their ears.

To their left, the Dordovans advanced, the well-marshalled column defended by mage fire, mage ice and three thousand swords and shields. The College had sent an élite.

Hirad made to join the attack, seeing the chance to inflict more suffering but The Unknown would not let his horse yield to the barbarian's pressure to turn.

"Not this time, Hirad," he shouted. "This is one fight we have to leave behind."

And, with the running remnants of the Wesmen siege force ignoring or avoiding them on their way to join the last battle for the College of Julatsa, The Raven galloped through deserted back streets and out onto the trampled, muddied green of the open mage lands.

Noon. And on the walls beyond the Long Rooms, the defence broke, Wesmen pouring on to the ramparts through the breach. Below, a back up team of Julatsan guard raced up the stairs, yelling defiance, charging head-long into the enemy, allowing those around them the time to regroup.

Across the courtyard, men, women and children ran in all directions carrying the wounded away from the battle, shipping water to the dozen fires that crackled where Wesmen flaming rounds had fallen, and carrying wood, weapons and food to the defence.

From the Tower, Kard's flagmen passed orders from the field Captains while the General himself strode the walls, his words boosting morale and his sword running with Wesmen blood. And at six points stood a Council member, directing spell offence, maintaining shields and simply being visible. All but Endorr, who was conscious but helpless.

Outside the confines of the College, the Dordovan force, while deflecting significant attention from the beleaguered Julatsans, had not reached the walls. Their progress, halted for over three hours, was grindingly slow and every passing moment brought the fall of the College inexorably closer.

The Raven's escape, half a day previously, had raised the hopes of Balaia as a whole but Julatsa was paying the price.

Barras orchestrated a barrage of HotRain which fell among the Wesmen attacking the north gate, scattering those not too damaged to run. He was desperate for some respite but, under a near cloudless sky, the fog of battle assaulted his every sense. The clash of weapons, the thud of catapults, the shouts of orders, the cries of children and the screams of the terrified, the wounded and the dying battered his ears. Colour flooded his eyes, a mist of ash and blood filled the sky, myriad weapons glinted in the sunlight, the ramparts and wall caps ran red, standards moved in the throng clamouring to gain the walls, flames sprang from the ground and the light of attack spells flashed and seared across open spaces around the College.

He could taste and smell fear and power, sweat and blood; he could feel the pain of every Julatsan who died and the desperation in all those that yet lived. They were not stopping the Wesmen and every invader that died made no dent in the mass still to come.

Despite their spirit, their spells and their obdurate strength, the Julatsan rear guard was simply not big enough and the Dordovans' failure to break the Wesmen lines and reach the College would surely prove fatal.

As he watched, a shout rang out to his right. Thousands of Wesmen were pouring into the square in front of the North Gate. Beyond them, the dust of the Dordovan battle still filled the air but something was wrong. Next to Barras, one of his mages sat in the lee of the battlements, accepting Communion. It was brief and at the end, she looked into Barras' eyes and the tears in them told him everything.

"The Dordovans are beaten," she said. "They're retreating." Barras felt a knot tighten over his heart and fought to keep his despair from his face. He reached down and helped the woman up.

"Come on," he said. "Don't give up. We can beat them." But as he turned to give his next orders he knew Julatsa was all but finished.

Alerted by the warnings fed around the walls, Kard dashed to the North Gate, the sweat pouring from his tired body but his spirit unbowed. Shouting encouragement as he went, he arrived next to Barras, made his assessment and leaned close to the old elf negotiator.

"This is it, my friend," he said. "When the time comes, I'll take you to the Heart."

Barras nodded. "But let's delay that time as long as we can, eh?"

Kard smiled and began barking orders to his men, standing beside them as they fought to stave off the endless tide of Wesmen. With reinforcements flush with victory over the Dordovans, there came more ladders, a second battering ram and an increase in the intensity of the battle.

In four places Wesmen had gained the walls, their ferocity driving back the defenders. Too close for spell assault, the walls had to be cleared by men alone and, as the Wesmen surged, it quickly became clear there weren't enough.

Yelling for reserve teams, Kard flailed about him, his unmistakable frame and voice a rallying point for his men. In tandem, Barras and his mages poured FlameOrb and HotRain on to the clamouring masses waiting below. But while the death toll was awful, they merely regrouped and came again.

"The gate!" yelled Kard. "Hold the gate!" As if to reinforce his words, the powerful thud of a battering ram shuddered through the stone of the north gatehouse. Immediately, spells arced out and down, but barely had the fires died than the scattered Wesmen were back on the ram, sensing victory.

From the south, the roar of attack grew as Wesmen forced further inroads on the walls and a woman screamed as one found his way to the inner court-yard before being felled by a townsman.

The defence crumbled so quickly. Catapult rounds smashed anew inside the College, the ram thumped again and again into the North Gate, its iron-clad timbers creaking, WardLocks fizzing and repair crews fighting desper-ately to reinforce it. A dozen wall breaches of varying severity had left the defenders ragged when Kard turned to Barras, wiping blood from his face.

"Now is the time," said the General.

"No, we can hold them," said Barras, eyes searching for hope but finding none. Kard gripped his arm.

"No, Barras, we cannot. Now go. I will shield you." The elven mage clasped arms with Kard, his face grim.

"Goodbye, old friend."

"Do what you have to do," said Kard gruffly. "I am a better man for knowing you."

But still a dead one, thought Barras. He ran for the stairs and as he did so, five mages detached themselves from the fighting and made their way to join him. They were the chosen whose task guaranteed their deaths but enshrined their memories forever.

As he ran to the Tower, the calls of Kard ringing loud in his ears, the tumult all around him a muted roar, Barras scanned the southern ramparts for Kerela, smiling as he saw the High Mage pointing out over the city, directing spell and soldier alike. As if feeling eyes on her back, she turned and caught sight of Barras who slowed to a standstill. For a moment, the two elves stared at one another, every time they had shared passing between them.

Barras felt a warm gentle ManaPulse bloom against his body. Kerela smiled, nodded slightly and waved. Barras returned the gesture then ran on to the Tower, drinking in everything and knowing he would never see any of it again.

Chapter 28

Lord Senedai sauntered among the ruins of the College while his warriors readied themselves for the fast march south. He'd known the boy mage would talk. Good with his magic but weak-willed under torture. It had been a bonus that he had been found weakened and in the infirmary. The others of the Council, old strong-heads, he'd simply put to death. It was the only way to reduce the danger. All except Barras. He had eluded them so far but then the College was vast underground—any coward could run and hide.

But before he left Julatsa, Senedai would keep his promise. He would have the head of the elf negotiator. Only then would he ride after The Raven who held the weapon to win the war, the weapon to bring dragons to Balaia. The weapon that would fulfil the myth of doom for the peoples of the West. His bird was already flying to alert Tessaya.

"Barras, where are you hiding?" Senedai was walking across the courtyard surrounding the Tower. His men marauded through the College; the cobbles were awash with the blood of mages. Their bodies littered the ramparts, the ground at his feet and the halls of their burning ancient buildings while their beloved people cowered under guard at the South Gate. For those who had so recently been released from the grain store the swift return to captivity was almost too much to bear and the weeping from men and women alike spoke everything about the mood of the surviving Julatsans. Crushed without hope of rescue. No one would come to save them now and every head was bowed in miserable submission.

Their soldiers, brave in the face of overwhelming odds, would, those that still lived, be given the honour of choice. To die a warrior's death or take enslavement. For the townsfolk, no such honour would be bestowed. They would rebuild their city for their new masters.

Senedai stopped walking. The answer to his question stared him full in the face. The Tower.

It alone stood undamaged by fire and force of Wesmen. Any mages left, those not running scared in the catacombs, and he had no doubt there were some, were plainly hoping the Wesmen fear of magic would keep them away from the hub of the College. Wrong. The College was broken, the Tower now just another building awaiting clearance.

Senedai smiled to himself. At least, that was the theory. The practice, as its unblemished stones testified, was very different. Every Wesman feared the power within a mage Tower but it was surely a power that had been lessened by the deaths of so many of its mages. He summoned half a dozen men to his side, dismissing their anxiety with a wave of his hand, so bolstering his own fragile confidence.

"The College is ours," he said. "Any inside are scared and beaten. Follow me and we will secure the ultimate victory."

Almost immediately on entering, the weight began to build. Senedai's men could feel it too. An oppressive atmosphere that pushed on the shoulders and neck, constricted the throat and shot lead through the limbs. It only served to heighten their unease and Senedai fought not to stutter in his stride and convey his own thoughts.

The Wesman Lord feared having to search the entire Tower for his quarry but needn't have. Once inside and moving around the central column, he could hear voices coming from below, murmuring and chanting.

He led his men down a short flight of stairs which hugged the outer wall. At the bottom of the stairs, a single door, outside of which stood a man whom Senedai recognised. The Wesman advanced, sword in hand.

"Ah, the senile last line of defence," he said.

"And one that kept your gutless, brainless hordes at bay for twelve days," said General Kard. "And I will personally see to it that you get no further." Kard's sword was at ready but he made no move to attack.

"This is a time for honourable surrender. The fight is over," said Senedai.

"How little you know." Behind the closed door the voices rose in volume and pace, cut off sharply and were replaced by one; strong, confident, determined. Barras.

"Get out of my way or I will cut you down," snarled Senedai.

"So be it." Kard lunged forward, his sword flashing in the lamp light. It was a quick strike but his age and exertion told against him and Senedai was able to block it aside and return a stab Kard moved smartly to avoid. To either side of Senedai, his men moved to attack, axes falling simultaneously. Kard's sword diverted one but the other thudded into his shoulder, driving him to his knees.

Kard's sword clattered to the floor and he fell back against the door, free hand clutching at his wound as the blood poured down his arm and chest. His eyes flickered and he gasped with pain. Senedai squatted in front of him.

"You are a brave man, General Kard. But foolish. There was no need for you to die."

Kard shook his head but was unable to raise it to face Senedai. "Wrong," he mumbled as his last breath rattled into his lungs. "There was every need."

At a gesture, one of the warriors pulled Kard's body to one side. Behind the door, the voice had ceased. The Tower shifted gently, dust drifting from timbers and stone.

"The door," snapped Senedai. "Quickly."

It was locked but an expertly placed boot had it shivering back on its hinges. Inside, six mages knelt in a circle in the centre of a room covered in books and parchments. Again the Tower moved, a more definite displacement this time. The sound of pottery breaking on stone was heard. The atmosphere of dread washed out into the corridor. Senedai stepped back a pace, his warriors more. The air was chokingly thick, deadening thought and muscle. Now the Tower shuddered, lamps fell from the walls and the sound of breaking glass echoed through the building. The Wesmen staggered; one fell, cracking his head against a wall; others exchanged anxious glances, tongues licking dry lips.

"My Lord?" The plea was drenched in fear.

"I know," said Senedai through gritted teeth. He looked again into the room, straight into the eyes of Barras. The old elf smiled.

"You can take our buildings and our lives but you can never take our Heart."

"You owe me your head, Barras."

"The deal has changed. Now I suggest you leave my Tower before it becomes your grave too." He raised his arms above his head and shouted words the Wesman Lord could not understand.

The Tower rocked violently, coving crashed down, timbers splintered, ceilings cracked and shifted, floors subsided. In front of Senedai's wide eyes, the chamber in which Barras and his mages knelt began to sink. Wood groaned and squealed against nails, stone and brick shattered like thunder. Everything vibrated.

"Leave, Senedai. Leave my College." The door whipped shut, thrust by an unseen hand. It thudded into the frame, crackling across its panels. Senedai turned to his terrified warriors.

"What are you waiting for? Go! Move!" As if to hurry them on their way, a tortured groan of timber, brace and stone tore from the sinking room. The warriors turned and ran, Senedai hard on their heels, while the walls rattled around them, the dust filled the air and, one by one, the lamps and braziers guttered and fell, the darkness spreading up the stairs behind them.

They burst back into the sunlit courtyard to join a circle of Wesmen staring up open-mouthed at the shuddering Tower. Tears ran up and down its length. Networks of cracks were scattered around it like carelessly woven spider's webs and, here and there, holes had been gouged in the stonework, the debris littering the courtyard.

It was a sight that brought fear but ultimately cheers as the Tower of Julatsa collapsed in a tumult of tumbling stone, billowing dust and shattering glass. But, as the dust blew away and the echoes died to silence, Senedai turned and walked away back to his command post, knowing that what he had witnessed was far from the end of Julatsan magic.

The march had been swift and proud, Darrick's cavalry at its head, Blackthorne and Gresse flanking the young General. Having dispatched three thousand back to Gyernath to help rebuild and defend the damaged port, Darrick organised his force, numbering just shy of eight thousand, into centiles each under a Captain. He built eight regiments from those centiles and each marched behind a mounted commander.

The mood was determined and confident yet light for all that. Each part of the army had won important victories; the port defence had held Gyernath, Blackthorne and Gresse had stopped a force four times their size from reaching Understone and Darrick had aided in the sacking of Parve, destroyed a Wesmen supply line and had either burned or taken every craft he had found.

But now the defence and harrying was over. Now the Eastern Balaians were on the attack and the talk was of liberation, not survival. It had taken them two hours to march from the beach to the rises surrounding Blackthorne's town and castle. They had expected to see the Wesmen barricaded in the town, their standards flying on the battered walls and from the castle battlements. They had expected to feel the fear pulsing from the helpless enemy and they had expected to march victorious.

What they saw, though, took the songs from their hearts. Blackthorne had been destroyed. A pall of ash from fires long dead still hung in the sheltered dip in which the town had stood. And beneath the dark cloud, barely one stone rested on any other. Blackened wreckage was strewn over a massive area. Here and there, timbers stood proud from the earth, scorched yet defiant, but of the walls there was nothing. Of the streets, the houses, the inns and businesses, nothing. And of the castle, Blackthorne's ancestral home, nothing. Just scattered stone in slab and fragment. It was a sight of devastation that literally took the breath away.

Gresse rode to Blackthorne's shoulder and dismounted to stand beside his friend who stood pale and silent, a tear from his left eye drawing a track through the dust on his cheek. This was not a time for words, it was a time to stand with your friend. To lend all the strength that you had.

And as the army crested the rise, the silence spread. Gasped expletives echoed hollowly and, here and there, Blackthorne's men fell to their knees, the will drained from their bodies, their dreams of a return home snuffed out. Blackthorne was gone.

The Baron stared down unmoving at the ruins of his town. Gresse saw the thoughts chase themselves across his face, on which anger flourished and spread. Behind them, the army waited, those native to Blackthorne stunned, those of Gyernath respectful of their anguish.

Eventually, Blackthorne turned to address all that could hear him.

"I'll be brief," his voice echoed out over the massed ranks. "Down there, you see my town. Torn apart by Wesmen. And among you are those who can see only ruins where their houses once stood. I am one of them. That is why we must pursue the Wesmen and that is why they must be stopped and driven from our lands forever. Yes, I want revenge but more, I want none of the rest of you to feel the way I feel now.

"Now let's get moving. General, if you please."

The mist was just as Hirad remembered it. Like dust across the sun but this time on a day plagued by showers and a cold wind. The dreary light merely added to the sense of wrong that the mass of static mana Septern's ailing rip generated.

But the weather was not all that was different. In front of the ruins of the Septern Manse stood Styliann and the Protector army, visible as a dark mass of barely human stillness through the mist and five hundred yards of distance. And to Hirad's left, riding so slowly he barely moved The Raven on at all, was The Unknown Warrior.

During the four days of their ride to the Manse, his mood had changed by degrees from one of hard determination to tetchy introspection, and now angry confusion. And as The Raven neared the low barn where he had met his death, his lack of focused thought led to snarled exchanges with Hirad that were merely exacerbated by the nearness of the Protector army.

"You should just ride on by," said Hirad. "Put it behind you."

"And that demonstrates exactly how little you understand." The Unknown jabbed a finger at the Protectors. "They know. They understand but they cannot say anything."

"Would it help if they could?" asked Hirad a little shortly.

"Yes, damn you, it would," snapped The Unknown, reining to a halt. "Try and get your head straight. Have you really no conception of how I might be feeling?"

Hirad shrugged. "But you're here," he said. "Here and breathing. Under the earth there isn't you. It doesn't have your soul."

The Unknown flinched as if struck. "'Soul?' Gods in the ground, your mouth will be your undoing one day," he growled. "You know nothing about my soul. By all that's right, it should be with those of my ancestors. At peace. Not back in a body that isn't the original and exposed to all this . . . this shit!" He swept his arms about him expansively, taking in everything: the Protectors, the Manse, The Raven.

"If you want to leave, go right ahead," said Hirad. "Desert the only true friends you have. I won't stop you."

"For God's sake, Hirad, listen to what he's trying to tell you," said Ilkar before The Unknown could speak again. "Unknown, you need time alone. I suggest the barn is the right place. Hirad, we have Styliann to deal with."

Hirad felt his anger surge but he kept it in check. Ilkar's expression had hardened. The Unknown simply nodded at Ilkar, shot Hirad a withering look and urged his horse to a walk toward the barn and the grave he should never have had to face.

"Hirad, we need to talk," said Ilkar.

"Now?"

"If Denser and Erienne will talk to Styliann on behalf of The Raven, I think now is a very good time, don't you?"

Hirad raised his eyebrows. "You think I've been a little insensitive?"

"You haven't lost your gift for understatement, have you?" said Ilkar. "Ride with me, Hirad Coldheart. Ride and listen."

The Unknown Warrior slid from his horse well before the long barn and let the animal wander away to trail the others to the ruins of the Manse.

Memories flooded into his head and his heart beat loud and wild in his chest, neck and ears. He pictured the Destrana war dogs running at him, their teeth bared, their saliva dripping and their eyes rolling. He felt his sword biting their flesh, the hot breath on his face, the clamp of fangs on his shoulder and the blood pouring from his torn throat.

He clutched at his neck with a gauntleted hand, his vision dimming as it had done before, the taste of his death in his mouth, the sounds around him diminishing. He fell to his knees and forward on to his free hand, gasping for breath, tears fogging his eyes. He coughed and retched, took the hand from his neck and stared at it while his vision cleared. No blood.

No blood, no dogs, no death. He raised his head, saw the barn dimly but found his gaze locked solid on the raised mound of earth just to the side of its doors.

"Oh dear Gods," he said. "Save me from this."

But there could be no salvation. For while The Unknown lived and breathed, his body still lay there. He retched again, bile flooding his mouth which he spat to the cracked earth.

"Why couldn't you let me have my death?" he growled, hauling himself to his feet. He cursed Xetesk. His home for his youth but the place that had stolen his death from him. Given him a hideous perversion of life behind a mask. He cursed the city and its masters, the mages who still retained the abominations that were his brethren.

With his every footstep like wading through thigh-deep mud, he ground his way to the grave, his eyes stuck on the dusty mound, unmarked save for the vague imprint of The Raven symbol burned into its surface—mostly gone now, eroded in a few short weeks by the incessant breeze.

And when at last he stood there, gazing down at his own lonely grave, his tears fell unchecked from his cheeks, patterning the dirt at his feet. He knelt down and brushed his hand across his grave, knowing he could touch his own bones, see his own body and face. Take a good look at the true Unknown Warrior, whose body lay where his soul wanted to be. At rest. Free.

He breathed deep and closed his eyes, placing both hands on the grave. He dropped his head to his chest.

"By north, by east, by south, by west. Though you are gone, you will always be Raven and I will always remember. Pity me that I breathe while you do not." He fell silent, unwilling to move. Knowing he had spoken the mantra to a soulless bag of bones but finding a curious peace in the Vigil he held.

Eventually, reverently, he stood up and backed two paces from the grave before turning toward the Manse. In front of him stood a Protector, Cil, and behind him, all of them. Silent ranks of understanding and respect, impassive behind their masks but with their minds ablaze at the wrong The Unknown suffered.

Unable to speak, Cil placed a hand on The Unknown's shoulder and squeezed, his head inclined very slightly. The Unknown locked eyes with him for a moment, then looked past him to those behind, a shiver running through his back at the power standing there in utter quiet. His eyes misted again, this time in gratitude.

"You can escape your calling," he said. "But the price is high, believe me. The pain of separation is great. I can still feel you though I can't be with you. Your choice will come."

He walked through the Protectors who turned and followed him back to the Manse. His choice was made but, leaving his grave without another glance, he realised he had another but he had no idea whether he had the courage to make it. Time, as always, would tell.

"If you think you're taking hundreds of Protectors through the rip, you're wrong," said Hirad once Denser had summarised thus far his fruitless discussions with Styliann. The former Lord of the Mount had flatly refused to let the Raven mages have sight of Septern's texts and Hirad considered it was only a matter of time before Styliann decided he could create and cast the magic himself. Hirad, like the rest of The Raven, was uncomfortably aware that they were hopelessly outnumbered.

"I would be keen to hear how you propose to stop me," said Styliann.

"It isn't a question of what I can do now," said Hirad. "It's a question of what the Kaan will do when you arrive. They don't need your Protectors and what they don't need, they tend to destroy."

Styliann gestured around him. "Destroying almost five hundred Protectors isn't easy."

Hirad stared at him. He felt a constraining hand on his shoulder. Ilkar's. He nodded and breathed deeply before speaking.

"You saw the size of Sha-Kaan, Styliann. He could do it on his own and you know it. I am just trying to save you wasting their lives, such as they—"

The Protectors moved, came to attention and marched slowly away toward the long barn, Cil at their head. Denser and Styliann stared slack-jawed. Hirad, when he realised where they were going, chuckled.

"Perhaps they won't listen to you anyway," he said, breaking the spell of silence.

"Come back!" ordered Styliann. "Now. Cil, you know your calling. Return to my side or face your nemesis."

"I don't think you want to do that," said Denser quietly.

"I beg your pardon?" Styliann stared on at the retreating backs of his erstwhile Protectors.

"You heard me," said Denser. "It would make The Unknown very angry. And right now, you're very much alone. They'll come back."

And come back they did, with The Unknown at their head, his face set, his determination returned.

"I take it we're ready to go," he said. "Styliann, you may take six Protectors with you. The rest will guard the Manse."

Styliann's jaw moved but no words came. His face, flushed and reddening, quivered with rage.

"Guard against what, exactly?" asked Hirad.

"*I may?* Who, by the Gods bleeding, are you to tell me what I can and cannot do with my Protectors?"

"You will understand soon enough," said The Unknown shortly.

"Unknown," said Hirad. "Guard against what?"

"The Wesmen are coming here," said The Unknown. "They must not bury the entrance to the workshop or we will never get back."

"Why would they do that?" asked Ilkar.

"Julatsa has fallen," said Cil, breaking the conditions of his thrall. "They know everything."

"How could you possibly know?" demanded Ilkar of Cil. "I have felt nothing." His voice was desperate, his eyes searching that mask for any clue and his ears reddening as he fought the emotion that washed over him.

"And maybe you won't," said Styliann. "Your mages fell one by one under the swords of the Wesmen; their mana ripples won't combine. And we must presume the Heart was successfully buried. I am truly sorry Julatsa has fallen but perhaps you are the lucky one. After all, you are about to leave this dimension."

"Lucky?" spat Ilkar. "Those bastards have destroyed the home of every living Julatsan. Lucky, my arse."

Denser cleared his throat. "Styliann's words were ill-judged but accurate, I suspect. Any ripples through your spectrum at all are unlikely to carry as much force where we are going."

"Well you'd better hope there's some, otherwise this spell, whatever it turns out to be, won't get cast." Ilkar stared meaningfully at the sheaf of papers in Styliann's hands.

"Eh?" Hirad frowned.

"No ripples, no mana," explained Erienne.

"It's all irrelevant conjecture," said The Unknown. "What we have to do is go. Now."

"Not until I find out how you know Julatsa is lost," said Ilkar.

"Cil, you may speak freely," said Styliann, plainly interested. Cil was silent for a time, his breath controlled as he thought through his reply. When it came, it was short and efficient.

"The demons are watching. When we are together as one, we can sense what they see."

"Fascinating," said Styliann. "The side effects of creation are an endless surprise."

"Enjoy them while you can," said The Unknown, his face a blank to mirror the masks of his former brethren.

Styliann half smiled. "Are you threatening me, Unknown?"

"Call it heartfelt advice."

Hirad came to The Unknown's shoulder and demanded attention. "All right, that's enough playing around. There're a few things you should know, Ilkar and Denser excepted, about what happens when we enter the rip."

He reassured them about the pain of travel, the drop on landing and the devastation of the Avian dimension The Raven had encountered in their search for Dawnthief. He described the walking dead lest they should rise again, the silence though the sky boiled with cloud and lightning above and below, the disorienting height and the other platforms in the sky, standing atop rock columns. And he reminded them that it was Kaan dragons that had caused the destruction and that the same fate awaited Balaia should the Kaan falter or the spell, when it was determined, fail to close the rip.

Finally, he told those that mattered that they were Raven and that, strange though it may appear, not just Balaia but countless dragons depended on their success.

"And now," he said, "now we will go."

But inside the Manse ruins, there was a new problem.

"What the hell has happened here?" Ilkar looked squarely at Styliann and away from the open entrance to Septern's dimensional workshop.

"It wasn't always like this?" replied Styliann, seeming genuinely surprised.

"No it wasn't," said Ilkar shortly. He crouched by the entrance, set in the middle of the floor. Denser dropped to his haunches by him and was joined by Erienne.

"I don't think Styliann is responsible," whispered Denser.

"So what has happened?" asked Erienne.

Ilkar scratched his head. "Without a key or forcing, there's only one answer to that. Septern's spell has collapsed."

"A consequence of the rip, you think?" said Denser.

Ilkar shrugged. "Can you think of anything else?"

"What does it matter?" said The Unknown. The mages turned to him, plainly irritated at the interruption. "The fact is that we can no longer seal the rip against the Wesmen. If they should defeat the Protectors, they can travel it too and I have no doubt that they will."

"We can't afford a Wesmen force in the dragon dimension," said Hirad. "No matter the power of the dragons, they could still find and catch us."

Ilkar rose and dusted down his knees. "So what do you suggest?"

"Reinforcements," said Hirad decisively. "It's our only option. Darrick must be heading north by now." He turned to Denser. "Sorry, Denser, but we need a Communion from you."

The Dark Mage sighed and nodded. "What do you want me to say?"

The Raven stood at the rip to a new dimension under a boiling sky and in the remains of the devastated Avian village. Below them, far below them, harsh red lightning sheeted and flared. It was a rip through which only Denser had passed, returning in terror, jabbering about dragons. For Hirad, it was a case of already seen. His union with Sha-Kaan gave him clear visions of what lay before them and, with a memory of curious clarity, summoned a subconscious thought that had lain hidden since Denser's ill-advised journey. Even then, he realised, he had known he would have to travel the rip himself. To face his nightmares and beat the demons of his mind.

Hirad turned to the company, Raven to the front, Styliann and his six Protectors behind.

"Are you ready for this?" He really only asked it of two of them. Of Ilkar, whose courage in the face of the loss of his College was extraordinary but flawed. And of Styliann, whose determination to minutely examine the wreckage of the Avian dimension had frayed tempers during the short walk between rips.

The former Lord of the Mount nodded stiffly. Ilkar managed a smile.

"As ready as I'm going to get," he said.

"I wish I could say the same," said Hirad. "Denser? Anything we should know?"

"Just be ready to fall backward. The place was a mess and I doubt it's got any better."

In fact, it was completely different to Denser's description. He had spoken of blackened earth, a sky heavy with dragons and fire splashing from the air. But through the rip they emerged *inside* a cave. And though it was dark where they landed, a gentle grey-green light filtered from around a sharp left-hand corner a few paces ahead of them.

"What in all the hells is this?" Denser dusted himself down. "The rip must have been moved."

"I don't think that's possible without the casting mage," said Erienne.

"Well, this bloody rock wasn't here before."

"Anyone got a torch?" Hirad was smiling.

"Dare I ask why?" asked The Unknown.

"Perhaps the dragons are painted on the ceiling, or something."

"You really are hilarious, Coldheart," snapped Denser. "I know what I saw."

"Then," said Styliann, the quiet authority of his voice cutting through the still air, "someone must have built it."

Hirad looked askance at Styliann but before he could speak, the power of Sha-Kaan's mind gripped him.

"Welcome to my world, Hirad Coldheart. Now you will see what your carelessness has caused. Jatha will guide you from the enclave." As fast as the power had come it was gone and Hirad found himself looking into The Unknown's puzzled face.

"You all right?"

Hirad nodded. "It was Sha-Kaan. He knows we're here. He—" He was interrupted by movement from ahead of them. A shadow moved in the light.

Seamlessly, The Raven formed up. Hirad, The Unknown and Thraun, responding automatically, unsheathing swords and spacing themselves centrally in the chamber. Ilkar, Denser and Erienne stationed themselves behind. A heartbeat later, the Protectors joined them on either flank.

A short man, simply dressed, and with a sheathed weapon at his side, walked into view. He showed no fear at the line of warriors facing him, his face breaking into a smile above his long braided beard. Hirad relaxed and put up his sword.

"Jatha?" he ventured, knowing he was right. The man nodded and with vocal cords sounding unused to regular speech, said:

"Hirad Coldheart. Raven."

CHAPTER 29

The Lord Tessaya received two messages via carrier woodruff within the space of an hour around midday, and they led him to preside over a slaughter he had thought to avoid.

The first message, from the remnants of Taomi's force fleeing northwest toward Understone, confirmed all his worst fears about the state of the invasion of Gyernath and the defiance of the Baron whose wine he so enjoyed. But worse, it informed him of the destruction of the southern supply base and that Darrick not only still lived but still fought hard.

And the second, while giving him the news he had craved from Julatsa, left him plagued with doubts because it spoke of a small force breaking through the siege line a few hours before the College fell. It spoke of a mission to a land of dragons, it spoke of cataclysm and death from the sky greater than any the Wytch Lords might have unleashed. And, coming so hard on the heels of the rout of his men chasing the cursed Xetesk mage, he felt uncertain for the first time since he rode from his village.

Hating himself for doing it, he called on Arnoan to help him. The two men sat inside the inn, ate and talked, the old Shaman's eyes sparkling and mischievous. Tessaya knew Arnoan felt a great wrong had been righted and was happy to let the idea ride.

"It will pay you to be calm," said Arnoan, breaking bread and soaking it in his broth.

"Calm?" echoed Tessaya. "The Raven, damn them, have escaped a siege city and apparently go to speak with dragons, to form an alliance against me. Styliann and his dread force which now numbers somewhere around five hundred have massacred, *massacred*, thousands of my warriors at precious little cost and, if my scouts are correct, appear to be travelling to meet The Raven. And now I find my southern brethren are fleeing from a town they thought was theirs and have now been forced to destroy to prevent its recapture. Their spirit is broken and those that are left are coming here expecting my sympathy. Something they will not get.

"This is not a situation in which I see any reason to remain calm." He drained a goblet of wine, Blackthorne red ironically, and refilled it, pushing a hunk of bread into his mouth with his free hand.

Arnoan smiled gently. "But how much of it is true, my Lord? Darrick and Blackthorne, yes, I can see that. But *dragons*? And death from the sky? Are we not beyond these wild stories? I rather suspect that much of Senedai's report is the hysterical claims of a mage knowing his life is about to end and wishing to strike fear into his tormentor."

"He succeeded." Tessaya regarded Arnoan over the top of his goblet.

"But we must discount dragons. They are creatures of nightmare with no hold on the real world. They do not exist," said Arnoan.

"And supposing I accept that, why did The Raven leave, and where are they going? And why has Styliann not remained in Xetesk to defend his own city, taking with him their prime fighting force?" Tessaya drummed his fingers on the table.

"It seems clear to me that, knowing the College was falling, The Raven ran. They have no allegiance, they are mercenaries," said Arnoan. Tessaya almost smiled, though irritation at the Shaman's dismissal of circumstance lent his mood anger, not levity.

"I would sooner believe dragons exist than that The Raven ran from a fight. Don't try to smooth over what is going on. Senedai's message was quite clear that they broke through with the aid and, I must presume, the blessing of the Julatsans." He held up his hand to silence Arnoan's next utterance. "Something is going on. I can feel it. And we are sitting here just waiting for the storm to break. I will not wait any longer."

"We can track them and watch them as we are doing now," said Arnoan. "Understone is important to us. We must not desert it."

"Perhaps you have lost your stomach for the fight now you are toothless, my Shaman, but I have not." Tessaya's voice was quiet and cold. "Let me tell you the way it is. The Raven are riding to parley with dragons and if not them, something equally powerful they believe can stop us. Styliann and his bastard creations will join them. At the very best, if we do not hunt them down and kill them, they will advance the defence of Korina and I do not want that. At worst, they might just find an ally we cannot beat.

"Lord Senedai has treated it seriously enough to give chase with much of his army, Lord Taomi is running here with Baron Blackthorne and perhaps General Darrick in his bootprints. Our goal is to control Balaia through the capture of the capital and we will not achieve that sitting here waiting for Taomi to lead trouble to our door.

"You will instruct Riasu that he is to man the eastern fortifications of Understone Pass. No mage must get close enough to cast the water magic. He has enough men and he can call on the reserve. We will march first to The Raven and then to Korina. Time is slipping from us, my old friend, and we must grasp the opportunity while we still have it."

Arnoan was quiet for a time, sucking his top lip and nodding his head as he thought. "It is a bold move, my Lord. But what of Understone itself? We have expended such effort securing it."

Tessaya glanced around him at the almost complete stockade and tower system. He shrugged. "Its purpose has been served. It has kept us safe and our warriors busy. We are under no threat of losing the pass again. The Colleges do not have the will now that Julatsa has fallen and Styliann is absent. We will leave it."

"For Riasu?" said Arnoan.

"No." Tessaya shook his head. "We will leave no building standing."

"And our prisoners?"

The Lord Tessaya sighed and passed a hand over his face. "We are warriors, not warders. And they must not be allowed to rejoin the battle."

"My Lord?" Arnoan's face had paled.

"They have no value to us and they have become an encumbrance. I wish to be unencumbered." Tessaya rose and walked away down the street toward Understone Pass, his heart not matching the chill of his voice. This was not how he wanted it to be. But too much was happening and conquest by any means was now the only way. He stopped and turned, his eyes coming to rest on the billets where the prisoners were held. He breathed out heavily and marched to give the orders.

Perhaps sensing their urgency, or feeling pressure of his own, Jatha hurried The Raven plus unwelcome guests from the rip, moving quickly through several turns of the man-made cave before coming to a blank wall. Pausing only to glance over his shoulder and beckon them on, he disappeared into it. The Raven pulled up short.

"Ilkar?" asked The Unknown.

The elf stepped forward. "Illusion, I should think." He placed his hand on the wall. It was solid. "And an exceptional one at that. I'm not sure . . ." His voice trailed off. He pushed again, this time his hand sank into its surface. "Extraordinary." Denser came to his shoulder.

"Interesting," he said. "This isn't a mana construct." Erienne and Styliann crowded the end of the passageway, probing at the rock illusion.

"What do you think?" asked Denser.

"Well, it's actually rock, isn't it?" said Styliann. "But modified."

"Perhaps it recognises certain people or something," ventured Denser. He sank a hand through up to the elbow, feeling his fingers reach open space beyond it. "There's only token resistance here."

"How would it know to recognise me?" said Styliann. "There was no word of my coming." He too probed the rock.

"Good point," said Erienne. "To me, it feels fluid, though I agree with you that it's rock. The question is, how does it maintain solid appearance and form?"

"I suspect it's a bounded magic, a little like the rip," said Ilkar. "It has clearly been placed here deliberately to hide the rip."

"So has the whole cave system, come to that," said Denser. "Though the rest of it is solid enough."

Hirad, who had been leaning against a wall, idly scratching his chin, blew out his cheeks, winked at The Unknown and stepped forward, a smile on his lips.

"All this wisdom and none of you have a bloody clue, have you?"

The quartet of senior mages turned as one, their supercilious expressions mirrors for each other.

"Hirad, do you mind?" said Ilkar. "We're trying to solve this before we walk blindly through it. That is our way, isn't it?"

"Oh yes," said Hirad. He placed a hand on the construct and leant hard. "But you're missing the point." He pushed himself away then leant in again, more gently this time, his hand moving easily through the rock.

"Oh no." Ilkar's face betrayed a brief comical alarm. "You know exactly what this is, don't you?" Hirad nodded. Ilkar sighed and addressed the mages. "You'll just have to live with the fact that he knows something we don't. It doesn't happen often but you'll never be allowed to forget it."

"Well?" demanded Denser.

"It's not magic. Not like you know," said Hirad. "It's a piece of interdimensional material carrying the signatures of the Kaan and Balaia. No one outside of those groups can go through it. To them, it's solid rock. Clever, these dragons, aren't they?" He walked through the wall.

Outside, the accuracy of Denser's memories of the landscape was confirmed. They emerged into a vast valley of blackened earth and scorched trees, dead trunks reaching for the sky, fingers searching in vain for rescue. Only the most tenacious of undergrowth grew on the blasted ground and an acrid burnt smell permeated the air.

Behind them, the rock appeared like an area of tumbledown crag, indistinguishable from a dozen like it scattered along the valley slopes. Above, the sky was a deep and beautiful blue, blown through by wisps of high cloud. Nothing stirred. No animals nosed under the trees, no birds twittered in the boughs or swooped through foliage. The atmosphere was heavier here, thick and moist, every smell alien in their nostrils; and the air settled uncomfortably in their lungs, though there was no ill in it.

"It's so quiet," breathed Erienne. The Raven stood together a few paces distant from Styliann and his half dozen Protectors, the latter seeming just a little distracted; a fact not missed by The Unknown. To the left, Jatha stood with two dozen of his people, all small men by Balaian standards, similar in height to poor Will but stockier, powerful in the shoulders and legs, their bodies used to hard physical labour. All were men and all wore beards of varying lengths tied with braiding, Jatha's being the most complex.

While The Raven studied the devastation, Jatha's people scoured the sky or held their ears to the ground, listening for attack, never letting their hands stray too far from their weapons; flat-bladed stubby broadswords and short maces, weapons designed to deliver uncultured power in battle.

"What now?" asked Ilkar.

"Now we travel to Wingspread. To the Kaan homeland," said Hirad.

Jatha came to Hirad's side and turned an anxious face in his direction.

"Come," he said, uncomfortable with the speech. "Bad place." He gestured away along the valley floor with his left arm. In the distance, hills shimmered in the sun's haze. "Home," he said.

"It's time to go," said Hirad. "Looks like we're walking it."

"No dragons to give us a lift?" asked Denser.

"Never," said Hirad, his face stony.

They set off after Jatha and his people, the Kaan's servant race setting a brisk pace, their eyes always tracking the sky above. Underfoot, the ground was baked hard by sun and fire and, here and there, as they crossed the valley floor, the white of bone showed bright against the earth.

"How far is it?" asked Erienne, her hand on her belly, eyes troubled. Hirad shrugged.

"We're very short of time," said Ilkar. "We have a great deal to learn if we are to cast an effective spell."

"Or anything at all," agreed Denser. He placed an arm around Erienne's shoulder. "Are you all right?"

"Tired, I think." She smiled up at him. "I'll be fine."

The party continued along the valley floor for over an hour before Jatha turned left and scrambled up a dried-up watercourse that wound up the slope, alternately steep and shallow in the climb. He and his men halted at the top where the line of blackened trunks thinned out. The sight that greeted The Raven was breathtaking.

In front of them, and sweeping away for mile after unbroken mile, lay a softly undulating plain of tall grass that whispered in the breeze. Gusts of wind played across its red- and blue-flecked straw yellow surface, driving dark colour in swirling patterns that ebbed and flowed like eddies on the sea. Here and there, unmoving dark scars spoiled the totality of the plain and the land rose and fell in gentle rolls until it butted against the foothills of a cloud-shrouded mountain range that ran across the horizon, its ends lost in mist.

But it was the scene above and ahead of them that caused hearts to flutter. Staining the cloud-flecked blue of the sky like a monumental smear of dirt on fine cloth, was the rip. Around its edges, cloud bubbled and roiled; across its surface, red lightning flared and coursed and the whole rippled, its periphery agitating ceaselessly at the blue.

And then there were the dragons. Hirad counted forty flying in complex but ordered patterns in front of the rip while two dozen more circled in groups of three at wider distances, plunging through the thin cloud, wheeling left and right, their cries echoing faintly to the ground.

Jatha pointed. "Kaan," he said.

"Can it be done?" asked The Unknown with another glance at the Protectors, none of whom stood ready to defend Styliann, their eyes also fixed on the rip and its guardians.

Styliann let out a long hissing breath. "Magic has an answer to everything."

"Eventually," added Ilkar. "But time is something we don't have. I suggest we get moving and work every break. Just look at the size of that thing."

Hirad looked, and the short time they had pressed on him like never before. He almost believed he could see it growing as he watched. Perhaps he could.

"Hirad?" It was The Unknown.

"Hmm?" He tore his eyes from the rip and its attendant Kaan to focus on the big warrior. "What?"

"It's time to go." He gestured at Jatha who was staring at Hirad reverently. Hirad nodded.

"Jatha. Wingspread?" The Great Kaan's attendant frowned then beamed.

"Wingspread," he said and pointed away across the plain to the distant mountains. His smile faltered a little. "Careful." He indicated the sky and made swooping motions with his arms. "Careful." He indicated his eyes then pointed in all directions around him.

"Got that, Raven?" Hirad asked. Their silence told him they had. The party set off down the slope toward the seductively swaying plains grass.

The grass was taller even than Cil and The Unknown but its dense growth made travel tortuously slow. It smelled of fresh fields but also contained a beguiling sweetness, like ripe fruit on a hot day. And while it gave them good protection from ground threat, none of them were under any illusion about how the path they left appeared from above.

Jatha had been more optimistic, gesturing to them how the strands sprang back. But even his expression turned to worry as he saw the damage the heavier Balaians were causing.

He kept them moving at as fast a pace as was possible for the entire afternoon, stopping only briefly for food. As the evening drew on, Jatha and his men began to look for something, though to Hirad there was no break from the monotony of the grass.

At a signal from one of his men, Jatha brought the line to a halt. He turned to Hirad and made exaggerated tiptoe. The barbarian nodded and turned to The Raven.

"Try not to break too much grass, eh?"

Jatha led them from their path, moving very slowly, watching his every step as he handed the grass aside. His men mimicked his careful movement, Hirad shrugging and doing likewise, knowing The Raven would follow his lead. The deliberate movement continued for a good half hour but again the result was obvious—it would take a tracker of Thraun's skill to find them.

As it had been for much of the day, their destination was unclear until they were on it. Hirad, following the last of Jatha's men, almost walked into the back of him as he stopped abruptly. In front of him, four of them crouched in a loose half circle. Each man grasped at the earth, lifted and moved back a soil- and grass-covered wood and sacking lattice some three feet on each side. Without pause, Jatha led his men down into the gloom.

"Neat," said Ilkar, standing by Hirad.

"I'm amazed they could find it," said Hirad.

"Don't be," said Thraun, his voice flat and emotionless. "The trail is well marked." The Unknown patted him on the shoulder.

"Come on, let's get inside and set up that stove. I could murder a coffee."

With the ground covering pulled over and lanterns lighting their way, The Raven descended a steep set of rough-hewn mud and stone steps into a natural cave. The space rose thirty feet from the floor to the ground above and the main body was perhaps forty feet each side. Opposite the stairs, the roof tapered down sharply to a narrow alcove through which a steady draft blew, indicating a passage.

The floor of the cave was covered in dried leaves. Stacks of wood, metal bowls and plates and four big water butts stood to the left. Woven dried-grass matting was pulled from its position to the right and spread across the floor to provide comfort from the cold stone. Jatha's men set their lanterns in carved hollows in the rock walls, illuminating ragged edges and shelves which jutted into the cave above their heads, and gently swaying strands of liana which grew from above. It was damp and chill, the smells of mould and rot mixing into an unpleasant cocktail for the nose, but at least it was safe.

The centre of the cave was dominated by a shallow pit in which Jatha's men expertly laid and lit a fire, the smoke disappearing through the porous ceiling. Heat spread quickly outward and soon the party began to relax, stretching tired limbs and leaning back on the matting, forming it into surprisingly comfortable bedding.

"Choul," said Jatha, opening his arms wide to indicate the cave. Hirad nodded.

"Choul," he repeated. Jatha and his men had taken the area opposite the stairs and were readying food. Dried meats and root vegetables appeared from backpacks and sacks, and metal stands held pots of water over the fire.

In the space in front of the stairs, Thraun bolted the stove together. Nothing would get in the way of The Raven's coffee and The Raven themselves gathered around it, a familiar sight in unfamiliar surroundings.

That left Styliann and his six Protectors to sit against the wall to the right of the fire, quiet, contemplative but changed somehow. The former Lord of the Mount, with a brief word to Cil, walked to The Raven, a sheaf of papers in his hand.

"We have much to do," he said.

"Yes," said Hirad. "There's coffee to be drunk, food to be eaten and The Raven to talk. Alone. Then you four can start your work."

Styliann stared down at Hirad, his lips thinning. "Have we not moved beyond our petty parochialities?"

Hirad's expression was blank. "I've no idea," he returned. "All I know is you're holding us up. During a job, we talk each night, review and plan. It is The Raven's way."

"Yes and I would hate to get in the way of your precious rules," spat Styliann. "After all, all we have to do is save two dimensions."

Hirad regarded him coolly, shaking his head. But before he could speak, Denser's weary voice filled the cave.

"Styliann, for the Gods' sake, please sit down before he trots out his 'that's the reason we're still alive' speech."

Ilkar laughed aloud, the sound echoing from the walls. Hirad glared at him. Styliann shrugged and returned to his Protectors.

"Thanks for backing me up," muttered the barbarian.

Ilkar smiled. "Some day, Hirad, I'll follow up our chat about sensitivity with one about tact."

The glorious smell of rich stew slowly replaced those of the mould and rot, and quiet dominated the travellers. Jatha's men communicated in gesture and what appeared to be a highly developed telepathy, leaving the clanking of plates and spoons, the crackling of the fire and the shifting of tired limbs as the only sounds.

After their short meeting, The Raven drank coffee in silence. There hadn't been much to say though all of them had been comforted by the feeling of normality it brought them.

Later, with the fires stoked for warmth and the bowls, plates and spits stowed back next to the water butts, the quartet of mages examined the texts and papers brought from Xetesk and Julatsa.

For hours, all that could be heard was the turning of pages and the odd sigh or heavily indrawn breath. Occasionally, though little of the text was in lore script, one or other would need help translating certain terms or phrases, and hurried whispering would fill the chamber.

Initially intrigued, Jatha and his men had stared intently at the Balaians but the interest soon waned and, as the time drew on, most slept but for the two guards who sat just under the ground covering, at the top of the stairs.

Hirad leant against a wall, The Unknown next to him, legs stretched out in front of them. Idle talk had fallen to nothing and Thraun, who hadn't said a word since they descended into the Choul, remained lost in his own thoughts.

Eventually, the mages had read everything and, resupplied with coffee, placed the texts in a pile between them and began to talk.

"Styliann, how long have you known this information was in Xetesk?" asked Erienne.

"From the start. The only reason for my silence was the trouble I discovered I was going to have liberating them from the College."

"But have you studied them before?" she pressed.

"Not like this, I am ashamed to say. They've been in the locked vaults."

"And what do you think?"

"Hold on," interrupted Ilkar. "We'll get nowhere voicing random opinion. Let's identify the task and try to solve it piece by piece. All right?" The others nodded, a smile playing across Styliann's lips.

"Ever the diplomat, Ilkar," he said.

Ilkar shrugged. "We just don't have the time to waste. Now, who wants to outline the problem?"

"All right," said Erienne. "We have an unbounded rip linking two dimensions and drawing power from interdimensional space to grow at an exponential rate. We believe that because it was formed through conventional magic, it can be closed by the same method. However, there is no lore-defined spell for dismantling such a rip and we are left with having to piece together what will effectively be an untested best guess from the fragments of Septern's writings we have here and our own small knowledge. The risks are unbelievable, success is uncertain and the power needed is unknown. How does that sound?"

"You've been framing that for some time, haven't you, my love?" said Denser, drawing a hand through her hair. Ilkar chuckled, more at the sparkle in Denser's eye than at his words. This was the old Denser and he was very glad to have him back. He wondered on the change in the Xeteskian and knew Erienne had much to do with it though he suspected much of the strength had lain trapped within the man all the time. All it had needed was freeing.

"I think it's a very accurate summation," said Styliann. "Now if you will allow, Raven mages, I believe the first part of the puzzle to be determining whether we can construct a mana shape capable of forming a linkage with interdimensional space. Because if we can't affect it in the region of the rip, we can't hope to sew the sky back together, to use slightly emotive language."

Ilkar looked at him. "Sew. Sew." He leaned forward and shuffled through the pile of texts. "Septern used that very word to describe something to do with bounded gateways. Here we are." He grabbed a slim leather-bound volume they had found in Julatsa and leafed through it, his eyes scanning quickly. "Listen to this. It's part of a student lecture script on thought process. It isn't enough to simply understand the theory of a mana construct when dealing with dimensional forces. One must attempt to build into that shape, a flavour of an earthbound activity, something mundane and every day that can keep your thoughts focused during not merely formation, but deployment.

"You must realise that interdimensional forces affect mana in very different ways than Balaian space does. A spell you cast to tame or mould its power will develop what can only be described as a mind of its own and a shape you have fashioned to, say, open a bounded gateway, can quickly run out of your control. So, how to remain focused and in control? Think through your action and, as I said, link it to something ordinary. For instance, to take on the bounded gateway example, the deployment of the spell takes the material of Balaian space, the material of the target dimension and pulls them together before fixing them to one another.

"So, focus one, imagine pulling two pieces of cloth together. And to fasten them? Why not sewing? We have all seen people sew cloth so build that into your thought processes as you form your mana shape." Ilkar passed the book to Denser. "He goes on to describe a practical casting the students have to do but the meaning is clear. What are we doing but darning a hole in the air of this dimension and our own and cutting the one from the other to close the corridor?"

Styliann nodded. "Thoughts, Denser?"

"I think that's all very well but I don't recall reading anything about how you build your needle and thread into the construct. I can imagine it might introduce instability."

"It might well but we're still getting ahead of ourselves," said Erienne. "That piece we all read concerning basic construct theory is incomplete. We have no idea whether what we build will have the power to link to the edges of the rip. Septern, after all, was standing right next to where he cast. We have a range of God knows how far."

Another nod from Styliann. "It is a point well made but one we don't need to concern ourselves with. The DimensionConnect spell we used at Understone Pass had a range element which I understand very well. The four of us have enough strength between us to cast a linkage construct. Only just, I suspect, but enough."

"We have to be sure," said Ilkar.

"It will become clear, Ilkar," said Styliann. "Now, to introduce Denser's needle and thread into the construct."

From his position next to The Unknown, Hirad yawned and stretched. It was going to be a long night.

His name was Aeb but it was the only mark of individuality he had. He did not consider himself singular in any way, not when he was singly assigned and not when, as now, he stood with all of his brothers. He could feel every one of them who readied to defend the house as he had been directed by his Given, the mage Styliann. The reasons were unimportant, the order was everything.

Aeb was a powerful man who dimly remembered his calling at the age of twenty-three. Garbed, as they all were, in heavy black leather and chain armour, stiff boots and ebony mask, carrying both sword and battle axe, he watched his segment of the land in front of him with complete calm. It was a calm that no non-Protector would have felt, because the horizon was full of Wesmen.

The Protectors had watched the approach of the enemy army for several hours, first through the thoughts of a dozen scouts and latterly through every eye as the force from Julatsa moved into position, encircling them at a distance of around one hundred and fifty yards. But as the day waned toward a warm dusk, Aeb sampled the feelings of his brothers, none of whom thought an attack would come before dawn.

"*We will stand down in turn,*" Aeb thought, the message passing instantly among the Protectors. He looked left and right, the ruins of the house at his back. From all parts of the defensive formation that left no gap to attack the building, brothers took three paces back and walked to a series of laid and lit cook-fires beside which fuel, food and water stood ready for use. The Protectors would stand down a third at a time for four hours or until the threat changed the order and they all came to ready again. At no time would there be an opportunity for surprise attack by the Wesmen. The night time was dangerous but more so for the Wesmen. They needed light by which to fight effectively; the Protectors did not.

Feelings, thoughts and ordered statements from his brothers moved through Aeb's mind, all of them filtered in the part of his mind just behind his battle consciousness. At any time, he knew everything that they saw and heard, he felt every spark of their bodies as they breathed, he knew every weakness, every muscle that pained them, and every injury that they had sustained. Damaged brothers were protected on weak fronts by those most suited to the task. None would be lost through lack of preparation.

The only fragment of concern that played across the soul-consciousness was that Cil and the five who had travelled with the Given could not be felt though their souls still remained in the tank. It was as if they were dormant somehow. Alive but not one with the brethren. The whole would be made stronger on their return.

"*The lost can still not be felt,*" signalled Ayl, a brother who had been detailed to search the souls of the six for signs of reawakening.

"*Yet they still live,*" came a response. "*When you return to stand ready, think of them no more in the battle.*"

Aeb let his eyes rove over the massing ranks of the enemy. Sampling the thoughts of others, he estimated there were around ten and a half thousand of them, all hardened fighters and men who had been victorious over magic and soldier alike. They would believe in their strength and their ability to sweep the small force facing them away.

The Protectors could not allow that to happen. Their Given relied upon them. As did the One who knew them but was no longer among them. Aeb let his thoughts for the man, Sol, drift out to his brothers and felt a strong urge to protect form around him.

There would be no failure.

CHAPTER 30

L ord Senedai ordered the halt to make camp and give his men a rest after three days' hard march. A rest and a chance to align the spirits for the battle to come. There was no rush to attack the men surrounding the ruins of the house that had become an icon for all the evils of magic in the minds of all Wesmen. Many of the warriors now sitting around their standards and fires would never have believed they would arrive here. The Spirits had brought them and the Spirits would have to give them the strength to win. The Shamen, though disarmed of their destructive magic, found themselves the centre of respect and attention for every tribe.

Senedai should have been supremely confident. Those defending the mansion were surrounded. They had nowhere to go and they were outnumbered by about twenty to one. Dawn would herald a slaughter and, following it, the chase to catch The Raven, wherever it took them. They would be caught, so ending The Raven's desperate attempt to bring mythical aid and, as a bonus, remove them from the war.

That was what he had told his Captains and any of his warriors as he swaggered past, his smile the brutal expression of a Tribal Lord in complete command.

But now, standing alone, the doubts began to assail him in a way they never had when he stood before the gates of the College. And he found himself wondering whether the eight thousand he had left to marshal Julatsa, guard its prisoners and tend its wounded, weren't the lucky ones. They saw themselves as denied the chance of more glory, almost of being dishonoured. Senedai half wished he had stayed with them as was his right as a victorious Lord. Julatsa was his city for all time.

He stood at the edge of the Wesmen encampment, beyond his furthest guards, and looked toward the ruins. There, one of his doubts was manifest. There were four hundred and seventy-six of them. He had ordered a tracking scout to count them the day before. All in identical armour and carrying identical weaponry. All powerful and all in those dread masks. And now all standing.

Silent, unmoving.

Senedai shuddered and glanced behind him to make sure nobody had seen him. There was something deeply disturbing about their stillness, their ramrod-straight stance and their hands clasped in front of them. Only their heads betrayed any movement at all as they watched the massing of the Wesmen forces. They would be formidable opponents and Senedai was absolutely sure that they wouldn't stand and wait when he ordered his archers to fire. That was his best chance of forcing a weakness in their formation yet the thought of them running toward him, despite their light numbers, worried him. Still, like everything else, it would wait until dawn tomorrow.

He turned his back on the mansion and in the dying red glow cast by the setting sun, imagined the mark over Parve. The Hole in the Sky. The young mage had blabbered endlessly about dragons pouring through it to consume them all and Senedai wasn't confident enough in their nonexistence to disbelieve him. That was, after all, why he was here and why Lord Tessaya had ordered him, at all costs, to destroy the manse ruin through to its foundations and chase The Raven to their deaths. Tessaya understood there was a gateway there. To another place. He had been quite specific about Senedai's responsibilities.

Another shudder and Senedai walked toward his tent. The whole place smacked of magic and evil. It made his skin crawl. Perhaps Tessaya would arrive before he had to attack alone.

The Barons Blackthorne and Gresse, with General Darrick, rode slowly through the wreckage of Understone with a close guard of thirty cavalry, though all three men knew instantly that no guard was necessary. The army had continued its march east toward Korina, giving Understone Pass itself a wide berth but expecting and encountering no resistance as it joined the main trail. The men they were chasing had not headed west to their homeland.

Trotting through the burned gates of the freshly built and burned stockade, under the empty gaze of a pair of torched watchtowers, Darrick had seen the first splash of red and had turned to his men, saying:

"Keep what you see here to yourselves. It will not be pretty."

And now, pulling to a stop in the centre of the town, or what they guessed to be the centre, his words rang so hollow. Not pretty. The magnitude of his understatement would have made him laugh but laughter would have been the ultimate insult.

Darrick thought he had seen everything during his years of soldiering. Warfare was an ugly business. He had witnessed horses' hooves crushing men's skulls as they lay crying for help. He had seen young men clutching at their stomachs, entrails spilling between their fingers as their wide eyes sought hope in the faces of their friends. He had seen limbs struck from healthy bodies, jaws hacked away, eyes pierced by arrows and axes jutting from the heads of men who still walked, too shocked even to register they were dead.

He had seen the horrific burns from fire and cold that magic could bring at the whisper of a word and, more recently, he had seen the terrible devastation of water flooding Understone Pass, leaving torn and beaten bodies folded into cracks in the rock.

But always there had been a certain justification. War was an engagement both sides entered into in the knowledge of its likely outcome in terms of suffering.

Here in Understone, though, it was quite, quite different.

Blackthorne Town had been destroyed but its natives had long since fled to the countryside or joined the Baron's army. The same choice had not been granted the inhabitants of Understone and their slaughter had been utterly deliberate.

Darrick shook his head. It didn't add up. He knew Tessaya's mind and this wasn't his way. The Wesmen had fortified Understone considerably, if the scorched ruins were anything to go by. A stockade had all but encircled the town, studded with armoured watchtowers. Pits and trenches had been dug outside the wooden walls and strong points had been placed in tactically perfect defensive positions throughout the town itself. Tessaya had been planning for a long occupation.

But something had radically and appallingly changed his thinking. Every building had been burned to its foundations, stone had been knocked from stone and all that the Wesmen themselves had built lay in splinters and ashen piles. And everywhere, *everywhere* were strewn the bodies. It had been a ritual massacre, each man taken to a particular place in the town after it had been burned, and murdered, throat cut, eyes put out and stomach split, the corpse spread-eagled toward the rising sun.

There had to be more than three hundred of them. Understone garrison soldiers and those of the four-College force. Some, Darrick recognised; others he counted among respected colleagues. They had been dead for a day and the clouds of flies filled the air with an evil hum while the carrion birds and animals waited for the riders to leave them to their unexpected feast. The stench of putrefaction was rising.

"What, by all the Gods watching us, has happened here?" Gresse's voice was a hoarse whisper. He slid from his horse to stand reverently on the ground. The rest of the riders followed suit.

"It's a warning," said one of the cavalry, echoing Darrick's own reaction. "They want us to fear them."

"No," said Blackthorne. "And it is they who are scared."

"You've seen this sort of thing before?" asked Gresse, his expression disbelieving.

Blackthorne shook his head. "It is documented in the Blackthorne library, or rather, was. Don't forget, we have been in the front line against the Wesmen before."

"So what drove Tessaya to do this?" asked Darrick.

"The burning, I think, is just to stop anyone else benefiting from what he had built and I expect the pass to be very heavily defended now. The sacrifices, because that is what they are, are something else entirely.

"When the Wesmen go into battle, their Shamen call upon their spirits to align behind them and bless them to give them strength. But when they fear an enemy is stronger than they are, they sacrifice enemies to ward off the evil they think is chasing them. These poor bastards are victims of a Shamen ritual and they are laid facing the rising sun because the Wesmen say the dawn brings sight to the eyes of the gods of their enemies and what they see will take their courage." He shrugged.

"They're scared of us?" Gresse frowned.

"I don't think so, not us," said Darrick. "Something has scared Tessaya very badly to cause him to abandon his plans. He is normally a very careful man. He must believe the invasion could fail and wherever he has gone, he must believe it critical to his campaign."

"And wherever he goes, his lackeys will follow," said Gresse grimly.

"Yes," said Blackthorne. "It looks as if we now chase the lynch pin and not merely a strut."

Darrick pursed his lips. "But before that, all these men must be given the honour of a pyre."

"Time is of the essence," said Blackthorne a little sharply. "These men would not thank us if their murderers eluded us while we burned their bodies."

Darrick regarded him bleakly. "And catch Tessaya we will. We have eight thousand men marching east. Join them and send back my cavalry. We will see these men are accorded the respect they deserve. We will catch you before nightfall."

"I apologise, General," said Blackthorne. "My words were not intended to—"

Darrick waved a hand. "I understand, Baron, and my respect for you is undimmed. But I cannot leave my men to fester where they lie in this grotesque slaughterhouse. You would feel the same."

Blackthorne raised a smile and remounted his horse. "I would indeed, General. You are a good man. Please, take your time."

"Time is something of which we have very little. But for us, at least, it has not run out."

The Raven, with their escorts and the Xeteskian contingent, left the Choul well before dawn. The mages had talked long into the night, Hirad hearing their low tones as he moved in and out of a strangely broken sleep. And when they had been woken by Jatha, he felt tired and irritable and saw his mood reflected in the eyes of all of his friends and Styliann.

Though the sun had not breached the plain, which was still cast in shadow, there was enough light in the sky to see by and nothing but tall grass in every direction. Indeed the semidarkness was comforting in its way and Hirad experienced a feeling of safety that he knew to be false. Though they could hide themselves in the dark from other humans, neither Jatha's people, nor dragons, had any trouble piercing the gloom. All that travelling at night would do would be to put The Raven at a further disadvantage. He said as much to The Unknown who simply nodded as if he had suspected exactly that.

The travellers' formation was altered from the day before. While Jatha and his people still led the way, The Raven mages had fallen back to keep talking with Styliann, leaving the Protectors to guard the rear, and Hirad, The Unknown and Thraun looking after the flanks. Thraun looked no better. Locked in his own world of misery and self-guilt over Will's death, he functioned and would no doubt fight but that was about all. He ate what was put in front of him, slept and watched when asked and responded to questions about terrain and tracking. Otherwise, he had completely withdrawn.

Midway through the morning, the land, previously flat and level, began to rise. Gently at first but then more steeply, and though the rises and falls were never more than twenty feet, they sapped the strength. The plains grass grew as before, its density undiminished, but now even Jatha, who forced the pace hard, flattened and broke stalks in his hurried passage.

Hirad watched him for a little, noticing the way he glanced up continually toward the rip while his men, frowns on their faces, scoured the land either side.

"Ever get the feeling all is not well?" asked Hirad, finding himself shoulder to shoulder with The Unknown.

"Very much so," said The Unknown. "We should consider the possibility of attack." He tapped the as yet sheathed sword in his back-mounted scabbard.

"Let me have a word with Jatha." Hirad moved forward and tapped Jatha's shoulder. The Kaan servant looked around and forced a smile though his eyes betrayed his worry.

"What's wrong?" asked Hirad. Jatha looked blank. "Danger?" Hirad pointed to the sky and gestured around him before flapping his arms as Jatha had done to indicate a dragon.

Jatha nodded vigorously. "Sky battle coming," he said. "Careful." He pointed to his eyes and then to the area immediately surrounding them. "More battle." He shrugged. Hirad nodded.

"All right Raven," he said, dropping back. "We might be getting company from the sky and the ground. Let's get prepared. Thraun, Unknown, left and right flanking positions, Ilkar the shield, Denser and Erienne, offence, please." Up ahead, two pairs of Jatha's men left the main group, disappearing into the grass to either side, swords drawn. Jatha himself continued onward, upping the pace still further until he was almost at a trot. Hirad looked back briefly toward Styliann. "I presume I can leave it to you and yours to organise our rear defence?"

Styliann nodded. "Nothing will get through from behind," he said curtly.

Up in the sky, the defence of the rip had strengthened. Hirad estimated seventy Kaan dragons now flew, their patterns close, their calls echoing down over the plain. It was a haunting sound that set him on edge. The brackish barks and muted growls were alien in his ears and he shifted his shoulders as the back of his neck tingled. Involuntarily, he looked behind him and it was then that he saw the shapes.

At first they were a group of black dots, high in the sky, coming from beyond the forest valley they had travelled through the day before. But as they drew closer, he saw their shapes, long slim and fast. They numbered in excess of twenty and they flew in a single chevron, heading directly for the rip. The calls of the Kaan became more urgent and the defending dragons, half of them at least, switched from set patterns into attack groups of five or six, moving out to meet the enemy.

It was Jatha's voice that made him realise that they had all stopped to look.

"Go," he was saying. "Careful." He made to move off but a change in the movement in the sky caught his eye. Hirad followed his gaze to the attacking dragons. One had cut away from the main group and was angling downward across the plain and coming straight for them.

"Raven, put up your swords and forget the spells. We're going to have to run. Protectors, likewise, believe me or die." He pointed up to the shape barrelling toward them. It would be on them in no time.

"Hirad!" Jatha was tugging at his arm, his voice distressed, his men agitated behind him. Hirad looked down to him. The little man spread the fingers of his hands wide then moved his arms apart. "Go," he said, repeating the gesture. He shouted an order to his men who instantly scattered away into the grass, no two in the same direction.

Hirad got the idea. "Raven!" he shouted. "Line abreast, three yard spacing. Raven with me!" Not waiting to see if Styliann was with them, Hirad ploughed off through the grass, sensing The Unknown and Ilkar flanking him. Glancing left and right, he could just about see them but couldn't make out the rest as they stumbled and fought their way through the tall thick grass that impeded their every step.

They were running blind and it was all a game of chance. As he thrashed through the pliable stems, he imagined the dragon rushing down, laughing at the pitiable attempts to escape it could see as it chose its first victims. None of them had a chance. It could wield its fire at will and soon they would all be so much ash floating up into the sky.

He felt anger that Sha-Kaan could leave them so unprotected and he called the Great Dragon's name in his mind, demanding assistance, pleading for rescue. Stumbling and almost falling, he choked back a cry, a stark realisation thumping through his skull. This was his nightmare made real. In Taranspike Castle he had dreamed that he was running on cracked earth and going nowhere but the result would be the same. He would be caught and the skin would be burned from his bones as he stood helpless.

A wave of heat washed across the plain from away to his right accompanied by red light as flame scoured into the grass. No one screamed but then they wouldn't have had the time. Hirad prayed it wasn't Jatha and increased his pace. Crackling noises filled the air and a dense smoke flooded into the sky as the dry grass was enveloped by fire. Through a swirl in the smoke the dragon, something like seventy feet long and no more than forty yards away, peeled back into the sky to prepare for another run, its sleek blue body slipping easily through the air, its wings beating in graceful time. Its shadow was black on the ground, those huge wings snapping like sails as they dug at the air, pushing it aside with great sweeps, the noise like wind howling around buildings. With cold certainty, Hirad knew it was coming for them next time.

He plunged on, shoulders hunched and arms up and protecting his face. No more than a dozen paces ahead, the ground fell away. It was their only chance.

"Raven!" he roared over the noise of the fire, the shouts of other men and the calls of a hundred dragons. "Slope dead ahead. Let's get down it. Stay low!" He could sense the dragon wheeling behind them. He ran on, took his last pace at a half dive and plunged to roll down the slope, turning over and over, grass, earth and loose stones filling his sight as he went.

It was a steeper slope than he had anticipated and he struggled to control his speed. A great scorch of flame lashed overhead, incinerating the grass at the top of the slope and sparking another fire that raged and consumed the vegetation all around. Heat washed down the slope, the shadow of the dragon passed over him, he splayed out his limbs to slow himself, hit the bottom of the slope and came to a sudden halt against The Unknown, dust filling the air and a run of dirt and broken stems sliding behind him.

The two men helped each other to their feet. Ilkar lay a few yards away, shaking his head as he dragged himself to a sitting position, dust clouding around him, smoke fogging the air above. An acrid, burning smell filtered down and the noise of the dragon-induced fire was close.

"Raven!" called Hirad. "Sound off if you can hear me. Be moving this way."

Denser and Erienne both called that they were all right. Thraun appeared at Hirad's side, nodding curtly.

"Assessment," said Hirad.

"The smoke in the sky will obscure us but the fire will kill us if we hang around," said The Unknown. "We need to move away and up the other side of this slope. The prevailing wind is blowing east to west, I suggest we push east."

Denser and Erienne came into view, the Dark Mage with an arm around Erienne's waist, she with blood running from a cut in her chin.

"Not exactly the entrance recommended for a pregnant woman," she said. Hirad's concern must have shown as she quickly smiled. "But it takes a lot more than a slide in the grass to hurt a mage child."

"Good," said Hirad. "Come on, let's move away from the fire. Cover your mouths if you can." He moved off, fetching a cloth from his pocket and tying it over his mouth and feeling instant relief from the smoke that smothered the sky overhead and was moving to fill the shallow cleft in which they were hiding. The fire burned on two sides of them, making its way steadily down the slope behind them and to their right as they trotted quickly along the base of the cleft.

Angling slightly upslope in the direction of their travel, Hirad strained to hear the attacking dragon or some sign of other life from the sundered travelling party but couldn't. Worried by the sudden apparent withdrawal, he unsheathed his sword almost reflexively, turned to tell The Unknown to do the same, heard a whisper through the grass and was calling for Ilkar's HardShield before the short arrow struck Thraun in the left shoulder.

"Shield up," said Ilkar.

"Raven, watch those flanks. Denser, I think your blade will be more use in here. Thraun how are you?" A second arrow bounced from the shield, then a third.

"Flesh only. I'm bleeding but I can fight." His flat-toned voice held no hint of the pain he had to be feeling.

Hirad pushed onward, The Unknown two paces to his right, Denser coming to his left, leaving Thraun as rear guard behind the casting mages. He could hear Erienne muttering as she built the mana shape for a spell he prayed held no fire. Another three arrows bounced before shouts from in front of them preceded the cracking of grass and the running of feet.

Hirad stopped and hacked the grass flat in front of him. "Here they come. Expect short swords; you know what Jatha was carrying."

Three shaven-headed men burst forward, all less than five feet tall and carrying stubby spiked clubs two-handed. As they charged, they shouted in a language Hirad couldn't understand, their faces suffused with hatred. Behind them, others were coming.

Hirad swayed backward and caught a surprisingly powerful blow on his blade, moving it left to right and down, exposing his enemy's right side. He rebalanced swiftly and snapped his blade up to slice the ear of the man as he tried to dodge the blow. The man cried out in pain and Hirad brought his sword back down in a killing blow through his shoulder, crashing through bone.

He stepped back again and waited, seeing Denser stabbing his victim through the chest while The Unknown had made even shorter work of his opponent. The chasing pack faltered. Where their companions had run on in a hate-lust, they stopped to look at those they faced, taking in their height, strength and the size of the blades ranged against them.

"Move up," said Hirad. "Keep an eye on those flanks. Erienne, I think another demonstration if you're ready." The enemy, perhaps a dozen of them, were backing off, Hirad watching them every step. He could see movement either side. "They're going to attack again. Not frontal. Erienne, ahead is yours."

Erienne stepped up to Hirad's shoulder, opened her palms and spoke a single command word. IceWind howled away into the grass, destroying man and vegetation over a twenty yard spread. The Raven warriors advanced quickly into the chill behind it. Shouts of pure terror erupted from all around and suddenly the sound was all of running feet as the enemy fighting men turned and fled.

"Excellent," said Hirad. He pushed on, trotting through the dead zone Erienne had created, poles of grass shattering at his passing, the bodies of half a dozen men, forever frozen in fear, scattered about him. Moving on up the slope, he could see the ground levelling out again. To his right, a pall of smoke covered the plain. The question was, where were Jatha and Styliann?

He brought The Raven to a watchful halt. Immediately, Erienne turned to tend to Thraun's shoulder. He scanned the sky. Around the rip, a furious battle was in progress. Flame lit up the sky which was full of dragons swooping, diving and climbing. As he watched, a pair of what he thought were Kaan by their size, chased down a lone enemy. One breathed a long gout of flame over its wings while the other dived down to grab its neck, twisting violently before dropping the victim who plummeted from the sky.

From three directions, more dragons were coming to join the fighting but of The Raven's assailant there was no sign. For a time, they all stared up at the sky, taking in the immense and raw animal power clashing overhead. So much force, speed and agility. It was a sight quite without equal and to Hirad it was a stark reminder of their stature in the conflict. They'd been lucky so far but, for the first time since they had faced the Wytch Lords, he felt their destiny was not in their hands. If a dragon wanted them dead, they would die.

"What now?" asked Denser, his gaze turned to Erienne as she tended to Thraun.

"We keep vigilant," said Hirad. "Above and around. We need Ilkar to maintain the shield for now. Erienne might have scared them off but they might come back. Meanwhile, we have to think how to find the others."

"Assuming they're there to be found," said Erienne. She had placed a pad of cloth around Thraun's wound. The shapechanger had grasped the shaft with his right hand and at her nod, tugged it once, hard. It came free. Thraun grunted his pain and blood spread over the cloth, running over Erienne's hands. She quickly stemmed the flow, muttered a few words and pressed a little harder. "Keep pushing," she told Thraun, placing his hand on the pressure point. "I've knitted the wound inside but it's still weak. Try not to use that arm for the rest of the day, all right?"

He nodded. "Thank you."

She caressed his cheek with her bloodied hand. "Dear Thraun," she said, and her troubled face said everything her words did not.

The Raven had stopped just below the lip of the cleft. There were enemies in the grass and enemies in the sky above and they had no idea where they were.

"Options?" asked Hirad.

"We need to push away from here," said The Unknown. "We know we have to head to the mountains. We can still do that."

"I'll go up," said Denser. "Take a quick look around, try and spot the others and our erstwhile attackers. What do you think?"

"Risky," said Ilkar, his voice faint with concentration on the HardShield.

"No riskier than staying here blind," reasoned Denser. "And we need Styliann. He has the writings."

"Do it," said Hirad.

"Be careful," said Erienne.

Denser nodded. "I won't be long."

With ShadowWings trimmed for speed, Denser shot into the air, aware immediately of how vulnerable he felt in a medium so totally dominated by dragons. Though they were far away, battling over the rip, with their cries, their flame and their power an incredibly alien backdrop to his flight, Denser felt all their eyes upon him. He shuddered and looked at the scene below him.

The area around The Raven's position was clear, their attackers still moving off to the east, their progress marked by the erratic waving of the grass. He couldn't tell how many there were but they represented no significant danger. The biggest risk he could see was from the fire which raged in three places, sending billows of smoke into the sky as it ravaged the plain unchecked. The blaze nearest to them had taken much of the cleft in which they had hidden and moved steadily in all directions, the breeze slowing but not stopping its progress toward them.

Two larger areas of fire burned fiercely away to his right and Denser could see so easily how the dragons had ruined their land. Nothing but torrential rain could stop this blaze completely engulfing the entire plain which had to cover hundreds of square miles and, looking about him, he saw nothing but blue sky and light cloud. No respite would come today.

He flew on beyond the flames, in the direction of the mountains, reasoning that any survivors would try to move onward. He was quickly rewarded by the sight of grass swaying and flattening in a careless swathe ahead.

"Styliann," he breathed. He swept down over the grass, calling for them to stop. Close to, he could see three Protectors in a wide arc and, though they appeared to be shadowing no one, the movement of the stems ahead told him that Styliann was there but under a CloakedWalk. Not a bad idea when you didn't care for the safety of your companions.

"Styliann, stop. We need to regroup." He overflew and wheeled in the air.

"No," came the disembodied voice, breathless with effort. "We need to get away. I've lost Jatha and three of my Protectors have been killed."

"Calm down, the dragon has gone."

"Don't you believe it." And as if to give credence to his words, a roar from his right told Denser all was not good. Bursting through the smoke, the dragon pounced to the ground and grabbed one of Jatha's men, or possibly Jatha himself, soaring back into the air and tearing the man in two with his front claws, feeding each piece into his mouth, blood spraying and scattering.

Denser's heart hammered in his chest and he twitched reflexively away, fighting to hold on to his concentration, his breath ragged, his mouth dry. A shudder coursed through his body and his hand was shaking as he moved it to wipe his sweating forehead.

"Get out of the sky, Denser; you're a sitting target. And get Hirad to call his bloody dragon friends in or we're all dead. Understand? Now stop giving away my position." Styliann and his Protectors changed direction and Denser soared away, very aware of his total exposure. Hugging the top of the grass, he flew hard to The Raven's position, surprised at how far he had come, and trimming his wings for more speed.

With a note of surprise in its tone, he heard the dragon bark. Looking back over his shoulder, he saw it bank and wheel, all the while its eye fixed on one thing.

"Oh dear God," muttered Denser. He was closing on The Raven and he and they only had one chance. He could hear the dragon's wing beats as it raced toward him, he dived deeper still, his body skimming the tall fronds of grass. He flew into the smoke of the fire ravaging the cleft, holding his breath and turning a sharp left, flying along the line of the fire. Arrowing back into fresh air, he saw that the dragon had carried straight on, missing The Raven in its search for him.

Seizing the only time he had left, Denser flew hard back to them, pulling up to land just as the dragon realised it had been fooled and turned again in the air. It wouldn't be long in reaching them.

"Quick," he said, talking as his feet hit the ground and he dismissed the wings. "Back down the slope. The dragon's coming back. Erienne, we need anything that may keep off fire. More HardShield. I'll try an IceWind defence. You never know." They cast as they scrambled down, keeping themselves in close formation, with Hirad cajoling them all the way.

As they descended, they knew it was hopeless. They were running back into the flames, the dragon's shadow passed over them once more, the force of its wings loud and terrifying and, this time, they could all see it bank and turn to fly down the length of the gully, opening its mouth to breathe.

It never reached them. At the top of the gully a huge set of jaws clamped around its neck and drove it into the ground which shuddered violently underfoot. Flame lit up the sky, a dual roar split the air, one was abruptly silenced. There was the sound of wings in the air and the shadow of Sha-Kaan hung over them, huge and comforting. His mouth dripped blood and he heaved great lungfuls of air as he hovered. The Raven's relief was palpable.

"I heard your call but I was far from you. Get away from the fire and head toward the mountains, I will bring Jatha and your people to you. You must be ready to close the gateway when our orb reaches its height thrice from now." And with that, he was gone.

Denser collapsed on to the ground. "Give me a moment," he said.

"Move when you get too warm, eh?" said Hirad, indicating the flames and smoke scant yards away. "Good move into that smoke, by the way, but a pity he saw you landing. Work on that for next time."

Denser looked up, anger in his eyes, but it evaporated when he saw the smile on Hirad's face. "Funny, Coldheart. Very funny."

Hirad reached down his hand. "Come on, Denser, we've still got a long way to walk."

CHAPTER 31

Lord Senedai awoke to the smells of campfires, cooking meat and damp, and the sounds of Shamen leading their warriors in songs and chants calling for the alignment of spirits and the ancient lords of war to be with them this day.

He rolled over on his low pallet, eyes to the slightly billowing roof of his tent. He listened to his men, he caught the whisper of the wind through the camp and he sighed, a deep slow exhalation, before sitting upright and rubbing a hand across his face and through his knotted hair.

"Attendant!" he shouted, and his tent door was pulled back immediately to admit a tall young warrior, barely more than a youth. His tanned frame was hard-muscled beneath a tight-tied sleeveless grey shirt and his hair was cropped to his scalp as his rank dictated.

"My Lord."

"Battle furs and breakfast," ordered Senedai.

"My Lord." A half bow and he left.

Senedai dragged himself reluctantly from his bed, walked a little stiffly to the door flap and pulled it open a crack. Outside, the predawn gloom was deepened by a misty rain that fell from a heavy sky, punctuated only by the cook fires dotted around the camp. He set his jaw and moved back into the relative warmth of his tent.

"So much for the songs of fortune," he muttered. A damp battlefield was all he needed. Yes, blood would slick the ground underfoot but rainfall on grass would make the ground slippery from the very start and he had a feeling they would need every bit of help they could get despite their overwhelming numerical superiority.

During his sleepless night he had gone over every option, wishing fervently his catapults weren't still in Julatsa, awaiting the move to Dordover. He could attempt to simply overrun the enemy, sheer weight and press of numbers driving their bodies into the mud, but that was a charge he would have to lead himself and he found no desire to die this day.

He ate and dressed quickly and walked outside into the slowly lightening sky, to be accosted by a tribesman who thrust a message into his hands. It was unopened.

"Who brought this message?"

"A fast rider from Understone, my Lord. He arrived just before you awoke."

Tessaya had sent word. Excellent. Senedai turned away and unsealed the message on his way to the nearest cook fire with enough light to see by. He made his way through a mass of warriors sharpening weapons, hefting furs, practising strikes or just talking among themselves, and everywhere the sounds of a camp coming to life filled his ears. Dogs snarled and barked, orders were shouted, fires crackled and popped, tent sides thumped, loose guys snapped and song filtered from all sides. It was hard not to feel confident. The enemy had nowhere to run and it was obvious to even the untrained eye that they were too few.

Yet Senedai felt doubt deep in the pit of his being. And reading the message from Tessaya multiplied his fears. He had hoped to see his Lord marching over the fields to make victory certain that very morning. But there had been a change of plan. Tessaya had had word from the remnants of Taomi's army that a large force was marching from the south. Senedai was to complete his task with no further help, the message said. Tessaya would join Taomi's forces and crush the southern enemy. They would then muster on the road to Korina while reinforcements shored up the defences of Julatsa.

Victory was assured, the message ended. The Spirits smiled on them and the enemy gods would look away. Tessaya had made certain of that.

But Tessaya wasn't facing what Senedai faced. And as the sun lightened the sky to reveal the masked force standing stock still on the ground in front of the ruins just as they had as night fell, the Wesman Lord quailed inside and prayed for an answer to present itself that could save him from humiliation.

Behind him a dog barked and a harsh voice silenced it. At least there was part of the answer. He dropped the message in the fire and summoned his Captains to issue battle orders.

In the light of late afternoon, General Darrick sat around a hastily erected map table with Blackthorne, Gresse and a tired Communion mage. The Wesmen had stopped and dug themselves in, scouts reporting that Tessaya and the southern force remnants had managed to connect.

"What is all this about?" asked Gresse. He'd just heard the Communion report and both he and Blackthorne faced Darrick blankly.

"Look, there's things been going on you know nothing about. I'm sorry not to have told you but there didn't seem any point and we all had axes to grind against the Wesmen anyway."

"What exactly?" asked Gresse carefully.

"This is going to sound preposterous but it's all true, I swear it," said the General. He looked round to make sure they weren't overheard. "There's a . . . a hole in the sky over Parve. It's growing and when its shadow covers the city at noon, dragons will invade. Don't ask me how or why, but they will. The

Raven and Styliann have ridden to find a way to close the hole. He went back to Xetesk, and they went to Julatsa. I was left praying they would make it and now it seems obvious they have.

"But now the Wesmen are threatening even themselves, ridiculous though that sounds, and we clearly have to stop them."

"But why have the Wesmen chased them? I mean we're talking about ten plus thousand running after what they think is six people."

"Yes, but they think that The Raven are going to bring back dragons. I mean, they've got it hopelessly wrong but that's what they think. And it makes them very difficult to deal with.

"More than that," continued Darrick. "It explains why Tessaya went on the move. Look." He indicated the map. "Tessaya's plan was to march on Korina when his southern army sacked Gyernath and his northern took Julatsa, thereby removing supply all the way, north to south, from the strongest Colleges, Xetesk and Dordover. Lystern he can leave until later. He has thousands of men in reserve to defend both cities and the pass so he is relaxed. He also knows, or thinks he knows, that coordinated defence of the East is nonexistent so even though Dawnthief has removed the Wytch Lords and his own magic, he still believes he can take Balaia. So he wants Korina next to cut off principal west—east supply and break Balaian morale.

"But not everything went right. For a start, Gyernath survived its onslaught and still stands. To add insult to injury, you two and your motley band of farmers' boys—" he imbued the term with complete reverence and respect "—have taken the rest of the southern force apart, something he has only become aware of very recently. Next, The Raven reappeared in the East as did Styliann and I, and they desert a siege situation and presumably through torture in Julatsa he has answers to why, but the wrong ones.

"He knows he has to move fast so he begins to destroy as he moves, knowing we still can't take the pass and having to hamper our resupply at every stage he can, hence Understone. He is on his way directly to Korina but he doesn't want to lead us straight past Septern Manse and leave any chance that we can stop his other army—also on its way to Korina, by the way— from catching and killing The Raven. I'd do the same if I held the superstitions they do. On their own, The Raven have already destroyed apparently indestructible forces and he'll be sure they can do it again. Best not to take chances. Best to see them dead."

"So he'll fight us just to stop us reaching Senedai?" Gresse's expression was sceptical.

"For one, but also because it's better to fight us there than outside Korina where he thinks, again mistakenly, that we would get significant help. Possibly even enough to defeat him." Darrick's heart was racing and he could see the pieces slot themselves into place in the minds of the Barons.

"But all that is immaterial if Senedai kills The Raven," said Blackthorne. "Because, if you're right about these dragons . . ."

". . . the only chance any of us, Wesmen or Balaians, have is if Senedai is stopped," finished Darrick.

"And Tessaya won't believe us," said Gresse. "Gods falling, I'm not even sure *I* believe us."

"Just say all this is right, how long can the Protectors hold out? Long enough to see The Raven complete their task? Long enough for us to skirt Tessaya and hit Senedai ourselves?" asked Blackthorne.

Darrick shook his head. "As to The Raven, I don't know. All I do know is that we won't get around Tessaya, not an army this big. He already has us scouted."

"So we're going to fight him?" Gresse looked less than upset at the idea.

"If we fight and win, it'll take two days minimum. No." He smiled at what he was about to say. "We've only got the one choice and, farfetched as it is, we have to have his help."

"So?" asked Blackthorne, though Darrick could see he knew the answer and was already fighting with thoughts of placing his need for vengeance to one side, much as Darrick himself was doing.

"So, we're going to march right up to him, as quickly as we can, look as powerful as possible and then we're going to persuade him to send a message to Senedai."

Hirad had known it would be beautiful, the feelings in his mind when Sha-Kaan had spoken of it told him that, but he hadn't imagined the half of it. They had climbed several hundred feet up a steep-sided rocky slope with the deep orange sun beating down from the same blue sky that had lain above them ever since their arrival in the dragons' dimension.

The remainder of their journey had been a nervy rush across the fire-ravaged plain. The surviving travellers had reformed an hour from where the Veret dragon's attack had taken place and while The Raven were unhurt, barring a few scratches, only Cil and two Protector brothers remained of the six that had come through the rip, and Jatha had lost seven of his people.

Styliann had remained quiet about what he had seen as his Protectors died but the flinch he had given when a Kaan dragon overflew them on the way back to its homelands was all the information Hirad had really needed. The Xetesk Master had been pale and clearly shaken and, for the first time, Hirad had actually felt a little sympathy for him.

The battle in the sky had been won, just, though Hirad had felt Sha-Kaan's sorrow as he had spoken of singling out one Brood, the Veret, for attack until the Kaan had driven them off, breaking their spirits and a fledgling alliance between enemy Broods. But, in a notable change to his attitude, he had detailed a quartet of Kaan to shadow their journey despite the extra attention the action would inevitably bring.

And so they had travelled, humbled by their experience and all too aware of the awesome destructive power of even a single dragon. No more was that evidenced than by the plain they left after a further day's travel to move into the rocky foothills of the mountains they had seen from the dead forest. Looking back, they saw the scars and open wounds that would probably live on forever.

No longer did the plain shimmer in its pale blue and red frond-topped light as far as the eye could see. Now, beneath a huge shifting pall of smoke and ash, a yellow and orange glow told of the fire still burning, consuming the stunning vegetation, voracious and insatiable in its appetite. Where it had burned itself out, the land was blackened and smouldering, laid waste to its roots and beyond in the heat of the consumption. The vegetation was resilient and would sprout again but that thought made the sight no less terrible.

"Just one dragon," The Unknown had said as they watched with hypnotic stillness the countless miles of smoke and flame. "Just one." His words had speeded their ascent.

Now here they stood, The Raven, apart from the rest as befitted the Dragonene of the Great Kaan and those pledged to help him, and looked down for the first time on the Kaan homeland. The slope they had climbed had flattened into a pitted rock plateau which swept to a point jutting out over the homeland. As they stood at its edge, the rock beneath them formed an overhang, arcing down and out of sight the Gods knew how far below. And all around them was a different world.

Left and right below them, a carpet of shifting green lay covering a wide valley, the walls of which were just visible through the veil. Massive leaves waved gently, attached to huge boughs that sat darkly beneath the surface and Hirad could only imagine the size of the trunks from which they grew. Across the undulating surface, the sun's orange light shot delightful rays of colour through pale strands of mist, and the stark backdrop of white peaked mountains tumbling down to dark flatlands completed the serene picture.

But that alone wasn't the beauty Hirad saw. In the sky above the canopy, the Kaan wheeled and dived, lazy beats begetting long, graceful glides as they circled while those entering the trees from above swept their wings back and shot past, golden bodies sparkling in the orange glow as their bodies spun, dragging vortices of mist after them as they disappeared.

And they called to each other. Sounds of welcome, of farewell, of sadness, of love and of enduring devotion. To the Brood, to each other and to their home. The calls were brackish and guttural, or haunting hollow cries that echoed from the valley walls. They tugged at Hirad's heart and senses, filling him with the warmth of belonging and the emptiness of the war that stole Kaan from the sky each day.

Hirad felt the strength falter in his legs and he crouched, one leg under him, his right hand on the ground as he rocked forward, watching. He could have stayed there all day, such was the majesty of the Kaan and their homeland. He felt a hand on his shoulder and looked up. It was Ilkar.

"Can you believe it?" asked Hirad, gesturing at the awesome view all around them, his eyes again on the Kaan and the trees and mist covering their valley, a warm moist breeze blowing in his face.

"If I live to be five hundred, this will be my abiding memory as I die," said the elf, the magnitude of it all plain in his voice.

"Never mind Balaia. They're too busy grasping for themselves, most of them. This is what we're really trying to save. And this is why we can't fail." Hirad stood up, wiping damp eyes. To his left, Jatha gazed down on the homeland with an almost stupefied expression on his face.

"Home," he said.

"See what it means to them? He must have seen this a hundred times but just look at him."

Ilkar nodded. "We all want this to work, Hirad, and your reason is probably more compelling than most but I think you need to be realistic about our chances."

"Tell me on the way down. I think Jatha is anxious to get there, as am I."

Jatha led them to a stairway carved from the stone of the mountain on which they stood. Steep and moss-covered, it swept under the overhang, twisting and turning through cleft, behind waterfall and around the enormous boles of the trees whose leaves hemmed in more strands of mist, building clouds the further down they went.

Descending through the dancing, orange-striated cloud, the atmosphere closed in hot and damp, vision was impaired and the stairs became slick and wet, treacherous to the unsure foot. Ahead of The Raven, Jatha and his men scampered down with practised confidence, Jatha's voice at odds with his movement as it periodically echoed "Careful!" up through the mist.

But for the Balaians the way was far slower. Leaning into the rock wall, which ran with water or was covered with a thin film of slime, they kept away from the far edge which plummeted down through the mist to death on the valley floor.

Hirad, walking behind Ilkar, had decided not to ask any questions until they breached the mist but when they did, it was a long time before he could find any words. In a few paces, the mist had thinned and cleared beneath the leaf layer, giving them their first view of the Kaan homeland.

A vast flat space of rock, grass and river stretched under the mist which reflected a gentle, warm light on to the land below, giving the homeland a tranquil aspect, easy on the eye. The river which meandered through the centre of the valley was a sparkling blue and the sounds of water reached them across the still, humid air from falls which fed the river in a dozen places he could see. The grassland was a luxuriant deep green tipped with red and blue just like the plain and, given the connected squares of close-cropped and waist-high stalks, was clearly tended and harvested for some purpose.

The buildings scattered along the valley sides, some low, flat and half-buried, others dug deep into the rock of the valley itself, seemed purely functional. But one magnificent structure dominated the Broodland. With its polished white stone gleaming in the filtered sunlight, its dome and towers striking toward the sky yet dwarfed by the extraordinary sculpted wings whose tips all but touched the mist above, Wingspread was a simply staggering monument to Sha-Kaan. And his carved face looked out at his domain, eyes forever watching for danger. Nothing like it existed in Balaia and, for all their magic, nothing ever would. This was a construct born of consummate respect and veneration for a leader the Kaan and their Vestare honoured freely and with a fervour lost to the peoples of its kindred dimension.

All the Balaians had stopped to drink in the view. Glancing across at Denser, Hirad saw the awe on his face while Erienne's held an enraptured smile that had as much to do with the atmosphere of peace and safety as the sights before her. For Hirad, it was like coming home and he closed his eyes and let the feelings of the Kaan wash over him, his limbs tingling, his mind suffused with the thoughts Sha-Kaan let drift through his mind.

"Tell me we won't let this be destroyed," he said eventually.

"We'll save it or die trying," said Ilkar. Hirad looked at Ilkar, seeing that the determination that had bound him to The Raven for ten years had not dimmed.

"Well, I have no intention of dying," said Hirad. "Tell me about our chances." He motioned that they should follow after Jatha and his men who had continued to the base of the stairway and were wading through a square of grass, their walk becoming a run as they approached the river and a set of crossing stones.

Calls of welcome from human mouths echoed across the Broodland and from a dozen small stone-and-thatch dwellings set in a hamlet close to the river came more of the Vestare. Children squealed with delight, men and women came together in embraces, splashing through the shallows to welcome home those who had been gone from sanctuary so long.

Laughter floated across the air but with it the sounds of crying and sorrow as those whose men had not survived learned of their loss. The mood broke quickly and solemnity returned. All faces turned toward The Raven as they, Styliann and the Protectors strode toward the river, crossing the same stones Jatha had danced across so recently.

"Raven, welcome," he said. "Hirad, home."

"Home," agreed Hirad. He pointed toward Wingspread. "Sha-Kaan?"

Jatha shook his head. "Wait," he said. His face cracked into a smile. "Eat? Drink." He clapped his hands and some of the Vestare scampered away, disappearing into their houses. He sat on some close-cropped grass and motioned his guests to do the same. Fruit and strips of meat were brought out on platters by some, while others brought pitchers of water and juice and carved wooden cups out of which to drink. From somewhere nearby, music from a set of pipes drifted across the air.

The scene and the atmosphere were idyllic but Hirad couldn't forget why they were here. A handful of dragons sat on the ground outside, massive hulking bodies resting part in the river or on the flat rock, heads sweeping lazily to grab Flamegrass or the carcasses their Vestare brought them. They all ignored the arrival of the strangers completely. Most, he presumed, were flying around the rip, injured in melde-corridors or cavorting in the skies overhead. Sha-Kaan, he was sure, was inside Wingspread and he thought it curious the Great Kaan had not come out to greet them. But, as always, he would have his reasons.

"Hirad," said Ilkar. "Before you speak to Sha-Kaan—"

"Yes, our chances," agreed Hirad.

"Or lack of them," said Ilkar. "And don't bridle like that, I'm only being realistic. You need to know exactly how far we've got."

Hirad tore at a piece of meat with his teeth, washing the food down with the pale green, sweet fruit juice.

"You aren't going to tell me anything good, are you?"

"It's not quite that bad," said Ilkar. "It's just there are so many unknowables and guesses we're having to make. But let me start at the beginning. Unknown, you ought to listen to this."

"I am," came the reply. "Thraun?" The shapechanger moved closer to Ilkar. He had a cup in his hand but hadn't taken any food.

"The theory is relatively simple but, without definite parameters, the power of any spell we cast is going to be a guess. Educated, but a guess. What we have to do, and the four of us are strong enough to do it from beneath the rip, is form a mana lattice that binds with the edges of the rip. This is all based on Septern's spells designed to border rips and contain them."

"So you're going to effectively border this rip," said The Unknown.

"Absolutely," said Ilkar. "And then we have to draw it closed. Now that would be reasonably easy if we only had one end to contend with but we don't; we have a corridor and another end all of the same massive size. You all right with this so far, Hirad?"

"Anything I don't get I'll ask The Unknown to explain when you've gone," he said.

"Gone where?" asked Ilkar.

"Gone where you can't hear me complaining how complicated you make things," said Hirad, smiling as Ilkar's ears pricked.

"Fine," said the elf mage. "Now, returning to reality for a moment, we're sure that Septern must have opened and closed dimensional corridors and there is theory that discusses the weave, if you like, that is required to close a hole in interdimensional space. What we believe we have to do is set up what is best described as a mana shuttle which, anchored at this end of the rip by the border we create, flies down the corridor, looping through its sides to come out the other end and effectively pull the sides together, closing the rip and corridor on both sides."

"Can that be done?" The Unknown took fruit from a platter offered to him and smiled his thanks at the woman serving. "I have to say, Ilkar, it sounds very farfetched."

Ilkar sighed. "It is. Look, we don't know if we can do it, yet. The lore theory is there in Septern's texts, Styliann and Denser are trying to link it to some Xeteskian dimensional theory and we do have a spell that will close a gateway."

"But it's the shuttle bit, isn't it?" said Hirad.

"Yes," said Ilkar. "It's certainly an extension of the mana lattice we'll make to contain the rip on this side but at the moment we're guessing and that's very dangerous."

"I don't want to worry you but we don't have the time for you to do anything else," said Hirad. "We have to cast this thing in the next day or so or it'll be too late for the Kaan and you know what that means for Balaia."

"I am aware, Hirad, but we did always say it would be difficult." Ilkar's eyes narrowed a little and his ears reddened. "Developing new spells isn't easy, you know."

The Unknown held up his hands for calm. "And bickering isn't going to help. Now, am I missing something or can't you cast the lattice that borders the rip this side, pull it closed, if that isn't too simplistic, and then go back to Balaia and do the same in Parve?"

Ilkar raised his eyebrows and smiled. "Lovely idea but we had to discount it. Even assuming we'd make it back to Parve from the Manse, it wouldn't work. The power in interdimensional space is too great and you have to remember that the corridor would still be there, just with no second opening. We have to close the corridor too and the lattice is inherently unstable and wouldn't survive to give us the time to reach Parve. That's why we had to come here. We have to close the rip against the flow of the way it was made."

"So sum up our chances in a way I can understand," said Hirad, his plate still full but his appetite fading fast.

"If Denser and Styliann can't find any help in Xeteskian dimensional theory, we have next to no chance because we'll have no idea of the forces operating beyond the rip. If they do, we're still making a best guess at a mana construct brand new to us all and will have no clear idea if it'll work until it either does or doesn't. It'll require all our combined strength to cast from the ground anyway." He paused and looked at Hirad solemnly. "There is less chance of this succeeding than there was of defeating the Wytch Lords."

"Sha-Kaan isn't going to like that," said Hirad.

"Well, he'll just have to live with it."

"Or die with it," returned Hirad, and he got to his feet, dusted down his trousers and leather and set off to Wingspread.

"Who'd be a Dragonene, eh Unknown?" Ilkar tried to smile.

"Who'd be any of us, Ilkar," he replied. "Who'd be any of us."

CHAPTER 32

*T*hey *attack.*

The thought pulsed around the Protectors in the dawn light. The Wesmen were advancing, their dogs and archers before them. This was no charge and Aeb questioned the tactic with his brethren.

Dogs in the vanguard, archers to weaken us, army to follow up.

As one, the Protectors brought their weapons to the ready, each masked man unsheathing double handed sword and battle axe.

We are enough to shield effectively. Aeb drove the idea around them. *Concentration is everything. We are one. Fight as one.*

We are one, fight as one. The mantra echoed around their minds bringing them the strength of the Soul Tank and the belief in their invincibility. They were ready.

From all sides, arrows flew and the dogs were unleashed. Their howls were drowned by the roars of the Wesmen. *Think shield.* They thought and the arrows bounced. The Wesmen roars faltered but the dogs drove on. Huge beasts, the size of newborn foals, their mouths thick with teeth, saliva dripping as they came. Another flight of arrows; no more than five pierced the shield and no Protectors fell. The dogs hit them.

They had counted seventy Destranas, all hungry for the kill but all fighting on their own. Those at the front of the charge leapt for neck, thigh or stomach but the Protectors saw every angle of attack. Aeb struck down with his axe at the skull of a dog that leapt at the brother next to him. Two more blades thudded into the beast's neck and back. It died with a whimper.

Aeb, blade left lower quarter.

Aeb struck without looking, feeling his sword bite into a Destrana midriff. The thought had come as he sensed the animal, it was merely direction but it was all he needed. He pulled his axe clear to hammer it through the jaw of a third dog while his sword still skewered the terrified, crying animal on the ground to his left.

Around the circle the orders flew and the blades and axes followed them. Seventy dogs was too few by at least three hundred and those that didn't run to hide behind the legs of their masters died without landing paw or fang on a single brother. Too slow, too obvious, too individual. It was why animals would never beat Protectors.

Quiet fell over the ranks of the army and their commander hesitated before ordering more arrows. Again the shield held and but one Protector took a wound in his thigh. He fell back to tend and direct until bandaged. Now the horns sounded and the encircled Protectors faced not a headlong charge but a careful, closed advance. Aeb could sense the nervousness as they advanced and pulsed his brothers to note it.

Their commander has no heart for this fight. We scare him. Seek those who command. Fight as one. We are one.

Fight as one, we are one. The second mantra echoed through their bodies. No thought was given to the overwhelming numbers who advanced toward them, only to the totality that was their being. The dogs were dead, their blood slicking the ground in the damp, drizzling morning. Their masters knew as never before that those first to the battle would die. It was inevitable.

As is victory. We are Given, we may not fail.

Lord Senedai fought to keep his mouth closed as he watched his war dogs slaughtered. Destranas were feared by all men, their ferocity and desire for the kill legendary. But these men, whatever they were, didn't so much as flinch, only taking a pace back when it gave them a better angle to strike. They seemed to know where an attack was coming from before it came and, though the distance might have confused his sight, he could swear some of them struck without looking. Struck and hit. This was no wild flailing, it was ordered, accurate power.

And that scared Senedai more than anything else.

The dogs had raced on in tight howling packs and had died whining, their bodies chopped and twitching. Senedai dragged himself back to the immediate with the baying shouts of his men dying to echoes in the mist and rain. An uneasy, fidgeting quiet gripped his army. None of them had seen a single enemy fall. Now they looked to him for orders, his signallers ready, standing expectant to his left.

"My Lord?" prompted a Lieutenant. "We should not lose the impetus."

"I know!" snapped Senedai, then calmed himself. "I know. Signal an advance from all quarters. Slow march. Let's have them watch us massing right under their noses and fear what is about to overwhelm them. Front ranks only. Rear stand ready for my command."

The flags went up, the horns sounded and the Wesmen advanced. Senedai's heart thudded in his chest as he moved up behind the front ranks, shouting encouragement, exhorting them to keep a slow pace as if any near him desired to charge to certain death.

From the ruins of the Manse there was no reaction. The small force stood ready, blood dripping from swords and axes, masked faces offering nothing, bodies exuding controlled aggression. Behind Senedai, an order signalled more arrows. More waste. A flight of one hundred turned aside by the cursed invisible barrier. But there was no mage.

"What in all the hells is going on?" Senedai shouted, frustration burning hot. "Who are these men?" he muttered under his breath, afraid again.

Forty paces from battle, the spirit chant began. Rumbling from the front lines in every direction, it rolled over the Wesmen army, setting Senedai's skin tingling and refreshing his flagging confidence. It was the song to greet enemy steel, the song to accept death like a warrior if it should strike and the song to bind the spirits to the Wesmen nation forever.

Over and over, the growled words, only twenty in all, emitted from the lips of the army, rising to a cacophony that drowned the clashing of weapons and the tramp of many thousands of feet. At the last, the march broke, the tempo of the chant increasing, driving the warriors on. In front of them, the masked force moved, axes raised, swords pointed to the ground, prepared to repel as the Wesmen wave broke over them.

Threat hung heavy in the morning air, lowering dark with the clouds above that dispensed a light drizzle but promised a downpour.

Darrick had marched his army directly toward the waiting horde, demanding order and speed. He knew they would be watching, just as his scouts watched them, and he needed the Wesmen to report determination and confidence. So he drilled them as they marched, the cavalry marking time ahead, never once breaking stride.

In open fields a little over a mile from where Tessaya's army camped, he brought the column to a halt. A single horn blast was followed by a tumult of orders from a hundred mouths and each man, elf and mage knew what they had to do. Defensive positions were set, a perimeter established, the command post erected and regimental lines drawn up. Mages stood by sword guards, elven eyes scoured the Grethern Forest to the south and the bare rises north. Fire and cess pits were dug, tents sprouted, animals were picketed and guarded, the quartermasters' and armourers' wagons emptied and stores and forges were in operation less than an hour after their arrival.

Darrick turned from the preparation with a smile tugging at his lips. "Not bad," he said, "when you consider that less than a thousand out there are seasoned campaign soldiers."

Blackthorne chuckled. "Well, Blackthorne farmers and winegrowers have always been practical."

Darrick looked hard, unsure if Blackthorne was joking. Gresse confirmed it for him.

"And the victorious defenders from Gyernath just stand and admire, eh Blackthorne?"

"They've been allowed to assist my specialists," said Blackthorne, his eyes twinkling beneath his dark brows. Darrick cleared his throat.

"It should give the Wesmen scouts something to think about," he said.

"I expect Tessaya will be scared rigid when he hears of the construction efficiency of Blackthorne's vintners and vintagers," said Gresse. Darrick scowled at the levity and Gresse's expression hardened. "Sorry, General. Tell us when you plan to ride in?" He sat on one of the six chairs unfolded around the map table in the command tent.

"We'll have lunch, then I will raise the parley flag and leave here with a small guard of a dozen cavalry."

"And us," said Blackthorne.

"I beg your pardon?" Darrick frowned and again looked hard at the tall stern Baron. He saw no hint of humour this time.

"I know Tessaya. He buys, or rather bought, my finest wines. He might listen to me," said Blackthorne.

"And you, Baron Gresse?"

"I will ride with my friend and you to add support and gravitas. Tessaya must not see this as merely a gambit. A deputation of three senior Balaians might sway him."

Darrick nodded. "Very well. I'll not say I couldn't use the support. Tessaya will be a difficult man so far into our lands." He felt a relief he knew he shouldn't as a General but there was some physical aspect about the two Barons that inspired confidence. He saw it as a matter-of-fact determination to succeed, a refusal to accept the possibility of defeat. Surely it was what their people saw and why a handful of soldiers and an army of farmers could have such a bearing on the war.

"Will he respect the parley flag?" asked Darrick.

"Yes," said Blackthorne immediately. "And not because he is particularly honourable. But he is an intelligent man unwilling to sacrifice his people if he can secure victory by negotiated surrender."

"But given to poor judgement at crucial times," said Darrick. "For instance, he could have faced us at Understone in a far stronger position. I believe he panicked."

"Possibly," said Blackthorne. "But don't assume he'll err again."

Two hours later, the three men rode from the camp, their guard in echelon formation behind them, a single rider ahead carrying the green and white halved flag to indicate peaceful parley.

A quarter of a mile from the Wesmen army, they were flanked by thirty

Wesmen axe-bearers who trotted beside the horses, melting wordlessly out of the forest. It was an honour guard and Darrick paradoxically felt a little easier than when they were alone though he indicated that the two mage riders maintain their shields.

Shortly afterward, they reached the top of a rise and the Wesmen were below them. Covering an area probably a quarter of a mile on a side, the camp sprawled across pasture and cropland. Dozens of fires burned into the damp early afternoon sky, banners and standards hung limp and tents hugged the ground in carefully spaced order. Forsaking their trademark towers and stockades with time against them, the Wesmen instead had mounted a heavy border presence of warriors. A sneak attack on this camp would not work and Tessaya wanted them to know it.

Passing into the camp, Darrick's ease evaporated. Thousands of eyes turned to stare, the hum of work and talk fell away and a savage hostility pervaded the atmosphere. From all parts of the camp, Wesmen warriors ran to get a closer look at the enemy in their midst and, here and there, Shamen in cloak and paint issued forward, gazing malevolently at the parley group, their hands and mouths moving, cursing.

But none broke the honour guard which shouldered its way through the increasing press, heading for a tent like all the others save the heavy security surrounding it and the dozen standards driven into the ground either side of its entrance, forming a tight walkway.

A short walk from the tent, the honour guard brought the parade to a halt, indicating that the Balaians dismount.

"Stay with the horses." Darrick instructed the squad leader, an elven mage. "Don't look any warrior in the eye and keep those shields firm."

"Yes, sir."

Darrick looked beyond the elf, whose curt confident nod belied the fear that had to be crawling in his belly, and saw the gathering mob of Wesmen pressing in toward the command tent on all sides. If the talks went wrong, there would be nowhere to run.

"Have faith," said Blackthorne, picking up his mood. "Should we die, your army still has everyone it needs to win."

"How comforting to think they don't really need me," said Darrick.

"You know what I mean."

The brown canvas of the tent flap was pulled aside and an old Shaman beckoned them in.

The tent was plainly furnished. To the left, a low pallet, tidy and made up. To the right, a serving table decked with meat, bread, jugs and goblets. To either side of the door, a Wesman guard and, in front of them, a table with a single chair. The old Shaman, dressed in plain brown shift, moved to stand behind Lord Tessaya who sat upright, gazing at them over a half-eaten plate of food.

"Welcome to my lands," he said, a harsh smile cracking his tanned features.

"I thank you for granting us audience," said Darrick, ignoring Tessaya's crude attempt at baiting. "There is a critical matter to discuss that affects both our peoples."

"Yes," said Tessaya. "Your surrender that confirms Wesmen ascension in Balaia and stops pointless death." He looked past Darrick. "Baron Blackthorne, it is as ever a pleasure."

"I trust we shall soon be able to share the finest bottle from my cellars, my Lord," responded Blackthorne. "Assuming your departing force failed to find the way in. But unless you hear General Darrick, that pleasure will be denied us all."

The Shaman leaned in and whispered into Tessaya's ear. The Wesman Lord nodded.

"I am already aware of your desperate search for help beyond this world. And even if you delay me here with meaningless talk, my kin Lord, Senedai, will destroy the Manse and then your precious Raven. He will soon overwhelm the Xeteskian unmen and, when he does, Balaia and another world will be open to my conquering armies. Speak, General Darrick. Let us see if you are as good a talker as you are a soldier." Tessaya leaned back in his chair and took a deep draught of the goblet at his right hand. At a snap of his fingers, a door guard ran to the table to grab a jug for refill.

"Balaia is under threat. There is a hole in the sky that hangs above Parve. It links our world to another and it must be closed if we are not to be invaded by dragons. The Raven go to complete that task. If Lord Senedai stops them, we will all die. I have come here to ask you to stop him before he commits a monumental crime in the name of the Wesmen nation." Darrick searched Tessaya's face for signs that he was really listening. He felt his face go cold as the contempt spread across the Wesman Lord's features.

"You must think me a stupid man and that makes me very unhappy," he said. "You should have respect for all I have achieved and yet you invent tales that a backward child would not believe."

"He speaks the truth," said Blackthorne. "And you know me as a man of honour. I would not lie to you."

"What I know is that desperate men will set aside their principles when death is the reward for keeping them," said Tessaya smoothly. "And I will tell you what is the truth. Indeed dragons will come here, completing a prophecy of our ancients unless I can stop them. And stop them, I will. There is no threat from the mark in the sky. My messengers tell me it is merely the fire mark of Parve, destroyed by your hands. I will not listen to you while your allies seek the only power that can halt the Wesmen march to Korina.

"And yet I will show you more respect than you show me. If you want to stop the Wesmen and you refuse honourable surrender, it will have to be on the battlefield. So go and prepare for the fight, if you have the stomach for it. Under the terms of parley, you have three hundred counts to leave my camp. That count has started." He turned his attention to the food remaining on his plate.

Behind Darrick, the tent flap was pulled aside but he ignored it, striding forward to bang his hands on the table, shaking the plate and upsetting the goblet which pirouetted over, spilling its liquid on the grass.

"And what if I do tell the truth and your men stop The Raven from closing the hole? It will be too late to ask for forgiveness when dragons are laying waste to Balaia, and they will fly over Wesmen lands first." Darrick felt his anger burning. He heard a weapon drawn but ignored it. "What will you do?"

Tessaya met his stare, waving a hand to keep his guards back. He smiled. "If that is what you believe then you had better hope The Raven can outwit my northern army. The count continues."

Blackthorne and Gresse came to Darrick's shoulders and gently drew him back.

"I understand your scepticism," said Blackthorne. "Yet it doesn't change the reality. As a gesture of good faith, Gresse and I will remain here as your prisoners. Should what we say turn out to be untrue, we will be at your mercy."

Tessaya pushed a spoonful of meat into his mouth and chewed, talking around the food and pointing the spoon at Blackthorne.

"You are a brave man, Baron, and I have nothing but admiration for your defeat of my southern army. I almost lament the destruction of your town but such are the necessities of war. You make a generous offer but what hollow victory will it be, placing your two noble heads on spikes while my people are killed by your dragon allies?

"Do you not understand? I am soon to march to victory in Korina once I have defeated you here. I will rule Balaia. So you see, you are already at my mercy." He turned to his Shaman who nodded and moved quickly to the tent door.

"Arnoan will escort you to the borders of the camp. I will see you in battle."

The three senior Balaians looked at each other. Darrick felt a sense of desperation sweep over him and, for a moment, considered breaking the parley to kill Tessaya. But he could not and he knew Blackthorne and Gresse would move to stop him. Tessaya's point-blank refusal to believe him was quite predictable but it left The Raven helpless should Senedai defeat the Protectors.

Stalking from the audience, he found himself praying that Xetesk's abominations would live up to their reputation.

Sha-Kaan flew from Wingspread with the orb beginning its fall from the sky. The Great Kaan, tired from his exertions in battle and without a melde-corridor now Hirad Coldheart was in his domain, stretched aching wings to catch the winds in the heights, heading again for the Shedara Ocean to find Tanis-Veret, if his *altemelde* was still alive.

The cold air brought a clarity of thought to the Great Kaan, his speed driving ice into his lungs when he opened his mouth to breathe, serving also to quell his anger at Hirad Coldheart's words. He found he could see through the haze of his own mind at what his Dragonene's words actually meant.

And that hatched unusual feelings. Sha-Kaan was used to having his orders fulfilled without question or error. Yet The Raven had told him there was no certainty of success in their mission and Hirad had introduced him to a Balaian concept quite alien to him—that the best a man could possibly do had to be considered enough, even if it meant ultimate failure or even death. Sha-Kaan had let his contempt show. He should have killed the puny human then and there but once again Hirad had managed to stay him with irrefutable logic.

"Kill me and you'll never know if we would have succeeded and you will die. If we do fail, we'll all die in the attempt anyway and you will have your wish." Spoken calmly. Sha-Kaan had laughed but it hadn't dampened his anger. Not then.

Now, flying to a meeting that had to bear fruit, he could understand the effort The Raven had made. He could feel their desire for success and he knew they were aware of the consequences of failure for themselves, for Balaia and for the Kaan. But knowing isn't the same as doing.

Another new emotion flashed through his body. Deep fear. He had been scared before; of injury, of facing the anger of his kin, and of his spawn dying before reaching maturity. But this was different. The fear marked the possibility that the entire Brood Kaan might become extinct and more, that they no longer wielded the weapons that could change that possibility. The Raven did.

They had to be protected at all costs which meant peeling defence from the gateway. He had too few healthy dragons. Elu-Kaan shimmered on the borders of death without his Dragonene to help him, reliant on the ministrations of the Vestare; and every melde-corridor was in use. The Kaan needed help and there was only one Brood that might turn. The tragedy was that it had been the Veret they had targeted in the last battle, knowing that to drive them off would break the Naik stranglehold. It had worked, but if the Veret refused him now, the death and maiming would have been for nothing.

Stooping from the heights with night full in the Shedaran sky, he feared the Kaan had done too thorough a job. No guard flew to meet him, no Veret sought revenge. None patrolled their air borders and the water below was still.

He landed on the meeting rock, pushed his head beneath the surface of the ocean and roared into its impenetrable depths. With his mind, he sought Tanis-Veret, pulsing his sorrow and his desperation at what had occurred in the skies over Teras. He pulsed his need and roared his urgency. He could only pray to the Skies that his *altemelde* heard him.

Sha-Kaan withdrew his head and lay flat across the rock, neck stretched in front of him. It was to keep his muscles extended and to appear in an attitude of deference from above but more it allowed his body sensors to cover the sea-drenched dark island, searching for vibrations from the water around him.

He waited for what felt an eternity in another's Brood space, exposed and vulnerable should attack come. Ultimately, though, he was rewarded. A thrumming through the rock told of the approach of a large dragon, powering up from the depths. Sha-Kaan sat up, neck to the formal "s" to greet Tanis-Veret as he exploded into the sky, water flying in all directions, waves rippling away from his exit point.

Water cascaded from his black-smeared body as he rose into the sky, trim wings angled for lift and tattered on the trailing edge. He bellowed his displeasure and fired a long breath into the air during a slow circle of the rock before landing heavily, tail sweeping water over his scarred lower back. His neck reared up, his eyes skewering Sha-Kaan with a malevolent stare.

"Here to preside over the final destruction of the Veret, Sha-Kaan?" He took in the sky as if expecting it to fill with enemy dragons.

"No, Tanis-Veret, I am here to offer your Brood a chance of salvation," said Sha-Kaan, allowing his head to bow slightly in a fractional expression of humility.

"Hollow words," spat the old Veret. "Your eyes have not seen what you have wrought."

"And now we—"

"Beneath our feet, the remnants of my Brood cling to the faint hope the Naik will honour their promise and leave us in peace when the Kaan are destroyed. Fewer than seventy of us remain, many near death in our melde-corridors. Of those that can still fly, I am the least wounded and the scales of my back will never knit, such was the ferocity of Kaan fire, claw and fang." Tanis-Veret met Sha-Kaan's gaze again and his voice became an echo of itself, broken and exhausted. "I cannot even spare the kin to defend my borders. Leave us, Sha-Kaan; you have done enough."

But Sha-Kaan did not move, an open act of aggression should Tanis-Veret choose to take it that way. But the damaged dragon merely shook his head.

"I see," he said.

"Skies above, Tanis, no you do not!" thundered Sha-Kaan. "I came here and begged you not to ally with the Naik, to trust us that we would protect you from them but you would not listen and so we were bound to fight you and you were the weaker link.

"It is of no succour but the Kaan took no pleasure in your destruction. And now, we have the chance to help you survive."

A laugh rumbled in the chest of Tanis-Veret and he growled in his throat. "How can you help us? The Kaan are finished too. This meeting is a meeting of the dead. The gateway is too big for you to defend any longer. We can all see it. When the Naik next muster their allies, you will be destroyed and your melde-dimension with you."

Sha-Kaan inclined his head. Tanis-Veret's incomplete knowledge led to his only possible conclusion. "But we now have the means to close the gateway and we need you to give us the time to do it."

"I can think of no reason why I should trust your words."

"I make you this offer, Tanis-Veret," said Sha-Kaan. "It is your decision if you accept. I will place no pressure on you. I have travelled alone and at great risk to talk with you and am honoured that you still grant me audience. Natives of my melde-dimension have travelled here to use their skills to close the gateway in my sky. It was forged by their magic and can be undone by that same magic. But they will be on the ground and vulnerable while they work.

"If you join the battle on the side of the Kaan, we can defend them. And should they succeed, the Kaan will return to strength quickly. I do not believe the Naik will leave you be, should they triumph. What I can promise you, and you know my words can be trusted, is that we will protect you after our victory. We will keep enemies from your borders while you heal and keep you safe while your numbers recover. Never again will the Veret and the Kaan fight. Our lands do not cross, we have no reason to be in conflict. So it shall be with the Kaan.

"I do not expect you to answer now. It is your gamble and the fate of your Brood rests on your decision. I need your help. The Brood Kaan needs your help. And now I must leave. I have to prepare for battle, as do you. Perhaps I will see you dive on the Naik."

"The Skies go with you, Sha-Kaan," said Tanis-Veret, his tone enigmatic, thoughtful. "I will respond to the call from the Naik as I must. But that is all I must do."

"As you wish, Tanis-Veret." He unfurled his wings, barked a farewell and flew for the Kaan Broodland, his heart a little easier while his mind turned to battle.

CHAPTER 33

A s evening gathered, the mist closed in and the pace of the Kaan Brood-land, already sedate, slowed even further. No dragons remained outside, choosing Chouls, melde-corridors or private dwellings if they were of sufficient rank. The Raven sat outside near the river. They hadn't been given any quarters and were clearly expected to sleep outside in the open. But the night was warm and humid and sleeping by the river would present no problem.

The real problem lay in the uncertainty of the mages and Hirad felt that keenly. He saw the anxious look in Ilkar's eyes and the fidgeting of Denser's lips as they worried at the stem of his unlit pipe.

On the one hand it was extraordinary, he thought, as he watched the four of them arguing and practising a short distance away, sitting on a flat rock near the river, books and papers held open and down by small stones and pebbles. Here, four of Balaia's most talented mages, including the most powerful man in Xetesk, struggled with a problem for which they had practically all the information.

And on the other, it was no surprise at all. They were being asked to close a hole in the sky, the size of a city, hundreds of feet above their heads. Hirad could only guess at the skill that must take. Again, he felt helpless. He knew his role as warrior meant they got here at all, but now, with the most important work still to be done, he was sitting around drinking coffee.

Across the stove sat Thraun, silent and brooding, his long blond hair lank in the humidity, hanging in thick clotted strands around his head. The shapechanger had barely acknowledged his own existence since Will's death, coming to life only when The Raven were threatened. But, like so much of The Raven of the recent past, the man he had been was gone.

"Thraun?" ventured Hirad. The young man lifted his gaze from the grass he'd been studying and looked squarely at Hirad. There was no strength in his eyes. No determination. Nothing but a brooding sorrow. Now he'd got Thraun's attention, Hirad had little idea how to go on, knowing only that he had to get through somehow, that the silence could not be allowed to continue.

"How are you feeling?" Hirad cringed inwardly as he asked the lame question. Thraun ignored it.

"Will would have loved this place," he said, his voice a low growl. "He was quite nervous, you know. Strange that, for such a talented thief. This place is so tranquil. It would have calmed him."

"Despite the large number of huge dragons flying about?"

Hirad was rewarded with the ghost of a smile on Thraun's lips. "Despite that. Funny, isn't it. Something as small as Denser's Familiar scared him so badly while something as large as dragons hardly even ruffled his feathers."

"I don't know," said Hirad. "There's much good in dragons, or the Kaan anyway. Nothing too holy about the Familiar."

"I suppose." Thraun fell silent, resuming his study of the ground. "I can't bear this," he said suddenly, catching Hirad off guard.

"Bear what?"

"Only he knows what it's really like." Thraun indicated The Unknown who stood near the mages with the three surviving Protectors. "Having something in you that you hate and love in equal measure. Something that you wish didn't afflict you but could not live without. Only his friends didn't die while he was a Protector."

"Richmond did."

"But The Unknown wasn't standing next to him, was he? You thought him dead. He had gone and Richmond couldn't be saved."

"And neither could Will," said Hirad earnestly, leaning forward. "Listen, when Sirendor Larn died, I felt the same. Like I let him down by not being stood by him at the moment of the attack. I had to accept quickly that there was nothing more I could have done. Yes, I had my revenge but you know something else? It doesn't make the pain any less. You just have to go on as best you can. Enjoy the things you still have, don't dredge up the things you don't."

Thraun looked at Hirad again, nodding gently, tears brimming his eyes. "I know you mean to help, Hirad. And I thank you for that. But Will was my only link to the human world when I was in wolf form. He was the only one I could trust to bring me back. The only one brave enough to stand up to me at my wildest. And I let him down. I hid inside my invulnerability because I was scared. It cost Will his life.

"It's something you can never really understand. He was my family and I loved him because he knew what I was and refused to judge me because of it. Now the only ones who won't judge me, the only ones who are my family are the pack. When we get back to Balaia, I will find them."

"The Raven are your family now," said Hirad. "We're strong and we care. Stay with us." Thraun's words had shaken Hirad. He felt the shapechanger slipping away from him.

That ghost crossed Thraun's lips again. "That is an offer and a commitment stronger than you know. But I don't belong, not really. Not without Will." He gazed deep into Hirad's eyes for a moment. "But I won't let The Raven down."

"I know," said Hirad.

It was curious, the force that drew The Unknown to the Protectors. But he saw their loneliness, their anxiety at separation from their brothers. He knew how they felt. And so he stood with them, lending them his immediacy. There were no words at first but The Unknown could sense the same lack of focus he had observed earlier. But stronger now, verging on confusion. He broke the silence.

"Cil, Ile, Rya. I am Sol. You knew me. You know me still. You are troubled."

Cil inclined his masked head. "We cannot feel the brethren. Or the chain that binds us. Our souls are distant. We fear their loss."

"Is the chain broken?" The Unknown was startled. To remove the DemonChain binding Protector to the Soul Tank would be to kill the body and lose the soul. But no Protector had ever travelled the dimensions and these Protectors were very much alive.

"We cannot feel it," said Rya. "It is not there."

"But you can still feel your souls."

"Distantly," confirmed Cil.

"Then . . ." began The Unknown.

"Are we not free?" continued Cil. "We will only know by removing our masks. And if we are wrong, torment is eternal. And how can we truly be free when our souls are not within our bodies."

"Does Styliann know?" asked The Unknown, wondering whether he was truly free himself. Yet his hope for his brothers rose even as he feared their reaction to permanent separation from the totality.

"We are still his Given," said Cil. "We will not undermine his belief."

"I will support you in whatever you choose," said The Unknown.

Cil, Rya and Ile nodded, an exact movement.

"We are one," they said. "It is ever so."

Darrick had decided his course of action before the parley team had reached their camp at a gallop, the hooting abuse of the Wesmen loud in their ears. Shouting for his regimental commanders, he slid from his horse and strode into the command post, Blackthorne and Gresse on his heels, a little winded from the hard ride.

The General stood behind the map table and his senior ranks were arrayed in front of him awaiting his words. His orders were swift and sure. Never show weakness. Never hesitate. Ask for comment. Prepare to adjust but never change.

"Tessaya will not yield, which we can't say is too surprising though I was disappointed in a man of his apparent education and intelligence. He thinks he has us where he wants us. We cannot break through his lines to reach the Manse and we cannot beat his march to Korina. We will, of course, attempt neither.

"We will move to engage his army immediately but with no thought of breaking it, merely occupying it. This is because we will not be attacking with our full strength. It is estimated that the army pressing the Manse is eight to ten thousand strong with only the Protectors keeping them away. Here is what will happen.

"The second, third and fourth regiments, under the command of Regimental Commander Izack, will depart immediately, heading south before turning east through Grethern Forest, aiming to attack the Wesmen at the Manse from the south tomorrow at first light.

"Tessaya will naturally anticipate this move. He is not a stupid man. Therefore the balance of the army under my command will meet them head on. We will try to draw them into the forest where our lack of numbers will be less of a disadvantage. Specifically, we will break the regiments into their component centiles and each Captain will have a particular area to guard. It's a risky strategy but will allow us to cover a wider front. It will be a running battle unless we can convince Tessaya he has us all trapped in the forest. Comment."

"Sir," said Izack, a black-haired middle-aged soldier with small brown eyes and an impeccably trimmed moustache. Darrick motioned for him to continue. "The way through the woods is slow. If you are creating a diversion in Grethern, should we not march north and turn east beyond the first crag?"

"But then if the Wesmen threaten to overwhelm us, you could not help. By the time you're far enough south to turn east unseen, we'll know if we can hold them without you. And you aren't to travel the forest all the way. A mile beyond the Wesmen encampment, you should rejoin the main trail. Overall, a quicker journey than by crag." Darrick had considered and dismissed Izack's thought earlier. But at least the man had the balls to speak up and the brain to speak well.

"General, you are trying to hide a great many men in the forest. Do you really think they can escape the Wesmen?" asked Gresse.

"Yes, but only if we make ourselves appear larger than we are. We must make full use of our mage strength to block the gaps. That is also why we need them in the forest to fight us and why Izack must travel three miles south before turning east."

"And if we don't hold them?" asked Blackthorne.

Darrick shrugged and gave the answer he always did to such a question. "Perhaps that is something you should ask Izack because I will not be here to issue new orders." The fact was that he never considered failure or defeat. He had never experienced it. And he firmly believed there was nothing lucky about it. "Anything else."

Heads shook and "No sir," rippled around the tent.

"Then come to me in turn to receive your area orders. Barons, I would be obliged if you would brief your farmers and vintagers, who built the camp so expertly, to defend it in a similar manner."

Gresse's laughter echoed back as he and Blackthorne left the tent.

The night was full when The Raven gathered around the stove to talk briefly before grabbing what rest they could. Tomorrow, the fate of two dimensions would be decided. Around them, the Broodlands were quiet. Light shone from the odd opening in one or two dwellings but the Balaians were the only people outside.

"Can you do it?" asked Hirad, yet another mug of coffee warming his hands.

"In theory," said Erienne. "We can construct the shapes."

"There's a but in there somewhere," said The Unknown. "A big one."

"Several," agreed Erienne. "We have no idea how much stamina will be needed to close the rip this side, only that we have the ability to project the casting from the ground. Just. If the draw is too great, we won't be able to close the corridor. We have had to estimate the effect of randomisation in interdimensional space on the mana construct. We have had to guess at how much strength the knit construct needs to seal the corridor rather than cause collapse. The list goes on and grows in technicality."

"Meaning those were the simple ones," said Hirad dryly.

Ilkar chuckled and patted his leg. "Poor old Hirad. Magic will always be a closed book to you, I'm afraid."

"Less of the old," growled Hirad. "I'm not having that debate start again. All I wanted was a yes or no answer."

"We'll do it," said Denser. "We always do."

"Has Hirad been teaching you what to say?" asked Ilkar.

"You have to believe." Denser shrugged. Erienne put an arm around his neck and kissed him on the cheek.

"Clearly he has," said Ilkar.

"And what about him?" Hirad nodded his head toward Styliann who sat with his back to a hut, Septern's writings clutched hard to his chest. "Does he believe?"

"With a zeal I find hard to credit," said Denser. "Frankly, it worries me. His eyes are wild at times. I don't know whether he's scared or excited."

"Well, we need him," said Erienne. "So don't go upsetting him."

"And he needs us," said Hirad. "Don't forget that. He dies just as much as we do if this fails."

The Raven fell silent. Hirad sampled the heavy, warm atmosphere. The Brood Kaan were at rest. But they knew, as their minds recovered from their last fight, that the next would decide whether they prospered or ceased to exist. They knew the Naik were coming back. They knew more of them would suffer the pain of flame and claw and they knew that no matter how hard they fought, their destiny was not in their hands.

The Raven's responsibility weighed heavy on Hirad very suddenly. Sha-Kaan was returning from his mission to the Veret and would want an answer from Hirad more certain than that he had been able to give earlier. And despite Denser's apparent confidence, Hirad could not shake his anxiety. Before he faced the Great Kaan, that was something he would have to rectify.

"Still you try and talk your way out of extinction, Sha-Kaan. Still you choose your mouth to speak rather than breathe the fire that makes a true dragon. Few will lament the passing of the Kaan. You preach that which no other Brood wants to hear."

Sha-Kaan continued his lazy circling. The Naik's leader, Yasal-Naik, flying with two escorts had intercepted the Great Kaan on his journey back from the Veret Broodlands of the Shedara Ocean. It was clear he had not come to fight. It was also clear that he had not come to talk of peace. Sha-Kaan was not surprised though he was disappointed in himself that he hadn't chosen to vary his route back to Teras.

High above the cloud in the chill streams where he could let the wind do the work to speed him home, he had seen the Naik trio by the light of the stars and had decided not to try and evade them. He felt able to defeat three of the smaller rust-brown Brood despite the weariness in his bones, scales and wings.

As they neared, he had picked out Yasal by the v-shaped cut in the wedge of armour behind his head. Sha-Kaan had put the damage there himself over a hundred cycles before, in a battle over Beshara. If Yasal was flying it meant only one thing. He had come to gloat over his impending victory.

The two elder dragons circled each other, their minds meeting to speak, while the escort stood off below.

"The Naik are the only Brood whose minds remain closed to the havoc we wreak on our lands. We cannot battle forever. If we do, there will be no land left to win. There will come a point where even you will have to recognise that."

Yasal-Naik growled a laugh. "But the battle is already won, Sha-Kaan.

With your Brood destroyed and your melde smouldering, we will have dominion and all other Broods will furl wing to the Naik. The Veret are already doomed to subservience. The Gost will follow, and the Stara will follow them, until every Brood does the Naik bidding."

"Your overconfidence will be your downfall, Yasal," said Sha-Kaan, though he knew the Naik's summation to be correct. "Don't preside over victory before it is assured."

"It is assured!" thundered Yasal. "The Kaan are now so desperate that not merely do they seek alliance with the weak water-dwellers but even bring Balaians to their aid. Do you really believe they can stand where you are failing? We will make ash from their bones before your very eyes and I will lead the Naik triumphant through the gateway while you lie dying on the ground, never to lift your wings again. We will drive the water from their oceans, tear down their puny towers and crack the fabric of their mountains. Any who survive will be food for my young. I will not stop until every insect in Balaia is dead. When I am done, nothing will grow, walk or fly there again."

"So much hate," said Sha-Kaan, his tone carefully measured. "So much venom that it blinds you. Since you have found me here, I offer for the final time. Cease your attacks and we will not pursue the Naik to destruction when the gateway closes."

Yasal-Naik swooped in from his circle to fly alongside Sha-Kaan, his flat green eyes burning with contempt, his mouth unable to contain his drool which was whipped away from him in the winds.

"The gateway will never close." His voice was a rasp in Sha-Kaan's head. "Perhaps your age has defeated your mind at last. We have won, Great Kaan. All I am here to do is remind you that you preside over the demise of all your Brood. I am here to look upon the face of failure."

"Then fly to the ocean and look upon your reflection, Yasal. Tomorrow the gateway closes and the Naik will feel the wrath of the Kaan every cycle until they are no more. Take your escort and go. For all your might, you have not the courage to face me alone. You are small, Yasal-Naik, and your passing shall signal the moment when the Broods begin to respect the lands they so carelessly destroy."

"I will feast on your flesh myself," said Yasal. Sha-Kaan opened his mouth and roared his frustration, his wings beating hard, his body angling upward, taking him above his enemy.

"Leave, Yasal!" he cried. "Leave before I take us both from the sky. Dare not to trespass in Kaan space when the orb lightens the sky or face your death."

Yasal summoned his escorts to him. "You are an old fool, Sha-Kaan. Pray to the Skies for your Brood and your melde. Before the orb sinks again, you will all be gone and the Naik will rule. Until tomorrow, Great Kaan." He turned and sped away, his escorts flanking him.

Sha-Kaan thought for a moment to give chase. To kill Yasal now would swing the battle around. But to die himself trying would seal the Kaan's ultimate defeat. He roared again, this time blasting the air with fire, before dropping into the clouds and heading home.

Feint left, strike right, axe. Sword flat defence, midriff, axe overhead. Drop sweep, axe, sword head high, angle left defence. Half pace forward, sword drive, axe back right quarter, block low. Drop off, strap wound, space filled. Rest. Fast strike upper left quadrant, drive on axe, pace back. Hold.

Every strike sure, every move deliberate, even and accurate. The Protectors fought with a terrifying silent ferocity, their souls communicating at the speed of thought and their eyes interlocked, missing nothing. The thundering force of the Wesmen assault was met with steel and fist. Their roars and shouts with the clash of weapons and the thud of blade in flesh. And their shifting orders and tactics with measured strike and unyielding strength.

Brother fallen. Grieve for the body, comfort the soul. Prepare for uplift.

The waves of Wesmen broke time and again against the flashing metal barrier and blank masks, their numbers huge, their dead rising and their confidence ebbing and flowing, such that each single Protector kill transmitted through the whole army. But the Protectors fought far beyond their numbers. In ranks three deep, spaced to allow maximum use of weapons, they deflected attack after attack, resting and switching as the Wesmen lines fractured and reformed under the orders of their commanders.

And where the Wesmen bodies littered the ground packed too close to fight around, the Protectors simply waited while their comrades pulled them from the front, gore and blood slicks tracing their last journeys.

Aeb could respect the Wesmen energy but not their disorder in the fight. Each man fought alone or with just one or two others, leaving defensive holes to exploit and making block and thrust a long-term plan for defensive success. He had no idea how long they must hold, just that their Given had ordered them to do so. He and Sol whom they all held in awe. The Protector who became a free man again.

And all the while, the messages, advices, orders and warnings flooded through his mind, filtered for relevance or tagged for his attention. He struck the axe arm from a Wesman, blocked back a strike from his comrade and sent warning five left to Fyn whose flank defence was temporarily opened by a stun wound to Jal.

Lower quadrant axe sweep Aeb.

He responded automatically, feeling the axe clash against a Wesman weapon. Placing his sword to block forward he turned his gaze on the wide-eyed enemy who couldn't hope to match his speed. He leaned in, smashed his elbow into the man's face and brought his axe back up and right, feeling it bury in his midriff, lifting him from his feet. He shook the corpse off, his attention already on the warrior attacking his left flank.

Falling back, rear Manse elevation. Front rank rest, third to line. Weapons ready. Joining.

Aeb savaged his sword into an exposed neck.

It was midafternoon.

"Balaia, let's march!" Darrick roared, swinging his sword arm in a wide circle over his head, and his desperate move began. Eschewing his horse in favour of walking at the head of the exclusively footborne army, Darrick nonetheless made himself as visible as possible. He knew that the Wesmen scouts would report back to Tessaya almost immediately and he wanted them all looking for him.

He'd been at pains to make his Captains understand that an attack could come at any time, at which point they were to scatter in centiles into the forest, heading for their allotted grid positions. They were not to engage on open ground unless absolutely necessary. Indeed, if the Wesmen stayed out, Darrick was happy to develop a stand off. He had warned of the chaos of forest warfare and of the importance of continued communication along the fragmented front line. He knew it was a gamble but he considered it the only chance they had.

Darrick would have loved to have spoken to the assembled army but that luxury was denied him by the pressures of time and organisational necessity. Instead, he had impressed very hard on his command team the importance of that which they undertook. Once again, Balaia could not afford for them to fail. Once again, The Raven deserved their unflagging courage and energy. There was no sense in saving themselves for the next fight because failing in this one would mean there were no other fights. Not for them, not for the Wesmen.

The army set off in tight formation, mage assassin pairs ahead under CloakedWalks, searching for enemy scouts. In his heart, Darrick knew their task would bear little or no fruit but there was no sense in holding them back; and at the least, they would provide an element of early warning.

They were less than an hour from total chaos in Grethern Forest and he wanted to squeeze out any advantage he had. His regiments marched quickly along the main trail, making good ground toward the Wesmen camp a mile distant. They had travelled less than half distance when a roar like rising thunder grew ahead.

It echoed off the far crags, fell away down the gentle slopes into Grethern and hung above the rise they approached, like a cloud of sound. The Wesmen. And they were charging. Darrick heard the sound of running feet approach and two pairs of mage-assassins dropped their Cloaks and appeared near him.

"Wesmen seven hundred yards and running, General," said one, a willow-framed elf, very tall, bald and dressed in tight-fitting cloth.

"Spread?" asked Darrick.

"Three hundred to three fifty, touching the first north rises and down closing on the first trees south."

"Thank you." It was a wide front but nothing more than Darrick had anticipated. He assessed their terrain.

To his left and north, the trail broke into small rocky undulations that cut up to high crag and scree slopes a mile distant. South, the Grethern Forest stood, dark and dense. Its first boles were scattered no more than a hundred yards from them but Darrick's preferred battleground was the thick growth that burgeoned a further two hundred yards distant. He could see the darkness within, could sense the restrictive snags of bough and branch and prayed to all the Gods that he'd made the right decision.

Behind his army, Izack would be leading the Manse relief column south. Now was the time of greatest threat to the plan. Darrick could not afford a single Wesman scout to report the split of the army. Tessaya had to believe he was fighting all of the last Eastern regulars outside of Korina. Mage-assassins from Gyernath swept the forest behind and the crags and rises north. It was time to move.

He raised a hand and the order sped down the column to halt. Next, he clenched the raised fist, splayed his fingers and shouted the order to split.

"Centiles, detach, crescent formation by number. Running. Now!"

Slight unevenly, the result of a lack of drill time, the centiles broke formation, cutting away from the main trail in sequence, leaving a strong line defending the trail. Darrick called it a crescent and in his drawings, that's how it appeared. In reality, however, it was a more uneven cascade. He could be nothing less than satisfied that they understood his orders at all.

Darrick nodded his appreciation and set off with his own double centile, angling only slightly from the main trail. He was little more than bait. Acting as running vanguard, he hoped to bring Tessaya's army to the forest before they had a chance to work out the weakness of the defence leading to his camp. They could, he knew, be quickly surrounded but he was relying on the Wesmen desire for battle. And though Tessaya was tactically aware, Darrick remained confident he would see their move into the forest as an attempt to skirt around to the Septern Manse.

Behind him, the army ran down toward the forest, breaking its borders. Orders rang out, centiles switched directions and from the morass came order as each found its feet and space from its adjacent centiles. A wall half bricked and a temptation surely too much for the Wesmen to ignore.

Darrick would not be disappointed.

Ahead of him, the leading Wesmen crested a rise, bellowing out cries as they surveyed the fragmented army below. For a while they gathered, like a dark stain spreading on the near horizon, then a blast from a hundred horns sent them flooding down on the Balaians, their battle cries and chants splitting the air, Tessaya plainly visible at the centre.

For a moment, Darrick considered attacking him but, though he was in the front line, he would be very well defended. And Darrick had better things to do than commit suicide. He took his twin centile and ran for Grethern, the first arrows of the Wesmen falling short.

"Stand ready!" he shouted, seeing his men ranked inside the confines of the forest. "Fall back three paces. Make them break stride. Mages, fill those gaps."

The orders were relayed through the forest as the Wesmen swept toward them, no more than half a minute behind. Arrows skipped and snapped against trees and branches, howls and taunts echoing darkly into the depths of the forest. Darrick turned, drew a line in the leaf mould in front of him, his men forming around and behind him.

The sky, brooding and grey, spilled rain, and the wind whipped up beneath the cloud, whistling through the trees. Somewhere, Izack and his men raced to the aid of the Protectors. Darrick watched the Wesmen pour on toward the forest, so far taking the bait laid for them. But the Balaians were outnumbered and would have to work very hard to remain unbroken. It was going to be a long afternoon.

CHAPTER 34

Senedai brooded over the reports from his army surrounding the pitifully small band of masked warriors defending the Septern Manse and its gateway to the land of the dragons. As his warriors tired, the enemy seemed to grow in strength. Their movement was smooth, their fighting ordered, like nothing he had ever seen. He knew there was magic involved but he couldn't see where. There was no mage, of that he was now certain.

Yet that hardly mattered. What mattered was what was before his eyes. The bodies of his men covered the ground, in places so thickly that the dead and injured had to be dragged away through the legs of the fighting front line to give them solid ground. And as the afternoon wore on, with the rain increasing in intensity hour by hour, Senedai's desperation increased with it. The enemy left no gaps, the numbers of their dead could be counted on the fingers and toes of a single man; and even though his warriors had injured a good many, they simply melted back from the battle to bind their wounds while others took their place.

Their strength and endurance were extraordinary, their courage something Senedai could admire. But his failure to overwhelm them despite massive odds in his favour gnawed at his confidence and at the belief of his men. It should have been a quick victory and yet, with the afternoon waning, he was now faced with returning to his camp as night fell, to face another day of humiliation.

He could force his warriors to fight on by fire and moonlight but somehow those masks would be even more terrifying in shadow. And to fight at night was not the Wesman way, though he had done so at Julatsa. It displeased the spirits. He growled, silently cursed Tessaya's failure to appear, called up more reserves and ordered another push.

Fire bloomed to Darrick's right, the injured Wesmen shrieking in pain, the burning trees casting stark light on the confused battle scene. As the General had hoped, the Wesmen line had been forced to slow and break by the density of trees and the early exchanges had been even as he had foreseen. And with his mages calling FlameOrb, HellFire and IceWind from the mana, the Wesmen charge was blunted.

Now, though, the tactics had changed, Tessaya had broken off the frontal attack, sending a sizeable force toward the Balaian encampment and concentrating on an area of Grethern perhaps seventy yards wide, daring his enemy to close ranks. So far, it was a temptation Darrick had been able to resist. He'd quickly reorganised mage teams to prevent flanking and keep the

Wesmen line ahead thin, left four centiles in reserve to provide emergency cover and brought in all of his mage assassins to maraud outside the flanks.

A barrage of metal on metal had him moving smartly forward. Ahead, the Wesmen had forced a triple centile back and were pushing their advantage to the limit. Calling reinforcements to him, Darrick raced in from his overseeing position, too late to save a knot of Balaian swordsmen and mages, caught against a wall of trees and cut to pieces by triumphant Wesmen.

"I want fire behind the front line! First centile right flank, attack at will!" roared Darrick as he crashed into the battle. With veteran swordsmen either side of him and a trio of mages behind, he waded into the Wesmen line, hundreds strong, his blade flashing down on a defensively placed axe. "Second centile, mage protection!" The axe was knocked aside and Darrick followed up with a boot to the abdomen and a reverse sword strike to the bowed head.

Left and right, Wesmen were cut down before the main body reacted to the attack. Darrick blocked a thrust with a spear, driving his free forearm into the face of his attacker, splitting his lips and nose. He trod on the spear tip before the Wesman could pick it up and drove his sword through the undefended midriff. Behind the fighting line, howls abruptly cut off, the clatter of metal and the unmistakable sound of shattering ice told of an IceWind ploughing its awful course. Further back, HellFire smashed in from the sky. Bodies flew, the explosion of spell on soul battered at the ears and a tattered arm flopped down next to Darrick.

In front of him, his next opponent quailed at the sight and hesitated fatally. Darrick didn't pause and the Wesman was chopped through the side to his spine, the Balaian General feeling his sword score bone, the blood surging on to the grass.

The Wesmen began to back off. Darrick held his line. They had no need to chase and, with the afternoon light fading quickly in the shrouded forest, they didn't have to hold out too much longer.

We tire. It is understood. Light fades. Lower right quadrant, block, axe. They will not pursue the attack after dusk. Be strong. Strike left, pace back. Rest. Hold the line. Our Given requires it. There will be no failure.

Aeb's limbs protested but he refused to allow the fatigue to show. The Wesmen were ragged. It had been a hard day and their organisation was lacking, their warriors not cycled for maximum efficiency. Yet there were many thousands of them and, despite their lack of victory, still they came on. It was less than two hours until full night and already, with the sky dull and grey, the light was fading fast.

The gloom made no difference to Aeb and his brothers. They had no need of illumination to see the fight. Aeb chopped downward, crashing his axe through the shoulder of a tiring Wesman, his blade already positioned to block the blow he knew was coming in from his upper left.

Beside him, a Wesman broke the guard of Oln. The Protector took a savage cut to his right thigh, the enemy axe wrenched clear with a gout of flesh. Oln staggered, unable to maintain balance.

Crouch.

Aeb backhanded his axe across the space left open by Oln and the Wesman who had so recently tasted victory, tasted violent death instead.

Withdraw. Aeb covers.

Oln half fell backward. He would not fight again unless the brethren survived to give him strength. Aeb shattered a Wesman skull with the pommel of his blade and turned to his next opponent, mind full of the words of his brothers. They had lost thirty men this day and another fifty were unable to fight on. They would survive the day but would not take another. Aeb had to assume it would be enough.

Tessaya, Lord of the Paleon Tribes, broke from the forest, axe dripping blood, to take quick reports. The Easterners fought a guerrilla action that he could not fathom, surely having enough strength to meet them head on. The Wesmen met them on a broad front in the trees and on a shorter side across the trail, where the fighting had ebbed and flowed, the Easterners unwilling to move up to force home the advantage they gained early on. It was as if they were waiting for something but Tessaya could not think what. There were no reinforcements coming, of that he was certain.

He shook his head and stared up at the quickly darkening sky. Rain fell on his face and pattered on the ground as it had done almost all day. Away in the forest, fires burned in half a dozen places and he could feel the heat of the closest though he knew it would not last. The rain let nothing last.

His men, bloody and brave, had torn away at the Easterners throughout the afternoon, never quite breaking through and never drawing them on to open ground. But the enemy had put up stout resistance and their damned magic made up so much for their apparent lack of numbers.

"What is it they are guarding?" Arnoan, ever at his side, asked the question Tessaya had never asked himself.

"Guarding?" He frowned, and the ice cascaded down his back as realisation snapped through his body. "How long have we been fighting?"

"Perhaps three hours, my Lord."

"I am a fool," he muttered, then raised his voice to a roar. "Paleon! Disengage! Revion! Hold position! Taranon! Push eastern flank!" He turned to

Arnoan, snatching at the old man's collar, drawing his face close. "Find Ade-sellere; he's in charge here. He is not to let them after us."

"What is it, my Lord?"

"Don't you see? Are you blind? Darrick's sent men south to drive around while he occupies us. He's guarding an army that's heading for Senedai. Now go."

Tessaya sprinted back toward his camp, calling his tribes toward him. They were the only people he could trust now. Taomi had failed and his Liandon Tribes were shattered by Blackthorne. He wasn't even worth a defensive command. Once again, the Paleon held the fortunes of the Wesmen and if he had to run all night to catch the Easterners, that is exactly what he would do.

Darrick lashed a kick into a Wesman knee, felt the bone crumple, hurdled the man whose axe had fallen useless from his hands and ran at the fleeing enemy. Shouts had echoed throughout the battlefield and the Wesmen had pulled away from his section entirely. Their move back toward their own camp had the hallmark of a phased retreat and for a second he was happy to let them go.

But the weight of enemy left in the centre of the line and flooding across the front of the forest to block a chase Tessaya must know they wouldn't mount told a different story.

Darrick stopped his charge and called his twin centile, what was left of it, to a halt.

"He's worked us out," he said to his Lieutenant. "We need a tactical withdrawal all the way back to the camp. I think they'll let us go. Find me our best Communion mage. I have to get through to Izack."

"Sir." The Lieutenant set off at a run, ducking back into the depths of the forest.

All around Darrick, the fighting was still fierce. FlameOrbs splashed through an area of dense brush to his left, scattering the Wesmen attackers. From either side of the fire, Balaian soldiers poured onto the stunned enemy, swords rising and falling, their dull thuds and occasional clashes telling where they bit. Right, a Wesmen surge had pushed back an isolated centile. As Darrick watched, a mage was felled by an arrow, depriving them of key attack.

"To me!" yelled Darrick, leaping across the charred branch from a fallen tree, his men at his heels. "FlameOrb the back of the line, we'll take the flank." He called as he ran.

The Wesmen saw and heard them coming. Arrows whipped through the boughs, one flicking Darrick's hair on its way to bury itself in the eye of a man behind him.

"I need those archers down!" Darrick thudded into the fray, his sword clashing with a Wesmen axe, sparks flying into the damp air. The General rotated his sword two-handed, loosening his enemy's grip, forced his weapon to the ground, leaned in and butted the man in the face. Blood surged from his nose and he staggered back. Darrick swept his blade up, knocked aside the half-made block and followed up with a straight thrust to the throat.

Over his head, FlameOrbs sailed into the back of the line, splashing down and spreading mayhem, destroying man and brush alike and putting the shadows to flight. The unearthly orange flame licked at everything within its compass, sticking to fur and leaf, eating into it until beaten out by flat of axe or leather gauntlet.

The beleaguered centile found renewed strength, stepping forward to take the attack to the Wesmen. To Darrick's left and right, the strikes went in with terrific ferocity, forcing the Wesmen into a desperate defence. Another FlameOrb dropped among them, Darrick split a skull, spraying gore and brain over his victim's companions and the Wesmen broke and ran.

"Leave them," ordered Darrick. He turned to his centile Captain. "Stay here, keep this flank free then withdraw slowly at your discretion. Don't chase anyone and keep a HardShield up."

"General." The man nodded and swung round to issue orders. Darrick ran back to the centre of the now much subdued fighting.

"Lieutenant! Where is my mage?"

Hirad's dreams were troubled. Time and again, he awoke with a sense of falling, his heart hammering in his chest and painfully in his throat. And while he slept . . .

Adrift in a vast sea of nothing. Below him, fire laced the land. Calls of pain and anguish flooded his mind and a sense of desperation suffused his wracked body.

He was alone. Last and lost.

Around him, the air was empty. No stars shone though it was dark, no cloud filled the sky. The only light flickered far below. And down there it was dead. He had nowhere to go.

To stay above was to die. So was to move down.

He fell.

"Dreaming again, Hirad?" asked Ilkar from nearby. Night was full, warm and very quiet.

Hirad nodded and sat up. "Emptiness," he said. "I felt I was flying but nothing else was alive."

"Let's hope it's not prophetic in any way," said the elf. "We're all anxious, Hirad. You're not alone in not sleeping." Ilkar indicated himself. "Probably best you don't dream, eh?"

Hirad nodded again. "Easy to say, hard to do. Anyway, I don't think I am. I think it's Sha-Kaan's dream."

He lay back down, smiling inside at Ilkar's raised eyebrows. This time, the Great Kaan soothed his mind into deep, dreamless sleep.

"Damn it, I didn't think he'd tumble us. At least not so soon," said Darrick.

Blackthorne smiled and leaned back in his chair. "I told you he wasn't stupid," he said.

The command tent was a beacon of light in a darkening camp in which Darrick had forbidden all but vital fire light to give the Wesmen as little sight of them as possible. Dusk was upon them, the Balaians had been allowed to withdraw and an uneasy calm had settled over the camp.

The Wesmen had stationed a hefty presence a respectful distance from their borders and were clearly unwilling to move in, fearful without their Lord to drive them.

Darrick had sent mages out to check the surrounding numbers. The Wesmen covered the main trail, the forest and crags with squads and scouts but had chosen not to encircle the Balaians. Their remit was clear enough.

The only good news was that Izack had not planned on stopping until within striking distance of Senedai's forces. He would however, have to move to a different position than planned in an effort to avoid Tessaya.

"How many will he take with him?" asked Darrick.

"Well," said Blackthorne. "From your reports, Tessaya was separating his forces along tribal lines. The Paleon are numerous though they'll have taken casualties both in the battle for Understone and today. Even so, if he takes them all, it could be as many as four thousand."

Darrick gaped and his body felt hot. "Izack'll be slaughtered."

"Not unless Tessaya finds him," reasoned Gresse.

"He won't be hard to spot once he starts fighting," said Darrick grimly. He passed a hand over his face, seeing his plan collapse. "What a shambles. We can't waste time taking them on here, there's no point. Look . . . How dense is the cover cragside?" He looked over to where a pair of his mage assassins awaited his next order.

"Not as dense as in the forest, sir," said one, scratching at two days' growth of stubble. "We could clear it a little." He smiled slightly.

"You'd have to clear it a lot to make a difference to our route," Darrick said, seeing the man get his train of thought.

"There are eight of us," said the assassin. "Anything is possible. They don't have cross-reporting, they are merely expected to shout if they see anything."

"Make them unable to shout, will you?" asked Darrick.

The assassin nodded. "We will prepare immediately." He gestured his companion to follow him from the tent.

Darrick turned back to find the eyes of the Barons and his surviving centile Captains wide on him. He shrugged.

"What choice do we really have?" He spread his arms wide, shrugging.

"They will see us and they will follow us," said Gresse. "It can't work."

Darrick shook his head. "If we all trooped out together, yes. But we won't. Here is what I want done. I want every able-bodied man brought to the rear of the camp. No injured will be coming. I need a token presence to remain here, highly visible. I suggest the cavalry.

"We will walk a mile back down the trail before turning up into the crags, using the mages to assess threat ahead. We will run all night if we have to but I will not let Izack die uselessly."

"And what about the wounded and those you leave behind?" asked Blackthorne. "Even should you succeed in this harebrained scheme, when dawn breaks they will be overwhelmed and suffer the fate you so wish Izack to avoid." His voice, low and stern, was tinged with anger.

Darrick smiled, hoping to defuse it. "There's more. Once the runners are away, I need volunteers to help the injured to move out of the camp and hide elsewhere." He stared squarely at the two Barons.

"And the visible force?" asked Gresse.

"When the Wesmen work it out and rush in, ride like the wind." His smile broadened as he saw Gresse's eyes sparkle with the thought of it all. "Well? What do you think? If we pull this off, we can make a real difference, maybe even turn the tide and give The Raven the time they need." He looked around the assembled command team. "Are you with me?"

To a man, his Captains nodded. "Yes, sir."

"Baron Blackthorne?"

"A nursemaid to the sick, eh?"

"I prefer to see it as a defender of the helpless," said Darrick. "Far more glory in that, I think. Baron Gresse?"

"Young man, you are an outrageous risk taker. Outrageous enough to win. I'll have the horses ready as dawn cracks the sky."

Darrick clapped his hands together, feeling the excitement surge within him, banishing the aches and tiredness of the afternoon's fighting. "Then let's get moving, because we really don't have the time to waste."

CHAPTER 35

Fires were alight all across the Broodlands when Hirad awoke, rested but still tired. He rolled over and sat up, joining The Raven in complete bemusement at what he saw.

The fires were strung, three dozen strong, along the banks of the river, casting an eerie yellow light that reflected from the mist, covering the Broodlands in pale luminescence.

And what the light showed was thousands of Vestare in groups and teams, some examining weapons and stitching armour but most tending to the hundreds of dragons covering every inch of free space. Vestare fussed about necks, wings, heads and talons, applying balms, singing songs and saying prayers to the Skies for Brood victory. They were tiny against the immense bodies of the Kaan, who stretched out their full lengths, many reaching well in excess of one hundred feet, their hulking bodies towering sometimes as much as fifteen feet. Great heads rested on the ground, some with jaws wide while the Vestare crawled in to spread their protective and healing creams on the flame ducts.

The sense of size was awe-inspiring and The Raven stared on, eyes roving the massive flanks, the twitching wings bigger than the largest warship sail and the muscled necks that carried those huge skulls.

"How long has this been going on?" asked Hirad.

"It seems like ages," said Ilkar. "And I cannot believe you slept through it for so long."

"Kept that way, I think," said Hirad. He nodded in the direction of Wingspread, outside of which Sha-Kaan had just appeared. "Come on, he'll have a few things to say to us."

"And I shall have some to say to him," said Styliann, striding off, his three disinterested Protectors in his wake.

"What's got into him?" asked Ilkar.

"He's been muttering about 'organising things better afterward' ever since he woke up," said Denser.

"And he's planning on telling this to Sha-Kaan now?" Hirad looked after the hurrying figure.

"I expect so." Denser shrugged.

"Mistake," said Hirad, heading for Wingspread. "Big mistake."

The set of Styliann's shoulders told of a no-compromise showdown with the one-hundred-and-twenty-foot Great Kaan who was preparing for the ultimate battle. Hirad knew he'd talk to The Raven because of their immediate role. Aside from that, he would be tended for flight and fight. Nothing else was open to conversation.

Hirad, trotting quickly ahead of the rest of The Raven, caught Styliann before he reached Wingspread.

"Styliann, I think I should be doing the talking," he said. The Xetesk master hardly broke stride to look at him.

"Ah, Hirad the Dragonene. There are matters of great importance to iron out. Now is a keenly appropriate time. I think I can make myself heard."

"Styliann, you don't understand," said Hirad.

The Dark Mage stopped, he and his Protectors surrounding Hirad. "Oh, I think I understand very well. And this one-way deal is about to be changed."

"What?" Hirad gasped.

"Stop him," ordered Styliann, his eyes wild. He set off again only this time the Protectors barred Hirad's path. He tried to push them aside but they wouldn't yield.

"Get out of my way," said Hirad, anger rising.

Silence.

"Don't you get it? Just who is it you're protecting? Because if you don't move, it certainly won't be Styliann, unless you want to guard a smouldering corpse." He tried to push past them again, one shoved him back roughly. Hirad's sword was out in a moment. The Protectors came to ready.

"Hirad, no." The Unknown's sharp tone stopped him in his tracks. "They'll kill you." He was at Hirad's shoulder. "Ile, Rya, Cil, he speaks the truth. Let him pass."

The Protectors sheathed weapons and stepped aside. Hirad ran through, The Raven behind him, and was quick enough to hear Styliann begin to speak. Vestare fretted around Sha-Kaan's head. The old dragon had his eyes closed, his neck resting on the ground and his body half in the river. Styliann stood silent for a while, Septern's texts clutched to his chest, as if summoning the courage to speak.

"Sha-Kaan," he said. He was ignored. "Great Kaan, I must be heard."

Sha-Kaan's head moved and his eyes opened. He took in Styliann with his cool blue gaze, in a lazy sweep that encompassed The Raven running up behind. He settled on the Xeteskian, his jaws stretching a little.

"This is not a granted audience," said Sha-Kaan, his voice low and sonorous. "Leave."

"No," said Styliann. "Make it granted."

Sha-Kaan's eyes narrowed and his head shot forward, bowling two Vestare from their feet. His snout all but touched Styliann's waist. "Never presume to speak to me in that manner," growled the Great Kaan. "You are not, and never will be, my Dragonene."

"My tone was not meant to offend," said Styliann. "But there is little time and—"

"I must prepare. Leave."

"—there is a chance the spell will not be cast," continued Styliann smoothly.

That stopped them all. Sha-Kaan drew back his head sharply, his eyes blinking slowly, breath hissing into his cavernous lungs. Hirad turned and shot Denser and Ilkar a glance. Both shrugged their ignorance while Erienne frowned deeply, mouth moving wordlessly. Sha-Kaan grabbed Hirad's attention with a sharp mind-jab.

"How is this possible?" he demanded.

"Great Kaan, I have no idea. It is not a problem raised by The Raven's mages," said Hirad.

"I understood there to be a certain casting but that there were risks as to its outcome." Sha-Kaan's voice was flat, cold and very angry. Hirad shuddered. It was Styliann who spoke.

"That is indeed the case. It is merely that there is a feeling that Balaia needs assurances of your continued support and future aid in legitimate struggle." The air temperature seemed to cool. Sha-Kaan moved his head back in close to Styliann.

"Assurances," he said.

Hirad noticed the Vestare had backed away from the dragon's neck and head. He turned to The Raven and muttered:

"Just in case. Give yourselves room. That goes for your Protectors too, Unknown."

"You don't think—" began Denser.

Hirad shook his head. "I would doubt it but, you know . . . Let me try and sort this out, all right?" He walked briskly up to stand beside Sha-Kaan's head, facing Styliann, whose face was set stubborn.

"I feel there must have been a misunderstanding, Great Kaan," he said, feeling the dragon's ire hot in his mind.

"Let us hope so," replied Sha-Kaan. There was menace in his voice that Styliann clearly did not read.

"No misunderstanding," he said, a slight smile on his face.

"Styliann, I'm warning you to back off. This is not the time," said Hirad, hand back on the hilt of his sword.

"Hm." Styliann lifted a finger, apparently framing his next words. "I realise that time is of the essence so let me make myself very clear." His eyes locked with Sha-Kaan's. "I take it, your honour is not in question."

"I am a Kaan dragon," came the reply.

"Exactly. Here is what will happen. You, the Kaan, will agree to help me regain my College. You will also help me in negotiating treaties with the Wesmen and the other Colleges. If you do not, I fear I will be unable to assist in the casting of the spell to close the rip; a fact that will render it uncastable."

"But if you do not assist, you will die," said Sha-Kaan.

"And so will you all," said Styliann. "So I strongly suggest you agree to my terms. Either that or I walk away." There was a madness in his darting, wild eyes that Hirad had not seen before. It was like a crazed zeal and Styliann really believed he would get what he wanted; as if the Great Kaan, one hundred and twenty feet of animal power, would crumble to his crude blackmail. The Xeteskian's hands were shaking and his tongue licked incessantly at his lips as he waited for Sha-Kaan to respond.

Hirad could not put into words what flowed through his body at that moment. The silence of The Raven told him they all felt the same. Disgust did not do it justice. Revulsion merely scratched its surface. Sha-Kaan, however, felt able to do more than glare his utter contempt.

"You, little human, are willing to sacrifice the lives of everyone in Balaia and my entire Brood if you are not promised help to further your own personal ends?"

"I prefer to think of it as fair recompense for my personal sacrifice in saving all of Balaia from certain death," said Styliann. "Though I can see where you might acquire your perception."

"But we are asking nothing," said Hirad, the words dragging themselves from his throat. "We do it simply because it has to be done."

Styliann raised his eyebrows. "Then you have clearly not thought it all through quite as deeply as I have."

"Styliann, think about what you're saying," said Denser from behind them. "You can't walk away. You know that."

"Can't I, Denser? I've already lost everything." Styliann didn't turn round. "So just you watch me."

"But you'll be killing us all," said Hirad.

"So persuade your dragon not to call my bluff."

Hirad wanted nothing more than to wipe the smug look from Styliann's face but he knew the mage could kill him before he struck. Sha-Kaan growled far down in his throat, the sound rumbling like a distant avalanche.

Styliann smiled again. "It seems a fairly open and shut matter. But please do me the courtesy of answering my request in the affirmative. Your word being your honour."

"My answer," said Sha-Kaan, a slight nod of the head accompanying his words, "is exactly as you should expect."

Styliann's smile broadened.

"Oh dear Gods," breathed Hirad. What possessed him he didn't know but he dived forward, snatching Septern's texts from Styliann's arms, hitting the ground and rolling on to his back.

Twin gouts of flame blasted from Sha-Kaan's mouth. Hirad's abiding memory was of the smile disappearing from Styliann's face as, in the instant before his destruction, he saw his death coming. His body was blown backward, a mass of fire, his chest a hole where his organs had once been and his head blackened and scoured.

He landed thirty yards away, his torso separating from his relatively undamaged legs, his chest and face gone, a scattering of ash in the breeze all that remained.

"Impudent human," said Sha-Kaan.

The Unknown helped Hirad to his feet, the barbarian's legs shaking, so close had he come to being caught in the fire. Denser had a hand over his mouth, his face ashen, exuding the nausea they must all feel. His other arm supported Erienne whose breath came in shallow gasps. Hirad turned to Ilkar, the elf regarding him blankly, his head shaking gently from side to side, ears pricked and reddening.

"I hope you can use these," said the barbarian, handing him the writings, parchments and books. "You know, to do something." He shrugged. "Something else."

"I will continue my preparation," said Sha-Kaan, all anger gone from his voice. "I expect your new solution presently."

Ilkar opened his mouth to protest but Hirad shushed him with a quick hand gesture. "Not now," he said. "Come on." He led The Raven away. The trio of Protectors wandered over to stand above Styliann's destroyed body, exchanging glances and looking over at The Unknown.

"What about them?" asked Hirad.

"I really don't know," said The Unknown. "But we have more pressing matters. Ilkar, Denser, Erienne, what options do we have?"

The other two turned squarely to Ilkar, who spoke.

"We have one. We read about the theory in Julatsa's library but dismissed it out of hand, particularly when Styliann arrived with so much more information. And thank the Gods you did what you did, Hirad," said Ilkar, tapping the texts.

"So you can still close the rip and the corridor?" asked The Unknown.

"Technically," said Erienne.

"It's like this," said Ilkar. "We no longer have enough strength to cast as we intended. And we can no longer sustain the spell long enough to knit interdimensional space correctly."

"So what can you do?" asked Hirad.

"We can trigger a collapse," said Ilkar.

"Excellent, so no problem!" Hirad clapped his hands together but his confidence drained when he saw Erienne shake her head. "What?"

"We can't know what a collapse will do either here, in Balaia, or anywhere in between. It'll cause ripples in interdimensional space and Septern is very clear on the potential risks of causing them. We could force dimensional realignment, we could tear the fabric of any or all dimensions, we just don't know." Erienne pushed a hand through her hair.

"But we don't have a choice, do we? Sha-Kaan has seen to that," said Hirad.

"No we don't," agreed Denser. "But there's one more thing. We have to be inside the rip to collapse it."

The shock swept through them though they were far removed from him. For those on watch, it was like a tornado in the mind, reaving the promise from the subconscious and threading turmoil through the conscious.

For those at rest, it was a nightmare come to haunt. The removal of security in sleep and the awakening of anxiety. Moans escaped from two hundred pairs of lips.

Any Wesmen watching would have seen the physical symptoms but would never have guessed the cause. The watch-line swayed, free hands clutched heads, legs quivered and feet sought new purchase. And behind them, the rest stood, staring in every direction, not believing the reality so rudely thrust upon them.

The shock had passed in a few moments but the aftereffects would rumble on.

Aeb rocked his head, trying to clear the muddle encasing his mind. He could feel his brothers, he would always feel them, but he could not feel their Given.

He is gone. We have failed. The thought chased itself across the Protectors' minds, accompanied by an acute feeling of loss and a dissolution of purpose.

It is not our failure. Aeb urged his response into the cacophony of sending. *We are resolute in our mission. We have not surrendered the Manse.*

But as he said it, he realised the futility of their position. They were guarding the Manse for the return of their Given. He was now dead. Their response now was surely to return immediately to Xetesk. The Wesmen no longer needed to be fought or kept at bay but they were still there and would surely prevent any Protector move to leave.

Aeb felt the confusion flood the Soul Tank. They were trapped but with no reason or drive to fight. Yet fight they would have to, hoping for salvation from other quarters than their Given.

Sol. We can fight for Sol, came a random thought.

Aeb flared. *Our goal is to survive until such times as we can return to Xetesk to await further Givings.* He paused, aware that the flow of other thought had ceased. He was the only one communicating. He felt them all. *We all respect and revere Sol. He was a brother Protector. He alone among men understands our Calling. But without our Given, we can only fight for ourselves. Each of you fight for his brothers. Hold that ideal in your soul and we will still triumph. Return to your positions. The night is not over.*

But he wondered. He wondered at the break in the linkage the Given had provided them. Had they enough belief in their own right to survive alone to win? Dawn would give him his answer.

Darrick could see the glow of the fires of the Wesmen camp around Septern Manse an hour before they were within striking distance. Forward mage scouts were dispatched to assess the strength of Senedai's outer defence, only to return to say there was none beyond the camp perimeter, which completely encircled the Manse and its few fierce defenders.

A brief Communion with Izack's forces set the attack time. They would both move in, half an hour after the Wesmen had resumed their fight with the Protectors, Darrick deciding that the noise of battle was the best cover for any surprise strike. He and Izack between them commanded a little in excess of six thousand men and mages. It still left them severely outnumbered, given Tessaya's tribes in the vicinity, but it was not a straight stand-up fight; and Darrick, master of spoiling tactics against the Wesmen, felt it gave him the edge.

Darrick could still hardly believe his plan had worked thus far. Under a strict silence order, with weapons and armour tied down, the fittest elements of the remaining regiments had run out of the back of their encampment, traversed north three miles and turned east, heading over rough ground toward the Manse.

Under the sure eyes of elf scouts and mages, they had covered their advance from any watching eyes, their intimate knowledge of the terrain allowing them to keep a high pace throughout the night, stopping for just five minutes in each hour.

Finally, they halted, an hour's march from the Wesmen, in a shallow valley part sheltered from the wind but not from the intermittent showers that still fell from a lowering sky. Darrick had personally toured every centile, thanking them all for their incredible effort and exhorting them for one more when dawn broke.

And now he sat alone with his thoughts, stretching the muscles of his legs. To sleep was fruitless with dawn so close but rest was vital for what could be a long day.

It was only now that Darrick felt the enormity of his gamble. He knew the day was dawning with the noon shade over Parve completely covering the city, if the calculations had been correct. It was the beginning of the time when the Kaan would be too few to protect it effectively and when enemy dragons could potentially fly through to attack Balaia. But when or if The Raven would appear, he had no idea. If they didn't, he supposed it didn't matter, because it would mean the rip over Parve couldn't be closed and, sooner or later, they would all die in flames anyway.

And if they did appear, what difference did it make if Septern's rip was still in Eastern hands? The Raven were just a few when the opposing sides were drawn up and, good as they were, if the battle wasn't going the way of the East by the time they returned, they would merely have saved Balaia for the Wesmen to rule.

He had always known it, he supposed. This wasn't merely an exercise in stopping Wesmen from gaining the rip and the opportunity to defeat The Raven. It was a fight for Balaia. He knew exactly why he hadn't communicated it. Something inside him had prevented him from believing it himself until now. While they had been trapped by Tessaya, he hadn't wanted to let any desperation creep into his men. The desire to break through might have deflected them from the task of seeing at least some of the army through to the Manse.

But now they were largely all here, they should know the whole truth. Indeed they had to. If they were to fight and win against the odds they faced, they had to know what exactly was at stake. And Izack had to deliver the same message.

He got to his feet and went in search of a mage.

Sha-Kaan's eyes blazed and he turned his head from Hirad who looked anxiously at The Raven gathered behind him.

"Find another solution," said the dragon flatly. "This that you suggest will not happen."

"Great Kaan, there is no other solution. We are out of time. There is no room for more research. The rip has to be closed now or by your own admission it will be too large for your numbers to defend."

Dawn had broken, though the fires still cast their mist-reflected light, and the day was beginning to warm.

"No human will ever ride a Kaan dragon. It is submission. It is forbidden."

"It isn't submission, it's necessity," implored Ilkar.

Sha-Kaan's head snapped back around, enormous fangs dripping fuel. "I do not recall inviting you to speak, elf."

Hirad took a deep breath. "Sha-Kaan, I am your Dragonene. May I speak freely?"

"It is your right," said Sha-Kaan.

"Right." Hirad strode around to face the Great Kaan square on. "I understand your feelings about the situation but it is our only chance. I know it wasn't your desire but, in killing Styliann, you removed a great part of our casting strength. Let's face it, you created this mess.

"But never mind that. Do you really think that we *want* to sit on dragons and fly into the middle of a battle to cast a spell? Do you think this is what we planned to happen? The furthest I have ever been in the air is as high as I can jump. Gods falling, Sha-Kaan, I can think of nothing worse than flying. Mages do it under their own power, warriors do not. And none of us, believe me, want to experience flight this way."

Sha-Kaan regarded him solemnly. "And that is to convince me to accede to your request."

"Well, yes, but more than that, it's to tell you that we none of us want this. Not you and certainly not The Raven. But it's the only choice for your Brood and for Balaia. We're prepared to try it. Are you?"

"But the shame of the submission." His head dropped.

"Damn the bloody shame!" Hirad raised his voice. "If this doesn't work, there'll be none of you alive to feel the shame. And if it does, you'll be strong enough to shove shame down the long neck of any Brood that taunts you. What in all the hells are you worrying about?"

"I think there's history here," said Denser, attempting to placate both parties.

"At last, wise words from the thief," responded Sha-Kaan. Denser smiled thinly.

"Yeah, and it'll be us that's history if we can't get up to the rip," said Hirad. "Sha-Kaan?"

The Great Dragon closed his eyes and drew his head back, his neck making the formal "s." For a time, he was silent, then he opened his eyes to speak.

"No dragon will submit to being ridden by a human. It is the ultimate sign of defeat for it signals that the dragon has become subservient to the human. But the Kaan understand that it is not to rule us that you wish carriage by us. It is to save both our races. For this reason alone, we agree to this partnership. Three dragons will each carry one mage. Those dragons shall be Nos-Kaan, Hyn-Kaan and Sha-Kaan. Elu-Kaan shall remain in his Choul, to rule the Brood should I fail to return." It was a speech made in the language of Balaia but Hirad knew that his mind had pulsed the same message to every Vestare and Kaan dragon in the Broodlands. The total silence was testament to the enormity of what had been decided.

"Great Kaan, your faith will be repaid by The Raven saving your Brood from destruction," said Hirad, bowing his head.

Behind him, he heard The Unknown relax and he turned, a smile on his face. "Calmer now, Unknown?"

"Naturally." He frowned. "Missed something, have I?"

Hirad nodded. "Just a bit. I mean, we all know the mages have to go up there but who do you think's going to hold them on while they're casting?"

The colour drained from The Unknown's face and beside him Thraun's jaw dropped.

"Oh dear Gods in the sky," muttered The Unknown. "I wondered why you kept talking about yourself and flying in the same breath. Is there no other way?"

Hirad shook his head. "Unknown, I am surprised at you." He winked at Ilkar. "And anyway, The Raven never fight apart, remember?"

The Unknown cleared his throat. "I think I'd better go and find some rope."

CHAPTER 36

Darrick's men moved closer and his scouts reported via Communion that Senedai was again taking the fight to the Protectors. Dawn had cast its gloomy light across Balaia, illuminating a tableau of rock, brush and scrubland soaked by steady rain.

Darrick brought his men to a halt near the head of a gentle rise. And, with the sounds of many thousand Wesmen voices raised in chant just carrying on the wind, he jumped up on a rock and begged for attention.

"You all know why we're here, and I must first thank you all for the determination, faith and courage you have displayed ever since we came together on the shores of the Bay of Gyernath.

"Our march has changed from one of liberation to one of revenge. It is now one of defence. But not merely defence of Septern Manse to thwart the Wesmen and give The Raven and Styliann the time they need. There is far, far more at stake and I need you all to understand this before we march to battle."

Darrick saw a ripple pass through the small army, a murmur like wind across calm ocean. He had them. Now he had to inspire them into fighting for the lives of every man, woman and child east of the College Cities.

"Consider our situation. Gyernath stands but it has no reserves. Blackthorne is gone. So too is Julatsa. The remaining Colleges face enormous threat from west of the Blackthorne Mountains and a Wesmen army stands ready to strike Korina. Unless we stop it.

"Korina has a pitiful regular guard. It has no walls. Baron Gresse might have mounted resistance but he is here with us. The other Barons hide in their castles, defending what is theirs and fragmenting our defence by so doing.

"Who is left? You. You are Balaia's final hope of victory and salvation. Nothing else stands in the way of the Wesmen. And if you believe in your land and your people—your family and those who you will never meet—we will be victorious.

"The Wesmen may have the greater numbers but we have the greater heart. We have the fire inside of us, we have the belief. We are fighting for our land and the people we love.

"The future of Balaia will not be decided at the gates of Korina, nor at the walls of Xetesk. It will be decided here at Septern Manse today.

"And I know that every one of you will play his part. I believe in you. Do you?"

The roar that greeted his question lifted Darrick's heart and made him very happy that the Wesmen had already begun their attack.

Great words, he thought, but the truth would be told by the stroke of the sword and the play of the mana.

Time to believe. Time to fight.

"Sol?"

The Unknown spun round at the sound of his given name. It was Cil. He, Ile and Rya were standing over the mound of recently-turned earth under which the remains of Styliann's blasted body now lay. There had been no reverence, indeed no interest from any but Denser who had felt a collegiate responsibility for the ex-Master's burial.

No grand ceremony for Styliann in the crypts of Xetesk. No lying in state, no train of mourning, no ritual entombment. No honour. Just a rude grave dug in the soft ground away from the river under a rock overhang in an alien dimension. Dug by Protectors using Vestare tools and infilled the same way.

The Unknown walked toward the trio. Vestare woven rope coils over his shoulders.

"What is it, Cil?" he asked.

"The decision has been made. We won't travel back to Balaia. We are staying here, to live among the Kaan."

The Unknown nodded. "I thought you might. Now, you are sure you can still feel your souls."

"And should the loneliness become too much, we can return," said Rya.

"The masks?" The Unknown touched his cheek, a painful memory returning unbidden.

"You are the one chosen to be first to see," said Cil. "The demons can't harm us here. They have no control in this dimension. Here, we are free."

Without hesitation, each Protector unstrapped and lifted off his mask and clutched it in his hands.

The Unknown held his breath but the wonder in their eyes told him all he needed to know. They were feeling the air on their faces for the first time in months, maybe years. They took in huge lungfuls, shook their heads and drank in a world where their sight was unencumbered by the edges of their moulded eyeholes.

Rya, Ile and Cil were all young men, none of them older than twenty-five. Their faces, white but for the dark areas around eyes and mouth, were striped by red weals and marked by boils and sores that, though treated by Xeteskian healers to prevent infection, were never able to fully heal under the masks. Now they would and Cil's young, handsome face, strong-featured with deep green eyes, would be a loss to the women of Balaia. The Unknown smiled to himself; at least that was one less in competition with him when he returned.

No words were needed to express their feelings. Their eyes said more than the longest text in Xetesk's library. The Unknown, Sol, walked to the men, free while they remained in the dragon dimension, and hugged each one. He looked deep into Cil's eyes, seeing the hope of every Protector reflected there.

"One day, we will all be free and you can return unmasked as you are now. Our brotherhood will never be forgotten and, though we all once again own our souls, we will never be parted. Believe me, I still feel you."

Cil nodded. "You'd better go. We're joining the second wave of ground defence with the Vestare."

"Good luck," said The Unknown.

"And to The Raven."

The Unknown trotted back to where The Raven stood by the dragons that would carry them to the rip. Each stood in the shadow cast by an enormous body, looking along the neck and up to the head that was held high and proud. Ilkar and Hirad would sit at the base of Sha-Kaan's neck, the warrior behind to hold the mage in place when his casting took all his concentration. The Unknown and Denser would ride Nos-Kaan and Erienne would be held by Thraun on Hyn-Kaan.

"Ready?" asked Hirad.

"Yes," said The Unknown, glancing back again to the free men. "There's a lot of work to do back in Balaia. Let's get going."

There had been a feverish discussion about how best to attach themselves to the dragons. Sha-Kaan and Jatha had joined them and, in the end, the solution chosen was a relatively simple one. Each member of The Raven would have a rope looped and tied around their midriff, leaving both arms and legs free for grip and balance. The rope would then be tied hard around the dragon's lower neck.

The idea wasn't that the rope should hold them firmly in place but to stop them falling should they slip. The lower neck would move the least while still being narrow enough to sit astride. The mound of the body would provide anchor against slipping backward and if the dragon dived . . .

". . . we'll just have to hang on," said Hirad. "Right, let's be aware that communication's going to be very difficult. Sha-Kaan will lead the flight, keeping the dragons as close together as possible. We'll have as much defence as they can spare from the rip cordon. Denser, I think you should lead the casting. Thraun, Unknown, you know what you have to do. Don't let your mages go."

"What if we're forced to break formation?" asked Erienne.

"Well, I'll know through Ilkar whether it breaks spell concentration, meaning a restart, and Sha-Kaan knows to bring the formation back together as soon as he can. We have to trust them to fly defensively as necessary. What can I say? Don't fall, any of you."

With back slapping, shaking of hands and hugs and a long, lingering kiss between Erienne and Denser, the three pairs split to their respective dragons, allowing Vestare woodsmen to fit their ropes. As they climbed on to the dragons' necks, laid flat on the ground, Hirad could feel the ire rise from the chosen Kaan carriers.

"This is most uncomfortable," grumbled Sha-Kaan.

"Yeah," said Hirad, "and not just for you." He adjusted himself behind Ilkar, feeling the rough scales against his trousers and stretching his legs around the broad neck. It was like riding a bull. "I'll not father children after this."

"I don't understand," said Sha-Kaan.

"Never mind," said Hirad. Ilkar looked around at him and shook his head.

"You are quite unbelievable," he said.

"Scared, Ilks. Very scared."

The Vestare tied the ropes under necks, using nicks in bone and scale to provide anchor points. Hirad found he could move but, so far, not loosen the rope enough to slip. In front of him, a second loop of rope gave him something to hang on to.

Now astride Sha-Kaan, he felt a new sense of the immense power of the dragon. Breaths shuddered down his neck to fill his lungs; everywhere, muscles bunched and relaxed beneath his scales, rippling his entire body, and the rumblings and gurgles of the gargantuan internal system reverberated through his legs and up his back. Looking over his shoulder, Hirad saw the mound of Sha's body arch up, blotting out everything behind him. He couldn't even see its tail. Below and just to the rear of his feet, the roots of the wings sprang from the torso. They too twitched, the wings slapping quietly against his body. Sha-Kaan was a flying mountain and he was an ant tied to it. The notion didn't bear close consideration.

"Whose idea was this?" he muttered. He looked across at The Unknown, who sat silent and pale as he was fixed to his dragon. "Hey Unknown!" he called.

"There's nothing you can say that'll make this better," growled the big warrior.

"I'm looking forward to shaking your hand in Balaia," said Hirad.

"What is it they say?" said The Unknown, and then a smile flickered for the briefest moment across his features. "See you on the other side."

"Hirad Coldheart."

"Yes, Great Kaan."

"Are you and The Raven ready?"

Hirad took a deep breath. "Yes. We are."

"Then let me introduce you to the Skies." Sha-Kaan's deafening bark ripped through the relative peace of the Broodlands. From the high ledges, Vestare called back before setting off to the plains. dragon calls answered the Great Kaan, flights of the huge beasts took to the air and Sha-Kaan lurched to his feet, sending Hirad's stomach tumbling end over end. The dragon's wings swept out and extended with a noise like a wave dragging on a pebbled shore. Hirad clasped Ilkar's shoulder, the mage's hand covered his and, with a beat of those wings, Sha-Kaan propelled himself into the air.

Barons Blackthorne and Gresse stood by one of the forward watchfires as dawn crept across the sky. The cloud kept the day dark but they could now just about see the shapes of Wesmen moving about. With the injured helped or carried to a hiding place deep into the crags to the northwest, Darrick's cavalrymen divided themselves into saddling their horses and appearing to be many more than they actually were.

"Ever feel like you've been left out, Blackthorne?" asked Gresse, taking a swallow of coffee in the chill damp of the morning.

"I've been given more exciting orders," agreed Blackthorne. "But I think he's right. I'm too old to run through the night."

"What do you think they'll do?"

"The Wesmen?"

"Yes. Stand or come on?"

Blackthorne scratched at his immaculately tended beard. "Well, they're too late to join the fight at the Manse today so if I was them, I'd make sure we were definitely all gone before I tried to join my colleagues. Then I'd go."

"So saddling up's a good idea for us," said Gresse.

Blackthorne nodded. "But I don't think they'll chase us down. We need to be visible enough to be counted but out of range of arrows."

Wesmen were around a hundred and fifty yards distant and spread from crag to forest. And while those visible numbered less than three hundred, Blackthorne had no doubt that the weight of Wesmen would be positioned not far behind. Had Darrick made it through? He had to assume so. No alarms had been raised in the Wesmen ranks and no one had returned with news of disaster.

With light growing, he knew they couldn't maintain the illusion much longer and he was relieved to hear that the horses were saddled and ready. His heart beat faster. It was going to be an exciting first half of the morning.

Beside him, Baron Gresse had swept the dew from a stone and sat down, a refill of coffee in his gloved hand. Every man and mage was ready. Packs were tied to saddles, swords cleaned and scabbarded. They'd have to abandon the forge, the armoury and hundreds of yards of canvas but it didn't matter. Equipment could be replaced. Able Balaian fighting men and mages could not.

"Ready to run?" asked Blackthorne.

"Absolutely," said Gresse. He placed his mug on the ground and pulled off a boot, emptying out an imaginary stone.

"Gresse, I will not hesitate to leave you to die," said Blackthorne.

Gresse laughed. "Everyone else in this war is experiencing tension and fear like never in their lives. I didn't want you to feel left out."

Beside Blackthorne, a cavalryman cleared his throat.

"Yes, Captain," said Blackthorne. The man, mostly hidden under nose-fluked helm, heavy cloak and leather armour, bowed slightly.

"My Lords, I believe we should be ready to move." He gestured toward the main trail which was rapidly filling with Wesmen. Shouts rattled across the whole front with answers bouncing back, the anxiety and urgency clear in the tones though the language was alien.

The cavalry still patrolled as they had all night, moving in and out of sight behind tents, making great play of stoking perimeter watchfires and calling out that all was well each half an hour.

"Gresse, get that boot back on," said Blackthorne.

"Trouble with the lace, old friend," came the reply.

"Gresse, your boots have no laces. Get it back on. This game of chicken is fast reaching a conclusion." He looked down to see Gresse take a glance at the opposition and ram his foot into his boot and stand up, his drink forgotten.

Wesmen were advancing.

"Cavalry!" called the Captain. "Ready the retreat. Eyes backward. Slowly!"

"I've got an idea," said Blackthorne as they moved slowly away, the Wesmen taking ground cautiously. "If we can, let's mount up, keep a respectful distance and HardShield ourselves. I'd like to talk to whoever's in charge."

"What by all the Gods for?" asked Gresse.

"Just trust me, all right?"

Gresse shrugged. The cavalry Captain issued his revised orders.

Hirad had vomited his stomach dry well before Sha-Kaan levelled out to fly directly for the rip. They would arrive there in no more than an hour, such was their speed, Nos and Hyn-Kaan tucked in behind, the mass of the Kaan dragons either circling the rip or flying on ahead.

The roar in his ears of the wind whipping past his head dragged all sense from him and it had been a long time before he had been able to open his eyes more than slits. Below him, the ground was impossibly far away. It was a mass of colours and textures fogging before his nauseated vision and the confusion of Sha-Kaan's banks and turns as he oriented himself left Hirad with no idea where they had come from. Only the size of the rip ahead gave him any sense of direction and even the sight of that was punctuated by the clouds that he knew worried Sha-Kaan more than anything.

He felt a warming pulse through his mind and Sha-Kaan was there, cooling his blood flow and slowing his heart rate.

"Calm, Hirad Coldheart. I will not let you fall."

"Small comfort," mumbled Hirad. He felt mirth, then seriousness.

"The cloud will hide our enemies. We will have to be careful."

In front of Hirad, Ilkar turned round, his face bright and alive and full of the excitement of the flight. But then, of course, if he fell he could cast ShadowWings before he hit the ground.

"How are you, Hirad," he shouted, leaning back as far as he could. Hirad just shook his head and gripped harder at the rope the Vestare had looped around Sha-Kaan's neck. "You're doing fine."

"It doesn't feel like it." He shouted back. He risked a glance behind him, seeing the other two dragons in close formation. Denser waved but The Unknown didn't see him. His head was tucked in, his hands gripping his rope as hard as Hirad was.

Facing forward again, he saw the gentle flying of the dragons around the rip change. Calls echoed distantly and trios of Kaan formed up and shot away. He followed their direction and felt his body quail at what he saw. Heading their way, the sky was black with hundreds of small dots quickly resolving into enemy dragons. Sha-Kaan roared and stepped up his pace, the sound rumbling through his body and shaking Hirad to his very bones.

"Hang on, Hirad Coldheart. Soon it will start."

Sha-Kaan powered through the air, the beats of his wings a thundering tumult assailing Hirad's ears. His legs ached from their grip around Sha-Kaan's thick rough neck and his hands were cold through his gauntlets, his grip on the rope that of a dead man. He only hoped he could lever his fingers free to hold Ilkar when the time came.

The cohesion was no longer there. The messages flew through their minds with the speed of the day before but somehow the thought was not converted to the instant action they had taken as right. And it cost them lives.

Within half an hour of dawn, Aeb heard twice the number of his brothers fall as in the whole of the previous day. He sported a deep cut on one arm, making his axe little more than a defensive pole while his sword arm worked double time just to keep him alive.

The Wesmen could sense it. They pushed all around the circle and the first cracks began to appear as the reserve stepping up to take the place of the dead and wounded were themselves already damaged.

Think and act. Let it happen. Aeb pulsed urgently but now they were all face to face with the truth. Without a Given to bring them to one entity, they couldn't retain the driving force that made them the awesome force that was their earned reputation. Still the Wesmen died five to their every one but at that rate they would have gained the Manse by midafternoon.

By the time the first fire flared in the Wesmen encampment, Aeb was already facing the alien concept of defeat.

Darrick's mages launched a ferocious attack on the Wesmen reserves. Simultaneously, Izack delivered his first strike. The Balaians ran through burning carts, tents and wooden barricades, Wesmen struggling to understand what was happening even as they died under magic and sword. FlameOrbs sailed out over Darrick's head, HotRain fell in a torrent from the drenched sky, fizzing as it came, and DeathHail roared across the enemy ranks, its razor-sharp edges slicing and rending through to a thousand bones.

"Centiles, detach!" ordered Darrick, his order carried away through the army by his Captains. The force split along drilled lines, scattering through the bemused arc of the encampment they attacked. The General led his depleted double centile of yesterday, storming up to the hastily forming defensive line, chopping through the weaponless and clashing with those a little quicker to arm. Opposite, across the battlefield and beyond the Manse, detonation after detonation told of Izack directing fire on to Wesmen positions. Darrick swung his blade through, waist high, its edge cleaving stomach to the spine. His victim fell, too shocked even to scream.

"Break this line, come on!" he yelled. All around him, his forces drove hard, harder than ever in their lives. Blood clouded the air, the acrid smell of smoke laced with burned cloth, wood and flesh floated in the rain and the screams of the wounded, the howls of attackers and urgent shouts of defenders filled his ears.

He exulted, deflecting a well-aimed axe blow to his chest, pushing the enemy back and drilling his sword straight through the man's heart. He crumpled. Darrick kicked the body aside and stepped forward. Ahead of him, he could see the line attacking the Protectors. If it was the last thing he did, he would get to them.

Senedai swung around in complete amazement, staring back a hundred yards to where his tent dissolved into flame and his second line were suddenly engaged in battle with an enemy that should be lying dead on a field far away. Caught on the precipice of fatal indecision, he called a Captain to him.

"What, by the Spirit, is happening?"

"My Lord, the Easterners have launched a surprise attack. They are here on two fronts."

"I can see that!" Senedai snapped, grabbing the Captain's furs and dragging his face close. "Just tell me we can hold them. I must have the Manse before the sun reaches its zenith."

"We will hold them—"

Another series of explosions, this time on the opposite side of the Manse.

"What is happening here!" yelled Senedai to the sky. He turned on the Captain. "If one of those bastards runs across this grass to attack me, I shall personally tear out your heart and eat it. Stop them." Unsnagging his axe, he pushed his way through his front line.

"Fight you dogs, fight! I will not suffer failure." A space opened before him and he was face to face with the masked enemy. This one dragged his axe low but his sword whipped into ready with unnerving speed. "I will not suffer failure."

He raised his axe in trembling hands and struck down, the sword blocking his blow with ease. From nowhere, the axe swung up and he leaped back, feeling its keen metal edge whistle past his nose. The sword came down again but this time he was ready, parrying it aside with his axe and punching through with its spiked head, feeling the point enter flesh.

The masked man backed up a step and the point came free, spilling blood. Senedai smiled, fetched back the blade to finish the job but instead felt dread heat in his side. He looked down to see the man's sword buried under his rib cage. He hadn't seen it coming. Hadn't considered the possibility as he delivered his disabling blow. Yet it was he who would die.

Lord Senedai's axe fell from nerveless fingers and, falling that great distance to the ground, he heard a name taken up in a triumphant, exultant roar.

Tessaya.

They should have run days ago but the scientist inside them all kept them rooted. There had been no need to measure the shade for days now but they had done it anyway, marking its rush across the city peripheries and logging it for future eyes to read, should any of their writings survive.

Jayash looked up at the hideous black-brown mass that covered the sky, keeping Parve in perpetual twilight. Clouds grated at its edges, sending rain the like of which he had never seen or felt and, inside the rip itself, lightning flared and spat. Away in the distance, a bolt sang to earth, rattling the ground. They were getting more common now.

But it mattered very little. Because today was the day that it all began to end. Today the noon shade would cover Parve completely. It was clear that The Raven had failed, that no help was coming and that the rip would continue to eat the sky.

And so they all stood in the central square, eyes locked on the rip as it hung above them and the shadows lengthened with the rush of midday. They waited patiently. There was nothing else for them to do now. Except die.

They waited for dragons.

CHAPTER 37

Hirad could feel Sha-Kaan straining as they flew into the battle. The Great Kaan was desperate to fight but knew he couldn't. Nos and Hyn had caught them and now they flew, three abreast, entering the mêlée zone that spread for over a thousand yards left, right, above and below.

It gave a terrifying aspect to the conflict. Death could come from any angle.

Ilkar had said they needed about two hundred counts of uninterrupted concentration to prepare the spell which, when cast, had to be released just at the rip's surface. It had to be followed up by a charge inside the corridor where the original spell could be used to trigger collapse all the way to Balaia. The Raven mages had worked out a way they might control the collapse but it was yet another risk on top of everything they chanced already. Hirad wondered if one more roll of the dice would make any difference.

Below him, Hirad saw two dragons locked in combat, spilling fiery breath over each other as they sought to bite and tear. Heedless of all else, they fell through the sky, dwindling toward the ground so far below until one found the death grip, used it, and came surging back up. It was the Kaan that fell all the way.

"Hirad!" yelled Ilkar. "We're beginning casting. Hold me upright."

Hirad passed the message on to Sha-Kaan, knowing he only had to think it clearly for him to pick it up and relay it to the other dragons in the flight. The barbarian unlocked his fingers from the rope he'd been clutching with such desperation and grabbed Ilkar's waist, leaving his arms free to weave if they had to. He couldn't let Ilkar slip sideways, it would break his concentration. He tightened his thigh grip, felt Sha-Kaan's scales chafing his skin and concentrated on keeping himself as still as he could.

Abruptly, Ilkar stiffened and then relaxed, his body sagging backward as he began preparing in concert with Denser and Erienne. Hirad leant in, his head to one side looking around and down, searching the sky for likely attack.

Riding on the biggest animal he'd ever seen and so high it took his breath away, Hirad had never felt more vulnerable in his life. His sword, strapped down, was useless in its scabbard and he considered himself open to attack from anywhere at any time.

The sky was full of dragons. Sha, Nos and Hyn powered toward the rip, their mage charges forming the mana shape for a spell that might save the Kaan. The rip itself, cloud-bounded and huge, dominated the sky. Light flickered and flared inside its brown mass and it ate at the blue with fearsome speed.

Stretched across its surface, the Kaan flew in desperate defensive patterns while flights patrolled further afield, looking to break up attacks before they threatened the rip.

Without warning, Sha-Kaan veered away, angling steeply and climbing sharply, a great bark escaping his mouth. Simultaneously, a shadow swept over them and a Kaan dragon whipped across Hirad's vision. It opened its jaws and flame gorged out. For a moment, Hirad couldn't see the target, but then what he knew to be a Naik darted into view, evading the flame and spiralling down. The Kaan gave chase.

"This isn't going to be easy!" shouted Ilkar, his concentration broken by the sudden move.

"We'll go again," said Hirad, head pressed to Ilkar's, their skulls making communication easier.

The trio of carrier dragons reformed, heading back up to the rip. On reaching it, they would circle its periphery until the spell was released. All tasks were easier said than done.

Hirad's terror was gone now, replaced by a morbid fascination, a gnawing fear and a detached disbelief in where he and The Raven found themselves. Sha-Kaan estimated that over seven hundred dragons fought in the sky, the Kaan outnumbered by their enemies but more keenly organised. Against them, the Naik, Gost and Stara, all disparate but all fighting Kaan rather than each other.

Sha-Kaan drilled through a cloud bank and once again the rip was before them. Ilkar tensed and relaxed. Hirad clung on to him and prayed.

Closer to the rip, the noise was extraordinary. Over the rushing in Hirad's ears, the calls of dragons raged all around him. Wings beat, flame tattooed the sky and the sounds of snapping jaws and claws rending flesh and scale were as clear as they were awfully close.

Hundreds of dragons fought, their bodies colliding with extraordinary violence, the reports echoing across the sky. Their speeds were impossible yet still they dodged, breathed fire as they passed each other and turned acute angles in the air. They were monstrous animal machines with the grace of dancers and the sky was their domain.

Six Kaan hammered past them, their bodies close enough to touch, their power and size causing Hirad to hunch down into his shoulders. His fixed gazed followed them as they dropped on their quarry, four Gost flying direct for the rip. Fire poured from ten mouths and both formations split to dodge the flames. A single Gost caught the brunt of the Kaan breath. Its wings flared briefly, its head a mass of burning scale, and it dropped squealing from the sky.

The Kaan wheeled and reformed, chasing two Gost survivors. But the fourth came on and, with a sickening lurch in his aching stomach, Hirad realised it was heading right for them.

Automatically, he signalled a warning with his mind, feeling Sha-Kaan's calm thoughts cover his fear. But the Gost came on, large, deep green wings beating, its jaws agape, its eyes fixed on its prize.

And then it was gone. Taken from the side by two smaller Kaan, one clamping jaws on its neck behind the head, the other digging talons into the mound of its body, the impacts sounding like flat thuds, shivering in the air.

Sha-Kaan flew on, Ilkar was oblivious, Hirad quaked.

Tessaya had his targets trapped. The Easterners had rushed into the poorly defended back of Senedai's forces, causing huge damage with their swords and magic. But their desperation to break through to the Manse attackers had made them careless of what lay behind.

The Lord of the Paleon Tribes had been forced to wait for their strike before he could be certain of their position. Now he moved in quickly, sending pincers to wither the flanks while leading the central prong himself.

To his left, he knew General Darrick was making quick progress. Only the courageous Easterner could have made up such ground during a rough night and Tessaya had nothing but respect for him and his powers of leadership. It wouldn't save him from death but Tessaya knew he had to destroy the other force quickly before Darrick's surge undermined the confidence of Senedai's men.

He clicked his fingers and his hornsmen stepped up. A single blast and the attack drove in. Tessaya unsnagged his axe and raced at the head of his tribesmen, storming into the Easterners' flimsy rear defence. His first swing half decapitated a man, his second shattered ribs and split heart and his third slashed a thigh open to the bone.

All the enemy mages were concentrated ahead and he had no fear of spell attack. He drove on and on, batting aside a sword thrust and burying his axe in another exposed skull. He roared his delight, ordered his men on and swung once again.

Sha-Kaan had wheeled away again under a concerted Naik assault. Too many Kaan were covering them, not enough held the rip against determined attack and Hirad could feel his anxiety as much as he could Ilkar's.

"We can't keep on breaking off," shouted Ilkar. "We're using stamina. Sha-Kaan has to stay on course. He has to give us time."

"He'll do all he can," replied Hirad, his voice hoarse, the spittle whipped away as Sha-Kaan bucked and turned back for another run at the rip.

For a third time, Ilkar tensed and relaxed, for a third time, Hirad held him steady. For a third time he prayed.

Sha-Kaan barrelled through the thickening cloud, ignoring a fight between two Kaan and a Stara that fell past him. Wings, talons and heads writhed, the trio locked together, none with any care for the speed at which they plummeted groundward.

At the face of the rip, a dozen Kaan broke from their holding pattern and raced directly out, calls urgent, bodies shaped for as much speed as they could muster. In the distance, but growing rapidly, at least fifteen dragons, resolving themselves into the russet brown of the Naik, headed in, and Hirad read something in their formation that spelled real danger.

They split into three groups of five, each in arrow formation. One pushed upward, another lost height while the third drove on, aiming for the heart of the defending Kaan, who couldn't afford to split their force into three to fight them all.

They chose to halve themselves, five heading on, five up, leaving the third Naik flight unmolested. With a multiple roar that ricocheted across the sky, the factions met. Fire exploded in all directions, wings beat, talons flashed and bodies thundered together. Naik and Kaan fell, one with a wing torn to shreds, another with a hideous wound all along its underbelly. Others followed, jaws snapping, roars shuddering through Hirad, orange afterglow on the back of his eyes.

But the third Naik flight came on. At first, Hirad couldn't be sure that they were coming for Sha-Kaan and The Raven. But they changed their direction, no longer diving for the rip but on an intercept course with Sha, Nos and Hyn and their helpless charges.

Hirad searched the air, looking for the Kaan that would take them out but everywhere was confusion. dragons clotted the sky in chaotic pattern, the gold of the Kaan melded with the russet Naik, the brooding green of the Gost and the startling burgundy of the Stara. He was sure no one had seen the onrushing Naik and he pulsed an urgent message to Sha-Kaan whose only reply was to fly harder.

"It must be this time. We can hold no longer."

If they reached the borders of the rip, the remaining defensive net would catch the enemy Brood but Hirad could see they weren't going to outpace the Naik. He looked left and right, taking in his friends. The mages' arms held in front of them, palms cupped, their eyes closed, heads thrust back as they built the shape that would close the rip and end the war in the sky. And the warriors, both big men and terrified, holding on to their charges as Hirad did, as much for comfort as to keep them upright.

Closer they came to the rip and closer came the Naik. He could hear their barks, confident and bold, and watched their formation spread slightly to give them maximum breathing arc. In seconds, they would be as much flame as flesh. Sha-Kaan had misjudged fatally. No help was coming.

To Hirad's top left, the clouds parted, three dozen dragons scorching through, blowing the puff aside. His heart leapt but fell harder. They were Veret, not Kaan. Hirad closed his eyes, waiting for the end knowing he would feel the heat for an instant but not wishing to see it coming.

The Veret raced past the Kaan and drove straight into the unsuspecting Naik, scattering them in a fury of wing and fire. The quick, slim Veret wheeled with incredible agility, each Naik the prey of an overwhelming number of the aquatic dragons.

Sha-Kaan exulted, his wings beat a little quicker and the trio shot the last distance to the rip. He barked the defence net away, banked and circled, Nos and Hyn in close attendance. In front of Hirad, Ilkar spoke words he couldn't understand, aimed his palms up into the rip and, with a shout that quivered through his whole body, released the spell. Three streaks of visible mana leapt the gap and attached themselves to the edges of the rip, one deep blue, one orange, one yellow. Like grappling ropes, they flailed and arced as the dragons circled, crossing strand over strand, plaiting into a rope of mana that fizzed and bucked, its ends still held by the Raven mages.

Sha-Kaan roared, his cry answered by Nos and Hyn. Around them, the air filled with calls, barks and cries.

"Ready Hirad!" called Ilkar.

"What for?"

"The ride of your life!" yelled the Julatsan mage.

The three dragons and their charges stall-turned and plunged into the rip.

Hirad screamed as the rip dragged at them, forcing them inward. Behind them, the lines of mana lashed at the corridor, attaching everywhere they touched. A noise like thunder in the mountains grew in intensity and, abruptly, Ilkar dismissed his mana line. It whipped up and burrowed into the corridor, sending multicoloured lights fizzing through its grey-flecked brown sides, tearing great rents through to a black void filled with a vicious howling wind.

Ilkar turned and shouted something but it was lost in the tumult. Everywhere, the brown corridor was dissolving and behind them the edges of the rip were collapsing in on themselves, sending down gouts of pressure that washed over the dragons. Sha-Kaan's body was swatted from side to side, tossed like a bird in a gale.

Hirad leaned in as far as he could, gripping the rope so hard he felt sure he would tear it from its moorings. He would have screamed again but the air was being beaten from his lungs as fast as he could drag it in to feed his quaking body.

Sha-Kaan steadied and beat his wings again. Hirad risked a look behind and saw blackness rushing at them faster than they were flying.

"Sha-Kaan, faster!" he pulsed, feeling nothing but a crazed mass of thought in return. The light was fading, the corridor disintegrating all around them. In a few heartbeats they would be swallowed into the nothing of interdimensional space. But a few heartbeats was more than they needed.

They burst into Balaian space, Sha-Kaan banking hard away from the rip and flying even faster perpendicular to the great stain in the sky. Hirad punched the air and whooped in sheer joy.

The Raven were back.

Jayash saw the edges of the rip ripple and the lightning stop flashing in its depths. Out from the darkness came three dragons who angled away as they dropped into view. But he hardly noticed them. Because the rip was tearing all across its surface, black replacing the brown he had come to see almost as normality. The edges fell back on themselves with a speed faster than the eye could follow and then the centre punched out, a huge fist of void washing toward the ground.

He could feel the force as the wind picked at his cloak, sent spirals of dust whipping across the square and pushed his hair into his face.

"Oh dear Gods," he said.

The blackness enveloped the ground.

Hirad looked down at Parve. The centre of the rip punched outward, deluging the ground beneath with the unimaginable power of interdimensional space. It roared among the buildings and howled across the open spaces, a great blackness tearing at Balaia. And, almost as quickly as it had come, the blackness was gone, sucking back in and disappearing with a detonation that would ring in all their ears for days.

Parve had been swept clean. Barely a stone remained to tell of its ever having been built there, just a patch of blasted rock, strewn with dust and the echo of ages.

"Dear Gods," he whispered.

"Justice," said Ilkar.

"Not for the noon shade monitors," said Hirad.

Ilkar, silent now, looked forward along Sha-Kaan's neck.

Not pausing, Sha-Kaan himself turned and flew hard for the Blackthorne Mountains.

"We are heading for the Manse of Septern," said Sha-Kaan in answer to Hirad's unasked question. "Your forces fight there. Your enemy must not be allowed to destroy the site; it is precious to the Kaan."

Darrick felled a Wesman warrior with a savage cut to the chest, feeling the strength surge through him. He bounded on, his warriors and mages at his heels. Spells fell less frequently but with no loss of intensity on the defenceless Wesmen and now he had the Manse attackers in his sights.

"Army to me!" he shouted and drove across the open land.

A shudder in the ground flung him to his knees. It was followed by another. He looked up to see most of the battle lines ahead sprawling. The Protectors were up quickly but the Wesmen facing them scrabbled to their feet and backed away.

The walls of the Manse were falling.

A third shudder rocked the ground and the Manse wavered, ruined bricks collapsing backward, tumbling into a gash in the earth where light flashed and darkness grew. A plume of dust shot high into the sky, followed by a column of darkness that snatched it back, licking at the air and driving back into the ground, the sides of the gash closing with a grating thump.

The Manse was gone.

From the Wesmen, a ragged cheer grew, picked up by voice after voice. Axes flew in the air, warriors embraced and songs of victory ripped from a thousand mouths.

Darrick held up a hand and his men stopped moving. He watched silently as the Protectors, weapons now sheathed, stooped to collect the masks of their dead, picked their way among the fallen and moved away. The Wesmen saw them and backed off, letting them go, as if sensing the passing of something. Or perhaps they were just happy not to be fighting the masked killers any more.

Slowly, the singing died away as more and more of the Wesmen gathered to one side of the now empty battlefield by Septern Manse. It wasn't over. Victory was not yet theirs. Darrick and his army still faced them, and they weren't moving.

The two sides watched each other closely, the Wesmen ranks parting to allow a man through to stand at their head. Tessaya.

"General Darrick!" he called.

"Lord Tessaya," returned Darrick across the gap of some one hundred yards that now separated the two armies. Any survivors from the Wesmen second line had run to join their kin; at least Darrick wasn't surrounded but he was outnumbered.

"Perhaps we should parley again, discuss your surrender."

"I don't think so," said Darrick and behind him, his men cheered. "After all, you didn't believe me last time and I do consider myself a man of my word."

He gestured west, far across the Blackthornes where the rip had dominated the sky like a second menacing moon.

"You see, The Raven were trying to save us all and I'll be damned if I let them return to a land ruled by you, Tessaya."

"Brave words for a man in your delicate position," said Tessaya. "You are not in a position to make demands and even your best warriors have given up." He wafted a hand at the Protectors who, walking away toward Xetesk, had stopped and were looking into the sky even as he indicated them. He shrugged. "And how, might I ask, will your Raven return at all? The hole to your allies has been most effectively plugged."

An alien sound echoed distantly. It was a sound Darrick had heard before but, this time, he gambled it did not signal an enemy.

"There are ways, Lord Tessaya."

The Protectors had not moved on, their masked faces still scouring the sky. Three dots had appeared on the horizon, high up and closing incredibly fast.

"I do believe they are coming now."

"As if it would make any difference," said Tessaya. "Meet me in the middle and we will discuss your surrender. Refuse and I shall bleed every last one of you."

"The Raven might not make a difference. Their friends, though, might." He turned to his nearest Captain. "Gods, I hope I'm right. Those are dragons coming this way. Pray The Raven are aboard them or we'll all be dead momentarily."

He walked toward the waiting Tessaya.

In no man's land between the opposing armies, the two men met, their bows respectful, the distance between them deferential.

"It is a complex situation, is it not?" noted Tessaya, his face smug.

"Not particularly," responded Darrick. "Your armies have invaded our lands, we have stopped you every step of the way and now you seek to negotiate a surrender to ease what would otherwise be a very uncertain path."

Tessaya folded his arms across his broad chest. Darrick could see drying blood on his forearms and furs. "An interesting view but, given the fact that I have already forced the surrender of the pitiful band you sent through my forest yesterday, I feel you are both outnumbered and hold no cards. I hold many lives and I will not hesitate to crush them."

Darrick risked a glance to his right and saw the dots increasing in size. He wouldn't have long to bluff now.

"Very well," he said, allowing his head to drop very slightly. "State your terms. Let me hear your version of honourable surrender."

Tessaya chuckled, a breeze ruffling his hair, the rain easing to a stop as he spoke. He spread his hands wide.

"Even the rains await my words," he said. "I do not wish to see any more fighting. All those standing behind you will lay down their arms and place themselves under the control of my Captains. They will be held here until suitable work can be found.

"You will accompany my victorious army to Korina where you will negotiate the surrender of the city to me. You and all of your soldiers will be well treated. Third—"

A ripple of consternation ran through the lines of Wesmen and Balaians. Tessaya half turned, a frown crossing his face. Now it was Darrick's turn to look smug.

"Sorry, my Lord but those terms and any that follow are unacceptable," he said. His heart was pounding and again he sent a silent prayer that it was Kaan dragons approaching.

"You are under no—"

"Be silent!" thundered Darrick, the power of his voice rolling over Tessaya, who flinched visibly. "You questioned my word, Wesman, and now you are about to regret that decision. You asked where The Raven might come from. Look to your left and look in the sky. There you will find your answer."

Without looking himself, he pointed, seeing Tessaya's head turn as if against his will. He watched the Wesman Lord pale and his mouth drop open. All around them, the consternation turned to shouts of warning and fear. On both sides, men broke and ran, the Balaian commanders shouting for calm; their Wesmen counterparts fleeing with their men.

To his credit, Tessaya did not bolt, choosing instead to back away to where his men once stood.

Looking at last, Darrick saw the dragons losing height as they rushed in, still coming at extraordinary speeds. And there was no doubting the flashes of colour against the radiant gold that he could see on each neck.

He opened his mouth and roared with laughter.

The Wesmen had launched arrows, they had made dummy charges and they had taunted, denouncing the courage of the Easterners. But the four-College cavalry, with Blackthorne and Gresse at its head, had faced them down, knowing they could wheel and outdistance their enemy at any given moment.

Eventually, as Blackthorne had guessed, the Wesman commander's curiosity had got the better of him and, under the red and white Wesmen flag of truce, he had come forward alone. Blackthorne and Gresse had ridden out to meet him. The conversation had been short.

"I am Adesellere. I would have your names."

"Blackthorne and Gresse, Barons," Blackthorne had replied.

"Where are the rest of your forces?" Only then had Gresse worked out Blackthorne's theory and why the Wesmen hadn't simply charged in, putting the cavalry to flight.

"Well now," Blackthorne had said, his tribal Wes all but faultless. "It is possible that they are dispersed around this camp, waiting to strike at you as you advance. Alternatively, they may have marched from here in the dead of night, north across the crags to fight your army at Septern Manse.

"You can find this out by advancing in here and you know we will ride out of your way. But then you might die. Or, you can march toward the Manse. You should be there before dark. Which is it to be? I know which I'd choose."

Behind them, tent flaps snapped in the breeze. The rain still fell. Adesellere had looked past him to the rows of tents. All silent but all potentially containing sudden death.

"You will not halt the march of the Wesmen forever," Adesellere had said. And he had turned and led his warriors from the battlefield.

Half an hour later, Blackthorne and the cavalry still sat on horseback. The odd scout had ridden out, reporting back that the Wesmen were indeed marching east at a healthy pace.

"Well, my friends," said Blackthorne. "I think it's time we went to collect our wounded. They would be so much more comfortable here."

He wheeled his horse, the cavalry following suit. It was then the cries went up. Forging toward them, three shapes came out of the shadow of the sky over the Blackthorne Mountains, travelling at extraordinary pace. Gresse thought to turn to ask an elf but it was clear to them all what was coming.

"Dismount! Dismount!" The Captain roared as the horses, sensing new and awful danger, began to stamp or buck. The order was obeyed immediately and the horses, once free of human control, took flight, scattering in the face of the threat from above.

"Dear Gods," said Gresse, a painful lump in his throat, his heart beating wildly. He was sweating. The backs of his hands, his forehead, his back and his breath stuttered in his lungs. He couldn't move and beside him Blackthorne didn't either.

The dragons closed, the gold of their bodies sparkling in the muted rain-swept sky. Lower they came, and lower, and one emitted a piercing bark as they raced overhead, swooping by. Gresse spun around, almost losing his footing. He could have sworn he heard laughter as they passed.

He shuddered as they disappeared behind the hill line and turned back to Blackthorne. The Baron's smile split his face and he clapped a trembling hand on Gresse's shoulder.

"What is it?"

"Didn't you see them?" he asked, pointing after the dragons.

"See them? I could hardly bloody miss them. I almost filled my trousers."

"No." And Blackthorne began to laugh. "Riding them. Oh my dear Gresse, we've done it. That was The Raven."

"You're . . ." Gresse looked again. The dragons had disappeared. Relief flooded him.

"My Lords?" It was the cavalry Captain. His helm was off and his face pale beneath it. He held a small, ornate presentation case in his hands.

"Yes, Captain," said Blackthorne.

"I thought perhaps we could all do with some of this." He opened the case to reveal a small bottle of Blackthorne grape spirit and four shot glasses. "I've been keeping it. For a special occasion. I think this qualifies."

"My dear boy," said Gresse, his mind singing, his head light as if he'd imbibed a good deal already. "You have made an ageing man very happy."

Hirad could see the opposing armies but he couldn't see the ruins of the Manse. Sha-Kaan arrowed down, sending one more chill of fear through Hirad as he felt himself slide just that little bit further down the neck than was good for his heart. He could see where the Great Kaan was going to land and so could those on the ground. He cheered as men scattered, hearing terrified cries and hapless orders for calm float up on the wind as they closed.

Sha-Kaan lifted his neck, angled his body and thumped his legs down. Hirad immediately snatched a dagger from his belt and cut at his ropes, suddenly desperate to feel the grass beneath his feet, slicked with blood though it may be. The Great Kaan lowered his neck and Hirad slid off, his legs failing to hold his weight. Immediately, arms were about his shoulders, helping him to his feet, every muscle in thigh and calf screaming for rest.

He turned around and came face to face with Darrick. He smiled and the two men hugged, Hirad thumping the other's back.

"Still alive then?" he said as they separated.

"Still alive," agreed Darrick. "Listen, celebrations later. For now, there's a Wesmen army just the other side of this dragon."

Hirad laughed until tears streamed down his cheeks. "Sorry," he said, wiping his eyes. "What a choice of phrase." He steadied himself. "Look, the war's over. You need to negotiate Wesmen withdrawal from east of the Blackthorne Mountains. If they don't want to play, I can arrange a demonstration, if you get my meaning."

Darrick smiled and clapped him on the shoulders. "I'll see what I can do." He strode off to meet the Wesmen.

Hirad ambled to Sha-Kaan's head where the rest of The Raven had gathered to watch Darrick talk to Tessaya. He laid a hand on the dragon's head.

"Thank you, Great Kaan."

The old dragon opened one eye and fixed him with a myopic stare. "You have saved the Kaan, you and your Raven. It is I who should be thanking you."

"So why the sadness? You don't sound at all happy."

"We have lost the Manse and that is a great loss to us for it contained a gateway and that gateway, like the one in your sky, has gone. I am unsure where to look for more."

"I don't think I understand," said Hirad.

"He's saying he thinks they're stuck here," said Erienne. "At least for now."

"But you can get them home, can't you?" asked Hirad. "Soon?" His eyes took in all three mages. Their heads shook.

"I don't know," said Ilkar.

Hirad faced Sha-Kaan once again. "You knew this might happen, didn't you? That's why you came here, to see if Septern's rip still worked?"

"Of course," said Sha-Kaan. "But what are the lives of three dragons in the cause of a Brood. It was a small sacrifice."

Hirad was lost for words. "We'll get you back. Somehow." He smiled. "After all, we are The Raven."

"Does your conceit know no end?" asked Denser, his eyes shining.

"No," said Hirad. He took it all in. Darrick talking to Tessaya, the Wesman Lord nodding, his eyes fixed on the trio of Kaan that rested in front of him. The Unknown, shaking hands with every surviving Protector. Denser and Erienne in each other's arms, their faces alight, their eyes speaking love. Sha-Kaan, his head up and surveying his new home, his bright blue eyes missing nothing, his thoughts dominated by triumph, sadness and great hope. And Ilkar, arms folded, smiling to himself and shaking his head at the thought of it all.

They had done it. The Raven. Again. He conceded it was hard to take in.

Only Thraun was missing. The big blond warrior had disappeared almost immediately after they had landed, slipping off the dragon and moving soundlessly away. He needed to be alone. Hirad understood that. He'd make himself known when he was ready.

A shout of alarm rang from the Balaian army. Fingers pointed back toward the demolished Wesmen camp. Hirad followed their line.

"Leave him," he ordered. "He'll not harm you."

Thraun loped up to Hirad, who crouched in front of him and stroked his head.

"Wouldn't have done that if you were in human form," he said. A sad smile touched his lips. "Oh, Thraun, what the hell have you done?"

The wolf regarded him solemnly, his yellow-flecked eyes moist. He sniffed the air and growled, a friendly sound that went right through Hirad. For a moment, he thought he might cry.

"I don't know if you can understand me, Thraun, but remember this," he said, his voice thick, the rest of the world gone for a moment as he stared at the shapechanger. "You will always be Raven. And we will always remember you. Good luck, both now and in whatever faces you. May your soul find peace." He felt a hand on his shoulder. It was Ilkar. The hand squeezed but the elf said nothing.

Thraun stepped forward, licked Hirad's face, turned and trotted away.

ACKNOWLEDGMENTS

Support, help, and encouragement are so important and thank you to all those who gave them so unstintingly. But there are some I should mention in person: Tara Falk who keeps me going; Peter Robinson, John Cross, Dave Mutton, and Dick Whichelow for being there any time; Paul Fawcett and Lisa Edney for tolerance and patience above and beyond the call of duty; William Holley who sent me my first piece of "fan mail"; and Simon Spanton whose sympathetic editing improves everything I write. It wouldn't be any fun without you all.

I thank you all.

ABOUT THE AUTHOR

JAMES BARCLAY is in his forties and lives in Teddington in the UK with his wife and son. He is a full-time writer. Visit him online at www.james barclay.com.

NOVEMBER 2009

"Barclay writes with power, pace, and a wonderful sense of humor. Better than that, he creates novels you want to read again and again."
—DAVID GEMMELL

NIGHTCHILD
CHRONICLES OF THE RAVEN

JAMES BARCLAY

"Packed with all the spell-chucking, city-smashing, limb-hewing violence you could want."
—*SFX*

Pyr®, an imprint of Prometheus Books
716-691-0133 / www.pyrsf.com